THE VEGAS LEGACY

THE VEGAS LEGACY

A NOVEL

OVID DEMARIS

DELACORTE PRESS / NEW YORK

Published by
Delacorte Press
1 Dag Hammarskjold Plaza
New York, N.Y. 10017

Copyright © 1983 by Ovid Demaris

Manufactured in the United States of America

First printing

Designed by Richard Oriolo

LIBRARY OF CONGRESS CATALOGING IN PUBLICATION DATA
Demaris, Ovid.
The Vegas legacy.
I. Title.
PS3554.E4555V4   1983   813'.54   82–13019
ISBN 0–440–09172–1

For My Attorney

Richard C. Leonard
whose friendship and wisdom I deeply value

I
TODAY

CHAPTER

1

The city faced an invasion. It started with a trickle in midweek and by Sunday it was a flood. For the first time in its history, the Grand Old Party was staging a convention carnival, its quadrennial, in Las Vegas and the delegates had come to do bloody battle in its searing July heat.

Sixteen hotel-casinos, along with two dozen motels, had set aside thirty thousand rooms to accommodate the onslaught of Republicans determined to have fun in sin city. They sported buttons that asked, "Who Says Republicans Don't Have Fun?" and they wore funny hats and carried horns and noisemakers to prove it. They attacked Las Vegas with the determination to dispel forever all rumors that Republicans were dull.

Ten thousand out-of-town prostitutes converged on the Strip and Glitter Gulch, the city's downtown neon jungle, and the police, used to protecting their own hookers, tried to control the "floaters" by asking them to abstain from propositioning delegates when they were with their wives. None of the floaters were permitted to work inside any of the casinos, which were the exclusive preserve of the local hookers.

The city fathers saw the convention as a golden opportunity to sell the world on the virtues of Las Vegas as a God-fearing town, no different from Des Moines—in fact, with far more churches per capita. Gambling, they suggested, was like any other business providing a service. Compared to the other forty-nine states, Nevada was a bastion of freedom. It permitted its citizens to enjoy life with a minimum of taxes, regulations, and irritation. It was the last free state in the Union.

The vicious propaganda that the so-called Mafia was skimming gambling profits was curtly dismissed as ancient history. Part of the gambling mecca's mythology. To use the favorite cliché of the publicists, the town was clean as a whistle.

In its own way, Las Vegas was the ideal convention city. The convenient cluster of its Strip and Glitter Gulch hotels and motels made it possible for the delegates to huddle together without having to travel great distances. They could whisper and gossip, wheel and deal in fancy restaurants and cocktail lounges, and while away the long dead hours at the gaming tables. When the urge struck them, at whatever the hour, all they had to do was crook a finger to get serviced by the world's greatest professionals.

The Monarch II, which was to serve as the nerve center of the convention, claimed to be the world's largest resort hotel, and its 150,000-square-foot casino, the size of three football fields, was likewise the world's largest. It had the world's finest restaurant, the world's largest swimming pool, the world's biggest jackpot, the world's largest display sign—all of it proclaimed in indelible neon. It was the perfect place for the world's greatest political party to meet to select the most powerful leader of the world's greatest nation. Somehow it all seemed to blend in raucous harmony.

CHAPTER

2

Aboard Air Force One, President Truman Abbott looked grim as he read the latest polls gathered by Pat Daley, his political consultant. Abbott's rating had tumbled eighteen points in the past four months, but there was nothing mysterious about it.

The persistent challenge of Hamilton Foote, a former governor of California and the chief spokesman for the ultraconservative wing of the party, who had waged internecine warfare through twenty-eight primaries and caucuses, had been rewarded, according to his count, with enough delegates to prevent Abbott from getting a solid lock on the convention. Coupled with that were the machinations of the backers of Senator Randolph Godwin, who had entered Godwin's name in several primaries, allegedly against his wishes, to test the political waters. The results had been surprisingly promising. Abbott knew that Senator Godwin's so-called secret forces were controlled by his father, Henry Godwin, and his grandfather, Rufus Boutwell, the wealthiest and most powerful man in Nevada history.

It was a tribute to Boutwell's national clout that Las Vegas had been chosen as the site of the convention. It was the first time that a political party had dared come here to select its Presidential candidate on national television. The seven-member site selection committee for the Republican National Committee had unanimously picked Las Vegas and Abbott hadn't exercised his veto power. Later, when he learned that the committee had been wined and dined in questionable fashion by Rufus Boutwell, it had been too late for him to do anything about it without causing a scandal.

Abbott carefully filed the report in his briefcase, which he kept on a table at his side. He leaned back in his seat and closed his eyes. At fifty-six, Abbott was completing a successful first term as the nation's chief executive, having reduced taxes, inflation, and unemployment in a peacetime economy, and his chances for reelection seemed assured if he could again secure his party's nomination.

"Mr. President, Joe Alcorn would like to see you," Pat Daley said. "We thought you might spare him a few minutes to keep him happy. He's pretty thick with Godwin, but still he's going to write his book with or without our cooperation."

Abbott looked out the window, the glare of sunlight accentuating the deep furrows etched around his eyes and mouth. "Yes, Pat, I suppose one must respect the wishes of an institution." A twinkle came into his hazel eyes. "Joseph Alcorn is a self-made institution, the first of its kind, the instant historian. He ranks with fast-food artists like Colonel Sanders as a modern innovator." He paused, his expression turning serious. "Give me about ten minutes, then send him in."

Joseph Alcorn was the dean of political convention coverage. Every four years he wrote a ponderous tome entitled *The Election Process in Action*, followed by the appropriate date, in which all the rumors, gossip, scuttlebutt, and hallowed words spoken by candidates and high priests of television journalism were recorded for posterity.

It was his life's work and he loved the money and prestige that flowed from it. At convention time he became the resident oracle for National Television Network (NTN). Staring straight into the camera, he pontificated at great length on the importance of rumors that floated up to his television booth from the chaotic convention floor. Though he was tall, with a whiplike body, his high cheekbones and sunken cheeks gave his face a certain ascetic flair that concealed a gargantuan appetite for all the good things in life.

When Pat Daley tapped him on the shoulder, Alcorn quickly closed his steno notebook and stood up. He was one of the few journalists left who preferred taking shorthand to using a tape recorder.

Escorted into the President's presence, he bowed his head, coming down so low that for a moment Abbott thought he was going to kiss his hand.

"Ah, Mr. President, how kind of you to allow me a few moments of your precious time. I realize you have many weighty matters on your mind and I'm doubly grateful for the audience."

Abbott waved him to a chair facing him. "Joe, it's always a pleasure to see you. I presume, as in former years, you'll be in the NTN booth analyzing things as we Republicans fumble along with the business of selecting the next President of the United States."

Alcorn smiled as he opened his notebook and poised his ball-point pen over an empty page. "Yes, I've been retained again as a consultant-commentator. I must say I look forward to it. It's an exciting challenge. Mr. President, if I may, sir, I would like to start by asking if you have the nomination locked up."

Abbott gazed out the window and wondered idly what the people directly under his airplane were doing at this moment. "Joe, we said some ten days ago that we had eleven hundred and forty-two delegates, and nothing, as far as we can see, has changed the tally."

"Mr. President, are you speaking of committed delegates? Is that a hard count?"

"It's a count that to a substantial degree was confirmed by objective tallies. We had it ten days ago and we think we have it now. That gives us a bonus of twelve delegates. So I think that's as locked up as one can have it at this point in time."

Alcorn coughed politely. "You know, Mr. President, there are those who will regard your arrival in Las Vegas on Sunday as an expression of weakness. An incumbent President usually stays in Washington until after his nomination is tendered by his party."

"Well, Joe, I've never been too interested in the habits of other Presidents. As you know, I'm a take-charge kind of leader, especially in areas that personally concern me."

"There's some talk you may be planning to meet with Hamilton Foote's delegates at the convention in an effort to unify the party. Is that your plan?"

Abbott smiled thinly. "Joe, I'm going off the record on this one. It's a distinct possibility. I plan to press flesh and make the necessary symbolic gestures wherever I find softness among Foote delegates."

Alcorn chuckled softly. "Ah, Mr. President, it will be an historic convention. As for Senator Godwin, have you assessed his situation?"

The President decided it was time to play the game. "To some extent, Joe, but I'm still uncertain as to what actually took place there. What have you heard about it? Have you had an opportunity to speak with Godwin?"

Alcorn grinned in anticipation. He knew the President was strictly a quid-pro-quo man. He never gave information without expecting some in return. But this was part of Alcorn's plan. This was the opportunity he needed to do his number for Randolph Godwin. Besides, it meant he'd have more time to bask in the Presidential glow. He knew the other correspondents on the plane were clocking him, and it was these small victories that marked him as the supreme chronicler of Presidential elections.

"Ah, yes, Mr. President, I did indeed interview Senator Godwin last week. He professes—in eloquent terms, I might add—to be one of your most loyal supporters, no doubt realizing I would transmit this information to you. I, for one, am a little dubious, Mr. President. He claims to know nothing about the people who entered his name in the primaries, but"—and Alcorn paused here for effect—"I have it from a reliable source that his grandfather, Rufus Boutwell, engineered the whole scheme with some of his associates in the Eastern financial establishment. Boutwell has powerful banking contacts on Wall Street. For a rube from Nevada, a man without any formal education, he's managed to climb up in the world of high finance to a dizzying height. Most men would get a nosebleed halfway up there." Alcorn smiled, pleased with what he considered a clever analogy. "My information is that Boutwell wants his grandson on the ticket in the Vice-President slot."

The President pursed his lips, his eyes narrowing. "My response to that one, Joe, is that Boutwell wasted his money. Orville Fowler has been a popular Veep, loyal to the bone. There's no man I'd trust more a heartbeat away from the Presidency than Orville Fowler. He has my total support, and rank will have its privileges, I assure you, at this convention."

"In other words, you're not going to leave the choice to the convention?"

Abbott smiled. "Again I must go off the record, Joe. As to your question, not on your life. Rufus Boutwell got his way in getting us to meet in Las Vegas, but that's the limit to what his money will buy him this week."

Alcorn stuck his tongue in his cheek and gave Abbott a sly look. It was time for some solid body blows. "Now, Mr. President, this may be just scuttlebutt, but I hear that Boutwell's battle plan is to attack you with one ideological challenge after another on the party platform, to confront you with alternatives you can't accept, and force you into an untenable position. His supporters' passions burn hot, and they're hoping to ignite the convention floor. It's been done before. They believe there are enough uncommitted delegates and 'soft' supporters supposedly committed to you to turn the convention around. If they flame their emotions, they can block your nomination on a first ballot. After that they feel it's their ball game."

The President casually looked at his watch. "Well, Joe, you haven't disappointed me. You always do your homework. What are your personal feelings about Senator Godwin?"

Abbott watched carefully as Alcorn's dark eyes narrowed in concentration. "I quite like the man. He's been a decent senator. Works hard for his state, and he's not afraid to stand firm on controversial issues. I could think of a worse Vice-Presidential running mate."

There was a hissing sound from the President's chair. "Senator Randolph Godwin is the last man in this country, or any other country, for that matter, that I'd want on the same ticket with me. And don't ask me to elaborate. Now, if you'll excuse me, I must get on to other pressing matters."

Alcorn pocketed his pen, closed his notebook, and stood up, leaning perilously forward from the waist, and thanked the President for the interview. He bowed out of the small compartment and went back to his seat. He couldn't wait for the plane to land so he could report to Randolph what the President had said about him.

3

He stepped into the headquarters tent and the General handed him the sealed message to be delivered to General Robert E. Lee, who was marching toward Gettysburg. The mission was the most important of the war, the General told him. The fate of Vicksburg was in his hands.

First on horseback, until his horse died under him from exhaustion, then on foot, he climbed mountains, swam rivers, crawled across enemy camps, and ran through forests, the leather pouch with the sealed message slapping against his hip.

Suddenly it was night and he was mired down in a sea of mud, his feet making sucking sounds as he struggled to lift them, but he was sinking deeper into the mud, until finally it was waist high. He knew he had to push on—the General had placed the fate of the South in his hands—but the fear of drowning rooted him to the spot. Hours later the first rays of sunlight broke on the horizon and he found himself trapped in a sea of blood and gore, of dismembered arms and legs, of mutilated torsos and faceless, decapitated heads.

Henry Godwin awoke in a cold sweat, his arms and legs twitching, his eyes searching the darkness of his room. He rolled over and sat on the edge of the bed, his hand reaching blindly for his cigarettes and lighter. The red digital numbers of his radio-clock showed that it was a few minutes before five.

How long had it been since he'd had that nightmare? He lit a cigarette and filled his lungs with the smoke, exhaling slowly, trying to get himself under control. Gradually it was coming back to him and he stood up, shaking his head. He didn't want to think about it. That was another place, another time, and another person had been there. He extinguished the cigarette and reached for a pair of jeans on a chair and a light wool shirt. Walking barefoot on the cool terrazzo tile of the hallway, he made his way to the kitchen to make coffee and smoke his first cigar of the day. In a few minutes daylight would break on the horizon and he'd go for a horseback ride in the foothills on the outskirts of Carson City before the July sun turned them into an inferno. Later in the morning he would fly to Las Vegas and get ready for the struggle ahead. But, for the moment, he would enjoy his coffee in the large kitchen that he'd loved for so many years.

The nightmare had taken him back to his youth in Vicksburg and the Godwin plantation. It seemed a million years away.

He got up to refill his cup, and when he turned he found his grand-daughter, Alicia, standing in the arched doorway smiling at him, the first rays of sunlight glinting on her strong white teeth.

She came forward and kissed him. "I heard you moving around and thought I'd ride with you this morning, Gramps."

He patted her shoulder. "Have some coffee. I'm not ready yet."

She poured herself a cup and lit a cigarette. "Even for you, isn't this kind of early?" she said, sitting next to him at the table.

She was beautiful and he loved her. She had strawberry-blond hair that covered her head in tight curls. Blacks called it an Afro, but it reminded Henry of Ingrid Bergman in *For Whom the Bell Tolls*. She had the limpid green eyes of her mother and the same sweet disposition, though she could be tough at times. A graduate of Berkeley, she was a liberated woman. Her twin sister, Eileen, was Radcliffe and more feminine than feminist, and she was her daddy's girl. In personality the twins were total opposites. It was as though they both were determined to break the mold.

"You feeling all right, Gramps?" Alicia asked, leaning forward to peer more closely at him in the dim light.

He smiled. "Just had a disturbing dream. Kind of shook me up."

"Want to tell me about it? I love to hear the dreams of others, but I hate to talk about my own. They're mostly X rated."

Henry shrugged. "It was about the General. The same nightmare I had on my thirteenth birthday. It was precise in every detail. Nightmares have a way of shaking you up. They bring back memories best forgotten. Did your father talk much about your great-great-grand-father?"

"Not really. He never knew him and I don't think he cares all that much. All I know is what you told us when we'd visit the ranch here as kids. I used to love those stories. You made the Civil War come alive."

Henry smiled tolerantly. "The War Between the States, darling.

When I was a little boy, the General used to sit by my bed every night and talk about the war. He was in charge of the Confederate forces during the siege of Vicksburg. And I remember his telling me stories about the children—'teeners,' he called them—who fought with the bravery of grown men. He said I reminded him of one of his couriers, a thirteen-year-old boy, who was executed as a spy by the Yankees because he refused to betray his cause. That was what triggered the dream then, but why repeat it now after all these years? The mind is a baffling contraption."

Henry paused to consider his last remark. "Anyway, that morning of my thirteenth birthday, even before I woke up, I knew the General was standing by my bed. I opened my eyes and leaped ten feet in the air, yelling, 'You did it, General. You put on your uniform.' God, he looked so beautiful standing there, ramrod straight, with that twinkle in his eyes. He took a step back and snapped a salute as he came to attention. 'The troops are ready for inspection, sir,' he said. 'At ease, soldier,' I replied, returning his salute. As long as I can remember I'd wanted him to wear his Confederate uniform, with his saber, field decorations, and the three stars that marked his rank as a lieutenant general. He was the most beautiful human being in the world. Then we went for a ride along the bluffs of the Mississippi. It was the kind of morning that makes a lasting impression on your senses. Even today I can recall the heavy musk of the wet grass, dead leaves, and tree bark, soaked by a night rain, steaming under a hot summer sun. And the sweet fragrance of jasmine and magnolia. I suppose I'll never again feel the way I did that morning. That image of the General is burned into my brain forever. He was resplendent in his gray uniform, with his saber catching the sun, his wide-brimmed felt hat worn at a rakish tilt, just the way I'd always pictured him."

"God, Gramps, how old was he anyway?"

Henry sighed. "He was pushing ninety, but he was sharp as a tack. An incredible man. Well, anyway, that's enough about ancient history. Let's talk about today. What are your plans? Flying with me to Vegas this morning?"

"Oh, shit, do I have a choice?"

"I don't think so," Henry said. "The next few days are going to be extremely important for your father. Wouldn't you like him to be Vice-President of the United States?"

"You want an honest answer?"

"Of course, always."

"I couldn't care less. There's only one thing I care about and that's to be left the fuck alone. I'm all done being part of his macabre sideshow. The bereaved widower with the darling twin daughters. 'Ah, the poor man, what a lovely father he is, and him so handsome.' After all these years, I'm sick of it."

Henry placed an affectionate hand over hers on the table. "Darling, there are times you sound unfairly bitter about your father. I know he hasn't been perfect, but he's done his best for you girls. It hasn't been easy."

Her green eyes flashed. "Christ, Gramps, you really disappoint me. Your dear son has never given a damn about anybody but himself. He's the world's most egotistical, selfish, self-centered bastard, which puts him heads up on all other crawly creatures."

"Your sister Eileen doesn't share your hostility."

"My sister Eileen suffers from an Electra complex. Someday I expect to find them in the same bed."

"Oh, Christ," Henry sighed. "You do carry on."

"And Eileen's every bit as selfish and self-centered. You only see the sweet side, but there's another side to her that would surprise you."

Henry shook his head. "Pure sibling rivalry."

Alicia smiled. "Dear sweet Gramps, you're cute and pretty sharp in most things, but you've got one hell of a blind spot when it comes to people you love."

Henry squeezed her hand. "Well, darling, perhaps that's what you need. More love and less critical nitpicking. Besides, most of us have to deceive ourselves sometimes to keep from going stark raving mad."

They walked to the stables and Moses Grimes was there waiting for them, his large white teeth gleaming in his black round face. He was a few years older than Henry Godwin, but unlike the younger man's his face was without wrinkles. Henry often kidded him about having had a secret face-lift and Moses would point to his hair, which was snow white while Henry's was turning a silver gray. "You got some mileage left," Moses would remind him, and Henry would say, "I'd still like to know the name of your doctor. That man's a magician."

"What are you doing up this time of the morning?" Henry asked.

Moses laughed. "Well, Henry, I had a feeling you'd go riding this morning. And Miss Alicia. So I just thought I'd come over and see how old White Lightning's feeling. Been a little pokey lately."

"He looks fine to me," Henry said as Moses led the Arabian stallion out, already saddled, and a smaller Arabian mare for Alicia.

"Thank you, Moses," Alicia said. "You're a dear, sweet man."

"Thank you, Miss Alicia. Have a nice ride. It's a beautiful morning, but it's going to get mighty hot real soon."

"Shall we ride out to the north pasture to see how some of the new colts are coming along?" Alicia asked.

"My very thought," Henry said as he brought White Lightning to a smooth gallop.

"Don't you just love Arabians?" Alicia said, riding next to him. "I think they're the most beautiful horses in the world. And the most lovable. How many do you have, Gramps?"

"Oh, I don't know—close to a thousand, I guess." He laughed. "I hate selling any of them."

She slowed her horse to a trot and Henry pulled in to stay alongside her. "What's the matter, darling?"

"Nothing, Gramps. I just want to talk. I feel freer out here." She paused and looked directly at him, her green eyes bringing a lump in his throat. "Did you know my mother real well?"

"Well, yes, I think so."

"Gramps, did she confide in you? It's important, really."

"Darling, we've gone over this before. As far as I know, your mother was happily married before the tragedy."

"I don't think so, Gramps. You know, you have your nightmares and so do I. There's one I just can't understand. I don't know if it really happened, or I just dreamed it, but it keeps repeating itself."

"You want to tell me about it?"

"Yes, I do. You see, in my dream I hear this terrible fight. My mother and father are yelling at each other. At least, I think it's my father. It's a man's voice and in my dream it's really him. Then there's a loud slap, like a pistol shot almost, and I hear my mother scream—you know, like a person does when they're really terrified and on the verge of hysteria. Then there's another sound, more like a gurgling, and then just silence. In my dream I lie in bed, too afraid to move, and the next thing I see is my mother lying in her coffin, and I'm bending down to kiss her, but she's staring at me with eyes full of blood. Christ, Gramps, it gives me the creeps to even talk about it. Do you suppose that was when she was raped and murdered, that I actually heard it happening?"

Henry's eyes narrowed as he gazed into the distance. "It's possible, darling. But your father was in New York with Rufus when it happened."

"I know that and that's why I think I'm confusing events. Eileen's and my bedrooms were on the third floor in the Georgetown house and Mother was murdered in her bedroom on the second floor. What puzzles me is why I wouldn't have gone to her bedroom if I'd really heard her cry out instead of it being in a dream. I was young but I was never a coward. They had fights before, you know, with him shouting, but it never came to blows that I know of. So the dream is really weird."

"We can't help what we dream," Henry said, uncomfortable by the turn of the conversation. "It doesn't help to brood about them in daylight. Let's forget it, shall we, and go see the colts run. All right now, get the lead out—let's give these Arabians a workout."

4

The white limousine with the black windows waited as the Learjet taxied to its private apron and the pilot cut the engines. When the plane's door opened and the steps were lowered, the chauffeur, who was standing with his hand on the right rear door, quickly opened it and a man of medium height stepped out of the limousine. He had the lithe figure and slim hips of a dancer but his long, curly hair was snow white. His nose was long and blade thin under a high intelligent forehead. His face was deeply tanned and his dark eyes behind the sunglasses were reptilian cold.

He walked with the grace and arrogance of a man who has been in control of the world around him for a very long time. Vince Bacino was the supreme arbitrator in Las Vegas on all matters involving Cosa Nostra members and their fronts.

By the time he reached the steps, a woman appeared in the plane's doorway. She stood a moment. Her sunglasses were pushed back into her thick russet-gold hair and the gold flecks in her emerald eyes sparkled in the sunlight. In years past many writers had described her as the world's most beautiful woman. Her face had graced more magazine covers than Jackie Onassis' and for many more years. No one was certain as to her age, but her career as a jazz and pop singer had started when she was a teenager in the last years of the Roaring Twenties. As she walked down the steps, there remained the sensuousness of a young woman in her movements.

They hugged and blew kisses and walked to the limousine with their arms around each other's waist.

The chauffeur, who had an ominous bulge under his left armpit, was grinning happily. "Welcome back," he said, bowing as he waited by the opened door.

"Thank you, Carlo," she said. "Europe was wonderful, but it's always great to come back home."

"Baby, you look fantastic," Bacino said as they stepped into the car. "How was the concert tour? SRO?"

She leaned back in the soft cushions and lowered the sunglasses. "Yes, but exhausting. Them ole bones ain't what they used to be. They're getting bitchy."

He laughed. "Them old bones look pretty damn good from where I'm sitting, baby."

"Well, you ain't sitting on them. But you're looking mighty spic and span yourself, and them ain't chicken bones you're sitting on, *baaaby*." Because she was so articulate and could phrase her sentences with precision, she enjoyed using slang and slurring words for effect. Her sophisticated audiences ate it up.

"I feel great," he said. "Been playing golf every day, do a little exercising with Nautilus machines, keeping the old muscles toned up, and I try to screw a little chickie every night. Can't ignore that muscle —don't want it to dry up and fall off, right, baby? How's your love life?"

She patted his knee affectionately. "Shifted it into idle," she said in a voice that dismissed the subject. "So the staid old Republicans are really coming to this green felt jungle for their convention. That's simply incredible."

The limousine was rolling down the Strip. Ahead were ten miles of towering neon signs. They revolved, rotated, oscillated, spiraled, pulsated, and boomeranged like a giant fireworks display that never ended. In Las Vegas the creation of neon signs had become the ultimate art form.

"Ain't this beautiful, baby?" Bacino said. "You know, whenever I ride the Strip I think these hotels with their signs are a big fleet of sailing ships and mine, the Monarch II, is the queen of the line."

She laughed lightly. "It's a busy harbor."

"Yeah, well. Wait till you see the surprise I've got for you. Ain't nothing like it in the whole world. Guaranteed to blow your mind. Wait, we're coming to it now. Yeah, look, see ahead there?"

She leaned forward to peer through the windshield and there it was. Her name, Daisy Miller, in thirty-story type. "Holy shit," she gasped. "Christ, Vince, you're nuts."

He laughed. "Ain't it gorgeous, baby? Didn't I tell you it'd blow your fucking mind. The sign's the same height as our hotel, thirty-six stories. That makes it the tallest single-support structure in the world. We're putting it in Guinness's. It's got five miles of fluorescent tubing and ten thousand bulbs and it's all controlled by a solid-state computer. I'm telling you, that sign can do everything but give head."

"Yeah, baby, it sure is gorgeous, all right," she said. "And *très* vulgar."

"What do you mean, vulgar? Every performer in Vegas will be demanding the same size billing from hotels with ten- and fifteen-story signs. Fat chance. As for the Monarch, only our Daisy Miller gets thirty stories. The other headliners will get fifteen stories, maybe twenty for super superstars like Sinatra and Streisand, but never thirty for nobody but you, baby."

She sighed. "I'm duly honored," she said as the limousine swung up the curving driveway of the Monarch II and stopped under a striped canvas porte cochere reserved for VIP cars. A perspiring doorman, dressed in what could have been the uniform of an admiral in John Paul Jones's navy, had the rear door open before Carlo had come to a complete stop.

"Good morning, Miss Miller—it's a pleasure to have you back at the Monarch II."

She stepped out and the heat hit her like a blast from an open-hearth furnace. "Thank you, Alfie," she said, looking closely at his wet, red face. "You're acting chipper for a man working the first circle of hell."

He laughed. "Come back around noon," he said as Bacino alighted. "I'd like to know what circle I'm in then."

"Hey, the way you live, Alfie," Bacino said, "this is good training for the hereafter. *Ciao.*"

Bacino took Daisy's arm. The glass doors slid smoothly open and they passed into the frigid air of the lobby.

"It's like going from the frying pan into the deep freeze," she said. "What a god-awful place for a vacation."

Bacino smiled and led her to a private elevator that went directly to the penthouse floor without any stops. He opened the door with a key and they stepped in. The doors closed and they were lifted up four hundred feet in a matter of seconds.

"This is the best place to have gambling casinos," Bacino said. "People get in the hotel and it's so nice and cool they don't want to go out. Don't worry, baby—we know what we're doing."

The elevator doors opened and he held her elbow as they walked down the carpeted hallway. Again he produced a key and unlocked a door. He stepped back and waved her in with a grand gesture.

"*Entrate, principessa*—your castle awaits," he said proudly.

It was a palatial suite, two stories with a sweeping staircase, and the decor was white and gold with a subtle touch of pale lavender. It had been redecorated since the last time she'd been there.

"Oh, Vince, it's exquisite," she said as her feet sank into the thick white carpeting. "It looks bigger."

He laughed. "It *is* bigger. We knocked down a couple walls. You've got three bedrooms upstairs, plus the master bedroom, and down here you've got separate living and dining rooms, kitchen, maid's quarters, library, and a playroom with a great antique pool table. Out on the lanai there's a Jacuzzi to get those kinks out of your tired bones. And it's all very private. How's that for consideration?"

She kissed him, on the lips this time, and he patted her shoulder. "Glad you like it, baby," he said, winking at her. "And your friend Henry's suite is just down the hall at the same old place and I'm at the other end. Now listen to this. The President's got the whole thirty-fifth floor for his command post. He wanted the penthouse floor but no dice. The Secret Service's been all over this place. They're guarding the fire doors, so don't try to sneak down there. The penthouse floor is reserved for Boutwell's forces. So everybody's afraid the other guy's going to tap into his phone lines." He laughed. "You've never seen so many scramblers."

Daisy went to a sofa and sat down. "Look, honey, if you don't mind, I'm going to use the Jacuzzi and take a nap. I've got a big night ahead. Two shows. And tomorrow evening I'm officially opening the convention with the National Anthem."

"Okay, baby, *ciao*—I'm on my way." He went to the sofa and kissed the air above her head. "Have I thanked you for cutting your European tour to do this for me? Well, thanks a million. I'll drop by your dressing room before the show tonight."

She took his hand and kissed it. "Dear, sweet Vince. You know I'd do anything for you. You're the kindest, sweetest man I know."

He raised an eyebrow. "You mean after Henry Godwin."

She waved and closed her eyes. "*Arrivederci*, Roman."

"I'm gone," he said, and in a moment he was.

5

At a hundred forty miles an hour, the red Ferrari had the shrill whine of a jet fighter Garfield Stone had once heard at an air show. The pilot had swooped down for a pass close to the grandstand before suddenly shooting straight up in the air. The whistling sound of the jet's engines had been electrifying.

Garfield Stone wished he could get his hands on a jet fighter. He'd buzz Rodeo Drive and scare the shitheads right out of their Gucci loafers.

He bounced his bony chest against the steering wheel as his foot tried to coax more speed from the Ferrari. But the sound of the Ferrari's internal combustion engine was of metal anguish as furiously moving parts neared the climax of disintegration.

At one time its V-12 engine would have cruised smoothly at a hundred sixty miles an hour, but its day had passed and metal fatigue had set in. The red Ferrari was twenty-two years old, a classic whose intestinal parts had not moved in nearly a decade. It was a family heirloom, a priceless objet d'art that Garfield's father, movie star Rocky Stone, had lovingly restored to its original splendor with his own precious hands. He had purchased the Ferrari the week he'd completed his first starring role. It was his good luck charm and in some ways his first and only love. He lavished more attention on this mechanical toy than he ever gave his wife and son, or any other human being.

The shimmering, undulating ribbon of black asphalt seemed to vanish in a pinkish haze as Garfield peered myopically through the thick lenses of his horn-rimmed glasses. The speedometer needle vibrated violently at one hundred forty-five and the RPM was at eight thousand, having red-lined at sixty-five hundred. Still he demanded more speed. He passed cars that were doing eighty, but seemed like they were barely crawling, and he laughed maniacally at the shocked expressions on the stupid faces of the drivers and passengers as he flashed by them like a bolt of red lightning.

All the windows were closed to avoid drag, and his body was drenched in perspiration. His glasses were fogging up and he kept sliding them down his nose to let them clear up. For those few seconds he was a blind man inside a red bullet looking for a target to impact.

"Why the fuck didn't the cocksucker air-condition this motherfucker?" he cried angrily, again pushing the glasses down his nose.

The Ferrari was reaching the top of a steep grade when Garfield replaced his glasses and a huge semi materialized a hundred feet ahead. For a split second Garfield wanted to smash the Ferrari into the back of the trailer and could actually hear the sickening sound of exploding metal, but in the next moment he spun the wheel and the Ferrari shot out into the open lane, missing the trailer by inches. He went fishtailing wildly past it, the tires shrieking as he gunned the engine for more traction. A moment later he had it under control and the truck had disappeared in his rearview mirror.

He lowered the window an inch and was hit by a blast of hot air. At least now he could breathe. The inside of the Ferrari was like a sauna.

"That was fucking stupid," he yelled at the top of his lungs. "What a fucking waste. Do it, dumb ass, do it, but grab the headlines. Make the fucking front page and the seven o'clock network news." He laughed and slapped the wheel. "Show the old man who's got the real balls in the family."

Then it happened. It sounded like a bomb. The hood and several metal parts shot up into the air, followed by boiling oil and water, which quickly covered the windshield. Still he managed to stop the car safely on the side of the road. Then he leaned back in the seat and laughed until tears were streaming down his cheeks. His father's jewel had exploded under the crushing weight of a sledgehammer. Nobody would ever put this Humpty-Dumpty together again—not with the original parts they wouldn't.

He opened both windows, removed his glasses, and flicked perspiration from his face with his fingers. He sat there, forcing himself to wait, denying himself the pleasure of viewing the steaming carnage until he couldn't bear it another second. The longer he waited, the greater would be the pleasure. How he'd hated this red Ferrari through all the years of his childhood and youth. His father had either been away making movies, mostly in Europe, or going off to Palm Springs or Santa Barbara in his Ferrari with one of the starlet whores he kept changing every week. Then, when the Ferrari was put to pasture, he spent what little time he had at home working on it in a garage that was off limits to his wife and son. Once Garfield had sneaked in to offer his assistance and his father had knocked him down with a slap across the head. When he'd started crying, his father had picked him up by the scruff of the neck with one hand and had bodily ejected him with a warning not to come back. Garfield had not returned to the garage until this morning. Now he had his revenge. But that was only the beginning. Before the week was out he would show the world what he thought of his old man.

Without his noticing it, the truck he'd nearly collided with had stopped behind him and the driver, a tall, heavyset man in his mid-thirties had walked to the Ferrari and was staring incredulously at what was left of the engine.

"Are you okay, kid?" he said, bending over to peer inside the car.

Garfield nodded. "Yeah, I'm fine. What are you doing here?"

"Just checking if you're okay. That was a harebrained stunt you pulled back there. You missed me by a coat of paint. Otherwise they'd be picking up pieces of you for a week and still not get all of them."

Garfield forced a smile. "Thought I'd give you a little thrill. Must be pretty boring sitting in one of them cabs all day long."

Garfield pushed the door open and stepped out. "Let me look at that fucker," he said. "She really blew her top."

"Never saw nothing like it," the truck driver said. "Looks like the crankshaft went and the pistons took the head right off. Everything's gone. Man, that's really something else."

"That's right," Garfield laughed. "It is something else. It's never going to be what it was, that's for damn sure."

The truck driver was shaking his head. "Must have been doing one fifty when you passed me. Want me to call for help on my CB?"

"No!" Garfield shouted. "Leave the fucker right where she is. How far are we from Vegas?"

"Seventy miles or so."

"You going there?"

"Yeah."

"Well, I could use a ride."

The truck driver laughed. "One minute you're doing one fifty in a Ferrari and the next you're hitchhiking. Well, that's the ups and downs of life, kid."

"Yeah, how would you know, you dumb truck jockey?"

The truck driver looked closely at Garfield and saw a boy not more than seventeen who was nothing but skin and bones. His brown shoulder-length hair looked like it hadn't been combed in a year. There were deep hollows in his cheeks and dark circles under large brown eyes that had a wild, furtive glint behind thick lenses.

"Kid, shut up and get in the truck before I change my mind."

"Forget it, shithead. Who needs you?"

The driver put his hands on his hips and further examined Garfield. "My name's Gus. What's yours?"

"None of your fucking business."

A car went by doing about ninety and sent a *whoosh* of hot air that brought tears to Garfield's eyes.

"Hey, come on, get in, will you," Gus said. "You won't last two hours out here. You got any idea what this desert sun can do to you?"

Garfield walked around the Ferrari and a grin twisted his thin lips. "All right, let's move it," he said. "I ain't got all day."

Gus shrugged, climbed in, and watched the kid pull himself up on the passenger side. It seemed to take every ounce of his strength. He was sweating profusely and he gasped with pleasure when the cool air inside the air-conditioned cab hit him.

Garfield sat quietly as Gus shifted through the various gears and transmissions until finally the rig was cruising at seventy.

"This is pretty neat," Garfield said. "Like sitting in the catbird seat."

"Not bad," Gus said. "It's a living."

"You got kids?"

"Yeah, eight—four boys, four girls."

"You spend any time with them?"

"All I can when I'm home."

"Where's that?"

"Kokomo, Indiana."

"Home's bullshit, you know that?"

Gus shrugged. "Not all homes."

Garfield looked out his window at the gray sagebrush and yellowish sand. "My name's Alfie," he said, deciding to use an alias. "I live in Beverly Hills. I don't have a home. Just a place to support my father's image."

"What does your father do for a living?"

Garfield laughed. "He flexes his fucking muscles. To him I'm a fucking physical disgrace. The cocksucker hates my fucking guts for it, too. Like it was my fucking fault. I can't help it if his fucking semen's defective. But it never stopped him from fucking, that's for sure. He fucks anything that moves—except my mother, of course, who's been fucking her mouth with junk food and looks like a sumo wrestler. His prick must be made of genuine cowhide. I'd like to skin it and use it for a baseball cover. I'll bet you could throw a mean screwball with it."

Gus was shaking his head like he couldn't believe his ears. "Good God, that's your father and mother you're talking about. Don't you have any respect—"

"Shut up!" Garfield screamed, his hand reaching for the door handle. "You start preaching and I'm jumping out of this fucking rig, you understand?" His huge eyes seemed to vibrate behind the magnifying lenses.

"Hey," Gus said. "I'm sorry, but don't try anything like that. You'll kill yourself."

"So what? Who gives a shit? Just don't you start lecturing me. I've had that shit for seventeen years and I'm not taking no more of it. So you watch your mouth or you're going to have to explain why a kid jumped out of your truck. Wouldn't look too good to the wife and kiddies in Kokomo, would it?"

The palms of Gus's hands were soaking wet and he could feel the perspiration trickle down his back and chest. This kid was a psycho. He wished he'd left him back there with his Ferrari. Somebody else would have picked him up. He felt like stopping the truck and kicking the kid's ass out, but he was afraid that if he started slowing down the kid would spook and jump out. Anybody who drove a car the way that kid did was capable of anything.

"Okay, Alfie, no more lectures. I'll just drive, and if you feel like talking, be my guest."

"Don't you patronize me, you motherfucker," Garfield shouted. "All you fucking adults are in the same bullshit bag. I'm goddamn glad I'll never live to be one." He chuckled smugly. "Being an adult is the pits."

Gus looked straight ahead, his foot growing a little impatient on the accelerator, pushing the needle to eighty. But what if a cop stopped him? No telling what the kid would do or say. His foot became less impatient and the needle dropped back down to seventy.

"Hey, Gus, you ever play Russian roulette?"

Gus shook his head and kept his eyes on the road.

"Man, that's cool. I started playing it when I was fifteen. I knew where my old man kept his thirty-eight and when he was away I'd sneak it in my bedroom. I'd put a bullet in one of the chambers and spin it maybe a dozen times before I'd put it in my mouth and pull the trigger." He laughed. "The first time I really shit my pants. I can't describe the feeling. Every nerve in my body was jumping. But the more I played it the more I wished it would blow my brains out. Then I did it with two bullets, cutting the odds in half, or whatever. Did it three times in five minutes one night. But then a lot of other kids got into it and some made it, but they couldn't even get their fucking names up front in the funny papers. It was always the son or daughter of actor or actress so-and-so died today, blah, blah, blah. You had to read way down into the story to find out if they really had a name of their own. So I gave up that bullshit."

"Well, that's good to hear," Gus said, not knowing what else to say to this strange boy.

"Why? It's no skin off your ass. Hey, you're a big man. Shit, you must weigh two forty and what are you—six three, maybe four? Look at me—five eleven and a hundred sixteen pounds last time I weighed."

"You ought to eat more," Gus said.

"Why? So I could have a fat belly like you? I don't like food. They sent me to a shrink and he said I was suffering from anorexia nervosa."

"What in the world's that?"

Garfield removed his glasses and cleaned them with the tail of his Christian Dior sports shirt. He looked at Gus and smiled. "Just a fancy word that says the flaky patient is systematically starving himself to death. Man, that's pretty hip stuff in Beverly Hills and Bel-Air." Garfield pointed to another semi coming toward them. "Hey, big man, let's see how brave you are. Go across the divider and let's play chicken with that rig."

"That's not brave, it's crazy," Gus said. "And so's playing Russian roulette."

"You think I'm crazy? Is that it? Well, just keep reading the funny papers, big man, and you'll see. What I've got waiting for Lost Wages will blow your mind. I'm going to steal the show from everybody. Wait till you see what I'm going to do. They'll be talking about *me* for years—not my fucking old man, but *me*. *Me, me, me*."

Gus kept his eyes straight ahead. From the way the kid was dressed, with the tight-fitting jeans and sports shirt, it was obvious he wasn't armed. So if he was planning on some stunt, it would probably be harmless. What he wanted was attention. Grab some headlines.

"You don't believe me, do you?"

25

"Alfie, I don't know what you're talking about. It's obvious you've got a grudge against your father, but what has it got to do with Las Vegas?"

"Forget it, turkey. Just keep reading the funny papers—you'll find out quick enough. I've got it all worked out. I'm really going to steal the show, wake up the horny old Republicans. Buy your tickets, folks, hurry, hurry, come see the one and only Alfie, the great daring weirdo, make his historic debut into the history books."

He paused and removed his glasses. "You know, my old man's got the eyes of an eagle," Garfield said. "That motherfucker can actually see around corners."

"And you don't see too good yourself," Gus said.

He laughed shrilly. "Without these fucking ugly specs I need a cane. But I won't need them for long. Some guy once said, 'When you shoot at a king, be sure you kill him.' What I say is, Be sure you kill yourself, too. Then you're not dragged through all that bullshit."

By now they had reached the airport and were caught in bumper-to-bumper traffic on the Strip. Ahead were the miles of neon signs, brighter than the desert sun itself. Gus thought of grabbing the kid and turning him over to the cops. He was a nut, but that could get Gus into all kinds of complications. Besides, it would be unfair to the kid if he was just spouting off for kicks.

"Hey, man, dig that white limo with the black windows," Garfield said, pointing to two cars ahead of them.

"Where do you want to get off?" Gus asked, keeping his voice calm, not wanting to reveal how anxious he was to be rid of the kid.

"Wherever that limo goes, that's where I'm going," he said, clapping his hands together. "It's a good omen. The Lone Ranger rides again. Get it? The good guy with the black mask. Ah, fuck it."

They rode in silence until the white limousine swung up the driveway of the Monarch II.

"Right here," Garfield cried, clutching at the door handle. "Couldn't be more perfect."

"Thanks for the company," Gus said, but the boy was already running up the curved driveway. Gus sighed in relief and drove toward the first freeway on ramp.

6

As Air Force One was landing at Nellis Air Force Base in Las Vegas that afternoon, a royal blue L-1011, with a golden crest on its tail, was still five hundred miles away. The wide-bodied jet, which had been equipped and decorated to the specifications of Senator Randolph Godwin, had been a Christmas gift from his grandfather, Rufus Boutwell.

Randolph's private quarters at the rear of the plane were three times larger than those of the President on Air Force One. They consisted of a sitting room, a bedroom, and a control room containing the latest in electronic wizardry. Unknown to the crew and most of his aides, for the control room was kept securely locked at all times, there was a panel of small television monitors that kept him aware of what was going on in every part of the plane, including the flight deck. The telephone system, equipped with scramblers, gave him easy access to any part of the world.

When bored with his electronic gadgets, his favorite place was the bedroom, where the focal point was an enormous water bed with a black mink spread. The floor was covered with wall-to-wall polar bear skins. The walls and ceiling near his bed were paneled with blue-tinted mirrors. Hidden television cameras and infrared lights made it possible for him to view his lovemaking on a large television screen, and he could video-record the sex play of others without their knowledge. For special effects, strobe lights and a ten-speaker stereo system could make the place really jump. His collection of pornographic cassettes and discs was impressive.

The first time Rufus Boutwell saw the bedroom he laughed until tears rolled down his cheeks.

"Christ, sonny boy, what I wouldn't give to be young again," he'd said. "Imagine, fucking on black mink. I'm getting a hard-on—I mean it—just looking at this poontang nest. Goddamn, that bed's big enough for one of them orgies."

Randolph had laughed. "That's the general idea, Rufus. Care to try it out with a couple of little sixty-niners I know? Eighteen years old—knock your eyes out."

Rufus had given his grandson a quizzical look. "Fun's fun, sonny boy, but that's strictly out of my league."

Randolph had quickly retreated. "Well, I'm just pulling your leg, Rufus. That's a little out of my league, too."

But it was precisely in his league and had been for many years. Along the way he'd picked up other habits and there were times in the middle of the night when he'd start perspiring and trembling at the thought of Rufus finding out. Randolph's greatest fear was of being disinherited. Rufus was capable of cutting him out of his life without blinking an eye if the provocation was strong enough.

Just thinking about his grandfather and what awaited him in Las Vegas had started him perspiring. The next few days were crucial. They would decide his future. It was his one shot at the brass ring. It had been conceived and orchestrated by Rufus, his last hurrah for his grandson. If Randolph had to wait another four years, there was no telling what could happen to Rufus. Even now there were signs of his failing health. He was grossly overweight and often short of breath. No, there was no time to wait. It had to be now.

In the control room Randolph reached for a handkerchief and dried his hands, then stood up and went to a wall safe. He took a vial of cocaine and brought it to a glass-topped table. Working carefully, he made two thin lines of the white powder. He stared at them, almost hypnotized, as he rolled a new dollar bill into a small tube. Then he leaned forward and sniffed the coke into each nostril. Even as he returned the vial to the safe, he could feel the cool numbness spreading across his cheeks. When he sat down again he wasn't perspiring anymore. He felt a penetrating sharpness in his thinking and he smiled when he thought of how foolish he'd been to worry about the next few days in Las Vegas. Everything would work out as Rufus had planned it. There was nothing that old man couldn't do once he set his mind to it. Hadn't he turned a whole state into his private corporation?

Randolph leaned back in his chair and his fingers started absently moving over the control console built into the arm of the large leather chair. Colored images flashed on the television monitors. He paused a moment for a zoomed-in view of a stewardess's buttocks as she leaned forward to serve a drink to one of the fifty journalists in the front section of the plane. All the stewardesses wore bikini-style shorts and snug-fitting T-shirts with WIN-GOD-WIN stenciled across the front. As they bobbed up and down the aisles on high heels, bare-legged and braless, it was frustrating for the passengers to decide which fatty masses to watch.

He pushed another button and there was Blair "Hoppy" Hopkins in the kitchen with Clorice. He had both hands inside her T-shirt. Their hips were locked together and grinding away. He was mauling her breasts and she had her tongue in his ear.

Randolph was enjoying the performance. Hopkins's face was turning red and he was perspiring profusely. Randolph knew he was struggling on tiptoes and his legs were probably cramping. Even with her high heels removed, Clorice, a recent *Penthouse* centerfold, was at least four inches taller than he.

As Hopkins was nearing his climax, Randolph buzzed the kitchen. They both stopped and looked wildly toward the wall telephone. Without disengaging, they moved sideways until Clorice could reach the instrument and speak into it.

"Yes, Senator Godwin."

"D.T., honey," Randolph said, using the initials of his private name for her: Deep Throat. "See if you can get Hoppy to round up the brain trust for a meeting in my quarters."

"Right away, Senator."

"And D.T., keep yourself available for later tonight. I may need a sleeping pill."

She laughed. "Yes, sir. I'm registered at the Flamingo. Have you any particular time in mind?"

"Be on call from one o'clock on."

She lowered her voice two registers. "Be waiting with bated breath, lover."

He chuckled and hung up. Then he leaned back in his chair and turned up the sound on the monitor. Hopkins was already zipping up his fly and Clorice was straightening her shorts and T-shirt.

"My God," she said, "that man's timing is uncanny. That's at least the seventh time he's called me while I'm making it with someone. He's not called God for nothing. He sees and hears everything that goes on in this plane."

Randolph smiled and turned off the television console. He tapped one key on the telephone console and waited for its computer to find Rufus Boutwell and complete the connection.

"Hi, sonny boy, I was just about to call you," Rufus said.

"What's happening, Rufus? Abbott arrived yet?"

"Yeah, just left Nellis. In fact, his motorcade is right ahead of me."

"Get a chance to talk with him?"

Rufus chuckled. "I took it upon myself to officially welcome our President to our fair state. There was a lot of hoopla, with the Air Force band blaring away and the press in full force, but I managed to impart the poop that it'd be to our mutual advantage if we had a little private chat. He promised to consult his agenda and get back to me this evening or tomorrow morning. So I said, 'Mr. President, please don't inconvenience yourself on my account. Still I feel duty bound to remind you that numbers are numbers. A contested convention is like a crapshoot. You may want a natural on the first pass but sometimes you get snake eyes and no amount of wishing will change their spots. If you blow the whole bundle on the first pass, there's a good chance you won't get the dice back for another roll.'

"I think he got my point, but I didn't press matters any further. He gave me his icy little shit-eating grin, the sanctimonious bastard, but don't worry, sonny boy, he'll come around. Whatever he is, stupid he's not. He knows we've got a tight hold on his precious ass. If he wants to shake loose without too much pain or aggravation, he better come to terms. So we'll be hearing from him."

"He'll come around," Randolph said, "unless he knows something we don't."

"Now, now, sonny boy, don't give me that negative jazz. You're in good hands. I've got the Las Vegas High School band waiting for you at the airport and a large crowd of city, county, and state workers and their families to lend you moral support. After all, you're our favorite son candidate. The media will be there in full force. Just play it cool. Make sure Eileen's at your side."

"What about Alicia? Did Henry bring her down?"

"Yeah, she's here, and we'll all be there to greet you at the airport. Now don't forget to say something nice about Henry. Say something like although your dad has been a Democrat all his life, you respect his views and he yours, and that's what democracy's all about. Lay it on thick. People and the press eat that cornball shit right up."

"That's a laugh," Randolph said. "I've never known Henry's views on politics. You had him work the Democratic side of the aisle while you worked the Republicans, so no matter who lost, you were always winners. But I don't think I better get into that, do you?"

"Save the jokes, sonny boy, until after the convention. Are you getting prepped for your appearance on the 'Today' show tomorrow?"

"I'm getting together with the brain trust soon as I hang up."

"So hang up already. See you at the airport."

The line went dead.

CHAPTER

7

Garfield Stone paused by the fountain and looked up at the Monarch II's soaring thirty-six stories and wondered which floor the President and his party would occupy.

He dipped his hands into the fountain's water and splashed it on his face. The water was tepid. There was no relief from the desert heat. Garfield felt suddenly depressed. The forecourt of the Monarch II was packed with people elbowing each other in their rush to get inside the hotel's air-conditioned lobby.

Then Garfield noticed the doorman in the old-fashioned admiral uniform. He had a voice like a bullhorn as he ordered cabs away from the VIP entrance where limousines were lining up like VW buses at a rock concert.

Garfield laughed. Big shots around here were a dime a dozen this week. But there were a lot of creeps, too. As he approached the doorman, he noticed that he wore a silver nameplate on his chest with the inscription ALFIE. An incredible coincidence. If the doorman noticed Garfield staring at him, he gave no sign of it.

"Hey, Alfie, you're going to get a stroke in that outfit, man."

The doorman gave him a sidelong glance, smoothly assisted a beefy politician and his wife from their limousine, and deftly pocketed the proffered tip.

"All right, let's keep it moving," he bellowed as the next limousine came to a stop in front of him and he assisted another couple from the back seat, again pocketing a tip.

"Hey, Alfie, you got long pockets, man?"

The doorman turned toward Garfield, but instead of scowling, as Garfield had expected, he was smiling. "You here trying to make my day, kiddo?" he asked. "Or are you looking for a handout? You look like you could stand a square meal."

Garfield laughed wildly. "A handout from you? Man, you nuts? Can't you tell I'm a rich kid? Look, turkey, them are Guccis on my twinkle toes."

Alfie opened another door and this time four people popped out of the back seat. He pocketed the tip and motioned for Garfield to move on. "You're interfering with my work, kiddo," he said without looking at him. "So be a good fella and move on."

Garfield looked at Alfie's blue wool jacket, which was soaking wet, and reached into his pocket.

"Hey, Alfie," he said, slapping a hundred-dollar bill in his hand. "Buy yourself a limo, old man."

Alfie looked at the bill, his eyes widening in amazement. "What the hell, kiddo—what's this all about?"

Garfield shrugged. "Better get inside pretty quick or you're going to have a stroke. I'm not kidding. This heat's fucking dangerous."

"I'm okay. I'm used to it," he said. "But why the C-note?"

Garfield shrugged again. "Don't worry, I can afford it. Look, on your break, maybe I'll see you inside and we can have a drink or coffee— whatever you like."

"Are you a delegate?"

"You betcha, Alfie. See you later."

The lobby was bedlam. A number of delegations were snake dancing and blowing horns to call attention to their posters proclaiming their choice of candidate. Hundreds of young girls, dressed in the colors of their candidates, seemed to be everywhere, giggling and pinning badges on anyone within reach. TV cameras were catching it all, their heavy cables like huge prehistoric umbilicals strewn along the floor.

A pretty girl in a short red-white-and-blue-striped dress with a straw skimmer tilted at a rakish angle on her blond head grabbed Garfield by the arm and quickly pinned an Abbott button on his shirt. She had laughing blue eyes and very white teeth and her tongue looked as pink and soft as a rose petal.

"Now, don't you take it off or let anyone else pin you," she said, "or I'll never talk to you again."

Garfield looked her straight in the eye and carefully removed the button. "Do you do this to everybody?"

"Oh, you—what are you, a Foote man?"

"No, not really," he said, holding the button before her face. "I'm pretty much a tit-and-ass man, but I've heard of foot freaks. They get off sucking on somebody's big toe."

She raised an eyebrow. "Oh, hell, you read that in *Penthouse*."

Garfield slowly unbuttoned his shirt and opened it. "See the blood running down my bony chest?"

"I didn't, did I?"

"Yes, you did, right through my little tittie."

She frowned. "You putting me on? Come on, you didn't even wince. That's cool. Want me to put something on it so it won't get infected?"

Garfield buttoned his shirt. "No big deal," he said, handing her the badge. "Now, do it again, but this time just the shirt."

She carefully pinned it on his shirt and looked up smiling. "See, practice makes perfect."

Garfield laughed. "Hey, how about a drink? I'll tell you the story of my rotten life."

"I can't go now," she said, and she genuinely looked sorry. "I've got a lot of people to pin."

"Okay, but you're going to be around here for a while?"

"All day and night, it looks like. Most of the week, too, I guess."

"I'll catch you later, then. You've got to eat sometime."

"Are you staying at this hotel?"

"I am now," he said, and hurried toward the front desk, which had people lined up five and six deep its entire length. Scores of disappointed travelers sat on every available sofa and chair, some on their suitcases, all looking forlorn and defeated, the reservation slips clutched in their fists meaningless. The Monarch II, as was its practice, had overbooked its 5,500 rooms by fifteen percent, but thanks to the convention there had been no cancellations.

Garfield looked the desk clerks over carefully before getting into line. It didn't take long because everyone in front of him was summarily dismissed by the young clerk with the slicked-down black hair and pencil-lined mustache.

"I'm Garfield Stone. I've got a reservation for a suite on the thirty-fifth floor."

The clerk's eyebrows raised slightly. "I doubt that," he said, purposely leaving out the customary "sir." "The thirty-fifth floor is reserved for the President of the United States."

Garfield's eyes seemed to vibrate behind the thick lenses. "I said the twenty-fifth. What the fuck's the matter with you—hard of hearing?"

"I think you better leave."

Garfield leaned across the desk. "Look here, asshole, I'm going to tell you one more time. I'm Garfield Stone and I've got a reservation in this fucking joint for a suite on the twenty-fifth floor. You got that straight, now, or do I have to pick up this fucking phone and call my Uncle Lew?"

The desk clerk had worked Las Vegas long enough to know that when anyone talked that tough he usually had the muscle to back his play. But this was probably just a creepy kid. Still, he couldn't take a chance.

The clerk's fingers flew over the computer keys of the console before him, his small dark eyes watching the screen. "I'm sorry, uh, sir, but I have no record of your reservation. Perhaps your travel agent booked you in another hotel."

"Hand me that fucking phone," Garfield shouted, his voice carrying the entire length of the front desk. "I'll call Uncle Lew, have him straighten out this fucking bullshit. I'm tired of talking to you."

"But who is Uncle Lew, sir?" The customary "sir" came out without hesitation this time.

"Lew Spark! That's who Uncle Lew is, you asshole."

That was what the clerk was expecting and yet it startled him. He looked at Garfield, looked back at his computer panel, and began tapping the keys again. He looked up and smiled as though he were seeing Garfield for the first time and couldn't be more delighted. When he spoke the unctuous tone he reserved for superiors and special guests was rich in texture.

"I'm terribly sorry, Mr. Stone, it's right here in the computer. Please forgive the inconvenience." He raised his hands in a helpless gesture. "Computers can be awfully frustrating at times. I have a lovely suite for you on the twenty-eighth floor, facing the front, if that is satisfactory. Just sign this register card and I'll have a bellman take you there immediately."

"Forget the bellman," Garfield said. "My bags are still in the car. I had to leave it at a garage down the Strip—a little problem with the head gasket."

"I hope it's nothing too serious."

Garfield finished filling out the card and took the key from the clerk's hand. "Nothing to it," he said. "Just a slight oil leak."

"Well, enjoy your stay, sir."

"I will—don't worry," Garfield said, leaving the desk and heading for the elevator. The moment he reached his room, he looked through the telephone directory and called a garage that specialized in foreign cars.

While waiting for someone to answer, he cleared his throat a couple of times, getting himself ready to do a much-practiced imitation of his father's voice.

"European Car Service," a man said.

"Hi, this is Rocky Stone. I need a big favor."

"Yes, sir, Mr. Stone. Be glad to help you any way I can."

"Left my Ferrari on the side of the road about seventy miles out toward L.A. Blew the damn engine. I'd appreciate it if you'd pick it up immediately before the vultures get to it. I've got to fly out of here in twenty minutes—going on location for a new movie. I'll send you a check for five thou by the end of the week. All I ask is that you repair it and keep this transaction to yourself. I had that baby at one fifty when she popped and I'd rather keep that as our little secret."

"No problem, Mr. Stone."

"Tell you what. Remove the plates and write the ticket under some phony name. How about John Stevens?"

"You've got it, Mr. Stone. But this may run into some pretty stiff costs. Might have to get some of the parts handmade."

"Don't worry about cost. Just put it back in mint condition and name your price."

"Yes, sir, Mr. Stone. Don't worry—we'll do an A-one job."

Garfield hung up and threw himself headlong on the sofa, rolled on his back, and kicked his feet up in the air. Everything was going like clockwork. "Hurrah for the creeps of the world," he shouted. "It's time to rise and shine."

8

His Madison Avenue competitors called Sam Rosen an unscrupulous manipulator, a ruthless con man, the world's greatest barker of snake oil politics. But to the candidates fortunate enough to secure his services, he was the heavyweight champion of media politics.

"He's an obnoxious little Jew," Rufus had told Randolph, "but he's the best there is, period. He'd kill for two votes. He wages campaigns the way Patton waged war. He goes for the groin like a fucking pit bulldog. Once he gets his teeth into anything juicy, he tears the living shit out of it. And another thing—he'll go to the wall for you."

Although Randolph had stayed out of the primary campaign, he'd had several meetings with Rosen in planning the strategy. His first meeting with Rosen had been in Rufus's office in Carson City.

Puffing on a huge cigar, Rosen had explained the rules of the game. "Every candidate who runs for office needs a political pollster and a political consultant. From then on, the candidate's every movement, every word, every gesture, every attitude, every smile or fart is dictated by these two experts. The pollsters will tell the candidate what the people want to hear and the adviser will tell him how to say it."

"In other words," Randolph had said, "campaigns are really battles between consultants, not candidates."

"I couldn't have phrased it better myself," Rosen replied. "Let me tell you a story, Senator. Back in fifty-two, BBD and O created Eisenhower's commercials around the 'I Like Ike' theme. Adlai Stevenson refused to run political commercials, said they were beneath the dignity of the office. Well, you know what happened to Adlai. Since then the word *dignity* has never again reared its ugly head in Presidential politics."

Now Rosen was standing in the middle of Randolph's sitting room on the L-1011, surrounded by Randolph's brain trust: Danny Arnold,

Randolph's chief of staff; Guy Charest, speechwriter and legislative aide; and Bryce Silver, the senior senator from Louisiana and one of Randolph's closest friends and advisers.

Rosen pierced Randolph with his fierce gaze. "Senator, Abbott will be watching tomorrow morning. You've got to give him a terrific show. You've got to make him realize that instead of being a thorn in his side you could be a feather in his cap."

Rosen shot a couple of quick left jabs and a right hook. "Knock the fucker out with a good right hook to his fucking head. Ring the bells in his belfry. See, he'll stagger away, shake his head, and say, 'Holy shit, that's my man. Let Orville go back to milking cows in Iowa or wherever the fuck he's from.' Show Abbott a touch of class, baby. Remember, that's what grabs the voters. After all, Americans receive about seventy percent of their news from television. So you've got to go for their head and body and solar plexus. Boom. Boom. Boom. You knock 'em dead with a terrific combination."

Randolph was smiling, enjoying the performance. "Give them the old snake oil treatment," he said.

"Absolutely, baby, you beat them at their own game. You learn to use the tube. You go for the image. The viewer sees a decent human being, a man who's suffered a great tragedy but who survived to bring up two lovely young ladies, who is brave and strong and yet gentle and caring and soft-spoken and mature and handsome enough to be a movie star, who has poise and charm and a sense of humor, but not witty, not intellectual, not cynical, not opinionated, not uppity, not flashy, not vain, not controversial, not argumentative, not flaky, not bigoted, a man with independent wealth, who is incorruptible, beyond the clutches of dirty bosses in smoke-filled rooms. In other words, your everyday, clean-cut American millionaire you'd love to take home to dinner."

9

It was a family dinner and Rufus Boutwell felt expansive. He sat at the head of the table in the dining room of his penthouse suite at the Monarch II. On either side of him were the twins, Eileen and Alicia, with Henry seated next to Alicia and Randolph next to Eileen. It was a candlelight dinner prepared and served by Rufus's personal chef and butler.

There was a smug grin on his battered face, his gray eyes mere slits glinting in the candlelight as he waited for the butler to fill their champagne glasses. He was in high spirits. The brief ceremony at the airport had gone off smoothly and a later meeting with the brain trust had further reinforced his optimism. It would be an easy victory at the convention. And if that failed, there were alternatives.

When the butler left the room, Rufus stood up and raised his glass.

"Come on, up, everybody—let's drink a toast to the next Vice-President of the United States."

They stood up and clicked glasses. Rufus downed his drink in one gulp and threw the glass into the fireplace, the fine Bavarian crystal shattering with a popping sound, and the others quickly followed his example.

The butler returned with new glasses, refilled them, but this time he poured Perrier in Rufus's glass.

Rufus grinned at Henry. "That's the first drink of real booze I've had since nineteen thirty," he said. "But I had to drink this toast with the real McCoy."

"I feel like a character in a Russian novel," Eileen laughed.

"Now that you mention it," Alicia said, "Rufus does remind me of Feodor Pavlovich Karamazov."

Eileen's green eyes flared angrily. "That's horrendous, Alicia. You're really bitchy, you know."

"Who's this Karamazov character?" Rufus asked, looking from one twin to the other.

"It's not important," Randolph said. "What's important is that I want these girls to start behaving like sisters and stop this goddamn haggling. It's getting to be a royal pain in the ass."

"But, Daddy," Eileen said, "she's such a flake. Always putting people down. Especially her own flesh and blood. Who does she think she is, for God's sake?"

"Whoever I am," Alicia said, "thank Karma I'm not like you."

"You're not like her," Rufus said, "that I'll grant you, but you sure as hell look like her. Which reminds me of a great story. Back in nineteen thirty-one, when we introduced the bill to legalize gambling, I had this assemblyman, Harry Butz, a miner I'd known in Goldfield, sponsor the measure. As you'll remember, Henry, we ran into some pretty stiff lobbying against it. So Harry called in his identical twin brother, Larry, to lend him a hand. Harry worked the Assembly all day, building support, and Larry, posing as Harry, would work on them in the bars most of the night. Next morning, Harry, fresh as a daisy from a night's sleep, was back in the Assembly, chopping away at them until finally they just collapsed and we got our bill."

Randolph laughed heartily. "Christ, they must have been fantastic days."

"They were, sonny boy, some of the greatest days of my life. As the kids say today, we had a ball. Right, Henry? When the gov signed the bill, the whole nation was horrified. One preacher, who was a big temperance leader, called for the 'dethroning of the renegades who run the state.' Of course, he meant me and your daddy. Oh, there were references in the press to 'Nevada's infamy,' and one newspaper wanted us separated from the Union."

"And today," Randolph said, "the Republicans are here in Las Vegas for their national convention. Times do change."

"Only if you work at it," Rufus said. "And we're going to change it even more with your nomination."

"From a state with three electoral votes," Eileen said. "That's truly incredible."

"Not so incredible," Alicia said, "when you consider the forces involved. But what I'd like to know, Dad, is why you'd want to be Vice-President. Who was it—John Nance Garner, FDR's first Veep?—who said the office was 'not worth a bucket of warm spit'?"

"Oh, God," Eileen groaned, "here we go again."

"Just one minute," Rufus said before Randolph could answer. "Let me straighten her out. Alicia, any fool knows that in most cases the Vice-Presidency is mostly a ceremonial job. But the same fools know that the Vice-President is a heartbeat away from the Presidency. That's one hell of a springboard right there. And even if the President don't die in office, we're still way ahead of the ball game. With the proper guidance and exposure, the Vice-President becomes a viable candidate in the next election." Rufus paused and looked around the table. "It's the only stepping-stone offered a Nevadan and by Christ we're taking it. All Abbott needs to be reelected President in the fall is the blessing of this convention without too much bloodshed. And to get that blessing, he's going to have to come to terms with certain realities. You get the picture now?"

Alicia shook her head. "What realities?"

Rufus laughed harshly. "It's called horse trading, darling. Don't worry your little head about it. One final point. Four of the last six Presidents were once Vice-Presidents. That's what I call damn good house odds."

By now the butler was serving the main course of a rack of lamb, but Alicia was not even aware of him. She gave Henry a quick glance and he smiled approvingly.

"That's ghoulish. Still, why pick Dad? Ike took Nixon as VP in fifty-two because he wanted to win California. Stevenson took Sparkman in fifty-two and Kennedy took Johnson in sixty to stroke the South. Goldwater took Miller in sixty-four because, for Christ's sake, he said, Miller 'bugs' Lyndon. The Veep is a straw man, a gimmick, something to seduce delegates or balance the ticket, or whatever, but he's never chosen because of his qualifications. So why will they pick you? What have you to offer? What's the gimmick?"

"Your father," said Eileen, "is a most attractive candidate. He has a fine record in the Senate and his reputation is international."

Alicia ignored her, turning her attention to Randolph. "I guess I really know the answer. I'd have to be pretty retarded not to appreciate Rufus's wealth and connections with the powers that be in this country—or in this world, for that matter."

Rufus smiled, his gray eyes amused. "So you're finally realizing that your great-grandfather has amounted to something in life."

"Oh, Rufus, I've never doubted that for a moment. Only the amount of the weight is in question."

"Why I permitted you to attend Berkeley I'll never know," Randolph interrupted angrily. "The freshman economics course must be Hate Capitalism, One and Two."

"Speaking of economics," Alicia said, "I read the Multilateral Commission's last report, 'Crisis of Capitalism,' and found it quite enlightening, considering that you're one of its commissioners, and particularly the Appendix entitled 'Targets for Action.' I assume everyone here has read it."

"Not I," said Eileen. "I leave economics and political science to the experts."

Alicia looked directly at Randolph. "Do you honestly believe there's an excess of democracy in this country?"

"I sure as hell do," Randolph said. "And it's a threat to itself. This country needs to restore a more equitable relationship between governmental authority and popular control. There can be no progressive change without a strengthening of the capitalist system."

"And how do you plan on going about achieving this goal?"

"Hey, enough already," Rufus said. "This is a celebration, not a goddamn political debate."

Henry pressed his knee against Alicia's leg and she nodded in understanding. "Yes, of course, you're right. Let's celebrate. Bring on the wine and the music and let's raise hell. That's what the delegates are doing tonight before they start their little *danse macabre* in the morning."

"Speaking of the morning," Randolph said, "I'd appreciate you and Eileen appearing with me on the 'Today' show."

Alicia shrugged. "Why not? But may I wear a mustache or ski mask. Just in case I ever want to visit old friends at Berkeley again?"

"You're sick," Eileen hissed through gritted teeth. "Sick."

10

Garfield Stone walked to the VIP entrance under the striped-canvas porte cochere and there was another admiral opening and closing doors of limousines. The guests were dressed in elegant evening clothes, many coming for Daisy Miller's midnight show. He remembered her coming to his house one Sunday afternoon with Vince Bacino and Lew Spark, who was then head of Talent Corporation of America (TCA), the largest talent agency in the country. His father, Rocky Stone, had been one of Spark's most important clients in the early days of TCA. Garfield had been hardly more than a toddler when he'd started referring to Lew Spark as his "Uncle Lew."

He went to the fountain in the forecourt and sat on the rim of it, looking up at the front of the hotel's thirty-six stories, trying to locate his room. Then he wondered which of the windows on the thirty-fifth floor belonged to the President's bedroom.

As he sat there, enjoying the sound of the cascading water, dipping his hand into its coolness, yet deep in thought, a cheerful voice addressed him and he looked up, startled by the interruption.

It was the blond girl who had pinned the button on his shirt that afternoon. She was dressed in a light blue silk blouse and deep blue skirt and looked as fresh as though she had stepped out of a shower after a full night's sleep.

"Fancy running into you," she said. "How's your chest? I hope there's no infection."

"Naw, it's okay, but I feel kind of weak. After all, I lost at least a dozen drops of blood and that's more than I can spare."

"Well, you're in luck," she said. "I'm loaded. I'll buy you a raw steak, a real juicy one, rebuild your hemoglobin, or whatever. If nothing else, it might put some meat on your bones."

"Forget it, I like my bones just the way they are."

She blushed. "Sorry, I didn't mean—"

"Wait a minute. All I'm saying is that people are nuts. They're always trying to stuff junk down your throat until you look like a blob, then they send you to a fat farm. You can't win."

"I'll see you later," she said, starting to move away.

"Wait up," he called, starting after her. "Where you going?"

"No place you'd want to go," she said.

He took her arm as they went into the lobby. "How do you know? Try me."

She bit her lower lip. "I want to see Daisy Miller. I've got most of her stereo albums. My mother used to go see her when she was my age. She's been at the top for ages. Her singing gives me gooseflesh."

"You've got a date, or a reservation?"

She shook her head. "No, but I've got the money and my fingers crossed."

"Leave it to me," Garfield said, leading her into the casino. The entrance to the Imperial Room was past long banks of slot machines. A long line of people waited, hoping to be admitted to the show. The line snaked around several banks of slots until it finally spilled out into the lobby.

"Oh, good Lord, look at that line," she cried. "We'll never get in."

"Have no fear, my little blond-haired, blue-eyed chickadee," he said as they reached the elegantly decorated entrance and were met by a group of hard-faced attendants in formal attire. Garfield walked right up to the maitre d' with the girl in tow.

"Ah, my good man, how nice seeing you again," he said, reaching to shake his hand and pressing a bill into it.

The maitre d' shook his head, his fist closing, refusing to accept the tip. "Sorry, sir, we're booked solid this evening."

"We'd appreciate a table for four, center front, please," he said, again proffering the bill, but the maitre d' kept his hand at his side. "Don't you think you should look at it?" Garfield said, turning a corner of the bill to reveal the hundred-dollar figure.

"Do you have a reservation?"

"Absolutely. The name's Garfield Stone. My father, Rocky, and mother, will join us later. Listen, if Uncle Lew comes in, show him to our table, will you?"

"Do you mean Mr. Spark?"

"Right on, friend."

The maitre d' consulted his seating chart and beckoned to one of the flunkies. "Table twenty-one C," he said as he and Garfield again shook hands. This time, however, he pocketed the bill with a smile.

"Holy smoke," the girl said as they were taken to their table, which was a blue velvet booth in the third row, center. "I can't believe this. Who are you? Are you really Rocky Stone's son?"

"Shit, no," he said. "All these guys are on the take and insecure. Greed and names is the game."

A waitress informed them they had to order now because there was no service during the performance. Garfield ordered a bottle of Dom Perignon.

"I'm impressed," the girl said after the waitress had left. "Is your name really Garfield?"

"Yeah, and yours?"

"Kathy Raines. Oh, I can't believe I'm sitting here. Oh, my God, look who's sitting in the row in front of us. It's Senator Godwin and the twins. Aren't they beautiful? And that man with them must be Senator Godwin's father—they look so alike. Aren't they handsome? And boy are they ever rich. I can't believe my eyes. Look, my hands are trembling. This is so exciting. Oh, wait until I tell the girls back in Omaha."

Garfield quickly removed the Abbott button, stood up, and walked to the Godwin booth. For the first time this evening he was glad he'd taken a shower and combed his long hair, which curled at the tips. He was wearing his ingratiating smile when he reached across their table and offered his hand to Randolph.

"Senator, please excuse this intrusion, but I just had to come shake your hand and wish you luck at the convention," Garfield said, his eyes gleaming.

Randolph accepted the handshake. "Well, thank you, son," he said, his voice conveying a finality to the greeting.

Garfield's eyes swept the table and noticed an amused glint in the eye of one of the twins. "I'm Garfield Stone. My father, Rocky, is a great admirer of yours. I came here looking for a chance to work for your campaign, whatever I can do."

There was a fleeting glimmer of interest in Randolph's eyes. "Well, Garfield, I don't really have a campaign, but if you're truly interested in helping out, give Blair Hopkins a call tomorrow. Suite thirty-six twelve. May I introduce my daughters, Eileen and Alicia, and my father, Mr. Henry Godwin."

Garfield enthusiastically shook hands with each one. "Thanks a million, Senator Godwin. I'll call him bright and early. This is going to be great. Wait until I tell my dad. He's going to be so proud of me."

"I know your father," Randolph said. "In fact, I've been to your home with Lew Spark. Is your father here?"

"No, he's on location in Italy, making another one of those great spaghetti Westerns."

Randolph laughed. "See you later, okay?"

"Yes, sir, and thanks again."

As Garfield returned to his table, the waitress was filling their champagne glasses. Then the lights dimmed and the orchestra began playing "I Want To Be Happy." Kathy grabbed his hand and let out a shrill squeal. "Oh, I'm so excited."

"Ladies and gentlemen," a voice said from offstage, "the Imperial Room proudly presents Miss Daisy Miller."

Green and blue spotlights followed her as she swept across the stage. She stopped in the middle to remove the microphone from its stand and did her characteristic fast little shuffle. The audience exploded in applause and whistles and screams.

She wore a full-length dress of sheer white silk that changed colors with the spotlights. It had a high Grecian waistline, with clinging layers of pleats falling in soft folds and long billowing sleeves with tight cuffs. The décolletage left little doubt that this was a lady still in top physical form.

After the opening number she extended one elegant arm to the audience, palms up, as though returning the ovation, and then proceeded to sing, belt, lament, whisper, wail, baby-talk, blast, and gyrate her way through a dozen popular standards, conveying a range of energy and vocal artistry that was simply astonishing. Between songs she talked and kidded with the audience, going from her crystalline diction and lavender vocal shading to guttural slangs and slurred words.

In introducing the Paul Madeira-Jimmy Dorsey classic "I'm Glad There Is You," she looked directly at Henry Godwin and said, "Baby, I'm gonna wrestle this one till it's taken all the falls it's got."

During the second act she paused to introduce "Our handsome senator from Nevada, Randolph Godwin, and his lovely family," then went into an original composition, "Miracles I've Seen." Finally, in a *coup de theatre* she launched into "Magical Times," a song she had written after she and Henry were reunited as lovers. At its conclusion the audience, as one, leapt to its feet for a rousing ovation that would have had her taking bows for an hour if she hadn't left the stage.

Kathy Raines was jumping up and down, squealing like a teenager at a rock concert. "Oh, I'm just drained," she gasped, squeezing his arm. "Isn't she absolutely divine?"

"Christ," he said, as they joined the others reluctantly leaving the room, "that's one foxy lady. She really freaked me out."

"Do you have a room in this hotel?" Kathy asked, pressing against him.

"Yeah, but you wouldn't like it. It's nouveau riche ghastly, with silver curtains and a gold quilted bed. I nearly puked when I saw it. Anyway, I've got to get to work early in the morning and there's not much time left."

"Well, okay," she pouted. "I was just trying to show my appreciation."

"Hey, don't bug me, okay?" he said, pulling away from her when they reached the casino. "See you later—maybe."

And he left her standing there with her mouth open and her soft pink tongue hanging out.

CHAPTER

11

They stood naked at the foot of the bed. Randolph took one last drag on the joint and handed it to Clorice, who went to the bathroom to flush it down the toilet.

He felt great, which was a miracle after a miserable dinner with that hostile brat, Ali. A real put-down artist. He was her father, damn it. Why couldn't she show a little respect? She sure knew how to take the wind out of his sails.

Clorice came back and stood before him. Randolph leaned forward and carefully examined her breasts.

"Has somebody mauled your tits?" he said, pinching her nipples. She gasped, clenching her teeth, and he said coolly, "A little pain makes it more erotic. Besides, slaves shouldn't complain. Theirs is to do or die for the master."

She assumed a servile expression and he reached down between her legs and grabbed a handful of hair and tender flesh. "Has anybody fucked your little pussy?"

"No, master."

He pulled hard and again she gasped but refrained from clenching her teeth.

"Slaves never lie," he said.

"Yes, master, somebody fucked my little pussy."

"That's more like it," he said, sliding a finger inside of her. "How does that feel, slave?"

"Delicious," she moaned, pushing against him, her hands reaching around to clutch his buttocks.

"Don't touch until given permission," he said, "or the master will whip your ass—you hear, slave?"

"Oh, master," she giggled, "you know all the right things to say."

Randolph laughed. "Okay, on your knees, let's get it on. I've got more important things to do than fuck around with a slave."

She took him in her mouth and he grabbed her head and pulled until he could feel his scrotum touching her chin.

"Baby, you give the best head in the world."

For a wild, compulsive moment Randolph wanted to drive his fist on top of her head with all his strength, or smash his knee into her chest. But the grass had taken hold, cooling the edges of the brain that sometimes drove him to violent outbursts as he neared orgasm. He laughed and held on to her head. In a moment it would be over and he could go to bed and enjoy a full night's sleep.

CHAPTER

12

Henry lay on his side in the large bed, leaning on an elbow to have a better view of Daisy's animated face as she told him about her European tour. He loved to watch the subtle changes in her eyes as she spoke, the gold flecks sending off sparks—it was like punctuation, he thought.

She paused and pulled his head down to plant a kiss on his chin. "You're not listening to me," she said. "You're just staring at me as though you lost something and think perhaps I have it hidden somewhere in my eyes."

He kissed her on the mouth, a long searching kiss. "Next to making love to you, my greatest pleasure in life is looking at you." He lowered his head against her breast. "You have no idea how much I miss you when you're away for long periods. It seems the older I get the worse it becomes. I get awfully depressed at times. I guess without you I'm just a lonely, empty old man."

"Oh, my, such self-pity," she teased. "You're certainly not an old man and there's no reason for you to be lonely or feel empty. Look at that marvelous son of yours. I saw him on TV this afternoon when he made that touching short speech at the airport. How proud you must be of him. And the lovely twins. Henry, you're a most fortunate man. I even understand there is a real possibility that Randolph will get the Vice-Presidential nomination. How can a man with all that going for him feel lonely or empty?"

"Oh, I don't suppose it's all that easy, but I do try hard."

Her words had brought him back to the dinner earlier that evening and the private discussion he'd had afterward with Rufus. When Henry had cautioned Rufus about premature optimism, Rufus had impatiently waved his remark aside. "There's nothing premature about it," he said. "We've got a lock on Abbott. We'd like to do it the easy way, by forcing the issue on delegate votes, but one way or the other, though, we'll make sure he comes across."

Henry had been as much shocked by the tone of voice as by the words. "That sounds ominous," he said.

"Henry, I'm going to the wall on this one. It's my last shot and it sure as hell ain't going to be a blank. There's no way the Republican Presidential candidate, whoever he may be, is leaving here without Randolph as his running mate. That's all I've got to say on it, but you've known me long enough to know I'm not blowing smoke."

That was fire he was blowing, Henry thought, as he listened to Daisy's heartbeat through the firm, warm mound of her breast.

"Perhaps you've started coasting," she was saying. "I know you've lost interest in some of the important work that kept you busy for so many years. Remember when I tried to retire six years ago? Bought that house in Carmel and we got to spend more time together? Well, I've never told you this, but without my work I began to feel like I was dying inside. So one day I thought, For Christ's sake, what are you doing out here trying to bake a cake and singing in the shower? Who are you kidding? That's not you. Get back out there in the real world where you belong. Go do it, baby. I sold the house and got the hell back to my work. It was the best decision of my life."

"Maybe I should start a singing career," he said. "Or I could learn to juggle and warm up your audience for you. You know, be your second banana. At least that way we'd be together all the time."

"Darling, you can travel with me as my lawyer-manager anytime you decide to make the move. I'd love it. But I'll tell you quite frankly, I don't think it'd change a damn thing. Loneliness comes from within. Henry, I think I know you better than anyone. You're disappointed with the way your life has turned out. You'd like to sneak back into the past, to reshape events, but it's all dust, and no amount of wishing will ever bring it back to life."

II
YESTERDAY

CHAPTER

13

They lay in the large bed in the upstairs bedroom, exhausted by their lovemaking, uncovered in the sweltering heat, the Mississippi air heavy with the sweet fragrance of jasmine and magnolia. Their hands were touching but their minds were lost in private worlds.

Suddenly Camilla sat up and took Henry's face in her hands, looking deep into his eyes. "I'm pregnant," she whispered.

He felt a quickening of his heartbeat and wondered what she could see in his eyes. "How long have you known?" he asked, his voice faltering. "I assume you're certain?"

"Nearly four months."

Henry sat bolt upright. "Four months! For God's sake, Cami, why?"

"I waited for the right moment," she said, her eyes still searching his. "I need to know how you really feel about it."

He reached for her, but she avoided his arms. "Let's talk this out," she said. "I'm keeping the child, whatever you say, and it's going to be born in San Francisco, as a white person, a member of the human race."

"Now, just a minute, one problem at a time," Henry said. "What makes you think I'm against keeping the child? Did you see the word *abortion* in my eyes just then? Well, if you did, you're nuts. Cami, what in hell's gotten into you?"

"I didn't like the look in your eyes."

"Oh, nonsense—what are you talking about?"

"I saw rejection, fear, confusion—"

"Come on," he interrupted, "what are you, a mind reader all of a sudden?"

"No, Henry, I'm only a pregnant nigger with a white baby in my belly and no husband."

Henry moved to the edge of the bed. "You look in my eyes in a dark room and tell me what I think, what my eyes say. That's a cute trick. You could make a fortune with your crystal ball."

She looked at him. "Well, ain't you afraid? Ain't you confused? Don't you wish I wasn't pregnant?"

Henry hesitated and she flew off the bed. There was fire in her eyes as she started dressing, moving furiously about the room.

"Where're you going?" Henry shouted, also starting to dress.

"Nigger Avenue in back of this mansion—where I belong."

Henry slipped into his trousers and jammed his feet in his shoes. "All right, so I'm confused, and a little angry you kept it from me for four months. And, yes, you're right. I can't say I'm overjoyed you're pregnant. Are you?"

"It's your child I'm carrying in my belly. That makes me happy even if . . ."

She never got to finish the sentence, for at that moment their words were drowned out by the heavy pounding of hooves coming up the road leading to the front of the house. Shots were fired, followed by rebel yells and coarse laughter. Henry sprang to the window. The road for as far as he could see was lined with riders wearing flowing white robes, their faces masked by high-pointed hoods. Many carried torches.

As they reached the portico of the antebellum mansion, seven men lined up their horses facing it while the others split up into two columns and rode down the paths on both sides of the house as though they were about to surround it. The seven men fired more shots and then the man in the middle, who was obviously the Klan leader, shouted for the General to come out.

"Stay here," Henry ordered. "I've got to get down there ahead of the General and get them the hell off this property."

"Be careful," she warned, but he was already out of the room. She could hear his footsteps down the hall and stairway, the front door slamming behind him, and then she saw him walk to the very edge of the portico's top step.

"What are you men doing here?" he asked in a firm voice. In the eerie dancing glow of the torches Henry could see their eyes shining behind the slits in their hoods.

"You don't much look like the General to me," the leader drawled. "Hey, this ole boy look ninety-four to you?" He laughed, and leaning forward in his saddle, he uncoiled a long black bullwhip.

"What are you doing here?" Henry repeated.

"Well, now," the leader said, "I'll tell you. We're lookin' for your young buck, that high-steppin', rapin', stealin' nigger bastard, Gabriel."

"What for—what has he done?" Henry asked.

The leader slowly recoiled the bullwhip. "Your nigger Gabriel Stowe stole the purse of a white woman when she fought back his filthy attempt to rape her," he said, pausing to let the gravity of the offense sink in before continuing. "We plan to make an example of that nigger rapist of yours. Now, where's he?"

"He's not here," Henry said. "He hasn't been here for a week or more."

Before the leader could respond, a rider came galloping up the path. "We've got somethin' for you boys back here," he shouted. "Follow me."

Without another word, they followed him at a full gallop, with rebel yells and more shooting.

Henry ran back to his room and Camilla threw herself into his arms. He could feel her trembling against him and all he could think about was the General. What would he do when he saw that these men had dared invade his private domain? There was more shooting and shouting coming from the back of the house. Henry and Camilla ran to a back bedroom that afforded a view of the Stowes' cottage. The men had it surrounded.

"My God, what are they going to do?" Camilla cried.

"They're looking for your brother, Gabriel. They'll go away when they see he's not here."

A woman screamed and Camilla's eyes went wild. Henry's grip around her waist tightened. "Let go of me!" she screamed. "What are they doing to my momma?"

There were more piercing screams from the cottage, followed by a frightened bellow from Camilla's father, Thaddeus Stowe, and whoops of shrill laughter as one of the riders who had brought his horse right up to the opened door of the cottage suddenly galloped away, dragging Thaddeus behind him. Thaddeus's hands were tied behind his back, the rope pulling him wound around his feet, his head bouncing every time it hit a rock or tree root. Camilla's mother, Alva, came running after Thaddeus, screaming hysterically.

The leader came riding up, his whip cutting into Alva's back, knocking her down. She scrambled to her feet and continued her pursuit of Thaddeus, who was being dragged in a circle around a large clump of oak trees.

Henry was transfixed at the window, the spectacle below holding him spellbound in horror. Camilla let out another shriek and broke out of his arms, running from the room.

Henry swore and turned from the window. As he ran from the room, he heard the leader shout, "All right, tie 'em to them trees over there. Let's get organized around here."

Camilla burst across the yard, shrieking wildly at the hooded men, her arms outstretched as she tried to reach her mother. A Klansman grabbed her and cried, "Lookit here, boys. Who wants a fancy piece of nigger ass? Anybody in favor step in line behind me."

Henry waded with flailing arms into the group of men gathering around Camilla. He could see her, kicking her legs and jerking her arms, fighting to her last ounce of strength.

Just then Henry felt something explode against the side of his head and he pitched forward on his hands and knees. He turned his head, blinked with pain, and saw the blur of a big yellow boot just as it caught him in the chest, flipping him over on his back, his head bouncing off the ground. He tried to raise his head, to look up beyond the yellow boot, but there was no strength in his neck.

"Hey, nigger lover," the owner of the yellow boots shouted. "I'm gonna reshape your pecker and give you a new set of balls."

The boot came down hard into his groin, and he felt the heel grinding into his scrotum.

"Lookit here," yellow boots shouted, "this ole boy's cryin'."

Henry fought to sit up and there was another explosion against the side of his head and he blacked out.

Later, as Henry regained his senses, he saw Camilla lying unconscious not more than ten feet away from him. Her clothes had been torn from her body. He tried to move but he couldn't. All he could do was turn his head slightly so that he could see Alva and Thaddeus, both of whom were tied to trees. The Klan leader, who had dismounted, was poking them with a long sharp stick. Standing next to him was a Klansman holding a hunting knife.

"Okay, you fuckin' niggers," the leader said, poking each in turn with the stick. "Every thirty seconds one of you's goin' to lose a finger until you tell me where Gabriel's hidin'."

"But, I told you, sir, we don't know," Thaddeus cried hoarsely. "The boy's been gone a week."

"Then we'll get to other things," he said, poking the stick into Thaddeus's eye. "Start with the black bitch."

Alva's mouth was open but no sound was coming from her throat.

Only the whites of her eyes shone in the eerie light. Henry saw the movement of the knife and the quick spurt of blood. "Who wants the first souvenir?"

"Not me," one ghoul shouted. "I'm waitin' for a tit."

Henry closed his eyes. "Merciful God," he intoned.

"Hold up there a minute," another ghoul shouted. "See what I've got here." He reached under his robe and pulled out a large corkscrew. "I'll open this nigger up for you." Moving quickly to Thaddeus, he began twisting it into his thigh while the others gathered curiously around to watch. "That's a dandy idea," the leader said. The shrieks tore from Thaddeus's throat until Henry wished he could put his friend out of his misery.

The ghoul jerked out the corkscrew and another asked if he could try it on the nigger bitch. Already some ghouls were preparing funeral pyres. Henry made one final effort to get to his feet, getting as far as a sitting position. It was then that he saw the General hobbling down the path, using two shotguns as canes. Henry tried to stand up, to signal the General to give him one of the shotguns, but his head started spinning and he knew that he was going to pass out again. His body twisted to one side and he tried to break the fall with his hands but fell on his face just as the first explosion came from the direction of the path.

Sometime in the night he felt cool water on his face and opened his eyes to find Moses Grimes, who had been Thaddeus's young assistant, sitting beside his bed. There was a strong scent of burnt flesh in the humid air, and it all came rushing back to him like a horrible dream.

"How's the General?" he asked, trying to sit up. The pain in his groin was so intense that perspiration broke out all over his body.

"Now, don't fret yourself," Moses said, his broad forehead covered with huge beads of perspiration.

Henry fell back on the pillow and closed his eyes. Suddenly he lurched up again. "Where's Cami?" But the effort was more than his body could sustain and he lost consciousness again.

14

With the wind a living force that flattened skin against bone and whipped fiercely at his clothing, Henry Godwin, his eyes protected by goggles and his tall frame hunched over his motorcycle, sped along country lanes, leaving great billowing clouds of dust in his wake, and floated over hardtop, the tires whirring, his eyes narrowed as he maneuvered around dangerous chuckholes.

He stopped at late dusk when he could no longer see the chuckholes to eat his one meal of the day in a small-town roadside diner or an obscure restaurant on the outskirts of a large city. He avoided human contact as much as possible. After his meal, he would ride out of town and find a spot to sleep a mile or so from the main road. He slept under the stars, wrapped in a wool blanket, fully dressed except for his boots.

Almost every night, before going to sleep, he would take out a small leather case in which he kept three pictures. The first was a snapshot of his mother taken on his ninth birthday, only days before her death. The sad, sweet smile and the haunted look in her deepset eyes reminded him nightly of the agony she must have endured before that final desperate moment.

Although his mother's suicide was never mentioned by anyone in the Godwin household, Henry had known even as a young child that she had never recovered from his father's accidental death when Henry was only three. Sometimes after awakening from the recurring nightmare that haunted him for many years after her death, he would run downstairs to look again at the large oil painting of his mother that hung over the mantel. But no matter how often he looked at the painting or the snapshot, he always had trouble recalling her features in his mind's eye. His memory of her was more sensory than visual. He remembered her fragrance and tenderness, her laughter, the feel of her warm lips on his, the softness of her voice, the touch of her hand on his cheek.

Also in the leather case was a daguerreotype of the General astride his legendary stallion, Black Lightning, which had been taken during the siege of Vicksburg. Henry loved to study the strong handsome face with its piercing dark eyes, stubborn jawline, and straight aristocratic nose. The expression was of such implacable determination that it was startling to realize that when the picture was taken the General had known that the battle was lost. It could have been the picture of a young prince on the way to his coronation.

Henry was proud of his paternal grandfather. Although General Randolph Harrison Godwin had failed to save Vicksburg from the hordes of Ulysses S. Grant, he had managed to negotiate the release of twenty thousand Confederate prisoners of war before surrendering the city.

The General's name was legend in Mississippi. There was a bronze statue of him astride Black Lightning at the entrance to the Vicksburg National Military Park. And Henry had delighted in the General's renown. In his day the Klan wouldn't have dared invade his privacy, but times had changed. Most of the people who had admired him were dead. He was a hero to Henry, but to Klansmen he was now a powerless old relic, waiting for death.

For many years after Henry's mother's death the General was the most important person in his life. They would sit on the back porch swing, the old man with his bourbon and huge cigar, the boy with lemonade, and talk endlessly. They never seemed to run out of conversation. They played chess, horseshoes, fished and hunted, and went horseback riding on the bluffs overlooking the Mississippi. In the evening at bedtime the General sat by Henry's bed and, while again sipping on his bourbon and puffing on his cigar, would vividly describe the military strategy of the great battles in the War Between the States and what life had been like for him as a boy in the antebellum South.

The General had lived through the golden age of the South and through the agony of its demise. He had wielded great power over men, black and white, and his decisions had meant the difference between life and death for many of them. There was something about that kind of raw power that excited the young boy.

But as Henry had grown older, his attention had gradually shifted to Camilla, whose skin was not black like that of her father, Thaddeus, but a light bronze, her eyes deep emeralds flecked with gold. Her hair was auburn, glossy and straight, reaching halfway down her back, her lips were full and inviting, and her nose as delicate as Dresden china. Many thought there was a white man in the woodpile, but since her mother, Alva, was probably a quadroon, old Thaddeus, thirty years her senior, could have been the father, though Camilla's brother, Gabriel, also light-skinned, had distinct Negroid features.

The last picture in the leather case was a snapshot of Camilla and Henry taken that spring at an amusement park in Vicksburg. Henry was standing behind her, his arms around her slim waist, pulling her against him.

He had been fourteen when he first realized that Camilla, who was a year younger, was no longer a silly little girl. The sight of her breasts pressing against her thin cotton dress made him feel funny inside. Sometimes when she rode behind him on Old Baldy, Thaddeus's plow-horse that also doubled as Henry's riding horse, she held on tightly to his waist as they jounced up and down, and the pressure of her breasts against his back made his penis stand straight up. The sensation made his cheeks burn with embarrassment.

It was not that he was a complete innocent. The General was always talking about the beauty of a well-turned ankle and perky ass. Henry had caught the General with his hand inside Alva's dress, fondling her breasts, and whispering in her ear. She had giggled, her white teeth flashing, her eyes sparkling with a strange light, the corners of her mouth curving in pleasure.

Once he had heard the General say, "My God, woman, I feel something stirring," and at the time he had his hand up between her legs.

"Lawdy," Alva had laughed, "ain't you the dreamer, though."

"I mean it, woman," he had said, his voice growing strangely hoarse, his hand moving deeper between her legs.

Her head had fallen back as she leaned against him. "Oh, General," she moaned, "you is as horny as the devil hisself." She kissed his ear and he pressed her hand against the front of his trousers.

"Feel it," he cried.

"Oh, sweet Jesus, I swear that gristle of yours ain't never gonna quit."

Then the General had seen Henry, and instead of being embarrassed, he had winked at the boy. "This old gal's been trying to rape me for years," he said, removing his hand from between her legs. "She says old Thaddeus is all worn out in that department."

"Now, if that ain't the Lawd's truth," Alva laughed. "His gristle's sure 'nuff dead, and that ain't no way to treat a lively woman."

Not long after this incident, when Henry and Camilla were riding Old Baldy, her hands had slipped down against his erect penis and he had experienced a strange burning sensation in his loins. For a moment he thought he was going to wet his pants. Then his penis began to throb and he had to grit his teeth to keep from grabbing himself and moaning out loud.

The two-cylinder tandem bike performed admirably and he found the experience exhilarating, except for the flat tires, which happened far too often on gravel, washboard roads. With gas stations few and far between on those long western stretches, he began carrying an extra five-gallon can of fuel, which he secured in the sidecar's passenger seat.

At that very moment Camilla was somewhere over the distant horizon. Of that he was certain. Word of her departure from Vicksburg had flowed back to Moses Grimes. Camilla had taken a bus to Jackson and the train from there to Memphis. That was all Henry knew. Except that she had taken Alva's paltry savings and left in the night. Some of her clothes, the ones Henry had bought her, and Alva's old cardboard suitcase were gone. He wondered what she was doing. How was she providing for herself and protecting their unborn child? He had no doubt that she was in San Francisco. That was the only city she had ever talked about. It was her dream city, a city without rednecks and Kluxers, where a beautiful octoroon girl could pass for white without raising an eyebrow. It was a city teeming with speakeasies and night-clubs, movie theaters and vaudeville houses, where a pretty girl with a voice could make her mark in the world.

When he closed his eyes that evening, he was transported back to the old fishing hole the summer he turned fifteen. That was the first time they had made love, two virgins exploring undreamed-of pleasures.

That fall Henry had matriculated at Virginia Military Institute, the General's and his father's alma mater. He loved the General's war stories, but he found little pleasure in the strict discipline of a military college. By the middle of the first semester he decided to leave at the end of the year. He then turned his attention to what appealed to him: reading, chess, and wrestling, the latter because he wanted to put muscles on his six-foot skeleton. Camilla had called him Daddy Long-legs. He kept away from girls, wrote to Camilla every other day, and sent her books to read. Just prior to Christmas vacation he discovered Clarence Darrow and resolved to become a lawyer.

That next summer, while they were out riding along the bluffs, the General fell off his horse and broke both legs. His recovery was slow. It was a year before he could hobble around on crutches. That year in bed took its toll. He was pale and suffered from dizzy spells. The timbre of his voice had lost its intensity. He spent most of his days sitting in a wicker rocking chair on the back porch staring off into space.

When Henry told the General he had quit VMI and was enrolling at a small law college in Jackson, the General had shrugged and said simply, "Do as you wish, it's your life."

Their old intimacy was slipping away and Henry was at a loss to do anything about it.

But Jackson was only about forty miles from home, which meant that Henry could be with Camilla every weekend. It was during his first semester in law school that he bought the tandem motorcycle to facilitate his commuting. On weekends, with Camilla in the sidecar, they roared down country roads at blinding speeds, her hair flying in the wind.

Thaddeus and Alva never said anything to discourage their romance, but some of the white neighbors were furious at the liaison and the word soon spread to Vicksburg.

It was left to Aunt Caroline, the General's only living daughter, to speak to Henry. Still a spinster at forty-six, Aunt Caroline was a thin, long-legged woman with anxious eyes and a quick nervous smile. Her greatest pleasures in life seemed to be in helping those less fortunate and irritating politicians. She was a self-appointed social worker, a bleeding-heart busybody in the opinion of the critics she ignored as she went about devoting her boundless energy to trying to improve the beastly conditions in orphanages and poor houses throughout Mississippi.

Alarmed by the talk in town, Aunt Caroline had turned her anxious eyes on Henry and got directly to the point. "Henry, I realize that sexual relations between a white man and a colored woman is tolerated when kept in its place, but you're flaunting it."

"But she's just as white as I am," Henry protested. "Besides, I love her."

"My God, Henry, where is your God-given common sense? What will you do if she gets pregnant?"

Henry shrugged. "Marry her and leave the South. She can pass for white anywhere in the world where they don't know she has Negro blood."

"What about her speech and manners and habits and all those other little significant details?"

Henry's eyes flashed angrily. "You don't know what you're talking about. In the past three years she's educated herself to the point where she knows more about literature than I do. She loves Edna St. Vincent Millay and Emily Dickinson, and she's read all of Henry James."

"Now, don't get on your high horse," she said, her voice rising. "I don't care if she can recite Milton's *Paradise Lost*. It wouldn't change the situation one iota. Flaunting your relationship is foolhardy. I'm sure you're aware the Klan is again on the rise and getting more violent all the time, with lynchings now practically every week."

The attack came only a few months later, one week after Henry's graduation from law school.

The General was dead. Alva and Thaddeus were dead. And Camilla was gone. At first light the morning after the attack, Henry and Moses had built a pine box and buried the charred remains of Thaddeus and Alva Stowe in the Godwin cemetery. Then they had knelt and Henry had read from Alva's Bible the passages that had given her and Thaddeus comfort in life. The pages were frayed and slick from use. Then he had said a prayer of his own. When he stood up, he saw that most of the Negroes who worked on the plantation were kneeling behind him, their heads bowed in silent prayer. Bent over with pain caused by the enormous swelling of his scrotum, Henry cautiously made his way back to the house.

The General's body lay on his bed with a white sheet over it. Moses' wife, Holly, was sitting by the bed, reading from her Bible. Henry reached down and pulled the sheet from the General's face. It looked peaceful in death. "After the General started shooting, everybody went crazy," Moses told him. "They all emptied their guns at him and rode out of there like the devil was at their heels." Although many bullets had pierced the General's body, Henry was grateful that none had touched his head.

Then Aunt Caroline had arrived, followed by Dr. Olin Botts, who had been the General's doctor for forty years. While Aunt Caroline made arrangements with a mortuary, Dr. Botts took Henry to his bedroom for an examination.

"Henry, I know this is a terrible day for more bad news, but I think you have a right to know where you stand," Dr. Botts said, as he jotted down notes on a pad. "Your head wound is not too serious. You may have occasional double vision for a few days, but it'll clear up. The problem's with your testes. Both are badly ruptured. I don't think there's much residual functioning testicular tissue remaining. I've seen a few stompings in my day, but this is probably the worst."

"Are you saying I've been castrated?"

"Not exactly, Henry," he said, sitting on the edge of the bed. "The testes have two functions, one hormonal and the other the production of sperm. Now you're a fairly well matured young man, so the hormonal is not much of a factor. As to the manufacture of sperm, I feel that's quite dubious."

"You mean I'm going to be sterile?"

"I'd say yes, but you'll be able to have sex. No problem there. You'll have an ejaculation, but there just won't be any sperm in the semen fluid."

Henry started to dress but Dr. Botts stopped him. "I want you in bed for at least a week. Give the swelling a chance to subside. You may go to the funeral, but otherwise I want you in bed."

After Dr. Botts had left, Aunt Caroline came into the room carrying a large bouquet of red roses, which she arranged in a white china vase. She placed them on a table next to his bed and leaned over to kiss his cheek.

"You poor boy, I'm so sorry," and her big anxious eyes were moist with tears. "What an ordeal it must have been."

Henry wanted to scream, to beat his fist against the wall, to leap from the bed and run berserk through the house, but he gritted his teeth and lay in stony silence, listening to the soft weeping of his aunt.

She rubbed at her eyes with a man's handkerchief and loudly blew her nose. "I promised myself I wouldn't do this," she said, sitting next to the bed. "But there's something I must say to you. I don't know what's going on in your head right now—God knows you're bearing a heavy burden—but I want to caution you not to do anything foolhardy in the heat of the moment."

"Like what?"

"Don't raise a legal fuss about this. Sheriff Turner and most of his deputies are Kluxers. The leader is Albert Pike and the way it looks he's just about got the whole county terrified. The boldness with which they invaded the General's sanctuary only goes to show how powerful and reckless they've become. No one dares stand in their way."

Henry nodded, his mind inflamed with the disclosure that Albert Pike was the leader. Now that he had heard the name, he realized there had been something familiar about the leader's voice. He was positive that his aunt was absolutely correct. Pike owned the biggest feed and grain store in Vicksburg and knew everybody in the county on a first name basis. He was a tall, gaunt man with sunken cheeks, a hawk nose, fishy blue eyes, jug ears, and a thin, cruel mouth. Henry had never liked him, but he had never thought of him as a man capable of such evil.

"Don't worry," Henry said, "the sheriff is the last person I'd trust."

The governor, whose father had commanded a battalion during the siege of Vicksburg, delivered the eulogy at the General's funeral, a moving oration that never once mentioned the nature of his death.

Through it all, Henry had stood with his face drained of color, his eyes stony, his jaws set firmly, and his hands clenched tightly at his side. Then suddenly his attention was caught by a movement in the valley far below the cemetery. His eyes narrowed as he focused on the figures of three riders moving in his direction. As they drew closer, his concentration grew even more intense, until finally he could discern their features. All three of them were craning their necks, trying to make out the mourners on the hilltop. Henry felt his gorge rising as he recognized Albert Pike and his two sons. They turned away and Henry redirected his attention to the governor.

Two days after the funeral, Henry was in the dining room for the reading of the General's will. The attorney skipped the usual legal preamble and said, "Here's what it boils down to. There's a bequest of five thousand dollars to the Stowes, a thousand dollars of which is to be set aside for Camilla. Miss Caroline is to receive twenty-five percent of the net profits of the estate, paid on a semiannual basis, and in the event of the sale of the real property, her share will be twenty-five percent of the proceeds. The remainder of the estate has been left to Henry, who retains complete control over it. All cash, stocks, and bonds, amounting to eighteen thousand dollars, and all personal effects, except for specific items listed in the will as bequeathed to Miss Caroline, are left to Henry to dispose of as he sees fit."

"I've already made a decision in this regard," Henry said. "I plan to leave here in a few days, and I'm turning over the house and land to Aunt Caroline."

"But you can't do that," Aunt Caroline cried. "It's your inheritance."

"Here's your chance to start your own orphanage," he said, gently touching her shoulder. "It's a large house. Do with it as you wish. Spend whatever is necessary to operate it. Use the balance for repairs and improvements. Buy modern equipment, and if there's still a profit, I'd like it to be distributed in bonuses to the sharecroppers."

"What about you, dear heart? Won't you need any money?"

"I have the cash bequest and I intend to earn my own living from now on."

The next morning, with Moses' help, Henry built a canvas enclosure for the bed of his Ford pickup. Then he removed the rear window so that he could crawl from the driver's seat into the back without having to leave the truck. That evening, after it was completed, he unlocked the General's gun cabinet and selected a Spencer carbine, one of a collection of rifles and handguns the General had not surrendered at Appomattox.

It used to be said of the Spencer carbine that Yankees loaded them on Sunday and shot all week. It was the best breechloader used in the war, with a rate of fire of up to twenty-one rounds per minute. Effective at four hundred yards, its .52-caliber ammunition made it an ugly weapon at close range. Sitting in the General's rocking chair, Henry cleaned and oiled the carbine, and then fresh-loaded a dozen cartridges, capping them with flat-headed lead slugs.

For the next five days Henry drove to town at daybreak and parked the truck directly across the street from Albert Pike's feed and grain store. Making sure there was no one about to see him, he would crawl through the window opening and then cover the hole with a piece of cardboard. Seated on an old mattress, he observed the activity at the feed store through a slit in the tarpaulin, taking careful notice of the routine followed by the Pikes in the course of the day. As the hours dragged by, he wondered how many of the farmers who traded there were actual Kluxers. How many had taken part in what had happened at his home?

On Saturday morning, the last day of his vigil, Henry carried a large package wrapped in old newspapers when he left his room. All day he sat on the mattress and thought of how he would do it.

He counted the people going in and out. By six thirty he knew that only Albert and his two sons remained in the store. He crawled back into the cab of the truck and looked up and down the deserted street. The store was in a warehouse district of town and Henry knew from his observations that no one came here after six o'clock. He also knew that the Pikes never left before seven. Having peeked through a back window three days running, he knew that they always got together in a back office, with Albert going over the day's accounts, while his boys amused themselves with a jug of corn liquor, passing it to their father for an occasional swig.

The scene when he came through the opened office door was exactly as he had pictured it those long nights he had slept with the carbine at his side. Albert was seated behind his desk, engrossed in his ledgers; George was slouched in a straight-back chair, with his yellow-booted feet on top of a corner of the desk, his chair tilted back, the jug covering the lower part of his face as he guzzled the liquor. Harry was standing next to him, his eyes on the jug, his hand reaching out for it.

"Pass the fuckin' ju—" was as far as Harry got before the first round smashed through his upper front teeth and splattered the back of his head against the wall. A fine mist of blood and bone and brain was gently settling on George when the second round struck him a half-inch above the right eyebrow and the top of his head disintegrated.

After the first shot, Albert Pike had screamed, "Hey!" and then when Henry was cranking the loading lever: "What the fuck's goin'—" That was as far as he got before George was hit.

"Retribution," Henry said in answer to Pike's unfinished question.

"Oh, Christ," Albert cried, jumping to his feet.

The slug smashed into his belt buckle, catapulting him over his chair, his head banging against the wall. He huddled on the floor, his hands clutching his stomach, the blood squeezing through his fingers. His eyes were glazing as he looked up at Henry, who had come around the desk, his hand automatically cranking the loading lever.

Albert tried to speak but blood gushed out instead of words. Henry put the next round between his eyes, then turned and walked out of the office. A few feet away, he picked up the carbine's leather scabbard and carefully rewrapped the weapon. Still moving normally, he walked across the street to the truck and drove home, his mind going over every detail of the three executions. By the time he reached the house, the tightness that had been in his chest all that week was gone. He found he could again take a deep breath without choking on it.

Early the next morning, Henry Godwin packed a few belongings in the sidecar of his motorcycle, including the General's saber, decorations, gray felt Confederate hat, and the Spencer carbine, and with eighteen thousand dollars in a money belt and the General's VMI class ring on his little finger, he drove down the gravel path to the state highway junction, where he turned west, slowing down to take one final look at that gray mausoleum of a mansion in the cemetery of his youth.

15

Around noon one day, a few miles west of Elko, Nevada, while riding through desert country of sagebrush and greasewood, with a merciless sun beating down and the narrow paved road shimmering in heat waves, Henry came upon an old man sitting by the road with a gray animal lying at his side.

The moment Henry spotted the old man, he began slowing down, trying to decide whether he needed help. From a distance, at least, the old man was sitting so still he appeared to be dead. His head was lowered and his arms hung loosely at his sides. Then Henry saw one arm move, the hand beginning to stroke the animal, which remained motionless. The old man seemed unaware of the approaching motorcycle. Even the terrible noise in that soundless desert failed to catch his attention. His head slowly came up, but he just stared straight ahead at the distant hills.

Henry shifted the bike into neutral and gunned the engine, hoping that the loud blast would evoke a response, but the man never moved. Henry coasted and brought the bike to a stop in front of the old man.

"Good morning," Henry said, removing his goggles and wiping the dust from his face with a soiled handkerchief.

"Howdy, stranger," the old man said, still not moving.

"Are you all right?" Henry asked, coming around the bike for a closer inspection.

The old man looked up at him and Henry was shocked by the intensely deep blue eyes in a face that seemed a hundred years old. Long years under a fierce sun had turned the skin to baked leather.

"I'm fine and dandy," he said, tears suddenly welling in those remarkable eyes. "It's Bessie, here," he said, pointing to what Henry suddenly realized was a dead burro. "She got snake bit and swelled up like a toad." He paused to remove his weather-beaten cowboy hat to scratch the top of his head. He had a full head of snow-white hair that reached down to his shoulders, but except for a couple days' white stubble, he was clean shaven.

"Dang old fool stepped into a nest of rattlers," he said, slapping his hat angrily against the ground. "A feller would have thought she'd knowed better after all them years in the desert."

His left hand was still absently stroking the burro's dusty hide as he talked. "Had to use my hunting knife on her—had to take her out of her misery." He paused again, putting his hat back on his head, his hand still stroking the dead burro. "I knowed she trusted me. The old gal and me have been a team since I come down from Nome in aught two. We prospected the big strikes in Tonopah, Goldfield, Rawhide, Rhyolite, Bullfrog—all them rich places—and dang near all the ridges of this whole dang state, and she never once stepped into a nest of snakes. I reckon her eyesight was getting poorly."

The old man got slowly to his feet. "I knowed she trusted me. Looked me right in the eye with them big sad eyes of hers when I stuck the knife into her heart. She didn't make a sound. Just pissed and toppled over." The tears were running into the dark creases of his face, making them look slick and deeper, and for a moment it seemed like he was going to lose control of himself, but suddenly he turned to look at the dead burro. "Dang your ornery hide, Bessie," he cried angrily. "Dang old fool was not only blind but had no sense to boot."

He looked at Henry and tried to smile. "Son, will you help me bury her proper? Had to drag her a piece and I'm plumb tuckered out."

"But why can't you just leave her here?" Henry asked.

The old man's blue eyes blinked in astonishment. "Why, son, me and Bessie, as I told you, been a team all these years and prospected all over creation. No buzzard's gonna feast on her bones. Not while I'm alive and kicking."

"If you have a shovel, I'd be proud to help," Henry said.

The old man handed Henry a shovel with the handle broken off in the middle and said, "Now you see why I need help."

By the time Henry got the hole dug through that sun-baked rocky ground, his back felt broken and his hands were bleeding from a half-dozen blisters. Picking up the burro by its legs, they lowered it gently into the hole. The old man insisted on closing the grave. It was only then that Henry noticed that he had a wooden leg. Henry had been so intrigued by those intense eyes in that ancient face that he had not really looked at the rest of the old man.

The old man stood over the grave a moment, his hat in his hands, his lips moving silently, and there were more tears before he finally slapped his hat on top of his head and turned away from the grave.

"I'm mighty grateful to you, son," he said, sitting down and pulling out a bag of tobacco, offering it to Henry. "Smoke?" he asked.

"Haven't picked up the habit yet," Henry said, declining the offer.

The old man smiled and deftly rolled a cigarette with one hand, licked the paper, and tucked the bag back in his shirt pocket. "Keeps a man peaceful on lonely nights," he said, lighting up. "Been smoking nigh on seventy-five years. Picked up the habit when I was seven."

"That was awfully young."

"Seemed like the proper thing to do at the time and I never regretted it."

Henry smiled. "I'm Henry Godwin."

"Walt Yuland, but everybody calls me Yulee. Glad to make your acquaintance, young feller."

"Can I offer you a lift?" Henry asked, moving toward the motorcycle.

"How far you going, son?"

"San Francisco."

"I'd be plumb grateful for a ride to Reno. Mean to get myself a grubstake and do a little prospecting around Virginny."

"You mean Virginia City? I thought that had been mined out years ago."

Yulee chuckled. "There are thousands of ridges not yet prospected. All I need is a burro and enough grub for a few months. I got me a special place I been meaning to look at since I was in Virginny in sixty-one."

While they were talking Henry was busily trying to make room for the old man in the sidecar. He had removed the gas can and was wondering what to do with it. "How far to the next gasoline station?" he asked, wondering if he could abandon the extra gasoline.

"Winnemucca, I think—quite a piece down the road."

Henry looked at his map and figured that it was about a hundred and fifty miles. If he filled the gas tank, he would have enough to get there.

"I can hold the can in my lap," Yulee said. "No problem at all."

"Not on your life," Henry said as he filled the tank and then poured the rest of the gasoline in the sand before tossing the empty can behind a sagebrush bush.

Yulee stepped into the sidecar with his good leg first, and with Henry supporting him swung his wooden leg inside without too much trouble.

"Been hopping around on this wooden stick since Nome," he said. "Kinda feels like part of me now."

Once settled in the seat, he took an extra pair of goggles Henry handed him and chuckled happily as Henry cranked the motor into life and they took off with a great burst of speed.

They made Winnemucca before sunset, and when Henry stopped in front of a cafe, Yulee stayed in the sidecar.

"Aren't you coming in?" Henry asked, coming around to open the door.

Yulee smiled. "Flat busted broke," he said. "Flatter than a sourdough's pancake. Not only that, but I left all my gear and grub up in the hills so I could drag old Bessie for a decent burial."

Henry was astounded. "You mean you actually dragged that dead burro all those miles."

"It was that or dig a hole with a short shovel. My back ain't what it used to be. I found the pulling a dangsight easier."

Henry shook his head in amazement. "It would be my pleasure to have your company for dinner."

Yulee grinned and gave Henry his hand. "Thanks, pardner. I never turned down a square meal in my life."

During dinner Henry listened, enthralled, while the old man talked about his adventures in the Klondike in 1897, and how he and his partner had climbed the legendary Chilkoot Pass twenty-two times to backpack two tons of supplies thirty miles to Lake Bennett. There they had chopped down trees and whipsawed lumber to make their own boat, which they had sailed six hundred miles up the Yukon River to Dawson City, safely navigating the treacherous White Horse Rapids in which scores had lost their lives that year.

His deep blue eyes kept smiling as he talked and Henry took a strong liking to him. He reminded Henry of drawings and photographs he had seen of old buffalo hunters. He looked like he had spent his whole life under the sun and stars and had probably fought Indians while the General was fighting Yankees.

As it turned out, Yulee had joined the gold rush at twelve after his family had been wiped out by Apaches. Later he had been a scout in campaigns against Geronimo in New Mexico and Arizona and was there when the Apache chief was captured by General Crook. He first struck it rich in Virginia City, but the money—over eighty thousand dollars—had slipped through his fingers faster than he could dig it out of the earth.

"You should have held on to it," Henry said.

"What for, son?" he asked. "So I could live in one of them fancy houses in San Francisco and dress up like them mucky-mucks?" He chuckled. "For me, looking for gold is like trying to seduce an ornery woman dressed in her Sunday finery. The digging and the getting is a dangsight more fun than the keeping."

They laughed and Henry asked him if he would like a drink of hard liquor. "Never turned down a free drink either," he said.

After the waiter brought them whiskey in coffee cups, Yulee downed his in one gulp and Henry ordered another. "Drank my share in my day, including that fancy warm piss they call champagne. I had me a gal in Dawson, a dance hall gal—oh, I was a dancing fool in them days—and we danced for three days and three nights, catching little catnaps here and there, and we drank a boatload of that warm piss, and when it was over somebody with nothing better to do added it all up and it came to fourteen thousand dollars." He waited to let that sink in, his eyes twinkling. "Tell you something else, young feller—I don't regret a nickel of it. When you cash in your last chip, it's not how much money you got in the bank that counts—it's whether you got what you wanted when you was around. That's been my motto all my life. I'm not one of them worrywarts about the future. I take her as she comes, good and bad, and I've had my share of both."

Henry motioned to the waiter to refill the old man's cup. Yulee took another gulp and exclaimed, "Dang, don't that hit the spot, though. I wish old Bessie was here to enjoy this good red-eye with us. She favored a little tipple now and then."

By the time Henry got Yulee into a blanket a few miles out of town, the old man was feeling no pain. Henry slept fitfully that night. Every time he closed his eyes, Camilla's disembodied face came floating at him in the darkness, and he would come awake with a start. Then it was the General hobbling down the path with the two shotguns. Suddenly he sat up and scratched his head. Today, July 2, was his eighteenth birthday. He lay back and stared at the dawning light on the horizon.

Yulee had made a strong impression on him. There were moments when the old man had turned his head a certain way or made a particular gesture that reminded him of the General again. It had given him an odd sensation, a feeling of emptiness in the pit of his stomach. He regretted not having been closer to the General in the last few years.

The ride to Reno was uneventful: more desert, the same sagebrush and greasewood, the same bare mountains in the distance. A searing wind came up in the afternoon and tumbleweed rolled across the desert floor like a herd of strange prehistoric creatures.

Yulee was quiet, his blue eyes contemplative when he looked at Henry. "That dang fool Bessie," Henry heard him say a few times, but it was impossible to carry on a conversation over the roar of the engine and the wind buzzing in their ears.

For the first time since he had left Vicksburg, when they arrived in Reno, Henry went to a hotel. He shared a room with Yulee in a hostelry that was frequented by prospectors. It was to be their last night together, and after dinner Henry purchased a bottle of whiskey to take to their room.

Yulee sat on his bunk and grinned at Henry. "Mind if I take McKenzie off?" he said, pointing to his wooden leg.

"Not at all," Henry answered. "Can I help you?"

"I can do her fine. Got the hang of it by now. But it was tough going at first." It took him less than a minute to unstrap the leg and drop it on the floor. The stub of flesh just above the knee was a dark purplish, the skin callused and slick.

After a couple of drinks, Henry said, "You say you lost your leg in Nome?"

Yulee, who wore his hat while sitting up in bed, reached under it to scratch his head. "Yep, in the winter of aught one. Some coyotes calling themselves undersheriffs tried to jump my claim on Badger Creek. Now claim jumping was not all that uncommon in the Klondike, but the yellow legs kept the peace pretty good in Canada. But in Nome, which is in the good old U.S. of A., we had the law robbing us. This big politician from Washington, D.C.—a coyote by the name of McKenzie—made himself a deal with some of the boys in our national Congress and they let him pick his own prosecutor and judge for the territory. He set up a company and went into the business of buying claims from jumpers. Made them undersheriffs and sent them out to steal outright what they couldn't jump."

Yulee paused to roll a cigarette and gulp down his whiskey. "Well, one day while I was in town fetching supplies, five or six of his under-sheriffs seized my property, moved right into my cabin, making them-selves to home. The minute I come into sight, they start shooting. I remember it was snowing pretty good and I hid behind a tree until night. Then I crawled to the cabin and let her have five sticks of dynamite. I knowed I killed one of them coyotes, but the rest took off after me across the tundra. McKenzie put a price on my head—a thousand dollars 'dead or alive or in pieces,' was the way he put it. So he sends nine more coyotes to track me down. Then like a dang fool, I fell through ice in a creek and lost my rifle and dang near froze to death. It was midafternoon and I ran till night before I felt safe enough to light a fire and thaw myself out."

He paused and looked down at his stump. "When I took off my right boot, the leg was black as the ace of spades and I knowed it was a goner. So I take out my knife, the same one I did old Bessie in with, and hacked the dang thing off, stopping the bleeding with a handful of moss, a trick I learned in my Indian scouting days.

"I hear tell that one of them coyotes threw up when he found the leg and said, 'I'll go to hell before I chase a crazy man like that.' The others agreed they'd rather chase the devil home than continue after me. So they bring the leg to McKenzie for the reward and he tells them to stick it up their ass. It was my neck he wanted. I stayed in the tundra until spring, living on porcupine and melted snow."

"Why porcupine?" Henry asked in a hushed tone, so shaken by the story that he didn't know if he could trust his voice. He stood in awe of the old man, whose youthful eyes were shining in the dim light of the room.

"The porcupine is the only animal you can kill with a club. Meat's sweet and tender, too."

"I'm sorry to have to ask you this," Henry said, "but how could you amputate your own leg?"

"It wasn't so bad," he said. "It was still kind of numb from the freezing and I just separated it at the joint, worked the knife through the kneecap the way you do a calf or turkey leg. It was that or die of gangrene."

Henry stood up and removed his money belt. "How much of a grubstake do you need?"

Yulee looked at him warmly. "I could do her for a spell with two or three hundred. I'd cut you in for fifty percent of the claim. I knowed there's gold and silver in that ridge. All I need is a little luck."

Henry handed him five hundred dollars. "Here, this should keep you going a spell longer. Luck, as I understand it, usually takes a pretty strong effort."

"Okay, pard, put her there," Yulee cried. "We're gonna be rich as Guggenheimer before you know it. Where do I send your share?"

"I'll write to you here after I get settled in San Francisco. Now if you need more money, just drop me a line."

"Pard, you just made the best deal of your young life."

Henry smiled, wondering how many others had heard the same words, but he didn't care about the money. Helping that grand old man made him feel good inside, the way it had been with the General in the old days.

16

Leaning against the railing of the ferryboat, Henry Godwin stared in fascination as the majestic skyline of San Francisco began to emerge from its morning shroud of July fog. He felt like a child entranced by a Grimms' fairy tale. One moment it was a mythical city rising on a magic carpet of fleecy white clouds, and the next it was a monstrous hydra-headed pterodactyl escaping from the depthless bowels of the sea. Henry was not moving toward it—it was coming inexorably toward him.

Through the ornate portals of the Ferry Building, Henry plunged into the noonday traffic on Market Street, San Francisco's gargantuan umbilicus that diagonally bisects the city.

After the dreamlike, almost mystical excursion across the bay, the chaos and cacophony of Market Street provided a stimulating return to reality.

Henry found himself in the heart of the melee, maneuvering his motorcycle through the maddening concourse of clanging streetcars, four tracks running down the center of the spacious street, bumper-to-bumper motor vehicles, and swirling eddies of fearless pedestrians swarming into the street at every intersection. People cascaded out of office buildings, department stores, and restaurants: smartly attired matrons, with the obligatory hat and gloves; young girls with shingle bobs and pony bangs in short flapper dresses and rolled stockings, their faces powdered and rouged, their bright lipstick kissproof; the men in light summer suits, straw boaters, and two-toned white shoes.

Thrilled one moment at the metropolitan atmosphere of this strange city and frightened the next at the prospect of trying to find Camilla in a city of such confusing magnitude, Henry kept riding up and down Market Street, unable to decide on his next move.

By midafternoon, with the traffic thinned out, he gradually began to get the feel of the city. He ventured northward, where the streets rose steeply to hilltops. Everywhere he looked were the manifestations of great wealth: fashionable shops, luxury hotels, enormous mansions, great theaters, tall apartment houses, imposing office buildings.

Henry soon discovered that the heart of the city consisted of the nine blocks between Hyde Street on the west and Montgomery Street on the east. Northward of Market was the city's social and commercial life. Southward, known colloquially as "South of the Slot," was the other profile of St. Francis's city: endless rows of pawn shops, greasy-spoon restaurants, shabby lodging houses, dingy transient hotels, slum dwellings, factories, railroad yards, and warehouses stretching to the bay's edge.

That evening Henry settled into a two-room suite in a residential hotel at the corner of Market and Powell streets, having unknowingly taken residence in the Uptown Tenderloin, a district filled with bohemian restaurants, fancy bordellos, speakeasies, gambling dens, all-night groceries and pawn shops, vaudeville and burlesque houses. Seated at his bedroom window on the fourth floor, he watched the parade of celebrants with keen interest. Every few minutes a south-bound cable car would come to a metal-screeching halt as it arrived at the turntable directly under Henry's window. After unloading its pleasure-seeking passengers, the conductor and a grip man would dismount and push the car around until it faced north for its return trip to the top of Nob Hill.

They all seemed so happy, carefree, while he sat there wondering what he was doing in this crazy city. One night of obscene violence had totally destroyed his world.

Early the next morning, as soon as the stores opened in San Francisco, Henry retraced his steps to Union Square, the city's most exclusive shopping district, and selected what he felt was the most elegant men's clothier. Henry bought one ready-made suit and had his measurements taken for two more suits. The tailor's advice was that the cut of the cloth should minimize the broadness of Henry's shoulders and accentuate his slender hips and great height. The fabrics selected by Henry were somber in color, a disappointment to the tailor.

"But, monsieur," he politely intoned, "you are too young and handsome for such *gris couleurs*. What you need is a little more flair, some checks and stripes, light summer fabrics in the finest linens that reflect the hot rays *du soleil* instead of absorbing them. And, of course, it is most complimentary and *très chic.*"

Henry smiled and the tailor smiled too, realizing that the young man knew precisely what he wanted. Further persuasion would be futile. Henry bought shirts, again disappointing the tailor by refusing silk, and he selected a straw boater and two felt hats, one a pearl gray, the other black. He bought two pairs of low-cut black shoes and refused to consider spats, which were then the rage. He bought ties, socks, underwear—a complete wardrobe, spending close to five hundred dollars.

Returning to his hotel, he sat down and wrote a cheerful note to Yulee. In the afternoon he found the offices of the American Bar Association and made plans to take the California bar examination in nine weeks. He was told that he could study in the law library on the fourth floor of City Hall, which was only eight blocks from his hotel.

That evening, for the first time since he had left home, Henry telephoned Aunt Caroline.

"Oh, dear heart, you are the most precious human being on God's green earth," she exclaimed the moment she heard his voice. "I'm so proud of you I could burst into a million pieces. The General, God rest his sweet soul, would have decorated you for valor. Henry, I think I would have died from anxiety if you had not called and given me this opportunity to express what is in my heart. God bless you, Henry, for it was a courageous deed you did. How I envy you the satisfaction of that climactic moment."

Henry was quiet a moment, relishing the words of praise from his aunt, but when he spoke, he said, "Well, that's quite an elegant speech for someone off on a little vacation."

Aunt Caroline reacted quickly. "Silly boy, I was thanking you for the generous gift of Godwin Acres."

"How are things working out?"

"Splendidly, Henry, just splendidly. Moses and Holly are such treasures. The renovations will begin next week. I have decided to create a home for unwed mothers and an orphanage for their children until they are either capable of supporting them or have agreed after due consideration to put them up for adoption."

"Will it be interracial?"

"But, of course, my boy—what a silly question to ask."

"You're right," he said cheerfully. "I should have known better."

"Now, I have a little favor to ask of you. Would you mind terribly if we named it Heartbreak Haven?"

"By all means," Henry said. "The place is yours to do with as you see fit."

"Thank you."

"By the way," Henry said, "I hear you had a little trouble in town. Something about Albert Pike and his boys."

"Well, strange that you should ask. I planned to write you at the first opportunity about that terrible shooting at the feed store. It seems, according to our local gazette, that there was a power struggle in what they call the Invisible Empire. The conjecture is that they were confronted by at least a half-dozen men, being that the Pikes were always so well armed and alert and so on. It is quite a mystery, I can tell you."

"Any word about Cami?"

"None, I'm afraid."

Henry gave her his address and asked her to contact him immediately with any news of Camilla. "Well, I better say good night. Good luck with Heartbreak Haven."

"Happy birthday, dear heart. It is belated, I know, but may you find what is most precious to you. Good luck and I wish you all the happiness this cruel old world is capable of giving a deserving human being. Take gentle care of yourself and please keep in touch."

Henry lay awake a long time that night. It was a relief to know that he was not suspected in the death of the Pikes. In his mind he never thought of himself as having murdered three men. He felt Aunt Caroline had been right. The General would have been as proud of him as he would of any soldier who had successfully carried out a dangerous mission, delivering a crippling blow to the enemy. In Henry's thinking it had been an act of war, a retaliatory strike, planned as carefully as any military operation.

Henry settled down into a routine that took him to the law library early in the morning and kept him poring over books until late afternoon. After dinner he prowled the streets of San Francisco in search of Camilla. He carried an enlarged copy of the snapshot taken at the amusement park, with his own image blacked out, which he showed to bartenders in speakeasies, waiters, waitresses, store clerks, cabbies, bouncers in dime-a-dance joints, even traffic policemen and those walking beats. No one recognized the smiling girl in the photograph.

During his first year in San Francisco Henry passed the bar exams and opened a small office in a building on Powell Street. In the evening he began distributing copies of the photograph along with his business card. At first he offered a five-hundred-dollar reward, then he boosted it to a thousand. Still there was no result. Gradually, however, he began to realize that his card was bringing a small trickle of legal business his way. He hired a secretary, a thirty-year-old spinster, whom he called Mrs. M. because he found her Polish name almost impossible to pronounce.

He climbed all the steep hills. Telegraph Hill, now called Little Italy, and North Beach, part of the Latin Quarter, and Russian Hill, the haunt of the city's artists. Henry trudged through Fisherman's Wharf in the shank of the night, trying to explore every foot of the wild city.

As he sat in his office reading law books and attending to the minor legal problems of walk-ins, and as he walked the streets in anxiety and loneliness, a change was coming over him: an awakening to the importance of money. There was the wealth and power represented by Montgomery Street, with its great banks and ticker tapes connecting it to world markets. Money was in such profusion all around him that it seemed the easiest commodity to acquire. He was living in a society of insatiable consumption, with new products rolling off assembly lines and immediately snatched up by eager buyers.

The opulence of Nob Hill overwhelmed him. It had started out as a "Hill of Palaces" in the bonanza days of railroad and mining tycoons long before the turn of the century, and it had continued afterward as the exclusive domain of the city's wealthiest families.

Walking by the canopied entrances, with their shining brass plates, red-carpeted sidewalks, liveried doormen, Henry could only shake his head in wonder. He was seeing a kind of wealth he'd never before even dreamed possible.

CHAPTER

17

By the end of his first year in San Francisco, Henry knew as much about the city's geography as any native-born son and more about its nightlife than the city's oldest vice detective. His resolve to find Camilla and his child never faltered, for he remained convinced that she had found a niche somewhere in this jigsaw puzzle of a city. Returning to his hotel after long fruitless hours of searching, he would sit by his bedroom window, in a rocking chair that was almost identical to the General's (he had found it in an antique shop), and drink straight bourbon from a tall glass and smoke big cigars, his mind deep in thought, his eyes automatically scanning the street below for any sign of recognition. When the glass was empty and he felt drowsy enough to lie down, he would stare at the ceiling, with his arms folded behind his head, and wonder how much longer the search would continue. His life hung in abeyance, arrested as it were in suspended animation. He moved like a robot, bereft of personal desires, his only emotions acute anxiety and loneliness. Yet he knew deep down that someday he would turn a corner and there she would be, running into his arms with little cries of joy and tears of relief rolling down her lovely bronze cheeks. He lived for that moment.

One night several months later, while passing an alley on Mason Street, he heard a young girl calling for help. Without hesitation he plunged into the semidarkness of the alley and came upon two short men who had the girl pinned against a wall. One had a handful of her hair, pulling her head back, while the other was pressing a knife blade against her throat.

Henry was on top of them before they realized he was there. Grabbing both by the nape of the neck, one in each hand, he dug his fingers into their carotid arteries, cutting off the blood supply to their brains. The moment their legs began to buckle, he quickly banged their heads together. They collapsed unconscious at his feet.

The girl threw herself into Henry's arms, trying to burrow her body into his. It was then that he noticed the deep knife cut across her cheek. The blood was flowing down her neck and staining her low-cut blouse.

"I better get you to a hospital," he said as he tried to disentangle himself from her frantic embrace.

"Oh, no, please, take me to Etta's Place," she cried, still fiercely holding on to him.

"All right, if that's what you want," he said, "but you'll need a doctor to close that wound."

She let go of him and felt at the cut with her fingertips. "The cock-suckers were gonna croak me," she screamed.

"You're safe now," he said, pointing to the two limp figures on the ground.

The next thing he knew, the girl had pulled away and was grinding the spike heels of her red shoes into their faces. It took nearly all his strength to pull the kicking girl away.

Grabbing a firm hold of her arm, Henry led her out of the alley, hailed a cruising cab, and just said, "Etta's Place." All night people knew that address.

Before Prohibition Etta Gold had been the reigning queen of the Uptown Tenderloin. Her red plush and gilt bagnio had catered exclusively to the carriage trade. Those were the days when Mason Street, one block west of Powell, was the "White Way," made famous by Kelly's Place, Jimmy Stacks's cabaret, the later Poodle Dog, and Billy Lyon's saloon, the "Bucket of Blood." In its heyday it rivaled the Barbary Coast for sheer debauchery.

With the passing of the Volstead Act, Etta's husband, Freddie Mack, had suggested, on advice from certain competitors, that they close shop and move to a suburban home in San Mateo. The air, he tried to explain, was healthier there, but Etta's response, overheard by a few customers, became an overnight classic in the city's folklore. "Why, Freddie," she had exclaimed, "I'd rather be an electric light pole on Powell Street than own all of San Mateo County." Not long after this witticism, Freddie was found in an alley, his body filled full of lead. The new vice lord, Francesco Bacino, who sat atop Telegraph Hill, sent his son, Vince, who was still in his teens, and some of his boys to put the squeeze on Etta, cutting himself in for fifty percent of her take.

But Etta Gold, who stood nearly six feet tall in her stocking feet and carried no fewer than three hundred pounds of bones, gristle, muscles, and fat, was a born street fighter, as Henry was to learn before the night was out.

Seated in a ruby-red velvet chair that was a perfect match for her dyed hair, Etta listened to the girl's story with a smile on her flushed face. She burst out in raucous laughter when the girl told about her stomping of the men with her spike heels. Henry noticed that all of Etta's upper and lower front teeth were capped in gold.

"That's my baby," she said, reaching to slap the girl across the buttocks. "Now get Eunice to put something on that cut—we don't want you getting an infection, do we?"

Henry, who had remained standing just inside the door to Etta's private salon, finally spoke up. "Not good enough," he said. "The girl needs stitches and she needs them right now. I wanted to take her to a hospital but she insisted on coming back here. I agreed, with the proviso that she get immediate and competent medical attention."

"Hey, what the hell are you?" Etta demanded. "First you're Kid Galahad and now you're some goddamn boy scout. How I treat my gals is my own fucking business, and you can take that both ways," she laughed, delighted with her double entendre.

Henry reached in his pocket and handed her his business card.

"Well, what do you know," Etta chuckled. "Henry Godwin, a mouthpiece tough enough to put two of Bacino's hoods out of commission in ten seconds flat. Grab a chair and sit down, counselor. Me and you have business to talk over."

Henry remained standing by the door. "Not before that girl receives medical attention."

She waved her heavy arms in resignation. "You drive a hard bargain, counselor. Come sit next to me." She reached for a telephone on a table near her chair and placed a call to her doctor. "Now, you satisfied?"

Henry smiled and accepted her invitation to be seated.

"By Christ, I like your style, counselor," she said, ringing a small golden bell to summon her maid. "There ain't no bullshit in you at all."

A Negro girl no older than thirteen appeared in the doorway and Etta ordered Napoleon brandy and Cuban cigars. "Don't you know that Kim will do good business with that scar? Some freaks go crazy over deformities. The uglier it is, the more excited they become. Some johns can't get it up unless they see blood flowing. I've got some Nob Hill johns who won't suck a girl unless she's having her monthly." Her eyes never left Henry while she talked, and he felt that she was deliberately trying to shock him. His face remained impassive.

The child maid brought the brandy in large snifters and the cigars in a jade humidor. Etta, whose slanted eyes reminded him of a tomcat's, watched Henry in curious amusement as he thanked the girl. "By Christ, counselor, you ain't been in here five minutes and already I'm head over heels in love with you."

Henry quickly took a long sip of brandy.

"So you ain't interested," she said, lighting up a huge cigar. "Okay, if we can't be lovers, how about you being my counselor? I need a guy with balls enough to fight the fucking dagos who are trying to take over this town. They've got the booze market locked up tighter than a drum, and the gambling, and now they want my business, too. They killed my poor Freddie, who never harmed a hair on anybody's head, filled his body with over fifty slugs, dipped in garlic for good measure, and now they're cutting up my tricks. They're keeping their distance from me because without me there's no Etta's Place. I've got the carriage trade, and I know more about running this business than that whole bunch of fucking dagos.

"First, they wanted a fifty-fifty split, but now that's not good enough. They want to start a shakedown racket with their little cameras, catch my johns in flagrante delicto." She paused, her cat's eyes gleaming. "Thought I was just a dumb old broad, eh? I told them to go suck their grandmothers, those old wop bitches in black sacks who walk around Telegraph Hill like a bunch of crows. They really should be up telegraph poles, sitting on the electric wires, getting their dried-up old asses heated up. Then maybe they wouldn't raise such mean fuckers."

"Sounds like you're in a dangerous business," Henry said. "San Mateo is a peaceful community. Might not be a bad idea to reconsider Freddie's advice."

"So you know about that," she said, her face hardening. "No fucking ego-crazy wop is gonna drive me out of business. So that's where you come in, counselor. The fixer in this town, the Mister Big, is Mike Feeney, chairman of the Board of Supervisors, a fucking little dwarf of a mick with mean beady eyes. I've heard he not only owns this building, but most of the real estate used for vice purposes in this town. The rent is goddamn high, but you get police protection along with it. He's made a fortune and lives high off the hog with his nabob buddies on Nob Hill."

Henry kept sipping his brandy and wondering what this wild woman had in mind for him. Whatever it was, it would be dangerous and unpleasant, and, to use her term, *goddamn* expensive.

"Well, counselor," she said, giving him a sly glance, "when are you gonna give me a gander at that picture you've been flashing all over creation?"

The sudden turn in the conversation caught Henry by complete surprise. "You mean you've heard about it?"

"Heard about it?" she shouted. "You've become a fucking legend around here. There are more mug shots of her floating around here than old rubbers. Come on, let's see it again. There's something about that face that rings a bell."

Henry reluctantly handed her a copy of Camilla's picture and waited anxiously while Etta studied it, her cat's eyes narrowed to slits. "Oh, shit," she exclaimed, returning the picture. "I know her name—it's on the tip of my tongue, but I can't get it out." Angrily, she rang the bell and ordered two more brandies.

"You're not trying to say that you think she's"—he hesitated, blood rushing to his face—"that she's in your line of work?"

Etta leaned back in the chair and closed her eyes. It was strange, Henry thought, how different she looked with her eyes shut—weaker, softer, more gentle, almost vulnerable, an idea that Henry swiftly discarded.

"You looking for yourself or a client?"

"Myself."

"Well, don't worry," she said, opening her eyes. "She ain't in this business, or I'd know about it. She'd be worth her weight in gold."

Henry visibly sighed and Etta laughed, giving him a coy glance. "Hell, counselor, I know people in all walks of life. All I'm saying is that I've seen her somewhere before, maybe in a different getup, and it'll come to me. Just be patient. Now, let's get down to cases."

"I was afraid of that," Henry said, laughing with relief, the weight that had been pressing on his chest suddenly gone.

"Here's what I want you to do. Check Feeney out, from top to bottom—find out exactly what he owns in this town. I'm sure he's using phony names and fronts, but he's a fucking cheap Irishman who wouldn't trust his own mother. So somewhere his real goddamn name is down on paper, and you, being a lawyer, would know exactly where to look for that bottom line. Get me a complete rundown on that sonofabitch and name your price."

"Suppose I can provide this information," Henry said, "which is not all that simple if he is using nominees and dummy corporations. What do you intend on doing with it, and how will it involve me?"

"Well, counselor, I'd like you to carry the ball over the goal line on this one. When we get the facts, I expect you to stick them right in Feeney's puss. I want them dagos off my back. If he leaves me alone, I'll leave him alone. Otherwise I'll raise one hell of a stink."

"If he's as important as you say, then the moment we start asking questions it's going to get right back to him."

"Yeah." Etta nodded, her slanted eyes pensive, the smoke from her cigar, which was clenched tightly between bared gold caps, covering her red head in a blue cloud. "That's the ringer, all right. Any way around it?"

Henry stood up and began pacing the room, his ordinarily smooth forehead furrowed in thought. When he sat down, he smiled at Etta and leaned back in the chair. "Let's reverse the process. Instead of looking at Feeney, let's look at properties. We'll start a company—how about something like the Alameda Real Estate Procurement and Management Company. You provide me with a list of the addresses of all the vice operations that you know of in this city. Prostitution, gambling, speakeasies, bookmaking backrooms—the works."

"Wait a minute, counselor, you're losing me."

"It's a very simple," Henry said, rather pleased with himself. "Once I have the addresses, I'll call various title companies and have them check out these properties on the basis that I have prospective buyers. That's where the procurement in the name of the company comes in. All perfectly legitimate and innocent."

She clapped her hands in delight. "You're a genius."

"Not so fast," he cautioned. "As I said, Feeney may have covered himself so his name won't show anywhere."

"I don't think that cocky little mick is that clever. He's a bum who thinks he has an easy racket, and I think once you get your list of corporations, you'll get down to bedrock real quick."

"I'm inclined to agree. But we'll need substantial capital for the company, a good bank balance as an added precaution."

"Name a figure."

"Quarter million should do it."

She never batted an eye. "Make it a half million," she said. "Let it never be said that we were sloppy or cocky."

"Of course, you'll get most of it back. We may have to forfeit a few small down payments and options, plus costs for title searches, but I'll do my best to keep expenses fairly nominal."

"Oh, Christ," she exclaimed, grabbing her bell and dangling it furiously until the Negro maid appeared. "Tell Rufus to jump into his pants and get the hell down here. I want to talk business with him."

Turning to Henry, she said, "In a minute you're gonna meet the richest and most powerful man in Nevada, even though he's only in his early thirties. His name is Rufus Boutwell and he's gonna put up the capital for our little enterprise. He's a dear old friend of mine and there's nothing he'd like better than to get his hooks into Mike Feeney."

18

The maitre d' at the Saturnalia smiled politely, bowing and offering his hand in greeting as he said, "*Bonsoir*, Monsieur Boutwell—your favorite table is ready for you."

Rufus shook his hand, slipping him a bill, and with Henry in tow followed the maitre d' to their table.

"They've got real Irish whiskey in this joint," Rufus said, settling his stocky frame comfortably into the gold-brocade armchair.

"Sounds good to me," Henry said, taking a discreet look at the lavishly decorated speakeasy. The statuary and murals portrayed the orgiastic pleasure of Saturn's festival as it had been celebrated in ancient Rome.

"Or would you rather have champagne and caviar?" Rufus asked, reaching over to give Henry's shoulder a friendly pat. "This is a celebration, my boy. The sky's the limit."

"The whiskey's fine."

"Goddamnit, I feel like really hanging one on tonight. What do you say, Henry?"

"I'm with you." Henry smiled. "With your help, I think we've got Feeney where you and Etta want him."

"Never mind my help," Rufus said. "All I did was make a few phone calls for you. You're the guy who thought up the scheme and dug up the records."

Henry shrugged. "The real estate and title companies did most of the work."

"That's right, but you fooled them into thinking they were going to make a killing. I like that, using other people to get what you're after—that's what it's all about."

Boutwell downed his drink in one gulp and motioned for another to the waiter, who stood attentively at a discreet distance from their table. The waiter, Henry realized, was charged with the sole responsibility of Boutwell's table.

"Christ, we've got that little prick pinned to the wall like some pretty little butterfly, except that he's an ugly sonofabitch." Boutwell downed that drink and another full glass appeared before him like magic. "When you lay that report on his desk tomorrow, he's going to shit a brick."

The more Boutwell drank, the faster and louder he talked. Henry was bewildered by the amount of whiskey he was consuming. His grayish eyes, partially hidden behind thick lids, were shining brightly, but he seemed to be breathing hard through his bent nose. He had a strong face, with a square jaw, bull neck, broad forehead, thick cheek-bones, and a wide mouth, with scars at each corner. He reminded Henry of a boxer who had been overmatched once too often.

In trying to calm him down Henry minimized his own achievement. "We were lucky," he said. "Feeney made it easy for us."

"You got him cold. Sure, he's a cocky little mick and he left himself wide open. But that's pure Irish arrogance. Thought he had the city by the balls. What the sonofabitch needed was a good lawyer. That's what we all need. Starting right this minute, I'm putting you on a ten grand a year retainer. Understand, of course, that I've got big law firms working for me all over this country. But all of it is so goddamn impersonal. What I need is someone I can turn to for special projects. I've got a lot of irons in the fire and I need good legal advice all the time. I want you right next to me in Nevada, and if things work out the way I suspect they will, someday you'll be my strong right arm. You'll tell those fancy law firms what I want and see to it that they get the lead out and do it right. I'm spending tons of money with brokers and lawyers and I know damn well that I'm not getting my money's worth. You've given me more for less than any fancy dan from any Ivy League school. All I can say is that Jackson State Law School puts out a damn good product."

Henry was so astounded he stammered. "You—you mean you've run a check on me?"

"Hell, yes," he said. "Rufus Boutwell never buys a pig in a poke." He laughed. "No insult intended."

Henry smiled and sipped his Irish whiskey. "No insult taken."

"Fine," Boutwell said, downing another drink. "Sure, I've had you checked out right down to your socks. I know about your granddaddy, the General, a damn fine soldier, and the Godwin name is respected in those parts." He paused and looked closely at Henry. "And I know there was some trouble with the Klan and the General was killed. That's when you left to make it on your own. I'm sorry about the General, but I admire a young man who strikes out on his own to make a new life for himself in a strange city. That took courage. You're my kind of man. I've made my own way in this world. I was on the road, on my own, at nine years old. Well, as you can see, I didn't do too bad for myself."

Boutwell excused himself and went to the men's room. When he returned Henry noticed that he was walking as though he'd had nothing to drink.

"Out in Creede, Colorado, when I was fifteen, I got this seventeen-year-old waitress pregnant. Two years later she ran off with some carnie snake oil grifter and left me with a little baby girl."

He closed his eyes a moment and rubbed his cheeks with his hands as though he were trying to stir circulation in flesh that was turning numb. "Ah, but what an angel she was and is, my little darling," he said, his face breaking out in a beatific smile. "By God, you've got to meet my Alicia, the pride and joy of my life. Studied *literature*," he laughed, effeminizing the pronunciation, "for two years at Stanford and quit. Says college boys are too immature. So now she's a flapper, a real vamp at eighteen, looking for mature men. Well, what the hell— what can you do with *literature*? Might as well be learning the Charleston."

He gave Henry a cunning look. "One thing, though—she'll never need to worry about money. She's got more than she can ever spend." He burst out laughing. "Are you mature, Henry?"

"Well, I'm not a college boy, but I can't do the Charleston."

Boutwell laughed and slapped the table, knocking his glass to the floor. He never even glanced at the waiter scrambling on all fours to retrieve it. In a flash there was a fresh drink on his table.

"Let's get the hell out of this joint," he growled. "Too classy for my blood. I want to howl tonight and I know just the place."

"Why don't we have something to eat and call it a night?" Henry suggested.

"Eat! Are you crazy!" he cried, jumping to his feet. "You want to spoil this glorious glow? Come on, I'll show you something really raunchy."

The limousine was waiting at the curb. They settled down in the back seat and before the chauffeur had started the engine, Boutwell had opened a small cabinet and was pouring drinks into huge tumblers.

"For the road," he said. "Hey, Jack, the Red Rooster, and don't spare the horses."

"What is the address, sir?" the chauffeur asked.

"The old Barbary Coast, down some little alley off Pacific Street." Turning to Henry, he said, "Used to be called 'Terrific Street' in the good old days. In its time it was more notorious than London's Limehouse and Marseilles's waterfront. I had me a checkered suit, a derby hat, and peach fuzz—ah, but that was long ago."

A tough seamen's hangout, the place was noisy and crowded, dense with smoke, and a foul stench greeted them as they came through the door. Boutwell headed for the bar, elbowing his way roughly through a group of men who were angrily engaged in a dispute over a wager. One of the men, a tall, heavyset Greek with a thick beard and dark smoldering eyes, reached out with one hand and spun Boutwell around.

"Hey, where the hell you think you're going?"

It happened so quickly that Henry was caught completely off guard. Boutwell screamed like a demented man and kicked the Greek in the groin, and as the man doubled over in pain, kicked him in the face. The next thing Henry knew there were gunshots and women were screaming and everybody was running for cover. Standing there with his back to the bar, his legs straddled like a gunfighter, Boutwell was waving a silver six-shooter, keeping the Greek's friends at bay, and taunting them with, "Come on, you suckers, come and get it—I'll bury the whole fucking lot of you."

Henry caught a movement behind the bar, a flash of metal in the bartender's hands, and he swung over the bar, feet first, catching the shotgun with his left hand as his feet smashed into the bartender's chest, knocking him against the shelves of bottles stacked against the wall.

Boutwell had stepped sideways when he saw Henry move and now he opened fire, hitting the man closest to him in the right kneecap. The man screamed and fell to the floor, writhing in agony.

Boutwell fired a shot into the ceiling and squealed with delight. "I'm the best fucking kneecapper in Nevada," he shouted. "Who's next? Come on, step up, you fuckers."

Cradling the shotgun in the crook of his left arm, Henry reached over and yanked the six-shooter out of Boutwell's hand.

"Give it back," Boutwell screamed, raising his fist just as Henry calmly clipped him on the side of the head with the gun barrel.

Still moving deliberately, Henry stuck the six-shooter in his belt. "There won't be any more trouble," he said to the crowd, "if you just keep your distance until I get him out of here."

Moving effortlessly, he tucked Boutwell under his right arm and, with the shotgun still in the crook of his left arm, walked out of the Red Rooster and gently deposited Boutwell into the limousine.

Henry dozed fitfully in a chair while Boutwell snored peacefully in a bed of such enormous proportions that he looked like an infant in it. Slivers of sunlight peeked through the edges of the drapery, creating a pattern of flickering bars across the royal blue carpeting and the gold damask-covered walls.

Henry was dreaming about the girl with the slashed face. She was standing naked before him and he was reaching with trembling fingers to touch the open wound, to feel the white bone that shone so brilliantly that it hurt his eyes. He came awake with a start and blinked, blinded momentarily by a sliver of sunlight. For an instant he was lost, a feeling of fear clutching at his heart; then he saw Boutwell and the events of the night came rushing back to him.

He stood up and stretched. The gilded clock on the wall near the fireplace indicated that it was three minutes before twelve. He went into the bathroom, urinated, and looked at his face in the gilded mirror. Everything in this palatial suite seemed to be gilded. That was as it should be, Henry thought, as he doused cold water on his face. After all, this was the Palace, San Francisco's most luxurious hotel, its reputation sustained over half a century.

Henry undressed, picked up the bathroom phone, and dialed the valet. "How long will it take to press my suit and wash my shirt and underwear?"

"Thirty minutes, sir."

Henry gave him the room number, hung up, stuffed his clothing in a paper sack, and placed it in the special compartment built into the door for this purpose. Then he drew a hot bath and stretched out in the biggest bathtub he had ever seen. A half hour later, he was dressed and back in the chair beside the bed. Boutwell was stirring. He groaned loudly a few times, rubbed his hand across his mouth, and opened his eyes.

"I've got more fucking cotton in my mouth than any darkie ever picked on your plantation," he said, moving his lips and tongue, trying to stimulate a trickle of saliva. "I need a little hair of the dog," he groaned, sitting up. "Would you mind pouring me a tumbler of good Irish. It's over there in the cabinet across the room."

Henry brought him the drink and Boutwell emptied most of it. "God, that feels good," he said, sitting up in bed. "I almost feel half human again." He emptied the rest of the drink and threw the glass across the room. It bounced on the thick carpet and came to rest against the far wall without breaking.

"That's it for a while," he said, burying his face in his hands.

"You all right?" Henry asked.

"I'm getting some nasty messages," he said. "Made a royal jackass of myself last night, right?"

Henry smiled. "Except for sterilizing a Greek and kneecapping another one, you were pretty well behaved."

"Holy Christ, it's coming back to me—the Red Rooster and that fucking Greek. Did you see the way he grabbed me, the bastard? He's lucky I didn't shoot him through the head." He paused and pointed a finger at Henry. "There was a time I would have in two seconds flat. I grew up with some pretty tough hombres. They didn't take shit from nobody." He smiled. "See? I'm improving." Then serious again, he said, "You know, I go for months holding myself in, being nice to people, polite as all hell, and then something happens. It's like an anchor chain inside me just snaps and I go wild." He stopped and shook his head. "I don't understand it."

Henry waited in silence.

Boutwell fell back on the pillow and closed his eyes. "I'll be okay for a while now," he said. "I got it out of my system. Kind of like taking a laxative—cleans out the shit in your blood. Anyway, nobody's perfect." He opened his eyes and grinned at Henry. "Maybe not even you, m'boy."

"That I'm sure of," Henry said.

"Okay, all bullshit aside, I want you in Nevada with me. I like the way you handle yourself. You're no ass kisser and, by God, there's a lump on my head to prove it."

They both laughed and Boutwell sat up again, a foolish grin twisting his mouth. "Do you realize that President Harding died in this very bed, in this very room. Know what he died of? Apoplexy. No wonder.

The poor sonofabitch was bamboozled by his most trusted aides. Played him for a sucker all the way. I knew him well and I liked the man. Played poker with him right here in the Comstock Room. Terrible player. No guts. As easy to bluff as a baby. Listen, let me tell you something. When I was just a kid, I played poker with the Nevada Four. The games opened with a takeout of seventy-five grand in ivory chips. The first time I played with them I busted their ass."

He fell back on the bed. "Enough already. What time is your appointment with Feeney?"

"Three o'clock."

"Does he have any inkling of what's coming up?"

"Gave no indication of it when I phoned him."

"Good. Kick him in the balls. Take care of Etta, and when that's straightened out I'll take care of Feeney my own way. I'll twist that sonofabitch's tail till he begs for mercy. Okay, when can you leave for Carson City?"

"I can't go to Carson City," Henry said. "I can't leave San Francisco."

Boutwell nodded. "Etta told me. That girl must mean a lot to you, giving up the future I'm offering you. There's no limit to how far you can go. I'll make you a millionaire before you're thirty."

"I'm sorry," Henry said, "but the subject is not open for negotiation. I came here to find Camilla and I'm not leaving until I do. It's just that clear-cut and final."

"Okay, I respect that in a man. I still want you on my payroll. There are things you can do for me right here. Meanwhile, let's get some outside help. I'll get the Pinkertons."

Henry's eyes flashed angrily. "No! Just stay out of it. It's my responsibility and nobody else's."

Mike Feeney dropped the report and looked across his desk at Henry.

"It's a piece of shit," he said, flipping his fingers disdainfully across the report.

"I quite agree," Henry said. "It stinks, all right."

"Don't pop wise to me, young man. I'll have you in iron so fast your head will swim."

Henry crossed his legs. "I didn't make this investigation to come here and be intimidated by some phony theatrics. You're going to do what I ask. You have no options."

Feeney's face looked like it was made of stone, his eyes cloudy little agates glinting without depth.

"This is extortion, pure and simple."

"Some newspapers would consider it a scoop. It all depends on your perspective."

"You turn that over to the press and you'll get your ass shot off by friends of mine who know how to take care of wise guys."

"I'm sure you're right, but it won't help your situation. Might even aggravate it. Certainly, I don't have to explain to you that others are involved in this project. I'm only an attorney representing a client."

"Well, who is your fucking client?"

Henry could not conceal the smile that curved his lips in amusement as he said. "Etta Gold. If you'll recall, she's one of your tenants."

Feeney leaned back in his chair but his eyes and face remained stony. "Well, now, that puts a different light on things. What's the grift?"

"Cut her rent in half and call off the Italians. Etta feels that Etta's Place is her place. And that's the way she wants to keep it."

"What have I got to do with the Italians? I'm a fucking Irishman."

"Feeney, I told you—it's not open for debate. Just give me a yes or no. If it's no, Etta moves to San Mateo and you go to prison. If it's yes, then it's business as usual for both of you, except that Etta becomes a little more unusual than the rest of your tenants."

Feeney crossed his little arms behind his head. "Okay, you've got a deal. For a while there, I thought you were either a blackmailer or some kind of fucking crusader."

"Not me," Henry said. "I'm only a lawyer earning a day's pay."

Back at his hotel late that afternoon, Henry found a message from Yulee. There had been three letters from the old prospector in the intervening two years, each a request for another grubstake, the last one for a thousand dollars to buy more blasting powder, a new windlass, and other equipment. But this was the first time that Yulee had asked to speak to Henry on the telephone. He had left a Virginia City number for Henry to call at nine o'clock.

Henry had dinner at a small Italian restaurant around the corner from his hotel and wondered what the old man was up to. That old one-legged sourdough must be pushing eighty-five. Perhaps he was ill, on his deathbed, with those kid's eyes of his anxious to see a friendly face. Henry resolved to go immediately if the old man needed him. The last time Yulee had written he'd said he had sunk a shaft over a hundred feet deep, timbering only the topsoil, and had tunneled some twelve hundred feet. He had used a shovel and an octagonal steel drill, which he held in one hand while he wielded a four-pound hammer in the other, turning the bit from an eighth to a quarter turn, depending on the character of the rock, with each hammer blow. He worked by candlelight in the unbearable heat.

"Well, pard," he'd written in a heavy scrawl, "a miss and there goes the old mitt for a spell. I drill them holes three feet deep and angle them for a good pop. Then I set the dynamite charge. I use forty percent gelatin and the trick is to put the fuse into the fulminate mercury cap, which I crimp with my teeth. That way I know how much pressure to use. One ounce too much and there goes the old noggin into a million pieces. Well, I always said I was partial to going with a bang. For exercise I trundle the tailings in a wheelbarrow to the shaft opening, load it into a steel bucket, climb the hundred-foot ladder, windlass it to the surface, load it onto another wheelbarrow, and dump it in a canyon a couple hundred yards away. By now that canyon is beginning to look like a small mountain. Believe me, if the ore's as rich as I reckon, even the dump could make us rich."

Yulee had gone on to say that he preferred to work alone, that his privacy was well worth the extra effort. Besides, he had young Bessie to keep him company. What more could an old sourdough want for companionship out there in the boonies?

When Yulee's voice came over the wire, it was jubilant and Henry smiled happily.

"Howdy, pard," Yulee said. "Thanks for returning my call."

"My pleasure," Henry said. "How are you, Yulee?"

"Fit as a fiddle," he said. "If it warn't for this dang wooden stick, I'd go dancing tonight and plumb wear out a dozen little gals before the night's out."

"You sound like a happy man."

"Well, I'll tell you what, pard. I think we got ourselves a little bonanza here that's gonna make history. I've been following the biggest and richest vein I ever did see and it's getting wider by the foot. I can reach up with my chisel and fill my pockets with high grade that might assay as high as fifty thousand a ton. Even my dump, which is just cleanup, is probably worth a hundred thousand. I'll tell you fair and square, pard—we are guldang millionaires."

"Why, that's fantastic," Henry said, not knowing what else to say.

The old man had lost his senses and the least Henry could do was humor him.

"I expect to strike the mother lode any day now."

Henry was speechless.

"Got you kinda tongue-tied, eh, young feller?" he chuckled. "Well, I plan to call it the Godwin, a right fetching name for a godsend, I reckon."

"I *am* tongue-tied," Henry admitted.

"It's a down-the-middle split for us, pard, with the survivor inheriting his partner's share. Now, being a lawyering man, I reckon you might know how to draw up that little scrap of paper for us. Of course, you understand, I plan to give you a go for your money on that survivor business. Finally decided to build me a real house up in the timbers above Lake Tahoe and live to a ripe old age, just smoking and watching the sun rise and set on that big old blue lake. Might go down to fetch some game and a fish or two now and then, but I ain't never gonna dig or drill another hole even if I live to be a hundred and eighty-five. I've got my bonanza and I reckon that's good enough for any man in one lifetime."

"Now, listen, Yulee, don't be offended, but I can't accept a fifty percent interest in that mine. Let's consider that money as a loan and you can pay me two or three percent interest, but that's as far as it goes. I don't deserve any part of that mine."

Yulee chuckled. "I'm gonna give you two days to get up here and file this claim with me. If you don't show up, then I'm gonna file it in both our names."

Henry was shocked. "You mean you haven't filed your claim?"

"Don't worry, ain't nobody knows where it's at. They couldn't find it in a million years. I ain't seen hair nor hide of another critter in them parts in two years."

"You haven't told anybody?"

"Not a soul."

"Where are you calling from?"

This time Yulee burst out laughing. "In a phone booth, pard. You reckon I was born yesterday?"

"All right, I'm taking the train in the morning. Where are you staying?"

"Mrs. Flanagan's boardinghouse. That old widow's been making goo-goo eyes at me for years. Might give her a tumble when I'm a millionaire." He hooted until he started coughing.

"Congratulations, Yulee. I don't know anyone in this world deserves a bonanza more than you do. As for my part in it, we'll talk it over when I see you, either late tomorrow or the next day."

"Good night, pard," Yulee said. "Happy dreams."

After saying good night to Yulee, Henry sat with the dead phone in his hand a long time, lost in thought. The old man had sounded perfectly rational. And he probably knew more about prospecting than any man alive. So it might well be that he was sitting on top of a bonanza probably worth tens of millions of dollars.

There was a strange gnawing feeling in Henry's stomach, and he found that the hand holding the phone was actually trembling, and there were beads of perspiration on his forehead. If the old man insisted on splitting it down the middle, would it be fair to deprive him of that pleasure? After all, there probably was more money in that hole than both of them could spend in five lifetimes. Like the nabobs of Nob Hill, their fortunes would be inexhaustible. Their dynasties would survive for generations—when merged as one, on the death of one of the partners, it would survive for centuries.

He hung up the phone and began rocking, lost in a reverie of wealth and power, shared with Camilla and their son or daughter, but he really always thought of the child as a son. His son would live like a prince, all the world opened to him to take and use as he desired.

The phone rang and Henry came back to reality. It was Boutwell wanting to know what had transpired in Feeney's office. God, Henry thought, that seemed like something that had happened a million years ago. His next reaction was one of embarrassment. He had forgotten to call Boutwell after he called Etta.

"I'm sorry," Henry apologized, "but I've just had the strangest phone call from an old friend in Virginia City."

Boutwell laughed. "Now, who in hell would you know in Virginny?"

"Oh, an old prospector I met on the road one day. His name is Yulee."

Boutwell exploded. "You mean Walt Yuland, the old pegleg sourdough. Christ, I thought he'd been dead for years."

"He's alive and kicking," Henry laughed. "He can kick higher than any two-legged animal around."

"If you don't mind my butting in, what's that old bastard calling you about?"

"I've been grubstaking him and he called to tell me that we're officially millionaires." Henry laughed nervously. "I still don't quite believe it, but he sounded so lucid, and he is an experienced prospector. I don't know what to think."

"What do you plan on doing about it?"

"I'm taking the train in the morning and I'm going to help him file the claim."

There was a long pause before Boutwell spoke. "I want to go with you. If that old boy says he's struck it rich, I want to see it, and I want a chance to bid on it. Look, I have my own private coach. The limousine will pick you up at six sharp in the morning. I'll show you what it's like to travel in the lap of luxury."

19

He was greeted by Rufus Boutwell, attired in a silk dressing gown and ascot, standing in the gilded vestibule on his own private railroad coach—a far different man from the one of the evening at the Red Rooster.

"Come in, Henry, and take a gander at what little Rufus has wrought."

Henry stepped into the vestibule as the train started moving. The opulence was staggering—on a level with that of the Astors and Vanderbilts. It was an exquisite coach, its outside painted a royal blue with touches of gold leaf and bearing a fancy crest of red, blue, and gold.

A Negro steward dressed all in white opened the door and Boutwell bowed Henry into the grand parlor. Here the walls were paneled in rosewood, the floor covered by an Oriental rug woven to the precise dimensions of the room. The large paintings on the walls, mostly of nudes reclining on red velvet settees, were in intricately carved gilded frames. The furniture had been custom made in Paris and covered in silk and the softest leather; the curtains were of sheer silk and the drapery of heavy brocade, the overhead lights original Tiffanys. There was a dining room, a kitchen of gleaming metal and tile, a conference room, and three bedrooms, each with its own bathroom.

Boutwell acted like a proud father showing off a newborn son. Henry could only shake his head in amazement when he was escorted to his private bedroom. There was a bed, a chair and small desk, a radio, and a bookcase filled with leather-bound classics.

"Well, what do you think?"

"I think you are who you say you are," Henry said, "and perhaps quite a bit more."

Boutwell laughed, pleased with the observation. "That goes for you, too," he said, leading Henry back to the parlor. "That's why I mean to have you at my side."

"That's not a bad side to be on," Henry said, taking the leather chair offered by Boutwell. "But for the time being, you know, there's something else I must do."

Boutwell plopped down on a velour sofa. "What if you never find her? What if she's living in Los Angeles, or New York, or what if she's dead?"

"Don't think I haven't thought of it, of all the possibilities. Someday I may give up, but not right now."

The steward brought them coffee in a silver pot with Haviland china cups and saucers. "Are you ready for breakfast, sir?" the steward asked.

Boutwell looked at Henry. "I'm starved," Henry said.

"You name it," Boutwell said, "and I'll bet we've got it."

Henry smiled. "Fresh strawberries and cream."

Boutwell roared. "You sonofabitch, this is mid-January."

"All right, I'll settle for blueberries or raspberries."

"Ah, shut up," Boutwell laughed. "How about a nice chicken-liver omelet, or crepes, eggs Benedict, pancakes, grits, caviar, melons, orange juice, grapefruit?"

"The omelet sounds just great, with a few slices of tomatoes and cucumbers."

Boutwell gave the steward a sharp look and caught the faint nod. "By God, Oscar, I'll have the same."

After Oscar had left, Boutwell lit a cigarette and smiled at Henry. "I've had three years of schooling. I was just a penniless kid when I hit Tonopah after the big silver strike. All I knew was how to deal faro. In less than six months I owned the Tonopah Club and had six hundred thousand in cash to invest in mining properties. A few months later one of the prospectors I was grubstaking was digging around a place called Grandpa some thirty miles south of Tonopah and hit a rich vein of gold. We renamed the place Goldfield. I've taken millions in gold out of lots of holes in the ground and have never once touched a shovel. I bought every claim in sight. I went into business with Charles M. Schwab, Frederick Augustus Heinze, John W. Brock, W. A. Clark, and the fucking Guggenheims. Bernard Baruch helped me incorporate all my major claims into the Nevada Consolidated Mines Company, which started out with ten million shares at a par value of twenty dollars. It sold like hotcakes. In seven years' time we grossed a hundred and two million dollars' worth of ore. But that was nothing compared to what we made on the stock deals. I had over fifty other companies selling stocks. Financial writers from all over the world came to Gold-field. You couldn't print stock fast enough to satisfy the speculative fever that swept the country. Ninety percent of the investors took a bath. There were hundreds of stock swindlers around. All they had to do was dig a small hole, register it, put a marker over it, and print stock. The suckers were snapping up everything that hit the exchanges.

"When the dust finally settled, I owned all the producing mines in that whole region, which included Tonopah, Goldfield, Bullfrog, Rhyo-lite, Rawhide, and a dozen other smaller places. The Guggenheims and those other smartass New Yorkers ended up with the tailings. Baruch, a damn smart corporation man, was the only one to come out with his shirt and that's because he played it square with me."

After breakfast, Henry asked to retire to his room to prepare for a lawsuit. He explained to Boutwell that a restaurant owner he knew on Powell Street was suing the *Examiner* for libel, and Rufus laughingly replied that "Willie Hearst will never invite you to San Simeon."

Propped up in bed with an open briefcase at his side and a foolscap tablet in his lap, he jotted down notes between glances out the window at the moving landscape. They had gone south to Palo Alto and were now headed northeast toward Sacramento. There was something hypnotic about lying in bed and watching fields and trees and build-ings moving away from him. After a while the pencil fell from his fingers and his eyes closed.

As he dozed, his thoughts turned to Yulee and the riches of his bonanza. He could see the old man whirling some young girl in a wild dance, his youthful blue eyes shining, his wooden leg thumping a staccato rhythm on the wooden dance floor. The girl's long hair was flying and her mouth was wide open in laughter as Yulee whirled her around and around until Henry got dizzy just watching them. Then suddenly Yulee was sitting by the side of the road, stroking old Bessie, the deep creases in his ancient sunbaked face glistening with tears. The old gnarled hand kept stroking, raising little puffs of dust from the short-haired hide.

Then Yulee was again twirling around the dance floor, his wooden leg thumping louder and louder until finally Henry came awake with a start—someone was knocking softly on his bedroom door. Henry jumped up and opened it.

"Mr. Godwin, sir," the steward apologized. "I'm sorry to wake you, sir, but Mr. Boutwell says lunch will be served in the dining room in fifteen minutes."

"Thank you, Oscar. Tell him I'll be there."

She was sitting at the table with her back to the window, and the sunlight glowing on her shoulder-length hair turned to gold. She was in a short, loose-fitting beige dress, with a Schiaparelli open cardigan in a matching tone of beige, as were her shoes and stockings.

She smiled, revealing straight, even, gleaming white teeth, and held out her hand in greeting. "I'm Alicia," she said, even before Rufus could make the introduction.

"Henry Godwin," he said, surprising himself by leaning forward to kiss her slender white hand. It felt warm and soft.

Rufus chuckled. "I love Southern gentlemen," he said. "They can get away with that savoir faire stuff."

"Rufus, be quiet," Alicia said, and she looked directly into Henry's eyes. The look startled him. He had never before seen violet eyes.

"Did you hear that?" Boutwell said as Henry sat down across from Alicia. "Calls me Rufus. Presidents have called me Mr. Boutwell, but my little darling here calls me Rufus. Not Father, not Dad, not Daddy, but Rufus. She's been calling me Rufus since she was six years old.

"She was such a chubby little tyke, cute as a bug in a rug, and one day I couldn't resist it any longer and I pinched her fat little bottom. Well, my God, she turned on me like a wildcat, fire blazing out of her eyes. 'Rufus' she said, stamping her little foot and shaking her little fist at me, 'don't ever do that again, you bad man.' For a minute there I thought she was going to slap my face. Well, sir, from that day forward I've been Rufus. Daddy died that day. Now ain't she the limit?"

"Rufus, you cut that out," she said. "I am tired of that story."

Henry saw that her cheeks had turned a fiery red and he held back the laughter that he felt. "I quite agree," he said. "She really is the limit—in grace and beauty and charm."

Boutwell fell back in his chair and howled with laughter. "You're the limit, too—brother, I'm seeing a side of you I didn't know existed."

Alicia was smiling, and the color in her cheeks seemed to accentuate the violet in her eyes. Turning to her father, she said, "Rufus, for the first time since you've bought this gilded cage, you have invited someone who acts like he belongs in it." She stopped, glanced quickly at Henry, and burst out laughing. "I think that didn't come out quite the way I meant it."

Both Henry and Boutwell were laughing so hard that tears flooded their eyes.

"That's what you get for studying *literature*," Boutwell squealed.

Oscar served the vichyssoise, and Alicia said, "I don't think Rufus will ever forgive me for not studying economics. What he really wanted in the family was an accountant he could trust, someone who wouldn't testify against him in the event the records were ever subpoenaed."

Boutwell smiled weakly. "She has a high opinion of her old man, all right. She's been reading all those fiction books about how corrupt millionaires and politicians are in this country."

"Rufus, I could have learned more about it as a history major."

"I know," he said. "Teapot Dome has everybody thinking there's corruption everywhere."

"We're living in a new generation," she said, and it was obvious the conversation was taking a serious turn. "This generation is in revolt against puritanism and organized religion, and it is also in revolt against the corruption of our elders, against ruthless financial pirates who have been bleeding the poor from the beginning of time. This new world belongs to the young. The world we are inheriting from our elders will be discarded."

"Well, sweetheart," Rufus said, now smiling pleasantly. "I'm just a farm boy, myself, who barely learned reading, 'riting, an' 'rithmetic. I never studied Darwin and his theory of the survival of the fittest. Didn't have to. Even as a little snapper I knew that cream always rises to the top. I knew how a bell cow controls the herd, that bands of horses have leaders, that chickens have their pecking order, that birds, dogs, cats, wolves . . . Look at any species of life, and you will find a king or queen of the hill. Somebody always rules, whether through financial power, or political, or brute strength, or cunning as in jungles or street gangs. Your generation is just another crop of kids going through normal growing pains. The difference is that the process has been interrupted by too much idealistic hogwash flying around those colleges. It only confuses a person's God-given common sense."

She looked at Henry and smiled. "This is par for the course in the Boutwell dynasty. We talk a different language—neither one of us understands the other, but we manage to communicate in other ways."

Boutwell reached over and gently touched her hand. "She's the love of my life," he said, his eyes suddenly glistening. He turned his head and furtively wiped his eyes with his napkin.

"Rufus, you big old pussy cat," she said scoldingly. "I think you've got Henry's tongue."

Embarrassed by the strange exchange between father and daughter, Henry said, "What do you think of Walt Whitman, Miss Boutwell?"

"I'll be damned," Boutwell said. "He calls me Rufus and calls you Miss Boutwell. I just can't win."

"Please call me Alicia," she said, giving him a brilliant smile. "As for your Walt Whitman, I think he's passé."

"I'm sorry to hear that," he said. "He's been my favorite since I first learned there were such miracles as poems."

"Now, that's truly lovely," she said, beaming at him. "Have you read Eliot or Pound or Cummings?"

"I'm afraid I'm not too well acquainted with their works."

"They speak for our new generation."

"Oh, yes, I've heard of Eliot's *Wasteland*. Sounds more like social criticism than inspirational. Whitman sings of the beauty of life and the miracle of a single blade of grass."

"Rufus, this hardheaded young attorney is nothing but a romantic."

Henry smiled. " 'COME,' " he said, quoting Whitman, " 'I will make the continent indissoluble,/I will make the most splendid race the sun ever shone upon,/I will make divine magnetic lands,/With the love of comrades,/With the life-long love of comrades.' "

She applauded, and Boutwell said, "Goddamn, that's beautiful."

Henry and Alicia looked into each other's eyes so deeply that Boutwell cleared his throat. "Well, I go for that kind of poem."

"All right, then," Henry said, "one more from him and I promise that's all. 'I believe a leaf of grass is no less than the journey-work of the stars,/And the pismire is equally perfect, and a grain of sand, and the egg of the wren, / and the tree-toad is a chef-d'oeuvre for the highest,/And the running blackberry would adorn the parlors of heaven,/And the narrowest hinge in my hand puts to scorn all machinery,/And the cow crunching with depress'd head surpasses any statue,/and a mouse is miracle enough to stagger sextillions of infidels.' "

"Rufus, you've got yourself one unusual attorney here," Alicia said.

"Would you care to quote Eliot?" Henry asked.

She shook her finger at him. "Touché."

"What's a piss-mire?" Boutwell asked.

"It's a reference to the acid smell of an anthill."

"I think the guy's a hundred percent right," Boutwell conceded. "Nature is really something to behold when you get right down to it."

Back in his bedroom, Henry tried to concentrate on his work, but he could not get Alicia off his mind. It was not that she was a great beauty. She had extraordinary eyes, lovely hair, and teeth that rivaled even Camilla's for perfection. But there were flaws in her face. The bridge of her nose was a little too broad, and her cheekbones were heavy like her father's. Still, she had a sensual mouth, with full lips that curved down slightly at the corners, and a strong chin. Even with the loose-fitting dress, it was obvious that she had well-developed breasts and her legs were long and muscular. She was rather tall for a girl— perhaps five eight, as tall as Rufus in her medium-sized heels.

What captivated him was her intelligence and her direct and stimulating manner of speech. She very definitely had a mind of her own. He concluded that Alicia Boutwell was a lot of woman.

He looked at the blue sky, at the white clouds floating in the distance, and for the first time in his life he felt a desire for a woman other than Camilla.

The sun was disappearing behind the snow-covered peaks of the Sierra Nevada when Henry stopped working on his brief and thought about Yulee working in the snow and freezing weather. He marveled again at the strength and determination of that incredible old man, and later that evening he was pleased when Rufus chose to tell them a story he'd heard about Yulee when the old man was up in the Klondike.

"This happened in Skagway," Rufus said, "a town bossed by Soapy Smith, a famous polecat. At the time Yulee had to be pushing sixty. As the story goes—and this was told to me by a good friend who was there at the time—Yulee was walking down a back alley at dusk when two sidewinders sidled up to him, each grabbing an arm, and while one smashed him on top of the head with his gun barrel, the other neatly stripped him of his money belt. They let him drop and took off for the center of town.

"By the time my friend reached Yulee, he was grabbing for his hat and trying to sit up. 'Them varmints coldcocked me,' he said, rubbing the back of his head. He felt at his waist and slapped his hat against the ground. 'Got my poke in the bargain,' he said. My friend gave him a hand and the first thing Yulee wanted to know was whether my friend could recognize them. He said he could, so they went looking in the various saloon and gambling tents. Meanwhile, Yulee had fetched his six-shooter and a blacksnake whip, which he carried coiled over his shoulder.

"It didn't take long. They were two of Soapy's boys, Yank Few-clothes and the Moonfaced Kid—most of Soapy's boys had funny nick-names like that. They were playing poker with Yulee's money. After my friend pointed them out, Yulee thanked him and looked over the situation. He noticed they were drinking beer and there was a rear exit in the tent. The problem, as he probably saw it, was whether their luck would hold out longer than their kidneys. He went outside in back of the tent to wait for them and my friend followed quietly behind to see what he'd do.

"This is the way my friend described it to me. Yank Fewclothes is the first to come out the rear exit. He staggers to his left, flips his cigarette away, and begins fumbling at the buttons on his fly. There's this low whistling sound and the snake whips around his neck, yanking him clear off his feet. His hands reach for his throat and his eyes are already bulging. He tries to scream but not a sound comes out as the snake tightens around his windpipe. Now he's flopping around like a fish out of water and Yulee raps him a good one on his noggin with his six-shooter. Then Yulee scoops him up, swings him over his shoulder, and begins walking toward the tidal flats to the north of town. He comes back, waits for the Moonfaced Kid to relieve himself, and gives him the same treatment.

"To make a long story short, the Moonfaced Kid's the first to wake up the next morning. He opens his eyes and starts screaming. You see, he's stark naked and literally hog-tied back to back with Yank Few-clothes. All that remains of their clothing and boots is a pile of ashes. From then on Yank Fewclothes was known as Yank Noclothes."

Henry loved the story. He thanked Boutwell for telling it.

"It only reinforces my feelings about that old man. He's a special breed, like the General, my grandfather. They don't make that kind anymore. God, I hope he's hit a bonanza. But I'll tell you one thing—I won't take a penny of it."

Boutwell was silent a long time and Alicia sat there watching them. "What do you mean, you won't take a penny? The deal is perfectly legitimate. It's the way the system works. You grubstake a prospector and, if he makes a strike, you split it down the middle."

"But I didn't grubstake him. I gave him the money because I admired and respected him. In fact, the act of sending the money gave me pleasure. It made me feel good inside to be able to do something for that grand old man. I had eighteen thousand dollars in a money belt when I found him in the desert and I would have given him the whole thing if he'd asked for it. With no strings attached."

Boutwell was shocked. "Stop talking like a sucker. You're blurring my image of you. You can read poetry all you want, but business is business. Charity begins and ends at home, unless it's for business purposes."

"That's the point," Henry said. "That old man is family. As much family as my own grandfather."

Boutwell stood up. "Okay, we all have blind spots, so if you want to throw away a fortune, that's your business."

"How can I throw away something I never owned?" Henry asked. "Putting a few dollars in an envelope is a lot different from digging a hole a hundred feet deep and a tunnel twelve hundred feet long with your bare hands."

"To each his own," Boutwell said, and left the parlor.

Henry and Alicia looked at each other and she shrugged. "You've just disillusioned a realist," she said. "Rufus has gobbled up old men like Yulee all his life. What you've said is so contrary to the rules he lives by that it's nothing short of heresy. Men like you are a threat to Rufus's world. If you were thinking of a future in Rufus Boutwell's great commercial ship of state, I think you've just scuttled your little dingy. If it's any consolation to you, I don't think I've ever admired anyone more than I do you at this moment."

"Thank you, but to be perfectly frank with you, I was sorely tempted for a while. I had visions of empires, of immortal dynasties. I think the story of Yank Noclothes was the straw that tipped the scale. If you'll pardon the vulgarity, I feel goddamn good about it. In fact, I would very much appreciate a cognac and cigar. I would like to bid farewell to this fortune in grand style."

It was dark when they crossed into Nevada just south of Lake Tahoe. The train was barely crawling over the pass. Snowdrifts rose twenty and thirty feet high, and the wind howled against the whole length of the train. The windows were frosted solid. Only thirty or forty miles north of them members in the Donner party had perished in a white wasteland not that many years ago, yet now Henry Godwin was sitting in a private railroad coach, drinking cognac and smoking a Cuban cigar, riding in the lap of luxury.

Alone in the parlor car, Henry was reading *The Great Gatsby*, the latest book by F. Scott Fitzgerald. Alicia had recommended it to him before going to her bedroom to rest and to pack for her departure in Carson City.

The book was lying on the coffee table when Alicia came out.

"I take it you gave up on it?" she said, and he could see the disappointment in her eyes.

"Not at all. I finished it and thoroughly enjoyed it."

"I wish I were a speed reader," she said. "I'm so glad you liked it. Don't you love his sophisticated cynicism? He's the voice of a new generation—our generation—which is more different from our parents' than any other that preceded it, regardless of Rufus's opinion that all new generations are alike. I found it particularly fascinating because Rufus is a Gatsby character himself, except that you'll never find him mooning over an old flame. Rufus tends to business first, last, and always. He's a dedicated capitalist, as though there were any other kind."

She laughed and picked up the book, holding it in her lap. "I'm so glad you like Fitzgerald. Besides him and Whitman, anyone else you enjoy?"

"Many," he said. "All the Russians, almost without exception, Balzac, Shakespeare's histories and some of the sonnets, Conrad, James, Dreiser, the Greek dramatists, and our own O'Neill." He sighed. "There are so many others."

"That's a nicely catholic taste," she praised. "I, too, don't conform to any particular period or style. As I don't always conform to the latest fashions. I live pretty much in a quandary."

Henry smiled maliciously. "I hope the environment is pleasant."

She looked at him quizzically.

"I mean in your quandary," he said. "I hope it's warm and comfortable and the furnishings are to your taste. You see, I've never been there myself, so I wouldn't know what it looks or feels like."

She gave him a coy look. "Well, big boy," she said, imitating a famous stage actress of the day, "maybe someday I'll give you a personal tour of the premises."

At that point the train came to a jarring stop and Rufus rushed out of the conference room with Oscar at his heels to announce that they had arrived in Carson City. Oscar went into the vestibule and there was a cold rush of air when he opened the outside door. He was followed into the parlor by a tall, broad-shouldered man with a black soft hat pulled low over his forehead, almost completely obscuring deep sunken eyes. The introduction by Boutwell was quick and perfunctory. His name was George Clews. What impressed Henry was the small, thin-lipped mouth in that heavy, large-boned face. It was the mouth of a prissy spinster. Boutwell and Clews went into the conference room and closed the door.

Alicia smiled enigmatically. "That's Rufus's strong left arm. If you ever become Rufus's strong right arm, you'll never know what the left arm is doing. Both arms, I may add, are firmly tied by strings manipulated by Rufus. George is the mystery man around here. Moves in dark shadowy places, the phantom of Rufus's silent opera."

She stood up and motioned to Oscar to bring her bags. "This is where I leave you. Good luck to you and your friend, Yulee. He sounds like a nice man, and so do you. If you're ever lonely some evening in San Francisco and would like someone to argue with, why not give me a ring at the Fairview. I have my own suite. If I'm not there, leave a message and I'll get back to you."

"I may take you up on that," he said, "if you don't mind associating with someone whose dingy has been scuttled."

Mrs. Flanagan's pleasant freckled face was swollen and red with grief. Henry introduced himself at her door and she burst into tears and sobs. She held a man's red handkerchief to her nose and stared back at him with blurred eyes.

"Oh, may the good Lord be praised," she sobbed, motioning him into the front parlor. She sat down and pointed to a chair with a wave of the handkerchief. "Sit and make yourself comfortable. 'Tis a hard, long journey you've had."

"Thank you, Mrs. Flanagan. I came to see Yulee."

She waved her fleshy freckled arms and shook her head as if the burden was too great to bear.

"The poor man's not here," she sobbed. "Been gone since yesterday forenoon. Went off to check the train schedule and never came back."

Henry felt like his heart had stopped beating. A cold sweat broke out over his body and for a moment he had trouble breathing.

"Oh, Mr. Godwin, something terrible has befallen that poor old man. I feel it in me bones. I checked all the saloons and gambling dens and even the dance halls, but not a soul could give me an encouraging word. 'Tis like he's vanished from the face of the earth, the good Lord help us. Oh, I tell you, something is surely afoul."

"May I see his room?"

"Oh, by all means." She trudged up the stairs ahead of him, a fat woman with thick, soft legs bulging in tight cotton stockings. "That poor man loved you. Called you his patron saint. Believe me, you made his life happier than you'll never know. Now, of course, that he's struck it rich, he couldn't wait to see the pleasure on your face when he filed that claim. He wanted to make you proud of him, to show you how your generosity was repaid a thousandfold."

She stopped at the top of the stairs and stood by a rough wooden door. "Of course, you know, he has no use for treasures. His work's been his life. His work and young Bessie—the new burro he named after the one he had for twenty years."

She opened the door and waved Henry into the room. "He was so happy he danced a little jig after he talked to you on the telephone. He even spun me around the parlor a few times. I tell you, that man has more life and spirit in him than ten youngsters. He spun me around so fast I thought me head was gonna fly right off me shoulders. Oh, a powerful one, he is, all right, and for a man of his advanced age. And so kindly and just as neat as a pin."

The room was so tiny that Henry could barely squeeze inside. There was a short, narrow bunk, a milking stool, and a small wooden box with an oil lamp on it. There wasn't a single personal object in the room.

Henry backed out, sorry he'd seen it. He could understand the old man's love of the outdoors, sleeping under the stars, where space was limitless and everything around him held a special meaning. "Could he have gone back to the mine for any reason?"

"And leave young Bessie behind?" Mrs. Flanagan shook her head.

"You mean you've checked the livery stable and young Bessie is there?"

"Oh, goodness, many times, and young Bessie was there each time big as life and twice as lonely. Even in town the old man went to see her a half-dozen times a day. He spoiled her rotten with sweets. If he was too slow in producing them, she slid her tongue into his pocket and got them out herself. She's a sly one, this young Bessie."

They were back in the parlor and Henry stood there, unable to decide on his next move. "Is it possible that he's already registered his claim and gone to Reno for a celebration?"

She shook her head. "Mr. Godwin, I've checked every possibility. The claim was not registered, nor has anybody else registered a claim around here in months."

"I don't know what to do," Henry said. "Will you keep looking for him?" He handed her his business card. "Please call me at this number, collect, the moment you hear anything. I'd appreciate it if you kept checking the claims office. If there's been foul play, it's very likely that someone will come along to register the claim when he thinks it's safe."

"Don't worry," she said. "Alfred—he's the government man—will keep me informed."

"Is it possible that Yulee had a couple of drinks too many and told somebody about the strike?"

She shook her head defiantly. "Not on your life. Yulee's not a gabber. He's been at this game too long for a slip of the tongue."

"Perhaps someone followed him there."

"Never, he's far too crafty and sly for any such silly shenanigans. I tell you, I feel it in me old bones—he was done in by thieves who suspected he had a strike. Yulee was spending some high grade in town. It don't take long for the word to spread when high grade starts floating around. God rest his kindly, sweet soul," she said, crossing herself and trying to keep herself under control. "Yulee, I fear, has gone to meet his maker."

"Then perhaps his body will be found?"

She shook her head. "Mister Godwin, there are a thousand abandoned shafts in these here hills and six hundred miles of tunnels under this town. No one will ever find his poor remains."

Seated in the back seat of the limousine with Boutwell—the limousine they'd driven up in from Carson City—Henry told Rufus what he'd learned from Mrs. Flanagan.

"I don't know what to do," Henry said. "I suppose I could stay a few extra days and look for him."

Boutwell quickly vetoed the idea. "If she can't find him, how will you, a stranger in these parts, do any better? I agree with her. Flashing that high grade probably got him killed. There're lots of desperate men stranded in this dying town. I'm sorry for old Yulee, but he's had a full life. If I can do as well, I won't be complaining at the end."

They drove back to Carson City in silence for a while. Rufus seemed to be lost deep in thought. "By the way, Henry, got any idea where the mine's located?"

Henry shook his head. "Not the foggiest."

"Well, think about it. Maybe he said something that would give you a clue. Listen, that mine's probably worth millions."

"I'm sorry, we never talked about its location. It could be anywhere in this area."

"That's the needle in the haystack answer," Boutwell said, closing his eyes. As they neared the outskirts of the city, he leaned forward to whisper directions to the chauffeur.

"I've got a little surprise for you, Henry," he said. "I know you have to be in court tomorrow and I want to get you back there in Boutwell style."

At this moment the limousine swung through the gates of Carson City's small airport. "I own one of the first trimotored jobs in the world. Its design is five years ahead of its time. Three big Pratt and Whitney engines that can carry a dozen passengers. It's all fueled up and waiting for you."

Henry was pleased. He'd seen airplanes in air circuses, but he'd never been inside one. Nor had he before seen one this enormous.

"Have you back in San Francisco in two hours."

"Rufus, there's just no limit to what you can pull out of the hat."

"That's right, Henry. Now you've got it. I'm the magician who makes all kinds of wondrous things come through."

Henry stepped out of the car and looked back at Rufus. "If you are truly a magician, find out what happened to Yulee. If he's been murdered, I want to see his killer punished."

"That's a big order."

"Not for a master magician with unlimited resources," Henry said, and walked quickly toward the plane.

20

They met for lunch on Nob Hill at the Pacific Union Club. Its membership was restricted to one hundred and was passed on like an inheritance from father to son. For many years it had been San Francisco's finest "gentlemen's club."

Although restricting himself to a white wine, Boutwell was still in a highly jubilant mood. "You won't believe what happened yesterday," he said, his eyes gleaming behind the heavy lids. "Willie asked me to call off my dog."

It took Henry a moment before he realized that Boutwell was referring to the libel action for Leon's Cafe he had filed against William Randolph Hearst's *Examiner*. Henry was appealing a ridiculous ruling by a judge who was blatantly biased in favor of the newspaper.

"He's committed several reversible errors and I've no doubt we'll win a sizable judgment somewhere down the line. And Hearst's lawyers damn well know it. By the way, how did Hearst know about our legal arrangement?"

"Why, I told him, of course," Rufus laughed. "You don't think I'd miss such a ripe opportunity to needle old Willie. Besides, his newspapers and magazines have considerable influence on Nevada politics. So far he's been most cooperative, particularly in our fight to keep raising the government's price on silver."

"It's going to cost him," Henry said.

"Now, now, let's not be too greedy. Be graceful in victory. That's the mark of a great man."

Henry laughed. "Will Willie be graceful in defeat?"

"Listen, old Willie's not a bad sort. Throws great parties at San Simeon, with all them hot-blooded little starlets, not to mention some of the big stars. Was there a couple of times and got fucked until I couldn't see straight. Of course, the old man pretends he don't know what's going on. He's against booze and fucking in his old age, except, of course, for his own little private sessions with his mistress, that actress, Marion Davies. She must really be some lay, because she can't act worth a fuck.

"Once old Willie had this whole country by the short hair. Goaded McKinley into fighting the Spanish-American War for him. This gave Teddy Roosevelt his opportunity to gallop up San Juan Hill and keep right on galloping until he reached sixteen hundred Pennsylvania Avenue."

He sipped his wine and licked his lips appreciatively. "Have I ever told you about the time we tarred and feathered the Wobblies in Goldfield?"

"Not that I can remember," Henry said.

Rufus shook his head, grinning. "The fact of the matter is that the miners were high-grading, robbing us blind. They weren't only filling their pockets and dinner pails with high-grade gold ore but were wearing special harnesses beneath their clothing that concealed fifty and sixty pounds of pure gold. To stop it I installed change rooms and forced the miners to change clothes in the presence of company inspectors. So they went on strike and their leader, a crazy Bolshevik, was actually encouraging them to high grade. I heard one of his speeches, sneaked into the hall in disguise, and the sonofabitch was telling them straight out to steal. 'Every time you can get your hands in a capitalist's pocket, do it. When you want a thing, take it. The capitalists are stealing ore, aren't they? The ore belongs to all of the people.' Well, I showed them suckers how much right they had to my ore. I got federal troops in there and a lot of Wobblies left town on a rail with more feathers than they knew what to do with."

"Those must have been exciting times," Henry said.

"It was the greatest period of my life. I was young and building a fortune. Of course, my ambitions now are grander and more complicated. I'm still in mining, own about every producing gold and silver mine in Nevada that's worth a damn, and in banking all over the state, ranching, real estate, hotels, feed and grain stores—in anything where there's a buck to be made.

"Henry, I'm going to give Hearst some competition of my own. I've decided to go into the newspaper business. I'll be the captain but it'll be a group effort. There're too many pieces on the board for one man to make all the right moves without some sound advice from experts.

So that's where you and other good men come into the picture. I'm still after you, even more so now that you've got Willie Hearst eating crow."

"What is Willie offering me to back off?"

"A retraction, generous attorney fees and expenses, and a moderate stipend for the plaintiff."

"How moderate?"

"Five thousand."

Henry looked directly at Boutwell. "I want a front-page retraction submitted for my approval, five thousand in legal fees, and fifty thousand for my client, Leon. Tell Hearst he's going to run out of friends on the bench long before I give up. Tell him also that perjury, conspiracy, collusion, and fraud merit high punitive damages, plus nationwide publicity, not to mention the criminal charges. Finally, tell him that it's not open to negotiation. He can take it or leave it, and he's got one week to decide."

"The only problem I can see is the retraction," Boutwell said, "Don't ask for too much. Remember, the editorial part of the newspaper is his baby, and for that control he'll fight you into bankruptcy and worse. Know when to push and when to ease off. I can't think of a greater business gift. It's strictly intuitive. Some men have it, while others try to bluff their way through blinded by greed and pride and end up, as the old saying goes, hoist on their own petard."

"I couldn't agree more," Henry said. "Besides, fifty thousand dollars will buy my client Leon a new restaurant as well as a new reputation."

On his twenty-first birthday Henry took Alicia to three Chaplin movies. During the several months they'd been dating they'd seen every Chaplin movie two and three times. The little clown poked fun at all the absurdities they disliked in life, and so they felt a great rapport with him and with each other. They did other things, too, that were of mutual interest. Alicia taught Henry to play tennis and he taught her chess. They went horseback riding in Golden Gate Park on Sunday mornings, and for brunch went to Leon's new restaurant, where they were treated like royalty. She took him to parties at the homes of her rich friends, and some nights she even walked the streets with him as he pursued his search for Camilla, of whom he would say only that she was someone he had to find.

Henry still sat in his rocking chair after every fruitless night's search, drinking straight bourbon and smoking his Cuban cigars, his eyes focused on the people getting on and off the cable cars. He was dreaming about the General more often now, but the dreams were often confused by the intrusion of Yulee, the two old men often melding. The General would fly off his horse and Henry would find Yulee's broken body on the ground, his bright blue eyes filled with pain as he tried to speak, his lips moving silently as Henry pleaded with him not to die.

Boutwell had hired the Pinkerton agency to look into Yulee's disappearance, but their report, a copy of which Rufus sent to Henry, was a depressing document. Mrs. Flanagan had died in a fire that had destroyed her boardinghouse, and Alfred, the government man, had retired from the claims office and had gone off to some unspecified city in Florida.

By summer's end, Henry was seeing Alicia three and four times a week. It became routine after a date for him to escort her to her suite in the Fairview Hotel, a grand pile of white granite on the summit of Nob Hill, and on occasion to accept her invitation for a nightcap.

On this evening Henry was stretched out full-length on the white carpet before the fireplace, his head resting against the base of a sofa, watching the flames lick at the burning logs.

Alicia had excused herself, and when she returned, Henry saw that she had changed to a red silk shift that came to just above her knees.

"You look divinely comfortable," she said, lowering herself to the floor, her dress crawling halfway up her thighs. It was clear that she had removed her stockings. A moment later, as she leaned back on her elbows and the dress pulled tightly across her breasts, he knew she'd also removed her brassiere.

"Don't you find it warm?" she said, and he could see her nipples clearly outlined against the thin silk of her shift. "Why don't you remove your tie and jacket and make yourself comfortable. I have something I want to read to you from a book banned in the United States. I bought it in Paris last summer and had to smuggle it through Customs. You may have heard of the book—it's called *Ulysses* and it's by an Irish writer named James Joyce."

"Yes, I've heard of him," Henry said, removing his jacket and tie. "His prose, I understand, has an unusual lyrical quality. And he's quite graphic about sex."

For three years Henry had lived without sex, as celibate as a monk except for the nocturnal emissions that left him more tortured than satiated.

Alicia leaned over and took his face in her warm hands and kissed him softly on the lips. "We live in a generation where the answer is always yes and yet you never pose the question."

She turned, the dress riding high on her white thighs, and picked up the book. "The heroine's name is Molly Bloom and in this passage she is dreaming of her first lover. ' . . . I was a Flower of the mountain yes when I put the rose in my hair like the Andalusian girls used or shall I wear a red yes and how he kissed me under the Moorish wall and I thought well as well him as another and then I asked him with my eyes to ask again yes and then he asked me would I yes to say yes my mountain flower and first I put my arms around him yes and drew him down to me so he could feel my breasts all perfume yes and his heart was going like mad and yes I said yes I will Yes.' "

With misty eyes Alicia looked deep inside of Henry and he reached for her with both arms and she came closer to him, gently pressing her soft breasts against his hard chest, her thighs touching him, feeling the stirring that was growing in him.

His mouth was on hers and he could feel her tongue pressing through his lips, seeking the warmth of his mouth, and his hand slipped slowly up inside her dress, moving across her thighs, exploring her body, ever so gently, until finally reaching her breasts, caressing each in turn. Her knee pressed between his legs, and her hand touched him, artfully releasing him from his painful confinement, and he was free and throbbing in her hand, as he had throbbed before in Camilla's, and his body moved over hers, her thighs swinging up to embrace him, drawing him to her, and her hand expertly guiding him inside her, lingering to caress him. Like Molly Bloom's lover, "his heart was going like mad" in the silent glow of the firelight.

In the bedroom, later in the night, as they lay naked on top of the sheets, she read snippets of erotic lines from Molly's soliloquy as he softly nuzzled her breasts. He listened to her voice, the words washing warmly over him, more sound than content. There was Molly talking about her breasts, ". . . 2 the same in case of twins theyre supposed to represent beauty . . . so beautiful of course compared with what a man looks like with his two bags full and his other thing hanging down out of him or sticking up at you like a hatrack . . ."

"Oh, Henry," Alicia said, "will you lend me your hat rack and tickle my behind with your finger so that I can come for about five million years?"

It lasted two days—two days of wild and frantic explorations, of tender, loving moments, of dozing in each other's arms, eating naked in bed, rolling on the crumbs, and feeling nothing but the pleasure of their bodies.

21

Henry hadn't been home an hour when Alicia called to invite him to the debut of a new jazz stylist who was opening in the Fairview's Starlight Room that evening.

"She's absolutely sensational. Just completed a fabulous tour of Europe and was SRO at the Waldorf Astoria for the whole month she was there."

"It's a date," he said. "Black tie?"

"Yes, and it gives me a chance to wear something *très sexuelle* I've been saving for a truly exquisite occasion."

She opened the door wearing a slinky white satin dress with a décolletage that left nothing to the imagination.

He held her at arm's length and shook his head in appreciation. "Keep your distance, pardner, or I might damage that little piece of satin ribbon."

She closed the door, shrugged her shoulders almost imperceptibly, and the dress slowly fell to the floor, leaving her naked. She stepped over the dress and came into his arms. "We have time," she said, unbuttoning his fly, "for a doggie boggie." She turned, reached down to hold her ankles, and waited for him, watching him from between her legs.

"Oh, God," she moaned hoarsely, when he entered her. In just a moment she was aroused almost to the point of climax. "Hard and fast, sweet baby—make the bags fly against my ass. Oh, mother of Molly Bloom, I'm coming, coming, coming," and her hips were moving so furiously that Henry could barely hold on to her.

From their table to the right of the stage Henry could look out the tall windows and see below him the city lights running all the way down to the waters of the Golden Gate. He felt as though he were looking down on the rest of the world from an eagle's nest.

Alicia touched his hand and leaned toward him to whisper that the people two tables to their left were Italian gangsters.

"It's Vince Bacino and his bodyguards," she said. "His father is Don Francesco, the kingpin of the local underworld, and he lives in a mansion on top of Telegraph Hill." She paused to glance quickly at Vince Bacino's table. "When I was a child, I thought that they really lived in the underworld, in dark tunnels under the ground, and came out at night to rob and murder."

Henry laughed and squeezed her hand. "Which is Bacino?" he asked.

"He's the one who looks like Valentino with curls. Sexy-looking little bugger, isn't he? I hear that Daisy Miller is his mistress, that he made her career, and that he pays for the lease on her suite here at the Fairview. He's married, of course, to Chicago royalty, the daughter of one of Al Capone's most powerful San Francisco associates. Like all wives of Italian kingpins, she cooks and washes clothes and dishes and cleans house and raises a brood of noisy bambinos while papa is out minding the store and pampering his mistress in a luxurious pied-à-terre."

"How do you know so much about gangsters?" Henry asked, giving her a mocked quizzical look.

"Rufus knows all about them. He says they're investing great chunks of their bootleg money in real estate all over the country, including Reno and Lake Tahoe. Rufus says that someday they'll own the whole state of Florida."

The waiter approached their table. "If you wish another drink, you'll have to order now. There is no service during Miss Miller's performance."

"I'll have a teapot of martinis," Alicia said, enjoying the bogus deception the hotel practiced by serving drinks in teacups and coffee mugs to pretend compliance with the Volstead Act.

"I'll have a coffeepot of Jack Daniel's, with a bucket of ice and a carafe of water," Henry said, taking a closer look at Vince Bacino. So this was the man who had ordered the beating and slashing of the young prostitute and had tried to start a shakedown racket at Etta's Place.

The waiter brought the drinks just as the lights dimmed and a master of ceremonies, dressed in white tie and tails, walked to the front of the stage and waited for complete silence.

"Ladies and gentlemen, the Starlight Room proudly presents Miss Daisy Miller."

With the stage in total darkness, the orchestra began softly playing the melody to "Easy Loving," a blues number Daisy had recorded that was sweeping the country. Then, suddenly, three cones of light from three directions merged into one on the woman standing in the center of the stage. Red sparks flew from sequins that started at the low point of her décolletage and snaked down the front of her dress to the hem, which barely touched the floor. Her platinum hair was shingled, her eyebrows plucked into thin lines, the eyelids darkly shadowed and sprinkled with glitter, her lips a bright red, her teeth gleaming white as she smiled in recognition of the ovation. Daisy Miller, San Francisco's own, they were saying with their applause, had come back home an international star.

She kept smiling at the dimly lit room, blinded by the three brilliant spots, waiting for the applause to stop. Finally, with the room again in complete silence, she said, "Thank you—it's so good to be home again."

The music started and she leaned toward the microphone, her hips gently undulating, and began singing "Easy Loving," her voice soft as silk, feeling each word, reaching each note with full intonation, and yet making it all seem so effortless, so weightless and free-moving, that it lulled the listener into a romantic trance.

Henry gasped in astonishment, the coffee cup slipping from his nerveless hand, the soft thud like an explosion in the silent room, bringing listeners out of their trance, their heads wildly swinging around, their eyes glaring. Alicia reached for him, for his face had turned deathly gray.

"Excuse me," he groaned, and lurched from the table, stumbling up the aisle, pushing away the helpful hands of waiters, his vision blurring, moving on frantically until he was safe behind the men's room door. He leaned over a sink, taking deep breaths, and splashed cold water on his face.

How stupid he had been all these years, searching for her in the pit of the city while she had lived on its pinnacle. *Daisy Miller*, her favorite James book, and he had even heard some of her records on the radio. He felt sick to his stomach and he leaned his head back and took more deep breaths until he felt his insides settle down and the strength coming back to his legs.

The door opened and he saw that it was one of Bacino's burly bodyguards. "Hey, what the hell's the matter with you, buddy?"

Henry waved him away. "I'm all right now."

"You sure you ain't drunk? We don't want no drunks ruining the show, understand?"

"I certainly do," Henry said. "It was just something I ate."

"If you go back in there, buddy, you watch it, see, or Vince will get your head busted. That's his skirt on the stage—get it?"

"I told you I was all right," Henry snapped.

"Hey, don't pop wise with me. You looking for trouble?"

Henry said, "Come here a minute."

The bodyguard took a cautious step forward and Henry took two quick ones. He landed one blow, an uppercut that caught the punk on the tip of his chin, sending him sprawling across the room on the seat of his pants, his head banging against a porcelain urinal. He sat there, listing to port, the seat of his shiny tuxedo wedged inside the urinal.

Henry felt his knuckles and went back to the sink to wash his hands. He knew he had to get Alicia and leave before Bacino sent his goons after him, but that one punch had released three years of pent-up frustration. The important thing was that at last he had found her. The rest was up to him.

Using a house phone, Henry said, "Miss Daisy Miller, please."

"I'm sorry, sir. Miss Miller doesn't accept calls from strangers."

"But I'm not a stranger."

"Sir, it's five o'clock in the morning."

"Listen, I'm Miss Miller's attorney, Henry Godwin, and it's imperative that I speak to her this moment. You call her. I assure you she'll take my call."

There was a long pause. "I'm not taking the responsibility. It's your fault if she complains to the management."

"Believe me, she won't complain."

"Well, okay, just a moment."

Henry sighed with relief. He'd waited in the lobby four hours for Bacino to leave Cami's room. As he sat there wondering what he would say to her, he could not help feeling sorry for Alicia, who had patiently waited for Henry to explain their sudden return to her suite. There, sitting on the sofa with her, holding her hands, he told her about Cami, saying that he'd known her a long time ago and that the last time he saw her she was pregnant with his child. Somewhere in this city his son or daughter was sleeping tonight without any knowledge of Henry's existence.

"Do you want her back?"

"I can't answer that right now," Henry said. "She was the first and only girl in my life until you came along. I—"

"Please," she said softly. "I'm sorry. I know how terribly mixed up you must feel right now. I just want to say I love you. That I loved you from the moment you walked into the dining room and kissed my hand. You quoted Whitman and gave up a fortune all in one day. I said then that I admired you, but what I meant was that I was madly in love with you. I know it sounds like silly dialogue from a Faith Baldwin romance, but I've had my opportunities and my love affairs, and more proposals, thanks to Rufus's money, than I would care to count. None has meant more than the moment when it was happening, and most of them not very much even then."

She paused, not bothering to wipe the tears that ran down her cheeks. "You kissed my hand and the world changed the pitch of its axis, and all the things I once cherished went flying off in a million directions. I was left with you and happier than I've ever been in my whole life."

She came into his arms and he held her a long time before the trembling and the tears stopped. She walked to the door with him and he said he'd call her later. He touched her cheek but they did not kiss.

"Hello," the voice said on the telephone.

"Cami, is that you?"

There was a deep intake of breath. Then he heard, "Oh, Henry."

"Cami, may I come up?"

"Yes, Henry," she said softly, and gave him the room number.

They sat at opposite ends of the sofa and looked at each other like relatives who have been separated a long time. She wore a delicate pink negligee and matching pink satin slippers.

"You're handsomer even than I remembered," she said, and her eyes were smiling now.

He hesitated, not quite knowing how to return the compliment sufficiently. She was a stunningly beautiful woman, groomed and polished until she glowed like a perfectly cut gem. But this was not the Cami he remembered, not the girl with the silky auburn hair that flew in the wind when she ran and covered his face when she made love to him. He looked at that mouth, still irresistible, the teeth straight and gleaming, and he longed to kiss it, to experience again the thrill of his youth. What would he give to recapture those moments? And he looked at her and smiled, saying simply, "You look sensational. I saw part of your opening number tonight and nearly caused a riot."

She laughed, throwing her head back, and it was the old Cami. "I heard something drop out there," she said.

"That was my coffee cup when I saw you. I nearly fainted."

"Oh, my God, are you the one who put Tony in the hospital with a broken jaw and concussion?"

He shook his head affirmatively, his eyes turning serious. "He called you Vince Bacino's skirt. Since I couldn't rearrange his vocabulary, I thought I'd at least try to rearrange his teeth. Now when he says *skirt* he's going to lisp."

She lunged across the sofa and grabbed his hands, pressing them to her lips. "Oh, Henry—I know what you did for Alva and Thaddeus, how you buried them and prayed over their graves, and I have an idea about the Pikes, and God how can I ever repay you for all that? I ran away and deserted my people, changed the color of my skin and used the wisdom you gave me to make my way in the white man's world."

"Cami, I've been looking for you ever since that night."

"I know," she said. "Etta told me." She laughed. "She recognized me from the picture you've been circulating. She came to see me a week ago and I made her promise not to tell you. I didn't know how to face you. Now that you know about Vince you can understand why."

"How did you ever get mixed up with people like that?" Henry asked gently.

"He's been very good to me, Henry. Kind and generous and loving. I owe my career to him."

"He kills people."

"Henry, compared to the Kluxers, he's a businessman in a highly competitive enterprise." She paused. "At least he deals on a one-on-one basis, only killing people who are trying to kill him. What did Alva and Thaddeus ever do to the Kluxers?"

He tried to put his arm around her shoulders and she moved away.

"I want to kiss you, to hold you," she said, "but I can't let myself do that. No matter how much I ache inside. I'm Vince's girl now."

"Well, that can change. You're not married."

"Maybe I don't want to change it. I like my life. It's exciting and fulfilling."

128

"What about our child?" Henry asked, finally finding the courage to ask the question that had haunted him for so many years.

"Randy's in a good home," said Daisy, betraying a trace of guilt as her eyes left Henry's. Henry smiled at the name. "He looks just like you."

"How big is he?"

"Pretty big now, but I haven't seen him in over a year."

Henry was taken aback. "Why not?"

"Vince doesn't know about him, doesn't know anything about my background, and that's the way I want to keep it. He was curious at first, but he got nowhere fast. I told him he had to take me as I am or find someone else. I won't stand for any bird-dogging. I'm free, *white*, and forever independent. He's gotten the message and everything's fine."

"Then I want the boy."

Daisy was overjoyed. "Oh, I hoped you'd say that, Henry." And she kissed his cheek. Just as suddenly she turned somber. "But you must promise me that you'll never say anything to him about me. Tell him his mother is dead."

"I promise," said Henry. "Thanks for naming him Randolph."

"Why not? Godwins are not ordinary people. They have roots and family names. I know how much you loved the General. And I loved him too. He was good to my mama and papa."

Henry stood up and looked around the room. "Could I have a drink?"

"Of course, the liquor cabinet is right behind you. You can fix me one too. How about cognac, for old times' sake?"

"You're reading my mind." He poured generous drinks and came back to the sofa, but he remained standing.

"There's something I'd like to know, but frankly I'm terrified to ask."

She smiled coyly. "Oh, go on and ask, Henry."

He bolted half his cognac down in a single gulp. "Are we related?"

Daisy threw her head back and howled with glee. "Oh, that horny old General with his hands up Alva's skirts all the time. You're thinking maybe he got it into her at least twice when no one was looking and, *presto*, Gabriel and Camilla."

Henry smiled with her, but would not be put off. "Come on, Cami, what about it? What do you know?"

"Oh, the General slipped it to Alva plenty of times back in New

Orleans, when she worked in a brothel in the Latin Quarter. Alva told me in those days he went there four or five times a year and spent several days at a stretch right in that brothel. Alva was his favorite. The last time he went there, Alva was already pregnant with me and the madam was trying to force her to abort me. The General had nothing to do with it, but he literally bought her right there and then, took her and Gabriel to Godwin Acres, and just gave her to Thaddeus. Just like that. And it was the best thing he could have done for both of them. They really had a good life together. That General was some man."

22

Henry sat on a hard bench in the high-ceilinged room, rubbing his hands nervously against his knees, his eyes glued to the door in the far wall. In a moment, Randolph, the son he had wished for and dreamed about for three years, would come through that door. What would Henry say to him? The boy was a month away from his third birthday. What did kids that age know anyway?

Fortunately, all the paperwork had been completed prior to Henry's arrival. He could not bear the thought of coming here for a visit and leaving without his son. Everything was arranged. Mrs. M. was packing his law books and personal property for shipment to Carson City. She herself would follow him to his new job within the week.

Much had happened in the past month. Alicia had accepted his proposal of marriage, the wedding to be "staged," as she put it, by Rufus as soon as he could put all the financial and political pieces together.

Rufus was not one to let an historic occasion go begging. He was ecstatic. During lunch at the Pacific Union Club, he promised Henry an annual salary of thirty thousand, with generous stock options, and an intricate bonus system that could be enormously lucrative if certain projects proved out.

"Listen here, Henry," he'd said, looking hard at his future son-in-law. "You'd get the same deal with or without marrying Alicia. I know she's nuts about you and she explained to me that you couldn't have any more children because of an accident. Well, Henry, I happened to have learned a little something about that accident long ago, but I never said a word to Alicia because I knew you were the kind of straight shooter who'd lay it right on the line."

Henry was pleased, but wary. "I'm grateful, Rufus. But I'd like very much to see that report. I don't feel at all comfortable about it. If you know this much about me, then so do your investigators, and some of the information may be inaccurate."

Boutwell dismissed the matter with a wave of his hand. "Don't give it another thought. George Clews personally checked you out and he's my original sphinx. But there's a question I want to ask you. Do you have any political ambition?"

"None whatsoever," Henry said with conviction.

"Good. Guys like us make better manipulators than puppets. But I'll tell you one thing, if that boy of yours shapes up, if he's got the kind of stuff it takes to be the man I'd want him to be, then we're going to make something special out of him—the best schools and grooming money can buy, and while we're grooming him, we're going to build up Nevada, kick out the outside sharks that have been feeding on it since the railroad came through—the San Francisco and Eastern bankers, the mine owners, the ranching corporations. I'm kicking their asses right out of the state, and we're going to build ourselves some money power and one hell of a political base. Before I'm done the whole goddamn state is going to be my private corporation."

"You make it sound pretty exciting."

"It is goddamn exciting, and not all that tough either, when you know how. Let me tell you something, Henry. In nineteen twenty-two I built myself a home on the highest hill in Carson City. It looks down on the governor's mansion, the state capitol, and the legislature—just to let those boys know who's boss. The house itself is an exact duplicate of the White House as originally designed by James Hoban and Benjamin Latrobe and approved by Jefferson. The Eastern newspapers poked fun at it, called it the White Cowboy House, but they're little men with no vision. Let them have their fun. Someday they'll wake up and there I'll be, Mr. Rufus Boutwell, reaching for the pie in the sky and getting it.

"The first thing on the agenda is to get Congress to raise the price of silver. That's going to take some lobbying and that's where you come in. My mines alone produce more silver than does any other state in the Union. Then we're going to get millions of acres of federal land granted to Nevada, and we're going to follow up by promoting the mining of coal, phosphate, oil, gas, potassium, and sodium in the public domain—meaning, of course, Boutwell's domain. Finally, we're going to get the Secretary of the Interior to lease certain lands for the purpose of increasing the potash supply of this country—all worthwhile projects in the national interest."

Henry was shaking his head and grinning. "Rufus, I don't know why, but I believe every word you say."

"This is only the beginning. We're going to legalize gambling and prostitution, make divorce simple, and just generally make Nevada a playground for the rest of the nation. The big boys, like Capone in Chicago, Bacino in San Francisco, and guys like them in every big city in this country, are loaded down with bootleg money they would love to invest in legitimate enterprises. We're going to provide them with that opportunity." Henry's smile of anticipation had faded. "I see you're frowning—any objection?"

"After three years in the Uptown Tenderloin, I'm for legalized gambling and prostitution, but you can't be thinking of going into business with gangsters."

"Not on your life," Boutwell said. "We'll be dealing with their fronts —legitimate businessmen—and we're going to run the show. I have a vision, Henry. It may be years before it's realized, but I'm still a young man, and you're even younger. Someday Randolph—if he proves himself, mind you—he'll inherit it all."

Then the door opened a tiny crack and Henry was brought quickly back to the present. He stood up. A small, dark, curious eye peeked through the crack, unblinking in its careful survey of the giant standing there.

"Hello, there," Henry called, smiling brightly, "could that little eye I see in the crack of the door by any chance belong to a boy named Randolph Godwin?"

Henry took a step forward and the door closed. He took a step back and waited until the door opened again, the crack now a little wider, revealing part of the boy's face.

"My name is Randy," the boy said. "What's your name?"

"Henry Godwin."

There was a long pause. "Are you really my daddy?"

"Yes, son, I'm really your father, and I've come to take you home with me."

The door flew open and the boy ran across the room into Henry's waiting arms. Henry dropped to his knees and hugged the boy to his chest and kissed him all over his face.

The boy quickly wiggled away. "I waited a long time," he said, his small face so serious.

"I know you have, son, but now I've come for you."

"To go where?" Randolph asked, his eyes still serious.

"To a new home in Nevada."

The boy took a step back and his lower lip began trembling. "I don't want to go to no more homes," he said, angrily stamping his foot.

"But it's our home, son, yours and mine."

"It's not a home like this one?"

"No, no, son," he said, reaching for him, the boy pulling back, his eyes questioning him.

"Why did you leave me here?"

"I'm sorry. Will you forgive me?"

"Okay, but don't ever do that again," and he stamped his foot again, his eyes flashing angrily.

"Don't worry," Henry said, finally getting him back into his arms, "you and I are partners forever. We'll never be separated again as long as we live."

The boy grinned. "Can we go now?"

"Right this minute," Henry said, "after you open these presents I brought you."

The boy ripped through the packages and found a fleece-lined sheepskin jacket, heavy corduroy trousers, a wool shirt and sweater, wool socks, and black cowboy boots—all of them identical to what Henry was wearing.

"Can I wear them now?"

"You bet, son," he said, and started undressing him right there in the reception room. The boy giggled and got his feet into the boots even before Henry could remove his old trousers. "Wait a second here, pard, I reckon we've got this arse backward. First the trousers, then the boots."

In two minutes flat the boy was standing next to his father, completely dressed. "Hey, Daddy, we're twinsies."

"That's us, the Bobbsey twins."

Taking the boy's hand, Henry led him away, abandoning his old clothes in a pile in the middle of the room.

Once outside, the boy saw the tandem motorcycle and let out a piercing squeal. Henry swung him up in the air and deposited him into the sidecar.

"I've got another present for you," he said, reaching beneath Randolph's feet and bringing out a small aviator's leather helmet and goggles.

A moment later the bike coughed to life. Henry looked at the boy who was holding tightly to the sides of the car, his little knuckles pinched white, and gave him the take-off sign. They roared away with the speed and noise of a thunderbolt. Randolph never once looked behind him.

23

It was still dark when he came awake with a start. He listened a moment to his wife's even breathing, then crawled out of bed. He slipped into a robe and tiptoed out of the bedroom, holding his breath until the bedroom door was safely closed behind him. The last thing he wanted was to waken Alicia. She already had reached twice for him in the night, and the plain truth of it was that after one year of married life Henry Godwin was a sexually exhausted man.

Switching on the kitchen light, he noted with relief that it wasn't yet five o'clock. The servants wouldn't stir until six thirty, which gave him some time to sit by himself, to drink coffee and smoke a cigar, and try to find a solution to the frustrating situation created by Alicia's voracious sexual appetite. There was a desperation to her needs that was beginning to alarm him. Even during the most intensely erotic moments he felt that he was being tested. Love was being equated with performance.

Once during their lovemaking he had murmured "Cami" instead of "Ali," and her body, so warm and soft under his, had immediately turned cold and rigid. Not knowing what to do, he had tried to continue, but had been betrayed by his own rejected body. Convinced that any apology would be hopelessly inadequate, he'd gently rolled aside and waited for Alicia to react, to say something, anything—to scream, cry, swear, even strike him—but she'd remained rigidly silent. In a split second her body had repelled him, her eyes had become empty of passion and rapture, and even anger.

Alicia was a proud woman, who had accepted the child of another woman, assuming that Henry was through with that woman once Randolph had become his. But now, because of an unfortunate slip of the tongue, Alicia felt she had the truth she'd never wanted to hear, the truth that her pride and vanity had refused to accept. He'd fallen asleep only to awaken in the morning to find her lying in the same rigid position, her eyes, now cold as slate, still fixed on the ceiling.

That moment, Henry knew, was the turning point in their marriage. That it had happened only two months after their wedding only exaggerated its importance in his mind. Their idyllic paradise on Catalina Island had turned as chilly as the January fog that had rolled in like a bad omen that very morning, to envelop them in its murky gloom for the remainder of their stay.

On their return to Carson City, they occupied separate bedrooms. Henry plunged into work. Alicia devoted her time to Randolph while the weeks and months flew by in a blur of travel and activity that saw him spending almost as much time in Washington as in Carson City. He'd begun the tedious process of lobbying the various Congressional committees that would help Rufus realize his "worthwhile projects in the national interest."

Then one spring day, after a particularly rewarding session on Capitol Hill, Henry had returned to his Willard Hotel suite to find Alicia there waiting for him. Her face was flushed and he realized that she was tipsy when she jumped up to greet him and nearly fell down. She'd found solace in gin, the aphrodisiac of the jazz age. For Henry, its distinctive odor on her breath would become as much a part of her as the exotic perfume she wore.

"Oops, Mr. Bloom," she cried, throwing her arms around his neck and pressing her hips hard into him. "I've come to inspect your hat rack."

The bluntness of her approach took Henry by surprise. "It's good to see you," he said, his arms going around her waist. "I missed you very much. I was beginning to feel like an old bachelor."

She licked his ear and purred. "Well, Mr. Bachelor, meet a hot old maid."

Henry kissed her neck. "Then I guess you've missed me, too?"

She pulled his head up and looked into his eyes. "Give me a big wet kiss," she said, "and let's go fuck our heads off."

The words excited him as much as the searching kiss, but even as he carried her into the bedroom, he knew that the old passions were dead and love had turned to crude wantonness.

Henry's hand tightened on the coffee mug as he recalled her latest fantasy. "One of these days when you get tired of me," she'd told him only hours ago as he lay exhausted on top of her, her legs holding him prisoner, "I'm going to be in a room with a dozen naked men, with their hat racks poking at me—all sizes, shapes, and colors—and I'm going to fuck them until they all run dry. It's one of my most titillating fantasies. I can come just thinking about it."

Henry could feel her trembling under him, but what could he do or say to this stranger?

"Know what I'm going to do?" she said, and her voice had grown hoarse as it always did when she became aroused. "I'm going to get fucked from behind and the front at the same time. God, that must be fantastic."

Her hips had started moving under him and he knew she was having another orgasm, and he lay there, immobile, letting her fingers dig into his buttocks. Instead of feeling disgust, he was filled with a terrible sadness, a gnawing emptiness in the pit of his stomach, a hopeless desolation that had been growing inside him for a long time.

He felt the hot coffee scald its way down his throat and thought of the wedding, of how Alicia's violet eyes had shone when he'd slipped the ring on her finger. The love and promise in her eyes had touched him so deeply that he couldn't bear to think about it. At that moment he'd felt he really loved her, loved her as much as he could love any woman after Camilla. But the marriage, he knew now, had been a mistake. What was worse, he couldn't understand how he could have deluded himself into thinking it would work.

He'd tried often enough to pinpoint the specific reason for the suddenness of his decision following the disappointing meeting with Camilla. She'd rejected his love, preferring the protection of a gangster. There had been his son, loveless all the years of his young life, who needed the security and love of a family life. There was Rufus and his promises of wealth and power. Finally, there was Alicia herself— bright, vivacious, sexually desirable—whose love for him had touched him deeply.

"Ah, you are a vain and greedy man, Henry Godwin," he told himself, "and it is others who must pay the price no matter how much you dwell in self-pity."

The wedding itself had been an extravaganza of the first magnitude, attended by a half-dozen governors, several United States senators and congressmen, and President Coolidge's own representative—the Secretary of the Interior. "The President has sent his prize chicken to Rufus's wolf den," Alicia told Henry, "and before he leaves Rufus will have the key to his hen house." Other guests included bankers from San Francisco, Chicago, New York, led by Bernard Baruch, and a sprinkling of artists, writers, and movie stars. Of course, Alicia's own young, highly nomadic, sophisticated, cocktail-bending, chain-smoking, wisecracking "cafe society" was also heavily represented.

As for Henry, the guest who pleased him most was Aunt Caroline, who arrived with his mother's brother, Uncle Avery Marsh, and Avery's wife, Harriet. Uncle Avery became Henry's best man, for Henry had lived his life in such total isolation that he had no close friends.

The summer following their lovemaking at the Willard Hotel there had been several parties at Rufus's Lake Tahoe mansion, which he called his Venetian *palazzo* for its façade was a scaled-down version of the Doge's Palazzo in Venice. It was Rufus's own version of Hearst's San Simeon.

Lake Tahoe was the scene of much social activity in the 1920s —dances, dinners, boating parties, picnics, regattas, and speedboat races. But the most elaborate affair of all was Rufus's annual Venetian Water Carnival, which began in midafternoon and lasted halfway through the night. The carnival was staged off a pier shaped like an Italian bridge. The grounds and boats were decorated with Venetian designs and lighted with lanterns. Musicians in costume sang and played Italian tunes. Under the great domed ceiling of the pavilion an Italian buffet supper was served throughout the evening, the tables placed in small alcoves around a dance floor on which dancers waltzed, shimmied, and Charlestoned to the syncopated rhythms of Paul Whiteman and his "symphonic jazz orchestra." The walls of the pavilion were covered with tapestries and friezes of Venetian scenes.

To Henry's utter amazement, included among Rufus's guests at Henry's first carnival was Vince Bacino, who brought Daisy Miller with him. Alicia too was shaken by their appearance. The color had drained from her face as she saw them approaching. Henry placed his hand on hers to steady her.

"Rufus, my old man should've come," Bacino said as he reached their table. "He'd have felt he was back in the old country."

Rufus jumped to his feet with such genuine enthusiasm that Henry was convinced Rufus knew nothing of Daisy Miller's background. For this Henry was grateful to Alicia, though he wondered again about the contents of George Clews's report. It obviously wasn't as thorough as Rufus had implied.

"You must make sure that he comes next time," Rufus said, shaking hands with Bacino, his eyes moving approvingly to Daisy. "I'm delighted you could make it and bring such a lovely companion."

Bacino looked proudly at Daisy, who was smiling pleasantly at Rufus. "This is Daisy Miller, an old acquaintance of mine. I'm sure you've heard of her."

"Yes, indeed," Rufus said, reaching to take Daisy's hand. "Your presence does us honor. May I introduce my daughter, Alicia, and her husband, Henry Godwin, who's also a close business associate."

Although Henry had stood, he did not reach across the table to shake Bacino's hand until it had been proffered in greeting. Bacino's flat dark eyes had moved quickly to Alicia, whose violet eyes were fixed on Daisy, whose own gaze had moved from Rufus to Alicia and back to Rufus without once looking at Henry.

Turning again to Rufus, Bacino said, "I can't get over this layout. I ain't never been to the old country, but I seen many pictures of Venice and this takes the cake. I tell you, the old man would get a real kick out of it."

"I'll confide a little secret," Rufus said, winking at Daisy. "I've never been to Venice either. Never had the time. But you know what they say about Mohammed?"

Bacino blinked his agate eyes in confusion. "You got me there, pal."

"It's just an old saying," Rufus replied. "If Mohammed won't come to the mountain, you take the mountain to him."

"Yeah, I get you, but who the hell's Mohammed?"

There was an embarrassing pause until Alicia spoke up. "Neither one of you has to worry about the competition. He's been dead about thirteen hundred years."

Rufus burst out laughing. "Well, you never know," he said. "I've moved a few mountains in my time."

Bacino's usually sleek Valentino brow was still furrowed, his dark eyes suddenly suspicious as they moved from Rufus back to Alicia, who said, "Well, if you promise to keep it secret, he was an old religious zealot who was a master of the art of persuasion, but he's not really significant to anything going on here tonight."

Bacino gave her a long hard look, his head nodding, and turned to Rufus. "College broad, right?" he said, his lips curling in disdain.

"You've hit the nail on the head," Rufus laughed. "*Literature* major at that."

Bacino exchanged knowing looks with Rufus, and then, taking Daisy's arm, said, "Let's take that gondola ride, baby."

140

Rufus sat down in disgust. "That dumb dago," he said. "How in hell does he rate a classy dame like that Daisy Miller?"

Receiving no response from either Alicia or Henry, Rufus said, "Well, the sonofabitch is riding high right now. His old man's got San Francisco and Oakland locked up and I hear he's got plans to move Vince south to Los Angeles, since the *padrone* down there is an *amico* from the old country. It's a damn smart move to consolidate their operations. Gets them away from the gang warfare going on in Chicago and New York. The Bacinos are worth keeping an eye on. May have some plans of my own for them one of these days."

Alicia's lovemaking that night had been more frantic than ever. Henry had understood, but the vision of Camilla was seared into his brain.

24

Henry refilled his coffee cup for the fourth time and looked at the clock. It was nearly six, just moments before daybreak. Once he finished this cup it would be light enough to go down to the stables for a ride on the white Arabian stallion he had named White Lightning.

The spring of his reunion with Alicia in 1927 he had bought a two-hundred-acre horse ranch some ten miles northwest of Carson City. The main house was a spacious old Mexican hacienda, with low rambling lines and wide porches of red tile. After six months in Rufus's White House West, it was a relief to be in his own home, to have his son grow up close to the soil, the way he himself had back in Vicksburg.

Rufus, who had grown fond of Randolph, had fought the move, hurt that Henry had rejected the splendor of his grandiose mansion, and puzzled by what he sensed as a deterioration in Henry and Alicia's marriage. Still Rufus had tactfully skirted the subject. Lately he'd started spending as much time at the ranch as at his own house, and when Henry was away on trips, Rufus would visit the boy every day, often staying overnight in a room directly across the hall from Randolph's. Although Rufus hated horses, he even went horseback riding across the desert with Randolph, took him sailing on Lake Tahoe, and filled his head with tales of the adventures of his wild youth.

Henry felt Alicia's arms go around his neck and her breath was warm in his ear as she murmured, "A kiss for your thoughts."

"Not worth it," he said, making a move to stand up, but she held on to him with all her strength, the nipples of her breasts pressing hard into his back. He turned his head slightly and saw that she was naked.

"Good God," he said, "don't you think you should put something on? What if Randolph or one of the servants walked in?"

She moved quickly in front of him and reached down, her hand sliding inside his robe, groping for him. "You worry too much," she whispered, her hand finding him and squeezing until he could feel himself growing hard.

Before he realized what was happening, she was kneeling in front of him, holding his erection, her violet eyes clouding with passion.

"I love your one-eyed cock," she said, squeezing the head. "See? It's winking at me." She placed the tip of her tongue to the hole and pressed hard. "I wish I could stick my tongue all the way in there, give you a good fuck, make you feel what it's like being a woman."

Her mouth moved down to his scrotum and Henry feared he would ejaculate on her hair. He started to push her away but she reached up and took him into her mouth not a second too soon.

Henry threw his head back and caught sight of Randolph, standing not more than ten feet away, his eyes wide as saucers, his mouth gaping in astonishment. Henry pulled back in the chair so quickly that he slipped out of Alicia's hand and had covered himself with his robe before she realized the cause of his alarm.

"What the hell—" she began. Then she saw Randolph, and a look of fear came into her eyes.

"What are you doing?" Randolph asked, his eyes fastened on Alicia's nude body.

"Oh, darling," Alicia said, now seemingly shy about her nakedness, her arms covering her breasts. "Daddy hurt his peepee, and Mommy was just kissing it to make it better."

The boy looked at her a moment, shrugged, and looked at his father. "Daddy, can I go riding with you this morning?"

Henry wondered if he could trust his voice. "You bet, son," he said. "Go get ready. I'll meet you here in ten minutes."

The boy smiled happily and ran away. Henry stood up and walked abruptly from the room without a word to Alicia.

One evening two weeks later, only minutes after Henry had said good night to Randolph, he decided impulsively to return to the boy's bedroom and tell him a story about the General that had been on his mind all day. He poured a bourbon and lighted a cigar before walking down the long hallway, pausing at the sound of Alicia's voice as he reached the bedroom. The door was slightly ajar and he looked in.

Alicia was leaning over Randolph's bed, her robe opened all the way down the front, her breasts hanging in front of the boy's face.

"Did Mommy hurt your little peepee?" Henry could see that her hand was inside the boy's pajamas.

"You want Mommy to kiss your little peepee?"

The boy's hands reached up and cupped both her breasts. "Oh, that's nice," Alicia murmured. "You like Mommy's titties?"

The boy giggled. "You tickle," he said.

"Well, Mommy is going to kiss your little tickle, like she did Daddy's."

Henry threw the door open so hard that it slammed against the wall. Alicia jumped up and stumbled away from the bed, her hands frantically closing her gown.

"Just get out of my sight," he said, "and be quick about it."

She scurried past him, head bowed, and ran down the hall. He heard their bedroom door slam and he walked slowly into Randolph's room, sitting down on the edge of the boy's bed.

"What's wrong, Daddy?" Randolph asked.

"Nothing, son."

"But you slammed the door."

"Well, I was so anxious to see you, you little rascal, that the door just slipped out of my hand."

"But Mommy's mad."

"No, she isn't," Henry said, smiling at the boy. "She was just scared by the door banging."

"It scared me," Randolph said.

"Me, too," Henry said, still smiling. "Tell me, son, has Mommy done this before?"

"You mean tickle my peepee?"

"Yes, that's what I mean."

"No, Daddy, but I tickle it sometimes. Is that wrong?"

Henry looked into his son's anxious eyes. "No, son, it's okay for little boys."

"What do you mean, Daddy?"

"Big boys don't do that."

"But Mommy kissed your peepee."

"I know, son, but I hurt it and she was making it well."

The boy nodded, his eyes widening. "It was swollen so big—boy, you must have hurt it real bad, Daddy."

"It's all right now," Henry said, standing up. "Okay, go to sleep and if you're up in the morning, you can go riding with me."

Henry leaned over and kissed the boy's forehead.

"Don't worry, Daddy, I'll be up," Randolph said.

Henry went to the library, which served as his office at home, and sat behind his desk without switching on the lights. The anger that had surged through him was still sending tremors down his legs and across his shoulders. He leaned forward and took several deep breaths. He'd never come so close to hitting a woman.

As his anger lessened, he began to feel concerned. There was something terribly wrong with her. There had to be. She was sick, and he had to do something about it. He couldn't allow things to continue this way. He'd gone along with Alicia's lust when he alone was involved, hoping that she'd change, that the drive would burn itself out. But now there was Randolph to consider. What effect would this have on his young mind?

Henry had read enough of Dr. Freud's theory of repressions to appreciate how traumatic childhood experiences could later affect the mental health of adults. Henry was thankful that he and Alicia had not made more of the moment than they had. Any violence on his part, or hysterics on Alicia's, could have resulted in precisely the kind of traumatic repression that Freud had discovered in so many of his patients.

There was a gentle knock at the door and Alicia slipped quietly into the room. She closed the door and leaned against it.

"Don't put the light on," she said. "What I have to say can best be said in the dark."

She paused and Henry remained silent. "I know it's pointless for me to say I'm sorry about tonight. Maybe I've had too much gin. All I know is something came over me. I can't explain it. Sometimes I feel possessed. I've thought about doing this to Randolph since the morning he caught us in the kitchen. Oh, believe me, I fought against it."

She lit a cigarette and in the flame of the lighter Henry saw that her eyes and face were swollen. "The worst thing is that I love you, and always will, as I told you the night you found Camilla," she said. "I hate her and have wished her dead so many times, but I know that her death would not change anything between us. You can't help being what you are any more than I can help being what I am. We feel what we feel and nothing can change that. We'll both continue in our own way, and all the wishing in the world won't mean a damn thing."

She paused again and Henry could see the tip of her cigarette brighten as she took deep drags on it. "I'm leaving for Paris in the morning, where I plan to live out my fantasies to the hilt." She gave a harsh laugh. "Paris is the perfect place for people like me. It, too, is a state of mind, a haven for disillusioned expatriates. It's quite chic. Oh, don't say it. I know I'm sick. I can feel your thoughts across the room. But the only cure for this sickness is to wallow in it until I either drown or learn to swim with the rest of the world."

This time when she paused Henry spoke. "How long do you plan on staying in Paris?"

"Oh, I expect to roam around Europe a bit. Oh, shit," she cried. "I'm going to stay there until I've burned you out of my system. It may take years, if ever—"

"That's crazy talk," Henry said. "If you know you're sick why not go to Vienna and see Dr. Freud?"

She lit another cigarette with the fire of the old one. "Now, wouldn't I make a classic case study? No, thank you, and that goes for Jung and Adler, too. What I've got to shrink is my vulva, not my head." She choked on her cigarette and began coughing.

"There's no need to be so rough on yourself," he said, his anger replaced by a deep compassion for her vulnerability. "I wish I could say or do something that would help."

"After what I did tonight?" She dragged on the cigarette. "You really are a good man, Henry Godwin. You've always been too good for me, and that goes triple for Rufus. All I can tell you is to watch him. Keep a sharp eye on his left hand, and never leave yourself open for a sucker punch. Rufus hates suckers. So you better hide your boy scout instincts and toe the line of winners."

"You're pretty rough on him, too," he said gently.

"If the truth be told, the best advice I can give you is to take your boy and go back to San Francisco or Vicksburg—just get away from here."

"You make him sound like a genuine ogre."

"You don't see it, do you? He's going to steal that boy out from under you and make him in his own image—which is really quite ugly, if you dare to look closely enough. And believe me, I know him close up."

"You don't make sense. Why in the world would Rufus want to steal Randolph from me?"

"Because he's the only grandchild he'll ever have and he knows it."

"You could divorce me and marry someone else, you know."

"I'll never divorce you, but I'll not stand in your way if you want a divorce. But, it wouldn't do Rufus any good. I had my tubes tied after Catalina." She snorted a laugh. "I didn't really lie about the scar. They did take out my appendix while they were at it. So Randolph is the end of the line for Rufus."

"Oh, God, why, Alicia?"

"Because if I can't have your child, I don't want anyone else's. It's that simple for me."

Henry leaned back in the chair, exhausted. "Go have your fling, Alicia. I'll be here when you come back. I can't promise how I'll feel then, considering what you have in mind, but I'm willing to wait before making a judgment. You may find that acting out sexual fantasies doesn't exactly result in castles in the sky."

"Will you answer if I write?"

"To the best of my ability," he said. "But remember, we have our own fantasies to work out here."

25

Henry's initiation into the political world of Rufus Boutwell had come a few days prior to his wedding, when Rufus had barged into the governor's office in Carson City with him.

Governor Fred Platt, who was in the process of pouring himself a drink, sat behind his desk with a whiskey bottle in one hand and a glass in the other. He had stared at them in utter astonishment.

"Put them down and shake hands with my prospective son-in-law, Henry Godwin," Rufus said gruffly.

The governor leaped to his feet, nodding obediently. He placed the bottle on his desk, but held on to the glass, as he came forward to shake Henry's hand.

"Pleasure to make your acquaintance, young man," Platt said, casting a nervous glance at Rufus. "May I offer you gentlemen a small libation?"

Rufus looked at Henry. "See? That's why he's called Friendly Fred." Then, turning to the governor, he asked, "Why small? Can't you afford a big one?"

The governor chuckled but his eyes were worried when they met Rufus's. "Why, of course, Mr. Boutwell. Let me fetch some glasses. Be back in a jiffy."

He scurried around his guests to the door of his secretary's office and disappeared.

When he returned, he held two empty glasses together by their rims. He was still holding his own drink in his left hand, and some of the liquid had spilled and was running down his fingers.

"You got your fingers inside the glasses," Rufus stated flatly. "How do we know you ain't been picking your nose?"

The governor chuckled again, his discomfort increasingly apparent. "Mr. Boutwell, I assure you, sir, that my hands are perfectly clean."

"Bullshit," Rufus said. "Nobody's hands are perfectly clean."

"Shall I have my secretary wash the glasses?"

"Forget it. Pour it—that rotgut will kill any germs."

The governor filled their glasses and brought them over, one at a time, still holding on to his own.

"Let's sit at the conference table," Rufus said, indicating a long table surrounded by ten chairs.

The governor waited until Rufus had seated himself at the head of the table before sitting to his left. Henry sat next to the governor.

"Henry, have I told you Friendly Fred once owned a butcher shop in this town? Do you have any idea how many times he sold those fingers he had in our glasses to little old ladies buying lamb chops or chicken liver?"

"Mr. Boutwell, you have a wonderful sense of humor," said Platt nervously. He turned to Henry. "Well, young man, you are marrying into our most prominent family. Mr. Boutwell and his gracious young daughter are highly regarded by the citizens of our fair state."

"What ever happened to the butcher shop?" Rufus asked.

"Sold it when I got a chance to be a conductor on the C and C Railroad. That, Mr. Godwin, was the old Carson-Colorado."

"That's right, now I remember," Rufus said. "That's how old Fred snagged himself the prettiest girl in Owens Valley. As the story goes, Freddy here saw this comely young lady driving a team and buggy and began flirting with her. Next thing you know, he stopped the train, jumped into her rig, and off they went to her home for lunch. So the passengers sat there and waited until finally Friendly Fred came back with this great big shit-eating grin on his face. That young girl today is our first lady, and, I might add, the prettiest one ever."

The governor smiled proudly. "Thank you, Mr. Boutwell."

Rufus smiled. "Freddy, since you're our governor, I thought I'd tell you what I've got in mind for Henry. Between the two of us, we're going to divide this state into two powerful political machines."

"But you already have that, Mr. Boutwell."

"Yeah, but now we're going to streamline it. In time Henry's going to take over the Democrats and I'm going to keep the Republicans. You being a Democrat, Friendly Fred, you better get mighty friendly with Henry. That is, if you're aiming to extend your future in this political business."

The governor smiled nervously at Henry. "Mr. Godwin, sir, I'd be honored to help you in any way I can."

"Now, friend, I'm going to tell Henry what I think about politics, but I don't want you to take this personally. I'm just talking theory."

"Of course, Mr. Boutwell, and it won't go past this room—you have my word on that, sir."

Rufus turned to Henry. "What you have to bear in mind, Henry, is that most politicians—and you can count the exceptions on the fingers of one hand—are nothing but public whores, put there by the bosses who rule their lives." Rufus paused. "Would you agree with that, Friendly Fred?"

"Yes, sir—there are some rotten apples, all right."

"Oh, they feel grand about their positions, Henry, their heads inflated by the royal treatment they receive, but they're men without any understanding of how business really works or of life on the underside. All they know is how to bullshit the public, and they feel no conviction about the things they preach—or, I should say, are told to preach—nor do they feel any compassion for those less fortunate than themselves. How does that strike you, Friendly Fred?"

"I agree with you completely. You know, of course, that I started out as a miner, and I worked in a stamp mill—nearly went deaf from the noise, so I know a little something about the underside. My daddy was a prospector all his life. All I ever got was four years of grade school and now I'm the governor. I wish my daddy could have lived to see me today."

Rufus winked at Henry. "See what I mean, m'boy?"

Henry had become increasingly embarrassed by Rufus's cruel performance. "No, I don't," he said. "I think you're being a bit too simplistic. Not to mention cynical."

Rufus stood up, leaving his drink untouched. "Did you hear that, Freddy? Not even married yet and already sounding like Alicia with that simplistic and cynical bullshit. But don't lose faith. Henry Godwin's going to be my strong right arm one of these days. You pay attention to him, Friendly Fred. When he says anything to you, he's speaking for me. Come on, Henry, let's go. I've got a wedding to plan."

After nearly two years of intensive lobbying in Washington, Henry had gradually begun to concede that there was something to Rufus's cynical viewpoint.

Then one evening at the ranch Rufus recalled the day Henry had called him simplistic and cynical in the governor's office.

"You've learned plenty in the last two years, Henry, so now I think you're ready to run Amos Rutledge's campaign for the United States Senate."

"You mean in the background."

"No, I mean up front. You're the Democrat and I'm the Republican. Next to the Holy Trinity, the two-party system's the most sacred political concept going. We recognize that fact and act accordingly. The politicians know I butter both sides. That way we don't create confusion. The time has come for you to become the clear moving force behind the Democrats in this state. We'll be Mr. Democrat and Mr. Republican, and between us we'll run the whole show. It's that simple if you've got the money to back your play. And that, m'boy, I've got."

"How did you come to select Rutledge?"

Rufus grinned. "He's the typical candidate, blinded by ambition and greed. And he's going to reach the top in government without once having experienced an hour's adversity. His whole life has been smooth as silk. Classy family, classy schooling, classy friends. The primrose path instead of the school of hard knocks. Consequently, no internal fortitude. One hard push and guys like him collapse, which, of course, makes it easier for us to control them. Not too bright, but bright enough to make an acceptable appearance and to know how to use opportunity. With proper prodding, guys like Rutledge find it easy to cut corners, wink at the law, bend it, or destroy it—all in the pursuit of their sacred trusts. So, like all greedy whores, they're pushovers for an easy buck as long as their asses are covered. That's where we come in. We show them how easy it is to fuck the system and not only get paid for it, but be admired in the bargain by the people whose votes they know we control."

"And what does that make us?" Henry asked.

"Power brokers," Rufus said, a gleam in his eyes as he glanced up at Henry from under his heavy lids, "who make the democratic system work the way it was intended in a capitalistic society."

The Forum Club occupied the entire top floor of the Capitol Hotel. Situated almost directly across the street from the Senate Office Building, it was a private club with a membership reserved exclusively for certain powerful senators, representatives, White House aides, cabinet members, and executives of regulatory agencies. Here in the luxury of the clubhouse they could meet with the country's most influential lobbyists, enjoy good food and drink, and be waited upon by skimpily attired waitresses who performed other services when so instructed by the management. Everything was on the house.

Conceived by Rufus, executed by Henry, and supported by a secret group of lobbies, membership in the Forum Club had soon become one of the most coveted prizes in Washington.

Seated with Henry in a red velour-upholstered booth, Senator Rutledge beamed happily as the waitress leaned forward to serve his drink, giving him a generous view of her creamy bosom. A moment later, another waitress serving drinks at a table nearby bent to pick up a napkin she had dropped and Rutledge's eyes nearly popped out of his head.

"I'll be damned," he said, turning to Henry, his eyes still unsure of what he had seen. "I'd swear that little gal's not wearing anything under that short skirt. She just took my picture."

"So I noticed," Henry said. "Not a bad-looking camera."

Rutledge nodded in approval. "I've never seen a shaved bush before. Damn intriguing."

Although Amos Rutledge conformed to Rufus's definition of a politician, Henry still liked him. He was an attractive man, energetic, a hard campaigner who knew how to follow instructions. His campaign had been aimed against the "moneyed oligarchy," a phrase that had delighted Rufus. Rutledge had promised to "stand at all times for the rights of the workingman." His father was a wealthy rancher and a stockholder in several of Rufus's corporations, but Rutledge assured his audiences that his origins were modest, a claim that was greeted by applause that grew louder as he kept pounding away at the "financial monopoly of Wall Street." The prosperity of Nevada depended upon the laboring classes, whom he pledged to protect by supporting laws so strong that monopolies would not dare disobey them.

He was equally forceful in affirming his belief in bimetalism. "If I'm elected," he told his audiences, "whenever any senator rises and offers a bill that is for the benefit and prosperity of his own state, then I will rise and demand that proper recognition be given to our greatest industry, and that some provision be made for the wider use of silver money."

Rutledge spoke out against high freight rates and the large landholdings of the Southern Pacific Railroad, castigated "the wealthy crooks who dispossess and rob the miners" (never acknowledging that the description fit Rufus Boutwell), endorsed the reduction of tariffs (except where they affected Nevada industries), the progressive taxation of incomes, effective corrupt practice acts, and the initiative, referendum, and recall—which he said were "the weapons the people will use to depose the trusts, special interests and privileged classes, who rule by virtue of wealth and might."

He said all these things with fervor and great sincerity. "The main issue," he would say, "is still the issue of justice and right. It is the issue of whether or not the people of this country shall be given the free voice in the control of their government that the Constitution guarantees to them."

Now seated with his mentor in the Forum Club, Amos Rutledge was reporting on his first month as the junior senator from Nevada.

"I couldn't be more impressed," he said, his attention now riveted on Henry. "My senatorial colleagues have made me feel at home. It's more like a club than a legislative body. I can't get over the deference paid to me. Doorkeepers bow and there are pages at hand to do my every bidding. Hotel and restaurant managers greet me personally. Waiters and bellboys can't do enough for me. I had no idea how prestigious a position a senator held. I believe it is affecting me. I seem to walk with more dignity. I have more poise. I certainly feel more confident. It is all very wonderful and I'm as happy as ambition could make me. And I owe it all to you and Rufus. What can I do to express my gratitude?"

"There will be ample time for that," Henry said, raising his glass in a salute to Rutledge. "You're here because we share the same goals for Nevada. What's good for our state is good for all of us."

"Precisely my sentiment," Rutledge said, saluting Henry in return. "I plan to move on some of these issues at first opportunity."

"For the time being, my advice is that you restrain yourself from taking part in debates," Henry said, turning to acknowledge greetings from the Chairman of the Senate Foreign Relations Committee and the Senate Majority Leader. They were being escorted to their favorite booth by the club's manager, Clara Cox, a statuesque redhead whom Henry had persuaded to sell her San Francisco brothel in order to accept this position. Henry returned his attention to Amos. "It is important for you to establish a reputation for modesty until we can arrange the proper committee appointments. In the next four or five months you will become a member of the most important Western committees: Mines and Mining; Public Lands, Irrigation and Reclamation; and Indian Affairs."

"How about Foreign Relations? I majored in international affairs at Stanford. I was thinking of a career in the State Department until Dad sidetracked me into his business."

"All in good time. For the moment, we're concentrating on positions that will be beneficial to your constituents. Legislative experts are preparing material for you to present to these committees. I assure you that your constituents will soon know that you are a busy man on their behalf."

"What exactly do you have in mind?" Rutledge asked, his eyes narrowing as he studied the glass in his hand.

"Rufus thinks of you as a 'frontier statesman,' and to create that image your concerns will deal with irrigation, Indian reservations, the control of rabid coyotes, and three major resolutions that we want you to sponsor. The first promotes and encourages the mining of coal, phosphate, oil, gas, potassium, and sodium in the public domain; the second authorizes the Secretary of the Interior to lease certain public lands for the purpose of increasing the potash supply; and the third raises the price of silver."

"That's quite an order for a freshman senator."

Henry ignored the thin edge of sarcasm that had crept into Rutledge's tone. "They are all worthwhile projects that will receive support from your colleagues, and we feel it will be to your credit to have your name associated with them. Unless, of course, you have some specific objection, in which case there are others who would be only too glad to author these resolutions. Perhaps you should hold back after all and let me talk to our senior senator. I'm sure old Elisha Toombs—"

"Just a moment, please," Rutledge interrupted. "I have no objection." His face had turned a delicate pink. "None whatsoever. In fact, I would consider it an honor to sponsor any bill that you feel will be beneficial to our state."

Henry smiled pleasantly. "That's very good of you. Meanwhile, I'd suggest again that you refrain from speaking out on controversial issues. This is not the time to antagonize colleagues whose support you will need on our local programs."

CHAPTER

27

For those knowledgeable about Nevada politics the real capital of Nevada was in Room 600 of the Bank of Nevada building at the corner of Telegraph and Carsons streets, two blocks north of the state capitol.

This was Rufus Boutwell's main office, atop the six-story building that served as headquarters for his major enterprises. It was here that the political and economic destiny of the state was charted. Beginning with his early days in Tonopah and Goldfield, Rufus and his aides had created a system of bipartisan politics in which the two main parties traded off political positions. The sole representative was a Republican, the governor was a Democrat, and the Senate seats were paired off, one to each party. Although the stated affiliations of the voters were predominately Democratic, Nevadans cast their ballots not so much for the party as for the candidate and the money behind him. Rufus Boutwell was the state's largest employer, and as the San Francisco *Examiner* had phrased it, "By reason of its small population and the transient character of some of its people, money has a powerful influence in Nevada elections."

Rufus had laughed. "They don't know the half of it," he told Henry. "For a state with a population under a hundred thousand, a fifth of whom are registered voters, Amos Rutledge's campaign still cost me a quarter million, which is more than they're spending in California for a senatorial race."

"We had to depose a stubborn old relic," Henry reminded him, "but Amos is well worth the investment. Less than six months in office, and he's already become an expert in legislative horse-trading, and he knows how to wage a campaign from the Senate floor. He's a tenacious, cunning debater and deserves much of the credit for pushing through the amendments and riders that raised tariffs on gypsum, clay, silica, manganese, and tungsten."

It was the first week of October 1929, and they were in Henry's office, Room 601. Rufus was sitting on a corner of Henry's desk, watching him with amused slits of gray shining through the thick lids.

"Don't bullshit an old bullshitter," Rufus shot back. "I know who's responsible for the tariffs, and I know that the last time Amos got up to speak on raising the price of silver he got only as far as 'Mister President' before the whole Senate chamber was empty. Even the Hearst reporter in the press gallery took a snooze."

Rufus was referring to a bill that would compel the Treasury Department to resume the purchase of silver at a dollar an ounce—thirty-five cents an ounce above the world market price. Since American mines were producing five and a third million ounces a month, the bill would yield a multimillion-dollar subsidy to silver producers, with the lion's share going to Rufus, the nation's single largest producer.

"It's true that he had to hammer at it pretty steadily, but the point is that he got the bill through the Senate," Henry said. "He was the only senator called to testify before the Committee on Banking and Currency. He did a superb job of pushing it through. The bill was favorably reported by committee, and it passed in the Senate over the repeated protests of Treasury Secretary Mellon."

"We've got to exert pressure," Rufus growled, "force Hoover to ditch Mellon."

"Our problem is with the House. The vote has gone against us every time."

Rufus shook his head. "The problem goes deeper than that. It really started in nineteen twenty-five when Britain put India on the gold standard. They melted the silver currency into bullion and dumped it on the world market. Then other countries got the idea that the best way to obtain funds to pay their war debts was by debasing their silver money. Last year alone, France, Belgium, and Great Britain dumped some forty million ounces of silver on the world market, and the bottom, as you well know, fell right in hell out."

Henry remained placid. "We'll try again this year. Several members of the House Banking Committee, including the chairman, are now members of the Forum Club."

"The House is always a pain in the ass," Rufus said, easing off the desk and slumping into an easy chair beside it. "Ah, fuck it. I'm just going to have to close down production at some of the mines."

"Probably a wise move, the way inflation is raising the cost of production."

Rufus stretched lazily and yawned. "Tell me, Henry, what do you hear from Ali?"

Alicia had been gone nearly two years and in all that time had not written a single letter to Rufus. Although Henry had written to her as often as he could, giving her news of Randolph, and had received a steady stream of letters, there was never anything in them that might give Rufus any comfort beyond the fact that she was having a good time and sending her love.

The letters were anecdotal and confusing. Alicia jumped from subject to subject, leading Henry to believe most had been written while she was more or less inebriated. She wrote about her "dearest friends," Scott and Zelda, Hem and Hadley, Ezra and Gertrude and Alice and Silvia and Isadora—an endless stream of first names. She implored Henry to read *The Sun Also Rises*, pointing out that Jake, the hero, who had "had his hat rack shot off during the war," was in love with a Lady Brett who "has my problem." Lady Brett had "flings" with various men, including bullfighters, "who have the world's tightest asses," but always "comes back to Jake, who has the patience of Griselda and the wisdom of Solomon. In the last passage of the book, they are riding in a taxi, and she snuggles close to Jake and says, 'Oh, Jake, we could have had such a damned good time together.' And he says, 'Yes, isn't it pretty to think so,'" At this point the letter had become illegible, and it was obvious to Henry that the blurred scrawl had been caused by a sudden flood of tears.

In another letter Alicia had bitterly denounced her way of life, recalling how "sophomoric" she must have sounded when she talked of a new generation, "when all the time it was a lost generation. Instead of creating a new utopia, we've ended up in the same dismal swamp." She alluded to unhappy love affairs and called herself a "rich bitch who can afford to be an international tramp."

But it was the last letter that Henry thought of when Rufus inquired about his daughter. She had written she was down with a "stylish disease," and the first word that flashed across Henry's mind was venereal. But she had gone on, quite gaily, to say that "Byron longed for it, Keats died of it, and it could even be argued that the decline in the arts can be traced to the decline in tuberculosis."

Henry had closed his eyes when he read that and leaned his head back in the chair, breathing through his open mouth. Cold sweat had broken out on his face and he had felt sick to his stomach.

Randolph, who had come into the living room at that moment, stopped to stare at his father. "Are you sick, Daddy?" he asked, his large dark eyes apprehensive.

Henry raised his head and opened his eyes. "No, I'm all right, son."

"What're you reading?" he asked, moving toward Henry for a better look at the letter in his hand. "Is it from Mommy?"

Henry nodded. "Yes, she sends her love."

"Is she all right?"

There was a tremor in Randolph's voice, and Henry tried to muster a reassuring look. "Of course, she's just fine."

Randolph hadn't forgotten his mother. Hardly a day went by that he didn't mention her name to his father or grandfather. He had kept every postcard she had sent him. At night, when Henry sat by his bed, Randolph would pull out the latest postcard and ask, "What's so nice about that place that she won't come back home?"

"Well, she has many good friends in Europe."

"Then why don't we go see her?"

"That's a swell idea," Henry would say. "One of these days we'll do just that."

"But when?" Randolph would insist.

"One day soon."

At first Randolph had cried, but in time he'd learned to control his tears. Once his eyes flashed and he looked challengingly at Henry and announced, "I hate her!"

"No, you don't," Henry said easily, refusing to rise to the bait.

"Yes, I do. She says she loves me in her letters and postcards, but she's a liar. Otherwise, why would she go away and leave us? She's selfish and I hate her. I never want to see her again. I'm gonna write and tell her to stay in Europe, that she's not wanted here anymore."

Henry tousled the boy's hair. "Don't be so hard on your poor mother. You don't want to break her heart, do you?"

At a loss for words, Randolph turned his head and glared fiercely at the opposite wall. Henry remained silently at his side until he fell asleep.

Now standing in front of his father in the living room, Randolph said, "Did she get the picture I sent her last month?"

"As a matter of fact, she says you look quite handsome. She's amazed at how much you've grown."

Randolph smiled. "I told her that in another year I'll probably be

159

taller than she is, and if she doesn't want to be my mother, she can come back and be my girl friend."

"That's quite a compliment," Henry said. "I'm sure she appreciated it."

"I was only joking around, but I wanted her to know how I feel."

"Of course," Henry said, looking down at the letter. "Was there anything special you wanted?"

"Can I ride White Lightning this afternoon? Charlie Fitch is coming over and we're gonna race."

"Sure, son—he'll enjoy a good run."

Randolph ran off, and Henry resumed his reading of the letter. "Keats was in the grip of tubercular fever when he composed his 'Ode on a Grecian Urn.' Some critics feel that the fever enabled the poem, and that the process of poem-making translated the fever into a benign passion. During a high fever there is a feeling of being out of one's own body that Keats called 'negative capability.' "

It was so typical of Alicia to dwell on the artistic aspect of something that was a serious personal tragedy. "In his 'Ode' he identifies the physical state as a 'burning forehead, and a parching tongue.' God, I can testify to that. He wrote the third and best of his volumes of poetry, which is rich in imagery and phrasing, when he was dying of the fever. At this point, dear Henry, you may well wonder as to my own artistic contribution. I've had some marvelous fantasies about you —a strange reversal, wouldn't you say?—but I think this shows that this bodily fever is a consuming passion. My fondest wish at the moment is more pragmatic than artistic. I want to outlive Keats, who died at twenty-six. When it comes right down to it, I find that I prefer life to art."

Henry dropped the letter on the coffee table and got up to make himself a stiff drink. What a pointless, incomprehensible waste. Yet somehow he felt responsible. His love had not been strong enough to satiate the passion that had driven her to the brink of madness. He would go to her at once. She was in a sanatorium in Zurich and had been there three months before she wrote. Returning to his chair with the drink, he picked up the letter.

"Oh, darling Henry," he read,

> this is not the time for heroic gestures. Please, and I emphasize the *please*, and underline it, don't come to Zurich. If there ever was a time in my life when I did not want you to see me, it is now, when

the ravages of this infernal fever have consumed what little youth and beauty I had left. Give me time to get back on my feet—the doctors are optimistic—then I will welcome you with open arms. We can tour Europe together and I will show you "divine magnetic lands." Oh, yes, my sweetheart, in the throes of my fever I relive that magic moment in Rufus's gilded cage and weep tears of repentance for our lost love. "Pride goeth before destruction, and an haughty spirit before a fall." It is truly the original sin.

Take good care of yourself, my true love, and of that sweet lovely boy, who writes such grown-up letters and still thinks of me as his mother. I count my blessings and hope for the best.

Love, Alicia

He sighed in anguish as he refolded the letter and slipped it into the inside pocket of his suit jacket. She had anticipated his reaction, and he admired her spirit and would respect her request. She was Rufus's daughter, all right—no question about that at all, and in more ways than one.

Now in his office, with Rufus waiting for a response, Henry said, "I heard from her about a week ago."

"Jesus Christ, what's she up to now? When the hell's she coming home to be a wife and mother? I tell you that boy's nuts about her." Rufus stood up and stalked to the window, staring glumly at the sparsely populated capital city. "This fucking town's not sophisticated enough for her. Alicia's like her mother. She needs the excitement of a big city. Bright lights and lots of fancy people."

"You're right, of course," Henry said, "but it's too late to worry about that now."

Rufus wasn't listening. "I loved her mother, goddamnit, and I fucked it up. Sure, she was oversexed, like Alicia, who handles it with a little more class." He turned to gaze sharply at Henry. "You look surprised. I've received reports—don't worry. But I should've done something about her, and you should've too. A woman's place is at her husband's side. You should have put your foot down. But don't get me wrong. I'm not blaming you for a goddamn thing. I'm grateful you stuck it out. I've grown damn fond of Randy and I've got big plans for him. He's bright and quick and plenty aggressive. He measures up. That boy's going places. There's no two ways about that."

Henry remembered Alicia's warning that Rufus would steal Randolph away from him. "You haven't been filling his head with your dreams, have you?"

"Sure, why not?" Rufus challenged, turning to face Henry. "You bet your ass I have. What's wrong with that?"

"He's just a little boy who misses his mother."

"Well, it's time he got over that and gave some thought to his future."

Rufus returned to the easy chair and plunked his feet on top of Henry's desk. "Why did you say it's too late for Ali?"

Henry took a deep breath. "She's in a Zurich sanatorium—"

"What!" Rufus exclaimed. "Taking the cure, is she?"

"Not exactly, Rufus. Ali is down with tuberculosis."

Rufus threw his head back in exasperation. "Holy sonofabitching Jesus Christ to hell. TB is a fucking killer. I've seen plenty of it in boom towns. That fucking fever eats you alive. Turns healthy people into ghosts right before your eyes."

"She says her doctor is optimistic. And you know she's a fighter. She's not going to give up. Her attitude couldn't be better. Even joked about it. Called it a 'stylish disease.' In fact, she said that Byron longed for it and Keats died of it but that he created his best work while under the influence of the fever."

"That's fucking nonsense. The fever drives people out of their minds while it eats up their lungs. You actually lie there coughing up pieces of your lungs."

Rufus was talking rough, but his voice was trembling. "That goddamn sweet, lovely, fucked-up little girl." And then he was weeping openly, the tears running down his ruddy cheeks. He took out a handkerchief and blew his nose loudly. "We've got to go to her," he sobbed. "I want the best goddamned doctors in the world looking after her. I want her cured and straightened out and back home where she belongs. By Christ, I've sat by long enough. She's gonna mend her ways if I have to keep her under lock and key twenty-four hours a day."

"I wish you would go see her, Rufus. I'm sure it would be the best thing that could happen to her."

"The best thing would be for you to come with me."

"That was my first thought, too. But she doesn't want me to see her the way she is now. Call it female vanity, but I can understand how she feels. When she's well again, I'll join her in Europe, and she's promised to show me the sights."

"Goddamnit, that's great. Make it a second honeymoon."

Henry smiled at Rufus. "Ali was right. You really are a pussycat."

Rufus closed his eyes and dug his fingers deep into his eye sockets. "Why do you suppose she's never written to me. Don't she know I love her?"

Sitting up in bed that evening, Randolph said, "Daddy, I wish you'd start calling me Randy instead of Randolph. All my friends at school call me Randy. Even Rufus calls me Randy."

"But your name is Randolph."

"I don't like it. It sounds dumb. Charlie Fitch's name is Charles but his parents call him Charlie."

"I don't care what Charlie Fitch's parents call him," Henry said, aware that his tone had grown sharp. "You come from a long line of distinguished Americans who took pride in their family names."

"I guess it's okay for a general to be called Randolph, but it sounds stupid for a kid. The other kids make fun of it."

Henry sighed and looked at Randolph. "General Randolph Harrison Godwin was a great man, a war hero, and you should be proud to carry his name."

"I'll bet he knew lots of great war stories," Randolph said, lying back.

"That he did, son. He told me the one I'm about to tell you now. It concerns a Negro man called Thaddeus. You see, after the War Between the States, Mississippi came under the domination of carpetbaggers and renegade Negroes. The governor was a carpetbag army officer. The lieutenant governor, as well as a United States senator, and most of the legislators in Jackson were Negroes. In Vicksburg, the entire city government was in their hands. Most were illiterate cotton pickers, who had no concept of government, and a few were cutthroats and thieves. The white folk, who paid all the taxes, which had multiplied fourteenfold, had no voice in their government. A Negro militia marched through our streets with muskets loaded and bayonets fixed. White men found on the street at night were searched and their weapons were confiscated. Then the Democrats put up a strong ticket and won the election, and the next day they kicked all the carpetbaggers and most of the Negroes out of the government."

"Were you there, Daddy?"

Henry laughed. "No, son, but I heard so many stories from the General that sometimes I feel like I really did live through those years."

Henry took a swallow of bourbon and puffed contentedly on the cigar. "Well, one time there was an armed insurrection. Negroes began marching on Vicksburg and the General had to rush to town to take command of a makeshift army of former Confederate soldiers. Your great-grandmother was left alone with my father, who was just a baby then. All the Negroes on the place, except for Thaddeus, had joined the insurrectionists.

"It was a Sunday night, and there had been shooting in the countryside all day, when finally your great-grandmother heard them coming up the road, yelling and shooting, and she could hear the impact of their bullets striking against the house, a few breaking through the parlor's front windows. Naturally, your great-grandmother was terrified. There had been some pretty gruesome stories about the fate of white families falling into the hands of Negro mobs, and she felt completely defenseless with no one there to protect her. Thaddeus, you see, was about seventeen or eighteen—just a kid.

"But suddenly there he was, rushing out the front door with two double-barreled shotguns in his hands. He stood on the porch, with a gun resting on each hip like one of those movie cowboys. Some of the Negroes had torches and there was wild talk about hanging your great-grandmother and burning down the house. But Thaddeus told them he was prepared to die on that porch, and he promised to take a whole bunch of them along with him unless they came to their senses pretty damn quick. 'If it's a white man's house you want to burn,' he said, 'there's a whole slew of them down the road a piece.' He told them he'd been born on this plantation and he was ready to die on it, if that was the way they saw it."

Henry took a deep breath. "From that day onward Thaddeus was the General's topkick on our plantation. He was his main man. He and his wife, Alva, and their two kids were family. The General wouldn't have traded a hair off Thaddeus's head for the whole state of Mississippi."

Randolph thought about this for a moment. "How much did the General give him?" he asked.

Henry gave the boy a sharp look. "What are you talking about?"

"Well, I mean, how much did the General pay Thaddeus for what he did?"

Henry could not conceal his irritation. "Where in the world do you get ideas like that? What does money have to do with it?"

The boy shrugged. "Well, Rufus would have paid him. He's got a whole lot of money. He's a millionaire."

Henry stood up. "Is that what you and Rufus talk about, money?"

"He says he pays you money," Randolph said, his dark eyes looking so innocent. Then he smiled and sat up in bed again. "Rufus said he's going to give me lots of money when I grow up. I'm going to be famous and rich. He's going to see to it that I get whatever I want. He promised me."

Henry shook his head and started for the door. "Go to sleep," he said. "We'll discuss this some other time."

28

He dreamed that a bell was ringing. Finally, the sound penetrated his sleep and Henry realized that it was the telephone on his bedside table. Without sitting up or opening his eyes, he groped for the phone.

A gruff voice asked, "Mr. Godwin, is that you, sir?"

"Who's this?" he said, his eyes still closed.

"It's Matt at the Golden Nugget, sir."

Henry opened his eyes and switched on the table lamp. It was two twenty in the morning. "Do you realize the time?"

"I'm sorry, Mr. Godwin, but I've got a situation here that needs your personal attention. It's Mr. Boutwell, sir."

"Well, what about Mr. Boutwell?"

"He's in a bit of a jam, sir. He's kind of under the weather, if you know what I mean, and kind of shot up the place."

Henry was wide awake now. "Anyone hurt?"

"No, sir—well, nothing too serious. There's some property damage, but I don't worry about that, Mr. Godwin, 'cause I know he's good for it."

"Where precisely is Mr. Boutwell at this moment?"

"He's in my office, tied to a chair, I'm afraid. He's not been harmed —that I swear—but we had to ditch the girl and gag him when the cops came to investigate the shooting."

Henry took a deep breath. "Ditched what girl—how does she fit into the picture?"

"Well, I'll tell you, Mr. Godwin, there's this young girl who works for me, hired her just last week, came in looking like a starved kitten—cute little thing, with big sad eyes—so I put her waiting on tables, and she's worked out just fine."

"Matt, for Christ's sake, get to the point."

"Well, when Mr. Boutwell started shooting, one of them slugs must've hit a nailhead in the floor or something, and kind of ended up in her whatchamacallit."

"Oh, God," Henry moaned. "Which whatchamacallit and how god-damn serious is it?"

"Well, you know, sir, her cunt, sir. Kind of creased it or something, but nothing serious. Got her stashed at Doc Sprague's place—every-thing's on the q.t. Nothing to worry about."

"That's what you think," Henry said, rising from the bed with resig-nation. "Untie Mr. Boutwell, but keep him quiet until I get there. I'm on my way."

While driving to the Golden Nugget in his Packard sedan, Henry thought about why it had happened. Baby-sitting Rufus was George Clews's department, Clews the one man who could cool him down without bruising his pride. So Clews must have been away on another of his secret missions.

Alicia had certainly been right when she predicted that Rufus's strong right arm would never know what his strong left arm was doing. "Both arms," she had said, "are firmly tied to strings manipulated by Rufus."

Henry had found this situation particularly troubling whenever he permitted himself to think of what Rufus demanded of him. He yearned for the day he could become his own man, build his own career, create his own destiny, without having to account to Rufus Boutwell.

Henry stood with his back to the closed door a long time before he spoke. Rufus appeared to be coming around. He sat slumped in a chair, his head rolled back, his eyelids flickering, the dark pouches beneath his eyes magnified by the harsh overhead light. His face was grayish and slimy slick, his mouth hung open, and his thick lips were coated with vomit.

"How much booze did you feed him anyway?"

"He already had a load by the time he got here around closing time."

"Then why the hell give him more?"

Matt shrugged, his eyes imploring the ceiling. "Nobody refuses Mr. Boutwell. Still, I tried to ease him out, and that's when he pulled his six-shooter. This is the third time he's shot up this place and I can tell you we're all lucky to be alive. Good thing we was nearly empty or we'd have a few dead bodies around here. He fired all six rounds before we could get the gun away from him. Even then, he put up a hell of a fight."

Henry moved to a small desk in the corner of the room, picked up the telephone, and placed a call to Doc Sprague. He listened while the doctor assured him that the girl's injury was not serious.

"Damnedest thing I ever saw," Doc Sprague said. "The spent slug just creased the lips of her pudenda. Damn near deflowered her."

"How's she taking it?"

"Asleep right now, but my advice is for you to be here when she wakes up in the morning. She may have some objection to being nearly raped by a gun, and I'm not the one to persuade her otherwise."

"Any permanent injury?"

"None whatsoever. Only a superficial wound, but painful for the time being all the same."

"Thanks, Doc. I'll be there in the morning."

Henry hung up and returned his attention to Boutwell.

"Want the boys to put him in your car?" Matt asked.

"Thanks, Matt—I'm grateful for all you've done."

Matt grinned proudly. "He's puked everything. He's gonna have a big head in the morning, but he can thank his lucky star nobody's dead. You tell him that for me, Mr. Godwin. We did the right thing by him, but next time ask him to go somewhere else, will you, when he feels like shooting up a place? Them Wild West days are gone, for Christ's sake."

No sooner had Henry gotten Rufus into bed in the room across the hall from Randolph's than he opened his eyes and reached for Henry's hand. "Get me some Irish—my head's killing me."

"Don't you think you've had enough for one night?"

"Jesus Christ, man, my head feels like it's gonna explode. The Irish will ease the pressure."

Henry left the room, and when he returned with the drink Rufus was sitting up in bed, his face contorted with pain. He reached for the drink and downed it in one gasping swallow. Then turning to Henry, his face now almost purplish, he cried, "Why hasn't she written to me? Not one letter in three years."

"I don't know," Henry said. "But forget it for now, will you, and try to get some sleep. You look like hell."

"I look like I feel," he groaned. "God, I wish George was here. He knows how to take care of me."

"Don't think I don't wish it, too," Henry said.

Rufus handed Henry the empty glass. "I need another and don't give me no argument."

"Why not?" Henry said, barely masking his irritation. "You're the boss, you pay the salaries."

Boutwell grinned. "In that case, get the whole goddamn bottle."

Henry brought the bottle, and Rufus drank directly from it. "I puked all that good booze, and all I've got left is a headache. I need a bun to sleep."

"Enjoy yourself. I'll see you in the morning."

"Sit down a minute and give me the bad news. How many people did I kill tonight?"

Henry sat down with reluctance. "I don't know. How many places did you shoot up?"

Rufus groaned. "How would I know?" He tipped the bottle, his Adam's apple bobbing, the liquor running out the corners of his mouth.

"I only know of one casualty—a young waitress. She's at Doc Sprague's house."

Rufus lowered the bottle and wiped his mouth with the back of his hand. "Give it to me straight."

"One of your wild shots ricocheted into her pudenda."

"Her what?"

"Let me put it this way. You nearly took her cherry."

Boutwell grimaced. "Have you talked to her? Is she going to make trouble?"

"I couldn't tonight—Doc had her sedated. But I'll see her in the morning."

Rufus hugged the bottle against his chest and Henry could see that he was quickly getting drunk again. "I need George," he whined. "What am I going to do?"

"What can George do that I can't?"

He waved the bottle impatiently. "You don't understand about George. He's been with me a long time. Knows what to do without my saying a word. Did I ever tell you how I met him?"

Henry stood up. "Rufus, go to sleep. That bottle's nearly empty, and that's it for tonight."

"Sit down, dammit," Rufus shouted angrily. "I want to tell you about this guy. This ain't no ordinary flunky, you know. This man would do anything for me. Don't you understand that, for Christ's sake?"

Henry remained standing. "Tell me tomorrow when you're sober."

"Don't give me that shit, Henry. Now sit down and listen a minute. What the hell's wrong with you?"

Henry sighed and sat down. "I hope you're not sorry in the morning."

Rufus laughed harshly. "Henry, you're my son-in-law. I trust you. We don't have no secrets, you and me—or do we?" He gave Henry a slanted look.

"Do you know what time it is?"

Rufus ignored him. "This happened nearly fifteen years ago. I was in some crummy bar in New York City. I'd gone slumming and I got in a fight with this big sonofabitch at least a head taller than me, and he yanked my six-shooter out of my hand and beat me over the head with it. Every time I got up, he knocked me down. I remember a woman pleading with me to stay down, but I kept getting up and he kept pounding me on the head. God, there was blood running in my eyes, I couldn't see anything, and I was crawling on all fours when he started kicking me in the ass and laughing like a loon." Rufus paused. "Then, after he had his fun, he kicked me in the head and the lights went out. I woke up outside in an alley and there was George bending over me. I was still pretty drunk and he picked me up like I was a baby and took me to a fleabag in the neighborhood to clean me up."

Boutwell leaned back in the pillows and closed his eyes. "He was just a punk kid of nineteen from Hell's Kitchen, a real rough-and-tough sonofabitch, but he was straight with me. All I wanted to do was go back to the bar and kill that dirty bastard. So George said he'd help me. He pulled out this blackjack, a leather job with lead inside, and said, 'I'll hold him and you use this. Why hurt your hands on this bum?' So back we went, but I stayed in the alley while George went inside to get him. The minute that guy spotted me in the alley, he tried to make a run for it. But it was too late. George got a headlock on him and I went to work with the blackjack. I smashed his face to pieces. All this time this guy's trying to scream but he can't because George's choking him. Then I hear this loud, cracking sound, and his head just dropped to one side, just hung there. I knew right away he was a goner. So George says to me, 'I'm sorry, he moved the wrong way.' And I said, 'Forget it, I only wish I'd done it myself.' That's the whole story. I got my gun back and George's been with me ever since."

Rufus sat up and emptied the bottle. "See, Henry, what I like best about George was that he knew how to pick a winner." He paused, handed the empty bottle to Henry, and lay back on the pillows, closing his eyes. "He could have rolled me in the alley. I always carry a bundle, and I wouldn't have been the first guy he rolled. But he had seen the fight, had seen how I wouldn't stay down, and he liked that enough to back my play without any preconditions. That kind of natural instinct is pure gold in my book."

Doc Sprague met Henry at the door and escorted him into the office in the front part of his home.

"Sure glad to see you," he said, sitting down behind a desk cluttered with medical books and folders, medicine bottles, and assorted instruments.

Henry didn't like the frown on the doctor's face. "How is she doing this morning? No complications, I hope."

Doc Sprague laced his fingers behind his head and leaned back in his swivel chair. "It's nothing physical, Henry—nothing you can put your finger on." Then he winked slyly. "I'm not saying you wouldn't want to. She's damn cute and it will heal soon enough. It's her mental attitude that bothers me. She's taking it pretty hard, I'm afraid."

"What precisely are you getting at?"

Sprague offered, "I'm glad you're here instead of George Clews. I'd appreciate it if you could arrange some form of livelihood for her. She can't go back to the roadhouse. This story will be all over the county by sundown."

Henry stood up. "Yes, well, the legend grows. Not much anybody can do about that. How about my seeing her now? I'd appreciate it if you'd leave us alone."

Henry tapped lightly on the door and slowly opened it. The girl lay on her back, the white sheet tucked under her chin, and all Henry could see were those big round, sad eyes Matt had told him about.

"May I come in?" he asked. "I'd like to talk to you for a minute. Doc said it was okay."

She nodded, her dark eyes not leaving his.

There was a chair next to the bed. "Mind if I sit down?" Henry asked.

She shook her head.

"How are you feeling this morning?"

She just stared at him with those big sad eyes. "You're not mad at me, are you?" Henry asked gently. "Look, I'm your friend. I want to help, if you'll let me. Doc says you'll be out of bed in a couple of days, and I thought maybe you'd be interested in a new job. Have you ever done any office work?"

She cleared her throat and held on to the sheet under her chin.

"I can type about forty words a minute, but my shorthand's terrible."

"Do you like typing?"

She shrugged. "Not all that much."

"Well, there's other kinds of office work. I'll bet you'd make a great receptionist. In fact, you know, we could use a pretty girl with a sweet voice. Dress up the place."

He winked at her and she almost smiled. "My name's Henry Godwin and I'm vice-president of Nevada Consolidated Mines. What's your name?"

She bit into her lower lip. "Iola," she said, pausing, uncertain for a moment, and then blurted, "Raintree. Iola Raintree."

They were silent for a while, each studying the other, Iola's big sad eyes never leaving his.

"Well, how about that job? Want to give it a whirl?"

She frowned. "Will I be working for you?"

"Yes. Well, more or less. Same building."

"How big is the building?"

"Six stories."

"Oh, I know that place. What floor are you on?"

Henry smiled. "Sixth. That's it. You'll be the receptionist for the sixth floor. That's where all the big shots hang their hats."

She was silent for a while. "Does that man who shot me work in that building?"

Henry took a deep breath. "Yes, he owns the building. Iola, please believe me, he's very sorry for what happened. He had just learned that day that his daughter is gravely ill in Switzerland. He felt terribly sad about it, and I'm afraid he tried to drown his sorrows. I suppose he thought it would kill the pain, but instead it kind of made him go a little crazy for a while there. Actually, he's really a good man, and he wants to do everything he can to make it up to you."

Iola's lips trembled and tears filled her eyes. "I forgive him," she murmured, and slowly turned her head away.

29

When the stock market crashed on October 29, 1929, Rufus Boutwell was two days at sea, on his way to see Alicia in Switzerland. Within a fortnight $30 billion in paper value of listed stocks would be wiped out. As bad as it was all over the United States, the Great Depression was cataclysmic in Nevada. The price of silver dropped so low that the cost of production alone would exceed its market value. Mining stocks plummeted, and Boutwell's Nevada Securities Company hovered on the brink of bankruptcy. Fourteen banks in which Boutwell owned a controlling interest failed within a month. This was followed by a drought that caused widespread destruction to farm lands. Water holes dried up, killing thousands of stock animals. Lumbering, railroad construction, and all mining activities came to a standstill, forcing countless workers to leave the state to seek more hospitable conditions elsewhere; there were no soup lines in Nevada—it was still a land of rugged individualism.

Henry wrote to Rufus every day, urging him to return before all was lost, but as the days and weeks slipped by without any response, Henry grew desperate. He sent cables, tried to reach him by transatlantic telephone, but Rufus remained incommunicado.

Henry sat in his office and stared out the window while ranchers, miners, bankers, and stockholders cooled their heels in the reception room. He knew what they wanted but had nothing encouraging to say to them. Their only option was to ride it out and hope for the best.

Throughout this ordeal Henry stayed away from George Clews, who had remained behind to continue doing whatever it was he did for Boutwell. Even if Clews were in communication with his boss, Henry knew he would never betray that confidence. Besides, Rufus had to be aware of the existing situation. It was worldwide. There was no escaping it. Unless, of course, Rufus was dead, a thought that Henry had quickly dismissed. The fact that Alicia had stopped writing was proof enough that Rufus was there with her. But why had he continued to ignore Henry's inquiries?

Henry spent hours staring at the distant mountain range, his view from the sixth floor unimpeded by any other structure, for Carson City was built low to the ground. No wonder Alicia couldn't stand it, Henry thought. It was a dismal frontier town, with nothing to offer but the crudest forms of gambling and drinking. There was no social life, nothing to stimulate the intellect, nothing to occupy the hours Alicia had to spend alone while he pursued her father's rainbows.

They had been in the process of building a solid political organization and financial base, but how ephemeral it all seemed now. In one letter Henry had warned Rufus that unless he acted immediately he would be left with nothing more than his Cadillac car and membership in the Cohisa Duck Club. It was hyperbole but there was a point to be made nevertheless. The political base was only as sound as the financial base. Or vice versa. One simply would not endure without the other. It seemed that even God was conspiring, withholding the precious water so essential to the survival of ranching and farming—two of the state's most vital industries.

Finally, unable to reach Rufus any other way, Henry contacted the Pinkerton's National Detective Agency and requested an immediate investigation. Within a week the head of the Pinkerton's San Francisco office was on the telephone with a report.

Afterward, Henry resumed staring at the distant mountain range. Once he understood what had happened, it was not altogether surprising. Rufus had gone on a horrendous bender, starting on the train that had taken him to New York, continuing on board ship and on European trains, until he reached Switzerland two weeks later. Upon his arrival, Rufus had been informed by the head of the sanatorium that Alicia was terminal.

Her appearance had so shattered him that he had vanished for another fortnight, the double-tiered bender culminating in a sudden hematemesis caused by incipient cirrhosis of the liver. The vomiting of blood had been a warning of the serious consequences that could result if he continued his drinking. The incident had so terrified Rufus that he had promptly signed himself into the sanatorium to take the cure—which explained his apparent inability to cope with the problems at home. But now, the Pinkertons had learned, the doctor claimed that Rufus was reading through his accumulated mail.

The call from Switzerland came three days later. It was a bad connection, with the static sounding like waves crashing against a rocky shore. Nevertheless, Henry was delighted to hear Boutwell's voice.

"All I've got to do is take off for a few weeks and the whole fucking country caves in." Boutwell had to shout to be heard over the static.

"I assume you've read all my mail, so I won't waste time repeating myself," Henry shouted. "What we need right now is some cash flow to keep us afloat until we can get our silver act through Congress." The act, Rufus knew, would force the Treasury to treble its silver deposits in order to raise the price.

"How're you doing on that deal?"

"We're making progress, but it takes time. Meanwhile, with stocks worthless and credit restricted, we just don't have any capital base. If you've got anything under the mattress, now's the time to produce it."

There was a long pause and when Boutwell spoke Henry could barely make out the words. "Listen, I'll talk to George. He'll get in touch with you later today and give you a pleasant surprise. Now you listen to him. He'll know what I want. If you need more financial details, talk to Harry Mitchell—he's got all the figures."

"Wait a minute," Henry shouted. "Before you hang up, how is Ali? I haven't heard from her in weeks."

"Not good, Henry, not good at all. That's why I'm staying. I can't leave her now. She's delirious most of the time, but she expects me to be at her side when she's lucid. It's the least I can do for the poor kid." His voice broke and he said, "I'll talk to you later."

"Want me to come over?"

"No, you stay put, keep the goddamn business going until I get back. That's the best thing you can do for all of us."

Late that afternoon Henry and George Clews met in a roadhouse halfway between Carson City and Reno. It was the first time they had ever been alone together. In the years he had known Clews Henry had barely spoken a dozen words to the man. It wasn't that Henry had deliberately snubbed him. George Clews was simply not the sort who invited the amenities.

Clews was already waiting in a back booth when Henry arrived. He sat there with the brim of his black soft hat pulled low over his Neanderthal brow, further obscuring his deepset eyes. Clews looked up at Henry but remained seated. Henry shrugged and slipped into the opposite side of the booth.

"You want something to drink, you've got to get it yourself at the bar," Clews said. "There ain't no waitress here till six."

"I'm fine," Henry said. "What did Rufus have to say?"

Clews sipped a tall beer and examined Henry from the dark sunken caverns that hid his eyes. "I talked to the boss today and he wants you to open up a new gold mine he's got."

Henry could not suppress the look of astonishment that tightened his facial muscles. "Run that by me again, will you?"

Clews's expression remained impassive. "I said the boss wants you to open up this new mine. What the fuck's so hard to understand?"

"I understand the words—it's the content that's giving me trouble."

"You've got me there, brother," mumbled Clews, half puzzled, half bored.

"Let me put it this way. I'm the vice-president of Nevada Consolidated Mines, and I'm not aware of any gold mine in the inventory."

Clews sipped his beer and wiped his mouth with the back of a beefy hand. "It's like this, see. There's this gold mine the boss bought a while back and he wants you to get it into operation, start digging out the gold. I'm told it's real high-grade shit."

"Where precisely is it located, and how long has he been sitting on it?"

"Which question do you want answered first?"

"Take your pick."

Clews shrugged. "It's someplace between Virginia City and Steamboat, off Route Twelve. You've got to pack in for about twelve miles." He paused and pursed his thin lips. "I'd say he's had it a few years, but I'm lousy with dates."

Henry felt a chill go up his spine. "How come I'm just finding out about this? What's the big secret?"

"I told you, the boss sat on it a while."

"But why did he want to sit on it if it's high grade like you say?"

Clews's heavy eyebrows furrowed in annoyance. "Look, brother, what's this bullshit you're pulling? Who are you to give me the third degree? You want answers, call the boss. I've told you what I know, period."

Henry leaned back and reached in his pocket for a cigar. He unwrapped it and struck a match, all the time studying Clews. "I don't know what you're getting excited about," he said, puffing on the cigar until he was satisfied it was properly lit. "You've got to admit, this is a rather bizarre solution, even for Rufus, who's pretty good at pulling rabbits out of the hat. This time it's right out of the blue. I'd just like to know where the company stands."

"I know what you're after, Godwin, but all I was told to tell you is where it's at."

"All right, play it your way," Henry said. "When can you take me to the mine?"

Clews shook his head. "Oh, no—not me, brother. I ain't going up in them hills full of fucking rattlers. See Harry Mitchell—he'll set something up." Clews downed his beer and stood up. He leaned forward, thrusting his face up close to Henry's. "If I was you, brother, I'd just do what the boss said and keep my nose clean. You go stick your nose up the wrong asshole, somebody's liable to fart your head off. Know what I mean?"

After the door had closed behind Clews, Henry went to the pay telephone on the wall near the bar. He called Harry Mitchell and arranged to have dinner with him at the Longhorn Steak House at eight that evening. He then drove home to shower, change his clothes, and relax for a few minutes. It was Friday, and Randolph, who was entertaining two school friends for the weekend, rushed up to tell him that Aunt Caroline had called and was anxious to speak with him.

In the years since he had left Vicksburg Henry had been too busy to keep in touch with Aunt Caroline. Still, she had made it a practice to telephone him every Christmas and on July 2, his birthday, while Henry occasionally sent cards with brief notes.

"Oh, dear heart, how kind of you to return my call so promptly," Aunt Caroline exclaimed, when she heard Henry's voice on the line. "I've been thinking of you all day, debating with myself whether I should call and blurt out my problems. It was an exhausting struggle, I assure you—the strong self against the weak self. And alas, I must confess the weak self was victorious."

"Well, I'm glad of that," Henry said. "You and I, Aunt Caroline, have an agreement."

She sighed and Henry could visualize her anxious eyes as she spoke. "I'm afraid, dear heart, I have a rather depressing disclosure to make. Heartbreak Haven served its last repast tonight. Twenty-seven deserving young ladies will have to find another haven. The Vicksburg National Bank does not indulge in charity. Nor does your Uncle Avery. They have foreclosed and Avery Marsh has bought the paper. You know, Henry, Avery's had his eye on this lovely old place a long time.

Oh, I remember years ago, when the General was having financial difficulties, Avery tried to buy it then, actually went so far as to make an offer. I swear to God if the General had had his saber handy, he would have run him through on the spot. I have never seen a man so angry in all my life. Well, now it's his to do with as he well pleases."

Henry was heartsick. "Caroline, for God's sake, why didn't you tell me all this before? Now it sounds like it's too late to do anything about it. Frankly, I thought the place was free and clear."

She sighed again and he could hear her breath tremble. "It was for a long time, but there were some necessary renovations, and the price of food and clothing kept going up. The inflation of recent years made it difficult. We just couldn't make ends meet. The bank was most generous. Well, the first thing I knew I was way over my head in debt. Then everything seemed to just collapse." She paused and he knew she was trying to compose herself. "Oh, Henry, it's all gone, and we were performing such a worthwhile service. My girls were truly marvelous. They were so happy here. What will happen to them now? Dear God, forgive my vanity. I should have come to you, Henry, but I just couldn't make myself do it. Pure Godwin obstinacy. That's all it was."

They talked for a long time, with Henry trying to relieve her feelings of guilt. Finally he said, "What are your plans now?"

There was a long pause, followed by a nervous laugh. "Well, I haven't given it a thought. How silly of me."

"Do you think it would do any good if I talked to Avery? Would he let me buy it back at a substantial profit to him?"

"Oh, no, Henry, he's been waiting such a long time for this moment. Dear heart, you can't buy back a dream, but thank you for offering. You are the dearest man I know."

Henry laughed. "Well, then I've got another brilliant idea. It's absolutely sensational. There's nothing I can do about your young ladies, but why don't you come live with us, help me bring up this hellion of a son. He needs a firm hand."

She gasped. "Goodness, what a lovely thought. Oh, Henry, are you serious? Could I be of service to you?"

"Absolutely. It's a golden opportunity. Randolph needs you. I'm away so much of the time. He's getting older and I'm not sure I like some of his ideas. He needs guidance."

"Well, what about Alicia—won't she object when she comes back from Europe?"

Henry paused. "She's gravely ill. Rufus is with her right now and it doesn't look promising. Please say you'll come live with us."

"I'm terribly sorry to hear about Alicia. She sounds like such a nice person. Do you think Randolph would accept me?"

"Of course—how could he do otherwise? It's the perfect solution. Then you will come?"

She hesitated. "But what about Holly and Moses? We've been together such a long time. I feel responsible for them. I know Avery will never tolerate a colored overseer. He's such a bigoted jackass."

"Bring them with you," exclaimed Henry, his enthusiasm for the notion growing by bounds. "I can use both here on the ranch. What an extraordinary development." He stopped. "God, I'm sorry, Aunt Caroline. I must seem to be taking advantage of your misfortune."

"Oh, but please do, dear heart. Take all the advantage your sweet heart desires. I've always been partial to being killed with kindness."

When Henry got to the restaurant to meet Harry Mitchell, the company's comptroller, he found Harry already there. Mitchell had been with Boutwell since his Goldfield days. Short and portly, with a freckled bald head, Mitchell was a friendly, garrulous man. If anybody in the company knew where the bodies were buried, Henry was sure it was Mitchell. There was no question that Rufus had entrusted Mitchell with secrets he would never impart to Henry. In fact, Henry had long suspected that Mitchell might be keeping second and third sets of books, which, to Henry's mind, would be essential to the intricate and devious financial machinations practiced by Rufus Boutwell. This probably explained why Rufus had so calmly accepted the stock market crash. Mines might shut down, banks might fold, but the Boutwell empire would survive. There would be secret resources to take care of all emergencies. Rufus would have seen to it.

Henry, whose nerves were still tingling from his talks with Clews and Aunt Caroline, asked for a double martini. Tonight he needed a quick anesthetic. It had been an incredible day, and things were likely to get even more bizarre before it was over.

"Henry, I didn't know you liked martinis," Mitchell said. "I always thought of you as a bourbon man." Mitchell's flushed face indicated that he had a pretty good head start.

"This is a celebration," Henry said. "How often does one come up with a new gold mine when you really need one? George told me about it and Rufus said you'd give me the details. How long have you known about this little pot of gold? Frankly, Harry, it's been a long time since I've seen any rainbows around here."

Mitchell laughed. "Little pot of gold?" He leaned forward and lowered his voice. "Henry, this is so big it'll make your head swim."

"But why the secret?" said Henry. "I don't get it, Harry."

"Well, you know Rufus. Man don't like to put all his cards on the table. Remember, this guy started out as a gambler, right? So he knows how to play them close to the vest, know what I mean?"

"Yes, indeed. I guess you and Rufus go back a long way," he said, determined to give Harry rope.

Mitchell smiled proudly. "You betcha, them were the days—everything wide open, sourdoughs pouring in from all over the place. It was a wild time. They worked with a pick and shovel and Rufus with a deck of cards and a pair of dice. They never had a chance."

"He was that good?"

"Good! He was the best. You believe me, now—I'm giving it to you straight. Nobody bluffed Rufus. Nerves of steel. And the best set of kidneys you ever saw. Could sit at a table twenty-four hours without taking a piss. I don't think he even took time to shit. He was something to watch, I tell you."

"Sounds like Rufus, all right. So now we've got ourselves a bonanza in the nick of time. Clews says it's high grade. Run it down for me, will you?"

Mitchell stopped smiling. "Well, Henry, I'll tell you what I know, which ain't all that much, really. See, Rufus has always grubstaked old sourdoughs, been doing it for years. That's how he made his first strike in Goldfield. What the hell, it don't cost all that much and the payoff can be fantastic."

Henry nodded. "I realize that, Harry, but this area has been gone over with a fine-tooth comb for the last thirty years. If you're talking about the Virginia City area, that's probably eighty years. Sounds like a pretty iffy bet for a cagey gambler like Rufus."

"You're going to knock success?" Mitchell laughed. "He's always got a dozen old-timers looking around for rich pockets still waiting to be taken. Maybe he just likes them, feels grateful. And of course he knows those old boys will shrivel up and die if they ain't out in the hills poking around for that yellow metal."

Henry smiled. "Interesting. I'd never thought of Rufus as a sentimentalist."

Mitchell guffawed. "Oh, well, I wouldn't go that far either. Being a smart gambler, he's usually got a little side bet going for him, with an ace in the hole, you know. He even made something out of the crash of nineteen aught seven. I remember the date like it was yesterday—October twenty-second—when the Knickerbocker Trust Company of New York folded. And the next day the Westinghouse Electric Company folded, and that kicked off the panic. Almost overnight money went completely out of circulation. Operators started paying miners with scrip, and pretty soon everybody was on scrip, which was only good locally. Later we had the trouble with the Wobblies. We locked them out of the mines, and you should have seen the rats deserting the sinking ship. The first to go were the pimps and whores, the dance hall floozies, the boomers and gamblers and bartenders and hustlers. The tenderloin was empty in no time. A couple years later the whole town hit the skids. But Rufus took a hundred million out of Goldfield in a few years at a time when gold was selling for sixteen bucks an ounce."

By now Henry was on his second double martini, but his nerves were still on edge. Ever since his talk with Clews Henry had been preoccupied with the suspicion that this fortuitous bonanza could actually be Yulee's mine—a possibility so unsettling in its ramifications that Henry hardly knew what to make of it. First, he had to get his facts straight. It was imperative that he not rush off half-cocked. Too much was at stake. The chance that this windbag, Mitchell, would blurt out anything useful was remote, but it was all he had to work with at the moment.

He forced a smile. "Oh, yes, I've heard a lot about those good old days from Rufus."

Mitchell slapped the table. "There'll never be another time like that again. I had me a little peach with an hourglass figure and skin smooth as satin. She called herself Merry Strumpet and she was the chanteuse at the Idle Hour. She sang all the good old tunes. You know, like 'Frankie and Johnnie' and she'd improvise some pretty salacious verses. Her favorite was 'Just a Little Rocking Chair and You.'" He laughed, waving to the waiter for another drink. "You can imagine what she did with that one. Her voice was low and husky and she was murder on those tearjerker ballads. When she and the 'Professor' at the tinny piano got properly lubricated, they could set a house full of drunks to weeping like babies. Her best number was 'Hello Central, Give Me Heaven, for My Mama's There.' Oh, Jesus, she could depress the whole audience with that tearjerker. Then there was 'The Pardon Came Too Late' and 'The Ship Never Came Back' and 'A Man Was the Cause of It All.' "

They ordered steaks, mashed potatoes, and peas, and Henry tried to steer the conversation back on course. "After I talked to Rufus today, I was wondering how we were going to work this out. Is Rufus thinking of printing stocks?"

"I think so, but we haven't got that far into it yet."

Henry cut a bite of steak and chewed meditatively as he buttered a piece of bread. "Harry, what exactly have we got out there? I assume it's lode."

"Oh, yeah, sure, a real rich vein. We know what we've got, Henry. Our engineer gave it a little pop a while back and loomed out a half ton or so. It assays out to nearly seventy-five thousand bucks a ton. I was in there before he popped it and you could see it with the naked eye. God, what a beautiful sight. The engineer thinks we're damn close to the mother lode."

"So you've dug a shaft and tunnel."

"Oh, hell, yes. Must be a hundred feet deep anyway and a long goddamn tunnel. Well, you know, Rufus has had a few guys working out there quite a while."

Henry felt like he was walking on eggs. One misstep and he'd have an omelet. "What kind of reading are you getting from the tailings."

Mitchell, who was cutting his steak, looked up with furrowed brow. "Hmm," he said, looking back down at his steak, spearing a piece with his fork, which he proceeded to chew in thoughtful deliberation. They ate in silence until finally Mitchell swallowed and patted his stomach. "That's a good steak. How's yours?"

"Fine."

"This's a great place. Even my wife likes it."

Henry was losing his patience. "Harry, I'm really enjoying this small talk, but if I'm going to act on Rufus's request I need information. Now if you can't give it to me, who the hell can? Just give me a name. Who's the engineer?"

Mitchell nodded and kept smiling. "Well, actually, Henry, there's not all that much for you to do. I think Rufus just wanted you to know where the needed funds would be coming from when this thing starts paying off."

Henry put his knife and fork down and leaned forward, his eyes narrowing in a hard stare. "Harry, I don't care how far back you go with Rufus. I'm vice-president of this company and when Rufus is away I'm the man in charge, you understand?"

"Wait a minute, Henry. I take my orders from Rufus."

"You wait yourself. You'll take your orders from me and damn well like it. You're a smart man, Harry. Don't make the mistake of locking horns with me."

"Hey, what's happening here?" Mitchell said, forcing a laugh. "We were having a good time and all of a sudden, boom, the table blew up."

"Harry, no more bullshit. Read me right. Don't force me into taking an action we'll both regret."

Mitchell stared back, a look of disbelief on his face. "You can't fire me. Rufus and me were out there when your mama was still diapering you. We're a team, Rufus and me, in more ways than you'll ever know. I realize you're his son-in-law, but that don't make you more valuable to the company, not by a long shot."

"Is that the way it's going to be?"

Mitchell downed his drink and signaled to the waiter for another one. "Henry, I don't want a showdown with you. It's silly. I don't understand why you're getting all hot and bothered over this mine. What difference does it make to you anyway?"

"One more time, Harry. I'm in charge of this company when Rufus is out of town. When I want information, you'll give it to me, or clear out. When Rufus comes back, if he wants me to go and you to return, that's fine too. But he's not going to get it both ways."

The waiter brought the drink and Mitchell gulped half of it down. "Well, what are you after, anyway? Maybe I can answer some of your questions. If I can, I will. Go ahead, shoot."

"Fine. I was asking about the tailings. Has the dump gone to a stamp mill, and if so, which one?"

The expression of indecision on Mitchell's face made him look like he was having bad gas pains. He leaned forward. "See, Henry, I can't talk about that. Rufus would kill me." He lowered his voice until Henry could barely hear him. "We didn't run it through the books. We had to keep it quiet, know what I mean?"

"That's obvious," Henry said. "And I must say you did a good job of it. You completely fooled me."

Mitchell winced. "See, Rufus has his ways, you know. It's no skin off my ass, it's not more money in my paycheck whether stuff goes on the books or not. I give Rufus what he wants."

"The name of the stamp mill?"

"Why, it's the company's, the one in Sparks."

"How much was it worth?"

Mitchell shrugged. "I don't remember the exact figures. Maybe ten thousand, not much more."

Just the way he said it, Henry knew he was lying. "Any of it go to the mills in Tonopah or Goldfield?"

"Oh, no, too far away."

"Not by train," Henry said, giving Mitchell a sharp look. "All right, who's the engineer?"

"Our own man, Al Grosbeck. He'll take you there whenever you're ready to go."

"Let's make it tomorrow morning, bright and early. When is it scheduled to go into operation?"

"Very soon. I sent Roger Spalding to San Francisco to recruit a bunch of Chinamen. They're the best. They're small, work hard, don't eat much, and can't speak English. We can get them for two bucks a day and grub—rice and fish—can't beat that. You know, we used Chinamen in the old days too. If the vein petered out, we'd lock them in the mine until we got rid of all our stocks. They didn't mind. Sometimes they'd be in there a couple weeks. An incredible people."

"Was that another of Rufus's bright ideas?"

"Oh, sure—this guy's thinking every minute. Anything else you'd like to know?"

Henry assumed a grave expression. "Yes, the name of the old-timer who discovered the mine."

The question startled Mitchell. His eyes, which were beginning to blur, tried to conceal his reaction. "Holy Christ, Henry, why—" he sputtered, and quickly downed the rest of his drink. "What difference does it make who found it?"

Henry bore down. "Just answer the question."

Mitchell fell back in his chair and threw his hands up. "I don't know, Henry—I swear it, on my honor. Rufus never told me."

"We're right back to square one, aren't we?" Henry said, the muscles along his jawline tensing.

"What do you mean? I told you I'd answer what I could. How can I tell you if I don't know?"

"Let's think about this a minute, Harry. The usual arrangement with a grubstaker is an even split. Is that right?"

"Normally, but in this case Rufus paid him off in cash. You've got to believe me, Henry. That's what Rufus told me and I never question the man."

Henry nodded. "Yes, that I believe. Who's doing the security at the mine?"

"Pinkerton."

"How long have they been on the payroll?"

"Henry, I'd have to look it up. I just can't give it to you off the top of my head. It seems to me, though, Rufus had some of his own people out there quite a while, but I don't think he was too happy with that arrangement. With the Pinkertons you know you're in good hands."

Henry ran his hand through his thick, dark hair, lowering his head to look Mitchell straight in the eye. "Where and when was the claim registered?"

Mitchell jerked his head like a boxer dodging a right hook. "Hey, holy Jesus, Henry, have a heart. That's completely out of my bailiwick. Rufus is the only guy that can give you that answer. I told you before, he plays his cards close to the vest." He stopped and again jerked his head. "What difference does it make to you? Frankly, I don't understand your whole line of questioning."

Henry decided it was time to retreat. "You're not thinking straight, Harry. I just want to make sure everything is in order before we make it public."

"Well, good Christ, you think Rufus would forget to register a mine? Not in a million years."

Henry smiled and Mitchell visibly relaxed. "How do you think a stock issue would go at this point?"

"Like hotcakes, Henry. Even after the panic of nineteen aught seven gold stocks sold all over the country. People will find the money for a good strike, even if they've got to tear up the old mattress. But we can't go public until Rufus returns."

Henry pushed back his chair. "Thanks, Harry. Sorry I had to come down on you like that. I hope you'll understand."

Mitchell smiled and scratched his bald head. "Oh, hell, forget it. Listen, want to get laid? There's a little cathouse near Genoa that's not bad."

"Thanks, but not tonight."

"I think I'll take a run up there. Talking about Merry Strumpet kind of got me in the mood. Ain't that a great name. The harlots really had themselves colorful monickers in them days. I remember there was Porcupine Nellie, Giggling Gussie, Big Tit Gertie, Big Hole Mabel, Swivel Bottom Sue—ain't that something?"

"Yeah, Harry," said Henry deadpan. "Kind of makes one wish he had been born sooner."

Henry had always liked Al Grosbeck. At least six-foot-six, slim as a rail, with an unruly mop of curly red hair and a beard like a rabbi, everyone thought Al was Jewish, but no one knew for sure—which was probably just fine with Grosbeck, since Jews and Negroes were about as welcome in Nevada as Mexicans.

Taciturn by nature, Grosbeck was the perfect person to be riding through the desert with Henry on this day. His silence gave Henry time to think, which was what he needed to do most at the moment. His future with Boutwell depended on his getting the right answers. So far the prospects were frightening. If this were really Yulee's mine, then Boutwell had to know what had happened to the old man. What was worse, he was probably responsible. If that proved to be true, Henry knew he would have to take some action, but that he couldn't think about now. His hope was that it would all prove to be a wild coincidence and that Rufus would offer a convincing explanation for everything.

During the long night Henry had remembered Yulee's last call in San Francisco and how afterward he had told Boutwell about it, had even told him that the mine was not registered. Then Rufus had offered to take him to Virginia City. George Clews had visited the train upon their arrival in Carson City, the two men going into the conference room for what could have been Clews's report on what had happened to Yulee. If there had been foul play, Clews would have done it. Of that Henry was certain.

He felt feverish. He had been up almost the entire night with dark thoughts eating away at his brain. Around daybreak he had fallen into a fitful sleep and had dreamed about Yulee up in Nome. He could see the old man fleeing in the snow, with the posse behind him, his bright blue eyes anxious as he struggled up snowdrifts high as mountains, slipping and sliding, with bullets whizzing over his head, sending little puffs of snow flying all around him. Then he was falling through the ice, into the freezing water of the creek, climbing out, shivering and pumping his arms to restore circulation. Henry had tossed and turned, not wanting to go on with the dream, but there was the knife cutting into the frozen flesh—the black, bloody stump dropping into the red snow—and Henry reached down in his sleep to touch his own legs. Sighing heavily in relief, he opened his eyes and stared at the ceiling, afraid to close them again.

The cutoff was almost midpoint between Steamboat and Virginia City.

"When do we walk?" Henry asked.

Grosbeck laughed. "Never, if I can help it," he said, shifting the pickup truck into low gear and taking off across the desert floor toward distant mountains. "We can make it partly up that mountain with this four-wheel drive, then I've got some burros waiting to take us the rest of the way."

"A man after my own heart," Henry said, holding on to the dashboard and door as the truck bounced and rocked crazily over the rough terrain.

"Sorry we don't have a gyro in this thing."

"Don't worry about it," Henry said, careful not to bite his tongue. "It's good for the digestion."

"Not so good for the springs, I'm afraid."

"Since it's a company truck, let her rip," Henry said.

They left a trail of dust a mile long behind them. Henry held on for dear life and hoped that the truck would hold together until they got there. He didn't relish the idea of hiking it. He looked at Grosbeck, his long body hunched over the steering wheel, his red beard whipped by the wind.

Henry had decided to wait until he'd seen the mine before questioning Grosbeck. This time he'd keep the tone casual, not get carried away like he had with Mitchell. That had been a mistake. While he'd gotten answers he wouldn't have otherwise received, he had to wonder what Mitchell would report to Rufus. His chances of solving this mystery were better if people up and down the line were not put on notice. There was also Clews's colorful warning to bear in mind. Must not stick nose up wrong asshole, Henry told himself.

They were climbing up the side of the mountain and Henry wanted to congratulate Grosbeck on his expert handling of the vehicle, but he was too busy holding on to say anything. With his beard flying in his face, Grosbeck looked demented. He furiously spun the steering wheel every which way as he maneuvered the truck up this intricate course of formidable obstacles. One wrong turn and they would vanish into the abyss awaiting them on either side of the path.

Henry saw a clearing ahead and Grosbeck brought the truck to a skidding stop.

"Whew," Henry said, opening the door and dropping gratefully to the ground. "By any chance, you related to Barney Oldfield?"

Grosbeck laughed. "Never could resist a challenge. Oh, there're our burros. The Pinkertons brought them down."

"I think I prefer to walk," Henry said. "Having entrusted my life to four tires, I'm not yet ready to entrust it to four spindly legs."

"Shall we leave them here? It's only about eight miles or so."

"I don't know, Al. I was kind of looking forward to seeing you sit on one of these stumpy creatures."

Grosbeck was pulling on his beard, trying to get it to hang down. "I've got to hold my feet up so the damn fools don't step on my toes."

"That's what I thought. Let's hike it. It's a nice day for walking. Air's just brisk enough to keep the rattlers in their holes."

They took the water canteens from the burros and Grosbeck led the way, his long legs covering ground at a fast clip. Henry stayed right with him and they made the mine in under two hours.

The first person Henry saw was the guard perched on the side of the hill. He wore an old army uniform, an infantry campaign hat, a Sam Browne belt with a holstered pistol, and he was holding a rifle in the air. Henry realized that he'd been in the guard's sights for at least a mile. The mine was another half-mile away, and there were two more guards, dressed and armed as the other. They were hard-eyed characters, probably war veterans, and they impressed Henry as alert and businesslike. Nobody was going to sneak up on this mine without inviting trouble. Fortunately, they also knew Grosbeck, and let the two men pass without interference.

"There's another guard up there on that hill," Grosbeck said. "They've got the place pretty well covered."

As Henry and Grosbeck reached the top of the rounded hill, Henry saw the windlass straddling the mine shaft. It was a strange feeling to be standing on this ridge, where perhaps Yulee and young Bessie had stood so many years ago.

Grosbeck had turned, his eyes thoughtful as he watched Henry, who seemed engrossed in the scenery. "Beautiful here, isn't it?" Grosbeck said. "You can see why these old prospectors never quit. Sometimes I sort of envy them."

Henry kicked at the loose topsoil. "How did he know where to dig the hole?" he said, shaking his head in bewilderment. "Look at this area—as far as the eye can see, one hilltop after another. Why here and not over there somewhere?"

"These old boys aren't geologists, but they know their business," Grosbeck said. "If you look closely at this hilltop, you'll find a network of narrow veins crisscrossing it. You can follow the veins by the line of quartz fragments exposed as residual float on the surface. In time rocks weather to soil, but quartz resists the elements. In this country, where rainfall averages about six inches a year, it's a slow process. But the prospector looks for the quartz and usually starts out by digging a trench to uncover a vein. In this instance, the float increased downward until he reached the vein at bedrock under about eight feet of topsoil. The vein was a good five feet wide and contained attractive mineralized quartz. A neophyte would need an assay at this point to determine traces of gold and silver, but the old-timers instinctively know when they're onto something promising. Of course, that's one of the problems of mining. On a good prospect you never find a quitting place. Well, here he could go two ways. Laterally along the vein or dig into greater depth. So he timbered a shaft through the topsoil, and since the walls are andesite, he tunneled the rest of the way without timbering. The vein was off vertical only ten or so degrees. Come, let me show you how far it took him and what he found when he got there."

At the top of the shaft Grosbeck handed Henry a miner's hard hat fitted with a calcium carbide lamp. "This shaft goes a hundred feet straight down, then drifts laterally for quite a ways. Watch your step on the ladder, and when we get below you're going to have to squat. The roof's a little low."

Henry followed him down the ladder, being careful not to step on Grosbeck's hands. In Henry's mind this was Yulee's shaft, and he marveled at his accomplishment. A chisel, a four-pound hammer, a shovel, a pick, a wheelbarrow, a windlass, and some dynamite. Not to mention a lifetime of experience and an indomitable will.

Grosbeck was waiting for him at the bottom and Henry looked up at the small square of light at the top. It was a long ways up there. In the tunnel it was pitch black and they turned on their lamps. Grosbeck also had a large flashlight and he pointed the beam to indicate the way. Squatting down to half their normal heights, they started down the tunnel, which was wider than it was tall. It wasn't long before Henry's thigh muscles were complaining.

"It's one way of finding out if you're in shape," he said.

Grosbeck laughed, the sound echoing along the walls. "Man hasn't had to walk like this for quite a few million years. Only health addicts would consider this a proper exercise."

"That's a consolation."

"Are you watching the vein above your head?"

"Oh, yes, and my neck is beginning to rebel."

"The answer, I suppose, is to train taller prospectors."

As he moved behind Grosbeck, Henry was counting the steps, trying to arrive at a figure that was reasonably accurate. When he thought he had counted a thousand feet, he was certain he could see large chunks of gold glittering in the cracks of the vein, which at this point was wider than the tunnel. They went about another hundred feet before Grosbeck stopped. They sat down and Grosbeck flashed his light on the vein.

"Is that pure gold I see?" Henry asked.

"As pure as God could make it. That's what miners call high grade. If you're a mine operator, that's what you want to protect. It's very easy for miners to walk out with a couple thousand dollars' worth of gold stashed in their clothing. You let a bunch of high graders loose in here, they'd carry a million bucks out in no time."

"That's something to bear in mind. Rufus told me he used to have change rooms in the old days."

"It's the only way to go. Want a souvenir?"

"Yes, let me do it."

"Wait, there's a short handle pick over there. Let me get it."

Henry got on his knees, crouching, and swung the pick. Sparks flew and dirt fell in his face, blinding him. He spat and coughed, his hand searching the floor for the specimen he had dislodged. It weighed nearly five pounds and rested comfortably in the palm of his hand.

"I had forgotten how heavy gold is," he said, examining it in the beam of Grosbeck's flashlight.

"That's a beauty," Grosbeck said. "I guess it's okay for the boss to high grade. Have you seen enough?"

"Yes, let's go. How much longer is this tunnel?"

"Another hundred feet or so."

"No mother lode yet?"

"Not yet, but I'll bet it's not too far away."

Henry waited until they had left the mine and were back on the trail before continuing with his interrogation. "I suppose quite a few people know about this place. By now the word must have gotten around."

"I don't think so. The security people are closemouthed."

They walked side by side, Henry matching his stride to Grosbeck's. It was midafternoon and the sky was a cobalt blue with fleecy white clouds drifting lazily over the barren mountaintops. This had been Yulee's world. Blue skies and starry nights in God's wilderness, where a man could still be his own master.

Henry tried to sound casual. "How long have you been involved in this?"

Grosbeck pulled on his beard. "About a year, I guess. But I haven't spent all that much time here. My work has been with the silver mines, as you know, finding more economical ways to produce ore."

"Yes, and you've done an excellent job. Both Rufus and I are pleased with your work."

"Thank you. With the price of silver dropping the way it has, lowering production costs is an even greater challenge."

"By the way, did all the tailings go to Sparks? It's been a long time and I can't remember if we sent some to Tonopah and Goldfield."

Grosbeck gave him a slanted look. "Henry, I don't know anything about the dump. It was gone long before I came here. In fact, that kind of intrigued me. I think I mentioned it to Rufus, but I don't recall his response, if he made one."

"Must have been worth a good piece of change?"

Grosbeck laughed. "I wish I had it. I could retire on a generous annuity."

Henry nodded. "I figure about a hundred thousand dollars."

"At least. This is a rich vein. I never could understand why Rufus didn't start production sooner. That mine could easily be worth twenty, thirty million. Maybe fifty million, with the way the price of gold keeps going up. Gold always becomes more precious in times of economic crisis. People shy away from paper money."

"What about the old-timer that discovered it? Have you met him?"

Grosbeck laughed. "No, but the way I heard it from Rufus, he's living the good life in Florida. Bought himself a lemon orchard. Partial to anything yellow."

"Oh, my gracious, look how tall he is," Aunt Caroline cried, hugging Randolph to her emaciated body, burying his face in the fur of her rabbit coat, refusing to let him surface for air. Randolph struggled to free himself, finally managed to pull away, his face flushed, his eyes a little wild in the fear that he was suffocating to death.

"Oh, darling, you're beautiful," Aunt Caroline chirped. "A true Godwin male. Why couldn't God have been equally as generous with the distaff side?"

"I'm over four feet tall," Randolph gasped, regaining his breath.

"Oh, dear heart, you're going to be so tall in a couple more years I'm going to have to crimp my neck just to look at your handsome face. Mind you, the sight will be well worth a crimp in the neck. Beauty is what we most admire in this world. Beauty of visage and body, and beauty of soul. Oh, yes, I hear that yours is lily white."

Randolph gave Henry a curious look. "Has he been talking to you about me?"

"Why, I should say. He's told me how sweet and precious you are. That's why I'm here with my good friends, Holly and Moses Grimes. They're going to live with us. Isn't that wonderful? All of us at your lovely ranch. Oh, I can't wait to see it."

Henry was shaking hands with Moses. He was a tall, powerfully built man with a gleaming shaved head, round eyes that showed a lot of white, and a square jaw that could have been carved out of granite. In his late twenties, Moses was a man with a booming voice and easy smile. His wife, Holly, was a strapping woman, with widely spaced teeth that gave her the happy grin of a Halloween pumpkin every time she smiled, which was more often than not.

Henry turned and called Randolph over. "Moses and Holly, this is my son, Randolph. What do you think of this boy?"

Holly said, "Come here, honey, let Holly give you a great big hug."

Randolph, who had never seen Negroes before, instinctively pulled away, his eyes shifting nervously between his father and his aunt.

"Come over here," Henry said, reaching out for Randolph's arm but missing it when the boy stepped back, his eyes filling with tears.

"Oh, now, come to Auntie," Aunt Caroline said, again enveloping the boy in the fur of her rabbit coat.

"What the hell's going on here?" Henry said, his perplexed gaze moving from the Grimeses to Aunt Caroline.

"Give him time," Aunt Caroline said. "This is his first experience and he's only a little boy, no matter how tall he is."

Chagrined and embarrassed, Henry turned to the Grimeses and held out his hands. "I'm sorry. It didn't occur to me that he'd never seen colored folk before. Don't worry—I'll talk to him tonight, straighten everything out."

"Now, Henry, you leave this boy alone," Aunt Caroline said. "He'll come around once he gets acquainted with them. These are good folk and he'll get to love them as much as we do. That's inevitable."

On the ride to the ranch in Henry's new Buick sedan they passed by the Bank of Nevada building and Henry pointed it out.

"That's a handsome building, Henry," Aunt Caroline exclaimed.

"It belongs to Rufus," Randolph said proudly. "He's the richest man in the world. Someday when he dies I'm going to inherit all his money. He promised me."

Once heralded by its builder, Rufus Boutwell, as the most modern and luxurious hotel west of the Mississippi, the Goldfield Palace had fallen upon hard times.

On the night of its grand opening, it was said, revelers had consumed five thousand bottles of French champagne. Each of its two hundred rooms had its own private telephone and private bath. The floors of the lobby, restaurant, and bar were of mosaic tile and the ceilings were covered with 22-karat gold leaf. There were brass beds, chandeliers, solid oak furniture, and Irish linen. The restaurant, which boasted of the finest English china, sterling table silver, and Bavarian crystal, could accommodate four hundred persons. But the hotel had died with the town. Now it had more rooms than there were citizens in Goldfield. Rufus kept it open for sentimental reasons. Even for a pragmatist like Rufus, it was hard to kill a queen he'd given birth to.

Ensconced in the Theodore Roosevelt Suite, named for the only President to have stayed in the hotel, Henry lay on the bed, his back propped up by pillows, his mind far from the faded splendor of his room. In the past week he had visited the stamp mills at Sparks, Tonopah, and now Goldfield, all of them owned by Nevada Consolidated Mines. On the pretext that he wanted to inspect production records for the past ten years, Henry had pored over the ledgers looking for some clue to the mystery of the missing tailing dump. He had found it on his second day at Sparks. In 1926 gold valued at $10,400 had been processed for the A. G. Ore Company of Reno. But when Henry checked the telephone and city directories, he found no record of this company's existence, past or present. At the Tonopah mill, the gold processed in 1926 for A. G. Ore amounted to $38,500. But it was at the Goldfield mill that Henry hit the jackpot. The gold processed that same year for A. G. Ore was valued at $72,100 for a grand total of $121,000, close enough to Yulee's own estimate to push Henry deeper into the investigation.

The superintendent at the Goldfield mill remembered that payment had been made by check to a post office box number in Reno. No one from A. G. Ore had ever visited the mill. Everything had been handled by telephone and mail.

While in Tonopah, Henry had checked A. G. Ore at the claims office with no results. There were no claims offices in Sparks or Goldfield.

On his drive back to Carson City Henry remembered Alfred, who had worked in the claims office in Virginia City. According to the Pinkerton report, the office had closed and Alfred had retired to Florida. If his search of the claims offices in Carson City and Reno proved negative, Henry resolved to visit the Pinkerton agency in San Francisco. At the same time he would inquire into the cause of the fire that had killed Yulee's landlady, Mrs. Flanagan. So far his meager results were more damning than exonerating.

The first thing Henry noticed when he walked through the lobby of the Fairview Hotel was the poster announcing the nightly appearance of Daisy Miller. He stopped and studied her picture. There were still telltale signs of the old Camilla, particularly around the mouth and eyes, but those days now seemed so unreal, the good and bad mixed together like a crazy dream. He had loved this woman when he was a boy, had loved her more than he could ever love anyone again. Of that he was certain. There had been sex with other women in recent years, brief and satisfying for the most part, but no one after Alicia had meant anything special to him.

It was a little after eleven o'clock in the morning and Henry sat on his hotel bed a long time before gathering the courage to pick up the receiver. He would invite her to lunch—that was straightforward enough. He had not seen or heard from her since that time at Lake Tahoe. They had a lot to catch up on.

The operator said, "Sorry, Miss Miller does not accept calls until one in the afternoon."

"I would like to leave a message," Henry said. "Tell Miss Miller that her attorney, Henry Godwin, would like a conference at her earliest convenience. I'm in Room Eighteen Ten."

A few minutes later she was on the line. "Henry, it's wonderful to hear from you. We must get together for lunch. Are you free?"

Henry laughed. "You bet I am. Anyplace special in mind?"

"Yes, a very exclusive place, my suite."

"Just say the time."

"Come right up. Room Twenty Twenty."

She opened the door. "Welcome to my lair," she said, holding out her hand.

He squeezed it gently and leaned forward to kiss her cheek. "You look absolutely stunning."

She laughed. "I was in the midst of my exercises when you called. I was so anxious to see you I didn't even bother to change." She was wearing a close-fitting Chinese red leotard, cut low at the neckline and high on the hips, her long shapely legs clad in sheer black ballet stockings, which made her legs appear even longer. Her platinum hair, longer now, was pulled back straight and swirled in a knot behind her head, accentuating the high cheekbones. Except for faint purplish eye-shadow, she wore no makeup.

"Want to join me in my exercises?" she asked, her emerald eyes teasing him.

"No, but I'd love to watch you."

"Same old Henry," she said, taking his hand and leading him to the sofa. "How about a glass of white wine?"

"Sounds wonderful."

"Make yourself comfortable. I'll be right back."

Henry leaned back in the cushions and unbuttoned his suit jacket. She returned with the wine and sat next to him, folding her legs under her.

"God, it's great to see you," Henry said. "You know, I've thought of calling you many times, but I didn't want to cause you any problems. I assume you and Vince are still together."

"Thank you, Henry—you've always been most thoughtful and I appreciate it. And yes, we're still together. But he lives in Los Angeles and is much too busy these days to accompany me on road trips. Which is just as well. I enjoy my privacy. I've learned a lot, Henry. I know how to take care of myself anywhere in this world. It makes me feel strong." She paused. "It's a good feeling."

He nodded, staring at his wine. "I can understand that."

She laughed. "Listen, Henry, know what I was thinking about after you called? The General's old horse."

Henry smiled. "You mean, the great-great-great-grandson of Black Lightning?"

"Yes, the one with the chronic gas pains. I remember Thaddeus talking about that horse. Most of its teeth had fallen out and his digestive tract was so shot that he broke wind almost continuously, even in his sleep. But—and this was what mystified Thaddeus, and everybody else, for that matter—that old horse never broke wind in the presence of the General. He'd hold it in, at times his stomach swelling so tightly he could barely move his hind legs. But the moment the General was out of sight he'd let go with all that gas and nearly knock the walls down. Thaddeus was afraid to strike a match in the stables. Claimed the one time he tried it the explosion knocked him flat and completely singed off his eyebrows. Isn't that incredible?"

"What's even more incredible was the one time he did it in the General's presence."

"Oh, I remember. That was tragic."

Henry shook his head, his eyes turning inward. "That was my thirteenth birthday, when the General came to my room dressed in his Confederate uniform. I had wanted to see him in that uniform all my life. It was his birthday gift to me. He wore his saber, his decorations, his three stars, and his wide-brimmed felt hat, with just the right rakish tilt to it. God, he was beautiful. I remember being so happy when we got on the horses and started for the bluffs that I let go with a rebel yell. It startled the gas right out of old Black Lightning. He let go a couple of boomers and bolted. My God, I couldn't believe my eyes. He was running toward the edge of the bluffs and the General was fighting to rein him in, trying to keep his voice steady not to alarm the animal further. When they got close to the edge, the General jumped off and hit the ground hard, rolling over several times. Next thing I knew the horse was sailing off into space.

"I jumped off Old Baldy and ran to the General. I thought he was dead. You can't imagine how scared I was at that moment."

"I remember. He'd broken both legs."

Henry nodded. "I bent over him and the first thing he told me was to take his saber and put Black Lightning out of his misery. See, the horse was on the rocks below, with its back broken, just raising the dickens. I hated to leave the General, but I climbed down there and pushed that sword into the horse's brain and ran back to the General. He was unconscious and I'll never forget this as long as I live. It was like seeing him for the first time in my life. The skin over his cheekbones was tight and yellowish, almost translucent. I could see all those little blue veins. They covered his whole face. His chin, which had always seemed so strong, looked as fragile as eggshells. His arms and legs were bone thin, his chest all sunken in, but I think it was his neck that really got me. It was so scrawny, with ropelike veins, and it was only half the size of his tunic collar. So this big bear of a man had suddenly been shrunk before my eyes."

"I remember how guilty you felt about the General."

"Yes, and I took my problem to Thaddeus. He knew how to say the right words. He would tell me it wasn't my fault. He said, 'The fool horse committed suicide. He was so ashamed of hisself for farting in the General's presence he just lost his head and decided there was no way out but suicide.' " Henry laughed. "I was eager to believe him."

"Good old Thaddeus. Had a heart as big as all outdoors."

"So did Alva. They were good people."

They were silent for a while, each deep in thought as they sipped their wine. "You wouldn't happen to have a picture of Randolph with you, would you?" she asked without looking up.

"Funny you should ask," he said, reaching inside his suit jacket. "It's about a year old, so he's a couple inches taller, but he still looks about the same."

She placed her wineglass on the coffee table and held the picture with both hands. She saw a boy standing in front of a huge white horse, holding the bridle over his shoulder, a big smile on his face, a cowboy hat pushed to the back of his head.

"Oh," she squealed with delight. "He looks so cocky and confident. He's beautiful. Not a care in the world. Is he really this carefree and happy all the time, Henry?"

"Well, yes, most of the time."

"Is that gorgeous animal his horse?"

"No, he's mine, but Randolph rides him more often than I do. By now I'm quite sure he thinks it's his. The horse's name is White Lightning."

"Isn't that nice. May I please keep the picture, Henry?"

"Of course."

"What is he like?" She stood up. "Come in the kitchenette while I fix us some lunch and tell me everything there is to know about him."

Henry talked while she fixed a cold seafood salad. He told her only the good things, what he knew she'd want to hear, the things that would make her happy. He didn't mention the habits and character traits that were beginning to worry him—the distorted importance the boy placed on money, the self-centeredness that seemed to guide so many of his actions, the inability to cope with the most minor disappointment, the quick temper, the way he could dissemble and lie, could evade and deceive with a look of artlessness that never ceased to astonish Henry. The boy needed guidance, but Henry was at a loss to provide it. With Aunt Caroline now running the household, it was Henry's hope that she would take the boy in hand and teach him proper values, get him back on the right track before it was too late.

Later, over coffee, Camilla inquired about Alicia and Henry mentioned her illness without going into details.

"Will you ever get together again?"

He shook his head. "I'm afraid she's terminal, and even before she was sick our marriage was almost over. Given a second chance, I would try my damnedest to make it work." He tried to smile. "How about yourself—planning on becoming an old maid?"

She smiled, arching an eyebrow. "Is a mistress an old maid? I suppose, but I don't feel like one. I really enjoy my life."

"I'm glad one of us is enjoying his life."

"Why, Henry, what a terribly defeatist thing to say. Are you trying to elicit my sympathy?"

He put his coffee cup on the table and reached for her hand. "I think so," he said, looking deep into her eyes. "Your sympathy and favors."

"Henry, don't," she whispered hoarsely, placing her other hand against his chest.

"Remember the legendary king of Cyprus," he said, pulling her close, his eyes never leaving hers.

"I remember, Henry."

"Called himself Pygmalion. He fell in love with an ivory statue he had sculpted. She looked a lot like you. Every day he would come and hold her in his hands and get very excited. So he begged Aphrodite, the goddess of love and beauty, to give him a wife resembling the statue, and instead she just flicked her wand and the statue came to life. Well, he lost no time impregnating his new wife and she bore him a daughter, whom he called Paphos. Do you remember what you said to me when I first told you this story?"

"Yes, I do, Henry. I said, 'I think Paphos is a beautiful name,' and you said, 'If our first child is a girl, we'll name her Paphos.'"

"How old was I at the time?" Henry asked gently.

"Sixteen."

He put his arms around her shoulders and pulled her tight against him. "How could you have believed I wouldn't marry you? I never once thought otherwise."

She kissed his neck. "I know that today, but I was so immature, so insecure. I was terrified I'd end up like Alva."

Henry shivered. "I still love you," he said.

Her head came up and her large gold-flecked eyes looked at him as though she were trying to determine if he really meant it.

"I've always loved you," he said, lowering his mouth on hers, his arms crushing her against him. Their mouths opened and she let it happen for a moment before turning her head.

"Please, Henry, let go."

"Cami, not now."

"Henry, you're not Pygmalion anymore and I'm not Cami. I'm Daisy Miller."

"What's the difference?" he groaned, releasing her from his embrace.

The struggle had loosened her hair from the knot at the back of her head and it fell around her shoulders, making her look younger, less sophisticated, more vulnerable. "Henry, I told you before, I may be a mistress, but I'm a one-man woman."

He nodded, picked up his cup and gulped down the cold coffee. "What is to become of us?" he asked, not looking at her.

"I don't know, Henry. All I know is I don't want to complicate my life. Why can't we be friends—two old friends sharing a mutual love for our son? I'd like to see you more often, but not if it means we must go through this every time."

"I'd be honored to be your friend," he said. "And I admire your ethics, though I'm not saying I approve of them—not in this one instance anyway."

She laughed easily and he reached over to pat her hand. "Is a love pat now and then permissible?"

"Yes, dear Henry, and even a little kiss might be in order on certain occasions."

Henry stood up, buttoning his suit jacket. "I've got to go," he said. "But, Cami, if you ever break up with Bacino, will you give my application top priority."

"Henry, you've got lifetime first dibs."

On the train that evening Henry's feelings were mixed. He felt good about his meeting with Camilla, delighted at the prospect they could be friends. He still loved her. There was no question in his mind or heart. Being with her had made him feel vitally alive and he wondered what their lives would have been like if the Klan had left them alone. He touched his lips, savoring the sweetness of her kiss, the warmth of her breath. "Oh, Christ," he intoned, "why did it have to happen?" Life could be such a pain in the ass at times. Did anyone ever get what he really wanted when he was ready for it. Or were the good things always deferred to another time, another place, another moment?

As the train neared Sacramento, he stared out his compartment window at the dreary landscape and sighed. The Pinkerton man had told him there was no record in their files of any investigation of Yulee's disappearance. The only conclusion Henry could reach was that Rufus had lied to him. There had been no investigation because Rufus already knew what had happened to Yulee. He was the last person on earth who would want investigators sniffing around looking for clues.

The evidence was in—all of it circumstantial, of course, but damn convincing. The A. G. Ore Company? Would it do any good to check state records for the date of incorporation and the names of officers? What did the A. G. stand for? Aggregate? Gravel? He took an engraved memo pad from his briefcase and began doodling, writing down words beginning with A and G that could have any connection with the type of work the company could be involved in. After a half hour he became disgusted at the futility of the game. G for goddamn, he thought, his eye moving up the page to his own name engraved at the top. Godwin. H. G. Then it hit him. Alicia Godwin! A. G. That had to be it. Rufus was pretty cute. But if Henry's suspicions proved out, he was also a murderer. Henry ripped the paper from the pad and tore it to bits.

Boutwell had not only procured the murder of Yulee but had cheated Henry out of a fortune. Why else had he waited this long to start production? He knew that Henry would suspect the sudden appearance of a new gold mine. Although Boutwell was wealthy, nobody was rich enough to ignore fifty million dollars. There had to be a reason and the only logical one, as far as Henry was concerned, was that it was Yulee's mine and Boutwell was a far more dangerous man than he had ever suspected. Alicia had tried to warn him, but he had interpreted it as her rebellion against a father figure, her new generation that had ended up a lost generation. But she had seen something he had not. Manipulating grateful politicians was one thing; murder for profit was something else entirely. A man who could do either with equal ease was a man out of control. Dangerous to all who opposed his will.

The question he could not answer, the one that kept eating away at the back of his mind, was the one that asked what he was going to do about it if his worst suspicions proved out, as he was now convinced they would? What would his move be? How far was he ready to take it?

The elevator doors opened on the sixth floor of the Bank of Nevada building and Henry stepped out and winked at Iola Raintree, who gave him a sweet smile, her big dark eyes not quite as sad these days. She was coming out of it, Henry thought, and making out remarkably well on her new job. Mrs. M., he had noticed, had taken her under her protective wings.

Instead of going to his office, Henry veered to the right and headed for Harry Mitchell's office. His secretary, a buxom redhead who was probably Mitchell's attempt to reincarnate Big Tit Gertie, smiled at Henry with that direct sensuous look she reserved for top executives.

"Is he alone?" Henry asked, moving across the room.

"Yes, Mr. Godwin. Is he expecting you?"

"More or less," he said, opening the door and peeking inside. "Got a minute, Harry?"

Mitchell, who was reading the morning paper and drinking coffee, waved him in. "To what do I owe this early visit?"

Henry went to the table behind Mitchell's desk and poured himself a cup of coffee. He sat on the leather couch to the right of Mitchell and lit a cigarette.

"I need some information on our subsidiary, A. G. Ore Company."

Mitchell carefully folded the newspaper and dropped it in the wastebasket under his desk. "You've got me there, Henry. Where did you come up with that name?"

Henry smiled, determined to keep the conversation friendly as long as possible. "Why don't you check the books. It may have slipped your mind."

Mitchell nodded. "That's possible but not too probable. As comptroller, I think I'm fairly familiar with the company's corporate entities. That one just don't ring a bell."

"Well, did we ever do business with A. G. Ore?"

"Frankly, Henry, I don't think I've ever even heard of that company."

Henry stood up and crossed over to the desk. "Do me a favor, will you?" he said, taking out his pen and writing down the three dates the stamp mills had made payments to A. G. Ore. "Check these for me. Like to have it soon as possible."

Mitchell shook his head. "Is there any purpose to this?"

Henry raised an eyebrow. "No, no—just thought I'd come in here today and see if I could waste some of your valuable time."

"Well, Henry, I mean, what am I looking for?"

Henry placed both hands on the desk and leaned forward until his face was only inches away from Mitchell's. "Harry, be a good fellow and check it out. Let's stop playing games. It's really a pain in the ass."

Mitchell shrugged and leaned back in his chair. "Okay, but I can't get to it for a couple days. I've got a bunch of meetings and appointments stacked up, and Rufus called last night wanting a report cabled to Switzerland within twenty-four hours."

Henry started for the door. "Well, I see you've got your priorities straight, as always."

"Well, just a minute, Henry, you're welcome to look at the books yourself."

Henry stopped with his hand on the doorknob. "Will I find anything, Harry?"

"I doubt it. A. G. Ore's a new one on me."

"How could that be possible, Harry? In nineteen twenty-six our stamp mills at Sparks, Tonopah, and Goldfield processed gold ore worth a hundred and twenty-one thousand dollars for A. G. Ore. Isn't it strange you're not aware of it? Have the ledgers for that year sent to my office. Or is this what you meant the other night when you said you hadn't run it through the books?"

Again the expression of indecision on Mitchell's face gave him the look of a man with severe gas pains. He winced and shook his head. "My God, Henry, what are you trying to do to me?"

"Never mind," Henry said, opening the door. "You've answered the question."

"Wait a . . ." he called, but Henry had already closed the door behind him.

It was late when Henry arrived at the ranch that evening. He had stayed in town to have dinner with Senator Amos Rutledge, whose efforts on behalf of the silver cause were faltering in the face of the economic crisis gripping the nation. After dinner they had repaired to a speakeasy for some serious drinking and talking, but Henry's thoughts had been elsewhere. As far as he was concerned, he had the proof he needed. It was Yulee's mine. The only question remaining was how

Rufus had gone about appropriating it. Knowing Rufus, he was sure that the answer, when it came, would be ingenious.

Henry stepped out of the car and heard the whinnying of White Lightning. He smiled and walked toward the corral fence, where he knew the horse would be waiting for him. No matter how late he came home, the horse always greeted him. He liked to think it was because the animal enjoyed seeing him, but he suspected that the reason was the cubes of sugar he always had for him. How many businessmen, he wondered, went about town with cube sugar in their pockets. No one else at the ranch was allowed to give the horse sugar. Otherwise, Henry reasoned, White Lightning was such a persuasive beggar that he would be toothless by now.

"Okay, big boy," Henry said, reaching over the top railing to stroke the horse's nose. "I know what you've been waiting for." He reached into his pocket for a cube of sugar and White Lightning suddenly bolted. "Whoa, baby," Henry said.

The horse reared up on its hind legs and a moment later Henry saw a blur of motion to his right and felt a rush of air. Instinctively, he leaped back, but not before something solid glanced off his right shoulder. The pain racing down his arm was excruciating and he dropped to one knee. His arm had gone numb. He raised his other arm protectively, for he knew that the weapon, whatever it was, was being wielded with deadly force.

There was another rush of air and Henry jumped back, falling flat on the ground and rolling in a backward somersault. He landed on his feet, his right arm dangling uselessly at his side, his left arm spreading out in the wrestler's stance he had learned at VMI, his body crouching, his eyes desperately searching the darkness of a moonless night for his attacker. Then he saw the huge black shadow moving slowly toward him, as broad as it was tall, and knew instantly that it was George Clews.

"Clews, have you gone mad?" he shouted, slowly retreating until his back was against the corral fence. He could feel White Lightning's hot breath on his neck. The horse, still whinnying, was furiously pawing the ground. "Clews, what the hell do you think you're doing?"

"I'm going to clean your nose for you," Clews growled, inching forward, his right arm raised above his head, his huge fist clenched around what looked like a long piece of iron pipe.

He braced one foot on the lower fence rail and waited until the last moment to propel himself headlong like a battering ram at Clews, his head striking just under Clews's rib cage. There was a loud gasp as Clews stumbled backward, his weapon momentarily forgotten as he struggled to regain his balance and breath. They both went down, with Henry on top. Henry jerked his knee into Clews's groin as hard as he could and quickly rolled away. Clews swung the pipe at his head, just missing him. As Clews struggled to his knees, Henry jumped up and aimed a kick at Clews's head. The blow caught him behind the left ear, knocking him sideways. He came to rest on all fours, shaking his head, dazed by the blow, and Henry moved in for the kill. One swift kick in the face would be the end of it. But he didn't move fast enough. The pipe caught him just below the kneecap and Henry heard the bone snap and felt a sharp stab of pain as his right leg collapsed under him.

Over the noise of his own heavy breathing, he could hear White Lightning whinnying and pawing the ground and he started crawling toward the fence, hoping to get on the other side before Clews could get to his feet. For a desperate, fleeting moment, Henry had the crazy hope that White Lightning would defend him, but the horse continued to dance on its hind legs, its eyes wild with fear. In his state of frenzy he was capable of stomping anyone who got in his way.

With a broken leg and a numb arm, Henry had been reduced to a defenseless victim. He was at the mercy of a man he had learned to hate more than anyone since the Pikes.

If he could have stood up, he would have leaped on White Lightning and ridden off to safety, saving his skin before his pride. Anything was better than being killed like a dumb, helpless creature in the dust and manure of the corral.

"Wait," he groaned, as he saw Clews moving toward him in a low, menacing crouch, the tip of the pipe trailing in the dust.

"Beg, you sonofabitch," Clews hissed through clenched teeth. "I'm gonna smash your fucking brains into a pile of shit."

Henry was frantically trying to pull himself along the ground with his left arm and leg, slithering sideways, but he was barely moving. He rolled on his back and saw Clews's face above him, the eyes glinting malevolently in the deep sockets of his beetle brow.

The pipe came up over Clews's head and Henry closed his eyes. He wanted to cry out, but no sound escaped his lips. Instead he found himself crazily thinking of what Yulee had told him about the porcupine being the only animal a man could kill with a club.

There was a loud thumping sound, followed by a great gasp of air and loud groan, and Henry opened his eyes to see Clews crash through the top rail of the fence, landing headlong in the corral. He lay there, motionless, his arms and legs folded under him, his face buried in the loose dirt.

To his right Henry saw Moses Grimes moving swiftly toward the limp figure, a shovel raised high over his head.

"Moses, stop!"

Grimes paused to glance at Henry. "You hurt bad, Henry?"

"Leg's broken. Get me in the house and call Doc Sprague."

"The bastid," Moses growled. "I'm gonna chop his fuckin' head off like I do them rattlers 'round here."

Moses took a step toward Clews but Henry said, "Don't do it, Moses. Let him be, but get White Lightning back in her stall before she stomps him to death. Then call Sheriff Webster. I want him locked up. And you stay out of it, you hear? You tell Webster you found us out here and that's all you know."

"Yessuh," Moses said, throwing the shovel to the ground. "I hope White Lightning stomps the son'bitch right to hell. Here, let me give you a hand."

Henry tried to sit up, to smile at Moses, to show his gratitude—the man had just saved his life. But Henry was overcome by waves of nausea and dizziness. He lay back and closed his eyes, letting the pain ease him out of it.

30

Henry lay flat on his back and stared bleakly at the ceiling. His leg, in a plaster cast from foot to thigh, was suspended by a jerry-built weight and pulley contraption that had imprisoned him in his own bed for the past three weeks. God only knew how much longer he would be at the mercy of Aunt Caroline and Holly Grimes. These two women kept pecking away at him like mother hens. One would have thought he was on his deathbed, the way they carried on. It seemed to Henry that every time the door opened one of them was coming in with a bowl of soup or a washbasin—by now he was convinced they were taking turns.

Another frequent visitor was Iola Raintree, whom Mrs. M. had delegated as her office messenger for bringing papers for Henry to read and sign. At first those big sad eyes appraising his cast had made him feel uneasy. He was not used to having people look at him as an object of pity. But gradually she seemed to have adjusted to his condition. In fact, she appeared to be coming out of her shell, actually blossoming in a way that was most appealing. Iola was a beautiful girl in a wholesome way, and yet sometimes her large sad eyes acquired a strange seductive look when she smiled at Henry. Once when she had leaned over to adjust his pillow—she too wanted to mother him—he had noticed a nest of tiny freckles on her nose that she was trying to cover up with face powder. He had commented on it, assuring her they were far too becoming to be concealed. She had blushed, but on her next visit he had noticed that she wore no makeup.

There was a brisk knock at the door and Aunt Caroline marched right in. "Henry, the office has just delivered this cablegram from Mr. Boutwell. I knew you'd want to see it immediately."

"Thanks, Aunt Caroline."

"Would you like to sit up, dear? Let me fluff a few pillows."

Henry sat up and she quickly arranged several pillows behind his back. "Now, try this. Is it comfy?"

"Perfect," Henry said, "as always. Thanks." He held the cablegram unopened in his lap. She glanced at it, smiled anxiously, and left the room.

This was the first message from Rufus since the fight. Except for the parties directly concerned, it had been business as usual at Nevada Consolidated. Sheriff Webster had kept the whole affair tightly under wraps. Rather than arrest George Clews, Webster had him taken by ambulance to a Reno hospital, where it was diagnosed that he had severe vertebrae fractures at the base of his spinal column. Doc Sprague had told Henry that Clews would be in a body cast for at least a year.

Henry opened the envelope and unfolded the sheet of paper. He closed his eyes, not yet ready to look at the bold printing. Intuitively, he knew it was bad news, and at the moment he didn't feel up to it. The three weeks in bed had given him time to reflect on his life, particularly his marriage, and he was not happy with his thoughts. He found himself brooding for hours on end, sinking into self-immolating depression—not because of anything Alicia had done, but because of his own thoughtless behavior, his own inadequacy in dealing with his wife's needs and desires. Her temperament had been delicate and volatile, yet there had been so many things he could have done to help her fulfill herself, to convince her of his love, to assuage her fears and insecurity. But he had done practically nothing. He had let her drown in her own lust. For that he would feel forever responsible.

He opened his eyes and glanced at the paper. It read:

OUR DARLING GIRL PASSED ON LAST NIGHT STOP LAST WORDS WERE OF HER LOVE FOR YOU STOP BODY CREMATED TODAY STOP ASHES TO BE SCATTERED AT SEA STOP RETURNING FORTHWITH STOP DEEPEST CONDOLENCES STOP RUFUS.

Henry turned his head, burying his face in the pillows, and wept. In the end he didn't know why or for whom he was weeping. It seemed as if all the tragic moments of his life had been wrapped into that small piece of paper.

There was his beautiful mother hanging from a rafter in the barn. He had been nine years old the morning Alva's screams had brought him running to the barn. Even now, with this latest tragedy, the intensity of that moment was so vivid in his memory that he could see every detail of his mother's body as it hung lifeless at the end of a rope. He had darted frantically backward, his vision blurred by the rush of tears, his legs buckling under him. In the far distance he could hear the General shouting for Thaddeus to "get the boy the hell out of here." He wanted to look, but his eyelids were glued shut. Thaddeus had lifted him in his arms and he'd lost consciousness. Later the General had come to his bedroom and even now Henry could hear his voice, so soft and comforting. Then he'd slept until the next morning, a full twenty-four hours, without once awakening.

That had been his escape then, but now he could only lie in bed and remember Alicia the way she had been in San Francisco the night she recited Molly Bloom's soliloquy. And he thought how terrible it must have been for her at the end, as she had awaited death in her Swiss hospital bed, in the final passion of her "stylish disease."

When Rufus Boutwell first walked into the room Henry barely recognized him. He had lost an enormous amount of weight and looked ten years younger. For the first time since he'd known Rufus, Henry could actually see his eyes, which previously had been buried in folds of puffy lids and pouches. His coloring had turned from pasty gray to pinkish robust. His whole being was that of a healthy and vigorous man. Even his nose looked straighter.

"What happened to you?" Henry asked. "You look like hell."

Boutwell laughed. "A little Swiss fresh air, a little Swiss medicine, and a little Swiss surgery—presto, a little Swiss magic."

Henry shook his head. "How're you going to explain this to the boys at the Cohisa Duck Club?"

"Might not have to," he said, moving to the bed to take a closer look at Henry's cast. "Those boys ain't too fond of teetotalers. You know what they say, Henry. There's no bigger wet blanket than a reformed drunk." He pulled out his pen. "Might as well add my monicker to this thing. Doc tells me it'll heal like new. That's more than they can say for poor old George."

"It's poor old George, is it?" Henry said, all pretenses at amiability gone from his voice.

"Well, Christ, Henry, you nearly killed the poor bastard. Webster tells me you hit him with a fucking shovel. That's a mean weapon. You could kill a horse with one of them things."

"Believe me, Rufus, I tried, but it's hard to give it your best effort when you've got a broken leg. That two-foot length of pipe he tried to kill me with was not exactly a toy."

"Oh, come on, now, Henry—he wasn't trying to kill you. Don't get carried away."

"What the hell do you know about it?" Henry shouted. "You weren't the one on the receiving end. But let me tell you something, Rufus, and I mean it. Keep that creep away from me. Next time I will kill him. Make no mistake about that."

"Henry, my boy, don't get yourself all riled up. It's no big deal. Just a couple guys having a little brawl. Where I come from it happens every day and twice on Sunday."

Henry's eyes narrowed angrily. "Drop the bullshit, Rufus. I'm in no mood for it."

Boutwell chuckled. "That shovel reminds me of the time this old geezer came at me with a pitchfork. Now, *that's* a nasty weapon. Found me in the barn with his little girl. She couldn't've been over fourteen, but she had all the right equipment in the right places and knew just what to do with it. At the time I was wearing her pink bloomers around my neck and had my nose buried in her sweet little snatch. Well, I'm rooting in there like a hog in slop when I hear this board creak and look up in the nick of time. The old geezer's coming at me with his pitchfork and it's aimed right at my ass. Christ, did you ever see a cat with its tail on fire? That's me, hightailing it out of there. I wore them bloomers around my neck until they fell apart. My pink badge of courage."

Henry tried to control his anger. "How much more nonsense before we get down to it?"

Boutwell walked across the room to a large window that looked out to the distant snowcapped peaks of the Sierra Nevada. "Where do you want to start, Henry?" he asked, keeping his back to the room.

"At the beginning, Rufus."

"That's a philosophical premise, Henry."

Henry gritted his teeth. "Start with Yulee's mine. Tell me how you came to own it. But first tell me what happened to him."

After a long pause, Rufus said, "I wish I knew what happened to old Yulee. And that's the truth, Henry."

"Rufus, don't talk to me about truth. Just give me the facts. For all our sakes, they better be straight. At this moment I'm this close"—he pressed his forefinger against his thumb until there was no space be-tween them—"to blowing this whole fucking company of yours straight to hell. Don't go mouthing off about truth—just don't goddamn lie to me."

Boutwell remained at the window, his back to the room. "I won't lie to you, Henry. I'll give you the facts and if you don't believe me then you do what you've got to do. But first let me spell it out my own way."

"Before you start, bear in mind that I know considerably more than you probably think I do."

"Makes no difference, Henry. I'm going to give you the whole story. But sometimes, you know, facts have a way of looking kind of different to different people. What may be a fact to me may look like a lie to you. I can't help it, Henry, if it comes out that way. So here goes."

He turned from the window and went to sit in a rocking chair near the bed. "Remember the morning we drove to Virginny and that old woman told you Yulee was missing? Then I drove you to the airport and gave you your first airplane ride. Well, when you flew away that morning I got this bright idea. I thought, Well, that old coot got himself done in by some bushwhacker right in town. But there's no way in the world Yulee would've told him the location of his claim. So I thought, Well, all I've got to do is find his tailing dump. And what better way to do it than with a small airplane. So I got me a map and made a bunch of circles around Virginny, starting about a hundred miles out and working in, and I told this pilot I wanted him up in the air every minute of daylight there was, every day of the week, until he found that dump. After six months, with no luck, I got me two more airplanes, and I kept them flying. I knew sooner or later they'd spot that dump. It was in the cards, right? Unless old Yulee made up the story, which I never considered for a minute, it had to be there. It was only a question of time before one of them pilots spotted it.

"Well, Henry, it took nearly a year. That old sourdough had hidden that dump in a way you wouldn't believe. They had to fly almost at ground level to spot it. He had all that shit graded out to make it look like the rest of the terrain. Where he got all his energy's beyond me."

"I want the names of the pilots," Henry said.

Rufus reached in his pocket and handed Henry a piece of paper. "Kind of thought you would. I wrote them down for you." He paused. "There's only one hitch. Two got themselves killed in one of them air circuses and the other's left town. They say he's somewhere in Florida. We can put the Pinkertons on his tail if you like."

"Yes, the way you put them on Yulee's? Aren't they also the ones who told you about Alfred, the government assayer in Virginia City, moving to Florida? Lots of people you know seem to be partial to Florida."

Boutwell ignored the sarcasm. "All right, that was a little white lie about the Pinkertons. I didn't need them to tell me what happened to Yulee. I knew he was at the bottom of one of them mine shafts and no one was ever going to find him. He wasn't the first miner to disappear in Virginny and won't be the last. Besides, I didn't want nobody nosing around. Keeping something like this quiet is hard enough without getting professional snoopers in it."

"Then why lie to me about it?"

"I had to tell you something, otherwise you'd have jumped in with both feet. Now, just wait a minute, Henry, and let me get my say in before you start firing questions at me." He pulled out a handkerchief and mopped his face. "Shit, I could sure use a shot of Irish right now." He took out a plug of chewing tobacco from his pocket and bit into it, tearing off a large chunk with his small yellow teeth. "Now all I need's a spittoon." He stood up and looked around the room. "Filthy habit." He got down on his hands and knees and peered under the bed. "Mind if I use your pisspot?"

Henry watched in silence as Rufus placed the porcelain chamber pot beside the rocking chair and sat down. "Now, where the hell was I? Oh, yeah. So I faked that Pinkerton report. I wanted to put your mind to ease. But once I had the mine, I didn't know how to tell you about it, your having such a suspicious nature and all. I did everything on the q.t., kept it locked up, so to speak, waiting for the right time, but now with the Depression hitting so hard we needed it real bad, and with me being out of the country—well, it all came to a head ass backward."

Rufus chuckled. "You've got poor Mitchell ready for a strait jacket. Gave him a pretty rough time, to hear him tell it." He spat in the chamber pot and wiped his mouth with his hand. "Before I go on, let me tell you about Alicia."

He leaned back in the rocking chair and closed his eyes. "I'm glad you didn't see her at the end. God, it was awful. That TB's vicious, ravages a being something fierce. I swear she got down to nothing but skin and bone. Her thighs were no bigger than my wrists. That poor, sweet, lovely child. Enough to tear the heart right out of you to see her in that condition. I cried myself to sleep more than one night, I'll tell you. Just to think how beautiful she was as a kid, so full of life and spunky as all getout. Oh, God, Henry, how that little gal suffered and how brave she was about it. No self-pity at all. Never a whine or a whimper. I was so proud of her I could have busted."

He looked down, his gray eyes glistening with tears, and rubbed them with his knuckles. "You know, I really loved that kid a lot, Henry. I was just a punk kid myself when she was born, and pretty much of a bum at that age, scrounging around for a buck, and her mother was nothing but a tramp. We didn't give her much to build on, if you know what I mean. I know she went kind of wild for a spell there. I gave that some thought. You know, it must have been in her seed. She never had a chance. God, college girl and all and it made no difference. Then there was this feeling she had about me. She had me pegged a certain way and there's nothing I could do to change it. Well, maybe it made sense to her. Who knows what gets into kids' heads when they're young.

"Anyway, at the end, she was hallucinating real bad. She was just burning up with fever. I'd hold cold compresses on her forehead and she'd talk a blue streak. Never saw nothing like it. Most of the time I don't think she even knew I was there. All she ever talked about was you and that Daisy Miller. At first, it made no sense to me at all. But, slowly, I began to sort out the pieces. You know, with what George found out in Vicksburg. Frankly, I don't know why I didn't make the connection sooner. It was all there. So one day I'm sitting by her bed and it all kind of clicked into place. You could have knocked me over with a feather."

He looked up at Henry and his gray eyes were hard as slate. "This Daisy Miller, this big-time singer, is actually Randy's mother." He scratched his head. "Everybody thinks she's from San Francisco and she's this gangster Bacino's—what do you call it in polite society— *paramour*? And her being a blonde and so fair skinned and all. Who'd have thought she was a little nigger gal from Vicksburg? Her name's Camilla, the same little gal you looked for all them years. What a small world this is." He spat again and moved the chaw under his lower lip. "Imagine Randy's mother being a little nigger gal. Oh, I tell you, it boggles the mind."

Henry's face had turned ashen and his eyes seemed to be having trouble focusing on Rufus, who stood up, spat out the chaw, and eased the chamber pot back under the bed with his foot. "Henry, don't say nothing just yet. Sleep on it. Just remember, I love Randy like he was my own flesh and blood. A little drop of nigger blood don't make no mind to me whatsoever. That boy's all Godwin where it counts. As far as he's concerned, Alicia's his real mother, and there's no cause for him to ever know no different. When he gets older, if you want to tell him, that's up to you. But I don't like to think what it'd do to that boy's mind to know the truth. Now, Henry, hear me good. As far as I'm concerned, for the time being, this is our secret, you understand? We forged his birth certificate."

He paused, his eyes narrowing until he looked like the old Rufus, just slits of gray glinting. "It's like with Yulee's mine, Henry. That's our secret, too. Just yours and mine. Nobody else's. And we'll go on doing important things for this state, make more money and gain more power than you can dream possible. And one day that boy of *ours* will be something real special for us to look up to. He will be everything we are and a hell of a lot more. Our progeny, Henry. Believe me, you'll live to be real proud of that boy. On that, Henry, you've got his grandfather's sacred vow."

31

Once he was ambulatory again, Henry quietly resumed his duties as vice-president of Boutwell's empire, which was to take quantum leaps in the 1930s and early 1940s toward the realization of Rufus's dream.

In 1931, at the height of the Depression, Rufus made good his plan to repeal the restrictions on gambling that had been enacted in 1915. The new legislation, spearheaded by Governor "Friendly Fred" Platt, was extremely liberal in its provisions. On payment of local license fees, club owners were permitted to engage in every form of gambling except the sale of lottery tickets. Other inducements offered tourists were a brief six-week residence requirement for divorce, instant marriages performed around the clock, and, subject to local option, legalized prostitution under police supervision, with mandatory registration and medical inspection—which, of course, meant that politicians controlled it.

Paying as little as fifty cents an acre, Rufus continued to purchase huge tracts of barren land around Lake Tahoe, Reno, and particularly Las Vegas, much of it along both sides of the ten-mile stretch of U.S. Highway 91 that separated the town from its airport. The land was in Clark County, and the highway was the only one connecting Las Vegas to Los Angeles and southern California, whose rapid growth Rufus was carefully monitoring.

Even during the influx of workers for the construction of Boulder Dam between 1930 and 1935, this land had remained totally uninhabited. In fact, after one look at the gambling, drinking, and prostitution in Las Vegas, Interior Secretary Ray Wilbur had decreed that the Reclamation Service build a model city for the dam workers. Wilbur named it Boulder City and forbade the sale of liquor and the operation of gambling houses there, but that didn't stop the workers from straying thirty miles northward on weekends to patronize the bars, casinos, and Block 16, Las Vegas's notorious red-light district.

To encourage their patronage Rufus had the governor make a speech defending the state's liberal moral attitude toward gambling, divorce, and prostitution, and its contempt for prohibition. "Nevada," said the governor, expressing Rufus's basic theme, "is the only free state in the Union."

Rufus knew the time wasn't yet right for him to realize his dream. Workers earning Depression wages weren't the answer to the state's real growth. In the long run they would only create greater problems, with the need to build schools and provide other costly services that the state wasn't prepared to offer. The state's future, as Rufus envisioned it, was as a tourist mecca, a place where a man with money could gamble, drink, and fornicate in plush surroundings. He would spend a few days, leave his money, and take his problems home to his own state.

By the end of the 1930s, Las Vegas was still a long way from achieving that goal. Reno, however, was already known as "The Biggest Little City in the World." But to its natives the cluster of gambling joints on Virginia Street was "Sucker Row." The city boasted deluxe hotels for gamblers and fashionable dude ranches in Carson Valley for wealthy patrons of its divorce mills. Rufus owned the Riverview, the largest hotel in Reno, but this was hardly what he had in mind. His vision was far more grandiose. Las Vegas, as he saw it, offered the state its greatest potential.

In 1939 Senator Amos Rutledge became chairman of the Foreign Relations Committee, making him the most powerful senator on the Hill. With President Franklin D. Roosevelt dependent on Rutledge to carry out his foreign policy program, there was a lot of room for Rufus and Henry to maneuver within the bureaucracy.

In late March 1939, Rutledge met with Secretary of State Cordell Hull and President Roosevelt in the White House. Having assumed his leadership position only a month earlier, it was a heady experience for Rutledge. Roosevelt entertained him with several colorful anecdotes and appeared in a jovial mood. Then the talk shifted to Hitler and the President's mood turned grave.

"Amos," said the President, as he carefully placed a cigarette into a long holder and lit it, "you and I have a momentous task ahead of us. This fellow Hitler is out to conquer Europe and he may well succeed a great deal sooner than we expect, unless we can persuade your colleagues to get off their isolation duff and repeal the mandatory arms-embargo provision in the existing neutrality legislation."

"A European war is imminent," Hull warned.

Roosevelt nodded, his gaze fixed on Rutledge. "First it was Austria and now he's annihilated Czechoslovakia in complete disregard of the Munich Pact. Poland is next, then perhaps France and England. Italy's already in the Axis camp. Hitler's on a rampage and nothing will stop him but the industrial might of this nation. It's time we stopped being bystanders. Our allies need us."

"I quite agree," Rutledge said, "but Congress is of a different mind. If you took a poll of this nation today you'd find, Mr. President, that most people want to stay out of it this time. We solved Europe's problem in nineteen eighteen at a great cost of American lives."

Roosevelt waved his cigarette holder. "Let's not rehash ancient history. What I want you to do, Amos, is push Cordell's new neutrality legislation through your committee. Let's get it on the floor. I assure you we've got the necessary votes to pass it."

"That's right," Hull said. "But first your committee must pass it with a convincing majority."

By the time Senator Amos Rutledge left the White House his head was in the clouds. During dinner in Rufus's Mayflower Hotel suite two days later, Rutledge was brought back down to earth.

"What do you mean this neutrality bill would be beneficial to England and France in the event of general war?" Rufus asked gruffly.

"Hitler's on a rampage," Rutledge said, looking at Henry for support. "We've got to do something about getting munitions to our allies. FDR's hot for this bill. He thinks we're probably already too late to save Poland and France."

"So," Rufus said, "what do we get in return?"

The piece of steak on Rutledge's fork stopped midway between his plate and his mouth. "I don't follow you. We're talking about stopping a world conflagration, not just business as usual."

"Save the two-bit words and listen to me. You say Roosevelt's hot for this bill. Right?"

"Absolutely determined."

"Then tell me something, Senator. How come he reduced the price of silver from seventy-seven cents an ounce to sixty-four cents on the very day you began your deliberations on this bill?"

"What does one have to do with the other?" Rutledge said, again looking at Henry for support.

"Never mind looking at Henry," Rufus said. "We're of a mind on this one. Listen, Amos, don't you realize the President just slapped you in the face. For Christ's sake, man, you're the fucking senator from the Silver State."

"But, Rufus, we're talking about the security of Europe, perhaps the world. He wants to start shipping munitions to England right away."

"Amos," Henry said, "we understand your concern and your responsibility as Chairman of the Foreign Relations Committee. All we're asking is for Roosevelt to horse-trade with you as he's done with everybody else."

"That's right," Rufus said. "When it comes to horse-trading, FDR's the world champion. So, here's what I want you to do. Ignore his request. Sit on the bill until he calls you in for another of his little chats, then lower the boom."

Rutledge blinked nervously, pursing his lips. "And how do I go about doing this?"

Rufus sneered. "Henry, what did I tell you years ago? Jesus H. Christ, Amos, look the sonofabitch straight in the eye and tell him that you're too busy worrying about the welfare of your own state to concern youself with this bullshit in Europe, which you think is exaggerated anyway."

"But it's not exaggerated."

"I don't give a shit. Are you getting fucking senile or has this job gone to your head? What the hell's going on here?"

Rutledge turned to Henry. "What do you think?"

"I agree with Rufus," Henry said. "Nothing's going to stop Roosevelt for long, but we might as well get something in the bargain, and at the same time strengthen your position with Roosevelt. Believe me, it's not going to affect events in Europe one iota."

"That's right," Rufus said. "Amos, you're the first Nevadan ever to be in this position. Show him your muscle. If he starts hollering to the press, tell him to shut up."

Rutledge laughed. "I'd like to see you do it."

"I'd do it in a minute. Use your head, will you? Tell him it's unwise to air this shit in the press. It tips our hand to Hitler. Keep that kraut bastard guessing as to what our government will or won't do about repealing the arms embargo."

A week later Rutledge again met with the two men in Rufus's suite. His head was again in the clouds, but this time it was because of his own achievement.

"I pulled it off, Rufus," he said, beaming. "First, as you've probably read in the press, I advised the President to keep quiet about what this government was going to do in the event of war in Europe."

"That's brilliant, Amos," Rufus said, smiling approvingly at the senator.

"Then, as you predicted, I was called in for another little chat, and this time Treasury Secretary Morgenthau was there. I knew then we were in good shape. The day before I'd told Hull on the phone that I felt I'd been stabbed in the back when the President lowered the price of silver. So, naturally, the word immediately got back to the President."

Rutledge chuckled. "Rufus, I wish you could've been there. Roosevelt says, 'Am I to understand that you will continue withholding your support of this legislation until the price of silver is raised?' Rufus, so help me, I looked him straight in the eye and I said, 'Mr. President, we've got eighteen votes and what are you going to do about it?' "

Again Rutledge chuckled. "He's quite an amazing man, our President. 'Well, Amos, how would seventy-one cents an ounce strike you?' he said. 'That would strike me just dandy, Mr. President,' I replied. He waved, kind of a half salute, and said, 'You've got it, Amos—now go pass my bill.' And by God we're taking it to the floor on Monday."

Rufus stood up and shook Rutledge's hand. "See, Amos? All it takes is a little gumption and people give you what you want. That's the whole secret to success, Amos. Don't ever let your balls go flat. Keep them round and firm all the time. Otherwise these polecats will eat you up alive."

Although the price of silver was important to Rufus, the war brought far greater rewards. Public lands in Nevada were leased to an assortment of corporations owned by Rufus, and the raw materials extracted from these lands were sold for the war effort at enormous profit. The most important materials were lime, titanium, and manganese, the rare metal that is lighter than aluminum and was desperately needed by aircraft factories for fighters and bombers and by ordnance factories making tracer bullets, flares, and incendiary bombs.

At a cost of $145,000,000 the government built a manganese plant twelve miles south of Las Vegas that stretched across the desert for a mile and three quarters. Each of its ten units was four stories high. It became known as "the plant that won the war." Thousands of workers lived in tents and army-style housing. The payroll was a million dollars a week.

Then, through the efforts of both Amos Rutledge and Nevada's senior senator, Elisha Toombs, the Army built an Air Corps gunnery school ten miles north of Las Vegas that was to develop into the giant Nellis Air Force Base. In time it would become the nation's major jet-aircraft-testing and pilot-training center and one of the world's busiest airports.

Dollars poured in by the tens of millions, providing Rufus with the wealth and political power he needed to become a member of the clandestine Century Committee, an exclusive society made up of the hundred most powerful corporate leaders in the nation. These were the men Rufus most admired—men without ideologies, without scruples, without religion, or allegiance to any nation. Their sole loyalty was to money and power. They were the heirs of the great robber barons of another era. The hundred members held interlocking directorships in thousands of industries and financial institutions. Their hirelings were some of the most powerful men in government. Membership was tantamount to sainthood in Rufus's world. Sworn to secrecy, Rufus never told Henry of his affiliation. It was to become his ace in the hole, the linchpin to the realization of his most fantastic dream.

32

On June 6, 1944, as Allied forces were storming the beaches of Normandy, Randolph Godwin and his new bride were in a Pullman bedroom heading west for their own D day in Carson City.

The train was somewhere between Elko and Winnemucca, following the same route Henry had traveled on his motorcycle many years earlier. Randolph knew the story of Yulee and old Bessie, but that was not what was on his mind as he gazed out the train window at the moonlit landscape of Black Rock Desert, a bleak wasteland that had given rise to colorful legends of lost gold mines. At his side his bride slept tranquilly, her voluptuous body curled snugly into his, her warm buttocks pressed tightly into the pocket of his hips. He could feel the heat radiating from the silky smoothness of her naked flesh and he gritted his teeth as he felt himself becoming aroused. He wanted to stroke her, to bury his face in her sweet-smelling hair, but there was no time for that now. He had a crucial problem to resolve before morning, one he could no longer postpone.

There was no telling what Rufus would do when told of the marriage. It was a terrifying prospect, considering his grandfather's zealous determination to control every aspect of his life. After weeks of agonizing over it, the moment of truth was finally at hand. Randolph had tried vainly to break the news by mail and telephone, but on paper the words were too banal and on the telephone they stuck in his throat. The only solution was a face-to-face showdown—psychological shootout. Yet, as the weeks had passed, he had gradually convinced himself that despite his wife's humble origins her great beauty and winsome nature would surely win Rufus over. If nothing else, it had to soften the blow, reduce the intensity of the explosion.

After all, Randolph thought, he was merely following the precepts Rufus had taught him while he was growing up in Carson City. You made up your mind about something you wanted and went out and took it, regardless of who got in the way. Success and moral ethics were contradictions. A man was what he chose to be. The world forgave everything but failure. Every day of your life you had to win. Money was the only god worth worshiping, the only earthly fortress against the horrors and perfidies inflicted on the unsuspecting by a mindless society. The worst crime was poverty. To lie and cheat with charm and boldness was a proven formula for success. The world loved a charming scoundrel and deified a clever manipulator. Honesty and back-breaking work were the roads to certain disaster. The clever man learned to plunder without dirtying his hands.

To illustrate his precepts, Rufus would recall fascinating anecdotes from the lives of his heroes, the great robber barons of the turn of the century. His greatest heroes were the two supreme potentates, John D. Rockefeller and J. Pierpont Morgan, the most ruthless of the lot. Teddy Roosevelt had called the robber barons "malefactors of great wealth." "They looted a whole nation," Rufus would proudly explain. "Every principle and institution was for sale, as they are today, and will always be."

Randolph, who had been in his early teens the first time Rufus had gone seriously into the subject, had listened in wide-eyed astonishment. Instinctively he had known that his father would not approve of Rufus's stories and had therefore never repeated them, but he found himself fascinated by the great wealth and ruthless power of these men.

"The rich are heroes to be emulated," Rufus liked to say. "See, sonny boy, everybody wants to be rich. That's the American Dream. Even John Adams, who was a true aristocrat, understood that right from the beginning. He knew the people would let the rich use all the tricks in the book to build great fortunes, because they wanted to keep things open in case they became rich themselves someday. Otherwise they'd have to face the reality of always being poor. Adams thought that the masses loved equality when they looked up to higher ranks and loved discrimination when they look downward. See, sonny boy, as long as you let these poor suckers think they've got a chance to reach the top, they'll let you get away with murder. Look at the tens of thousands that've been killed in industrial accidents, unsafe mines, unsanitary food, through all kinds of corporate shenanigans. For Christ's sake, Armour, Swift, and other Chicago meat packers killed more American troops with embalmed meat in the Spanish-American War than did the enemy. Teddy Roosevelt said he'd rather eat his old hat than canned meat. It's been the same with patent medicines. A few years ago they used to lace babies' pacifying syrups with morphine and cocaine, and they peddled heroin as a new miracle drug that doctors prescribed for everything from melancholia to constipation.

"Then along comes this bunch of rabble-rousing reporters, do-gooders, reformers—oh, they thought they'd change the world." Rufus laughed at this absurdity. "They had this Commie magazine, *McClure's*, and they wrote about graft, price fixing, bid rigging, kickbacks, secret rebates, dangerous products, child labor, race problems, prison abuses, church-owned slums—that was a good one—insider stock deals, monopolies, cartels, bribes, special interest groups, unsafe working conditions, false weights and measures in fancy packages, corruption in high places, and the looting of the nation's forests and other natural resources. They had a catalogue the length of both my arms—called the 'white collar' crimes. But Teddy the Trust Buster blasted them as socialists, sensationalists, agitators, puzzleheads, and muckrakers—that's the handle that stuck to their tail.

"They thought they knew everything, but they didn't understand the system they were trying to destroy, hadn't the foggiest notion of what really made it the most successful in the history of the world. Even Woodrow Wilson said it."

At such times Rufus would pore over books to find exact quotes. " 'The masters of the government of the United States are the combined capitalists and manufacturers of the United States,' Wilson said in 1913. 'The government of the United States at present is a foster child of the special interests.'

"Ain't that beautiful, 'a foster child.' Ah, the truth in that statement. Right from the start, the rich hog-tied the legislative process, cut its water off right at the source long before it could outlaw their methods. And you can forget about the Sherman Antitrust Act. It's dead as a doornail. It's never sent no businessman to jail and never will."

Rufus would usually end these sessions with his favorite question. "Tell me, sonny boy, if the ends don't justify the means, what in hell does?" He'd laugh uproariously, tousle the boy's hair, and be off on another one of his big deals that would net more millions for Randolph to inherit come that fateful day—a fact Rufus seldom failed to impress upon the boy.

"One of these days, sonny boy, old Rufus will keel over and make you rich as Rockefeller, and don't you ever forget it. I'm your fairy godfather. I can make you into a handsome merchant prince or turn you into a pumpkin with a scratch of my pen."

Even for a young boy there was nothing subtle about the implication. The effect was to create feelings of terrifying insecurity, particularly as Randolph grew older. One wrong word, one false move, and Rufus might pull the rug out from under him, turn him into a pumpkin. He became convinced that Rufus, like God, saw all, heard all, knew all, and forgave nothing. He told himself he loved him, that he enjoyed being with him and didn't in the least mind the effort it took to keep him in a happy frame of mind. Deep down, however, he was terrified that somehow he would inadvertently provoke Rufus, thereby destroying his one chance to gain Rufus's promised dream.

This created deep-seated anxieties, which he tried to conceal by being quick to smile even when he felt like screaming obscenities like a madman. As he grew older, his natural good looks, his strong muscular face became an important mask behind which he could hide his true feelings. It was one thing to feel emotionally vulnerable; it was quite another indeed to reveal it to others. He was soon taking pride in his ability to dissemble. In time he became a smooth operator, the epitome of the well-adjusted, typical all-American boy.

Meanwhile, as far as Rufus was concerned, his philosophy, the tenets by which he lived and prospered, appeared to be well received by his grandson, whom he considered to be bright, alert, and promising.

On the other hand, Henry had little to say to his son on the subject of success in a mercenary world. To Randolph his father's interest seemed to lie in the past, with a culture that had died with the General.

Almost from the moment she had arrived in Carson City, Aunt Caroline had started complaining to Henry that the boy was being spoiled rotten by a man totally bereft of moral and ethical standards. "He has the conscience of a guttersnipe," she would declare in moments of bitter frustration. "He's teaching Randolph to cheat at cards. Showed him how to deal what he calls 'seconds'—I think it's cards dealt from the bottom of the deck—and then he showed him how to mark a whole deck while holding a tiny piece of sandpaper hidden in the palm of his hand. I declare, Henry, that man has me at my wit's end."

Not wanting to further aggravate his aunt, Henry always tried to play the problem down during these conversations. "He's just having fun with Randolph, trying to entertain him."

"To hear that horrid man tell it, the world's made up of millions of nincompoops and a handful of smart crooks like himself. 'Takers and suckers,' as he coarsely puts it."

Henry shrugged. "We teach what we know, usually what has meant most to us as we were growing up. Rufus, you see, was never a boy. When children his age were still playing cowboys and Indians, he was scrounging around for food and shelter in an extremely harsh environment. He pulled himself up by his own bootstraps and he's rightly proud of it."

"I won't hear of it," Aunt Caroline cried, her anxious eyes darkening angrily. "That man behaves like the ruffian he's always been. You'd think he was brought up in a cave by wild animals. He's a predator and the worst influence imaginable on the innocent mind of a growing boy."

"Give Randolph credit for having some good sense," Henry said. "He understands the difference between tall tales and reality. He knows Rufus's past has nothing to do with his own future." Henry placed his arm across his aunt's shoulders. "Fear not, dear Caroline, Randolph will not become a riverboat gambler."

She pulled away angrily. "Don't patronize me, Henry Godwin. You should hear the things that man says about you. Sometimes it takes all my willpower to keep from walking up to him and slapping his impudent face. He calls you his *employee*, says it like it was a dirty word, and says you owe everything you have to him, and although you're a lawyer and come from a distinguished Southern family, without his help you'd still be struggling to make ends meet. But he's made you vice-president of the largest company in Nevada. Then he chuckles like an imbecile and says, 'See, your daddy had the good sense to marry the boss's daughter. That's how one gets up in the world if one can't cut it on his own.' Is that what a grandfather should be telling his grandson about his own father?"

Even Randolph could tell there was something wrong with the relationship between his father and Rufus. Randolph had noticed that whenever Rufus was around a subtle change would come over his father.

There was nothing specific, nothing he could put his finger on, except that Henry seemed to withdraw into himself. His eyes would turn cold and distant, veiling all emotions, never visibly reacting to anything Rufus said or did. He was polite, cooperative, but remained completely submerged. At times the silence hung between them, with neither seemingly aware of it. Randolph wanted to scream or clap his hands, anything to fill the deadly void. Henry's smile was more like a nervous twitch at the corners of his mouth that left the facial muscles immobile, his eyes still veiled. If Rufus was aware of this metamorphosis, he never let on. But his own behavior became more subdued in Henry's presence, his conversation restricted mostly to business matters.

Although all this mystified him, Randolph never broached the subject with either man. He had enough problems of his own without looking for more. Through the years, on the surface, at least, Randolph learned to cope with Rufus's moods and in the process managed to gratify his own needs. In fact, he came to believe that he could twist Rufus around his little finger with the greatest of ease. By assuming various poses, all calculated to seduce Rufus into a receptive mood, he had learned he could get his way on everything he desired, however capricious the need or extravagant the cost.

In his entire life Randolph could recall only one violent episode with his grandfather. It was the war that had come between them, causing an explosion with ramifications that had not only forever altered Randolph's attitude toward Rufus, but severely crippled the new self-confidence he had been so carefully nurturing since leaving Carson City.

It began on December 7, 1941. Randolph and a group of his Harvard classmates were guzzling beer in a Scollay Square dive when they heard that the Japanese attacked Pearl Harbor. When the news reached them, they rose as one and drunkenly marched out in search of the nearest recruiting station.

Saved by the fact that December 7 was a Sunday, the next morning Randolph telephoned Rufus, who was in Washington on business, to say that he was enlisting in the Army Air Corps with the idea of becoming a pilot.

Rufus's response nearly burst his eardrums. "You dumb bastard, don't you move a muscle until I get there!"

That evening, when Rufus's train arrived at South Station in Boston, Randolph was on the platform waiting for him.

Randolph would never forget the hiss of Rufus's voice or the feel of his fingers as they dug into his arms. "You big stupid shithead! Want to be a big fucking hero in a soldier suit? Is that it? Is that why I've worked my ass off all these years? So you could get your ass shot off in a stupid fucking war?"

By now they were at the Summer Street exit and a limousine was waiting at the curb, its engine running. As the chauffeur opened the back door, Rufus pushed Randolph inside and jumped in after him.

The ride to the Ritz-Carlton Hotel was the longest in Randolph's memory. The barrage of obscenities was a totally unexpected reaction, a side of Rufus he had never before even suspected, one that at first confused and then angered him.

"I thought you'd be proud of me," he shouted, trying to wrench his arm out of Rufus's viselike grip.

Rufus released his grip and slapped Randolph across the face. It was the first time he had ever laid a hand on him and the expression on Randolph's face was one of utter astonishment.

"That'll show you how proud I am," Rufus shouted back. "There'll be ten million monkeys like you jumping in there before it's over and you can bet your ass they'll shit their goddamn pants the first time somebody takes a shot at them with a real bullet. But by then it's going to be too late. Cannon fodder. That's what they called them in the first war. They buried millions out there with bulldozers. Great fucking fertilizer. You should see the flowers in Flanders in the spring.

"And most of the ones that got back from the front trenches were shell-shocked, gassed, blind, armless, legless, or both. They sold pencils in tin cups or pushed themselves around on little wheeled platforms. Who gives a shit about any of them today? To most people they're nothing but a fucking nuisance."

"But I'm not going to be in the trenches," Randolph tried to explain. "I'm going to be a pilot, an officer."

"Yeah, yeah, I know, a hotshot fly-boy. Big fucking deal. When they shoot you down, you won't have to worry about a tin cup or a wheeled platform. They'll mop you up with a blotter. Listen, sonny boy, you're just a fucking college freshman, a baby, barely seventeen, for Christ's sake. Wait three and a half years and then talk to me about the war. I'll set you up real good. Get you all the ribbons and promotions you want. They'll come in handy someday. But don't rush it—there's plenty of time."

"All my friends are joining up now. What'll they think of me?"

Rufus settled back in the seat, but his gray eyes remained fixed on Randolph. "I don't give a fart in a windstorm what they think of you. And don't you either. If you know what's good for you, you better worry about what *I* think of you, sonny boy. That's what counts where you're concerned, and don't you ever forget it."

Randolph shook his head in confusion. "I don't know what to do. What'll I tell my friends? It's not fair your treating me this way. I won't stand for it."

Rufus raised his hand. "I'll show you what's fair."

"Don't you dare hit me again," Randolph said, trying to keep his voice from shaking.

This time Rufus lashed out with even greater force. Randolph's hand came up to protect his face but he was too late. The blow caught him on the side of the head, knocking him back against the limousine's headrest.

"Listen good, sonny boy. I'm going to say this just one time. Don't you dare ever defy me again. Don't ever even think about it. You want to join the army? Just say the word. I'll get you in there where you'll get your ass shot off so fast you'll never know what hit you. You're either my grandson or cannon fodder. Understand? You do what I say and one day you'll end up a rich and powerful man. A man the whole world will respect and admire. You defy me and your life ain't worth spit. And that goes for your old man, too. Nobody crosses me. Nobody destroys what I've worked for all these years without paying the price. If you don't think I can do it, ask your father. Ask him who holds the power. He'll tell you goddamn quick."

Randolph stifled a sob and Rufus smashed his fist into the door frame with such force that he felt bone breaking in his hand. He cried out in pain and grabbed the hand, holding it between his legs. "Now, see what you made me do. I broke my fucking hand. You're goddamn lucky I'm a temperate man. In the old days I'd have shot this car full of holes." He paused and smiled at Randolph. "Now, you be a good boy and let's forget this little scene ever happened."

Randolph blinked away the tears, his head rapidly nodding in agreement. "I'm sorry, Rufus. I didn't mean to make you angry."

"It's okay, sonny boy. You just scared the living shit out of me. From now on, take it easy on me, will you? I'm too old for this kind of shit. The old ticker ain't what it used to be."

"How's your hand?" Randolph asked. "There's nothing broken, is there?"

Rufus smiled and reached up with his good hand to tousle Randolph's hair. "Everything's fine, sonny boy, as long as you and me go it together as a team, pals forever."

"You bet, Rufus. We'll always be pals."

"You love your old grandpa, sonny boy?"

Randolph reached for Rufus's injured hand and kissed it. "With all my heart," he said, holding on to the hand and staring straight ahead, his eyes veiled. At that moment, for the first time in his life, Randolph thought he knew how his father felt when he was with Rufus.

The train was highballing and the rocking motion wasn't conducive to serious thinking—not when her buttocks kept rubbing into him, a delicious friction, with every movement of the car. God, he thought, as he reached down to stroke her, to prepare her for his urgent entry, how do you argue with an erection? Rufus had never explained that part of it. In essence that had been Randolph's problem the moment he first set eyes on Betty Schurtz.

He was in his senior year at Harvard and his roommate, Blair Hopkins, along with what seemed to be half his dormitory, had taken a crack at this "sexy bombshell" and struck out. Although one icy look from her slanted green eyes had chilled their approach, it had not cooled their ardor. Nor had it stilled their need to articulate their frustration to Randolph, the dorm's acknowledged premier cocksman, a reputation he encouraged by having named his Cadillac convertible sedan his Cherry Chariot.

"Listen, old man, are you ready to be titillated by my latest dream girl?" Hopkins was saying, his usual preface before launching into familiar raptures. "If only you could see those sensual eyes and radiant red hair—à la Hayworth—that flawless milky white skin and those sculpted cheekbones—à la Lamarr—that delicate turned back tip of a nose and dimpled cheeks—à la Garland—not to mention those other unmentionable well-rounded and no doubt equally dimpled cheeks—à la Grable. The very thought of ever setting mere mortal eyes on such exquisite pulchritude literally takes one's breath away."

He kissed his fingertips and rolled his eyes. "Ah, *mon cheri*," he said, assuming a dreadful French accent, "it would take Charles Boyer, no less, to melt those icy green eyes and soften that stony *coeur*."

Randolph was sprawled on his bed, leaning on one elbow, with *The Wealth of Nations* lying open at his side, the convoluted economics of Adam Smith already making his head ache. It was Wednesday and he had a term paper due next Tuesday, but this idiot wouldn't shut up. He'd heard Hopkins's rhapsody so many times, delivered with the identical hyperboles and extravagant gestures, that by now he felt he could mimic it perfectly. Although he enjoyed Hopkins's performance, today wasn't the day. The student he'd paid to write the term paper had made an awful mess of it. Now he was stuck unless he could find someone else who knew something about economics and needed money badly enough to tackle this boring subject. It wouldn't do for Randolph to get low grades in economics. Rufus would kill him. It was the one course his grandfather cared anything about. Economics was a businessman's most important tool. And Rufus himself, one way or another, had been a student of economics all his life. To Rufus Adam Smith was a prophet. He was God's special emissary to the ruling elite.

"Old man, forget that dreary old fogy Smith for a minute and listen to your old uncle Hoppy . . ."

"Hey, Hop," Randolph said, slapping the book with his hand. "Go in the john and jack off, will you? Do us both a favor."

Hopkins jumped to his feet and clutched his heart. "How vulgar," he cried. "I speak of immaculate pleasures and you suggest unseemly semen down the drain. It's sacrilegious, that's what it is. You, old man, are an uncouth barbarian, a Neanderthal throwback. But, alas, what can one expect from an aborigine raised in the wilds of Nevada? The desert heat, I'm told by an unimpeachable source, sears the brain at a tender age."

Hopkins flopped back in his chair. "However, be that as it may, I shall forge ahead with my fantasy as though I were perfectly alone, a Trappist monk in the solitude of his sacred little cell. As I was about to say before being so rudely interrupted, one look, just one little peek at those fantastic legs and you're sunk, brother—a dead duck, ruined for life, her everloving slave for eternity. The very idea of glimpsing those long gorgeous gams, *sans culottes*, is enough, as old uncle Waltie so aptly phrased it, to 'stagger sextillions of infidels.' On the other hand, any normal, red-blooded Christian boy would gladly give his left nut for such a vision. Mind you, I speak not lightly of such momentous matters. I, for one, am peculiarly fond of my left nut—never mind that its contribution to certain illicit pleasures may be dubious. For me there's the more critical question of ballast, being something of a fanatic for symmetry. One, I presume, would have to go through his remaining years listing to port—or is it starboard? I always get the two confused. Whatever. Imagine, if you will, having to undress in the dark, not to mention the curtailment of foreplay, to avoid embarrassing explanations. This sacrifice, as anyone can see, considering its various adverse aspects, is nothing to sneer at."

Again he jumped to his feet. He was obviously enjoying himself.

"What do legs and Water Street have in common?" he asked, leaning forward to give Randolph an impish grin.

"That's a new twist in your shtick," Randolph said.

"Ah, you've noticed. Just making sure you're paying attention," he said, turning away.

"Well, are you going to tell me?"

He shrugged. "They both lead to the water works."

"Hilarious," Randolph sneered.

"Which leads me once more to those gorgeous gams. Have I ever truly tried to do justice to those marvelous members—what a crude word for such works of art. I suppose I must have, once or twice, but it's hard to know what one is talking about when such libidinal visions of loveliness keep dancing in one's head. No mere mortal poet possesses the language to describe their erotic dance of perambulation.

"Picture in your mind, if you will, these legs coming at you, elfin, nimble, muscular, and yet so delicate, a prima ballerina gliding across a stage, a belly-dancing prima ballerina, coming at you with her pelvis thrust forward until it seems that her pubis has been detached from its other parts and is floating up there all by itself, preceding her, as it were, a separate entity coming at you in heat waves, undulating, teasing, challenging, winking, inviting, until finally the rush of heat hits you like the sudden opening of an oven door."

At this point Hopkins was prancing around the room, exaggerating her walk and rolling his eyes at Randolph. "Absolutely heartbreaking. That's precisely the moment you cream your pants and slink away like a beaten cur."

"Sounds to me like she's swayback," Randolph said. "Where I come from, we shoot horses that look like that."

"Oh, mother of God, all women should be that swayback. Picture, in Technicolor, these succulent labia, suspended in midair, flaunting themselves before your very naked eyeballs, begging to be touched, to be patted, to be stroked, to be scratched, to be tickled—ah, dear God, to be kissed. The temptation, the urge, the compulsion, the itch to drop to one's knees and bury one's puss in the juicy fragrance of that pussy is positively excruciating."

Randolph slammed the book shut. "Okay, Hop, where do I find this iron maiden?"

Hopkins smiled. "She quits at five every afternoon, works in an office on Memorial Drive, about a half-mile from Lowell's Erection."

Lowell's Erection was an inside joke. It referred to the MTA kiosk in the middle of Harvard Square. When Harvard President Abbott Lawrence Lowell had opposed its construction, the old Boston *Examiner* had contributed its most memorable headline: "President Lowell fights erection in Harvard Square."

Randolph glanced at his wristwatch. It was five minutes past three. "All right, Hop, today I'll show you how us baked-brain aborigines operate in the big city."

Hopkins sat down. "Tell me honestly, old man, am I that repulsive?" He was smiling, but there was an anxious look in his pale blue eyes. "Why won't that delicious little witch give me a tumble?"

Randolph cocked an eye to simulate a serious appraisal of his roommate. "Well, the fact that you're a little runt . . ."

"What do you mean, 'little runt'? I'll have you know I'm five-eight and one-quarter, which means I'm a quarter inch taller than the average American soldier who's defending this great nation of ours against the dirty krauts and nips. In the First World War the average height was five-six, for God's sake."

". . . with an apoplectic complexion and fat little chipmunk cheeks and a roly-poly little body and more teeth than a barracuda." The teeth were Hopkins's greatest pride. He possessed the most dazzlingly white teeth Randolph had ever seen. Their glow added a certain strength to his face, made him appear a little taller, stronger—transformed him into an attractive boy, really, until he stopped smiling. Then he looked like a fat-cheeked teenager—pleasant and friendly-looking, but hardly a Don Juan.

"Okay, but you haven't answered my question. Let me put it this way. What if you were a girl stranded on a deserted island with me?"

"I'd cut my fucking throat," Randolph said with a straight face.

From where he stood on Memorial Drive Randolph could look across the Charles River to Boston and its Brahmin enclave on Beacon Hill. The last rays of a slowly sinking sun glinted off the golden dome of the State House. A gentle April wind stirred tiny whitecaps on the dusty slate water, impeding a half-dozen oarsmen in shells from ever achieving the synchrony they were so doggedly attempting. It made Randolph smile. He loved the river, having spent long hours in a shell working out the kinks in his powerful arms and shoulders. If Harvard had not abandoned intercollegiate sports for the duration of the war,

Randolph was certain he would have made the varsity crew. Next to polo, it was his favorite sport.

He enjoyed being alone on the river, taking pleasure in the tall buildings that grew out of its banks and the massive stone bridges that held its shores in place. Every time he looked at the Beacon Hill skyline, he couldn't help but think of the drabness of Carson City and the fact that he would be returning there in a few months to take his place in the family business, a prospect that failed to excite him.

For the past three summers he had enjoyed the lively conviviality of wartime Washington while working as an administrative aide in the office of Senator Amos Rutledge. Rufus had wanted him to learn the ropes, which meant everything there was to know about a senator's sphere of influence. Rufus had left no doubt in Randolph's mind that one day he would represent Nevada in the United States Senate, a far more appealing prospect than the family business, but rather remote at this stage in his life. Being only nineteen, he felt an eternity away from the minimum Constitutional age requirement of thirty. The problem was how to survive the next eleven years in Carson City. Perhaps he could persuade Rufus to let him continue in Washington with Rutledge, assuming greater responsibility, even to becoming his administrative assistant. But Rutledge was getting antsy around him, no doubt reading the handwriting on the wall, regardless of Rufus's assurances that his own tenure was secure. Whenever Rutledge broached the subject, Rufus would make cryptic remarks about Nevada having two senators, and one of them, he would say with a chuckle, "Has one foot in the grave and the other on a roller skate. First time somebody steals his cane, he's a lame duck."

There was always the possibility, Randolph mused, that he could persuade Rufus to rush things along by effecting a Constitutional amendment. Where Rufus was concerned, nothing was impossible. He had demonstrated his magical powers time and again. He was Svengali in a cowboy hat, Midas in cowboy boots, Lucifer in a string tie.

Randolph spotted her the moment she appeared at the door with a group of other emerging workers. His first thought was that she was the loveliest creature he had ever seen. She reminded him of a deer, timid and graceful, keenly alert to all alien sounds and sights without having to turn her head, which she carried proudly above a long graceful neck. Her dark reddish hair fell in soft curls across the padded shoulders of her three-quarter-length camel's hair coat, the belt cinched tightly enough to accentuate her slim waistline and well-rounded hips and bosom.

Contrary to Hopkins's exaggerated antics, she moved gracefully, her hips thrust slightly forward, like a model displaying the latest fashion.

As she reached the sidewalk, people separated in various groups and directions and Randolph was pleased to see that she was alone. She looked straight ahead, the fixed expression on her lovely face a signal that she was in no mood for any nonsense.

He quickened his step and caught up with her. He looked at her and cleared his throat. She continued walking, her eyes still fixed straight ahead, her expression unchanged. The message was plain enough: as far as she was concerned he didn't exist.

"Pardon me, miss," he said softly, leaning forward to smile at her. "Please excuse this intrusion. My name's Randy Godwin and I've been selected by the president of Fair Harvard to personally convey his profound apologies for any inconvenience a few of our more obstreperous students may have caused you by infantile exuberances that are inexcusable whatever the provocation."

She gave him an icy glance, and when he saw the depth of her greenish eyes his breath caught in his throat. "It's provocation, is it?"

"Oh, please, forgive me for being such a clumsy ambassador," he said, again clearing his throat. "I meant provocation only in the sense that your great natural beauty—through no fault of your own, of course—has led some of our more impressionable young men to drastic measures to attract your attention. I truly hope you will find it in your heart of hearts to forgive their trespasses, as we—well, I think you know what I'm trying to say."

Without slowing her walk or looking at him, she said, "What is the point of this little farce you're so set upon acting out?"

Randolph shook his head to indicate the enormity of his disappointment. "But I've just explained. I'm on a special mission for the president of Fair Harvard. Believe me, there is no greater honor and, I might add, none that I take more seriously. I beg you to forgive their impertinences. They're victims of their own youthful weaknesses. Well, let's face it. They're stung, I'm afraid, by the love bug. Spring, as you may have noticed, is early this year."

There was the tiniest crinkling at the corner of her eye in profile, but her mouth remained firmly set.

"We live in strange times, Miss . . ." He waited to see if she would fill in the pause, then shrugged and went on. "With many of our young men off to war and our young women available in rather plentiful numbers for the few of us left behind, it's a great compliment, indeed, that so many strapping young fellows would single you out to the exclusion of all others. As you know, Radcliffe, a bountiful girls' college, is just up the street, but none of its fair ladies, if you'll pardon an old cliché, can hold a candle to you. To that I would personally attest before the highest authority in the land."

The crinkling was widening and he thought he saw the corner of her mouth turn up. "I'm getting pretty desperate, you know," he said, encouraged by these outward signs. "In fact, I've thought of a solution to this dilemma I'd like to propose for your consideration. What if I were to rent them military uniforms of enlisted men and then escort these desperate young men to a USO canteen, where they could let their hair down, so to speak—get this pent-up frustration out of their systems, undergo an emotional catharsis, if you'll pardon the expression. Would you make a point of being there that evening? Just to give them a chance to look at you, to be in the same room with you. You wouldn't have to dance with any of them, unless, of course, you so desired. That would mean so much to them. I realize they're only college kids to you, but many of them will be in the service of our great nation the moment school lets out this spring."

By now he knew she was struggling to keep a straight face. "You realize, of course, that there's an element of risk involved. Impersonating military personnel may well be considered an act of treason in time of war, and the consequence could be a firing squad." He paused and shrugged. "Perhaps this would be the most merciful solution. Except, of course, that it's so final. Ah, well, who's to say what's best in the long run?"

She turned her head away, but he could see her shoulders begin to shake. Then he heard her laughter, deep and earthy, and it was the sweetest sound this side of heaven.

"You're really some kind of lunatic," she said between peals of laughter. "Was this spontaneous or is it something you've written and memorized?"

Randolph feigned shock. "Oh, please, fair lady, totally spontaneous. You are divinely inspirational. You make me feel like a babbling youth again. Cupid hovers in your shadow with a quiver full of golden tipped arrows, taking dead aim on every male who dares to cross your path. Ah, but it's a lovely sting."

She stopped laughing and her green eyes had softened when she looked at him. "You are full of the old blarney, aren't you? One would think you've kissed the bloody stone itself."

"So, it's Irish, you are, my comely lass," he said, assuming an Irish brogue. "It's true, I've been to County Cork, but the bloody micks hid the Blarney stone when news of my impending arrival traveled through that emerald land. 'Tis my hope to sneak up on it one moonless night and hug it to my bosom like a long-lost lover. Oh, the kisses I shall bestow." He paused. "I'm afraid that's one of my worst traits. I'm so terribly affectionate. But it'd be in a good cause. The way I see it, one can never have his fill of the old blarney in these dreary times."

They had reached Harvard Square and she waited at the curb for the traffic to stop before crossing over to Lowell's Erection. She turned squarely to Randolph. "Now, if you'll excuse me, I'll say good-bye. Please feel free to report to your president at Fair Harvard that everything is all right—or do they teach you words like hunky-dory at Fair Harvard?"

"No, but they do in Nevada, where I hail from. I'm just a little old cowpoke myself trying to git along in the big city. Won't you take pity and let me ride shotgun to your home?"

She shook her head, smiling, the deep radiant red hair glowing in the last rays of sunlight.

"This has been delightful," he said. "Do you have far to travel? By any chance do you live in Southie?"

"Well, being Irish and having a poetic soul, I much prefer the Irish Riviera."

She stepped off the curb. "Tell you what," he said. "Let's dream about each other tonight and compare notes tomorrow."

But she was gone, lost in the crowd hurtling across the street and into the concrete bowels of the subway.

Randolph stood a moment, deep in thought, undecided as to whether he should follow her. There was no question that he was determined to have her, but there was no sense in pushing his luck. What he needed now was a sentimental gesture. Something that would take her by surprise and break down the wall of resistance she had built around herself.

He smiled at this thought and started whistling "Green Eyes." The words echoed in his head and he could feel a great warmth wash over him. His step felt lighter and he found himself smiling at complete strangers. *"Your green eyes with the soft light, your eyes that promise sweet nights . . ."*

Holy Christ, he thought, I'm going balmy. Better watch your step, sonny boy, or Rufus will go apeshit.

He headed toward Church Street and the finest florist shop in Cambridge. There were several customers and Randolph waited until all had left before addressing the florist, a short, round man with bushy brows and trumpet-shaped ears that reminded Randolph of lilies. These, however, were scarlet and had patches of dark hair growing out of their orifices in rich profusion.

The florist smiled and when he spoke his ears seemed to vibrate from the shock waves. "Good afternoon. May I be of service to you?"

Randolph tried to concentrate on the man's small piercing eyes. "I want a bouquet of wild flowers, the kind I'd find if I went tramping through the woods tomorrow morning."

The florist chuckled and Randolph turned away, not wanting to see how his ears would respond to this movement. "Spring flowers? Now that's a tall order. Mmmm. Anything particular in mind?"

"Oh, daffodils and violets, I suppose—whatever grows wild around here this time of year. You can throw in a few dandelions, a cattail or two, a couple weeds."

The florist nodded. "I think I understand. When do you need this bouquet?"

Randolph hesitated. "Friday afternoon. Around three thirty."

"Excellent. I'll have a lovely bouquet for you."

"Oh, not too lovely," Randolph said. "Keep it simple. No ribbons or fancy wrappings. Just make sure they're all spring flowers. I don't want any ringer in there. It's got to be authentic."

The florist's eyes widened in appreciation. "I get the picture. Very sensible. Nothing touches the heartstrings of a young maiden more deeply than the thought that her young swain has tramped through the woods to pick a posy of wild flowers just for her." He paused and his ears seemed to inhale. "If I were you, I'd get a bit of mud on my shoes. Nothing like a little touch of realism, if you get my meaning?"

Randolph smiled. "You've got the picture."

The florist coughed politely and stuck the index finger of his right hand into his trumpet ear, pushing and shaking it until his entire finger had disappeared within. Randolph looked away. If that were a man-eating plant, the florist would promptly become a lefty.

He retrieved the finger and closely examined a glob of wax hanging from the tip before shaking it loose. "Unfortunately, I can't quote you a price until I know the precise time involved. I'll send someone out first thing Friday morning to a secret place where they grow in profusion. I'm sure you'll be most happy with the result. But it will be rather expensive."

"Cost is of no consequence," Randolph said, handing the florist a twenty-dollar bill as a deposit.

She was wearing the same camel's hair coat and her red hair again curled softly around her lovely graceful neck. Somehow she looked even more beautiful than the last time. Randolph waited until she had started down the sidewalk before coming up from behind and handing her the bouquet.

"A token of our president's appreciation," he said.

"Thank you," she said, her two hands closing over the stems as gently as butterflies. She lowered her head until her nose touched the flowers and closed her eyes as she inhaled deeply of their fragrance. "They're lovely. Thank you so very much. It was sweet of you, truly it was."

"You're more than welcome," he said. "Picked them myself this morning. Just took a little hike, one of my favorite pastimes. Tramping through the woods early in the morning is so invigorating. Then I saw the flowers and they reminded me of you—so fragile and beautiful. I simply had to bring them to you. I hope you don't mind. Honestly, I don't want to make a nuisance of myself."

"Well," she said, a happy lilt in her voice. "The way I see it, you were merely performing your duty for President Miles Standish of Fair Harvard."

He laughed. "That's me, John Alden. If I had a fine silk cape and could find a puddle somewhere, I'd gladly spread it at your feet."

"That's truly gallant."

She pressed the flowers to her breast, and when she looked at him, he felt his legs go weak, and nearly stumbled.

"I know you've been pestered by so many of us and I really wanted to do something that would show my true feelings about you."

She nodded and looked away. He noticed part of one ear through the thick tresses of her red hair and longed to kiss it. Again the song "Green Eyes" was reverberating through his head and he wanted to sing it to her.

They walked in silence for a while. As they neared Harvard Square,

Randolph said, "I hope you don't have too far to go before you can place them in water. I should have brought a vase."

"Don't fret about it. They're a lot tougher than you think. They'll be just fine."

A moment later she had again disappeared into the concrete bowels of the subway, but this time not before turning to smile and wave good-bye. He walked away humming.

He turned to stare at the MTA kiosk, and he suddenly gave vent to a great urge to jump in the air and clap his hands. She was gorgeous and she would be his forever. Of that he was suddenly convinced.

That evening Randolph called Rufus for their weekly chat. In the course of their conversation Randolph mentioned the problem he was having with his term paper on Adam Smith and Rufus didn't hesitate to offer advice.

"Sonny boy, the guy to read on Smith is Andrew Mellon. Wrote a neat little book called *Taxation: The People's Business.* He borrowed a lot from Smith, but added a few curves of his own that I particularly admire. Get a pencil and paper and take this down. Might give you a couple ideas for your paper.

"As far as Mellon was concerned, the middle and lower classes prospered the most when taxes on the rich were the lowest. Now that's important because high business taxes discourage the profit motive, which lowers production and the incentive to invest. On the other hand, high taxes on the workingman are beneficial to the economy because they discourage indolence and encourage industry. In other words, they've got to work harder if they want to keep afloat. That's what you call laying it right on the line, sonny boy. But, remember, the Founding Fathers were great admirers of Smith.

"The Founding Fathers agreed that business does best when government keeps its long nose out of it. They called it individual initiative. Competition does the trick, you see. That's the key word. If the price of certain goods goes up, then others will get into the act and produce more of those goods. That makes the price go down because the supply becomes greater than the demand. Okay? Now, take wages —if they go up in a certain industry, others will hear about it and train for those jobs, and so the competition for those jobs will reduce wages. The crux to Smith's thinking is that a man can concentrate on his own best self-interest and say fuck everybody else because the market is self-regulating. He called it 'the hidden hand,' which, he said, kept things balanced. It's the old saying about the rich getting richer while the poor get poorer. That's what keeps the wheels turning.

"See the beauty of it, sonny boy? A man can pursue his own selfish interest—as if anyone ever pursued anything else—and feel he's serving society at the same time. It's like substituting the marketplace for God—you know, He cares about social well-being and that makes the marketplace sacrosanct—in other words, don't fuck with it. Neat little theory, wrapped in pink ribbon and carried on angels' wings. It's a present from the Age of Reason, where they left nothing to chance, and Smith himself left no loose strings anywhere for anyone to unravel."

Rufus chuckled. "Got all that down like I told it to you? Make that professor of yours sit up and take notice. You know, I was a believer in Smith long before I even heard his name. With a little education I could have written my own book, might even have showed Smith and Mellon a few twists they never dreamed of."

"Thanks, Rufus," Randolph said sincerely. "I really appreciate the help. You're still the champ. I'll let you know how it comes out."

"Sonny boy, anything you want, all you've got to do is ask. I'm your pal."

"I know that, Rufus. And I'm yours."

"Getting enough spending money?"

"I'm loaded, really. I'm in great shape."

Rufus laughed. "How's the poontang? Dipping the old wick, are you? Keeping the old machinery oiled. At your age—ah, well, some other time."

Randolph nearly blurted out about the girl with the green eyes, but felt it would somehow denigrate her if raised in this context. "Well, you know, they keep us pretty busy out here. Not too much time for playing around."

"Hey, sonny boy, don't kid an old kidder. What about them Radcliffe gals? I hear them rich bitches will just gobble you right up. Some got pretty powerful daddies, too. If you need an introduction, let me know. I've got a couple business buddies with daughters over there." He chuckled. "If they look anything like their daddies, you might have to put a pillow case over their heads. But what the hell, pussy is pussy, and some of the uglier ones are the best fucks. Listen, I know what I'm talking about. Anyway, you're too young to be talking about anything but poontang. Remember the old motto: 'Find 'em, feel 'em, fuck 'em, and forget 'em.' That's the ticket at your age. Don't make my mistake. Got lassoed before I ever saw a condom. You've got your whole future ahead of you."

After hanging up, Randolph returned to his room and stretched out on his bunk. What had that been all about? Rufus was uncanny. It had to be mental telepathy. But over three thousand miles of telephone wires? It was incredible. Too eerie for comfort. He would have to watch his step, that was for sure.

He closed his eyes and in a moment the girl with the green eyes was smiling at him. He reached out for her and she glided softly into his arms. They were on a dance floor, swaying to the syncopation of Jimmy Dorsey. Colored spotlights reflected off a huge mirrored ball, sending colored spots whirling around the darkened room. He held her close as Bob Eberly sang about those green eyes that promised sweet nights.

He slept with his clothes on, flat on his back.

After six o'clock mass on Sunday morning Betty Schurtz took a streetcar, transferring several times before arriving at her destination. It was a lovely spring morning, with a fine dew still glistening on the sweeping grassy knoll with its rows of granite headstones. Some mornings, when the haze was still rising, they reminded her of rows of jagged and broken teeth, and she thought of the cemetery as a huge mouth that swallowed up the dead.

But on this morning she liked the peaceful ambience of the cemetery, the feeling that when she knelt on the soft mound of grass she was alone with her baby. She could pray without distraction from a living soul.

Now she knelt and placed the spring flowers in front of the small granite cross that marked the grave site and bowed her head to begin the prayer she had composed on the way over from church. She wanted to say something special this morning, words from the heart, words intended for the ears of Our Virgin Mary, Holy Mother of Jesus, who lost her Son on the cross and could perhaps be persuaded to intercede on behalf of Betty's own son, to help him through eternity until she was ready to join him herself. Michael would have been two today had he lived.

"Please, Holy Virgin Mother," Betty prayed, letting the words take form in this empty cemetery, "however long it takes, protect him and have him waiting when I arrive, so that we can once more be together, mother and child, as it should be." She knelt a long time, head bowed in silent prayer, fighting back the tears of self-pity that threatened her resolution.

On the streetcar later her thoughts turned to the handsome young man who had given her the spring flowers. She felt he was different from the others, that he truly liked her for herself and would continue to pursue her as long as she gave him proper encouragement. How tall and muscular he was, without an ounce of fat on his strong, straight bones. She thought of his eyes, so dark and piercing, with that glint that danced in them whenever he looked into hers. It made her quiver with desire when she permitted herself to think of the consequence of his meaning.

But what would he think if he knew the truth of it? That her body, so innocent in appearance, had been used and abused, sullied like a whore's—except that in her mind she believed herself pure, an innocent victim of mindless perversion.

She had been seventeen and crazy about dancing, the best jitterbugger in her high school senior class, and she loved the music of the big bands—Benny Goodman, Glenn Miller, Tommy Dorsey—all the great ones of the times. She'd have danced seven nights a week if her parents had not restricted her to Friday and Saturday. Instead of accepting dates with boys, she preferred going to dances with girl friends. That way she could dance with anybody she chose, only the best dancers, and she never missed a number.

Paired with a partner who could really swing, she'd let herself go until the other dancers would stop, forming a circle around them, and clap in appreciation while she and her partner went through all the intricate gyrations and acrobatics of jitterbugging—everything from the Big Apple to the Lindy—at times her skirt twirling up around her hips to reveal long shapely legs.

Once caught in the rhythmic excitement of the music, with her head thrown back, she thought of nothing but keeping step with the beat. She became a different person on the dance floor: daring, uninhibited, sexual. It was as though her mind went blank and she was left alone with a body whose nerve ends responded to every nuance of the music. In bed sometimes after a night of dancing, with the rhythms still pounding in her head, she wondered how she could get so totally lost in the music.

One hot July evening she had gone to Revere Beach to dance to the music of Duke Ellington. Her girl friend's parents had taken them and were to pick them up at one o'clock sharp. During intermission she accepted the invitation of a young sailor, a terrific dancer, to go for a hotdog on the boardwalk, while her girl friend went off with another boy.

The sailor's name was Ezra Cohen and there was something about him that reminded her of the skinny boy who sang with Tommy Dorsey's band. Ezra's friends called him Izzy. She had noticed that he was with three other sailors, all older men, tall and heavyset, who obviously were not dancers. They seemed satisfied just to watch her, shouting and whistling encouragement whenever Izzy twirled her around, sending the skirt of her light summer dress flying around her hips.

After Izzy bought her the hotdog and a root beer, he said, "How would you like something a little stronger to drink? I have a bottle of Green River in the car."

"No, thanks," she said. "Root beer will quench my thirst just fine."

"Mind if I have a little snort? It'll only take a minute. The car's just around the corner of the next block."

She gave him a sharp look. Boys were always pulling that dumb stuff on her. "I'm not getting in the back seat, if that's what you have in mind."

"That's okay, Betty, if that's the way you feel about it," he said, smiling pleasantly to show that he wasn't offended by her remark. He quickened his stride. "Let's make tracks, though, so we'll be back for Duke's first number."

But she never got back to the dance that night. The other three sailors were waiting for them when they arrived at the car. Izzy seemed genuinely surprised to see them. Instantly alarmed, she took a quick step back and nearly fell.

"Look out there, little lady," the biggest of the group said, grabbing her by the arm, his huge fingers bruising her flesh.

She looked up into his dark hard eyes and knew right then she was in serious trouble.

"Hey, Charlie, let go of her," Izzy said, his voice quivering nervously.

"Shut up, you little kike, and get in the front seat," Charlie said. "You, Oscar, drive." As he said this, he clamped his other hand over her mouth, stifling her scream, and the next thing she knew she was dragged into the back seat and the car was speeding away, the tires kicking loose gravel against the fenders, then squealing as they hit the pavement and headed up the coast highway.

The other sailor sitting next to her in the back seat was almost as big as Charlie. His name was Joe and he had a red beefy face and battered nose. Suddenly he reached into the top of her summer dress, his fingers slipping under her brassiere, and ripped it open with one vicious pull. The front of her dress and slip disintegrated and he came up with her bra in his hand. She tried to cover her breasts with her hands and he laughed as he waved the bra in front of Charlie's face.

"What the hell?" Izzy shouted. "Are you guys gone stark raving mad?"

Charlie reached up between her legs and ripped her panties off. "Here, Izzy, take a whiff of this. You be a good boy and we'll save you a piece."

"Charlie, for God's sake, this is insane," Izzy pleaded. "This is kidnapping and rape. You can get the firing squad."

Charlie laughed. "You, too, sweetheart. But first we're gonna fuck the living shit out of this juicy piece of ass. That's what we're all gonna do, you included. So shut up and watch how us big boys do it."

Joe began pulling and squeezing her left breast. The pain was excruciating. She screamed and tried to pull his hand away. He lowered his head and began loudly sucking on the nipple, still pulling and squeezing the breast.

"What the fuck you doing, milking her?" Charlie laughed.

Betty scratched at his face and pulled his hair with all her strength.

"Tell you what, Charlie," Joe said, raising his head and slapping Betty across the face. "You fuck her cunt and I'll fuck her tits. I want to shoot the load right in her fucking mouth. But first we've got to tie her hands up. She's scratching the shit out of me."

"Slap her again, for Christ's sake," Charlie said. "Teach her some fucking manners. And you, Oscar, find a deserted spot. We need some room for this maneuver. That's something I've got to see, brother."

Oscar giggled shrilly. "Hey, you guys, I get to fuck her in the ass."

Charlie laughed. "Yeah, you fat queer, just close your eyes and make believe it's one of your cute seamen."

"Now, don't get nasty," Oscar whined.

Charlie jabbed at her exposed pubis with stiff fingers and she closed her eyes and bit down on her lower lip until blood ran down her chin. She screamed, throwing her head back, blood spewing from her mouth.

Charlie laughed. "Hey, Izzy, want to smell my fingers? Don't worry, sweetheart, she's enjoying it. They cry and moan at first, but in the end they all love it. I got two fingers all the way in there and her cunt's all wet. See! Smell 'em. I've got this little bitch coming, hot damn."

"That's blood, you maniac," Izzy screamed. "You're raping a virgin with your lousy fingers. They're big as fucking bananas."

Charlie reached forward and wiped his fingers on Izzy's hair. "Never had me one of them virgins before. Hot damn, this's gonna be some fucking party."

They drove to a deserted part of the beach near Point of Pines. She had fought hard at first, slapping and scratching and kicking, using all her strength, but with the first painful penetration of Charlie's fingers and the brutal tearing of her hymen, she went into a state of trauma. No longer aware of sensations, she stopped fighting, letting them take turns at her, doing with her as they wished. And they did everything they could possibly think of doing to another human being short of killing her.

Finally, Izzy, who had refused to take part, was forced to suck her breasts and put his fingers inside of her, for he was incapable of doing anything else. He tried to whisper to her, to reassure her that it would soon be over, but Charlie grabbed him by the nape of the neck and yanked him to his feet.

"You fucking yid, don't think you're not in this up to your ass like the rest of us. So don't give her no bullshit. Remember, you set her up. You brought her to the car."

Charlie's fingers were digging into Izzy's windpipe and for a moment Izzy thought his lungs would explode; then Charlie released his grip and leered at him.

"See? I could kill you with one hand."

Tears were rolling down Izzy's face. "I know, Charlie, but let's take her home, please. You can't leave her out here. She's in no condition to get home by herself. Somebody will pick her up and take her to the cops. If we get her home safe and sound, maybe her family will just want to hush it up."

Betty was lying on a blanket, her face turned away from them, her eyes closed. Charlie leaned over her. "Listen, sweetheart, we're gonna take you home, so you better put your clothes back on. The party's over."

She gave them directions but by then she had lost all sense of reality. This had not happened to her. It was a nightmare and soon she would wake up in her own bed.

When the sailors dropped her off in front of her house early that morning, all she could think about was her torn dress and how to explain it to her mother, who would still be up waiting for her, as she always did when Betty came in late, chain-smoking and pacing up and down, getting angrier by the minute.

But her mother took one look at her and rushed to take her in her arms. "Oh, my poor baby," she cried. "Oh, Mother of God, what have they done to you?"

For weeks thereafter Betty spent hours every day bathing, scrubbing herself with the strongest soaps she could find. Her mother helped her scrub, gave her douches and enemas, doing everything in her power to help cleanse away the filth that had been heaped on her daughter by those animals. But she never told her husband about it. She knew he'd have gone straight to the authorities, more interested in revenge than in his daughter's public disgrace. So it became their secret, and when it was discovered that Betty was pregnant, her mother began looking for an abortionist.

Then one morning Izzy Cohen rang their doorbell and asked if he could come in and talk with them. Eileen Schurtz, knowing by now that Izzy was not responsible for the rape of her daughter, invited him inside her home.

He stood in the middle of the small parlor, his white sailor cap in his hands, shifting from one foot to the other, his eyes unable to look directly at the two women sitting on the sofa.

"I've been wanting to do this for a long time," he began, still not daring to look at them. "First, I'm sorry for what happened to you, Betty, but you've got to believe I didn't know nothing about it. They just told me there was a bottle in the car and what happened was as much a surprise to me as it was to you."

"We know that," Eileen Schurtz said. "I have to thank you for their bringing her home. In her condition she'd have died if left out there on the beach that night."

He nodded and bit his lower lip. "Well, I've made a decision. I'm ready to tell the police about it. I think they should pay for their crime."

Betty gasped, her hand going to her mouth. "No, please, don't do anything like that. I couldn't bear it." She jumped up and ran from the room in tears.

Eileen waited until her daughter had closed the door to her bedroom before inviting Izzy to sit down. She looked him up and down, her hazel eyes unflinching in their appraisal. "Look at me," she said. "You've nothing to be ashamed of except the company you keep."

He nodded again and looked directly at her. "They weren't even friends," he said. "Just guys I met at the beach, and they promised to give me a ride back to the yard. We're all on the *Arizona*. Honestly, I'd like to kill them all. I hate them that much."

"Where do you come from, Izzy? Where's your home?"

"Brooklyn." He smiled faintly for the first time. "Ain't all Jews from Brooklyn?"

"Not all of them. My husband was born in Germany, but he came to Boston with his family as a boy. I'm Irish myself—born right here in Southie—but there's lots of Jews in Boston. You're not ashamed of it, are you?"

His cheeks flamed. "No, but sometimes I wish I was English or German or Irish—anything but Jewish or Negro. We both catch it in the service, especially the Navy. We're the scapegoats for everything that goes wrong—even the weather."

She studied him in silence for a long time. "Betty's pregnant," she said, lowering her voice.

"Oh, Christ! I'm sorry, but, my God, what's she going to do?"

"I want her to have an abortion but she's dead set against it." She shrugged. "So now I've got to find her a husband and bloody damn soon, if you'll pardon my Irish."

His eyes were as wide as saucers and she was surprised to see that they were a soft blue, the eyes of a gentle soul, and the idea struck her like a thunderbolt. "Will you marry her, give her unborn child your name?"

He jumped up. "In a minute," he said. "If she'll have me."

Eileen Schurtz stood up and held out her arms. He stepped into them and she hugged him. "Don't worry, she will, and she'll make you a fine wife."

Izzy and Betty were married the next week but never lived as man and wife. Eight days later he shipped out. It was the last time she saw him. On December 7, 1941, he went down with the *Arizona* at Pearl Harbor along with the three rapists.

33

Aunt Caroline opened the door and threw her arms around his neck. "Oh, my goodness, Randolph," she squealed with delight. "You look absolutely splendid. Come in, dear heart, and give your poor auntie a big kiss and hug."

Randolph quickly stepped into the foyer and grabbed her around the waist. He whirled her around and set her down next to Betty, who was smiling, but the expression in her green eyes was uncertain.

Aunt Caroline straightened her dress and coughed politely as she tried to think of something to say to the young woman standing before her.

"Well, Auntie, what do you think of the new Mrs. Randolph Godwin?"

"Oh, goodness gracious," she cried, her anxious eyes shifting between them as if she couldn't believe what was happening. Then she laughed, her voice rising shrilly, and she put her hand over her mouth to stifle it. "Oh, Randolph, you always have your little jokes. Now, please, introduce me properly to this young lady."

Randolph took Betty's left hand and displayed the diamond ring and gold wedding band. "It's no joke," he said. "We're really married. Have been for nearly two weeks."

Aunt Caroline took a step back, her hand going to her throat. "Have you told your daddy and Rufus yet?"

Randolph shook his head. "No, just thought we'd drop in and surprise everybody."

"Oh, my," Aunt Caroline sighed heavily. "I must sit down before I faint dead away. Come, dear hearts, let's go in the parlor and get acquainted. But first I must catch my breath."

Randolph took her arm and helped her to a wingback chair. Then he and Betty sat on a sofa facing her, waiting for her to compose herself.

She sat with her head back, her eyes closed, taking deep breaths. Without opening her eyes, she said, "What a shame about commencement. Imagine canceling it because of the war emergency. Your daddy and I were so looking forward to attending your graduation. You know how very proud of you we both are."

"Well, I've got the sheepskin and that's what counts. What about Rufus? Is he in town?"

She nodded, opening her eyes. "They're both at the office. Don't you think you should call them?"

Randolph took Betty's hand and held it in his lap. "Now, honestly, Aunt Caroline, what do you think of her?" he asked, sidestepping her suggestion. "Isn't she the most glorious creature you've ever set eyes upon in your whole life?"

Betty could feel the blood rising to her cheeks, but she forced a smile. "They say that love is blind," she said softly.

"If that's what being blind is all about, I'm for it a hundred percent," Randolph said, kissing her hand. "Well, what about it, Auntie? Fess up."

"Oh, my goodness, she's lovely, just lovely, just lovely, oh, yes . . ." And she seemed unable to think of anything else to say.

Randolph stood up and knelt on one knee before Caroline's chair, taking both her hands in his. "I know you're worried, Auntie. I should have told Rufus about it. I'm not worried about Dad. He'll understand. He always does."

"Yes, yes, but Rufus has his own plans for you." She waved her hand weakly at Betty. "Pardon me, my dear, but he's a dangerous man to cross. My advice, Randolph, is for you to face him alone at the office and have it out with him right away. Spare your young bride the needless confrontation. Her turn will come soon enough."

Randolph laughed, but it sounded hollow to Betty. "Oh, now, don't make him into an ogre. He's just proud and set in his ways. But he'll come around. I have my ways with him."

She nodded quickly, raising her eyebrows. "I've seen your ways, dear heart. I know all about your ways. And so does Rufus. You've never fooled him for a minute. He enjoys letting you delude yourself. But enough of this dreary talk in front of your young bride."

"My name is Betty, Aunt Caroline," she said, her cheeks again flaming.

"I'm sorry, darling," Randolph apologized. "I guess I am a little nervous, after all. Yes, Aunt Caroline, I believe you're right." He stood up and smiled at Betty. "Don't worry, darling, I won't be long. Meanwhile, Auntie, will you show Betty around and have Holly unpack our things?" He took Betty in his arms and kissed her tenderly. "Everything's going to be just fine. Now you believe me. All right? If you feel a little tired, take a nap. Tonight we celebrate."

After Aunt Caroline had shown her around the house and introduced her to Moses and Holly, Betty lay down for a nap, but she couldn't sleep. The idea that Randolph had to explain her to Rufus made her uneasy. She had heard Rufus's name so often in the past two months. There was no question that he had been the most important person in Randolph's life. One time she had asked him if his father were dead and the question seemed to shock him.

"Of course not," he replied. "What makes you say that?"

"Well, you've never mentioned him. It's always your grandfather Rufus. I just assumed your father was dead."

Randolph had shrugged. "Haven't I mentioned him at all? That's strange. I guess it's just that I'm closer to Rufus. You know, we're like buddies. I can talk to him about anything. He's had no formal education, but he knows everything that's worth knowing, and every*body*, for that matter. And he's rich, I mean filthy rich." His eyes had shone with a strange light as he had gone on to say, "And someday it's all going to be mine. Do you have any idea what that means?"

She had nodded her head, unable to speak. His words filled her with an eerie foreboding she couldn't comprehend.

Henry was alone in his office when Randolph walked in unannounced. Although he had been expecting Randolph to return to Carson City any day, the sight of his son, so tall and handsome, walking across the room, smiling, his hand outstretched, thrilled him more than he would have thought possible.

Henry came around his desk. He wanted to embrace Randolph, but the movement would have been awkward. So he held on to his son's hand as long as he could without being obvious about it, steering Randolph to a leather chair facing his desk. For a moment Henry was reminded of the day he had first seen his son at the boarding school, of how Randolph had peeked at him through a crack of the open door, that big brown eye appraising him. Then they had become "twinsies" and roared away on his motorcycle, with Randolph in the sidecar, his little hands holding on to the sides for dear life.

God, Henry thought, sitting on the edge of his desk to be closer to Randolph, how the years had flown away. His son was now almost as old as Henry had been on that day.

"Well, have you been to the house? Your aunt's been anxiously awaiting your arrival."

Randolph nodded. "I brought her a little surprise. She nearly fainted dead away."

Henry smiled. "That would be a first. She's quite a sturdy Southern lady. No smelling salts for her. Remember, she pretty much raised you, and you weren't exactly the easiest child for an aging spinster to handle. She's had her share of surprises from you. Well, what was it this time?"

Randolph stood up. "I could use a drink," he said, crossing to the liquor cabinet. "Can I fix you one?"

"Sure, good idea, let's celebrate. It's not every day that a man's son graduates from Harvard."

They raised their glasses of bourbon and clicked them together. "And it's not every day that a son brings his new bride home for inspection and approval."

Henry nearly dropped his glass. For a moment he just stared at his son. "And where is the bride?" he asked finally, not yet sure how to react.

"Oh, tucked away at the ranch—secure in the bosom of the family, you might say."

Henry emptied his drink and went for a refill. "You're really serious, aren't you?"

Randolph kept smiling, but Henry could tell that he was beginning to feel the strain. "Dad, she's an absolutely glorious creature. I've never been happier. She's just what I've needed for a long time."

Henry swirled the brown liquid in his glass and then looked up. "Well, then, congratulations are in order. Let's drink a toast to the bride. May she remain absolutely glorious forever. And you, son—may your love never falter. I've not met the bride, but you have my blessings."

Moved by the words, Randolph reached out and the two men again shook hands. "I knew you'd be swell about it," he said, pausing to pour more bourbon in his glass, "but how do we handle Rufus?"

"Ah, there's the rub," Henry said, but he wasn't smiling.

"Maybe I should wait and just introduce them tonight at dinner. You know—we invite him over to the house, give him a chance to see her first, soften him up, if you will, then let him have it."

"Oh, it's 'we' now, is it?"

Randolph shrugged. "I can use all the help I can get. This is important. I know he has very definite plans for me, but this is the one area of my life where I must be free to do as I wish."

"That's academic," Henry said. "You've already done it. The question is how do *you* live with it?"

Randolph put his glass down. "Well, let's go in and get it over with."

"You sure you don't want to go it alone?"

"Hell, no, I want you at my side. If it gets violent in there, I'll need some physical protection."

For several years Rufus Boutwell had been eavesdropping on the office and telephone conversations of his son-in-law. During the remodeling of their office suites not long after he had returned from Switzerland, he had had the connecting door removed, making it impossible for Henry simply to walk in on him. Later, listening devices were concealed in the new wall, which contained bookcases and a fireplace for each of their offices. The listening device on Henry's telephone was installed at a more recent time. Whenever Henry's telephone was in use, a light flashed on the side of Rufus's desk. And when important people came to visit Henry, one of the receptionists promptly notified Rufus.

Now as Henry and Randolph were ushered into his office by his secretary, Rufus had himself under control. He knew the bad news and had already decided how to handle it. The one thing he wanted to avoid at all cost was for Randolph to have to turn to his father for support. That would be a reversal of roles that could prove disastrous to his long-range plans.

He was standing at the window and turned to face them. "Well, well, sonny boy's home." He came forward and grabbed Randolph in a bear hug, grunting as he squeezed with all his might, his face turning red with the effort. He let go and stood back. "This sonny boy just keeps getting bigger and stronger all the time. Maybe we ought to make a prizefighter out of him. A few lessons and he'd knock that nigger Joe Louis on his ass. Well, anyway, congratulations on your graduation. Imagine, having a Harvard man in the family. Now that's something to be proud of. Let's all drink a toast to your future. Henry, fetch this young man a drink. And bring me my usual Moxie."

Henry complied without changing expression.

"Now, you sit yourself right over here," Rufus told Randolph. "I've got some good news for you. Something I promised you long ago. Remember Pearl Harbor and how you almost ruined your life? Well, I promised you then that someday you'd get your chance to serve your country."

"Yes, I remember it quite clearly," Randolph said, smiling wryly. "You called me a stupid shithead."

"Did I now? Well, I meant it. That was a dumb play. But I told you I'd set you up real good when the time came. Get you all the campaign ribbons and promotions you'd ever want."

Henry brought the drinks and Rufus raised his glass of Moxie. "To Captain Randolph Harrison Godwin," he said, his battered face breaking into a smug grin. "They timed the Normandy invasion just perfect for you. Your new boss, Major General Sam Wheeler, deputy chief in the Inspector General's Office, will be landing in Europe as soon as our boys have cleared the area. You'll be with him, sonny boy, and that's going to look real good on your record."

Randolph smiled, pleased with the appointment. *Captain.* All his classmates would be going to OCS and coming out as second lieutenants. Rufus was incredible. There was no question about it. But how in the world was he going to broach the subject of his marriage? Rufus had taken the play away from him. He glanced at his father and found that Henry seemed intent on what Rufus was saying.

"When did this come about?" Henry asked.

Rufus grinned. "Been in the works a long time. Wheeler's an old friend. He'll be ready for retirement by the time Adolf rolls over and he's just the type of guy we need in our Washington office. Has the kind of contacts at the Pentagon we can use. So meanwhile he's going to take extremely good care of sonny boy here." Rufus reached over and patted Randolph's knee. "He won't let the dirty Nazis harm a hair of your fair head."

"Has he promised to stand in front of me if anybody starts shooting?"

"He goddamn better," Rufus laughed. "Now, what's new with you? Bring any of your buddies home with you this time?"

Randolph stood up and walked to the window, turning his back on the two men. "You might say that," he said, speaking to the window.

Rufus glanced at Henry, raising an eyebrow. "Oh, anybody I know?"

Randolph turned and looked directly at Rufus. "Look, Rufus, there's something I've got to tell you, but first you've got to promise to hear me out."

Rufus shrugged. "Go ahead. You make it sound like the world's about to come to an end."

"Not exactly. In fact, I've never been happier. Two weeks ago I married the most beautiful girl in Boston. I know you'll just love her if you'll only give her a chance."

Rufus's eyes narrowed into gray slits. "So you sneaked off and got hitched, just like any bohunk, not a word to your family? What's to be ashamed of?"

"Nothing," Randolph said. "I just didn't want anybody trying to talk me out of it."

"Hey, sonny boy, I'm not just anybody—get that through your head and don't never forget it." He paused, trying to regain control of himself. He had to watch it, make the right move at the right moment, but for now this scene had to be concluded quickly. "All right, so it's done. Radcliffe girl? Do I know her father?"

"Not exactly," Randolph said.

"I see. How will she stack up as the wife of a United States senator? Did you give that a second's thought before you tied the knot?"

Randolph smiled and came over to Rufus. "She'll knock 'em dead. She's gorgeous and bright and . . . well, she's got everything I'll ever want in a woman. Just give her an even break. You'll see, she'll grow on you."

Rufus's eyes widened. "Oh, you think so? Well, why don't we wait and see. When do I get to meet this glorious creature?"

Henry's head came up, a quizzical look in his eyes. Randolph had used just that phrase to describe her to him when they were alone. He had not used that expression to Rufus. Yet there it was and certainly not a phrase Rufus would ever use on his own. It was strange what he came up with at times. Absolutely uncanny.

Henry sat in his den at home and thought about the evening ahead. Things had gone too easily at the office. Rufus had capitulated far too quickly. He was up to something. Henry sipped bourbon and puffed on a huge cigar, leaning back in the swivel chair, his feet up on the desk. Betty certainly *was* a glorious creature. She had the kind of beauty that made men ache inside. Henry thought of Camilla, of her great beauty, but even more important what her love had meant to him when he was a young man. He could only hope that Betty's meant as much to Randolph. He was a lucky boy. How lucky he would never know. The twists and turns in the road that had brought Randolph to this moment were awesome. It was something Henry seldom allowed himself to think about.

At dinner that evening Rufus sat at the head of the table, with Betty on his right and Aunt Caroline on his left. Randolph sat next to Aunt Caroline and Henry was beside Betty.

Rufus appeared to be on his best behavior. He had greeted Betty with a kiss and warm words of praise, making a great show of congratulating Randolph on his good fortune.

Moses served the onion soup that Holly had prepared, which was Rufus's favorite. Everyone at the table waited for Rufus to dip his spoon and pass judgment. He sipped and raised his eyebrows.

"Ah, perfect, as always," he said. "Moses, give my compliments to Holly."

Moses smiled broadly. "Thank you, Mr. Rufus. I'll surely tell her."

Rufus turned to Betty. "I guess you Bostonians prefer clam chowder?"

Betty smiled. "Yes, and baked beans. Cod. Oh, we have all sorts of strange habits."

Rufus studied her as she delicately sipped from her spoon. She looked directly at him. "This is delicious."

"Betty, I've been sitting here trying to decide your nationality," he said, "and I'll be darned if I can. And I'm usually pretty good at it. It's kind of a game with me. I've never studied all that stuff about evolution, but there are certain characteristics and traits associated with various nationalities. Don't you agree?"

She glanced quickly at Randolph, to assess his reaction, and caught him frowning down at his soup. "I've never really given it much thought."

"Well, think about it for a minute. For example, take Moses—he don't look like the rest of us, does he? At least, I don't think so."

Henry leaned forward. "Are we in for one of your lectures on the supremacy of the white Anglo-Saxon Protestant?" He turned to Betty. "You see, Betty, Rufus is one of the few people I know who proudly admits to being a bigot. So arguing with him on that subject is a total waste of time."

"Now, wait a minute," Rufus said. "Let me go on. I'm trying to make a point here, pay this young lady a compliment. You see, Betty, the mixture of nationalities—even races, at times—can produce something completely different. I mean, result in great beauty. Like yourself. I'll bet my shirt that you're mixed. What is your maiden name?"

"Schurtz," she said in a small voice.

"Well, now, what sort of name is that?"

"German," she said, staring down at her soup.

"Oh, is that right? And your mother? What is her maiden name?"

"Donahue."

"Okay, you've made my point. German and Irish and I'll bet you don't look like either one of your parents."

"I take after my mother. We have the same coloring. I've seen pictures of her when she was young and there is quite a striking resemblance."

"So the German blood was weak," Rufus said. "Well, that's interesting for a people that call themselves the super race. I wonder what Adolf would think of that?"

He looked proudly around the table. "Sonny boy, you've met both her parents. Do you agree she looks like her mother?"

Randolph shook his head. "Rufus, what difference does it make? I married her, not her mother or father."

"Well, ain't we kind of touchy tonight," he said, returning his attention to Betty. "Where do you live in Boston?"

"Southie. I mean South Boston."

"Sounds like some kind of ghetto."

She nodded. "I suppose so. It's mostly Irish people who settled there many years ago."

"And what's your maiden name again?"

"Schurtz," she repeated, her voice rising slightly, her green eyes hardening.

"So that's a German name? What does your father do for a living? Is he a lawyer, doctor, a professional man?"

She shook her head. "He's a cobbler."

"Is that right? Repairs shoes, does he?"

"Yes, and he does a very good business. He's well liked in the community."

"That's nice to know. I presume your mother's Catholic, but what about you and your father?"

"We're all Catholics."

Rufus nodded slowly, as if he were giving it serious consideration. "I'm afraid you won't find too many Catholics up in this neck of the woods. Do you intend to raise your children as Catholics? That is, if you plan on having children?"

Moses came in and picked up the empty soup plates and they waited while he brought a large roast beef, already sliced, mashed potatoes, peas, carrots, and a tossed green salad in a huge wooden bowl.

After Moses left, Randolph turned to Rufus. His face looked pale in the candlelight. "The children's religion will be her responsibility," Randolph said. "This family hasn't been exactly what you'd call religious."

"Oh, but you're going to be," Rufus said. "You're going to be a good Episcopalian. That's the religion of wealth and power in this country. And we're going to touch all bases. Besides, there's not all that much difference between Episcopalians and Catholics. Except for the Pope and all that malarkey about infallibility."

Betty pushed her chair back and stood up. "I hope you'll excuse me. I don't mean to be rude, but I feel a little dizzy."

Aunt Caroline hurried to her side. "Let me help you, dear heart."

"Please, I don't want to spoil your dinner," she said.

Aunt Caroline glared at Rufus. "Don't worry, you're not, which is more than I can say for someone else in this room."

Randolph stood up and Aunt Caroline waved him away. "Good night, gentlemen."

When they reached the bedroom, Betty put her hand to her mouth and ran for the bathroom, dropping to her knees before the toilet bowl. Aunt Caroline held her forehead while her body was caught in the spasms of vomiting. Afterward Betty brushed her teeth and Aunt Caroline helped her prepare for bed.

"How do you feel now?" she asked, after placing several pillows to help Betty sit up.

"I don't know. I'm afraid to move."

"That evil man. He'll be the death of us all."

"Oh, please, it's not him." She hesitated, looking closely at Aunt Caroline. "I think it's morning sickness. I missed my last period."

"Oh, goodness gracious, does Randolph know?"

"Not yet."

Aunt Caroline shook her head. "You'll never convince Rufus."

"What do you mean?"

She shook her head sadly. "That it wasn't a shotgun wedding."

Betty started laughing, but when she saw the startled expression on Aunt Caroline's face, she became frightened.

"He hates me, doesn't he?" she cried.

Aunt Caroline took her in her arms. "Now, hush—you're Randolph's wife and carrying his child. I'm thrilled for both of you. Rufus be damned."

34

Captain Randolph Harrison Godwin sat at a sidewalk cafe in Place Pigalle—a nightclub area called "Pig Alley" by GIs—and watched the parade of whores, a nightly event that went on from eight until the eleven o'clock curfew for military personnel in Paris. He sipped watery cognac and felt like a buyer at a slave market. As far as he was concerned, it was a sad spectacle. He thought of them as diseased women who had probably screwed the entire German army and were now working their way through the Americans. Yet some of the girls were stunningly beautiful and incredibly young. It was hard to believe they were whores. He wondered what had led them to choose such a depraved way of life.

But Major General Sam Wheeler had a more pragmatic viewpoint. "They're the world's greatest cocksuckers," he had told Randolph. "The word Frenching didn't get in the language by accident. French whores are absolutely fantastic. They're great actresses. For twenty bucks they'll be whatever you want them to be. They love to play roles—you know, create fantasy—and some even dress the part. One will not only dress like a grand duchess but act like one. Another like an American bobby soxer, complete with dirty saddle shoes, and by God she'll make you think you're fucking some teenager in the back seat of the family car."

Randolph nodded gravely, aware that the general was about to give him his first assignment since they had arrived in Paris last August, only days after the German garrison had surrendered to the Second Free French Armored Division. Wheeler had set up headquarters at the Hôtel Ritz, and his suite of rooms on the second floor had become the focal point for officials, journalists, and celebrities on tour who liked to party with good booze.

Short, with a bull neck, broad shoulders, and a round head covered with a thick mat of tight salt-and-pepper curls, Wheeler had managed to rise through the ranks without ever exposing his precious hide to enemy fire. He was a champion politician and paper pusher.

Randolph sipped his cognac and lit a cigar. Most of the patrons were enlisted men and he felt compromised by having to be here. This was not what Rufus had promised him. The general seemed interested in only four things: talking, drinking, eating, and fucking, and preferably doing all four at the same time. His manner was expansive with superiors, but gruff and aggressive with subordinates, his temper explosive, his needs insatiable. So far he had treated Randolph as though he were a slow-witted flunky. There had been no reference to Rufus, and the only concession, if it was a concession, was that Randolph was billeted at the Ritz, his private room part of the general's suite.

Randolph noticed that when a soldier saw a whore he liked he merely crooked his finger and the girl came over to the table. Usually she had a drink while they completed the negotiation. From there they repaired to a cheap hotel down one of the side streets. The procedure seemed simple enough.

He had another cognac and tried to decide. He wanted to make sure he picked someone that would please the general. Finally, he selected a tall, slender girl with long dark hair who was dressed in a tweedy riding outfit and looked very British. She carried a riding crop under her arm and when she smiled she raised an eyebrow to maintain her aristocratic air.

Randolph crooked his finger and she came directly to his table. "Good evening, captain," she said, when Randolph stood up to hold her chair. "It is quite charming of you to invite me for a drink." She waved her riding crop and the waiter hurried to the table. She spoke in rapid-fire French and the waiter brought her absinthe.

"To your health, captain," she said, taking a delicate sip. "And how are you feeling, my dear captain? Looking for a little fun?" She spoke crisply, but the French accent was there, giving her words a certain elegance.

Randolph smiled. "Not exactly. But I know someone who might be interested."

She pouted. "What a shame. Is he as handsome as you?"

Randolph shrugged. "I didn't know you were particular about your customers."

She looked directly at him. "But of course. I do not go with just anybody. I am not like some of these French sluts. I am a British noblewoman. I have royal blood. After all, I have certain . . . what do you call them?"

"Standards?"

"Precisely, captain. One must maintain a certain decorum."

"That's admirable," Randolph said, keeping a straight face. "May I inquire as to your name?"

"Lady Belford."

"Well, Lady Belford, what is your fee?"

She raised that aristocratic eyebrow. "That all depends on the services required and the time involved."

"I don't know what my friend has in mind."

"No problem. Let us shoot the works for fifty American dollars."

"I presume you have a wide repertoire."

She laughed softly. "Yes, captain, you might say that. I assure you your friend will not be disappointed."

"Then we have a deal." Randolph said. "Shall we go? I have a staff car waiting down the street."

The concierge at the Place Vendôme entrance to the Hôtel Ritz gave Randolph a disapproving look but said nothing.

The general opened the door and smiled broadly. "Come in, come in," he said, taking her hand and leading her into the drawing room. He was dressed in a dark blue silk dressing gown, with a polka-dotted scarf tied at the throat, but his legs were bare and his small feet looked white as alabaster in their black patent leather slippers. "You caught me as I was getting ready for bed," he said.

"That is wonderful, darling," Lady Belford said. "Think of the time we will save."

The general laughed. "Thank you, captain. Mission accomplished. See you in the morning."

Randolph excused himself and crossed to the connecting door to his room. He poured himself a bourbon and stretched out on the bed, propping himself up with a couple of pillows. He tried to think of Betty, of the intensity of their lovemaking, but his mind kept coming back to the parade of whores.

Paris was a strange city. His mother had lived here for years. She had been a golden-haired flapper who had drunk herself to death. He still remembered her and sometimes he thought he recognized her in other women. But no one could live up to the image of Alicia he had so lovingly constructed as a child.

After a while he dozed off only to be awakened moments later by what sounded like a scream from the general. Randolph went to the door and pressed his ear against it. There was a cracking sound, like a sharp blow, and a loud groan. He gently opened the door a crack and put his eye to it. What he saw rooted him to the spot.

The whore and the general were both naked. She was on her knees and the general's engorged penis was in her mouth. As her head moved back and forth, she was whipping his fat buttocks with her riding crop. His head was thrown back, his eyes closed, the expression on his face pure ecstasy.

Two nights later Randolph returned to Place Pigalle. It was a lovely fall evening and the whores were out in full force. He sipped his watery cognac and puffed on his cigar, his eyes never wavering from the moving parade. After a half hour he became uneasy, wondering if she had already been taken for the night.

Ever since he had seen her with the general, he couldn't get the picture out of his head. No girl had ever done that to him. Radcliffe girls had thought he was a pervert the few times he had suggested it. Even Betty had refused to take him in her mouth. Somewhere in the back of his mind was the fuzzy image of his mother on her knees in the kitchen, with his father's penis in her mouth. Nor had he forgotten the time she had touched him and had been about to kiss his "little peepee" when his father had come into the room. He realized now that his father had been terribly angry and his mother had left for Europe not long afterward, never to return again. He had missed her and had thought about her and *it* often in those lonely years. He had indulged in fantasies that excluded his father on the night his mother had touched him. But in later years he had put it out of his mind.

Then actually seeing the act performed with the whore and the general had started the whole thing over again. This was his first real opportunity and still he hesitated. Something deep inside of him told him not to. He thought of it as a dark force that had been locked inside of him and he was afraid to release it. Afraid of the consequences.

A moment later he saw her, but before he could crook his finger a sergeant at a table in front of him had already signaled her. As she approached the sergeant's table, she looked directly at Randolph and he shrugged to indicate his disappointment. She smiled and he was surprised at how white and perfectly even her teeth were.

She passed the sergeant's table and he jumped up, angrily grabbing her arm.

"Hey, where the hell you going?" he growled, trying to spin her around. He was about her height but heavyset with a pronounced paunch.

Using her most imperious tone, she said, "Behave yourself, sergeant. Do not let what is in your pants go to your head." With that she playfully struck him in the groin with her riding crop. The crowd burst into laughter and applause.

The sergeant's face turned crimson and for a moment Randolph thought he was going to strike her in the face with his fist.

Randolph quickly stood up and took a step toward the sergeant. "I suggest you let her go and sit down. Relax," he said. "I signaled her first."

The sergeant released his grip on her arm. He gave Randolph a long baleful look, swore under his breath, spun around on his heels, and left the cafe.

"Well, thank you, captain," she said, sitting at his table. "You are most gallant."

Randolph gave her a questioning look. "Would you have gone with him if I hadn't been here?"

Her dark eyes sparkled. "Not that one, captain. He has a Boche goiter."

"What's that?"

She laughed. "A beer belly."

"And no doubt fat buttocks."

She smiled knowingly. "Did you enjoy the little show the other night? I saw you at the door. What is the expression? Peeking Tom?"

He grinned, trying to conceal his embarrassment. "Peeping Tom."

"Oh, that is even worse. Well, do we have time for a drink or is your general impatiently awaiting a repeat performance?"

Randolph frowned. "I don't know. We haven't discussed it."

She gave him a sharp look. "Then I will have a calvados," she said, giving her order to the waiter. She placed her elbows on the table and rested her chin on her clenched hands, looking up at him with her large dark eyes. There was a mischievous glint in them and he smiled, not quite knowing how to proceed. "For you, my dear captain, the fee will be only twenty American dollars, plus the rent for the room, unless you want to return to the Ritz."

Randolph looked down at his drink. "I just thought we'd talk and get acquainted."

"Of course, but I still must have my fee. It is my time that is valuable and not what I do."

Randolph nodded. "That's reasonable. I suppose you must know Paris very well. I thought perhaps you could show me some of the sights. Museums, churches, historical places—that sort of thing."

"Oh, a daytime tour," she said, a note of disappointment in her voice.

Randolph nodded again, more gravely this time. "I suppose working all night as you do you probably like to sleep most of the day." Then he smiled. "But I'll pay you enough so you won't have to work at night."

She laughed softly. "Why are you so generous? Paris is full of tour guides. You would not be trying to reform me, now would you, dear captain?"

"Not at all," he said defensively. "I just thought you'd appreciate a change of pace."

"I suppose you are wondering what a nice girl like me is doing in my line of work?"

"Something like that."

She emptied the glass and motioned to the waiter, who brought another. "Am I now on the payroll?"

"Certainly."

"Then I will tell you the sad story of my life, but not here."

"Any special place in mind?"

"First, I do not feel very tweedy tonight. I would like to change into something more suitable and then we could walk along the Champs-Élysées like two young lovers out for an evening's stroll. I do not get to do that very often in my line of work."

"I'd like that," he said. "Let's do it."

He waited in the taxi in front of her Left Bank apartment building on a narrow street off Boulevard Saint-Germain, a short walk from the Sorbonne. It was an ancient building but looked well kept. There was a doorman and Randolph guessed that it was probably reputable. She was back in less than ten minutes, dressed in a brown skirt, white blouse, and with a beige cardigan sweater draped over her shoulders like a cape.

The taxi dropped them off at the Place de L'Etoile and they walked under the Arc de Triomphe. She stopped before the small blue flame in front of the tomb of the Unknown Soldier.

"In 1938, when I was thirteen, I remember coming here with my parents. It was a celebration for the twentieth anniversary of the nineteen eighteen Armistice. There were searchlights and a huge flag, and a military band was playing patriotic songs. A crowd filled the whole square, and all the people sang. I remember my father's voice and the solemn look on his beautiful face. Two years later, the Boche were here and there was no more singing."

"You mean you're only nineteen?"

She smiled. "Yes, but it has been a very long life the last four years." She shrugged. "No matter—I look older in my tweeds. How about now?"

He looked at her and was surprised at how much younger she suddenly appeared. "You're like a chameleon."

"Yes, I know the word. That is true about me. As they say in America, that is my stock in trade." Her words were soft now, her accent more distinct, warmer, and he found it far more charming.

"Where in the world have you learned so much English?"

She took his hand and led him down the Champs-Élysées toward the Place de la Concorde.

She walked slowly, swinging his hand in hers. "My mother spoke fluent English and I grew up bilingual. By the time I was ten I was reading your Hemingway and Fitzgerald and Wolfe and Steinbeck. Now I am majoring in American Literature at the Sorbonne."

"Good God," Randolph exclaimed, looking more closely at her. "Then how can you demean yourself as a prostitute?" He paused, at a loss for words. "I mean, you're beautiful and bright. How can you just go out and sell yourself like a piece of meat?"

She walked in silence for a while. "You Americans are so bourgeois. Fucking for money is the least important thing in the world as long as there is no love in it. It is certainly no more demeaning than having to empty one's bladder or bowels. Frankly, I would much rather use those same organs for sexual ecstasy than disgusting excretions."

"That's one hell of a way to put it," he said. "But please, I'm not trying to judge you. It just doesn't make sense."

She squeezed his hand. "I know you are confused. It is not important." She turned and said, "Look at the beautiful silver moon over the Arc de Triomphe."

"God, that's some sight. Where are we? This looks like some sort of a park."

"Yes, Les Jardins des Tuilleries."

"I wish I'd studied French instead of German."

"Come, let us sit down on this bench and I will tell you all about my sad life."

"You don't have to, you know."

"But I want to. For twenty dollars you could buy many good books with truly fine stories in them. You are the only person in the world who would pay good American dollars for my story."

"Is it terribly sad?"

"Yes, but it is quite short. Maybe your Hemingway would make a nice little story with it. But nothing more."

It was dark where they sat, and when Randolph looked up the Champs-Élysées, the streetlamps seemed to flicker, their glow reflected in the large plate-glass windows of the shops and restaurants that lined the avenue.

"Well, where shall I begin?"

"Start with your real name."

"Why, do you not like Lady Belford?"

"I do, but tonight I'm out with a college girl and I'd like to know her name."

"My name is Justine Moreau. Now, see, that is not very exciting. I was born in Paris, in Montparnasse, and my father was a schoolteacher and he did not know anything about war. But he wanted to fight for France. So they put him in the Ninth Army and when the Boche broke through at Sedan, that is at the end of the Maginot Line. You have heard of our great invincible deterrent? Well, the Boche sent a hundred and fifty divisions, two million *cochons,* and they broke through what they called the 'vital hinge' and then attacked the French on the Maginot Line from the rear. The Ninth Army was ordered to retrieve the situation, but it was a hopeless gesture. My beautiful father was run over by a Panzer tank, squashed like a bug, and my equally beautiful mother joined the Free French underground."

She paused and looked up the avenue. "How quiet it is tonight. Do you truly want to hear this story. It is not very original."

"Please. Would you like a cigarette?"

She nodded and he gave her one and lit it. She puffed and he could tell she wasn't very expert at it. "I was fifteen in nineteen forty when the Boche came to Paris. Then one night the Gestapo broke down the door of our little flat and they took my mother away. They would have taken me away too if it had not been for a young captain with golden hair and pretty blue eyes who ordered them to leave me alone. An hour later he was back and he took me to another place. He told me my mother would be safe as long as I pleased him. Pretty soon he was shipped somewhere else, but not before I was pregnant, and he sent a major to look after me. After him there was another major, once there was a colonel, then another captain, and on like that for nearly four years. My son was getting bigger and finally one day I just took him and ran away. Instead of fucking the Boche for nothing, I started fucking Frenchmen for money, and now of course Americans, who are much more generous."

Randolph gently touched her shoulder. "I'm sorry," he said. "It must have been hell."

"Not always. But I worried about my mother for a long time, until I decided that she was dead. I used to have nightmares about their torturing her. She was a very strong woman, so stubborn, and I know she would not freely tell them the secrets they wanted to know."

"That's most admirable."

"You think so? I think it is stupid. I love Paris, but I refuse to die for any group of men who want to control it. I have no politics. No ideology. It is for fanatics and fools. You think my mother's little secrets made the slightest difference in the course of the war?"

"Maybe not, but she probably saved the lives of other patriots."

She flipped the cigarette away, the sparks bouncing off the gravel path like miniature fireworks. "Oh, I am tired of this story," she said. "I would like to eat and drink and just live for the moment. The past is always such a bore."

In the weeks that followed Randolph saw her many times. On weekends they covered all the interesting sights of historic and modern Paris. Then they went out into the countryside, to Bois de Boulogne, Versailles, La Malmaison, Fontainebleau, Barbizon, Château-Thierry, Reims. They took picnic lunches prepared by the Ritz, cheeses and bread, pâté maison, cold chicken, langouste, fruit, and some of the finest wines from the treasures of the hotel's incomparable cellar. One evening they dined on the *Bateau Mouche* as it cruised up and down the Seine.

They grew comfortable together, but the image of her with the general persisted in the back of Randolph's mind. He would wake up from a sound sleep and think about her doing it to him.

He knew the time was coming when he would not be able to hold back any longer. One evening, as they drank coffee in a large room facing the Champs-Élysées, she touched his hand and said, "Would you like to come home with me?"

They had come into the restaurant to escape a sudden cloudburst and Randolph looked out at the wet dark-gleaming avenue. The large plate-glass window was beginning to steam up. He nodded. "Yes, I'd like that."

"Come then, let us not waste any more time here."

The taxi dropped them off in front of her place. He followed her up the stairs to her apartment on the second floor. She unlocked the door and they walked into a lighted room. An old woman, dressed entirely in black, was sitting in a rocking chair, listening to music on the radio. She stood up, spoke a few French words to Justine, and left, wobbling on feet that seemed to shoot pain up her legs with every step.

It was a medium-sized room, with a bed at one end and a child's crib at the other. The room was cluttered with books and toys and cheap art objects. There was a small dining table with three chairs, an icebox, a small cooking stove, and a metal sink with cupboards above it. It looked clean and the clutter gave it the warmth of a place that is lived in.

She went to the crib and adjusted the little boy's blanket. "This one could sleep in a boiler factory."

Randolph laughed. "I haven't heard that expression in ages."

She smiled. "I am full of American clichés. It is the slangs that give me trouble. Each have so many different meanings. Would you like a calvados?"

"That sounds good," he said, watching as she crossed to the cupboard.

"Sit in the rocking chair," she said, bringing him the calvados. "Except for the bed, it is the most comfortable."

He sat in it and she took a pillow from the bed and sat on it next to his chair. "How do you feel?" she asked, resting a hand on his knee.

"Well, just terrific," he said, looking down at her hand, wondering when it was going to happen and whether he was ready for it.

She smiled and gently began stroking the inside of his thigh just above the knee. "Are you made of flesh and blood?" she asked. "Or snails and puppy dogs' tails?"

He shrugged and her hand moved a little higher. "Do you have anything between your legs?"

"Oh, yes," he said, and could feel himself becoming aroused.

"I'm glad," she said. "Do you mind if I see for myself?"

"You take your clothes off first," he said.

"Would you like a striptease?"

"Yes, nice and slow."

She stood up and her hips began undulating as she unbuttoned her blouse. She removed it to reveal a black lacy bra. "I am not very big in the tits but I make up for it in other ways. Are you big in the cock or do you make up in other ways too?"

"Big enough and getting bigger by the second."

"Oh, captain, it looks like you are definitely coming out of your shell." She reached over and unzipped his pants, her long slender fingers finding his hard penis and releasing it from its confinement. "Oh, you are beautiful, dear captain."

He looked down at himself and saw that he was in full erection. "Come on, hurry up, get your clothes off."

She smiled and slipped out of her skirt and he saw that she had not been wearing panties. She removed her bra and her small breasts looked hard as rocks, her nipples long and dark brown.

"Come, loosen your belt and I will pull your pants off. It would be a pity to soil them."

She knelt before him and removed his shoes and pulled his pants and shorts off. "Oh, my captain, do you want me to take you in my mouth and suck you like I did your general?"

"Yes, but give me the riding crop. I think it's time somebody smacked your bottom."

She stood up and brought him the riding crop. "Now, be gentle, dear captain—a little sadism goes a long way."

He pushed the crop up between her legs and moved it back and forth across her vagina. "How does that feel?"

"Wonderful," she said, swaying, her hands going to caress her breasts.

He reached out with one hand and cupped a buttock, his fingers closing over it with enormous strength.

"It feels like you would like to tear it right out," she said, her hands reaching for his penis and scrotum.

"How many cocks have you sucked in your life?" he asked, his voice growing husky.

She lowered herself to her knees and brought his penis up to her mouth, the tip of it barely touching her lips. "Thousands, dear captain—all sizes, shapes, forms, and colors. And I loved all of them."

"You're nothing but a dirty cocksucker," he said, and whacked her sharply across the buttocks with the crop.

She took him in her mouth and he could feel her tongue and teeth and lips working on him. He whacked her again, harder this time. She was really working on him now and the chair began to rock with the motion of her head, as her mouth slid up and down, her fingers gently squeezing his testicles, one long finger pressing against his anus.

"Oh, you fucking whore," he cried, and whacked her across the shoulders and then again against the buttocks. "I'd like to shove this fucking stick up your ass," he groaned, trying to hold back the eruption that was now inevitable. He looked down at her head, her long dark hair falling against his white thighs, and suddenly he wondered how many times his mother had done the same thing to men. She had been a dirty, filthy whore. He was seized with a terrible urge to hit his mother with his fist, to break bone, to crush her with his bare hands, squeeze the last ounce of life out of her. Then he exploded and he grabbed Justine's head with both hands, pushing it down until he could feel his penis pressing against the back of her throat. She struggled wildly, trying to come up for air, but he held on until he felt her teeth beginning to close over him. Suddenly terrified of what she could do, he released her.

She fell to the floor, gagging and gasping for air, her body trembling like the last spasms of a fish out of water. Randolph dropped to his knees beside her and gently touched her head.

"I'm sorry," he said. "I don't know what came over me. Please forgive me. I'm truly sorry if I hurt you."

She coughed, wiped her eyes with her knuckles like a child, and sat up. "What are you, dear captain, Mr. Hyde?" She looked directly at him and he turned away, unable to meet the pain in her wet eyes. "You better watch yourself," she said. "You do that with some whores I know and they will bite it right off. Then where will you be?"

Randolph nodded. "I know, I know," he said, but at the moment he didn't know what had happened to him. All he knew was that for a blinding instant he had wanted to hurt her, perhaps even kill her. And that realization terrified him.

In February 1945, as the Allies mounted their final offensive against a desperate German army, Major Randolph Harrison Godwin and Lieutenant General Sam Wheeler were in Rome, ensconced in another luxury hotel. They had made inspection trips to North Africa and

Sicily, and the campaign ribbons across Randolph's chest were beginning to look impressive. Both men could hardly wait for the day they would drive into Berlin.

In the meantime, Randolph found an ample supply of whores along the Via Veneto, which kept the general in splendid form. As for Randolph, he had two more distressing experiences with whores. In the first incident he squeezed her breasts until they turned purple before his eyes. In the other, he pressed a lighted cigar against her anus.

Shocked and frightened by his own compulsive behavior, Randolph had tried to make amends by giving the first whore five hundred dollars and the second a thousand. Both had greedily accepted the money, but not before castigating him in vociferous and indecipherable Italian.

On February 14 Randolph received a cablegram from Carson City informing him that he had just become the father of twin girls. Betty sent her love and wished him Godspeed in returning to them.

35

At first light on a cool spring morning, a beautiful young woman left her warm bed, went down a long hallway to a sweeping staircase leading to the entrance hall, slipped out the back door, and ran barefoot on the dewy grass, the air heavy with the fragrance of jasmine and magnolia, the breeze from the Mississippi bringing its own pungent scent. She moved gracefully, her breath coming in short gasps, her soft brown eyes moist with tears, her arms fluttering as she floated over the dark lawn in a flowing nightgown, a ghost caught in a ray of sunlight.

Henry Godwin came awake with a start, instantly grateful to be released from the dream. His body was drenched in cold perspiration and his hand trembled as he rolled over and sat on the edge of the bed. The large bedroom was cool in the darkness. The phosphorescent hands of the alarm clock showed that it was two minutes past four.

How long had it been since he had dreamed about his mother? Twenty years? He pressed his fingers against his eyes, his mind turning inward to the nightmare that had haunted him so many years ago. Her face had come floating through space toward him, a disembodied head, a hideous balloon carried by a soft wind, slow but relentless in its flight. Then it was right before his eyes, a purplish gargoyle with a mouth twisted by a swollen tongue, and sightless eyes bulging out of black sockets. He had cried out in his sleep, jerking his head back, his hands striking furiously at the balloon to push it away, but it bounced crazily around him before suddenly bursting and splattering him with *her* blood.

He shuddered at the thought and stood up. He was afraid that if he went back to bed the dream would come again. He slipped into a robe and went to the kitchen to make coffee. He wondered about his nightmares. The strange part was that they were always about his life as a boy in Vicksburg. If he dreamed about his present life, he was unaware of it.

He shook his head and filled his cup with steaming coffee. The hell with it. He had other things to think about. He sat down and lit a cigar. In a few hours he would be flying to Las Vegas with Rufus to meet with some men who were interested in building a modern hotel-casino that Rufus claimed would put Las Vegas on the map. Although Henry had been told nothing about these men, he knew from the way Rufus had acted that they represented underworld money.

He sipped coffee and his thoughts turned to the twins. He smiled. They were the most beautiful babies he'd ever seen. It was good to have babies in the house. Their arrival had rejuvenated everybody. Aunt Caroline and Holly seemed ten years younger. Even Moses cooed at the babies. Only Rufus seemed unimpressed.

"That's because they're girls," Aunt Caroline had said. "He can't shape them into his own image. Besides, he's still suspicious about Betty's peculiar German name. The way that man goes about, you'd think he was the handsomest and smartest man in the world, instead of the most ignorant and repulsive creature alive."

Sometimes Henry had to admit to himself that she was right on target, but he was careful never to express any thoughts that would confirm her opinion.

He finished his coffee and snuffed out his cigar. He walked down the hall and stopped at Betty's door. He suddenly felt a great urge to look at the twins. There was a light on in Betty's room. He gently opened the door and looked in. Betty was sitting up in the bed breast-feeding one of the babies.

"Hi," he whispered. "I thought I'd sneak a look at the girls."

She smiled and waved him in. "This one's always hungry," she said, looking down at the baby with eyes filled with love and pride.

"Which one is this one?" Henry said, moving to the bed for a closer look.

"Eileen, of course, the oldest. She's really demanding. If I had two like her, I wouldn't have enough milk. Alicia's far more contented. Such a sweet, easy baby."

Henry sat on the edge of the bed and watched the baby sucking on the nipple, Betty seemingly unaware that her breast was exposed. What a beautiful woman she was, Henry thought. Randolph was a lucky man. He could see the veins in the swollen breast and suddenly he was back in Alicia's apartment at the Fairview, lying in her bed as she read Molly Bloom's soliloquy, and he tried to remember the words about Molly's breasts being "2 the same in case of twins" and something about their beauty.

And they are beautiful, he thought, looking away to Alicia's crib. "You must be awfully proud of these girls," he said.

She nodded, tears coming to her eyes. "I can't wait for Randolph to see them. Do you think he'll love them the way I do?"

"Of course he will. How could he not?"

"How much longer before he comes home? The war's been over almost three months." The baby lost the nipple and began scratching at the breast with her small hand, her lips making sucking sounds as she searched. Betty laughed. "She's insatiable. Oh, she's going to be a demanding one, this Eileen." Henry impulsively leaned over to kiss the baby's cheek, his lips only inches from the breast. He could smell the milk. He stood up and went to Alicia's crib. A great surge of love swept over him. He wanted to pick up the baby and hold it against his chest. But he turned away and looked at Betty.

"I wish I could feed a baby. It must be very satisfying."

Betty nodded gravely. "I know what you mean. It's a wonderful expression of love. Makes you part of the baby."

"I better get out of here," Henry laughed. "I'm developing a maternal instinct."

He went back to his room and sat in his rocking chair. God, he thought, I'm getting to be a pervert. How can a normal man get an erection watching his daughter-in-law breast-feed her baby? What he needed was a woman. Any woman. Pretty damn quick.

Iola Raintree opened her eyes and looked at Rufus Boutwell at her side. He was snoring, with his mouth open, the air whistling through his battered nose. At times like this she often wondered how she had gotten into his bed when the man she truly loved was Henry Godwin. But he hadn't given any indication he knew she was alive as a woman, even years ago when she had visited the ranch daily when his leg was broken.

The years had gone by and then one day Rufus's secretary had told her that Mr. Boutwell wanted her to work exclusively for him. Her salary was tripled and she began spending considerable time in Rufus's office. Later he asked her to travel with him. He took her to New York and Washington and Los Angeles, and they stayed at the most deluxe hotels, occupying large suites, and ate in the fanciest restaurants. He bought her expensive clothes because he wanted her to look proper when he entertained business associates. She learned to mix cocktails and to leave the room at the proper moment without being asked.

He took her to the Stork Club, 21, Copacabana, El Morocco, Toots Shor's, and introduced her to celebrities. She dressed smartly and looked chic, but inside she was still insecure and vulnerable, still surprised at what was happening to her and wondering when it would all end.

Then one night six years ago, when they occupied a suite at The Plaza in New York, Rufus came into her bedroom moments after she'd gone to bed. He wore a royal blue satin robe with gold embroidery and tasseled belt. He looked at her, a strange light in his gray eyes, and sat on the edge of her bed.

"Hey, have I ever told you the story about the salesman and the farmer's daughter?" he said, rolling his eyes. "That's a hell of a hot story."

She shook her head. "No, Rufus, and I don't think I want to hear it."

"Come on, now, sit up. Sit here next to me on the side of the bed. This story needs illustration."

"What are you up to?"

He reached out and took her arm. "Come on, sit here right next to me."

She let him pull her to his side. Her silk nightgown had slipped up to her knees. She pulled it down as far as it would go and quickly clutched her décolletage.

Rufus smiled tolerantly. "Now, there was this salesman and he was out in the sticks selling farm machinery. So he comes to this farmer's house around dinner time and is invited to share a meal with him and his daughter, who's really stacked. This salesman looks her over and thinks, Wow, how do I get to first base with this old fart watching me?

"The daughter's sitting on his right, like you are now. They start out with soup and this salesman starts eating with his left hand, dropping his right on his lap. Now, slowly, he places his hand on her knee—like this, see."

She looked down at Rufus's hand on her knee. It felt warm and moist.

"Slowly, oh, ever so slowly, he starts pulling her dress up with his fingers, like this, just rolling the dress up, and the daughter goes on eating her soup like nothing's happening. All this time, the salesman's eating his soup and carrying on a conversation with the farmer, who's eating his soup with his right hand and resting his left elbow on the table.

"Hey, mister, something wrong with your right hand?'"

" 'Nothing,' says the salesman, now slowly inching his way up the inside of her thigh. 'I'm a lefty and it's not polite to rest your elbow on the table.'

"The farmer scratches his head. 'Yup, I think I heard that's so one time. Now, daughter, why don't you follow this gentleman's advice and take your elbow off the table.'

" 'Yes, Papa,' she says, and drops her hand—now give me your hand —on his knee and right away starts moving up his leg. Now they're both going at it and the old farmer beams proudly at his daughter."

Rufus's hand was moving up Iola's thigh and he began pulling her hand up his own leg. She tried to pull away but he held on, his eyes still smiling, but his jaw determined. She had known it would happen one day but had never been able to decide what action she would take. Now she felt almost paralyzed by her ambivalence. His fingers touched her through her panties and he pulled her hand inside his robe and placed it against his rigid penis.

"Take ahold, daughter," he said.

She gasped when she felt the heat of it against her hand. Slowly, her fingers closed around it and she was reminded of the number of times her stepfather had tried to make her do just that. When she had refused, he had masturbated in front of her. Finally, she had run away from home, but she was too old to run away again.

She shivered when his fingers worked into her panties and pressed inside of her.

"Please," she said, "I'm a virgin."

"My God," Rufus cried, "I'm coming. Pump."

And she did.

Later he had been gentle with her and that was the beginning of their relationship. She moved into his home and his bed and had been there ever since. Neither ever talked about marriage. Everything considered, so far it had been a good life. And there were bonuses. Today, for example, she would fly to Las Vegas with Rufus and Henry. Those were moments she cherished.

Rufus had bought a new DC-4 and had it completely remodeled. It reminded Henry of Rufus's railroad coach. The outside was painted a royal blue, with gold trim and the fancy crest. The walls were covered with a heavy damask and the chairs and sofas upholstered in silk brocade and the softest leather. The sofas converted into beds and accordion dividers could be drawn to make private rooms. There was a kitchen, two bathrooms with showers, and a small one up front for the crew. There was a library corner, with bar, and thick carpeting throughout. A crew consisting of a pilot, co-pilot, and navigator were on call twenty-four hours a day. The DC-4 was the best commercial airliner available, and when something better came along, Rufus Boutwell would put his crest on it.

It was a short ride from Carson City to Las Vegas, and after Iola served them coffee, she went to the library corner at the front of the plane and started reading. She knew that Rufus wanted privacy when he sat his guests in leather chairs at the back of the plane. She sat facing them, unable to hear what they were saying, but able to steal glances at Henry. All he had to do was look at her and her heart would start pounding in her ears.

Today Rufus Boutwell would take his first major step to implementing his dream about Las Vegas. The city's population was ten thousand, but there were only three downtown hotels. Two others had sprung up along U.S. Highway 91 at the town's edge: the El Rancho Vegas consisted of a casino surrounded by hacienda-type guest cottages, and the Last Frontier looked like an oversized Western ranch house, complete with old wagon wheels, steer horns, and cattle brands burned into wood. They certainly weren't what Rufus had in mind. His vision was of luxury hotels, something similar to Miami Beach's Collins Avenue. Big hotels filled with big spenders.

As the war was winding down in the Pacific, Rufus had pushed through an amendment to the gambling act, creating a seven-man State Tax Commission, which had the final say on the granting of gambling licenses. Appointed by the governor, who served at Rufus's pleasure, the commission also administered liquor laws, regulated public utilities, and performed other vital functions that gave Rufus the leverage he needed to control the gambling boom that he anticipated with the ending of the war.

Rufus had turned to his closest associate in the Century Committee, Jesse Stelk, a mysterious financier with close ties to underworld leaders in both New York City and Chicago. At thirty-six, Stelk was the youngest member of the Century Committee, but there was no doubting his credentials as a top financier. Tall and slender, with light brown hair flecked with golden streaks, a cleft chin, and deep blue eyes, he was a handsome man with the bearing of someone far older. There was nothing frivolous in Stelk's demeanor. He dressed conservatively and took his business and himself seriously. He had little patience for stupidity or nonsense. He was precisely what Rufus hoped Randolph would become one day: strong, intelligent, ambitious, aggressive, and totally unscrupulous.

For the first time, Rufus was explaining to Henry about his friendship with Jesse Stelk, while omitting the fact that they both were members of the Century Committee. Rufus had no intention of ever revealing his membership to Henry or anyone else, except, perhaps, Randolph one day, with the committee's approval. But that day was in the far distant future.

"This guy Stelk sounds interesting," Henry said, gazing out the plane's window at the ridge of mountains that appeared almost directly under them.

Rufus nodded. "That he is, a real live wire with all the right connections." Rufus lowered his voice. "He's got access to millions of untaxed dollars. Runs all this money through Swiss and Caribbean banks—kind of launders it—and it comes back as loans. There's nothing the tax boys can do about it. Henry, do you have any idea how much these guys make from illegal gambling alone? The net runs into tens of millions every year. What are they going to do with this money? They can't keep it in old socks. Stelk has shown the big guys how they can invest it and earn legitimate profit. Have something to leave for their kids."

"Who else is coming with him?"

"Meyer Lansky. I'm told the guy's a financial genius. He's in tight with the Italians."

"What is he, a gangster?"

"More a gambler. He's involved in gambling joints all over the country. Doesn't own them, but has a piece, and was instrumental in setting them up. He had the racetrack and a couple of casinos in Havana before the war, and he's still a close friend of Batista, who's now in exile in Florida but is expected to get back into power in Cuba before long."

"I've heard of Stelk," Henry said. "Owns a large hotel chain. He's a respected businessman. But do you think we ought to deal directly with guys like Lansky? I don't know the first thing about him. Could be public enemy number one for all we know."

Rufus shook his head. "Nothing to worry about. We're having a private meeting. Later, when we get things on track, we'll use a buffer when we need one. I just want to get this thing off on the right foot. It's important that we control it from the beginning. I don't want these guys to think they're getting a free ride. On the other hand, I don't want to discourage them. We're going to have to play this down the middle."

A limousine was waiting to take them to a cottage at the El Rancho Vegas. It was a special cottage, air-conditioned, and decorated by Iola. Rufus leased it by the year. A moment after they entered the room, the telephone rang and Rufus picked it up, listened, grunted a reply, and hung up.

"Iola, we'll be back in an hour or so. Come on, Henry, our guests are ready for us."

They walked to another cottage. It was only eleven o'clock on a fall day and already the temperature was over a hundred. In the distance Henry could see heat waves shimmering over the desert floor.

Rufus took out his handkerchief and wiped his face. "I'm out of shape," he said. "I've got to start doing some exercises. That's what Iola keeps telling me." He put the handkerchief back in his pocket and smiled crookedly at Henry. "She's quite a gal, Henry, quite a sharp little gal. I tell you, I'm a lucky man. Damn glad I didn't shoot her box off that night I shot up Matt's joint."

"I'm sure it's come in handy," Henry said.

Rufus chuckled. "That it has, laddie, that it has. Christ, one of these days we're going to have to hunt up a little gal for you to play with. It's good clean fun, Henry. Have you forgotten?"

By now they were at the door of the cottage and Rufus knocked. It opened and Jesse Stelk was standing there, smiling, his hand extended to Rufus, his gaze taking in Henry.

"This is my son-in-law, Henry Godwin," Rufus said. "He's my strong right arm."

"Good to meet you at last," Stelk said, giving Henry his hand. "Rufus has told me a great deal about you. Here, gentlemen—may I introduce my good friend, Meyer Lansky. I know he's been looking forward to this moment."

Lansky stepped forward and Henry was surprised at the size of the man. He couldn't have been more than five-foot-four and probably weighed less than one thirty. Hawk-faced, with hard brown eyes, he resembled a jockey.

"Hello," Lansky said, shaking hands with both Rufus and Henry. His brow was dotted with perspiration and he looked uncomfortable in his starched white shirt and blue and white polka-dotted bow tie. He wore a dark gray wool suit and vest, conservatively cut, and a white linen handkerchief with four points showing in his breast pocket. "It was cold enough to freeze your nuts in New York when I left yesterday. I had no idea this was one step this side of hell."

"Well, it cools off around Christmastime," Rufus said. "I've seen snow here, the whole desert just white, but it was gone in an hour. Sure was a pretty sight while it lasted, though."

Henry removed his jacket and loosened his tie. Rufus followed suit, but Stelk and Lansky kept theirs on.

"There's one thing for sure," Lansky said, sitting on the sofa next to Rufus, his small feet barely touching the floor. "Nobody should build a hotel here without air conditioning."

"I agree," Rufus said. "With a big swimming pool and lots of grass and trees and shrubs. You know, under this sand is perhaps one of the largest water basins in the world. You could turn Paradise Valley into a real paradise. You drill a couple of wells and you've got all the water you need for free."

"We drove up from Los Angeles last night just to see what kind of drive it is, and there's nothing to it," Stelk said. "You build a real first-class hotel and casino, with all the trimmings, and I think you'll get more tourist business than you can handle."

"That's what I've been saying for years," Rufus said, "but we had the Depression and the war. Now the time is ripe. The first ones in here get the edge."

Lansky nodded. "Any chance of getting an exclusive for five years? Give us a chance to recoup our investment. After all, it's quite a risky investment. This joint right here's not doing anything. Neither's the Last Frontier."

Before Rufus could answer, Henry said, "I understand you have interests in other gambling casinos in various states."

"That's true, but they're in or near big cities, not out in the desert. Also I understand you get bad sandstorms here. I'm told it takes the paint right off your car."

"That's a slight exaggeration," Henry said. "But your clubs must represent large investments."

"Oh, they're first-class operations."

"But illegal?"

Lansky glanced quickly at Stelk, who smiled and lit a cigarette. "That's true," Stelk said. "If I read you right, what you're getting at is that we could get closed down if the sheriff or whoever we're greasing goes out of office. Right?"

"Exactly. But you won't have that risk here. We're making you legal and we give you a license to prove it."

"You can always lose a license."

"Yes, but then you can sell out. We don't come in with axes."

Stelk leaned forward. "Good point, Henry. But there's something here that I've discussed with Rufus that you perhaps don't know. Meyer has his own people spread out in all the major cities of this country. And his people are connected with political organizations in all these cities. So he swings considerable political clout not only in these cities, but in state capitals and Washington as well.

"What we want, Henry, is to limit to some degree the competition to our own people. If there's business for more than one casino, then we want our people to build the rest. That way everything's going to be very friendly. In other words, we want Las Vegas as an open city for our people."

Rufus was shaking his head. "Las Vegas, or all Nevada, for that matter, is too big to permit any such limitations. Your people, Meyer, are welcome to do business in this state—of course, under the right arrangements—but others, I hope, will also want to invest. What I envision for the future is far bigger than what you're proposing."

Lansky shrugged. "Okay, you've made your point."

"Your best guarantee for success," Henry said, "is to build something so luxurious that no one can compete with you."

"That's precisely what Ben Siegel has in mind," Stelk said. "He's been dreaming about this for years. He even had an architect do renderings and they're absolutely outstanding."

"Do you mean Bugsy Siegel?" Rufus asked, his eyes narrowing as he waited for an answer.

Stelk nodded. "He's been called that in the press. But I assure you there's nothing bugsy about him. He's a levelheaded, hard-nosed businessman who's had considerable success in Los Angeles."

"You can't tell me about Bugsy Siegel," Rufus said. "He controls the wire service in this state and he's been muscling the bookmakers here, forcing them to give him a percentage of their operation. I've been meaning to have a word with that guy."

"Wasn't he indicted for murder in Los Angeles a few years back?" Henry asked.

"Bum rap," Lansky said. "He beat the case. As far as the wire service, I'll have him ease up on that score. Don't worry, we'll take care of it."

"I don't think he's what we're looking for," Henry said. "We don't want to start off on the wrong foot."

"Now, Henry, have no fear," Stelk said. "He's going to do a great job. He moves in top circles in Hollywood. Chums around with actors like George Raft, Gary Cooper, Clark Gable, Jack Warner. *La crème de la crème*. If anybody can get movie stars to perform here and draw big crowds—he's planning on a huge showroom, plus a lounge show—he can do it."

"Is this going to be his place alone or are there others involved?"

Lansky chuckled dryly. "Hey, we're talking about a couple million bucks. He's going to have partners who will keep him in line—don't worry."

"Have you picked out a spot yet?" Rufus asked, glancing at Henry, who knew from the question that he was accepting the deal.

"Yes, we have an option on a thirty-acre tract about five, six miles up the highway, closer to the airport."

"You mean that sleazy Folsom motel?"

"Right. We can buy it for peanuts," Stelk said. "You think we'll have any trouble getting a license?"

Rufus smiled. "You've got it. I'll have a nominee for our fifteen percent." He paused and grinned crookedly. "And we want it from the top—not after the skim."

"You'll have your own man in the counting room," Lansky said. "It sounds like you know something about gambling."

"You can say that," Rufus said. "Now, as to that Bugsy, just make sure he behaves himself. No rough stuff. We want to maintain a professional public image."

"No problem," Lansky said. "But just don't call him Bugsy. Otherwise he's a pussycat."

36

He lay spread-eagled on the wet deck, his face pressed hard against the slick brine-coated teakwood planks. Above him full white sails billowed out and the rigging moaned and groaned like some ginch making a mark.

Water splashed against his face, cold and stinging, and he laughed. "Let her rip, buddy boy," he bellowed into the wind.

He pounded the deck with his feet and hands, rolling over on his back to stare up at the darkening clouds. His hair was plastered against his head, coming down over his eyes. He pushed it back and shook his fist at the ominous sky. "Drop dead," he screamed. "You don't scare me, buddy boy."

Mister Benjamin Siegel, popular sportsman, man-about-town, Hollywood playboy, and now the swashbuckling master of a three-masted schooner, one hundred and fifty goddamn feet long from bow to stern. This was the big time, strictly first-class stuff. Even Meyer Lansky, who always acted so goddamn nonchalant, would be impressed—especially if he met the Countess. Genuine wop royalty and worth a cool fifteen million fish. And, buddy boy, she was stacked. A real platinum-plated piece.

"Mr. Siegel, you should be below." The words were spoken in a thick German accent.

Siegel rubbed the water out of his eyes and gazed up into the bearded face of the captain.

"It's my fucking crate, ain't it?"

The captain pointed at the sky. "The wind is coming up fast. Looks like big trouble. The barometer's been dropping all day."

"So you're the lousy captain," Siegel said. "Take care of it. That's what I'm paying you for."

The captain stood hunched over, trying to maintain his balance, but it made him look like he was about to lunge at Siegel.

"Go on, get the fuck out of here. Earn your dough."

The captain's fat lips pursed and his nose twitched, but that was all. He spun around on his heels and hurried aft.

Siegel sat there depressed. The bastard had spoiled everything. The wind, the water, the tossing and pitching of the ship. Nothing meant anything now. Not even his ginch below. "You prick," he hollered after him. "You lousy stinking kraut. Drop dead." Maybe he was a Nazi who had escaped from Germany before the Allies took Berlin. Probably had made soap out of Jews for years.

Siegel stood up and nearly went down. The deck wouldn't hold still for nothing. Carefully he made his way below.

As usual, the main lounge was blue with smoke and buzzing like a beehive. They were all there except for the Countess and Julian Stone. There was Vince Bacino and his fancy ginch, Daisy Miller—he'd like to get into her pants just once, show her what a real man was like, but that crummy dago kept the lid on tight. Bacino's lizard eyes never missed a trick. But someday, Siegel thought, when he had his fabulous joint in Las Vegas, he'd headline her and take his best shot.

There was Dr. Aaron Black, an old buddy from his boyhood days on the Lower East Side, who was now the physician at the Los Angeles county jail. Black had played it straight, studied and worked hard, while Siegel had quit school in the fourth grade and gone into the rackets. Today Black came to him for handouts.

Black was talking with Rosario Bellini, a little gray-haired dandy with a waxed mustache. Once married to the mother of a famous movie sexpot, he'd had his moment in the Hollywood spotlight, but following the actress's mysterious death, he had ditched the old lady and was now a two-bit character actor. Three days out at sea he had married the Countess's young nurse, Ruth somebody, and at this moment was holding her hand in his lap, way up in his lap, while he carried on a conversation as if nothing was happening.

Across the room from them, Alan Tulley, an expert card cheater, had his eye on Ruth's dimpled knees as she nervously crossed and recrossed her long legs. Next to him was Lew Spark, a young attorney whose influence with Talent Corporation of America (TCA) and various Hollywood unions was already beginning to be felt by the large studios.

Seated next to Bacino was Frankie Carbo, Siegel's number one henchman on the cruise, who had selected the crew and seen to it that Siegel's orders were carried out. Carbo had earned his reputation as a contract worker in the days when Murder Inc. was a going operation in Brooklyn.

In a corner by himself was Ape. Ape wasn't interested in conversation or in long legs. He was strictly a muscle. He had been with Siegel fifteen years. There was nothing he wouldn't do for the boss.

Siegel banged the bulkhead door shut and all eyes turned his way. Black jumped up and hurried toward him. "What in the world," he cried, shaking his head. "You're soaking wet, Ben. You been on deck all this time? I thought you were with the Countess. Get out of those wet clothes immediately."

"Relax," Siegel said, "it's only water."

"You don't want a chill, do you?"

"Fuck off," he said. "What are you? My Jewish mother?"

"I'm your doctor, Benny."

"Shove it," he said, turning his attention to Ruth. "Hey, nursie, come help the patient undress."

The locked hands on Bellini's lap stopped moving. They both stared at him with frozen expressions.

"I'll help you," Black said, taking hold of his arm.

Siegel jerked his arm free. "That's it, buddy boy. Go park your ass somewhere and stay out of it. All right, sweetheart," he said, beckoning her with his middle finger.

Bellini opened his mouth. "Now, Benny . . ."

"Shut up," he said. "What's the matter, puss? Ain't I using the right finger?"

Bellini gave a nervous laugh. "Go ahead, honey. It's all in fun. Benny's just having one of his little jokes. Aren't you, Benny?"

He didn't even look at Bellini. Ruth came to him and he said, "Start with the shirt and be careful with it. It's a hand-tailored job, worth twenty-five skins."

Red faced, with lower lip trembling, she carefully unbuttoned the front of the shirt, then slowly reached into the top of his pants to pull it out. He expanded his stomach muscles, trapping her hand inside, and leered at her. "What is it, sweetheart? Want to play more pocket pool?"

"Mr. Siegel," she said, her voice shaking, close to tears, "please stop it."

"I don't know," he said, looking down at her hand. "It kind of feels good."

He relaxed his muscles and she pulled her hand out. He looked around the room. Carbo was grinning like some skinhead at Minsky's. Alan Tulley looked amused, but Black seemed worried. Lew Spark appeared mildly interested. Bellini was smiling like a nut, his gray head bobbing like a yo-yo.

Daisy Miller was talking quietly to Bacino but his lizard eyes remained expressionless as they stared right through Siegel. That was the trouble with the wops, especially the fucking Sicilians. You never knew what they were thinking. They were treacherous.

Siegel himself had been forced to work with Bacino for the past seven years. Siegel had shown him how to organize various rackets in southern California. Although Bacino had listened to his advice, Siegel had felt left out of the internal planning of Bacino's Mafia family. The Italian "made guys" were kept away from Siegel. It was a close-knit operation and to this day Siegel wasn't sure who really belonged to the family.

"Go on," Siegel said, having suddenly lost interest in Ruth. "Beat it. Go back to your pocket pool. You bore me."

He nodded to Ape and hurried down the narrow passageway to his quarters. He had to hold on to both sides to stay on his feet.

In his cabin, he quickly slipped out of his wet clothes and stretched out on the bunk while Ape gave him an alcohol rub.

After Ape left, Siegel rode the bunk for a while, trying to recapture the exhilaration he had felt earlier on deck. It was hopeless. He thought of the Countess, his mind conjuring up all kinds of erotic images, until finally he could feel himself warming up a little.

He jumped up and hurried across the passageway, busting into her room without knocking. She sat propped up in bed, listening to Julian Stone read poetry. He sat at the foot of the bed, dressed in a suede jacket, complete with horn-rimmed glasses and pipe. A bottle of bourbon rested conveniently at his elbow. Julian was a certified lush.

The Countess gave a sharp gasp when she saw him. "My God," she cried. "Is the joint on fire?"

Siegel didn't get it at first. Then he realized that he was stark naked. "That's right," he said, "and I'm here to put it out."

Julian picked up the bottle, tilted it to his mouth. When he lowered it, there was no lip smacking or mouth wiping. He merely recapped the bottle, stuck the dead pipe in his mouth, walked to the door, and opened it.

"Man, I haven't walked this straight in years," he said before closing the door behind him.

Siegel laughed. The damn boat was rocking all over the place and this lush had walked a perfectly straight line. He had to admire the guy. He was a lush but he had class. He had started out as the Countess's jelly-roll and had soon been reduced to court jester. But like everything else Stone took it with a shrug of his shoulders. Nothing seemed to faze him. He had a Harvard accent and the big words to match it.

"How does that lush get it up?" he asked, sitting on the bed.

"Very slowly," said the Countess, reaching for him. "Not like you, my little jackrabbit. See? It's already coming to life. Come to mama, precious boy."

He lowered the covers and pressed his face into her huge warm mounds. She parted her gown and raised a breast to his mouth. When he took the nipple between his lips, she shuddered and reached for him with both hands.

It was like being on deck again, with the wind screeching in the rigging and the ship tossing him about as it leapt from wave to wave. Sometime during the act she had moaned and groaned, but he couldn't distinguish it from all the other noises of the ship. Moments later he fell into a deep hard sleep.

In the middle of the night he was aware of great claps of thunder and once it felt as though it had struck the yacht. The funny part was that he didn't do anything about it. He just lay there sleeping, or pretending to sleep.

When he awoke in the morning, bright rays of sunlight streamed through the porthole, flooding the room with cheerful warmth. The Countess was gone and he lay on top of the covers, still naked. He sat up, a queer feeling in his chest, his eyes darting wildly about the room. Something was wrong. He jumped from the bed and opened the porthole. Then it hit him. The boat wasn't moving. There wasn't a creaking sound anywhere, not a voice or a footstep. Just dead silence. The ocean looked as soft and calm as the water inside a bathtub. There wasn't a ripple as far as the eye could see, nor a breath of air.

Reaching inside the head, he grabbed a towel and hurriedly wrapped it around his waist as he threw open the door and ran down the passageway to the main lounge. It was empty.

"Goddamn!" he bellowed. "Where the hell's everybody?"

The bulkhead doors were open above the steps to the deck. That's it, he thought. They're all on deck. It's a beautiful day. They're probably fishing, or stopped to do some skin diving. Black is a bug for that junk. He clambered up the steps.

But the moment he hit the deck, he saw that the ship was naked. All three masts were gone, rigging, sails, the works. There wasn't even a piece of rope left. He just stared at it, his mouth open. Then his eyes found them, gathered around the wheelhouse, listening to the captain.

He saw Siegel and waved importantly, ordering him over. Feeling like a Roman soldier, Ben walked up the deck with the white towel tucked around his middle. It felt strange without all that racket overhead. It was as though some sneak thief had made off with the roof during the night.

All the guests were there plus the sixteen crewmen and the first mate, Max. Carbo was standing with the crewmen and Ape stood next to Black, a perplexed look on his broken face.

Siegel looked back at the naked deck. "What the hell happened here?" he asked, keeping his voice as calm as he could under the circumstances.

The captain looked as though he had been through a rough night. His eyelids were so puffed that his eyes were slits as he stared at Siegel. His tremendous black beard looked as wilted and soggy as the long hair that stuck out all around his cap. He shook his fist.

"Sir," he bellowed. The noise, the first Siegel had heard that morning, froze him to the spot. "These miserable filthy cowards standing here below me are responsible for what you see. I tell you we are most fortunate to be alive. Look at them. Look at their cowardly faces. But I'll fix them. I'll see them in irons."

"Wait a minute," he said. "What're you yapping about?"

"I'm talking about mutiny, sir. Mutiny!" He puffed out his chest and clenched his huge fists.

"Yeah. Well, if there's mutiny around here I'll do it," Siegel said.

"I am the captain," he bellowed at the top of his voice. He sounded like a crazy man. "In Germany these cowards would be placed against a wall and shot by a firing squad. Traitors, cowards, imbeciles, idiots, gangsters . . ."

Siegel turned away from him, motioning for Black to follow.

"Carbo and the boys refused to come on deck and help out last night," Black said. "The captain and Max had to fight the storm by themselves. Benny, believe me, for a while it looked like we were done for. You can't blame the captain for being mad. The guys should have helped out."

"Why didn't somebody wake me?"

"I tried, Benny, but you were out like a man in a coma. Anyway, it wouldn't have done any good."

"Next time wake me up. Understand? What's the damage here?"

Black scratched his head. "At least forty, maybe fifty thousand dollars. Besides everything you can see up here, they also fouled up the engine. They ran it without oil and burned out the bearings."

Siegel spun around and stalked off. The pounding in his head nearly blinded him. Somewhere along the way the towel fell off but he just kept going.

Then someone tapped him on the shoulder and he pivoted on his heels, his fists lashing out. He saw Carbo's grinning face, the towel in his outstretched hands. Siegel's left hand caught him squarely on the ear and his right slashed down across his big nose. Carbo doubled over and Siegel gave him a knee in the mouth. Blood gushed out and his eyes closed in pain.

"You goddamn, stupid, moronic sonofabitching bastard," Siegel cried. "I'll kill you." He grabbed a broken piece of wood lying on the deck, the size of a two-by-four, and smashed it over the top of Carbo's head.

He went down the steps and straight to his room. Fifty thousand bucks and not a penny's worth of insurance. The insurance company had been too particular about the makeshift crew of bookies and policy runners, small-timers on the edge of Siegel's organization who owed their livelihood to his continuing goodwill. So he had told the insurance company to get lost. And now he was stuck with the tab. The crate had cost him a quarter million dollars, much of the money borrowed from the Countess and movie pals like George Raft. It had been a dumb move. He wasn't all that crazy about the ocean. The image of being a sportsman, like Bogart and Flynn, that was what had really appealed to him. That was definitely big time.

"Fucking bastards," he cried, slipping into a pair of ducks and tennis shoes. He threw a sweat shirt over his head and furiously pulled out a trunk from under his bunk. He fished out a Thompson submachine gun and, holding it up with his left hand, snapped in a full drum of ammo.

They were all still on deck when he returned with the chopper.

"Now, you bastards," he screamed, running across the deck toward them. "I'll show you who's boss around here." He cradled the chopper in his right arm and pointed it directly at them.

"Good Lord," Bellini cried, pulling Ruth to his side.

"Everybody move back except the crew," he ordered. "I want to talk to the bastards personally. Go on, move!"

Most of them fell over each other in their hurry to get out of the way. From the corner of his eye he caught the captain moving behind him in a crouch. He spun around and punched the trigger. The captain went skidding on his face, his hat flying off, his long hair coming down around his ears.

"Freeze," he said. "Don't move an eyelash." The burst had been over the captain's head but not far enough for him to miss the message of the whistling slugs. Siegel saw the naked fear in his bloodshot eyes.

"All right," he said, turning to address the crewmen. "I've got a message for you crums." He lifted the chopper and sprayed a burst over their heads. They fell to the deck as one man.

"Up on your feet," he shouted. As they lifted themselves from the deck, he gave them another burst. Down they went again. He stood there, waving the smoking chopper at them, the wild, black anger leaking out of him like cold air from a balloon until there was nothing left inside of him but a dull headache and a leaden emptiness in his guts. It was too late to walk away. He had to do something to impress the jokers once and for all. Nobody was going to make a sucker out of Benjamin Siegel.

"Back on your feet, crums," he ordered. "Jump to it." He waited for them this time. Waited until they were all standing on shaking legs, staring up at him from bowed heads.

"This is a chopper," he said, holding up the tommy gun for their inspection. "I know a lot about this instrument. I learned to play it when I was a punk kid of seventeen. I can play any goddamn tune I want, see. My favorite is the 'Funeral March.' Get it, buddy boys?" He glared at them, his mind a blank. Where the hell did he go from here? He tried to work up the old anger but it was dead. Christ, he thought, what am I doing out here with a chopper in my mitts? Suddenly, he started to laugh. The more he looked at their stupid frightened faces the harder he laughed. The whole bit was very funny. By the time he turned away from them, tears were rolling down his cheeks and he had a catch in his side.

"Christ," he howled, grabbing Bellini's sleeve. "Did you see their lousy faces? I scared the living shit out of them bastards. Didn't I?"

Bellini nodded, swallowed hard, and gave him a sick grin. "Yes, Benny," he said. "You did that, all right."

"Well, buddy boy, why ain't you laughing? And that goes for you, too, Tulley. And you, Stone. All of you. Didn't you see their lousy faces? I'll bet they thought it was St. Valentine's Day all over again. Jesus, what a bunch of schnooks."

Without a glance at Siegel, Bacino took Daisy's arm and calmly walked away.

There was a peculiar expression on the Countess's face. "What's the matter, Countess? Can't you take a little joke?"

"Please," she said. "Put that nasty thing away." There was a tightness around her mouth that aged her.

"Don't worry," he said. "I know how to handle this baby. Come. I'll show you."

"No, thank you," she said.

"Okay, okay," he said. "Be a bunch of hard-nosed schlemiels. It's no skin off my ass."

He walked toward Black and Carbo, who by this time was sitting up while Black bandaged his head.

"How do you feel?" he asked, leaning forward to examine the dressing.

"Okay, I guess," Carbo said. "A little dizzy."

"Swell," he said. "How is he, Doc?"

"He's one of God's children. Got the skull of a true Neanderthal. That blow would have killed any ordinary civilized man. I wouldn't be surprised if his head was bulletproof."

"Don't make fun of him," Siegel said. "He's as smart as anybody."

"I was just paying him a compliment," Black said.

"Sure, if you say so," Siegel said, but Carbo looked doubtful.

Siegel went down below and stretched out on the bunk with the chopper resting on his chest. He loved everything about it. The feel, the look, the smell. When he was a punk kid on the Lower East Side, he would have given anything to own this baby. It would have made him a king. In those days the boys carried their choppers in violin cases and took better care of them than some joker with a Stradivarius. They spent all their spare time oiling and polishing, which gave them an excuse for caressing it. He knew one character who slept with his chopper. Even when he had a dame in bed, the chopper was right there at his side. He loved that weapon more than anybody or anything. For practice he used to shoot the heads off chickens. He was the best chopper man in the business. Then one night some boys caught up with him and blasted him while he slept with the damn thing cradled in his arms, fully loaded and the safety off.

When the knock came at the door an hour later he was still in bed with the chopper, dreaming about the old days. Hell, it wasn't that long ago, and yet it seemed like a million years. Times had changed plenty since the repeal of prohibition. Now a chopper man was about as useful as an old corn still. He was thirty-nine years old and he had been going at it for twenty-five of them. Most of the guys he'd started out with were long dead and buried, some in quicklime pits, others in cement overcoats at the bottom of the East River. They hadn't been tough enough or smart enough to survive in the concrete jungle. That, buddy boy, took brains and guts. Plenty of it. For every guy who made it big, a hundred were knocked off and a thousand served time. Except for the arrest on the Big Greenie murder rap, he'd never served a day of time in his life. He had plenty of arrests. Bullshit like carrying a gun, vagrancy, gambling, extortion, consorting with known criminals, maybe a half-dozen for homicide, then one for rape and a few for assault. Most of them were in New York, Miami, and Philadelphia. He thought there was one in Hot Springs. Then the murder trial in Los Angeles. But through the artful devices of expensive mouthpieces and the poor memory of terrified witnesses he was still clean. The knock at the door became more insistent and he finally told whoever the hell it was to come in. He stayed down on the bunk with the chopper. Ape came in and handed him a radiogram. "Just came in, boss," he said.

Laying the chopper at his side, Benny opened the envelope. The message was brief and to the point. It read:

THE DEAL IS SET. CONGRATULATIONS. M.L.

The initials, he knew, stood for Meyer Lansky. He stared at the message and felt the hair on the nape of his neck stand on end. It meant that he would get to build his hotel-casino in Las Vegas—the most fabulous gambling joint of all. He would become legit for the first time in his life. No more bullshit from the cops, or anybody else for that matter. It would be his joint and he would skim the shit out of it. And nobody would be able to lay a finger on him. He couldn't wait to get started.

He looked at Ape. "When are we getting out of here?"

"I don't know," he said.

"Well, for Christ's sake, don't just stand there. Get me somebody who knows."

Ape ran from the room and a few minutes later Tulley came in.

"We're in luck," he said. "There's an Italian steamship on the way. Should be here early tomorrow morning."

"Where are we anyway?"

"In the Gulf of Tehuantepec, about two hundred miles from Acapulco."

"How long will it take to haul us in?"

"Not long. Couple days at the outside."

That evening at dinner he sat at the head of the table with the Countess facing him at the other end. They were all there, but no one seemed in a very talkative mood.

"Look, everybody," he said. "I'm sorry as hell about today. I guess I just blew a fuse when I saw the damage to this crate. Here I'm paying those bums good dough to take care of things and we could have all been killed in our sleep. Can you blame me for being mad?" He stopped and gave them his most boyish grin. "Well, let's forget it. As the Countess says, 'C'est la vie.'"

"Oh, Benny," the Countess said, smiling warmly, her expressive hands forgiving him. "You're such a naughty boy. Sometimes I really don't know what to make of you."

There was laughter and the tension was broken.

"Hey, everybody," he said, "how about a swim after dinner? It's a perfect night for it. Warm and not a ripple in the water."

"Aren't there sharks in these waters?" the Countess said, looking around the table for confirmation.

"Only in the daytime," he said. "They sleep at night. Come on, any volunteers?"

"Count me in, pal," Tulley said.

"Anyone else? How about you, Rosie?"

Bellini shook his head. "Not for me, Benny. I'm not much of a swimmer."

"Well, Ruth?"

She glanced at Bellini and he nodded approval. "Sounds wonderful. Thank you."

That was all he wanted to hear. He looked around the table, caught Bacino's hard stare, and quickly moved on to Spark, Black, and Carbo, whose bandages looked like a turban. "Sorry, buddy boy. I'll talk to you later." He stood up. "Okay, last one in's a monkey's uncle." He stopped and grinned at Ruth. "Or aunt."

In his cabin, while changing into swim trunks, he took a good look at himself in the full-length mirror, arched a thick eyebrow, and smiled at his reflection. He knew he had a face that women considered handsome: bright blue eyes, long dark lashes, dark, wavy brown hair. He was almost five-foot-nine and his weight was only one sixty, which wasn't bad for a thirty-nine-year-old guy who never exercised and ate in the best restaurants. Besides, he had what it took to make a ginch cry for more.

He was the first one out on deck. Ape came up and Siegel said, "Skip down and tell Tulley I don't want him. He'll understand. I want that ginch all to myself."

After Ape hurried away, Siegel went to the starboard side and looked down at the cold black water. Maybe sharks didn't sleep at night. Those bastards were probably looking for food twenty-four hours a day. Jesus, wouldn't that be something? Having taken all them human sharks all his life, then getting taken by a real one. What a screamer. Fuck it. Everybody had to go sometime. Meanwhile, you lived it up.

Bellini and Ruth came on deck. She had on a one-piece black suit and all he could see were her white thighs coming toward him. When she got closer he could see the tops of her large breasts jiggling with each step. He licked his lips in anticipation.

"Hi," she said. "I guess Tulley's the monkey's uncle."

"The water looks cold," Bellini said.

"You crazy?" Siegel said. "It looks perfect. I'll bet it's warmer in than out. How about it, Ruth? You game?"

"It does look nice," she said. "It's so still. Are you going to dive from here?"

"Sure. I'm an old bridge jumper from way back. Want me to go ahead and wait for you?"

"All right."

"Here goes nothing," he said, and climbed over the railing. He took his time, wanting to impress her with a perfect dive. When he sailed out into the air, his muscles tightened, rebelling against the inevitable shock. He nearly had a heart attack. He had to get his breath back and come up for air. He kept his eyes closed until he hit the surface.

Jesus, he was deaf, blind, and numb. It must have taken him thirty seconds to regain his senses. When he looked up, she was staring down at him while Bellini was trying to tell her something.

"Come on," he hollered.

"How is it?"

"Fantastic. You'll love it."

She listened to Bellini a few more seconds and then took off, her white thighs sweeping back, her body arching, her arms stretched out like a graceful bird. It was a perfect swan. She hit the water clean as a whistle. He waited for her and she came up right in front of him. Her lips were trembling and he had to fight to keep his from doing the same.

"How do you like it?" he asked, pushing his hair back and smiling like he was having the time of his life.

"A little chilly," she said, her teeth clattering like broken china.

"You'll warm up real quick. Tell you what, let's swim out a bit. That should warm you up. Don't worry. I'll take good care of you."

"I'm not worried, really I'm not."

"Fine," he said, swimming away from the boat.

"Please, Mr. Siegel, not too fast. I don't want to lose you."

He swam into the darkness until he knew he was far enough away from those on the boat. He stopped and she was right beside him. He smiled and took both her shoulders in his hands. "I'm Ben. None of that mister stuff. I'm a lot younger than your husband."

She nodded, smiling, and he said, "You're still shivering. Come closer. Let me rub a little circulation in your veins." He began running his hands over her, up and down her back, touching her buttocks, then back up her waist, barely touching the sides of her breasts.

Her mouth opened and closed. She blushed but didn't say anything for a while, letting him touch her in all the private places.

When he reached between her legs, she said, "Please, don't do that."

"Do what?" he asked, smiling at her while his hands again moved across her buttocks, squeezing tenderly here and there.

"Please don't."

"Be nice," he said. "I go for you. You're really a sweet dish."

"It's not right. We shouldn't do that."

The *we* was like the flashing of a green light. He went. His mouth was against hers, and one of his hands had moved inside her suit to caress her breasts. It took furious paddling to stay afloat. She let him kiss her for a while, even permitted him to ease one breast out of her swimsuit. Things were just warming up when she pulled away.

"No, leave me alone, please. It's not right."

"I see your teeth aren't chattering no more," he said. "It warmed you up."

"Ben, please, be nice."

"I'm nice. Look, baby, face it, will you. I'm hot for you."

She stopped moving and looked squarely into his eyes. "I love Rosario."

"So? Love him. Who's stopping you? What does that have to do with us having a little fun? Come here, give me your hand. I want to show you something."

"No, thanks."

"Oh, you've got a dirty mind."

"I don't trust you."

"I just wanted you to feel my heart beat. See how excited you get me? That's not healthy for a man. You don't get Rosie all excited and then pull away, do you?"

"Well, that's different. We're married."

"Baby, don't kid yourself. Live like you travel. First class. Listen, I've fucked some of the biggest movie stars in Hollywood, and not one of them ever got me hotter than you've got me right now. Come on, give me a little fuck. It won't kill you. Nobody will know except you and me. What do you say?"

She was blushing but her eyes were shining. He knew that the rough language was getting to her. He put his arms around her waist.

"I'm afraid," she whispered hoarsely.

"Now, now, baby, just relax and enjoy it." Slowly, he pulled her suit down to her waist, his hands caressing her lovely pointed breasts. "Don't get upset now," he said. "I'm going down to pull your suit off."

"No, I don't want it off."

He leaned forward and whispered in her ear. "I want to fuck you, baby. I want to stick my cock into your juicy cunt and give you the best fuck of your life." He could tell by the brightness of her eyes that she was enjoying hearing the dirty words.

"You're awful," she finally gasped.

"Where I come from, baby, we eat little girls like you with a spoon."

"Please, don't say any more."

"Okay, you hold still, I'll be back in a jiffy."

He went down, his hands sliding along her body, making sure to linger on her buttocks, sort of a preview of things to come. The suit came right off. In fact, at the end she was helping him.

"That's beautiful, honey," he said, coming up for air. "Now you wait here for me. I'll be right back."

He swam toward the yacht with her suit in his teeth, like Fido with a prized bone. Bellini was peering over the side, his hands up to shield his eyes from the deck lights.

"Hey, Rosie, throw me a lifesaver."

"A lifesaver? Why? Is Ruth in trouble?"

"Hell, no. She just wants to float around a bit. Come on, throw it overboard. I ain't got all night."

Bellini hesitated only a moment before throwing one of the white rings into the water.

"Thanks, buddy boy. See you soon. You ought to jump in yourself. It's great."

"Where is she?"

"Just a little ways back there. Relax, we won't be long."

Ruth was just where he'd left her and she seemed happy to see him. "See, baby, Benny thinks of everything. It's big enough for both of us."

He ducked under and came up inside the ring. She followed him and came up laughing. "This is crazy, you know."

"Just put your arms back like this. Holds you up." He leaned forward and nibbled both breasts. They seemed to be floating all by themselves. He raised his head and smiled into her shining eyes.

"Ever fucked in the water before?" he asked, rubbing his feet along the outside of her thighs.

She shook her head.

"Good," he said. "I'm going to show you what you've been missing."

"Be careful," she said. "I don't want to get pregnant."

He laughed. "Silly, you can't get pregnant in water. It's like getting a fuck and a douche at the same time. Now, kiss me, baby."

Her wet lips were slightly parted when they closed over his. They were cool and soft and he could feel her warm breath against his teeth. As they kissed, he carefully pushed his own trunks down to his knees and pressed his body against hers. She pressed back and their mouths opened. When his tongue penetrated her lips, it was like a bolt of lightning striking her. Her body jerked convulsively and her breathing became harsh and erratic. Suddenly her legs opened and twisted around his hips, drawing him in. He felt her hand on him, furiously arranging things. She moaned and groaned and grunted and squealed. But he didn't know if she blushed. He was too busy to notice.

Later that night, while Siegel was resting on his bunk, Carbo came in with a worried expression. "Max tells me that stinking kraut captain's going to make trouble when we dock in Acapulco."

Siegel stared at Carbo. He should have thought of it. The captain had probably radioed the FBI about the chopper business on the deck. That was the trouble with life. You spent nine-tenths of your time fixing up and explaining the things you did in the other tenth.

He sat up. "Let's go see that sonofabitch."

The captain's quarters were at the stern near the wheelhouse. He was seated at his desk when Siegel and Carbo came in. The first mate, Max, was in one of the deck chairs. There was a half-empty bottle of booze on the desk and a dead one on the floor by Max's chair. Both looked drunk. Max rose halfway in his chair and fell back again with a wave of his arm. The captain stared at Siegel through glassy bloodshot eyes but didn't bother trying to get up. Siegel sat and Carbo stood behind his chair.

"What are your plans for the future, captain?" Siegel asked.

The captain burst out laughing. "Don't worry about that, mister. Just worry about your own future." The liquor had thickened his accent.

Siegel smiled. "But I'm worried just the same. I wouldn't want anything to happen to you. After all, you saved my life. I feel I owe you a special bonus. Five grand for each of you."

The captain's bloodshot eyes seemed to be laughing at him. "Now, that's very generous, considering what I have in mind for you, sir."

Siegel's eyes turned to ice. "Hey, buddy boy, let me tell you something. In my business we take care of pals. Know what I mean? But if somebody crosses us—well, you've seen some of them Cagney movies. Stool pigeons get it right in the head. It don't make no difference where they run. Our organization's international. Get it?"

The captain refilled his glass. "I'm not afraid of you," he said. "No Jew ever scared me, mister."

Siegel jumped up. "One fucking word from you and I'll personally blow your fucking head off. You can have the cops following you the rest of your goddamn life and I'll still blow your brains out. Now you better be a man with me. I've spent a bundle on this trip and I ain't going to have it ruined by nobody. I'm not going to have the goddamn newspapers play up this shit with the chopper." He pointed his fingers like a gun at the captain's forehead. "One word, kraut, and you're a goddamn dead man. Period. And that goes for you too, Max."

The captain leaned back in his chair. "In that case, mister, it will cost you ten thousand for each of us. Take it or leave it."

Siegel grabbed Carbo and pushed him toward the door. "It's a deal, but remember what I said."

When they reached the deck his whole body was shaking out of control. "I want that prick hit. You hear me, Frankie? When we reach Acapulco, I want you and Ape to lay back, wait for your chance, then hit and bury that cocksucker."

"Okay, Benny. We'll take care of it."

"Look, about this morning, I'm sorry I nailed you."

"That's okay, Benny. I should've gone topside last night. But it was wild. You know, none of us are seamen and we could've been washed overboard. You've got no idea what it was like up here. I was in a hurricane in Florida once, but that was nothing compared to last night. I never saw nothing like it. It's a miracle we're still afloat."

They paced up and down the deck until Siegel worked the anger out of his system. Back in his stateroom, he broke down the chopper while Carbo stood by the door watching him. He wrapped each piece in a towel and carefully packed all of them in a small suitcase.

"Okay, Frankie, get Rosie in here."

When Bellini came in Siegel was stretched out on the bunk. He waved and winked. "Hope I didn't interrupt any monkey business."

Bellini grinned, fingering his mustache. "Not tonight. The swim pooped her out. She went right to sleep."

"Nothing like a good swim to relax the nerves and muscles," he said. "That's quite a kid you've got there. Hell of a fucking swimmer. Tell me, Rosie, does she blush in bed? I mean, how is she, daddy?"

"C'mon, Benny, that's personal stuff."

"Since when? You've told me all about the others, including your sexy stepdaughter. So tell me, is she a lights on or off type?"

"That's different about the other broads. I love this kid. I really mean it, Benny. For the first time in my life—and I'm pushing sixty—I'm really in love. There's nothing I wouldn't do for this kid. I married her, didn't I? And she didn't have a nickel to her name. I could've married big dough. I've got the contacts. You know that."

"So what're you going to do for a living?"

"Well, that's a problem. I've got to give it serious thought."

"Tell you what. First, I want you and the bride to enjoy a week's honeymoon in Acapulco as my guests. Then maybe I'll have a job for you in Vegas. I'm going to build that gambling joint. Let's see how things work out."

"Benny, you're fantastic. I've never met anyone like you. Thanks a million."

Siegel fingered his chin. "Listen," he said. "Would you do me a little favor in return?"

"Sure, you bet. Anything. You name it."

He picked up the suitcase. "I'd like for you to keep this with you. Bring it to me in L.A. when you return."

Bellini frowned. "Is it something illegal?"

Siegel laughed. "It's the chopper."

"But how do I get it through Customs?"

He stood up and patted Bellini on the back. "I'm not worried. You'll think of something. Remember, this is important to me. It's not because it's worth all that much. You might call it sentimental reasons. So don't fuck it up."

They sat on deck, under a cobalt blue sky, and watched the rocky coastline grow larger and larger until they could see red tile roofs and shimmering alabaster walls perched like birds' nests on precipices far above the clean-swept sunny beaches.

"Countess," he said. "Have you ever seen anything to beat it?"

She squeezed his hand. "It's the most marvelous sight in the world."

He smiled. "Sorry about the trip. Coming to L.A. with me?"

"No, darling. I'm flying to Rome."

"Well, have a good trip," he said. "I'll miss you." Secretly, he was glad the cruise was over. That sex route was getting to be a bore. But who could spit on fifteen million skins. When he was that close to big money, he expected some of it to rub off on him.

37

The Honorable Elisha Toombs raised one fat buttock off the chair, farted three times, and grinned slyly at Randolph. He reached for a cigar and waited for Randolph to light it.

"Nothing like a good Havana to kill the stink of wet farts," he said.

Randolph reached in his pocket for a gold Dunhill lighter and held his breath while the senator puffed noisily to get the cigar going. Then he moved across the room to the window and slowly exhaled. It had been snowing since noon and the large spruce trees looked like huge snowmen. It reminded him of Germany and that reminded him of the months-old rotting corpses that had smelled less noxious than the gas expelled by that fat, ugly bastard he'd been humoring ever since his release from the service almost a year ago.

Moving him from Amos Rutledge to Toombs as a legislative assistant had been Rufus's latest ploy. As compensation for "cruel and unusual punishment," as Rufus had phrased it, he'd bought Randolph and Betty one of those slim, elegant three-story homes in Georgetown, along with a membership for Randolph in the Forum Club. "This will be your postgraduate course," Rufus had said. "Old Elisha won't like it. And neither will you. He's going to think you're after his job, but don't pay him no mind. He'll come around in good time or by God I'll know why. Meanwhile, pick up on some of his tricks. He's a shifty old coot, as crooked as the day's long, and been getting away with it for over thirty years. You couldn't ask for a better teacher."

"Hey, m'boy, wake up," Toombs called, "and pour me a real bazooka."

Randolph turned from the window and Toombs said, "And pour yourself one."

Randolph went to a file cabinet, fished out a bottle of bourbon and a glass from the top drawer, and brought them to Toombs's desk. "Say when, Senator," he said, holding the bottle over the glass.

"Fill her to the brim, m'boy, to the brim. It's been a long, strenuous day and I'm coming down with something that I want to kill real quick. Nothing like fine Kentucky bourbon to kill whatever ails a man. Now, you have one, hear?"

"Not tonight," Randolph said, handing Toombs the full glass. "The snow's going to snarl up traffic and I want to get going before it gets much worse."

"Watch it, there—don't splash none of that precious elixir on my Sunday-go-to-meeting suit." He grabbed the glass with both hands and carefully brought it to his mouth.

Randolph looked away. Everything about Toombs was repulsive. His farting and belching and spitting globs of tobacco juice in an old-fashioned copper spittoon that had turned a putrid green. It had been a long year and it was getting longer every day. Nothing that disgusting old man could do would ever again surprise Randolph. Once he had even caught him humping his secretary, Jenilee Ream, on the leather couch. All the senator had done was unzip his pants and push her panties aside to enter her. As Randolph had told Rufus, "You'd have thought the building was on fire and he had to tear off one last piece before meeting his maker."

Jenilee had been with Toombs twenty-two years, coming to work for him fresh out of a Reno secretarial school. She was a hard-faced woman with shrewd eyes and melon-sized breasts who serviced the senator and ran the office with an iron fist. Whatever power Toombs possessed, she exercised it with smug satisfaction. No one, except close insiders, saw Toombs without her approval, and no bill received his vote without her consent. When Randolph had reported his discovery, Rufus had dismissed it with a wave of his hand. "She works for me," he'd said. "She's my eyes and ears in that office. And she keeps that horny old fart out of trouble. When he wants to dip his wick in something younger, she pays for it and makes him think he's getting it for free because of his stately bearing. They all think they're members of a royal family in that Senate chamber. It's a kind of ego disease that weakens the brain. Let's hope it don't afflict you when your turn comes."

"So, m'boy, how do you like working with a Republican for a change?" Toombs asked, leaning back in his huge leather chair, blue smoke curling like a halo over his dyed-black fringe of hair. He'd asked that question a hundred times in the past year and each time he'd made it sound like he'd just thought of it. "Reckon Amos taught you all he knowed and now it's my turn. Well, how're you doing so far? Learning all my little secrets? Getting ready to usurp my office and make your granddaddy proud?"

Today Randolph felt like telling him what he really thought, but as always he said, "Rufus thinks most highly of you, Senator. The only reason I'm here is to do whatever I can to help you and our state. There's no conspiracy involved."

Toombs grunted. "You're not going to try to bullshit an old bullshitter, are you? You and Rufus figured old Elisha could educate you real good before you broke his tail. Now fess up—no need to be bashful 'round here."

Randolph forced a smile. "Senator, I'll be twenty-two next month. If I'm not mistaken, the age requirement for a senator is thirty. I'd say your tail is safe for quite a while—*yet*."

Toombs's eyebrows shot up on the *yet*. He emptied his glass and motioned for Randolph to refill it. Instead Randolph returned to the window, ignoring the request. The senator shrugged and did it himself.

"Ah, youth's so impatient. Always waiting like vultures for the old to pass on. In my time I've stomped a whole passel of bloodsucking pissants who tried to ride my coattails. The good folks back home keep reelecting me—with Rufus's blessings, naturally. You see, Rufus appreciates the privileges of seniority. Junior senators ain't worth a small fart in a windstorm to an ambitious man like Rufus."

Randolph watched the snow come down. It was getting dark and the streetlights had come on. It was the last day before the Christmas recess and he wanted to go home. "Everything and everybody comes to an end at some point in time," he said, keeping his back to the senator.

"Ah, so now out it comes," Toombs cried, splashing more bourbon on his trousers. "Well, let me tell you, m'boy, you've got a long wait coming. I'm only sixty-one and I have many good years left. I'll be here long after you've attained your maturity."

"I'm sure you will."

"I'm aiming to die with my boots on, preferably on the Senate floor in the course of a great debate. I've always been partial to dramatic exits."

Randolph turned from the window. "Senator, I hope you get your wish. But for now, if you'll pardon me, I'm going to head home."

"Sure, sure, go on home. That's the trouble with younguns today.

They're all clock punchers. First, though, tell me something, and be honest now." Randolph could hear the bourbon slur creeping into Toombs's voice. "Would you sneak up on an old man in the twilight of a great career and try to sandbag him?"

Randolph paused at the door and smiled. "Not me, Senator—I'm no bloodsucking pissant."

When Randolph arrived home that evening Betty and the twins were waiting at the front door to greet him. He scooped the twins up, one in each arm, as they squealed with delight, then leaned forward to receive Betty's kiss.

"Your nose is cold," she said, pinching it. "And your cheeks are rosy and your ears purple. Are you the multicolored monster I've been hearing about?"

"That's me, madam."

"Please, Mr. Monster, before you harm my lovely babies, be fore-warned. Their daddy is ferocious. He'll tear you limb from limb."

"In that case, madam, you can have them back. But there's a price."

"Oh, yes, I presumed as much."

He released the twins and they danced around him, trying to stick their hands in his coat pockets to pluck the tiny silver-wrapped choco-late Kisses he often brought home.

"I'll collect now," he said, and she came into his arms. While they kissed, Betty found the candy in his pocket and gave it to the twins.

They shouted with glee and Randolph released Betty. "Ah, been in my pockets again. Stealing my candy. I'm the one who buys it, I should get the reward for giving it."

"But I just gave you your reward," Betty said, touching his cheek. "Gosh, you feel so fresh and nice. How about going for a walk in the snow? When I was a girl I loved walking in the snow at night. Every-thing looks so pristine."

"Okay, get your coat and tell Martha to hold dinner. I'm game."

She took the twins to the kitchen and when she came back she was wearing a candy-striped stocking cap with a huge pom-pom, a green muffler the color of her eyes, and a navy blue pea jacket.

They went out into the snow, holding hands, their faces turned to the sky, delighting in the gentle touch of the snowflakes.

"Oh, this is so wonderful," Betty said. "Look, we're the only two survivors left in Lapland."

He leaned over and kissed her. Ever since his release from the army he hadn't been with another woman. The madness that had come over him in Europe was gone. When he thought about it, he couldn't imagine what possessed him. Sex with Betty was clean and good, as she was clean and good, and *his* only—not the property of every man who could pay the price. And the twins were *his* daughters, conceived in the womb that *he* fertilized with *his* sperm. It was an act of love as pristine as the snow itself, and he was proud of what he'd achieved.

"Oh, darling, I wish we didn't have to leave for Carson City tomorrow. Wouldn't it be possible for your dad and Aunt Caroline and Holly and Moses to come to visit us for Christmas?"

"Sweetheart, the plane's here already," he said. "If the weather clears up we'll take off in the morning. I hope we're all packed."

"We are. Your dad called today and I made the suggestion, but he didn't sound very enthusiastic. He and Rufus have to be in Las Vegas the day after Christmas."

"Oh, right, I had almost forgotten. It's the grand opening of the Flamingo."

"That's the one with that horrible gangster, Bugsy Siegel?"

Randolph laughed. "Betty, because somebody's called Bugsy it doesn't necessarily follow that he's a gangster. As far as I know Siegel is just another businessman."

"Well, that's not what the papers have been saying."

"You can't always believe the newspapers."

"Oh, but, darling, the plot thickens. There's this luscious redhead, Virginia Hill, but nobody actually knows her real name. They say she's a gang moll and gets oodles of money from gangster friends—her latest being Bugsy—which she uses to throw ritzy parties in Hollywood nightclubs. I tell you it's fascinating stuff you've been missing. This Bugsy's got a wild temper. Beats people over the head with a gun butt when they displease him. You either do what he likes or pop goes your weasel."

Randolph laughed and slipped his arm around her waist, pulling her against him. "Has anyone ever made love to you in a snowbank?"

"Not lately," she whispered, snuggling against him. "Find one quick and I'm yours for the taking."

Randolph looked up and down the street. "How about this one?"

"Looks nice and comfy to me," she said, letting herself fall backward into the snowbank. "All right, darling, mush."

38

He sat on the edge of the bed in a lethargic stupor. The whole thing was turning into a colossal disaster. Who would have believed that so many things could go wrong?

Virginia Hill came out of the bathroom and started rummaging through drawers. She was naked but Siegel looked right through her.

"Where's my fucking Benadryl?" she cried, tossing clothes out of drawers with the frenzy of a junkie looking for a fix. "This goddamn hay fever's killing me. I hate this fucking place."

Siegel ignored her. He had problems of his own. It was December 26, 1946, and that night was to be the grand opening of the Flamingo. It was the moment he'd been waiting for, had worked so hard to achieve, but nobody of any importance in Hollywood had accepted his invitation. George Raft would come, and Georgie Jessel, Charles Coburn, George Sanders, Sonny Tufts—all relative small-timers without the glamour to draw crowds or excite columnists. Daisy Miller had rejected his offer of $25,000 to headline the first two weeks and finally he'd signed Jimmy Durante, with Tommy Wonder, Baby Rose Marie, the Tunetoppers, Eddie Jackson, and Xavier Cugat's orchestra. It was a good show but not real top class like Daisy Miller.

But that was the least of his problems. He'd just received a call from Los Angeles saying that the Constellations he'd chartered to ferry customers would probably be grounded by weather. So now even the weather was conspiring against him.

It had been an incredible year. Had he been a religious man, he'd have sworn the gods had turned against him. His contractor, Del Webb, had broken ground a year ago, but though the main building housing the showroom, casino, restaurant and cocktail lounge was ready for business, the ninety-two hotel rooms were still unfinished.

And the cost, first estimated at $1.5 million, had spiraled to $4 million, and it would probably take another $2 million to bring it to completion.

Lansky and his dago backers were screaming at him, but what did they know about building a hotel in a postwar market where priorities still existed? When Webb couldn't furnish the necessary steel, copper, tile, fixtures, or piping, Siegel had gone into the black market and paid dearly for everything he bought. The plumbing bill alone was $1 million. Instead of the usual chicken wire and stucco, the hotel walls were of solid concrete. He had demanded imported woods and marble and bullied architects into supplying the latest in designs. Plasterers, painters, and carpenters were flown in from Los Angeles, San Francisco, Denver, and Salt Lake City and paid fifty dollars a day to get the place ready in time for the scheduled opening.

For a while it appeared that he might make it. Then everything went crazy. The solid-concrete boiler room was too small and had to be blasted out and rebuilt. The air-conditioning system had been incorrectly installed with intakes but no outlets. And to add insult to injury, his own penthouse suite had been spoiled by a heavy concrete beam running down the middle of the spacious living room, resting so low that he couldn't walk under it without lowering his head. The only solution was to divide the room in half, depriving himself of the romping space he'd grown used to since leaving the Lower East Side.

Driven into a frenzy by what he considered wholesale incompetence, he had fumed and cursed as he prowled the area with Ape at his side, prodding workers into making greater efforts. A cigarette butt on the ground or a fingerprint on a newly painted wall was enough to send him into a maniacal rage.

Virginia Hill found the Benadryl and went back into the bathroom. Siegel stood up and walked out on the small balcony overlooking the enormous sky-blue swimming pool and garden terrace that represented a quarter million dollars' worth of palm trees, shrubs, flowers, grass, and concrete. He'd personally selected the wrought-iron furniture and striped umbrellas. A great feeling of pride welled in his chest. It was pretty as a picture postcard. He'd transformed thirty acres of desert wasteland into an opulent vacation oasis that was unequaled anywhere on earth.

When Rufus and Henry arrived at the Flamingo that evening they found more employees than customers in the large casino. It was easy to distinguish between the two. The employees were the only ones wearing tuxedoes.

"The goddamn place looks like a convention of headwaiters," Rufus said as the two men went into the cocktail lounge and were seated by maitre d' Rosario Bellini, who signaled importantly for a waiter.

On the small stage that provided continuous entertainment a woman was singing a Cole Porter medley, accompanied by a jazz combo, the music clashing with the casino sound, a cacophony of whirring and clinking slot machines, the jingle of bells and coins, the smooth clicking of roulette wheels, the cries of players, the monotone of dealers.

From their table they could watch the action at the gambling tables.

"Ain't this great?" Rufus said with an edge of sarcasm. "All the gamblers at the crap tables are locals, guys Siegel drove out of Los Angeles years ago, so now they've settled here. It's an old custom for local operators to attend openings and try to bust out the new joint."

The waiter took their orders and a moment later Ruth Bellini came to their table. "Cigarettes, cigars, chewing gum?"

Rufus took one look and started beaming, his gray eyes glinting mischievously. Ruth was wearing a brief, strapless costume with black stockings and black garter belt, six inches of white thighs showing.

"Yes, Chesterfield," Henry said. "How about you, Rufus?"

Boutwell seemed in a trance, his gray eyes moving up and down her body, devouring the white flesh. "I'm set for now," he said, "but be sure and come back later, pretty little lady. You're a feast for these poor old eyes."

She smiled demurely and returned her attention to Henry. He gave her a five-dollar bill. She took the money and handed him the cigarettes, her fingers barely touching his hand. Their eyes met and Henry said, "Keep the change."

She looked surprised. "Well, thank you, kind sir."

"You're welcome," he said.

"Now, don't forget to come back," Rufus said. "We're heavy smokers."

She gave Henry a parting smile and he thought he detected an invitation in her lovely dark eyes. He watched her go, his gaze dropping to the seams in her black stockings, straight arrows pointing to barely concealed, well-rounded buttocks.

"I've got a hard-on that would put White Lightning to shame,"

Rufus said. "See that look she gave you? Boy, I'd fuck that little filly in two seconds flat." He paused and looked closely at Henry. "Here's your break. You can tear off a little piece, make a new man out of you."

Henry smiled as his eyes followed her across the room. Her back was to him and when she bent forward to hand cigarettes to a customer, he noticed she was wearing black panties. He looked away and thought of Camilla and wished that she were headlining here tonight instead of Jimmy Durante.

Only a month before they had met quite by accident in the lobby of the Jefferson, a small, sedate hotel in Washington that Henry preferred for its privacy. They had repaired to the dimly lit bar for a drink and Camilla had indicated that her relationship with Bacino was definitely cooling down.

"Oh, we're still close friends, and I do like and respect him, but he's found other playmates for his bed."

"The man's a fool," Henry said, "but I'm glad. Now maybe you'll come to your senses."

She smiled. "I hear you, darling," she said, patting his hand.

He looked deeply into her emerald eyes with the bright gold flecks. She never ages, he thought, and wondered about himself. His hair was sprinkled with gray and the wrinkles along his jawline were deepening.

Henry leaned forward and they kissed lightly. "I'm still waiting in the wings," he said.

"I know, darling, but I need a little time to get my own emotions straightened out. I was with Vince a long time. I just can't walk out of one situation and into another just like that."

Henry felt a surge of anger and fought to control it. "Cami, my love for you has been constant through all these years, but there are times when I don't think you feel quite the same about me."

She released his hand and leaned back in the booth. "Henry, to be truthful, and, God, I *do* want to be truthful with you and myself, I honestly don't know how I feel about you. I haven't let myself think about it for such a long time. I've blocked the old days out of my head. It wasn't easy but I've done it. That was another world, Henry. An ugly world that you made magical for a moment, but ugly nonetheless." She made a gesture of helplessness with her hands. "Let's not talk about it, please."

"All right."

She reached into her purse for a cigarette. "Oh, about that lunatic

Bugsy Siegel who's building that hotel in Las Vegas. Vince and I went to Acapulco with him on his yacht and you wouldn't believe some of the things that madman did." And she'd gone on to tell him about the cruise in great detail.

"Hot damn," Rufus said, bringing Henry out of his reverie, "what I wouldn't give to be young again. But next time around I'd like to look like you or Randy."

Henry ignored the compliment. "What's the matter, Rufus—getting tired of Iola?"

"Hey, what're you talking about? There's nothing wrong with a man getting a little poontang on the side once in a while. Keeps his wick slick."

Henry opened the pack of Chesterfield and offered one to Rufus. "Here, you better start smoking. You want her back, don't you?"

"Me?" Rufus acted shocked. "It's you she gave the eye to, pal. It's simple. Want to dip your wick in that little gal's poontang? Just say the word. Rufus will wave his magic wand and there she'll be in your bed."

"And how do you intend on accomplishing this magic?"

"Oh, I'm sure Mr. Bugsy would be more than happy to accommodate one of his principal benefactors, don't you think?"

Henry shook his head in disgust. "I'd be damned before I'd let a slimy character like Siegel pimp for me. What's wrong with you? You've been pulling people's pants down for years and making suckers out of them and now you want that gangster to do it to you?"

A hard glint came into Rufus's gray eyes. "Don't get carried away, Henry. No two-bit punk like Siegel will ever make a sucker out of me. If you don't want her, say so and I'll take her myself. I was just trying to do you a good turn. This living like a fucking priest ain't good for you. Sooner or later you're going to explode. I like for my people to have good dispositions. Lately you've been chafing at the bit and all you need's a good piece of ass. Straighten you right out."

Henry pushed his chair back and stood up. "Let's go try our luck at the tables. That's more in your line."

Rufus looked at him as though he had lost his mind. "Are you plumb loco? The only time I gamble is when I'm on the other side of the table. The house's percentage will grind you into dust."

"So what," Henry said. "Set a limit and quit when you reach it.

Win or lose, it's not going to hurt you. You could buy this place and give it to Iola for a birthday gift and it wouldn't even show on the balance sheet."

Rufus reluctantly pushed his glass of cola aside and stood up. "It's not a question of money but principles."

"Then watch me give it a whirl. I have no principles."

Rufus grunted. "Trying to get your mind off that poontang? You think losing a little money's going to help?"

"You know, Rufus, you're a devious old bastard."

Rufus chuckled. "First time you've called me old. Keep smiling when you say that, pardner."

"I wonder where our Mr. Bugsy's keeping himself tonight?"

"Easy on the Bugsy," Rufus cautioned. "I hear it's like waving a red flag in front of a raging bull. Now, since you've got your mind made up, let's hit a crap table. It's the best odds in the house if you know what you're doing."

For the occasion Virginia Hill wore an orange-red gown, which her designer called The Flamingo, and with Siegel at her side in a dinner jacket with a flower in his lapel she marched grandly into the showroom for the evening's performance. Others were already at their table, and once Jimmy Durante came on stage, Siegel excused himself and went into the casino to check the action.

When he saw Rufus and Henry at the cashier's cage, he hurried over to greet them.

"Rufus, Henry, glad you could make it. Where's the governor?"

Rufus smiled crookedly. "Has a little headache. Seems that all the commotion down here the past few months got him a little upset. Poor man worries about his public image."

Siegel frowned. "The fucking reporters wrote a lot of shit, you know. Blew everything out of proportion. Well, how do you like the place?"

"Absolutely first class, Ben," Rufus said.

Siegel twisted his mouth angrily. "All first class except for the trashy crowd. My planes are grounded in L.A. and all I've got here's a bunch of local jerks."

"Trying to bust you out? Are they hurting?"

He shook his head, a worried expression in his eyes. "Hurting? They're killing me. The house's down nearly a hundred grand. Well, what the hell, it's bound to turn—it's got to. That's the law of percentages, right?"

"Absolutely," Rufus said. "By the way, how come the big waterfall sign out front's dark? I thought you'd have that thing lit up like a Christmas tree."

Siegel rocked back on his heels and slapped his fist into the palm of his hand. It sounded like a pistol shot. "Everything's gone wacko. That sign cost me a fortune. When it's lighted up, with the color spots playing on the spray, you can see it a mile away. So it's dark tonight because a fucking cat crawled in the sump and had six kittens. The only way to get them out of there was to flood them out. I told the grounds keeper to leave them alone."

"I didn't know you liked cats," Rufus said.

"I don't. I hate them. But it's bad luck for a gambler to touch a cat." He paused and again punched his fist into his open hand. "The way things are going right now, I should've drowned the fuckers."

Rufus took Siegel's arm and moved away from Henry. "I'll be back," he said, winking at Henry.

He steered Siegel toward the cocktail lounge. "Listen, Ben, I need a big favor."

"Christ, anything, Rufus, just name it."

"That cigarette girl in the lounge. Think you could fix Henry up with her? He's kind of smitten. I think it'd do him a world of good to dip his wick in some cute dish like that."

Siegel looked uncertain. "Shit, Rufus, I don't know. She's no hooker. Besides, she's married to the lounge captain."

"That can be our secret," Rufus said. "I'd consider it a mighty important favor, Ben."

Siegel pinched his chin, his blue eyes deep in thought. "Okay, let me see what I can do."

"You got a room here he can use?"

"Sure, the room in back of my office. Got a big couch and I'll have some stuff sent up, champagne and snacks."

"Thanks, Ben. I won't forget this."

"My pleasure."

"Tell her it's the tall fellow that gave her the five-dollar tip for a pack of Chesterfield. She seemed attracted to him."

"Wait here, I'll be right back."

Ruth Bellini saw Siegel come into the lounge and she smiled when he headed her way.

"Ruth, honey," he said, his mouth close to her ear. "Remember the tall good-looking guy that gave you five skins for Chesterfields?"

"Sure I do, Ben. Wasn't it okay for me to accept it?"

"Oh, yeah, baby. But listen, he's stuck on you. Now, he's very important in this town. Him and the guy that's with him just about own the whole goddamn state. The old guy's probably one of the richest men in America."

She nodded, her eyes puzzled. "What do you mean, he's stuck on me?"

"What do you mean, what do I mean? You know what I mean. Look, I've never asked you to do this before, and I won't ever again, but how about giving this guy a little fuck?"

She gasped, her eyes widening in amazement. "Are you serious?"

"Of course. What's the matter with you? It's no big deal. Go to the room in back of my office, give him a little toss, and come back. He's not going to bite you."

She bit down hard on a thumbnail. "Gosh, I don't know."

"Look, there's a C-note in it for you. You can buy yourself something nice and no one will be the wiser."

"It makes me feel like a prostitute."

"That's bullshit."

She bit into the other thumbnail. "He is kind of handsome." She paused, her large brown eyes studying Siegel. "You promise you'll never ask me to do it again?"

"You've got my word, baby," he said, reaching down to cup her buttock in his hand. "And thanks a million. I won't forget it."

"When do you want me to go? And what about Rosario? Won't he get suspicious if I leave?"

"Don't worry your pretty little head. I'll send him on an errand. When you see him take off, just go to the room. And, Christ, smile. You're going to a fucking party, not a funeral."

Ruth tapped lightly on the door and opened it. A small lamp barely illuminated the room and she had trouble making out the man sitting on the couch. Somehow his silhouette didn't seem as tall as she remembered.

She stood in the open doorway a moment, undecided, then softly closed the door and stepped into the room.

"Better lock it," the man said from the shadows.

Even the voice was different. "I think I've got the wrong room," she stammered.

"No, you don't, little lady. You've got the right room and the right man. Come sit next to me."

"Aren't you the man that was with the one who gave me the five-dollar tip?"

"That's right, little lady."

"But Mr. Siegel said it was the other man I was to see."

Rufus laughed. "Mr. Siegel's a little confused tonight. Now you wouldn't want to upset him by making me unhappy, would you? Mr. Siegel values my friendship."

She took another step toward him, trying to make out his features. "But he said the other man was stuck on me."

"Well, so am I stuck on you, sweetheart. Come right over here and sit down next to me, and I'll tell you the story of the traveling salesman and the farmer's daughter."

In the next two weeks the Flamingo dropped $300,000. In a final act of desperation Siegel closed the casino, announcing that it wouldn't reopen until the hotel part was completed. Well aware of the house's edge in the law of averages, he began complaining that he'd been clipped by his own crooked employees.

In the next few months Siegel became a man possessed. He fired all the dealers and hired security guards to stop sneak thieves from stealing truckloads of furniture and fixtures. Meanwhile, his enemies in downtown Las Vegas were spreading rumors that the hotel was a hangout for Eastern gangsters and that Siegel was a man with a homicidal temper.

Giving vent to her own violent nature, Virginia Hill added spice to the unfolding drama. In a fit of jealousy she had swung a haymaker and dislocated the jaw of a British actress who claimed she was engaged to Siegel. In turn, Bugsy had swung on Virginia, knocking her down. "You ain't no lady," one story quoted him as saying. Virginia's response was to rush to their penthouse suite and swallow a handful of sleeping pills. Discovered in time, she was taken to the hospital to have her stomach pumped out.

At one time Siegel had four girl friends stashed in various rooms around town. The tension between him and Virginia grew so volatile that few dared approach the couple.

It wasn't long before newspaper and magazine writers were spreading the stories nationwide. It wasn't the kind of press Rufus appreciated and he let his feelings be known to Jesse Stelk, who confidently assured him that time and patience would solve all problems.

With the hotel finally completed, the Flamingo reopened its doors in late March. Even with the new dealers the casino continued to run in the red, a phenomenon interpreted by Lansky's Italian backers as high-handed skimming by Siegel. No other explanation satisfied them. They had been in the gambling business far too long to be made patsies of by a wild man like Benjamin Siegel.

The second week in May, Vince Bacino flew to New York for a sitdown with the three most powerful Cosa Nostra bosses in that city. All three—Frank Costello, Joseph Bonanno, and Tommy Lucchese—were in the prime of life and at the peak of their careers.

Although the press referred to them as Mafia bosses, they themselves never used the word Mafia. That was something they had left behind in the old country. Here in America they had adopted a new terminology, Cosa Nostra—Our Thing. There were twenty-six Cosa Nostra families in America and each was made up of a boss; underboss; *consigliere*, whose role was to advise the boss on matters of policy; *capiregime*, known as captains or skippers; and *soldati*, the soldiers, or buttons, who did most of the dirty work.

The four bosses met in a private dining room at the Villa Capri on lower Third Avenue. The owner, Jocko, a *soldato* in Costello's family, personally undertook the task of serving his guests. Bowing and beaming, his round face glistening with perspiration, he went about his work with the efficiency and humility of a man humbled by the presence of his distinguished guests.

The four bosses had entered through an alley door that led directly to their private dining room. Crash cars blocked both ends of the alley and *soldati* were posted at strategic spots in the alley and restaurant.

All was in order for the sitdown. The large round table was laden with a variety of steaming pasta dishes in silver casseroles, soups in exquisite china tureens, huge silver platters of antipasto with mountains of salami, dried sausages, cold sliced veal, artichoke hearts with sauce rémoulade, stuffed mushrooms with béchamel sauce, oysters baked in oil and covered with parsley, oysters baked in Parmesan cheese, cold salmon mousse, clams on the half shell, anchovies in oil and with peppers, shrimp and tuna stuffed in tomatoes, eggplant with prosciutto and Bel Paese, thin slices of tender bresaola, and zucchini, sweet peppers, radishes, asparagus, carrots, cardoons, broccoli, Roman garlic bread, and a seemingly infinite variety of cheeses and fruits.

There were jugs of red wine in wicker baskets, magnums of champagne in silver ice buckets, and bottles of mineral water. It was a feast fit for four Italian kings.

"Hey, Jocko, what's this, a fucking Chink dinner?" Lucchese laughed.

Jocko beamed happily. "I fixed all your favorite dishes. That way, see, everybody's happy." It was the first and last time he would speak to his guests that evening. Without having been told, Jocko knew that when the bosses met in that room everything had to be served at once. And no one was permitted in the room while they talked.

"*Ciao*," said Costello as he reached for a carrot stick.

Jocko bowed his way out of the room. There was a click from the other side and Bacino knew that one of the *soldati* had locked the door.

They nibbled at the antipasto and drank mineral water and talked about the coming season for the Dodgers and Yankees. They reminisced about Babe Ruth and Lou Gehrig and argued over the prowess of Joe DiMaggio and Ted Williams. Bacino listened in silence. Although he had met these men on various occasions and they had treated him as an equal, as all bosses were held to be equal whether or not they were on the commission—a body composed of ten bosses who arbitrated jurisdictional disputes between families—still Bacino felt like an outsider in this Eastern city, a feeling that sharpened his nerve ends to the point where he weighed every word spoken for double meaning or subtle insult. As the son of a boss and a boss himself for many years, he instinctively distrusted all men he could not rule through fear.

"Hey,Vince, when are you guys in L.A. going to get off your asses and get major league ball down there?" Bonanno asked.

Bacino looked squarely at Bonanno, his cold dark eyes expressionless. "Joe, you making money with baseball?"

"Plenty. Sports betting's big money these days. It used to be the bangtails got all the play, but now all the sports get plenty of action."

"When was the last time you fixed a game?" Bacino asked.

Bonanno laughed. "You don't have to fix games. Just balance the books and collect the vig."

Bacino nodded thoughtfully. "We've got the Coast League," he said, "and we're good for two fixes a week minimum, where we spread the action with the Jews and collect a bundle."

Costello coughed politely and wiped his mouth with a linen napkin. "Vince, that sounds great. Just take pity on our layoff guys."

"We don't move no action back East," Bacino said without raising his voice. "Nobody out here gives a shit about minor league ball."

"Sounds like a good racket," Costello said, smiling at Bacino to show that no insult had been intended. "Here, how about some of this clam soup. Smells delicious."

They passed the soup tureen around and each man helped himself. They ate in silence for a while, the only sound the slurping of the soup. Then the various pasta dishes made the rounds and the men exclaimed their appreciation of Jocko's culinary skills.

They passed the wine around and drank a toast to friendship. Bacino could tell that Costello was getting anxious to get to the point of the sitdown, but he said nothing to provide an opening. Finally, Costello said, "Now, Vince, we wanted you here because we've got to make a hit in your country, so we need your approval."

Bacino chewed on his pasta and kept a straight face. "Who's the mark?"

"Three guesses," Lucchese laughed.

"I don't need three guesses," Bacino said. "It's Bugsy and it's about time."

"Right," Costello said. "He's been fucking with our money and this guy's gone off the deep end. There's no talking to him. He no *capisce* English no more. Got bugs in his brain."

Bacino sipped his wine and slowly looked at all three men. "Why not hit him in Las Vegas?"

Costello shook his head. "The commission made a law. We don't want no gang killings in Nevada."

Bonanno laughed. "Not good business to shit where you eat."

Costello ignored him. "We've got a good setup in Nevada and we want to keep it clean. Of course, it's okay to clip somebody there if you can bury the body so nobody finds it, but that's out with Benny. There's no way to set this guy up. He knows how the fucking game's played. So we hit him in Los Angeles. I hear he goes back and forth a lot. So what's his routine over there? Got any idea?"

Bacino had been expecting this for a long time and had been monitoring Siegel's movements for months.

"I know this piece of shit's movements better than my own," he said, smiling for the first time. "I've got a couple good men planted in the Flamingo. One travels with him wherever he goes. When Bugsy comes to Los Angeles, he stays at Virginia Hill's house on North Linden Drive."

"Ain't she in Europe?" Lucchese asked.

"Right—she got pissed at Bugsy and took off for Paris. But he's got a key to her house. That broad is screwier than he is, if that's possible."

"She's fucking lucky she's in Paris or we'd clip her too," Lucchese said. "Never liked or trusted that bitch."

"So what's the routine?" Costello persisted.

"He never comes to L.A. without going to Drucker's barbershop. Then he usually fucks around town, visits George Raft, books a few bets, maybe lays one of his movie stars, goes out to dinner with a couple friends, and he's back at Virginia's house by ten, eleven o'clock. Got to get his beauty sleep. I'm told he smears cold cream all over his face and neck, wears an elastic chin strap and sleep shade. Goes to bed like a fucking actress that's over the hill. Drives him nuts that he's losing his hair. Scared shitless of getting bald."

"Well, that's one thing he can stop worrying about," Bonanno laughed. "We're going to solve that problem permanently."

"What kind of setup is Virginia's place for a hit?" Costello asked.

"Perfect. Lots of bushes where you can hide and wait for hours without attracting attention. The house's below Sunset so the Beverly Hills cops don't patrol there as much. All the big shots live north of Sunset. Now this Bugsy's real fancy. Never pulls the curtains—just walks around there like he ain't got a worry in the world."

"Sounds perfect," Costello said. "Can you provide a crash car?"

"No problem," Bacino said. "We'll take care of the whole package if you say so."

"Thanks, but that's Meyer's problem. Benny's his fucking man. He sold us a bill of goods on the idea he could control him. Now he's got to make good on the money and the hit."

"That's right," Bonanno said. "We've got to keep these fucking Jews in line."

Bacino poured himself a glass of champagne and passed the magnum around. He held the glass up and smiled. "To Bugsy—the sooner he goes under the better. He's been one royal pain in the ass for years."

They raised their glasses and drank the toast. Bacino lowered his glass. "My advice is don't send no more fucking Jews as advisers over to my country. One in a lifetime is one too many."

They laughed and Costello leaned forward and looked closely at Bacino. "Vince, you know, Bugsy fucked up, but we've got big plans for Las Vegas—all of Nevada. We're going to build a lot of joints and most of them will be fronted by Jews that we can trust, Meyer's people. Don't forget, Meyer's a sharp businessman. This guy's a fucking genius in his own way. Nevada's going to be an open state. Families from all over the country will want pieces of casinos. Now what we've got to do is make sure they go by the rules. We don't want no trouble. No hassles. Everything nice and smooth."

"That's right," Bonanno said. "It's a golden opportunity and we don't want nobody fucking it up. I know Chicago wants in right away. Then Cleveland's moving some Jews in to finish building the Desert Inn, a new joint just started by a two-bit hustler from San Diego, Wilbur Clark. Ran out of dough before the foundation even had time to set. Someday that goddamn strip of highway's going to be the biggest gambling resort the world has ever seen."

"And we're going to control all of it," Costello said. "And that's where you come in, Vince. We'd like for you to become the arbitrator. You're going to be the man, the guy that keeps the wheels greased, settles all petty bullshit that comes up on a daily basis. If a couple of families get at each other's throats, the commission will step in. Otherwise, you handle it."

Bacino could barely conceal his pleasure. "Sounds like a big job," he said, "but I'll give it a whirl. You know, I'm thinking of building a place of my own."

"You've got to have somebody else front it," Costello said. "You can't have one of us up front."

"I've got Lew Spark—he's real tight with Chicago. I'm going in with them and Spark will front for both our families."

Lucchese looked doubtful. "Hey, let's not overbuild. Let's test the water before we all dive in and drown."

Bacino shook his head. "There's no way you can overbuild that place. Every joint you build will multiply in value every year. Double and triple, no end to it. Bugsy had a great idea. His problem was that he got in over his head. He's a fucking lunatic. Knows shit about business."

Bonanno slapped the table. "And he's a fucking thief. Stole from his own people. Never mind this bullshit about no honor among thieves. We've got to be honorable with our people. You don't fuck friends."

Bacino nodded approvingly. "So who has Meyer picked for the hit?"

Costello shrugged. "Nobody yet. Got a suggestion?"

"Yeah, Frankie Carbo. He owes Bugsy one and he's a fucking good worker. He's got the balls to pull it off without a hitch."

"And he's Italian," Lucchese chuckled. "I like the twist. An Italian killing a Jew for a Jew for Italians. I'll tell Meyer."

"Okay, enough business," Costello said. "Let's eat and enjoy ourselves."

Bacino's eyes remained impassive, but deep inside he was rejoicing. For him the business at hand had been the real banquet.

On the evening of June 20, 1947, John "Frankie" Carbo hunched in the shadow of a rose-covered pergola. The barrel of a .30-caliber Army carbine rested on a crossbar of the latticework as he sighted and gently squeezed off the entire clip. Nine slugs slammed through a fourteen-inch pane of glass. Two of them tore apart the handsome face of Benjamin "Bugsy" Siegel. He died instantly, his blood-soaked body slumping sideways on a chintz-covered sofa in the living room of Virginia Hill's pink Moorish mansion at 810 North Linden Drive.

Twenty minutes later, two other Lansky fronts walked into Bugsy's Flamingo Hotel in Las Vegas and took over the operation. In Beverly Hills police cars hadn't yet arrived at the Hill house—they didn't know Siegel was dead—but in Las Vegas they knew that the city was finally coming to life. When the sun broke over the desert that morning, the whole town was bathed in gold.

39

It was a cool evening in November. Rufus stood on the balcony of his tenth-floor penthouse suite at the Monarch and gazed proudly at the miles of blazing neon that had transformed that stretch of U.S. 91 into what was now the famous Las Vegas Strip.

The Monarch was the latest in a string of plush casino-hotels that had risen from the desert floor in the seven years since the sensational publicity following Bugsy Siegel's murder had really put the town on the map.

Las Vegas was a boom town—the hottest in history. For Rufus it was a dream come true. But from his tenth-floor perch it looked more like a mirage—in Technicolor. When he thought of it, he knew there was something unreal about it. It was more a state of mind than a place. The tourists were flocking in by the millions. Eight million last year. Once an average American saw the place he was hooked for life. Where else could anyone get a steak dinner, drinks, and see big movie stars performing in person for ten bucks? Or enjoy the luxury provided by hotels like the Flamingo, the Sands, the Desert Inn, the Sahara, the Thunderbird, or the Monarch, the first high-rise on the Strip. A joint venture between the Chicago and Los Angeles Cosa Nostra families, the Monarch was fronted by Lew Spark.

Just last week Rufus had talked to Jack Dempsey, who was contemplating building a three-million-dollar casino-hotel. Then there were the plans for Mae West's Diamond Lil Hotel, and other movie stars were looking for suitable sites. They were the kind of people Las Vegas needed. Their names alone were worth millions in free advertising. They were great draws. Because of Bacino, the Monarch had signed Daisy Miller for a half-dozen two-week appearances a year. She was strictly standing room only.

The great thing about Las Vegas was the feeling of freedom people felt the moment they arrived in town. First they lost their inhibitions, then their money. Rufus was not sure that head shrinkers were right when they said compulsive gamblers got more pleasure from losing than winning. Hope was the true gambler's addiction. Each time he came to the table with a new stake he forgot all the times he'd lost. It was another chance to get revenge on Lady Luck. It was a vendetta to the grave. No winner ever knew when to quit and no loser ever quit until he was flat broke.

Rufus was grateful that he'd learned his lesson at a tender age. He knew what it felt like to lose every penny he owned in the world, the sickening feeling that he'd been a sucker. That was something he never could stomach and that was why he'd gotten on the other side of the table. He'd seen gamblers caught in the excitement of the game forget their bodily functions for thirty-six hours, stand at a crap table with swollen feet and bleary eyes. At such times they would rather pit themselves against Dame Fortune than go to bed with the world's most seductive woman. Gambling offered its own sexual gratification.

Rufus heard someone move behind him and Henry Godwin said, "Look out there toward Glitter Gulch. There's so much neon out there that from up here you'd think downtown's on fire."

Rufus chuckled. "Well, Henry, there's lots of money burning holes in pockets. There's your real sawdust joints. Gets the blue-collar dollar. Most of the people who gamble downtown wouldn't be caught dead on the Strip, and vice versa. This place's got them coming and going."

"It must be doing something right," Henry said. "A few years ago the only reason a tourist stopped here was to buy gas and take a leak."

"Yeah, and twenty years ago I bought thousands of acres along this Strip for peanuts and still people thought I was crazy. Now they think I'm a genius."

"Rufus, you had the vision."

"I sure as hell did. It was stuck in the back of my head and I just couldn't shake it loose. And someday it's going to be ten times bigger than it is right now. Hell, there's a half-dozen more places on drawing boards and even the ones finished are already adding on. There's no telling what the future holds." He paused and grinned crookedly. "I have to keep revising my vision."

Henry turned from the railing. "Have you seen Randolph?"

Rufus shook his head, a hard look coming into his eyes. "Last time I saw him he was with that Episcopalian Jew—the great senator from Louisiana, Bryce Silver. What do you suppose was his real name, anyway? Silverman, Silverberg? Something like that, I'll bet."

"I thought you liked him."

"What's there to like? He's a fucking degenerate in every sense of the word. I hear the stories, don't worry. Has a big dong and likes orgies. I like fucking as much as the next guy but I prefer mine in private. If you want my guess, Bacino and his gang probably have him on film—Technicolor, no less—with his dong in some whore's mouth while a chorus boy's fucking him up the ass."

"You've got a vivid imagination. Like him or not, Bryce has been one of our staunchest supporters in the Senate."

"Yeah, and he gets his payoff like the rest. I don't want Randolph hanging around him."

"Then I think you should tell Randolph."

"Don't worry, I plan to. But what's up? Why do you need Randy?"

Henry shrugged. "I came in on the plane with Toombs around five and he was pretty loaded. I told Jenilee to watch him carefully, but I think we ought to get Randolph up to his suite to make sure he shows up for the nine-o'clock rally. It's important. Tomorrow's Election Day."

Rufus looked at his watch. It was seven thirty. For the first time since Rufus had started backing political candidates, the election had turned into a real donnybrook. A young war hero, Philip Austin, who had lost an arm in Germany, had captured the Democratic nomination in the primaries and had gone out to campaign seriously against Toombs, which was something no other rival candidate had ever dared attempt before. Austin, who campaigned in a trailer, claimed to have shaken hands with every registered voter in the state. He promised to end the rule of the bosses. He claimed that his telephone was tapped, his mail opened, and that newspapers either ignored or distorted his speeches.

Austin's underdog approach had created a ground swell of grassroots sympathy that made the outcome unpredictable. As a consequence, Toombs had been forced to get out on the stump and campaign hard for the first time in his life. Randolph had been at his side, writing speeches, working out schedules, but the biggest job had been to keep Toombs from getting falling-down drunk in public.

The telephone rang. Henry answered it, then placed his hand over the mouthpiece as he handed the phone to Rufus.

"It's Jenilee and she sounds upset."

Rufus spoke softly. "What's up, Jenilee?"

"Oh, Mr. Boutwell," she whispered hoarsely, "you must come to the room at once. Please hurry, I can't say anything on the phone."

"We'll be right there. Just keep calm."

Senator Elisha Toombs's suite was also on the tenth floor, but at the other end of the hall. Rufus knocked once and Jenilee opened the door. She was dressed in a robe and her hair was disheveled and her eyes looked frantic. "He's in there," she said, waving toward the bedroom.

"Stay with her," Rufus said, crossing over to the bedroom. Toombs was stretched naked across the bed, his bloated belly a huge mound of gray flesh, his head twisted to the side, his mouth gaping open, his dead eyes frozen in an expression of annoyance. The bubble had burst at the wrong time and that was his final complaint about the vicissitudes of life.

Rufus swore under his breath. "Henry," he called, "come here a minute."

"What the hell," Henry said. "Is he dead?"

"If he's not, it's a damn good imitation."

Henry leaned over the bed and placed his ear against Toombs's chest. He straightened up and shook his head. "He looked bad on the plane."

Rufus sat on the edge of the bed. "Look at him," he said in disgust. "Looks like a beached whale that's been dead a month."

"So what do we do now? Concede the election?"

Rufus stared at him with narrowing eyes. "Not a chance. Listen, Henry, we can't announce his death until after Toombs wins his election. Then, after Randolph's thirtieth birthday on January second, I'll see that the governor gives him the interim appointment. That's been my plan all along. Toombs just moved the timetable up on me a little sooner than I expected."

Henry shook his head. "That means we can't announce his death until the day after tomorrow. How're you going to keep rigor mortis from setting in? Besides . . ."

Rufus waved his hand for silence. "Never mind that, just help me get him in the bathtub. Grab him under the arms and I'll get his feet."

"Let's use the sheet," Henry said, "to be on the safe side."

Rufus nodded and they struggled with the still limp body. Fortunately the bathroom was only a few feet away and they made it almost to the bathtub before Toombs's bowels emptied.

Rufus groaned like a man in pain. "Oh, the dirty bastard. Drop the sheet and let's get him in the tub."

They laid him out gently, careful not to cause any bruises, and Rufus grabbed handfuls of toilet tissue and furiously cleaned up the mess, flushing the toilet several times.

"You can never tell about life," Rufus said, shaking his head in disgust. "After all these years, who'd believe I'd end up on my knees cleaning his shit?"

Henry folded the sheet and tossed it inside a drawer of the sink cabinet. There was something unreal about the moment. The naked corpse in the tub and Rufus wiping up excrement.

Henry stood at the sink and carefully washed his hands. He wished he could walk out of there and just keep going until he was out of Nevada. He had thought of it often in recent years, but deep down he knew it was no longer possible. This was where he'd planted his roots, however shallow their structure, and there was no turning back now.

"Here, let me get in here," Rufus said, moving up to the sink to wash his hands.

"What now?" Henry asked, as he followed Rufus into the bedroom.

"You'll see," he said, grinning. "I've got it all figured out."

He went to the telephone on the nightstand by the bed and dialed. He identified himself and asked for Lew Spark.

"Rufus, what can I do for you?"

"Lew, if there's somebody there with you, just listen and I'll explain later. I need a couple hundred pounds of ice and a portable air conditioner, something really powerful. Send them to my suite right away. But send the ice first and then have someone bring the air conditioner. I don't want anybody making any connections between the two, understand?"

"Want me to come up?"

"No, I can handle it. I'll need more ice later, but I don't want it coming from the same kitchen or being delivered by the same person."

"Why don't I send a hundred pounds now and another hundred pounds in an hour or so—from a different kitchen, of course."

"That's fine. Thanks."

He put the phone down and gestured with his head for Henry to follow him into the living room. Henry went to the bar and mixed himself a drink. Rufus noticed that Jenilee already had a drink and looked like she was getting herself under control.

"Fix me a tomato juice with a shot of Tabasco," Rufus said, sitting in a chair next to Jenilee. "At times like this I wish I was a drinking man," he said, when Henry handed him his juice. "Got the picture?"

"Yes," Henry said. "It may work but it's dangerous. Want me to check the medical end with . . ."

Rufus waved his hand impatiently. "No, no, this is going to be among as few people as possible. I'll have a little talk with Toombs's doctor on Wednesday and he can make the announcement and sign the death certificate. He's a good old boy. No problem there. He may suspect something, but I don't want him part of the conspiracy. This way he'll take my word for it and that'll be it."

"All right, but while we're at it, let's keep Randolph out of it too."

Rufus looked at him as though he had lost his mind. "Keep him out of it? For Christ's sake, he's the one we're doing it for in the first place. When are you going to stop trying to protect that boy."

Henry persisted. "But why get him involved? What do we accomplish?"

"Hey, he's a big boy—he can face the hard facts. You know, Henry, there's a limit to how free a ride you can get in this world. If he'd been here I'd have had him clean up Toombs's shit. But I did it and I did it for him. Like everything else I've done for him. But now he's going to do his part, like we've been doing ours all these years. Listen, Henry, I know that boy a damnsight better than you do, and this won't faze him one bit."

"I think it's as pointless to have him here as it is for me to argue with you once your mind's made up."

The frantic look in Jenilee's eyes was gradually being replaced by a calculating shrewdness that had not escaped Rufus's attention. "Henry, go to my suite and wait there until they deliver the ice and air conditioner I ordered. When nobody's around, sneak them in here. We've got to get him on ice as soon as possible."

Henry left and Rufus said, "Now, Jenilee, this's going to be our secret, you hear?"

"Yes, sir, Mr. Boutwell."

"You wouldn't want Philip Austin to be our next senator, would you?"

"No, sir, Mr. Boutwell."

Rufus smiled. "I'd like to see you in charge of Randolph's Reno office. Be his administrative assistant. Come back to live where your roots are. That's a mighty fine-paying job and you'd have a chance to do a few patronage favors for your friends. Make you mighty popular. And Senator Randolph Godwin will be a good boss, or I'll know why."

"That sounds wonderful," she said, averting her eyes.

"Now, Jenilee, you want to tell me what happened?"

She looked away. "He was making terrible gasping sounds and his eyes suddenly glazed over and he just collapsed on top of me. I knew right then he was gone. I'm so glad you were here to take charge of things."

Rufus took the empty glass out of her hand and went to the bar. "What're you drinking, bourbon?"

She nodded and he fixed her a stiff drink. "Here, drink it all down and then I want you to get dressed and get yourself under control. I'm going to need you right here for the next few days. We're going to have to act like nothing's happened."

"What do we do about tonight? He's supposed to be at the rally. Austin's going to be there. It's not a debate, but they're both supposed to make their final speech of the campaign from the same platform. It's going to be broadcast on radio all over the state and everybody in the press is going to be there."

"I know," Rufus said, "and I've been giving it some thought. We need a good explanation for his absence. I thought of sending Randolph, but that may not be too good an idea, seeing what I have in mind for him later. I think it'd be best if you went there and told the people the senator's car broke down near Goldfield and he won't be in till late tonight. Then I think you should tell them the senator asked you to say a few words on his behalf and say something about the importance of seniority in the United States Senate and the important committee positions he holds because of his great experience and knowledge of how the system works in our nation's capital. And anything else you can think of along these lines. Now, I'm depending on you, Jenilee. You can do it. It's not the first time you've had to sub for him."

As he waited for the ice and air conditioner in Rufus's suite, Henry paced up and down the spacious living room. He still wished there was some way to keep Randolph out of it. What bothered Henry was the motivation. Was Rufus going to tell him to get Randolph further obligated to him, and further corrupted in the process, or was it that Rufus needed Randolph's appreciation, needed to have his own ego stroked for the risk he was taking on Randolph's behalf?

The more Henry thought about it, the more convinced he became that he should be the one to brief Randolph on Rufus's plans. He picked up the phone and called Randolph's room. When there was no answer he called Lew Spark.

"Lew, have you seen Randolph?"

There was a brief hesitation at the other end of the line. "Yes, he's with Bryce taking steam."

"Thanks, Lew. Could you leave a message for him to call me soon as he gets out?"

"No problem, Henry. Will do."

Lew Spark's private steam room on the executive floor was known to the in group as King Dong's Playroom. King Dong was Bryce Silver, the United States senator from Louisiana. Nature had so generously endowed Silver that women fled in panic when they saw him fully aroused. Even hardened hookers either fled or tripled their price. In certain swinging circles in Washington, New Orleans, and Las Vegas, Silver was referred to as the "cunt breaker."

Silver felt nature had selected him for special consideration. And he enjoyed sharing his gift with others, which explained his preference for group sex.

A staunch Republican, Silver was in his third term as a senator, having taken a leave of absence during World War II to fly fighter planes in the European theater. Now, as a colonel in the Air Force Reserve and chairman of the Armed Services Committee, Silver was permitted to fly Air Force jets whenever he traveled. He was a close friend of Jesse Stelk and was secretly supported by Carlos Marcello, the boss of the New Orleans Cosa Nostra family, which meant that Silver had the proper credentials when he visited Las Vegas. Everything was complimentary, including women, and five thousand in markers on each visit. All his comped expenses, of course, were being duly recorded in a private ledger for future reference in the event Silver ever gave his patrons cause to regret their generosity. This was standard operating procedure at all casinos, whether the recipient was a Washington politician or a local newsman. It was charged to public relations and sooner or later became tax deductible.

Randolph was sitting with Silver in the steam room, when the door opened and a young woman walked in and stood before them in a white ankle-length terry robe. Randolph took one look at her face and blinked in astonishment. For a moment he thought it was Justine Moreau and all he could think was "What kind of sick joke is this?"

Then she smiled and said, "I'm Ruth Bellini. I'm told you gentlemen want a little party."

After helping Rufus cover Toombs's body with the ice and set up the air conditioner in the bathroom, Henry decided to go look for Randolph. Although he'd never used the steam room, he had no trouble finding it.

He found the redwood door, opened it, and stepped into the room before he realized what was going on inside. Ruth Bellini, now naked, was leaning over Silver, who was sitting on a bench, and she was holding his enormous penis in both hands and licking the head of it like a child with an ice cream cone. Randolph was standing behind her, his hands gripping her hips, pulling her tightly against him, as he pumped away inside of her. His head was thrown back and his mouth twisted in a satanic grin, or so it seemed to Henry as he stood transfixed by the orgiastic tableau. He spun around and left without being noticed.

He took the elevator to the casino and went outside into the blinding incandescence of belching neon. He began walking at a rapid pace, his thoughts a jumble as he tried to sort them out.

He pounded his fist into his hand. Perhaps the problem was his. He was, as the popular saying went, square. Years ago he had tried to understand Alicia's sexual needs. She had talked about her fantasies, and perhaps had participated in group sex in Europe, but he hadn't let himself think about it. Had never visualized it. And now he wondered how he'd have reacted if he'd walked into one of her orgies.

Yes, there was no doubt about it, he was square. But what was the alternative. How different was he from his son? And how responsible was he for that difference? That little boy he first saw in that San Francisco home was not the man in the steam room. That little boy was brave and vulnerable, innocent, waiting to be shaped by those with the responsibility. Alicia had been right in her warning. Rufus had corrupted Randolph. Aunt Caroline had described the process in bitter terms, but he'd ignored her too. He had seen the greed in his growing son's eyes, heard the lies, and had felt helpless to change it.

The plain truth of it was that he'd lacked the courage to defy Rufus. Rufus was stronger, more reckless, and therefore more dangerous. He remembered how he'd fumed for days after the confrontation in his bedroom when Rufus had returned from Switzerland. If he could have gotten out of bed, he might have loaded his Spencer rifle and killed Rufus the way he had the Pikes. By the time his leg had healed, the anger had receded, and he'd done nothing. The only thing he prided himself on was that he never asked for a percentage of Yulee's mine. After all, Yulee had promised him half of it, and all of it after his death. He'd thought of it often in those days, especially when the mine went into production and millions in gold came pouring out, but Henry never could make himself say the words. As he saw it, to accept the money would have been tantamount to sanctioning the old man's murder.

Well, it was too late to change anything. Randolph would be thirty in two months. His life was in his own hands. Or rather in Rufus's. At any rate, it was out of Henry's. But he loved his son. Was there nothing he could do to help him?

By now he had left the developed area of the Strip and had run out of sidewalk. He walked along the edge of the road, facing the oncoming traffic, and ahead he could see the lights of the airport. Suddenly he realized why he was walking toward the airport. He had to get away. Away from the bloated corpse in the bathtub, from the sordidness of the steam room, from the sickness of Las Vegas itself. He ached for the tranquility of his ranch. He wanted to be with his horses. To ride and to mend equipment and fences, to chop wood, to do physical labors from sunrise to sunset, and to forget the images just stamped into his brain.

40

Years ago, when he was jitterbug king of Revere Beach, Joey Alongi was known as the Italian Adonis. Nearly six feet tall, with an athlete's physique, Joey had black hair that covered his head in soft curls, eyes like ripe olives under long eyelashes, a nose sculptured to the precise dimensions of his oval-shaped face, a generous mouth, gleaming white teeth, and a dimpled chin that would have done justice to Cary Grant.

But life had left brutal marks on Joey Alongi. Too much booze, too many women, and too many sleepless nights at gaming tables had taken their toll.

A day had come when an Irishman, with no respect for his Adonis features, had smashed him across the nose with a sash weight wrapped in a newspaper. The blow nearly killed him. He was unconscious twenty-one days and lingered in the hospital another two months while doctors tried to repair his jaw, cheekbones and the bridge of his nose with gristle taken from the lower part of his chest. Before leaving the hospital he was advised to return for plastic surgery when the repairs had healed, but he never went back. He knew his Adonis days were over and there were more pressing problems that required his immediate attention.

He stalked his quarry nearly four months before snaring him. By then he knew the Irishman's every movement and most of his habits. One habit that appealed to Joey was the urgency with which the Irishman often relieved himself in the bushes near his garage before entering his home after a long night of beer guzzling at his favorite pub.

Hidden in the bushes this one night, Joey waited until the Irishman started urinating before jumping up and sapping him behind the ear with a blackjack. Joey caught him as he was falling and gently lowered him to the ground. Working swiftly, he tied his hands behind his back with friction tape and dumped him into the trunk of his Oldsmobile.

It was late October and Revere Beach was deserted. Dragging the Irishman across the sand by his feet until he was under the pier, Joey threw a rope across a beam, tied it to the Irishman's neck, and pulled on it until the man's toes were barely touching the sand. By now he had regained consciousness and was trying to beg for mercy, but the rope cutting across his windpipe confined him to grunts and groans.

Joey loosened the Irishman's belt and lowered his trousers and underwear. "Go on and take another leak," Joey said. "It'll be your last one. Enjoy it. I'll be right back."

His Oldsmobile was parked on the road at the edge of the sand. Joey unlocked the trunk, felt around the spare-tire compartment, and came away with a brown paper bag. He closed the trunk and returned to his captive under the pier.

"Look at this," he said, pulling out a stick of dynamite from the bag. He held it up before the Irishman's eyes.

"Here, take a good look, smell it, make sure it's the genuine article. Then look at my fucking face, you motherfucking mick. You don't recognize me, do you? Well, say hello and good-bye to Joey Alongi— remember now? Rings a bell? They used to call me the Italian Adonis."

By now Joey was screaming and tears were running down his scarred cheeks. "You made me a fucking Frankenstein," he sobbed. "Why, you motherfucker, why? Did I fuck your sister? Your mother, maybe? Is that it? You rotten cocksucker."

The look of stark terror in the Irishman's eyes pleased Joey. "I'm going to blow your fucking ass all over Revere."

Joey spun the body around and dropped to his knees. Grabbing the Irishman by the testicles with one hand, he shoved the dynamite stick up into his rectum until only the two-foot fuse was hanging out. The Irishman was dancing on tiptoes and gasping for breath, his face purple and his eyes beginning to bulge.

Joey started laughing. "You dumb fucking mick, don't you know you can't tap dance on sand?"

Joey flicked his lighter and calmly lit the fuse. Without another word, he walked to his Oldsmobile and was already rolling down the street when he heard the explosion.

The brutal murder started a gang war that took the lives of nineteen Irishmen and thirteen Italians. But Joey Alongi's role was never discovered. No one suspected him because he was a mere punk, a gofer, who had been nickel-diming it on the fringe of what he suspected was the New England Cosa Nostra family of Ray Patriarca, who operated his crime empire from Providence, Rhode Island.

Patriarca's *caporegime* in Boston's North End was Carlo Russo, a forty-two-year-old Sicilian who ran his end of the operation with an iron fist. He used Joey Alongi as a policy runner, loan shark collector, and in recent months as a bumper of jukeboxes and vending machines found on the premises of competitors.

Joey seldom looked in the mirror these days. He knew his face was a gargoyle. Even his curly hair had deserted him, leaving a shining pate instead of a widow's peak. Pasta and meatballs had turned the muscles of his athletic physique into rolls of cascading fat that made climbing a flight of stairs more strenuous than a night of jitterbugging had been in the good old days. He had trouble breathing through his battered nose and any exertion started him wheezing. He felt and looked like an old man and he was only thirty-eight.

He was single, having lost interest in women—other than whores—at the time they'd lost interest in him, and that was when he'd gained a new appreciation for the delights of his palate.

Although he felt that life had dealt him a bum hand, he never lost hope that his calamitous streak of bad luck would change. The odds were with him. That was the law of percentages.

His dream was to get a sizable stake and go to Las Vegas. In the dream he would walk into the elegantly railed baccarat enclosure at the Monarch, and the croupiers and laddermen, in their evening dress, would welcome him to the table with smiles reserved for high rollers. "Mr. Joey Alongi's shoe," the croupier would say, and Joey would smile thinly as he dealt out the cards from the mahogany box, looked at his own two, and coolly turned them face up. He held a natural, invincible nine. At his request the house removed its two-thousand-dollar limit. Before he was through, gamblers were lined up twenty deep along the gray railing, and he could hear their excited whispers. All of them were wondering who he was. As banker, he ran out the shoe with straight passes. Within nine hours he hit the table for a cool million. He stood up, threw four five-hundred-dollar chips to the head croupier. "For you, gentlemen," he said, and smilingly pushed his way through the hushed crowd. His next stop was a fat farm where he dieted and sweated away two hundred pounds of excess weight. Now it was time for the plastic surgeon, the best in the world, to reshape his face to its original Adonis splendor. Then he was ready to start life anew, with a clean slate, in Miami. This dream had kept him going through many dark times.

The break that he'd hungered for had finally come while he was sitting in his dentist's waiting room. His lower plate had been left to be relined and the dentist's nurse had called to say it was ready. For the past week he'd been running around without it, which made him feel as though he were gumming it like Popeye the Sailor Man. While waiting he picked up a five-month-old copy of *Life* and began leafing through it without real interest until he came to a two-page spread with the headline: "Freshman Senator Takes Oath on 30th Birthday." Randolph Godwin stood very erect in the photograph, with one hand on the Bible and the other straight up from the elbow, and at his side were his wife, Betty, and their twin daughters, Eileen and Alicia.

Joey gasped in recognition and nearly dropped his upper plate. There were pictures of Senator Godwin at his father's ranch, the whole family riding Arabians, and a shot of Rufus Boutwell's palatial home on a hill overlooking Carson City. All three men were described as millionaires, and the grandfather as the most powerful man in Nevada history. There were also pictures of the senator's Georgetown house, a gift from his grandfather, along with his own private DC-6 airliner.

Joey was so excited that he tried to whistle and his upper plate fell out. He picked up the dentures, looked quickly around the room, tore out the two pages, and stuffed them in his pocket.

The maid answered the doorbell and stared incredulously at the fat man standing on the doorstep. His face looked as though it'd been crushed out of shape by a vise, and perspiration was oozing out from under a toupee that resembled a bird's nest. It ran into his eyes and he kept blinking as he tried to focus on her in the bright sunlight.

"I'd like to see Mrs. Godwin," he said.

"Is Mrs. Godwin expecting you?"

Joey Alongi flicked water from his eyes and tried to look past the maid into the house. "I'm an old friend from Boston. Just tell her Joey's here. Don't worry, she'll see me."

The maid hesitated. "Mrs. Godwin isn't home."

"Listen, you black bitch, don't you fucking lie to me. You go tell her Joey from Boston wants to talk to her. And no more bullshit."

He pushed the maid aside and stepped into the house. The maid opened her mouth to scream and he barked, "Shut up! Or I'll shove my fist down your throat."

"But I swear, she's not home," she cried.

Joey raised his arm in a threatening gesture and she covered her face with her hands.

"You skinny spook, do what I tell you."

Then he heard footsteps on the staircase and even before he turned he knew it would be Betty, because he'd been casing the house since six o'clock this morning. He'd seen the maid arriving, the limousine pick up the senator, and the station wagon pick up the twin girls.

He turned and his mouth fell open, revealing his cheap dentures. Betty was standing on the staircase in a light summer dress of beige linen and she was so stunningly beautiful that he couldn't believe his eyes.

"Yes, what do you want?"

"Hey, Betty, baby—it's me, Joey. Don't you recognize me?"

She looked at him, her soft green eyes perplexed. "I'm sorry, but you must have the wrong house."

"Naw, I don't. Look, tell smokey here to get lost. What I've got to say's private."

The voice was familiar but she was sure she had never seen that face before.

"Celia, please finish what you were doing in the kitchen. I'll talk to the gentleman."

The maid was wringing her hands. "But, Mrs. Godwin—"

"It's all right, Celia. If I need you, I'll call."

The maid left reluctantly and Betty stayed on the staircase, ready to take flight in the event of an attack.

Joey waited until the maid was gone. "Hey, Betty, it's me, Joey Alongi. Look, my face's all fucked up, but it's me—can't you recognize my voice?"

Betty stared at him in stunned silence. The nightmare had returned in the form of a monster. How many times had she thought and dreamed about him? How many times had she berated herself for having lacked the courage to tell Randolph the truth before their marriage. Afterward it was too late. She'd learned to live with the fear of discovery. But this was Judgment Day.

"Is this somebody's idea of a joke?" she said tensely, not yet willing to accept the inevitable truth. "You're not Joey Alongi."

"Beauty's only skin deep," he said bitterly. "One time you was nuts about me. In them days all the broads pulled their pants down for me. Remember how you loved to dance and was always giving me the eye when I looked over the line of wallflowers? I was the fucking ballroom king of New England. Remember that night at the Raymor-Playmor when we won the gold cup and I gave it to you? That's the first time I got in your pants, baby. Ah, you thought I was pretty special that night, all right. We was quite a team, me and you, like Astaire and Rogers, and the kids got in big circles and clapped like crazy when we cut loose. Them fucking days, I think about them all the time. I was beautiful. They called me the Italian Adonis. I was like a fucking work of art."

While he was talking, Betty came slowly down the stairs and he followed her into the library. She closed the door and leaned against it. "Please, what are you doing here? What do you want from me?"

Joey moved behind a library table and sat in a large leather chair. "Don't push," he said. "I'll get to it when I'm fucking good and ready. I was just, what do you call it, *remissing* about the past. About the good old days when me and you was an item, you know, like they say in them gossip columns. Now you're married to a rich senator and your picture's in *Life* magazine. The poor little slut from Southie is Mrs. Highshit Society. So don't get high hat with me. I know you from way back. Which reminds me. Remember the High Hat? That's where we decided to get hitched. And we got bombed and woke up in Connecticut. Don't tell me I ain't got class. And we had room service, the works, and you was hanging on to my prick like it was the family jewel and you was afraid somebody was going to come in and steal it."

"I remember you," she said, "but I don't recall your being this vulgar and obscene."

"What're you talking about? Don't give me this vulgar-obscene shit. My face is different but inside I'm still the same Joey Alongi. I've always talked this way. Don't worry, I remember. You used to like dirty talk when I was fucking you. You was one hot mama, sweetheart. If I'd been smart I'd have turned you out on the street and cleaned up."

"Why are you being deliberately obnoxious?" she said, trying desperately not to reveal any emotion. "Why don't you say what you came to say and go away and leave me alone?"

He smiled and she looked away. It was a hideous face, made even more so by those dead eyes. She remembered when those same eyes had luster and laughter in them. Whatever had crushed the face had killed the eyes and filled the brain with venom. This new Joey Alongi was a monster, an animal.

"I just thought I'd drop in and meet the hubby. How's he in bed? Pretty hot stuff? Got a big schlong like your Joey?"

"Oh, shut up," she said savagely. "I'm not going to listen to any more of this foul language. Say what you came to say and get out!"

He banged the side of his fist against the table. "You watch your mouth, cunt. Don't you go telling me what I can or can't do. I'm in the driver's seat and don't you ever forget it. Did you tell the senator about me? I'll bet you a hundred grand you didn't. What do you think *Life* would pay for this little story? The senator's wife and the Mafia hood. Or what would the senator pay to keep *Life* from getting it? The magazine said you married into a fortune. So, okay, cards on the table. I want a hundred grand. Now, do I get it from you, from him, or from *Life*?"

"You must be insane," she said, trying to conceal her shock. "Where would I get that much money?"

He laughed and stood up. "So the senator don't know. Good. I'll give you one week to come up with the dough. Next Wednesday, at this same time, I'm going to be on your doorstep, and you better have it. No fucking excuse will save your ass."

Without another word, he started toward her. She quickly opened the library door and he walked out of the room. She waited, afraid to breathe, until she heard the front door open and close. Then she collapsed into a chair and covered her face with her hands.

When the call came Henry Godwin was in Rufus Boutwell's office listening to him read the riot act to Governor Oscar Upstrom. The governor had dared to question Rufus's appointment of Roger Spalding as chairman of the newly created State Gaming Commission, which superseded the old seven-member Tax Commission. The Gaming Commission was empowered with the final authority on the granting of all gaming licenses—the word *gambling* having long ago been banned from all state statutes. And Rufus had set up the State Gaming Control Board, to act as the investigative arm of the Gaming Commission. The board held public hearings, many of which provided some of the liveliest entertainment in the state.

Rufus picked up the phone, nodded, and hung up. "It's Mrs. M. Says it's urgent. Take care of it and come right back. After all, Oscar here's one of your Democrats, so I want you to set him straight on the rules of the game."

Henry stood up and winked at Upstrom. "Oscar, I clearly recall telling you this before—several times, in fact, but I'll repeat it again. There is only one rule you must never forget."

"Yes, Henry."

Henry crossed to the door and turned to smile at Upstrom. "Never say no to Rufus Boutwell. Why can't you remember this simple little rule? When you consider all the people you're allowed to say no to, and do, with great enthusiasm, why can't you remember this one exception? I must say I'm surprised and disappointed. And on that note I will leave you to the tender mercies of your *padrone*."

Rufus's laughter followed Henry as he went out the door. Mrs. M. was waiting for him in his office and she looked uncharacteristically worried.

"Henry, it's Betty, and she sounds terribly distraught. She wants you to call her right away, but not from the office." Here Mrs. M. lowered her voice. "She said to use a pay telephone." Now Mrs. M.'s voice became a whisper. "You don't suppose this place is bugged, do you? There's a lot of talk about this sort of thing these days."

Henry smiled. "No, but there's a switchboard, and some of the ladies do get bored at times. One never knows. Look, if Rufus calls, tell him I had to run an errand and I may not be back today. Please don't mention Betty's call."

"Oh, gracious, no, Mr. Godwin. Never in a million years."

The next noon Henry was in Washington having lunch with Betty in his suite at the Jefferson. One look at her and Henry knew she needed stiff reinforcement. He had mixed double martinis and ordered a dry Chardonnay with the chef salad now waiting on the dining table.

Betty sipped the martini and fought back the tears brimming in her green eyes. In the years she'd been married to Randolph Henry had grown to love her as his own child. In recent years he had suspected that the marriage was not all it should be. His discovery in the steam room had confirmed that suspicion.

Whenever he tried to broach the subject to Randolph, he was brushed aside. There was no question in Henry's mind that Betty was still in love with her husband, but she now acted as though she'd been rebuffed enough times to know the precise distance Randolph tolerated.

Betty emptied her glass and Henry refilled it. "I don't know how to begin," she said, her voice faltering. "I'm sorry to involve you, but I really don't know who else to turn to. Henry, you're more than my father-in-law, you're my best friend. There's no one else in this whole world I admire and trust more. But I'm about to hand you a dirty deal you don't deserve. After today you may never want to see me again."

"Nothing could be that bad," Henry said.

The tears were flowing now and she caught them with her tongue at the corners of her mouth like a frustrated child. "Damn, I wasn't going to do this. I promised myself I was going to be strong and not muck it up."

Henry took her in his arms. "Go ahead, darling, let yourself go—then we'll sit back and talk. Whatever is wrong, I'm with you all the way. Don't ever doubt that. Whatever you need from me, you've got it. No questions asked."

She sobbed against his shoulder and he smelled the fragrance of her hair and thought again how fortunate his son was to have a wife like Betty, and how stupid he was to look at any other woman. Finally, she pulled away and he handed her a handkerchief.

She tried to smile, a valiant effort that ended in a grimace. She swallowed several times, then announced, "I'm not what you think I am." She paused and turned her head away. "I mean, Randolph was not my first husband." She bit down on her lower lip. "Nor my second."

Henry took her hand and said nothing as she told him of the night she was raped at Revere Beach and of the marriage to Izzy Cohen because her mother wanted a father for her baby.

"I was seventeen when I received the telegram he'd been killed at Pearl Harbor and I must have cried for a week. He was such a sweet boy and felt terrible about the rape. He was carrying this awful burden of guilt, and the marriage I think eased it some.

"After his death, though, something happened to me. The only way I can describe it, and I don't want to make excuses for myself, but I did go sort of crazy. After giving birth to my son, Michael, I stopped caring about anything except having a good time. I started going to dances again and that's when I met Joey Alongi. He was a fantastic dancer. Won all the jitterbug and waltz contests. All the girls fought to dance with him. And they were all in love with him. It was contagious, I guess. That's all they ever talked about. It was always Joey. Joey's so smooth, Joey's always the first to know the latest steps, Joey's so handsome, so sharp, and on it went.

"They called him the king of the ballroom and the Italian Adonis. And he danced like Astaire and made me feel like Rogers.

"And Joey Alongi, who could sweep any girl off her feet, had picked me out of the whole crowd. I became his favorite dance partner. We won many dance contests. The next thing I knew I was Joey's girl. And I was proud of it."

She looked at Henry with trusting eyes that said she knew he understood. "It was a form of madness. I know it now. It was the war and the way life was changing, the hysteria, with so many of the boys going off to war. One night Joey told me he'd been reclassified and they'd be calling him any day. I felt so desperate. All I could think about was what had happened to Izzy. We went to this nightclub, the High Hat, and I told him about Izzy and my son, Michael. We just sat there and got drunk. The next thing I knew we were standing before a Justice of the Peace in Stafford, Connecticut. I was so drunk Joey had to hold me up. The next day we drove back to Boston and my father wouldn't even talk to me. He hated Joey. Called him a bum. As far as he was concerned, I was dead. He thought I was a fool and he was right. I never went back to my home until after my father died about a year ago. Before his death my mother and I met secretly from time to time, and she'd come to the house to visit the twins, but my father knew how to carry a grudge. I know it affected their marriage and for that I'm truly sorry.

"One month as Joey's wife was like an endless cold shower. It brought me back to my senses. I discovered he was incapable of loving anyone but himself. In no time he was back at the dance hall—without me, of course, and chasing other girls. He spent his nights in ballrooms and his days in poolrooms."

"What did he do for a living?" Henry asked.

"Peddled lottery tickets and did odd jobs for the Italian hoodlums he hung around with all the time. He'd lied about being reclassified. Getting money from him to pay the rent and buy food was an impossibility. I got a job at Filene's as a salesclerk and studied secretarial work two nights a week. I had an older woman keep Michael in the daytime. The two nights I went to school Joey watched him until I came home around nine, then he'd take off and that was the last I would see of him until the next afternoon when I returned from work."

She picked up the martini and emptied it. Her eyes filled with tears and she clutched her hands together until the knuckles were bone white. "Oh, God, how I try not to think of this." Again she was sobbing, but Henry kept his distance. The strength, he knew, had to come from within her.

"One night—oh, dear God—I came home and the house was gone. It had burned to the ground. It was a pile of ashes and in those ashes were the charred remains of my son."

She covered her face with her hands and lowered her head, burying her face in her lap. Henry could hear the sobs and see the terrible spasms of grief that racked her body. He waited, helplessly, his hand on her shoulder.

Then he heard a small voice, a child's voice, muffled by her hands and lap. "Joey had fallen asleep on the couch, which was next to the drapes, and his cigarette caught them on fire. When he awoke, he ran from the house and never even tried to save Michael."

He let her cry it out, knowing that she was reliving a horror story that had been locked up inside of her far too long.

Much later, after she'd regained enough control to continue, she told him the marriage had been annulled and she had never again seen Joey Alongi until the morning he showed up at her Georgetown house.

They left the hotel and Henry's limousine followed discreetly as they walked up Pennsylvania Avenue, past the White House and toward Georgetown. It was a hot, muggy afternoon and Henry removed his suit jacket and held it over his shoulder by one finger. Her eyes, which were red and swollen, were concealed by large sunglasses.

"Betty, I've thought this out," Henry said, as they passed the White House. "I'm going to handle this for you."

"Oh, God, thank you, Henry. But please, be careful. He's been in an accident that terribly disfigured him. He's very bitter. He must weigh nearly four hundred pounds and he looks like a monster, something out of a horror movie."

"There are ways of dealing with blackmailers. Let me give it some thought."

"Thank you."

"Where was the marriage annulled? And who was the attorney?"

"A friend of my parents, James Cronin. He was an old man and he died a couple of years ago. His office was in Roxbury."

"Do you have the marriage license?"

"It burned in the fire."

Henry nodded. "Look, honey, for the time being don't mention any of this to Randolph. Give me a chance to see what I can do about it."

"Oh, dear God, it's the last thing in the world I want to do." She stopped walking and looked at Henry. "I think you know our marriage is not perfect. I'm not complaining. Randolph's a wonderful man, but life in Washington is fast and there are lots of temptations for a handsome young senator, especially one with his wealth."

She looked away. "There hasn't been anything meaningful between us in a long time. I've become part of his stage setting, along with the house, the twins, the dog, the two cats, the parakeet, and the goldfish."

Henry looked at her with sympathy. "I'm sorry about the marriage," he said, "but often these things have a way of working themselves out. If you love Randolph, hold on as long as you can."

"Don't worry, I'm a fighter," she said, and they started walking again. "I love him and I intend to hold on as long as my fingernails will support me on the window ledge he hung me out on to dry."

"Adversity sharpens your metaphors."

"That's the Irish in me."

"Well, darling, keep holding on. Together we're an invincible team."

When the doorbell rang the next Wednesday, Henry Godwin answered it. The perspiring fat man on the stoop appeared nervous. He wore a brown straw hat pulled low, dark glasses, and he kept glancing up and down the street, as though he expected FBI agents to leap from behind trees and bushes with cameras or guns.

Henry stood in the doorway, blocking it, determined to prolong his discomfort. "What do you want?"

"I'm here to see Mrs. Godwin. She's expecting me."

"No, she's not," Henry said.

Alongi's whole body stiffened and his lower lip curled in a snarl. "The fuck she ain't."

Henry's hand snaked out and tore the dark glasses from Alongi's face. "Let's take a good look at you," he said, glancing up and down the street, hoping to create the impression that others might be interested in a better look at Alongi.

"What the fuck you doing?" Alongi growled. "Give them back."

"In due course," he said. "You're not browbeating a woman now, big man. Your gutter talk doesn't intimidate me. I'm going to ask you again, what do you want?"

"I told you, for Christ's sake. Mrs. Godwin's expecting me."

"Why would Mrs. Godwin be expecting a gutter rat like you?"

"Hey, buddy, you better watch your mouth if you don't want it fucking busted. I'm telling you, she's expecting me."

"No," Henry said. "I'm the one expecting you. And I must say you're a disappointment."

Alongi snapped his fingers. "Now, I get it. You're the father-in-law. Well, you better come up with the loot, that's all I've got to say, Mr. Big Shit."

Henry stepped out on the stoop and closed the door behind him. "Is that red Ford across the street yours?"

"Yeah, so what?"

"Let's take a ride and discuss your problem."

Alongi followed Henry to the Ford. "Me, a problem?" He laughed harshly. "You've got balls, old man."

"Age is relative," Henry said. "Depends more on mileage than years."

Alongi started the engine and pulled away from the curb. "Where we going?" he asked.

"Just follow that black limousine ahead of us," Henry said. "It's going to National, and we better have your problem solved by the time we get there because I'm leaving for Las Vegas the moment we arrive."

Alongi chuckled. "Me, too. I've got my ticket right here in my pocket. I've got me a date with a baccarat table. But first let's have that hundred grand and no more stalling. I don't know what Betty told you, but if you don't want to get your son's ass in a sling, you better come across."

"Joey, hasn't anyone ever told you that blackmail is a felony? Ten years minimum."

"No more bullshit. I want my fucking money. Fuck the slammer. I've taken lots bigger chances for lots less."

"And it's a sleazy, dangerous business."

"Skip the violin routine. You're the one taking chances. Who's got the most to lose? I can do ten years standing on my head. But what about your son and Betty and the fucking twins? That's going to be a fucking nice story, right? Senator married to a fucking hooker who peddled her ass for a Mafia hood."

"Don't exaggerate your story," Henry said, "or I'm liable to add another dimension to your already fascinating nose."

Alongi turned to give Henry a hard look. What he saw was an unmarked face, which told Alongi that this man was a better talker than fighter. Probably had never been in a real fight in his life. Never had the shit kicked out of him in some alley. Joey Alongi had guys like him for breakfast without raising a sweat.

He scowled at Henry. "Take your best shot, Mr. Big Shit, and I'll tear your fucking arm out of its socket and jam it up your ass. Who the fuck you think you're dealing with, for Christ's sake? Some punk kid? I was mugging marks like you when I was sixteen."

He pounded the wheel and laughed. "While you was eating your oatmeal with a golden spoon, I was killing rats with my bare hands. Caught them by the tail and spun them around, you know, and banged their brains out against the wall. I was so fucking quick with my dukes that sometimes I caught two at the same time, one in each hand, and whirled them around like some stripper twirling tassels with her titties. How many rats have you caught in your life?"

"Never a four-legged one," Henry said, "but there are other species."

The black limousine drew up in front of American Airlines at National and Alongi pulled up behind it. He turned in the seat and for a moment he looked like he was going to lunge at Henry. "Okay, we're here, so where's the hundred grand?"

Henry shrugged. "There's no hundred grand. But there's fifty if you'll agree to certain terms." Henry reached inside his suit jacket and brought out a folded sheet of paper.

"What's that?"

"The terms are stated quite clearly. Sign it and I'll give you fifty thousand dollars."

Joey Alongi read the paper and started laughing. "What do you think I am, some fucking kind of schmuck?"

Henry motioned to the black chauffeur, who had stepped out of the limousine with a briefcase, to remain where he was. "Sign the paper and the briefcase is yours."

"Bullshit. This thing says I've blackmailed you for fifty grand on a phony story I made up."

"What are you worried about? I'm not going to use it unless you get greedy again."

Alongi considered. "Let's see the briefcase."

Henry again motioned with his hand and Moses Grimes brought the briefcase to the passenger side of the red Ford. He handed it to Henry and walked back to the limousine.

Henry gave Alongi a pen and opened the briefcase to display the stacks of greenbacks. "This is it," he said. "Sign the paper and take the money. Or go peddle your sleazy story somewhere else."

"Ah, fuck it," Alongi said, scribbling his name to the paper and grabbing the briefcase. "This piece of paper ain't worth shit. If I ever decide I need the other fifty grand there's plenty of records to prove my story."

Henry carefully folded the paper and stepped out of the car. "Don't ever try this again," he said, leaning into the opened window. "There's only one record, and I've got it in my hand. Have a nice trip. I'm sure they'll welcome you with open arms in Las Vegas."

CHAPTER

41

The first time Henry Godwin and Daisy Miller made love since leaving Vicksburg was in her suite at the Monarch. It was midafternoon, but with the closed blackout drapes used by all Las Vegas hotels it could have been midnight. Time had no meaning in this gambling city. There was no day or night—just the eternal flow of the action.

Their lovemaking had not been the thunder and lightning Henry had dreamed about these many years since Vicksburg. For the first time ever he called her Daisy instead of Cami. And now, as he lay on his side with her body curled against his back, he wondered how he could have kept that childish dream alive. Cami had been a passionate young girl and Daisy Miller was a sophisticated, experienced woman. And Henry Godwin was a clumsy, inexperienced lover, out of sync with the times, an anachronism in modern attire.

Besides everything else, he hated this place, this room, this hotel, and the men who operated it. Particularly the one man who had possessed Daisy Miller, Vince Bacino, the strutting Sicilian with the lizard eyes.

Henry couldn't help but wonder if this mating had received Bacino's blessings. He didn't want to ask, but he knew he must if things were ever to be right between them.

"Did you have to ask his permission?" he said quietly.

He felt her body stiffen against his, then slowly relax again.

"No, Henry, it's over between us. We go our separate ways and no questions asked."

"Does he know about me?"

"Not from me, he doesn't."

"Thanks," he said, and without turning his head he reached back beyond his own hip to stroke hers and marvel at the smoothness of the curve.

"It wasn't very good for you, was it?" she said softly. "Not what you expected after all these years of anticipation."

"And you—was it good?"

"Oh, yes, it was glorious."

"It was?" he asked incredulously.

She sat up and turned his head so that he was facing her. "Henry, I love you. I've always loved you and I'm so glad I can finally say it. I love you, Henry Godwin. I love you." And she planted kisses all over his face and neck. "Give me time to awaken your love."

"Oh, God, Cami—don't you know I've never loved anyone else?"

"Then love me the way a lover loves his only love. Slow and gentle and selfless. Just two people giving of themselves."

Closed blackout drapes had also turned day into night in a room five floors below Daisy Miller's suite at the Monarch. Outside a July sun was scorching the earth, but inside the dimly lit room it was cool and comfortable. On a table beside the king-size bed was a bottle of twelve-year-old Chivas Regal, a silver bucket of ice, and numerous plates and bowls that looked as though they'd been licked clean. Nothing remained of the two jumbo prime ribs, two giant baked potatoes with sour cream and chives, two Caesar salads, assorted vegetables, baskets of bread, two chocolate mousses, and two pots of coffee.

Contented for the moment, Joey Alongi sat propped up in the middle of the bed, watching an old Randolph Scott movie on television. Joey was naked and between his legs was a huge pile of greenbacks—twenties, fifties, hundreds—fifty thousand to the dollar, which he had just finished counting for the fourth time.

He gulped down more Chivas and smacked his lips. It went down smooth as velvet. This was the fucking life. From now on it was going to be first class all the way for Joey Alongi. No more hustling on the dirty streets of Charlestown, with the El trains breaking his eardrums while he tried to conduct business. No more suspicious looks from Carlo Russo, no more sad songs from degenerate gamblers in hock to their eyeballs to Carlo's shylocks, no more greasy spoons and dives, no more freezing his nuts off in the winter, no more trudging through dirty snow, looking for punks, while his feet went numb and felt like wooden stumps. And for what? Fucking nickels and dimes.

He ran his hands through the greenbacks and closed his eyes. Christ, it felt better than jacking off. In the morning he'd stop at the cashier's cage and exchange the whole bundle for a hundred pumpkins—orange $500 chips—the way high rollers did it. But for now, he would lie in bed, drink Chivas, order more food later from room service, watch television, and build up anticipation for the moment when he would sit at the large kidney-shaped table with the fancy green baize layout divided into numbered sections for twelve players.

Alongi pulled the greenbacks up into his crotch and closed his eyes. Now he would slip deeply into his favorite dream, and tomorrow or the next day, depending on how long he could withhold his anticipation, he would go downstairs and live it out.

Around seven that evening, Henry and Daisy waited in front of the Monarch for the parking jockey to bring Henry's car. They were engaged in conversation when they heard the sputtering of a motorcycle. Daisy turned and saw Henry's old tandem motorcycle come to a stop in front of her.

"Henry," she squealed, grabbing his arm and almost jumping up and down like a child in a moment of ecstasy. "It can't be the same one?"

"It sure is," he said, opening the small door of the sidecar and helping her inside. She was wearing a sunshine yellow pants suit and a pale orange silk blouse, opened at the throat to reveal a pearl choker. She reached into her purse for a pastel orange band and slipped it over her blond hair.

"This is a sweet surprise," she said as Henry got on the bike. He revved the engine and they roared away as they had done so many times ages ago. "You're incomparable," she screamed over the noise of the engine and wind.

"You ain't seen nothing yet," he shouted back.

"It runs really well for its age," she cried into the wind.

"Oh, I tinker with it from time to time. Keeps me out of mischief."

They rode up the Strip in silence for a while, each lost in the past that was their youth. Henry turned into the airport and headed for the helicopter area. He stopped in front of a Bell Ranger and Daisy seemed to be lost in thought.

Finally, she looked at Henry and her voice was filled with emotion. "Henry, this bike is a time machine. In the space of a few miles I was transported back to another world. And for the first time what I saw was good, very good—all the pain is gone. I feel like a new woman. I really do, darling."

Henry walked around the bike and opened the sidecar door. "Now for a trip into the future. Come on, give me your hand."

She looked up, seeing the helicopter for the first time. "What are you up to, Henry Godwin?"

"I'm going to take you to our secret hideaway, our mountaintop tryst."

"You mean in that little bubble-topped eggbeater?"

"Of course. How else can you get to an eight-thousand-foot mountain peak in Charleston Park in fifteen minutes? Besides, there's no road to our tryst."

"But what's up there?"

"Come on, let me help you into this little eggbeater."

She looked around, as if expecting someone else to join them. "Where's the pilot?"

Henry laughed. "You're looking at him."

"Oh, Henry, don't be ridiculous. You can't fly this thing."

Henry shrugged. "See those big Sikorskys? They're S-Fifty-eights. They used these babies in Korea, carried about fifteen troops, they can lift four thousand pounds of wet concrete. I'm using them to build a chalet on a mountaintop that's the next thing to a paradise on earth. Completely surrounded by tall firs. The air's so clean you get up in the morning feeling so happy and free you want to sing like a bird."

"Sounds marvelously primitive." She reached up on tiptoes and kissed him lightly on the lips. "Take me in your crazy-looking flying machine to this Shangri-la. Will we be young forever if we never leave?"

"Yes, darling, in spirit."

He led Daisy to the Bell with its bubble top and open framework fuselage. He strapped her in and she smiled bravely as he eased behind the controls.

"Aren't there any doors?"

"Yes, but it's so warm. Thought you'd enjoy the cool air."

"Oh, I will, believe me." She paused and bit her lower lip. "When in the world did you find time to learn all this?"

"Here and there. I've been flying fixed-wing aircraft for quite a while. This is a little different. Not as stable. After all, it's a lump of machinery. The rotor blades have the function of wings but they give you that monkey motion that's different than flying an airplane. The rotors won't trim and fly themselves. You've got to hold on to everything."

"What do you mean, for God's sake?"

Henry laughed. "Don't worry. I mean it takes two hands and two feet to fly this thing."

Her eyes were getting wider. "What's that little propeller in the back for—looks like it's aimed in the wrong direction."

"That's why you need two feet," Henry said. "The pedals change the tail rotor pitch to take care of the torque. It's only out there to counteract the torque of the main rotor blades."

She gave him her most brilliant smile. "All right, you've convinced me of your competence. Up, up and away."

He laughed and switched on the engine, waiting for it to warm up. Holding the cyclic in a neutral position, he gave it full throttle and pulled on the collective. The Bell shot straight up in the air for about two hundred feet before peeling off at top speed toward Charleston Park.

Daisy screamed and Henry smiled proudly. "This I don't advise on the first lesson. It takes all the power this baby's got."

"My teeth are chattering," she said, looking toward the Strip with its scattered hotels, swimming pools, and golf courses in the middle of this vast empty desert. "From up here it looks like such a pitiful, puny effort to tame nature."

"Look ahead to Mount Charleston. That's my idea of nature. Wait until you see it in the winter."

"Does it snow up there?"

"Plenty. I want my chalet finished before the first snow. Then I'll sit there, drink bourbon, smoke cigars, gaze contentedly at its beauty, and let the rest of the world go fly a kite. I wish you could be there with me."

"Oh, darling, I will be—you know that—whenever it's possible."

He nodded, refraining from saying what he felt—that she would be at his side whenever it didn't interfere with her career.

A few minutes later they were hovering over Henry's mountaintop.

"It takes your breath away," she said, leaning out for a better view of the magnificent forests and granite peaks. "But where's the chalet?"

"On the drawing board. That excavation right under you, with the steel posts, is the beginning of the foundation. The posts are buried in fourteen feet of concrete and the whole excavation will be covered with tons of concrete and steel. It will be as secure as the mountain itself."

"It's like building your own bunker."

Henry sat the chopper down on the circular landing pad and let the engine idle. Daisy unbuckled her safety belt. "Scoot down until you're away from the blades," he warned her. "On idle they have a tendency to droop."

"Don't worry," she said as she jumped out and ran in a crouch.

Henry followed and they stood on the site that one day he hoped they would share.

Daisy took his hand. "Henry, it's truly spectacular. It's another world."

42

The ladderman sat in his high-towered chair, his hawkish gaze never missing a single movement of the pit boss and three croupiers who worked the baccarat table. The eight decks of blue-backed cards were spread across the table and the two slot croupiers, who handled the bets, began shuffling them, each taking about two decks at a time and passing them on to the dealer croupier, who finally assembled all eight decks into one packet. Then the dealer croupier turned to Joey Alongi and handed him a yellow indicator card. "Cut, please," he said.

Alongi smiled and tried to hit dead center with the card. He watched as the croupier completed the cut. Taking a second indicator card, he inserted it about ten cards from the bottom of the packet, then deftly lifted the cards and placed them face down in the card-dealing box. Quickly, the croupier dealt three cards from the shoe and dropped them into the discard receiver through a slot in the table. That, Alongi knew, was called *burning* the top cards. The shoe was now ready for the first banker-player.

Since Alongi was sitting in the number one chair to the immediate right of the dealer croupier, the shoe came to him. He had spent three days in his darkened room plotting each move and expression. Now acting as he had in his dream, he placed four pumpkins (two thousand dollars) in the Bank's slot and waited with a serene smile for the other players to cover or, in gambling parlance, *fade* his bet.

As best as he could figure it, there were six players and three shills at the table. One of the shills, a flaming redhead with heavy-lidded bedroom eyes, was in the number two chair. She put a black hundred-dollar chip in the Player's slot, thus betting against Joey. The others all placed their bets in the Player's slot until his bet was faded. No one bet

Bank, which astounded Alongi, since Bank was the percentage bet even though the house extracted a five percent charge on all Bank winnings and no charges on Player's winnings.

Although he found their lack of confidence in his luck demoralizing, he kept his serene smile as he dealt out the cards from the shoe. One to the dealer croupier, one to himself; another to the croupier, another to himself, his hands as calm and steady as a barber's shaving a corpse. The cards were on the croupier's wooden palette and he looked around the table, dropping them in front of a skinny kid with a ducktail haircut who didn't look old enough to shave. He had bet the highest amount on Player's.

The skinny kid squeezed a quick look at his cards and scratched them against the table to indicate he wanted a hit.

"A card for the Player," said the croupier.

This meant that the kid was holding any of the numbers from one to five, or a ten, and the rules of baccarat required that he draw a card. That was what Alongi liked about the game. There was no agonizing over decisions. There were no options. You drew cards on certain numbers, stood pat on others, and turned your cards over when holding eight or nine. The idea was to get as close to nine as possible with two or three cards, with nine being invincible. The ace had the value of one point; kings, queens, and jacks were worth ten each, which meant they were valueless, and all other cards held their numerical face value. When the cards totaled two digits, only the latter digit had any value— for example, a jack and a seven, seventeen, had the value seven, or a five and eight, thirteen, had a value of three.

The kid drew a two and shrugged. Alongi looked at his cards and frowned. He had an ace and a two. He dealt himself another ace and tossed his cards face up. The kid giggled and revealed three twos for a value of six.

"What the fuck's this?" Alongi growled. "Poker? Pair of fucking aces and three deuces." This was not the way it was supposed to go.

"Had you beat either way," the kid said.

The shoe passed to the redhead, who produced another black chip, this time in the Bank's slot. Alongi, who hated to bet Player's, threw four pumpkins in the Player's slot anyway, because the redhead was now Bank, and there was something challenging in the disdainful look she had given him when he'd complained about his hand. Fucking cunt, he thought—nothing but a fucking shill.

Since Alongi had placed the largest bet against the Bank, the cards went to him. The redhead dealt two cards and he took his time squeezing a look at them. The first card he saw was a nine and he held his breath, hoping the next card would be a ten or a picture card. It was a five. For an instant, he felt like throwing his cards into her arrogant face.

"Hit me," Joey said to the croupier—as required with the fourteen he held.

"A card for the Player," the croupier called.

It was a picture card, and when the redhead turned over her cards, the value was seven.

"The Bank wins," the croupier announced.

In the next forty minutes the redhead ran out the shoe with winners, most of them naturals. When she left the table, a blond shill quickly replaced her. Surreptitiously counting his pumpkins, Alongi confirmed his worst suspicion. He was down thirty-eight thousand dollars, and in all that time he'd had the shoe for one play. The redhead had taken him to the cleaners, with that arrogant little sneer at the corners of her slashing mouth. Her light brown eyes under the heavy bedroom lids were laughing at him.

Rage swept over him and he fought to conceal it as he beckoned to the pit boss, who came promptly to his chair.

"I'm going up to my room for a shower and quick fuck to change my luck. Give me five minutes and send up that fucking redheaded cunt that just reamed me for thirty-eight Gs. I like getting kissed when I get fucked."

The pit boss's face was troubled, undecided, and Alongi reached in his money slot and slipped him a pumpkin. Without waiting for an answer, Joey nodded to the croupier, indicating he'd be back, and leaving his chips behind, stood up and ambled out of the enclosure with a smug grin twisting his fat lips.

Alongi was stark naked when he opened the door for the redhead. She looked at him, her face crumpling when she saw him standing there with his hands barely reaching hips that were protected by cascading rolls of fat. His penis, which was erect and of average size, was barely visible, tucked away as it was in convoluting folds of flaccid flesh.

She looked away, revolted by the grotesque sight. Although a soft hooker, performing only at the request of the pit boss, she'd been through several weird situations in her four years in Las Vegas. She'd fucked or sucked her share of creepies, old and young, handsome and ugly, but this one was in a class by himself.

She moved over to a chair and plumped into it, kicking off her shoes, trying to act nonchalant. She dug into her large hooker's purse and brought out a lighter and cigarettes. She lit one and returned the pack and lighter to the bag, without once looking in Joey's direction. Now she inhaled and exhaled clouds of smoke while studying her painted toenails, also the color of her hair and lipstick.

"Look at me, you cunt," he shouted. "And take them fucking clothes off. I ain't got all day."

"What do you mean, take my clothes off? Jack said to give you a quick blow job and get back to the tables."

Alongi took a threatening step toward her and she started giggling. "You look like a giant bowl of walking Jell-O."

Alongi moved so quickly she was taken completely by surprise. With one hand twisting into her hair and the other grabbing the front of her dress, he yanked her out of the chair and flung her across the room. She landed on all fours, her long red hair covering her face that was now contorted with fear.

"What do you want?" she cried, trying to stand up on trembling legs.

"Stay on the floor and strip, you cunt."

Alongi moved to the room service table, which still contained the dishes from his breakfast, grabbed up the tablecloth at four corners and swung it in the air, letting it clatter against a wall. The table had been swept clean with one motion of his enormous arms. Soon the redhead was naked and sitting on the floor, waiting for his next command. Alongi looked at her and sneered. There was no arrogance on her face now, only apprehension.

"Come on, get to the table and bend over."

She shrugged and went to the table. He wouldn't be the first to use her back door. As far as she was concerned, it was better than having this ton of shit lying on top of her. She felt his moist hands on her buttocks, separating them, heard him spit and felt his spittle on her rectum. She waited for the first painful thrust. Then it would be all right. Las Vegas was full of buggers. There were very few straight front-door tricks these days—everybody was after some new kick. But this guy wanted something more. He wanted to humiliate her, and if he thought this would do it, he had to be more stupid than ugly, which was all but impossible.

"How do you like it, cunt?" he hissed, his huge hands grabbing her breasts and squeezing them as he began to pound into her.

"Mmmmmmm," she moaned, trying to simulate pleasure.

He was pounding harder and harder, grunting and wheezing in her ear, then she felt him coming and suddenly knew this wouldn't satisfy him.

He shuddered and she could feel his masses of fat jiggling.

He pulled out and stepped back.

"On your knees, cunt," he ordered.

"What do you mean?" she asked, straightening up from the table.

"I mean take it in your mouth and wash off your shit."

"Oh, no, please," she pleaded, "that's dangerous. You can get some terrible infection."

He grabbed her by the neck with one hand and pulled her down to her knees in front of him. "Wash it with your fucking mouth or I'm going to pinch your fucking head off."

With tears running down her face, she reached for him and did as ordered, trying not to gag.

When passion again started stirring in his loins, Alongi pulled out of her mouth. "Okay, cunt, go lie down in the bathtub, on your back."

"What for—" she began to ask, but stopped when he raised the back of his hand. Joey followed her into the bathroom and waited until she was lying in the tub as directed. Then moving carefully, he climbed in and sat on her breasts, his penis touching her chin.

He laughed and started grunting. "I ain't had a good shit today and I ain't never saw a better-looking toilet. When I give you the word, start sucking my cock."

The redhead closed her eyes. "You're crushing me," she wailed.

"Shut up, cunt. Next time you run out a shoe on a mark, remember that you're nothing but a fucking toilet."

For eight hours a day, five days a week, Cecil was one of several chickens who roamed the rafters above the casino's ceiling to monitor the action through the two-way mirrors known in the trade as the eye in the sky.

Cecil's station was the baccarat table. For hours he lay on his stomach, watching the action, making sure there was no cheating on either side of the table. At his elbow was a telephone with two direct lines: one to the baccarat ladderman, the other to Gus, his shift boss in the rafters. His binoculars were so powerful that he could zoom in and see a hangnail on a player's hand.

Cecil was interested in other things, too. For example, the blond shill who had replaced the redhead had the kind of décolletage that made Cecil's mouth water.

"Hey, Gus," he called on his phone. "Lilly's showing her nipples again. I swear, they must be an inch long. I'd give a week's pay to suck one."

"You horny old bastard," Gus said. "Forget the nipples and watch the action."

"Hey, the fat man's back, but no Shirl. Must have given her a good working over."

"She's on her way to County General," Gus said.

"What happened?"

"Who the fuck knows. Something about a collapsed lung."

"He's a big bastard," Cecil said. "She's lucky he didn't squash her to death. I know he was pissed when he left to get serviced. How'd you like to get humped by a fat tub of shit like that, for Christ's sake?"

"Cecil, being a rooster, and not a chicken like you, the thought never occurred to me."

"Fuck you," Cecil said, and adjusted his binoculars for a better view of the blonde's nipples. "Okay, baby," Cecil said to the mirror, "bend over a little more—give old Cecil a real eyeful."

When the shoe finally came back to him, Alongi was down to his last four pumpkins. It was too late to start pulling back. He had to go all the way, show them he was a classy guy. Resuming the posture of his fantasies, he casually tossed the four pumpkins into the Bank's slot without a change of expression. Then slowly his face creased in a serene smile as he waited for the other players to fade his bet.

"Banco," said a short, thin man with a heavily lined face, a hooked nose, and thick steel-gray hair.

Alongi watched with interest as the man placed a two-thousand-dollar marker in the Player's slot. There was something familiar about him, and the way the pit boss hovered behind his chair, he had to be connected—probably Chicago, Alongi guessed—a capo with points in the joint. His black mohair suit was expertly tailored, as was his white-on-white shirt. A thin red line ran diagonally down his black silk tie. The only flash was the diamond on his left pinkie, which had to be at least five carats and absolutely perfect.

Alongi waited for the croupier's signal before dealing the cards from the shoe. This was his last shot and he was proud of his calm behavior. His hand was steady and there was no twitching at the corners of his mouth. Slowly, he squeezed a look at his first card and saw a queen of spades. His heart nearly stopped beating. All he needed was another picture card and he was finished. From the corner of his eye, he noticed that Chicago was standing pat, which meant he was holding a six or seven.

Suddenly, without even looking at his second card, he flipped both of them over and couldn't restrain a gasp when he saw a nine. It was his first natural and it was like a jolt of electricity administered directly to his heart. For a moment he was afraid that others could hear it. It was pounding in his ear, the way it did some nights when he lay on his side with his ear buried in the pillow.

"The Bank wins," said the croupier.

"Let it ride," Alongi said. He felt euphoric. Like the natural nine, he too was invincible.

"Sorry, Mr. A.," said the croupier. "The house limit is two thousand."

Chicago raised his hand and the pit boss nearly jumped out of his patent leather shoes. "Let it ride," Chicago said. "Let's get some action going here for a change."

"Yes, Mr. C."

"Banco," said Mr. C.

Then it hit Alongi. Chicago, Mr. C., was actually Frank Covelli, one of the top Mafiosi in Chicago, his career going back to the days of Al Capone. The rumor was that he was one of the shooters when seven of Bugs Moran's boys were mowed down in the 1929 St. Valentine's Day Massacre.

As in his dream, Alongi went on to hit seven straight naturals, but three were pushes—draws—when Covelli also hit naturals. Alongi's bank was now worth $32,000 and still he let it ride.

Although Covelli retained his composure, he asked for a break to stretch his legs. He stood up and the pit boss followed him. Alongi saw Covelli's lips moving and the pit boss nodding politely. Joey figured he was arranging for more credit. But the break in the tempo of play was bad for Joey's luck. The longer he waited, the more impatient he became.

Finally he couldn't contain his anger any longer. "Hey, what's happening?" he shouted at the croupier. "This guy's trying to chill my streak. Let's get this fucking game going."

The croupier glanced up at the ladderman and received a negative sign.

"One moment, Mr. A., please," the croupier said. "As a courtesy to a player who's dropped thirty-two thousand in a few minutes."

"Fuck that," Alongi growled. "I'm still eighteen grand behind."

The croupier's face hardened. "Unless you wish to continue with the house's limit, I advise you to wait a moment longer."

Some of the other players were also stretching their legs, but no one paused by Alongi's chair, or spoke to him, afraid that he would interpret their words as an evil incantation to change his luck.

He wished the punks back in Charlestown could see him now. Joey Alongi playing head to head with Frank Covelli. That would pop their eyes. He'd finally made it to the big time. He was a bona fide high roller. Even in this casino, the biggest and fanciest in the country, people had already heard of his streak and were lining the elegant railing three, four deep, all of them wondering as to his identity. He'd heard their exclamations every time he hit a natural and let the money ride.

Little did they realize that he was prepared to run it to a cool million and walk away as though nothing unusual had happened. They'd be talking about him for years. The big man who came to the Monarch with the invincible arm.

Covelli returned to the table. The pit boss went to speak to the ladderman, who reached for the phone at the side of his chair. He made a call, speaking softly.

"Okay, let's play," said Covelli.

"Let it ride," Alongi said.

Covelli reached back and the pit boss handed him a marker for the amount, which he placed in the Player's slot. "Banco," he said, and leaned back in his chair, waiting for the croupier to hand him the cards dealt by the fat man with the serene smile on his face and the invincible look in his eyes.

Lew Spark, president of both the Monarch and Talent Corporation of America, spent the first three days of every week in Beverly Hills attending to the agency's business and on Wednesday evening flew to Las Vegas. He loved the Monarch and Las Vegas and gladly would have given up TCA if the Chicago family had permitted it. But his influence with top stars and his power over movie industry unions made him too valuable to replace.

When the call from the ladderman reached him, Spark was at the Monarch Country Club with Vince Bacino, at their reserved table overlooking the eighteenth green.

The two men were in a good mood. They'd just completed nine holes of golf and were now exchanging golf stories while they waited for their lunch.

Spark said, "This one's for real. Happened to a good friend of mine at the Bel-Air Country Club. He was playing with Charley Jones, a character actor, and when they got to the fourteenth tee, Charley dropped dead of a heart attack. At that point my friend was under par and he's got a nine handicap. Christ, he didn't know what to do. He looked at Charley and at his scorecard. Then he looked toward the clubhouse, which was way the hell out there. So, he told me later, he said, 'Fuck it. I'm going to break par if it kills me.' From then on it was hit the ball and drag Charley. The son of a bitch shot a sixty-nine, first and only time in his life, and gave a rousing eulogy at Charley's funeral."

The phone buzzed and Spark picked it up. He was still laughing when he hung up the phone.

"You bastard," Bacino said. "You had me going for a minute there."

The waiter brought them each a Bloody Mary and they touched glasses in a friendly salute.

"I've got one for you," Spark said, pointing to the telephone. "That was Larry on the ladder. Frank Covelli's going head to head with some character named Alongi. They lifted the limit and this fucker's got Frank on the hook for sixty-four grand and this Alongi's still letting it ride. Looks like he's going to run out the shoe and bankrupt the fucking joint."

"You're right. Frank's a degenerate. He'd break the fucking house before he'd back away."

The phone buzzed again and Spark listened without saying a word. When he hung up he said, "They ran a check on Joey Alongi. This guy holed up in his room three days before hitting the tables. Ate and drank like a pig."

"Well, who the fuck is he?"

"Just a punk, not a made guy—works for Carlo Russo in North Boston, who's damn curious as to where Alongi got his stake."

"Okay, let's get The Weasel in there fast. Hand me the phone."

A moment later, Bacino was talking to the ladderman. "When The Weasel gets there, I want Frank to go take a piss and let The Weasel take his action. And you tell Frank for me that I don't want no more bullshit. I'll talk to him later."

Tony "The Weasel" Spicuzza was not only the best mechanic in Las Vegas, but probably the only sleeper there. Few knew of his talent. The chickens in the rafters had been watching him a long time and could predict the outcome whenever he got into action, but they were still unable to spot his moves.

Most of the time they didn't even recognize him, for Spicuzza was a master of disguises. He would use wigs, false mustaches, goatees, and eyebrows, various styles of eyeglasses, stuff cotton in his nose, use rubber cuds for his cheeks, paint dark circles under his eyes. He also could change his voice and assume various accents.

Today when he sat down at the baccarat table he was a Texas oilman, complete with cowboy boots, Stetson, Western shirt, string tie, and gray handlebar mustache. He'd grayed his hair and stuffed enough cotton up his nose to effect a proper nasal drawl. He carried a doeskin briefcase, which he casually handed to the pit boss.

"Howdy, boys, I see we got ourselves a man-sized game going on at this here table. Give me a half-mil in markers for starters. I'm aiming on injecting new blood into this little ole shimmy. Hot damn."

Alongi scowled. He hated Texans. Loudmouth bastards with their fucking oil wells. Thought they were king shit. Most were crap shooters. Bet like maniacs. Didn't know the first thing about gambling. Threw their money away like confetti.

After several pushes, Alongi had completed two more passes and was now holding $256,000, less the house's five percent commission taken out after each winning hand. Alongi resented the house's steep commission. He compared it to loan sharking. It was like lending someone two thousand dollars and collecting five percent interest every ten seconds.

Covelli's complexion had turned grayish. It was apparent that the old man was feeling the pressure. He was on the hook and beginning to wiggle. Two more losses would bring him to a million of the hotel's money. Even if he wanted to walk away, his pride would force him to continue the duel with the ugly fat man.

When the Texan walked in and went into his routine, the pit boss whispered in Covelli's ear that Bacino wanted him to take a piss and not return to the table.

Covelli waited for the moment the pit boss placed the markers in front of the Texan before standing up and speaking directly to Alongi for the first time. "Nature calls," he said. "I'll be back in five, ten minutes. You can wait or take somebody else's action."

Alongi sneered. "Go on, old man, before you shit your pants," he said, his voice dripping with sarcasm.

Covelli slammed his fist on the table. "Watch your mouth, you fucking punk."

Covelli's mouth was twitching and there was a murderous glint in his eyes as he leaned across the table until his face was almost touching Alongi's. Lowering his voice, he hissed, "You dirty motherfucker, I'm going to remember you." Then he straightened up and calmly walked away, the crowd at the gate parting for him in respectful silence.

For a moment Alongi felt like cashing in his chips and taking the first flight out of town. But the gambling fever was stronger than his fear. He looked at the croupier. "Let it ride."

"You're faded, pardner," the Texan said, pushing a quarter million in markers into the Player's slot. "Now deal them little ole cards and weep."

The croupier turned to Alongi. "Deal the cards, please." After the four cards were dealt, the croupier scooped up the Texan's two face-down cards with his palette and dropped them smoothly in front of him. The Texan reached for the cards with his left hand and held them face down for a split second, covering them with his right hand, then rapidly turned a jack of clubs and a nine face up. "Hot damn, a little ole natural. What do you know. This is easier than pumping oil and lots more fun." In that split second he had palmed the cards dealt to him without looking at them and substituted the jack and nine he'd brought to the table.

The croupier turned to Alongi and asked him to turn his cards over. Without first squeezing a look at the cards, Alongi flipped them over and saw an ace and a seven.

"No cards, Player wins," the croupier said. He scooped up the four dealt cards and swiftly dropped them through the slot into the discard cylinder under the table.

Alongi was breathing with difficulty as he pushed back his chair and stood up.

"Thanks, pardner," said the Texan. "I admire a good loser. Cash me in, boys. I think I'll give the crap table a whirl. Looks like the action at this here table has gone plumb dead, real quick like."

Alongi left the table, walking through the crowd at the railing as though he were in a trance.

"My God," a blue-haired woman exclaimed as he went by, "a quarter million dollars gone in two seconds. I'd die of a heart attack on the spot."

Alongi heard the words and reached automatically with his right hand to feel his chest. Through all that blubber he could feel his heart pounding against his hand. By the time he reached the elevators, his knees felt so weak he was afraid he wouldn't make it.

43

Vince Bacino was seated behind his desk in his corner office on the second floor when Frank Covelli came in. He stood up and the two men embraced.

"How're you feeling, Frank?" Bacino said, grabbing Covelli's hand in a firm grip. "Heard you got a little pissed down there."

Covelli shook his head. "Thanks for saving my ass, Vince. When I saw The Weasel walk in, I didn't know what to do. Come up here and blow your head off or kiss your ass. That fucking punk really had me on the hook. You've never seen so many fucking naturals. Then when I'd hit seven, he'd hit eight. I got six, he got seven. He was fucking invincible."

Bacino led Covelli to a chair beside his desk, went to an elaborate built-in bar and filled two glasses with Scotch and soda. "Here, *paesan*, drink up and relax."

Covelli studied his drink in silence for a while. When he looked up, his eyes were hard as flint. "I want that motherfucker hurt, Vince. Hurt real bad. I want him in the hospital. I want somebody to break his fucking legs at the ankles, the knees, and hips. I want him on his fucking back in a basket for the rest of his miserable life."

"What the hell happened?"

"Nobody, not even God, can talk to me like that and get away with it. I'd like to be there when they give it to that *grosso pezzo di merda*."

Bacino shrugged. Sicilians were nuts, he thought, including himself. Insults burned in the brain like hot coals. The only way to put out the fire was the vendetta.

Bacino's intercom buzzed and his secretary announced that Mr. Spicuzza was in the outer office. "Send him right in," Bacino said, jumping up from behind his desk and going to the door to greet The

Weasel, who came in with a big smile on his face. He had disposed of the Texan disguise and was wearing a blue blazer, gray slacks, and a light blue and yellow sports shirt.

The two men shook hands and Covelli stood up and waited for his turn. He embraced Spicuzza. "Tell me, how did it go?"

"Smooth as silk, Frank."

"What did he draw?"

"Eight."

"And you?"

"Why, Frank, a natural, naturally."

"Cut the bullshit, what did he deal you?"

"Look in your inside jacket pocket," Spicuzza said, winking at Bacino. "I haven't looked at them."

"You fucking pickpocket," Covelli said with admiration, "you slipped them in my pocket when we hugged." Covelli reached inside his pocket and pulled out two cards, a four and a three. "Oh, shit," he cried. "That cocksucker was on the biggest winning streak I've ever seen. It was fucking uncanny. Imagine, one fucking point for a half-million bucks."

Spicuzza went to the bar and poured himself a glass of Chianti. "Frank, there's luck and then there's skill. Me, I'll go for the skill every time."

"Tony, you're not a gambler," Covelli said. "You don't understand the thrill of hitting a streak. You, you go in there like God, knowing the outcome. Where's the kick?"

"Forget it, Frank, you can't beat the table. You don't have to be God to know the outcome. Me, I take pride in my talent, and that's my kick."

Bacino was nodding in agreement. "You're the best, baby. Frank, Tony's so good even the chickens ain't never spotted him."

Covelli smiled. "Give the devil his due."

Bacino reached inside his desk and handed Spicuzza an envelope. "Here's five big ones, Tony. The cage said you left the briefcase with them. It all checks out." He turned to Covelli. "Hope you don't mind, Frank, but it's coming out of your end. Now, as to the markers you lost, we'll have to work that out with Chicago."

"What the fuck, you've got your money back."

"That's not the point, Frank. The people have to know. It's out of my hands."

Covelli shrugged. "Fuck it. But you do what I asked, Vince, and there's ten big ones for the muscle."

"Thanks anyway, Frank, but except for Tony here we don't pay soldiers for work in my family."

"I know," Covelli said, "nobody does, but I want this cocksucker so bad I'd pay a cop to do the number on him."

Bacino laughed. "Here in Vegas that's the cheapest proposition in town."

Once his heartbeat was under control Joey Alongi sat on the edge of the bed, pondering his next move. The fifty thousand was gone but that was a minor problem, easily solved with another phone call. The real problem was Covelli. This was his turf and he was a mean son of a bitch. Alongi had been dumb. Incredibly dumb. He didn't know what had possessed him to insult a man like Frank Covelli. The goon squad was probably on its way to work him over this very minute—maybe even bury him out in the desert. He was sure they had checked with Carlo Russo and been given the green light. So now there was Russo to worry about too. He'd have to explain the fifty grand. And how could he do that without losing control of the best thing that had ever happened to him? They'd take over and cut him right out of it. By the time they got done with that senator and his old man and grandfather they'd own Nevada and he'd still be nickel-diming it—if they let him live, that is.

The only answer was for Joey to move fast. Hit the senator's father and grandfather for a half million each and leave the country. He could slip into Mexico, buy a phony passport, and take off for Rio. Invest the million and live like a king off the interest.

He stood up, removed his suit jacket, slipped off his tie, and tore off his shirt, the buttons flying in all directions. The room was air conditioned, but the shirt was soaking wet and the foul odor of his sweat disgusted him. He put on a clean white shirt, slipped on his jacket, and jammed his tie into his pocket. He had to get out of there. He opened the door, looked up and down the hallway, and hurried to the bank of elevators. He glanced at the indicator board and saw that two elevators were on the way up. A creature of instinct, Alongi suddenly bolted for the stairwell. He reached the fire door just as one of the elevators stopped and its doors opened. Leaving the fire door slightly ajar, Joey saw three burly thugs dressed in workmen's coveralls, and he knew immediately they were the goon squad. Two were carrying crow bars and one a pipe wrench. A moment later Joey was lunging down the stairs at breakneck speed. His heart was pounding, but he didn't have time to worry about it. He had to get his million and get the hell out of the country before these bastards made chopped liver out of him.

At six o'clock that evening Henry was in his office trailer at the airport. He had just returned from his mountain peak, the last worker having left for the day, when he received a call from Joey Alongi.

"Your secretary in Carson City gave me this number," he said.

"I told her to give you the number," Henry said quietly. "I thought you might be calling again. I hear you caused quite a stir at the baccarat table."

"Yeah, well, listen, can the small talk. I want a half million and no bullshit. I'm in no mood to argue, you understand?"

"Not so fast. We have a signed agreement."

"Fuck that lousy piece of paper. This is a new deal."

"And how much time do I have to raise this money?"

"Two hours."

Henry laughed. "You know what time it is? The banks are closed."

"Look, I told you, no bullshit. You and your father-in-law own most of the fucking banks in this state. If I don't get it from you, I call him. I got his number, too."

"Don't do that," Henry said. "I'll get you the money."

"That's more like it, Mr. Big Shit. Now how do we work it?"

"I'll bring it to you at the Monarch."

"I'm not there anymore."

Before Henry could answer, his other phone rang. It was his direct line to his office in Carson City. "Hold the line a minute," Henry said, putting him on hold and picking up the other phone.

"Henry," Rufus Boutwell shouted, "what's the story with this Joey Alongi. Says he was married to Betty and wants a half million from me or he'll tell the press. What's going on?"

"Rufus, I don't know what you're talking about. Look, I'm in the middle of a problem down here—let me call you later tonight."

Henry hung up before Rufus could object and released the hold button.

"Sorry to keep you waiting," he said, "but I just called our banks here in town and the vaults are on time locks. But I can get the cash in Goldfield."

"Where the hell's that?"

"Not far. We'll fly up and be back in no time. Where are you? I'll pick you up."

Alongi hesitated a moment. "I'm in a phone booth at the Five Star Motel parking lot."

"Be on the sidewalk. I'll be there in twenty minutes."

"What are you driving?"

"A blue pickup truck."

Alongi laughed. "You've got to be kidding," he said, but the line was already dead.

44

When Alongi spotted the blue pickup, he moved swiftly from behind a parked car in the lot and crossed to the sidewalk, arriving at the precise moment Henry pulled over to the curb and stopped.

"Let's go," he said. "Get up a breeze. This fucking heat's killing me."

Perspiration was pouring down Alongi's face.

"I've got the answer for you," Henry said, making a U turn at the next intersection and heading back toward the airport. "Ever been up in a helicopter?"

Alongi smiled. "Hey, that's great. Always wanted to try it out."

But at the airport, when he saw the Bell Ranger, he hesitated until Henry assured him that it was strong enough to lift three men his weight.

"Here, let me help you with the belt," Henry said after Alongi had climbed in. Henry pulled the buckle all the way out and it barely fit around Alongi's waist.

Without further conversation, Henry climbed in and switched on the engine. This time, instead of taking off straight up, as he had with Daisy, he started the helicopter moving forward like an airplane. The air moving over the rotor blades increased their speed, giving greater lift with less power.

Once they were airborne and had left Las Vegas behind them, Henry turned to Alongi and studied him without speaking.

"What the hell you looking at?" Alongi growled.

"When I was a boy," Henry said, "I once went swimming in the Mississippi during dog days, although I'd been warned not to by the General. When I came out of the river I was covered from neck to toe with leeches. I was about ten years old and I remember running home, screaming my head off."

"What the fuck you babbling about?"

Henry ignored him. "That was quite an experience. A leech is an interesting carnivore. It has a sucker at each end of its body and a mouth inside each sucker. It's got a large stomach with pouches at the sides. It's actually hermaphroditic. Anyway, to get back to my story, I was completely covered with them and they were sucking away my blood. You could actually see their pouches grow. The thing about leeches is that once they get their suckers into your bloodstream, they never let go. You can't pull them out without leaving their heads in your body. They'd rather die than give up their free lunch."

"How the hell did you get them out?"

"Only one way. With fire. The General touched them with his cigar and they shriveled up and dropped off. That taught me an important lesson that I'd forgotten lately."

Alongi's gaze narrowed as he studied the terrain below. "Where the fuck's this Goldfield? Up here in the mountains? This looks like Vermont."

"It's Charleston Park," Henry said. "It is beautiful, isn't it?"

"Yeah, if you like mountains and trees. Me, I'm a big-city boy. I go for the action."

"Tell me, Alongi—how much did you tell Rufus Boutwell?"

"None of your fucking business."

"Think again," Henry said. "Because if you don't tell me, I'll turn this chopper around and deposit you right in front of the Monarch. There are no secrets in Vegas. It's a small town. By now everybody knows you've insulted Frank Covelli and there's a good possibility they've got the posse out looking for you. I hear they like to break bones."

Although it was cool in the helicopter, with the wind coming through the open sides of the bubble, Alongi's face was again dripping wet. "All I told him was that I was married to Betty and before that she was married to this kike, I've forgotten his name, and she had a kid that died in a fire."

"A fire you started."

"What the fuck, it was an accident."

"You never even tried to save the baby. You ran out of there like a coward to save your own worthless hide. Like the leech, a little fire and you shrivel up."

"Cut that shit about leeches. I'm not fucking stupid, you know. I know what you're getting at. You keep insulting me and I'll double the ante."

"I don't think so," Henry said. "Look down there, about a hundred feet straight down."

Alongi leaned over to peer out the side. "It's just a fucking hole in the ground."

In a split second Henry flipped the Bell on its right side and Alongi went out the opening like he'd been shot from a cannon. He screamed all the way down, but Henry couldn't hear him over the noise of the rotor blades as he straightened the Bell and brought it down on the pad.

Alongi was lying spread-eagled almost dead center in the excavation. In the hole were various pieces of heavy machinery which had worked their way down to the bottom and would later have to be air-lifted out by the Sikorskys.

Before leaving the Bell, Henry removed the remains of the safety belt, which he had cut through with a knife before picking up Alongi in the truck. He replaced it with a new belt and threw the rest of the old one into the excavation before climbing down a long ladder to the bottom.

He examined Alongi, to make sure he was dead, and then went to a bulldozer. Within minutes he had dug an eight-foot-deep trench. Using the blade of the dozer, Henry scooped up Alongi's body and dumped it into the deepest part of the trench. Then, climbing down, he picked up all the pieces of the safety belt and dropped them into the hole. Filling in Alongi's grave went quickly. A few minutes later Henry was back in the Bell, on his way to the airport. Within a fortnight Alongi would be lying under five feet of steel rods and concrete.

The problem was solved, but not before Henry Godwin had committed murder. And, as with the Pikes back in Vicksburg, he felt more relief than remorse. It was something that had had to be done. He'd have paid the half million if that would have been the end of it, but Alongi's gambling spree had escalated the problem out of control. Once the goon squad caught up with him, he would have had to explain the fifty thousand dollars, and that would have placed the kind of power in the hands of Bacino and his henchmen that could have been catastrophic. By acting swiftly Henry had taken the play away from them. Alongi's secret had died with him. But there was still Rufus Boutwell to deal with and that presented a far more complex problem.

Except for the flight crew, Rufus and George Clews were alone in the cabin of Rufus's private airliner. They were seated in chairs facing each other, but Rufus's mind was elsewhere and Clews watched him from under his beetle brow, his small deepset eyes glinting in anticipation. He knew that Rufus needed his services, that he was Rufus's most trusted aide, and he was proud of his special position in Rufus's world.

At the moment Rufus wasn't even aware of Clews's presence. There were more important things on his mind. They were flying to Las Vegas for a prearranged meeting with Alongi at the Five Star Motel on the Strip near the airport. One discreet phone call to Lew Spark and Rufus had learned that Joey Alongi was a cheap punk from Boston who came to the Monarch with fifty thousand dollars in cash, which he had promptly lost at the baccarat table. In the process he had insulted Frank Covelli and the goon squad was looking for him. Rufus knew Covelli, who owned a few points in the Monarch, and he knew about Bacino's goon squad. Besides breaking bones, rumor had it they considered the desert an ideal burial ground.

Although trying to be subtle, Lew Spark had ruffled Rufus by inquiring about his interest in Alongi.

Rufus had been blunt in his reply. "Nothing that concerns you," he'd said. "He tried to muscle a friend of mine and I just wanted to know who I was dealing with, that's all. Talk to you later."

He'd cut his water off right there, but Rufus knew that if Alongi fell into the hands of the goon squad, he'd spill his guts. And if what Alongi had hinted at was true, that would be a different problem entirely, but nothing Rufus couldn't handle. Nobody would ever blackmail Rufus Boutwell and live to brag about it. As far as Rufus was concerned, that punk Alongi was as good as dead right now. But first Rufus would get the full story from him, every minute detail. It wasn't only Randolph's future he was tampering with, but Rufus's lifelong dream.

The desk clerk at the Five Star Motel had never heard of Joey Alongi. The meeting had been set for nine o'clock in the parking lot, and when Alongi hadn't shown up by nine thirty, Rufus had gone to the clerk to inquire. When Rufus returned to the limousine, he ordered Clews to take him to Henry's trailer at the airport. No man expecting a half-million dollars would be that late unless it was beyond his control.

Clews remained with the limousine while Rufus headed for the trailer. Ever since the night he'd attacked Henry at the ranch, George Clews had slipped more into Rufus's shadow than ever. He was still his strong left arm, but was now almost totally invisible. In all these years he'd not spoken one word to Henry Godwin. Although he'd seen him on various occasions, it was always from a position where he couldn't be observed. As far as Henry was concerned, George Clews had ceased to exist. But Henry had not ceased to exist for Clews. Someday he'd pay him back for the pure hell he'd gone through before he could again walk straight like a man.

Inside the trailer, Henry was seated on a stool before a drafting board, studying the blueprints for his chalet. He loved going over the specifications. This was the first time he'd ever built anything for himself and he'd picked an architect who believed in personalizing a home. Henry had no thought of abandoning the Carson ranch, but he needed a retreat, a place where he could be in total isolation. The human race had a way of pressing in on a person, and if one could afford to escape on occasion, why not? That was his rationalization for building his chalet and he could hardly wait for it to be completed.

Then Rufus barged in and Henry wished that this was one of the nights he'd taken his sleeping bag and gone to his mountaintop to sleep under the stars. But there was the matter of Betty to resolve.

Rufus stood in front of the drafting board and glared balefully at Henry. "Now, what's this bullshit you gave me on the phone about not knowing this punk Alongi?"

Henry looked away and reached for a cigar, offering one to Rufus, who refused it. Henry carefully unwrapped the cigar, clipped the end, and lit it.

"Rufus, are you referring to the fellow who dropped fifty thousand dollars at the Monarch?"

"Yeah, the dirty wop blackmailer who wants a half million from me."

Henry feigned surprise. "What in the world for? What has he got on you, Rufus?"

"Henry, cut the shit—you know damned well what he's got and it ain't on me, but on that slut your son married."

Henry leaned forward, resting his elbows on the drafting table. "Rufus, you may be getting on in age, but you're not old enough yet to call Betty a slut without getting your nose reshaped and your vision blurred for a while."

Rufus chuckled. "You sonofabitch, you'd do it, too. You've got no gratitude. After all I've done for you, you'd actually slug me."

"Never mind that, what's this about *my* son? Now that's a switch."

Rufus sat down and wiped his face with a handkerchief. "Why don't you air-condition this trailer? This place's hotter than hell."

Henry puffed on his cigar and said nothing.

"Okay, Henry, you win. I don't have time to argue with you. This Alongi, this guy you don't know, told me he was once married to Betty. He's a punk hood from Boston. Not only that, but he was her second husband. Her first was killed in the war, some Jewish kid. See, I've always suspected she was Jewish. Well, at least half Jewish. So this little virgin Randolph married had two husbands in the closet."

"That's rubbish," Henry said. "This Alongi sounds like a lunatic."

"You mean he made it all up, just like that?"

Henry stood up and leaned over Rufus. "Not alone. I'm sure he got help. Sounds to me like somebody's trying to get to you. If you give in on this, they'll really twist your arm. Call his bluff—tell him to go to hell, and I guarantee you that will be the end of it."

"And if you're wrong? Then what?"

Henry shrugged. "Have you seen him yet?"

"I was to meet him at nine o'clock but he didn't show up."

Henry forced a smile. "Then my advice is forget it. He sounds like a crackpot. Probably read in a magazine about Randolph and Betty, saw where she was from Boston, and that you're filthy rich, and thought he'd try a shakedown. I'm sure it happens every day."

"Maybe, but they usually make an appearance for a half million."

Henry laughed. "You've got a half million in the limo?"

"I was going to make him a proposition."

"Sure you were, Rufus, but I think Bacino's goon squad saved you the trouble. My guess is that he's probably already buried. Wouldn't be the first time around here that it's happened. This little paradise in the desert you've dreamed about all these years has some pretty tough angels watching over it."

Rufus stood up. "Henry, this is no time for jokes. If Bacino got to this guy, it could be serious. I don't want to give them an inch of shit they can rub on me."

"Rufus, my advice is let's wait and see what develops. If they've got it, or get it, they'll be at your throat soon enough. No need inviting it."

Rufus nodded. "Of course, you're right. No need tipping our hand. But I've got to warn Randolph before they get to him. It's better coming from me than from them."

Henry grabbed Rufus roughly by the shoulders. "Don't do it. Don't mess in their marriage—leave them alone."

Rufus shook himself loose. "No, if they go to him first I want to be there to handle it."

"Please, don't jump the gun."

"Henry, I don't care what you say—there's a ring of truth in what that Alongi said. I can't take the chance of leaving it in Randolph's hands."

"Then let me go with you. Let's do it together."

"No, you stay out of it. You're no good with Randolph, never have been. You're too soft, Henry, and you don't understand him. All you'd do is confuse him at a time when he's got to think straight and be strong."

Henry sat back on the stool and shook his head. "You're wrong about this and you should stay the hell out. But if you go on with it, I warn you—and I mean it, Rufus—don't you hurt Betty."

"What do you mean, hurt Betty?"

"I mean mentally or physically, or her marriage. Just stay out of their personal lives."

"Henry, it's a little late in the day for you to start giving me orders. I'll do whatever I think is right for Randolph."

"Well, you better tell Randolph to keep it to himself. Otherwise you're going to end up with a messy divorce, and I don't think that's what you want any more than I do."

"Don't worry about divorce," Rufus said, opening the door and stepping out. "That's not in Randolph's best interest, or he'd have ditched that Yiddish cunt years ago."

The trailer door slammed shut and Henry heard the limousine pull away. All he could do now was warn Betty and hope that she had the inner strength to withstand the assault.

CHAPTER

45

As the wife of a United States senator, Betty Godwin's life had taken on extra dimensions that she found on the whole quite distasteful. She didn't mind joining the Senate Ladies in projects like the Red Cross and attending their lunches, but she avoided socializing with the more aggressive wives who dined at the in places simply to bask in the reflected glory of their husbands' political power.

As her marriage cooled, Betty grew disenchanted with Washington, hoping for the day they would return to Nevada and live a quiet life in Carson City. But deep down she knew it was wishful thinking. After his return from the war, Randolph had seemed glad to be back. Betty had tried to pick up where they had left off, but gradually she'd noticed a subtle transformation. There were days, sometimes weeks, when he barely acknowledged her existence. He moved through the house like a robot, cold and impervious to her presence, and she felt she was living with a stranger. Then there were moments when he was like his old self, full of laughter and jokes, and she was carried back to those wonderful carefree days in Cambridge before their marriage. But his moods were mercurial and their sudden turns only added to her confusion. He was a man of contradictions.

At first she had blamed the stress and frustration created by the humiliation of his being a senatorial aide to Toombs, a gross and drunken fool. Upon Toombs's death and Randolph's elevation to his Senate seat, Betty had been certain that life would once more get back to normal. But if anything it had gotten worse.

That was when she really became conscious of Randolph's blatant philandering. He became the main topic of cocktail party gossip. It became so embarrassing that Betty stopped attending social events and spent the evenings with the twins while Randolph made the rounds accompanied by different young ladies every night. Washington socialites were more amused than shocked, and Randolph became in great demand, which refuted Rufus's dictum that a proper wife at the side of her husband was an essential rung on the ladder of political success. Washington inner circles were far too jaded for that kind of homespun homily.

Betty even curtailed her own social daytime activities. Randolph's womanizing was causing her pain she couldn't conceal in public. Hard as she tried, she couldn't ignore the harridans who thrived in the company of misery. Washington, the world's greatest power center, was in fact a small town, with every woman knowing everyone else's dirty little secret and using it to assuage her own humiliation.

Then there had been Randolph's insistence on finding the "right" private school for the twins; he wasn't satisfied until Betty enrolled them in the most exclusive girls' school in the Georgetown area.

Wealth-power-appearance was the holy trinity that now governed her life. Love, tenderness, warmth were alien emotions, forgotten in the hustle of creating a foundation for success.

Although Betty vaguely understood most of this, it was impossible for her to comprehend why one trinity should cancel out the other. She had seen happily married couples, senators and their wives, who were comfortable in their own old age, attentive to each other's needs, but perhaps that was the result of their having survived the hungry years with a selective memory.

There were times when she would sit alone in the library and drink until she started feeling sorry for herself. It was all so beyond her grasp, with her husband becoming a stranger to her in a city that was as cold and emotionless as the marble that decorated its shrines. How impressed she'd been those first few months in Washington, standing in awe before the memorials to legendary patriots, but now she wondered about their lives—whether they too had been men driven by insatiable egos to the brink of personal disaster while achieving their great national prominence. It was a game, really—a game that politicians played, the goal being to postpone failure to the very end. That, in essence, was the real success for a Washington politician.

But these thoughts, these problems were as nothing once Joey Alongi had rung her doorbell eleven days ago. Ever since that traumatic moment she'd been unable to keep any food down. She had taken to her bed, lying there all day with her eyes fixed on the ceiling, her mind a blank. She hypnotized herself into a trance by staring at a single crystal of the chandelier above her. Once focused upon it, watching the colors change with the intensity of the light coming through the windows, she made the hours pass like minutes. The twins would return from school, their chatter shrill as they raced up and down the stairs, while Celia tried to calm them down, but Betty in her trance was beyond exterior sounds. In the evening, by the time Randolph came home, she had retired for the night, feigning sleep if not already asleep.

Late in the evening of the eleventh day the telephone rang and it was Henry on the line."

"Henry, where are you?" she asked.

"Las Vegas," he said. "First, let me say that Joey will never bother you again."

"Oh, Henry, how can you believe him, no matter how much money you give him?"

"Betty, he's left the country and he's not coming back. He got himself in trouble with the wrong people here in Las Vegas. And he won't be back in Boston because he'd have to explain the money he's lost here gambling."

Chills ran along her spine. "It sounds too good to be true. How can I thank you for what you've done? I hope it didn't cost you too much money."

"Betty, forget the money—it's not important. However, there is something I must tell you, and please don't panic. Before leaving the country Joey called Rufus and told him part of the story. I don't know exactly how much he told him, but enough I'm sure for Rufus to get his bloodhounds on the trail."

"Oh, my God—"

"No, Betty, be tough. You've got to stand firm and deny any and all accusations. I know it goes against the grain, but it's the only way to handle it. You don't know Joey, never met him, have never been married before, don't know what they're talking about. Once you concede one fact, they'll be off and running."

"But they'll check the records."

"Let them, they won't find anything. Believe me, the slate has been wiped clean."

"How in the world did you accomplish that?"

"I have my ways," he said, forcing a laugh, not wanting to reveal that the day after she'd told him about Alongi he'd flown to the various halls of records and obliterated all references to her marriage to Izzy Cohen, the birth of the child, her marriage and annulment of Alongi— by the simple method of surreptitiously applying acid to all entries.

Then he had visited all the newspaper morgues in Boston and determined that none had a folder on Betty or Cohen. There were plenty of folders on Alongi, but only one newspaper had carried the story of the fire, a three-inch item, which was the only one that mentioned Betty. Henry had stolen it. The chance that anyone would go through all the issues of all the newspapers themselves for those years and find that tiny story was next to impossible.

"Betty, honey, Rufus has as much interest in preserving your marriage as you do. As you know, he's grooming Randolph for bigger things, and the last thing he wants is a divorce or a scandal. But that doesn't mean he won't tell Randolph about it. I'm going to try my damnedest to stop it once I get off this phone. So you collect yourself. Chin up, honey, the worst is over. If you need me, call and I'll come right away. Don't worry, it's going to work out."

In a little voice she said, "Why has Rufus despised me so all these years?"

"Honey, this isn't the time to go into it. It has nothing to do with who or what you are—and he doesn't really despise you. But you infringed upon his personal property by marrying Randolph without his permission."

"I know," she said, "that was a terrible mistake."

"No, it wasn't," Henry said, raising his voice slightly. "You never would have received his permission. I'm glad you married Randolph, and let's leave it there for the moment. I've got to run."

"Thank you," she said, and there seemed to be a new strength in her voice. "I will stand firm and fight."

"That's right, kiddo," Henry said as encouragingly as he could. "Get the old Irish up."

46

It was like waiting for the other shoe to drop. For three days, since Henry's call to warn her of Rufus's intentions, Betty had not seen or heard from Randolph.

She had called her mother to tell her about Alongi's threat and that someone might be coming over to ask her questions, but her mother, who had moved from the old neighborhood after her husband's death, had made a new life for herself in Quincy and doubted that anyone could trace her whereabouts.

"Somehow, darling," her mother had said, "I've always known deep down inside that the dirty Mafia dago would cause you trouble one of these days."

Betty had told her about Henry's remark that "the slate was clean," and her mother had blessed him.

Betty took the girls to the park in the afternoon. She sat on the grass and watched them play, never ceasing to be amazed at how physically similar and mentally dissimilar they were. Their personalities were totally different. Eileen loved hopscotch, rope jumping, and was never without a doll at her side, and Alicia climbed trees, tumbled, and preferred an old baseball mitt to a doll. Alicia rebelled against identical clothing, which Eileen loved and Randolph insisted upon on the premise that it presented a stronger family image.

Eileen was daddy's girl, always wanting to sit on his lap, or hold his hand, devoting hours to making personal cards and writing little notes to please him. Randolph rewarded her with hugs, kisses, and pats on her little fanny. While Alicia was polite, she kept her distance, showing little affection for either parent, although when she did kiss or hug her mother there was an intensity in it that was lacking in Eileen. As Betty saw it, Eileen did what she thought was demanded of her, and Alicia did exactly what she felt like doing when the urge struck her.

In a week the Senate would recess for the rest of the summer and Randolph would go off on an Asian junket. The minute he was on that plane Betty was going to be on the next one to Nevada, to stay at the ranch until school started in the fall. Randolph had asked her to wait until he returned from his junket in three weeks, but now she knew she couldn't stay in that house one more minute than she had to. She had an open invitation from Aunt Caroline and Henry, and she loved it out there, with the swimming pool, tennis court, and the beautiful Arabians and their darling little colts. It was a good life, easy and relaxed, and both girls enjoyed it.

For a man in his late forties, Henry Godwin was in remarkable physical condition. He could ride a horse all day, or could play furious, hustling tennis, charging the net on his first serve, and killing you with a crisp volley. She'd watched Henry and Randolph play three hard sets in scorching heat and at the end it was Randolph who was dragging.

When she was there, she swam laps with Henry every morning, rode horses, and played tennis. As a handicap, he gave her the alleys and took only one serve.

At times Betty wondered what her life would have been like if Randolph had been more like Henry. That was as far as she wanted to carry that thought.

At the ranch she was surrounded by people she loved. Aunt Caroline, so quick and birdlike, so warm and generous. And Holly and Moses Grimes were family and behaved like it. Aunt Caroline worked right along with Holly, and Henry worked with Moses, taking suggestions from Moses as often as he offered them himself. When Moses had been placed in charge of the ranch, the first and only Negro ranch foreman in Nevada history, there was some bitching and quitting among the hands, but Moses had proved himself to be every inch as much a man as the best of them. Grudgingly or not, they grew to respect him for his fairness, his enormous strength, hard work, and gentle ways.

Betty knew that unless there was company Henry and Aunt Caroline ate all their meals in the large kitchen with Holly and Moses. Their ties went back to Vicksburg, and in some ways Aunt Caroline and Henry seemed more comfortable with the Grimeses than with Randolph and Rufus.

It was Aunt Caroline who had explained to Betty that Rufus wasn't Randolph's real grandfather. Betty was told that Randolph's mother had died in San Francisco during childbirth and that Henry had married Rufus's daughter, Alicia, who died of tuberculosis in a Swiss sanatorium when Randolph was still a child. Afterward Betty had wondered why Randolph had never mentioned these things. Aunt Caroline had assured her that Randolph had been told the facts of his birth when he turned sixteen, but that he had continued talking as though Alicia and Rufus were his real mother and grandfather.

What intrigued Betty was that Randolph had never asked a single question about his real mother. That seemed abnormal to her. The only explanation, offered by Aunt Caroline, was that Randolph had so loved Alicia that he couldn't tolerate the thought that she wasn't his real mother. Not once during their marriage had Randolph ever broached this subject. It had been Randolph's idea to name the twins for Betty's mother and Alicia. It was ironic that Eileen had turned out to be Daddy's pet.

On the fourth night after Henry's warning call Betty sat in the library drinking Napoleon brandy. With each drink she became more morose and maudlin. Life was unfair. The things that had happened to her were beyond her control. She had loved Randolph and she knew he had once loved her—well, at least, loved her as much as he could love anyone. By now she was convinced there was something vital missing in Randolph's makeup. It was impossible to tell when he was being sincere or dissembling. And perhaps, Betty thought, by now he was incapable of knowing the difference.

He was like an actor going through life playing different roles. Even his lovemaking was an act. And a poor one at that. Perfunctory, arbitrary, and selfish, more demanding as the years went by in ways Betty considered perverted. His suggestions became demands, and when he was rebuffed his frustration exploded into a rage that drove him from the house, often for days at a time. Upon his return following each of these dramatic exits, Betty had acquiesced to his demands, each time feeling soiled by her capitulation.

Sex became a synonym for love and perversion a synonym for sex. In time Randolph had grown impotent for any form of straight sex. Whoever his mistresses were—and they were plentiful—Betty felt sorry for them. They were paying a steep price for their dalliance with this surrogate of wealth and power.

Pouring her fifth drink, Betty told herself that she didn't envy them. Let them wallow in their perversions. She pounded the arm of the chair with her fist. To hell with Randolph Harrison Godwin and be damned with his good looks. And his artful manners.

He was a two-faced liar and a cheat, who could invent a story on the spot and look her square in the eye as he lied his head off. And what was he anyway but a puppet for Rufus Boutwell, the most bigoted, narrow-minded, disgusting man she'd ever known? And to think that she once had trembled in his presence. How naive and stupid she must have appeared in those days. Or last month, for that matter.

She sat down and looked at her distorted image in the huge snifter and thought what a damned fool she'd been. A whole decade had slipped by, most of it downhill, at a head-spinning clip.

Why couldn't she have met the father instead of the son? God Almighty, what a husband and lover Henry would have made. She leaned back in the chair and closed her eyes. For the first time in nearly two weeks she felt the tension easing, the fear slowly evaporating, and a sliver of hope rising in her heart. She held the snifter against her chest and warm tears came to her eyes. Henry had solved the problem of Joey Alongi. A celebration was in order.

But had she thanked Henry for what he'd done for her? Had she really thanked him?

She looked down at the brandy snifter and was surprised to find it empty. She stood up, tried to take a step, and found herself reeling. "Whoops," she said, "am getting a little tipsy." Holding the brandy glass at arm's length in front of her, she tried to walk a straight line and nearly fell down as she reached the bar.

She returned to the chair and collapsed into it. "Napoleon, you miserable little twerp, you've been distilled into one potent bastard," she mumbled aloud, trying to place the glass on the end table, next to the telephone. She stared at the instrument for a while, then picked it up, dialed for the operator, and gave her the number of Henry's trailer in Las Vegas.

A moment later she heard Henry's voice. "Henry," she said, slurring her words, "it's Betty. I'm all alone and drunk as a skunk."

Henry laughed. "Well, that's better than being all alone and sober as a judge."

"Henry, have I thanked you for all you did for me—have I *really* thanked you?"

"Yes, darling, you *really* did."

"Oh, I'm so relieved to hear you say that, Henry." She paused and he could hear her breathing, as though she was trying to collect herself. "I never thought I would love to hear myself say the name Henry, but I do, I really, honestly do. Henry, Henry, Henry. It has such a sweet, gentle ring to it. Like the man himself."

"Well, frankly, I never really cared all that much for it myself."

"Oh, Henry, how can you say that? It's a beautiful name. I just love it."

"Thank you, Betty, and I love your name."

"Henry and Betty, names made for each other. Why didn't you name Randolph Henry instead of Randolph? I think that's the whole problem with him. That terrible name. Randy Randolph. And he's doing his damnedest to live up to it."

"Darling, have you seen Rufus, has he been to the house?"

"No, nor has Randolph. Four days now and not a sign of either one. Probably with their whores at the Forum Club."

"Now, Betty—"

"Never mind with the 'Now, Betty.' I know all about that place. Randolph spends more nights there than at home." She paused and took a sip of brandy. "Henry, have I told you that Napoleon is one potent little bastard?"

"Not recently."

"Have I told you that your son has peculiar habits?"

Instantly, Henry's mind flashed back to the steam room scene with Silver and Ruth Bellini, but he pushed it aside.

"Betty, darling, haven't you heard anything at all from him in the past four days?"

"Not a whisper," she said, and giggled. "That's not easy to say when Napoleon has you by the tongue and is pulling at it with a team of horses. Arabians. Have I told you I love your Arabians? And your ranch, and your pool, and your tennis court, and your sweet, darling aunt, and—oh, God, I'm really running off at the mouth."

"When are you coming out? Aunt Caroline and Holly and Moses are looking forward to it."

"And you, Henry, are you looking forward to it?"

The implied intimacy made him uneasy.

"Of course," he said, trying to steer her into something less sensitive. "Have you been practicing your tennis?"

"I'm going to beat the socks right off you, Henry Godwin. I'll give you the alleys this time, but I want two serves. I've learned the French twist for my second serve."

"Sounds awesome."

"Did you know your son learned lots of French twists during the war? Some place you in humiliating positions. Oh, I'm sorry, Henry, please forgive me."

"Don't be silly, there's nothing to forgive."

"It's the Irish in me. Have I told you the Irish are terrible drinkers."

"Is that Napoleon's opinion?"

She laughed. "I'm killing him. One more drink and he's going to be a dead soldier. How do you like that one, Henry?"

"That was the Irish, all right."

"Oh, my God! Someone just came in the front door. It's judgment day, Henry. The time has come for me to pay for my sins."

"Betty! Remember, now. Stick to your story."

"Henry, have I told you I love you?"

"Yes, darling, and I love you."

"No, Henry, I mean *really* love you."

And the line went dead.

47

Rufus and Randolph had spent four days in Boston trying to check up on Alongi and Betty without arousing suspicion. Their quest was in vain. Nobody in the old Southie neighborhood remembered Betty Schurtz. There were no records or news stories to indicate that Betty and Alongi even knew each other, much less were ever married.

Rufus was quiet on the flight back to Washington. After landing at National they went to the VIP lounge for a drink.

Rufus gulped down half his Coca-Cola while Randolph sipped at his bourbon and water. "You want to know what I think, sonny boy?"

Randolph had to struggle to conceal the anger seething through him. It had been building up ever since Rufus had told him about Betty's marriage to Alongi and the Jew. He was at the point now where he could have reached across the table and throttled Rufus for delaying his confrontation with Betty. That harlot posing as a virgin, with two fucking husbands, and she acting holier than thou when he asked for the simplest deviation from the boring missionary position she associated with true love.

"Your daddy got there ahead of us and cleaned the record."

"I don't get it," Randolph said, struggling to keep his voice calm.

"It's quite simple when you put the pieces together. Where do you think this punk got fifty thousand dollars? Santa Claus?" Rufus studied him through glinting slits of gray eyes. "Here's the way I see it. Alongi goes to Betty, wants money, she goes to Henry, who cleans up the record and pays off. Alongi comes to Vegas with the money, loses it at baccarat, gets in trouble with Covelli, and the goon squad buries him. Or—" He paused, his eyes widening. "Goddamn! Why didn't I think of this before? Your daddy buries him."

"What?" Randolph exclaimed. "Are you losing your mind?"

"No, no, listen to me. It's the only explanation that makes sense.

Henry wasn't the least worried about the goon squad. He tried to fake it, but he's no good at it. He knew they'd never find Alongi because he'd already beaten them to the punch."

"That's ridiculous," Randolph said. "Henry wouldn't hurt a fly. In fact, he doesn't kill flies. He doesn't kill anything—not even on the ranch. Holly doesn't mind wringing a chicken's neck and Moses butchers calves, but not Henry. He's nowhere in sight when that's going on."

"Listen, sonny boy, I could tell you things about your father that would make your hair stand straight up, but I won't. He's done us a big favor. We can forget about the goon squad and the dirty dagos. They're going to be looking for that punk until doomsday."

"Listen, I better get home," Randolph said, only half listening to Rufus, his mind already forming the words he would say to Betty when he walked in that house and looked at her, saw for the first time what she really was, a fucking lying whore. He'd given her his seed, conceived his daughters in her filthy cunt—what a fool he'd been. How she must have laughed at him behind his back. She'd made a sucker out of him. Women—all of them were nothing but snakes, crawling their way into your brain to loose their poison.

Rufus nodded, deep in thought. There was no judging Henry Godwin. He'd been with him all these years and he still didn't understand what made him tick. Who would have thought that Henry, at his age, would have the balls to pull this off? Alongi, Rufus had been told, weighed four hundred pounds and was a tough, bone-breaking hood, what they called a strong-arm.

Rufus finished his Coke and looked up at Randolph, who could conceal his anxiety no longer. "When I picked your father as a son-in-law and a partner, I made the best decision of my life. Oh, we've had our differences. His ethics get in the way and I have to do an end run now and then, but he's the straightest shooter I've ever known."

"I don't believe Henry's capable of violence. Besides, you've told me enough times that he's weak."

"He still is, where it counts politically. He don't have the stomach it takes to reach for the top and make it. He's complacent, satisfied with half measures, and too goddamn scrupulous when he should be ruthless. And that's why you're in the United States Senate and he's not. Oh, I thought of running him years ago, but I realized that the future was with you, sonny boy. You and me think alike. We make an unbeatable team. We're hardheaded sons of bitches and we don't bullshit ourselves with pious excuses. We don't mind kicking ass and stomping heads to get our way. But you can't get Henry to see it this way. Oh, I don't mean he was not a good man. He made his contribution, in his own way. He could handle a little bribery, vice, or corruption in high places, but his heart was never in it. And he lacked the guts to go all out. Go for the kill. Except in a special case like this Alongi character, who threatened his family. Henry has very strong loyalties. But usually too many qualms get in his way, blind him to what the real goals are in this world.

"Well, you and me, sonny boy, we don't have such qualms. Someday we're going to own this town, this country, this whole fucking world." Rufus laughed, banging his Coke glass against the table. "And you sure as hell can't say it's the booze talking, either."

Randolph stood up and tried to smile. "Rufus, I've got to get home."

Rufus nodded, pushing his chair back and standing up. "I know, sonny boy, but take it easy. Use your head. Don't create a situation you can't handle. Sure, you've been had by a Jewish slut, but nobody else knows that except you and me and your father. Let's keep it that way. Hell, you don't have to sleep with her—get your own bedroom, go your way and let her take care of the kids and house. Remember, politically we need Betty. Divorce is out of the question for where we're headed. Use your head and work it out. Be smart."

48

Randolph slammed the front door and crossed the foyer to the kitchen, which was empty, Celia having gone home after doing the dinner dishes. The girls, he knew, were already in their beds on the third floor. He walked through the dining and living rooms. Both were empty. Betty was either in the library or in her bedroom on the second floor.

He opened the library door and she looked up at him from the chair, the telephone still in her hand as she replaced it on its cradle.

"I was just talking to your daddy," she said. "He's worried about you."

Randolph glared at her. "You dirty fucking cunt," he shouted.

"How would you know?" she snapped back. "You've forgotten they exist. Isn't that what you think God made assholes for?"

"Ah, now I see you've got the mouth that goes with the reputation. What happened to the demure little virgin who trembled with trepidation when first making love? For a dirty slut, you're one fantastic actress."

Betty stood up and staggered toward the door. "I'm going to bed," she said. "You know what a bed is, don't you? People sleep on them when they're tired or drunk."

He stepped in front of her, a menacing glint coming into his eyes. "You shut your filthy whore's mouth."

"Other people," she said, trying desperately to keep her balance, "use beds for other purposes, but I wouldn't know about such things, and if I once did, I've long forgotten. Time erases all memories."

"You fucking kike."

"You forget mick. It's mick-kike or kike-mick—take your pick, you bigoted pervert."

Then he hit her with a vicious combination—a left to the solar plexus and a right to the side of the head. The blows propelled her halfway across the small room. She fell on her back and he heard her head crack against the marble hearth. A moment later the white marble began to streak with crimson. Betty's head was twisted to the side and her left cheek and eye were already swelling and turning purple.

Randolph stepped back, his hands automatically going to his mouth to hold back the hot vomit he felt burning in his throat. He ran to the kitchen, reaching the sink just in time. He vomited until his body was racked by dry heaves and even then he couldn't seem to stop it.

The phone rang and he jumped back in fear, wondering whether he should answer it, knowing it would prove he was in the house at the time of death, for he had no doubt that Betty was dead. Instead he picked up the phone and broke the connection with his finger. A moment later he dialed Rufus at his hotel.

"What the hell's going on?" Rufus asked. "I just called you and somebody picked up the phone and hung up."

"Oh, Rufus, please," Randolph cried, "you've got to get over here right away. Something terrible's happened. Please, hurry, please."

"Hold tight, sonny boy, I'm on my way."

"Rufus—"

"Don't say another word," Rufus shouted, and hung up.

George Clews stood in the library doorway as Rufus examined Betty, who was still lying where she had fallen. She was unconscious but alive, her pulse weak and her heartbeat erratic.

He looked up at Clews and motioned him over. Randolph was still in the kitchen, cleaning up the sink.

"Jesus Mother of Christ," Rufus growled. "What a fucking mess."

Clews sidled up to him, lowering his voice. "Randy thinks she's dead. Why don't we let him think it and make sure she stays dead? That's the cleanest, safest way out."

Rufus looked at him. "Damn, I needed her alive, but maybe you're right. She's a danger to us now. We can no longer trust her to behave. She'll be nothing but trouble. So go ahead. But wait until we're gone. Then finish her off. Make it look like some rapist broke in here and killed her." He paused and gripped Clews's arm firmly. "But make it quick and painless. She's suffered enough. I know this is asking a lot, but strangle her before you rape her. Do it upstairs in her bedroom. But wait a couple of hours. In fact, wait until I call you from New York. Then climb out her bedroom window and down the trellis. Go to a phone booth, call the cops, tell them you were driving home and saw somebody coming out the second-story window. Then hang up and go back to the hotel."

"What if she dies before you call?"

"You rape her anyway, then wait for my call. After that go through the same routine I've just given you. You got it?"

"Yeah, sure. Where're you going to be at?"

"The Stork Club, where we're going to be goddamn visible. By the time we get back it'll be early morning and most of the mess will be cleaned up."

Before leaving the room, Rufus suddenly grabbed Clews in a hug. "George, you're my good left arm. This is the most important thing you'll ever do for me. There's some danger in it. That trellis could give way, a cop could be going by at the wrong time—just be very careful. Everything we've worked for rides on you. That's how important you are to me, George. No one in the world has ever had a more loyal friend than you, George."

"Oh, hell, boss, don't worry, I won't fuck it up."

"I'm not worried. You never have and never will. You're not the fuck-up type. Good luck. I'll see you in the morning."

"Have a good time, boss."

Rufus stopped as he reached the library. "What do you mean?"

"I mean at the Stork Club, boss—that's a swanky joint."

Rufus smiled. "Remind me, George. Next time we go to New York I'll take you there."

"No kidding! Thanks a lot, boss."

Rufus smiled, shook his head, and left the room. George Clews was no Einstein, but then Einstein was no George Clews. In this world there was a need for all sorts of talents. The real geniuses of the world were men like Rufus Boutwell, who could pick the right one for the right job.

49

Eileen Schurtz insisted that her daughter be buried in Holy Trinity Cemetery next to a plot with a small granite cross that bore the name Michael and nothing else. At Henry's urging Randolph and Rufus agreed.

The press of the world was there, the focus of attention the bereaved widower—the handsome senator with the beautiful twin girls flanking him. One was crying and holding on to his hand and the other was dry-eyed and standing stiffly with her hands clenched tightly at her sides.

Henry had to support Aunt Caroline, now a paper-thin lady with snow-white hair and large anxious eyes blurred by tears. Henry had his arm around her shoulders and could feel her trembling. She had come against his wishes and now he worried about her. Rufus stood near Randolph, his head bowed in respect, as the coffin was slowly lowered into the grave. Betty having received a papal dispensation arranged by Rufus, the Catholic priest blessed the disappearing coffin with holy water and a final prayer.

When the first dirt was dropped on the coffin, Aunt Caroline collapsed in Henry's arms. She was gasping for breath and as Henry gently lowered her to the ground, kneeling beside her, he saw the anxious look glaze over, her mouth go slack, her pale lips turn blue.

Others gathered around them and Henry angrily ordered them away. No one should have to die with blurred faces peering down like ghouls. Her lips moved and he lowered his ear to her mouth.

"Oh, dear heart," she gasped, struggling for breath. "Please bury me next to the General."

"Of course, darling," he said, "but you're not going to die."

She opened her eyes, trying to focus, and for a fleeting moment her eyes turned anxious. "I love your ranch, but Vicksburg's my real home."

"Now, please, don't speak. Just rest."

Henry motioned to the funeral director, who hurried over. "We better get her to the hospital right away."

The funeral director knelt by Caroline and shook his head. "It's too late," he said. "She's gone."

Henry looked at her in disbelief. Then he lifted her gently in his arms and walked to the hearse. The funeral director opened the door and Henry stepped inside and sat down on a jump seat.

"Don't you want to put her down?" the funeral director asked.

"No," Henry said, "I'll hold her."

Before the funeral director could close the door, one of the twins jumped inside the hearse and sat on a jump seat next to Henry. "I'm Alicia," she said.

"I know," Henry said. "How in the world could I ever forget?"

50

High on a hill overlooking the Mississippi on one side and a vast green valley on the other, where once Henry had seen the Pikes riding during the funeral of the General, Henry watched another body being lowered into the ground. Uncle Avery and Aunt Harriet, as withered as the corpse in the coffin, stood beside him. It was a simple funeral, with a few neighbors, Holly and Moses Grimes, and the twins. Randolph had left for his Asian junket with the understanding that the twins would spend the summer at the ranch.

In the afternoon Henry walked to the old fishing hole and sat with his back against a willow tree. Here, with the bait drifting at the end of a bobbing cork, Henry had first read *Leaves of Grass* and marveled at the discovery that others had felt what he had felt, had thought what he had thought, had loved what he had loved. Henry closed his eyes and saw himself, a gangly youth, lying on the grass with his arms folded behind his head, gazing up at a blue summer sky and floating white clouds.

The words had echoed in the young Henry's head: "A few light kisses, a few embraces, a reaching around of arms."

The lines of Whitman's poem had brought the image of Camilla before the youth's eyes and he'd felt a stirring in his loins. As the teenage boy had done so many times before when the fantasies had come to him in the night, he pressed down hard with one hand, squeezing himself until the surging feeling inside him grew with such intensity that he could hear himself moaning.

Then he heard a twig snap and sat bolt upright, a guilty expression on his face as he looked wildly about him. He heard a giggle and Camilla came out from behind a bush.

"Hey, Henry," the girl teased, moving toward him, "was you pullin' your puddin'?"

"What are you talking about?" he asked.

"I saw you pullin' your puddin', so don't bother denying it, 'cause I saw Gabriel do it plenty times."

"I was doing no such thing," he insisted, but he could feel his face flush and his penis beginning to throb again. Her hot eyes were on him and he quickly rolled over on his stomach.

She came and sat next to him. "Turn over and let me show you how to pull your puddin'. I ain't never done it before, but I've been dying to try it with you. You can touch my pussy, if you have a mind to."

He was fourteen that summer and she was thirteen, and that was the way it had begun for them on that warm summer afternoon.

III
TODAY

51

President Truman Abbott woke up with heartburn. He sat up in bed and emitted a series of dry belches. The First Lady sighed in annoyance and reached blindly for the bedside lamp. She raised her eyeshade and blinked in the soft glow of the lamp.

"I told you about those mixed nuts," she said. "They do it to you every time."

Abbott ignored her. He remained hunched over, belched a few more times, and looked at his watch. It was a few minutes past four. Too late for sleeping pills, They worked so slowly they would leave him groggy all day.

Mary Abbott slipped the eyeshade back on and flopped over on her side, facing away from her husband.

Abbott felt the gaseous pressure burning its way through his stomach up to his chest, tightening around his heart, squeezing like a powerful fist, and for a moment he thought he was having a cardiac seizure. Finally the belch shot up his throat and burst from his mouth like rumbling thunder, bringing the First Lady to a sitting position next to her husband.

"My God, Tru," she said crankily, "how long must you indulge yourself with this gurgling display?"

Abbott smiled contentedly. "Mary, go back to sleep. The seventh wave just crashed to shore. I feel fine now."

Mary removed her eyeshade and looked closely at her husband. There was a grayish cast to his flesh that worried her. The primary campaign and now this convention had placed him under greater stress than he'd ever admit. He was a man who worked hard at presenting a relaxed demeanor under all circumstances.

"Are you sure you're all right?" she asked.

He leaned over and kissed her cheek. "Listen carefully, Mary. I'm issuing a Presidential Proclamation. No peanuts or mixed nuts are to be allowed within a one-mile radius of the President of the United States. And I will hold you personally responsible for any infraction."

"Same old song and dance. Your problem, Tru, is that you lack self-discipline when it comes to nuts."

He shrugged and rolled out of bed. "I don't care. The decree stands," he said, going to the window and parting the blackout drapes. Thirty-five stories below him the Strip was crowded with pedestrians shuffling from casino to casino, the neon lights so brilliant that the people cast no shadow.

"Mary, come here, you've got to see this to believe it."

She joined him at the window and peeked through the opening in the drapes. "Are they crazy?" she asked. "It's past four in the morning. What do they do in the daytime?"

"Sleep," he said.

"I hope they're not our delegates. What a hideous place for a convention," she said, moving back toward the bed. "Come on, let's get to sleep—you've got a hard day ahead."

He released the drapes, followed her to the large bed, and sat on the edge of his side of it. He shook his head. "Mary, can you give me one good reason why I ever got into politics?"

She reached over and placed a hand on his drooping shoulder. It was at times like this that she loved him most—when he opened himself to her, discarded the pose and became vulnerable like the shy boy she had fallen in love with in high school.

"You're a politician, darling, because you're damn terrific at it. You're a decent man with compassion for people and a great capacity for reducing complex problems down to their basics."

"Thanks, Mary, but you're wrong. Right now I feel more like a Chicago ward heeler hustling around for delegate votes. Have you any idea the kind of question they have the gall to ask when they suspect you need their vote? There are times, believe me, when I'd like to punch some of them right in their mealy mouths."

"I know, I know," she said. "I wouldn't mind slapping a few faces myself."

"I've got two hundred goddamn bush beaters meeting with delegations in state caucuses, urging them to stand firm. And still Foote's attempt to release the delegates from their pledges is gaining support."

"That man has more gimmicks up his sleeve than a used-car salesman," she said.

"Between the religious loonies and the Wall Street bankers, he's built himself quite a bizarre political base."

"Forget Wall Street, darling—they think you're a Bolshevik in Republican clothing."

He chuckled. "Reminds me of a story about Jack Kennedy and a banker. 'If I weren't President right now,' Kennedy said, 'I'd be buying stocks.' And the banker shot back, 'Yes, I quite agree. If you weren't President, I'd be buying stocks, too.' As far as the bankers are concerned, Hamilton Foote is a reincarnation of their beloved Calvin Coolidge."

"Does Foote really have a chance?"

He shrugged. "Who knows? Anything can happen in the next three days. At least, that's Joe Alcorn's opinion, for whatever his opinion is worth."

"The poor man's Teddy White. Alcorn's a disgrace."

"And a pretentious bore. Now he's a perfect example of the crap you've got to put up with to have a career in public life today."

"Tru, I know how self-serving this sounds, but the country needs you. So, like it or not, you're going to have to grin and bear it a little while longer."

He smiled. "Of course, you're right. I need a second term. The only President truly worth a damn is a lame duck with enough political appeal to convince members of Congress that his endorsement in their future campaigns would be helpful."

Abbott stretched out but kept his eyes open. "What time's the 'Today' show?"

"Seven, and we can't miss it."

He took several deep breaths, trying to relieve his tension. "Have you heard from Lisa?"

Now it was Mary's turn to take a deep breath, but she let it out softly. "No. I'd have told you if I'd heard anything."

He closed his eyes and tried to visualize his daughter's face, but it wouldn't surface. "I wish I knew where the hell we went wrong with her."

"Who says *we* went wrong? I, for one, have stopped worrying about her. She's a grown woman and responsible for her own actions."

He sat up again. "I never told you, but a couple years ago she dated Randolph Godwin. In fact, they spent a couple of weeks in Aspen together."

"Too bad it didn't stick," she said. "He's quite a catch."

Abbott looked at his wife. "Not you, too."

She shrugged. "I know you despise him, but he's terribly good-looking and charming, and it's not his fault his grandfather's Rufus Boutwell."

Abbott was too tired now to dredge up what he knew about Randolph Godwin. He looked at his wife, who was still an attractive woman, and impulsively embraced her. "If I'm reelected, I'll sign a proclamation that he must dance with you at the Inaugural Ball."

She kissed him and replaced the eyeshade. "I'm going to sleep."

"Okay. Put out the light."

She snapped off the lamp and lay there listening to her husband's deep breathing. She wondered what his reaction would be if he knew of Lisa's rapid deterioration in the past two years. She was heavily into drugs and appeared to have adopted a life-style lacking any decency or morality. But so far, thank God, she'd been discreet enough to stay out of the headlines by using pseudonyms and staying away from newsmen.

52

Shortly after four o'clock that morning a Learjet came to a whining stop in front of Rufus Boutwell's private hangar. Two men emerged from the plane and Rufus was there to greet them.

Jesse Stelk was the first to shake Rufus's hand. In the years since the two men had met, Stelk had become vice-chairman of the Century Committee, an honor that bespoke his financial success. His International Conglomerate, Inc. (ICI), presently controlled sixty percent of the outstanding stock of nearly five hundred major corporate entities, which made him one of the wealthiest men in the world.

Wealthier still was the man standing next to him, H. Russell Pierpont, who was chairman of the Century Committee and the founder of the Pierpont Bank, the world's largest commercial bank, with nearly four hundred domestic offices and more than two hundred in foreign countries. On its board sat the world's most powerful industrialists.

Their presence in Las Vegas signified to Rufus that the Century Committee was finally ready to take its first major step in achieving its grand design of establishing a new corporate world.

Moments after their arrival, Rufus had whisked both men by helicopter to Henry Godwin's chalet on top of an eight-thousand-foot peak in Charleston Park, which was protected by a half-mile-wide hollow, nature's perfect moat, making it accessible only to mountain climbers or helicopters with permission to land on the chalet's private pad.

It was the ideal hideaway. Boutwell's electronics expert had planted hidden microphones and video cameras with infrared lights in the caucus rooms and command posts of several of the important delegations and sophisticated listening devices in the headquarters of President Abbott and Hamilton Foote. The minuscule microphones had been installed at the time of the hotel's construction and immediately became dormant when sweeping equipment attempted to detect them. Ensconced in the chalet, Rufus's guests would be able to monitor on television screens and/or speakers a great deal of the behind-the-scenes drama taking place at the convention.

CHAPTER

53

Again Henry Godwin awoke in a cold sweat. He sat up in the bed and looked wildly about him. He was alone in the bed and was immediately grateful that Daisy hadn't witnessed his fear. Two days in a row he'd had the same nightmare. If there was a message, it eluded him. He left the bed and found Daisy in the kitchen, expertly breaking eggs into a bowl with one hand and humming happily as she worked. She was wearing a peignoir of sheer black silk that highlighted the golden tone of her skin.

She looked up and offered him her lips. He kissed her lightly and she went on with her work without interruption.

"I was just about to drag you out of bed," she said.

"What's for breakfast, woman?"

"Your favorite, chicken-liver omelet. Have some coffee and go turn the set on in the den. We'll eat there and watch the 'Today' show. I can't wait to see the twins together again with their father. Sometimes I can't believe he's really my son and they're my granddaughters. I've had so little to do with it." She looked up at him with misty eyes. "There are moments when I try to imagine what our life would have been if I'd left Vince in San Francisco and gone with you and Randy, wherever that would have taken us."

He took her in his arms. "I regret it, too," he said softly. "More than you'll ever know."

She looked up at him. "His life would've been completely different. He wouldn't have met Betty, the twins wouldn't be alive. Would he be a senator today? The possibilities are frightening and I try not to think about them. But sometimes I just can't help myself."

He held her tightly against him and for the first time since he'd left Vicksburg Camilla was weeping in his arms. The only good thing that had come out of the whole mess was his granddaughter Alicia, but he had to wonder if even she was worth it all.

Steve Adler sat in the makeup chair, studying himself in the mirror, and listening to Sam Rosen while the beautician prepared him for the camera, turning his largely pallid complexion to a robust tan.

Rosen kept up his patter, moving around the chair like a boxer stalking a weary opponent.

"The twins are with the senator in the green room, but go easy on them. Just the necessary amenities. This is the senator's show. Get him to explain the new ideological factions in the Republican party and where he stands in this struggle between Abbott and Foote. He'll give you a fantastic fucking show. You believe me, Steve. The timing's perfect. You couldn't have a better guest than the senator this morning."

The beautician stepped back admiringly and Adler stood up, moved closer to the mirror, and parted his lips to examine his clenched teeth.

"They sparkle, honey," the beautician said.

"They goddamn well should," he said. "They cost me nearly twenty thou." He smiled at her, his handsome twenty-six-year-old face crinkling just enough to give him a touch of maturity. He looked at his watch and turned to Rosen. "We're on after the seven-thirty news break. Go give him a pep talk. I want him to level and not get cute."

Rosen grabbed Adler's hand and shook it vigorously. "Steve, I'm counting on you. No fucking showboating from him and no sandbagging from you. Treat him right, pal." He let loose with a few jabs and uppercuts. "This means a lot to me, and for you it's just another fucking show. Tomorrow it'll be somebody else." He paused and looked sharply at Adler. "It don't pay to make enemies in this musical-chair business. Here today, gone tomorrow, and forgotten the day after."

Adler shrugged. "Sam, you do your job and let me do mine. If you want an honest opinion, I'm not all that crazy about the way you do yours."

Rosen again grabbed his hand and shook it vigorously. "Don't turn prima donna on me now, Steve. You listen to your Uncle Sam and everybody's going to be real happy."

The twins sat on either side of Randolph, and Steve Adler sat facing them. The technicians were attaching the small lapel microphones and Adler kept clearing his throat as he reviewed his cue cards.

"Ten seconds," the director said. "Five, three, two—you're on."

Steve Adler smiled and began talking, introducing Randolph, Alicia, and Eileen, referring briefly to the tragedy that had brought them international attention as children.

"I must say you've grown up into beautiful young ladies," he said. "Are you both actively engaged in the campaign?"

"Yes, very much so," Eileen said, turning to smile at her father. "I find politics not only exciting but a most rewarding career."

"Does that mean you have plans of your own for the future?"

She smiled enigmatically. "I've given it serious consideration."

"And you, Alicia?" Adler asked.

"Well, I haven't found a political party that'll have me." She smiled.

"That's interesting," Adler said, turning to Randolph. "But, Senator, before we move into the political arena, did you ever think you'd see Republicans holding their national convention here in Las Vegas?"

"That Alicia's pure Godwin," Daisy said.

"She's got a mind of her own," Henry said. "That's for sure."

"But, Henry, can't she bend a little at least for her father?"

Henry shrugged and took a bite of omelet.

"Absolutely," Randolph said. "Las Vegas is the ideal convention city. The concentration of hotels and restaurants, the world's greatest entertainers, and the gambling, if you're so inclined." With a perfectly controlled smile, Randolph made it clear to the viewers that *he* wasn't so inclined. "There's no other place like it."

"Granted that everything is convenient, but what about its reputation as 'Sin City, U.S.A.'"

Randolph smiled tolerantly. "That's old hat. Nevadans have always prided themselves on being citizens of the only truly free state in the Union. We don't, as the young people say today, get bent out of shape by words like *immoral*."

"You don't mean to imply that Nevadans are immoral or amoral?"

"On the contrary, Nevadans are realists. Remember that Will Rogers, one of our most famous political humorists and a man of great moral character, was one of the few outsiders to support us back when we legalized gambling in nineteen thirty-one. 'Nevadans,' he said, 'have shaken off the cloak of hypocrisy.' That was an astute observation, and one that I think applies equally to the fact that we were the first state to legalize public prizefighting in eighteen ninety-seven and to the fact that prostitution, the world's oldest profession, has either always been legal and licensed or openly tolerated in most counties of our state. Also we led the nation in the enactment of sensible marriage and divorce laws. Other states are coming around to our way of thinking, slowly but surely. Look at gambling today. It's now in Atlantic City, and a dozen other state legislatures are considering casino gaming bills. Today many of our leading social scientists and economists are predicting that by the turn of the century every major resort in the world will offer casino gambling." Randolph paused and smiled. "So progress marches on—it's contagious."

"And what has happened to those old rumors about the Mafia and profit skimming?"

Randolph continued smiling. "Part of the mythology, Steve. I hate to say this, but it's true—Las Vegas is so respectable that it suffers from an identity crisis."

"I'm afraid I don't follow you."

"I mean, the switch from the fable to reality. Young people don't come here. They think we're square. The point, you see, is that Nevada, which completely ignored Prohibition laws, is tough on drug users. To put it in street vernacular, any youngster who thinks he can come here and buy drugs is going to leave town with a monkey on his back. Our law enforcement people are vigilant. Oh, there was a time when Las Vegas was known as the swinger's paradise, but in the last twenty years this country has gone through some drastic and, for most of us, traumatic changes in morals and values. Our previous concepts of wickedness now seem almost quaint. Drugs and easy sex, the hardrock culture, pornography in movies, magazines, and books, the pervasive influence of television on young minds—all of these things have pushed our society into revolutionary social changes. In the process Las Vegas has become as respectable as apple pie, its appeal shifting to middle-aged, middle-class Americans."

"You make Las Vegas sound almost dull, like fun city for the Geritol set. Is that why gambling stocks dropped so sharply?"

There was the bare raising of an eyebrow before Randolph chuckled pleasantly. "The stock situation is stabilizing. There was a speculative fever a few years ago that drove stocks sky high, and gradually they've been coming back down to earth. They're once again an attractive investment. Not only does our Gaming Control Board have a backlog of applicants for licenses, but the present establishments keep expanding, adding on more rooms all the time—the boom has never stopped."

Steve Adler smiled up at the camera. "We're going to break here, and when we come back, Senator, we'd like you to give us your assessment of what we can expect to see here in the next few days. Is President Truman Abbott in trouble? That's the question that's paramount in everybody's mind at this moment. Stay with us, folks—we'll be right back with Senator Godwin and his lovely daughters."

Mary Abbott sat on the sofa next to her husband and stared blankly at the deodorant commercial.

"He's almost as smooth a talker as he is a dancer," she said lightly.

Abbott, who was watching the program alone with his wife, was deep in thought—about Alicia. There was a coolness toward her father that was almost glaring, particularly in contrast to her sister Eileen. He knew that some of his staff would want to follow up on it, exploit it, if possible, but that was something he'd never permit.

"What are you thinking, darling?" Mary asked.

"Oh, the old soft-shoe routine."

"I can't wait to hear his assessment of you and the convention."

"I can," Abbott said. "Soft-shoe dancers are low kickers. I think I'm about to get drop-kicked in the groin."

From his sky suite at the convention center NTN anchorman Alistair Baker was watching the NBC monitor as he prepared to go on the air in a few minutes with the convention's call to order by Republican National Chairman Bill Shockley. He swore under his breath, disappointed that Steve Adler's director was keeping the cameras focused on Godwin and Adler, with no close-ups of either of the girls since the opening sequence. Goddamn megalomaniac, Baker thought. Who gives a shit about the back of his head. Or his face, for that matter.

Baker would have enjoyed a closer look at Eileen. She was delicious. Having been a passenger on Randolph's L-1011 on the flight to Las Vegas, he had talked with her and found her most responsive. It was true that Eileen was probably young enough to be his daughter, but she nonetheless was a mature woman with perhaps more experience in the sexual arena than he possessed. Young women today were more liberated. That very fact intimidated him and made him feel his age. The look in her green eyes had been all the invitation he needed, but the problem was that he hadn't known how to follow through.

There was another angle to Eileen worth bearing in mind. His perception of her hostility toward her sister Alicia. Handled properly, it

407

might provide the kind of sidebar this convention needed to spark it up. He would make it his scoop, then sit back and give Cronkite, Chancellor, Brinkley, and Reynolds the old finger. That he hadn't forgotten how to do.

Steve Adler adjusted his tie and smiled. The red light on the camera came on and he started speaking, again introducing Senator Godwin and the twins.

"Senator, before the break I asked you for your views on this convention. How united is the GOP? Or perhaps I should say how disunited is it as it meets here to select its next standard-bearer?"

Randolph's expression turned serious. "I wish I could say that all four thousand delegates, half-delegates, quarter-delegates, and alternates will act in harmony, but that would be asking for a party's leadership to be composed of robots instead of human beings. Our party is in a constant state of flux. Just looking at the people who worked on the platform last week and the hard-line planks they'll be bringing to the convention floor today, we can see that harmony is not the keynote of this convention. First of all, I don't know of a single ideological liberal left in our party. The old Teddy Roosevelt-to-Nelson Rockefeller wing is finally extinct."

"Well, you'd think the loss of these liberals would unite the party."

"No. Actually, the party is split into two major factions. First you have the traditional conservatives, who include President Abbott and leading Republicans in Congress such as Senators Wiltz and Atkins. While in some respect they may be as conservative as Governor Foote, on specific issues they tend to be more pragmatic, more willing to adopt moderate positions to achieve certain goals."

Randolph paused and smiled. "You might say they carry the proxies of what remains of the party's Eastern Establishment. The other faction is made up of what we call ideological conservatives. Governor Foote exemplifies the type of leadership that entered into politics for ideological reasons and remains determined to use government to achieve those ends."

"Senator, you're sort of getting in deep water here, but what I think you're saying is that the traditional faction is willing to compromise while the ideological is not."

Randolph shook his head. "Nothing is ever that inflexible. The longer one plays the political game, the more pragmatic one becomes. The question, however, is how far will one go in compromising his basic beliefs in good government for momentary popular programs. It's a question of personal versus political integrity."

"You say there's a difference?"

"I certainly do say it. You have to live with yourself first as a person. We all make compromises in our personal lives for one reason or another, and it affects ourselves and perhaps one or two other persons, but in politics, when you compromise your principles you affect the lives of millions, and quite often in adverse ways. Phrased another way, it's a question of purists versus pragmatists."

"Could you give us an example?"

"Take national defense. It's imperative that we restore military balance with the Russians, who in the past decades have amassed arms in enormous quantities in all categories while we've been working in fits and starts. Their ongoing ICBM buildup is far superior in accuracy to our Minuteman and Titan Two missiles, which remain susceptible to a surprise strike. One scenario proposes a preemptive strike by the Soviet to destroy our land-based warheads. If successful, and our best minds acknowledge the possibility, then the President is faced with the awesome choice of responding with what is left of our nuclear capability, thereby inviting a second strike, this time against American cities, or capitulating."

"What is the other scenario?" Adler asked. "Another arms race?"

Randolph shook his head again. "Steve, this is not the time or place to get into this debate. The point, at this convention, is that the purists are going to stand firm on their defense plank, and I think they have the necessary votes, so whoever this convention selects as its standard-bearer will have to accept their position on national defense."

"Considering your voting record in the Senate for a strong military defense, is it fair to presume you'll be voting with the purists?"

"Steve, I've been a strong supporter of President Abbott and I respect him not only as our President but as a person. His personal and political integrity are beyond question. However, I'm also fond of Governor Foote and know from his successful two terms as governor of California that he is an energetic and brilliant leader."

"You sound like a person on the horns of a dilemma."

Randolph smiled, pleased that Adler had realized that he wasn't about to burn any bridges. "That's often the case in politics. You have to choose between good men and good programs and hope for the best."

"This convention is faced with a similar dilemma. It has to choose between two good men and some important platform planks. What about this business of opening up the convention? The President characterized it as a public relations gimmick. Is it an effort to dump Abbott on the part of those who favor it?"

"Absolutely not, Steve. I think for the President to release his delegates from their pledges would be one of the most unifying gestures he could make at this convention. Remember, we're talking about a popular President who can coattail a lot of Republicans to victory. Why should he feel threatened by his own party? There is no question in my mind that the Republicans will win in the fall, whoever is the standard-bearer."

"Aren't you contradicting yourself?"

"I don't think so. When I say either man can win, I mean if they're not bloodied on the convention floor. It's important for the Republicans to leave Las Vegas strongly united in purpose and dedication. And you're not going to achieve that by having a free-for-all that will provide the Democrats with issues we cannot later counter. A political party can be its own worst enemy at a convention. Remember the Democrats in Chicago in sixty-eight, or the Republicans in San Francisco in sixty-four? That we must avoid here at all cost. If it means opening up the convention, then by all means let's do so."

"What about your own aspirations at this convention? You did quite well in the few primaries your name was entered in."

"Without my consent," Randolph said. "Certainly, I'm touched by the enthusiasm and determination of the people who persisted in entering my name in these primaries, and I will not violate their pledges."

"That's interesting. Let me see—you have two hundred and thirty delegate votes, if I'm not mistaken, and what you're saying is that you won't release them on the first ballot."

Randolph nodded. "That's right. I can't betray their loyalty. Besides, my name is being entered as a favorite son, and although it's a token gesture, it's a proud moment for me. To be nominated for the highest office in the land, even though it is only complimentary, is an honor I shall always cherish."

"What about the rumors that you're making a bid for the Vice-Presidential slot?"

Randolph laughed good-heartedly. "Well, I'm afraid that's more pie in the sky. The people who believe in me are well intentioned and I'm deeply grateful and honored by their trust, but I can't really take it too

410

seriously. President Abbott seems perfectly content with Orville Fowler."

"Yes, the President has made that quite clear—but what about a Foote-Godwin ticket? Is it out of the realm of possibility?"

Randolph gave Adler his most sincere expression. "All I can say is that Governor Foote has not yet stated his intentions. And until he does I'm staying completely out of it."

Adler turned to Eileen. "What about you? How would you feel being the daughter of the Vice-President?"

"Oh, I think it would be divine," Eileen said.

"And you?" he said, turning to Alicia.

"As my father said a moment ago, until Governor Foote states his preference, it's futile to speculate."

"Oh, what a shame," Daisy said, flipping off the TV set, "to end a brilliant performance on such a sour note. Henry, what's the problem between them?"

Henry shrugged. "She's hurting, it goes back a long ways, and I don't know the answer. All I can tell you is that she's independent, has a sharp tongue, and refuses to toe any line but her own. But I love her and often find myself in sympathy with her."

"I don't care," Daisy said. "It was uncalled for."

"It's my fault. She didn't want to come down here in the first place. She did it as a favor to me. I shouldn't have asked her. But this is a big moment for Randolph and Rufus, something they've been talking about ever since Randolph was a little boy. Rufus had those dreams dancing in Randolph's head before he knew what any of it meant."

Daisy looked straight at him. "Isn't it a big moment for you? He's your son, our son, and I'm certainly proud of him. It's a big moment for me. Why not you? What is going on, Henry?"

Henry sighed and stood up. "Of course it's a big moment for me, too."

She grabbed his hands. "Now, Henry Godwin, you're a lousy liar, always have been, so level with me. I have a right to know, don't I?"

Henry looked at her and there was a sadness in his eyes. "Some things, yes, and some things, no," he said. "There've been a lot of years and a lot of things. I wouldn't know where to begin or end. Remember what I told you last night about reaping the whirlwind?"

"Yes, but you were depressed. I certainly didn't take it seriously."

"Right now, Cami, we're in the eye of the storm and there's not a damn thing either one of us can do about what's coming at us."

Blair Hopkins, whose primary function as a senatorial aide was to provide Randolph with drugs and women, came out of the elevator and the skinny young man stepped up and offered his hand.

"I'm Garfield Stone," he said. "Thanks for coming right down."

Hopkins looked him over carefully. "You're really Rocky Stone's kid?"

"Yes, sir—that's my old man, all right."

"Christ, can't they afford to feed you at your house?"

Garfield's first impulse was to spit in Hopkins's face, but instead he smiled. "They say I've got a tapeworm."

"Yeah, is that so?" Hopkins said, a worried expression creasing the pinkish skin above his chubby cheeks.

Garfield's fist clenched and unclenched. At that moment Kathy Raines came by. "Where's your Abbott button?" she demanded imperiously, her blond hair bouncing and her blue eyes snapping. "You promised to wear it. Don't tell me you threw it away."

Garfield looked at Hopkins, then looked at her, and threw up his hands. "Hey, fuck off, brat," he said, his voice rising. "What are you, my goddamn mother? Go stick pins in somebody else for a while."

"You really are a creep," she snapped, whirling around and into the arms of a fat Abbott delegate, who quickly pulled her tightly against his paunch.

"Sweetheart," he cried, puckering his lips. "Give us a big kiss for good luck."

"Let go of me, you ugly pig," Kathy screeched. She was holding a button with the pin opened and jammed it into his arm as far as it would go. The delegate screamed and fell back into the crowd as Kathy spun around and hurried off without looking back.

"Jesus Christ," Hopkins said. "What was that all about?"

"Some dumb chick. I let her pin me yesterday so I could ball her and now she thinks I'm an Abbott convert."

"Really?" Hopkins said, standing on tiptoes, trying to find her in the crowd.

"Did you see that little pink tongue?" Garfield said. "She knows how to use it."

"I'm going to keep her in mind," Hopkins said. "I know someone who likes little girls who can do things with their tongues." He turned back to Garfield. "Okay, let's get going. You ready to go to work? We'll put you on a phone for a while, see how you work out."

"Terrific, I'm the greatest with a phone," Garfield said, watching Hopkins use his special key to open the doors of the penthouse elevator.

"Am I going to get a key of my own?" he asked, trying to sound casual.

"We'll see," Hopkins said as the doors closed and they were *whoosh*ed to the penthouse floor.

While Garfield Stone was on his way to the penthouse floor, Gus Meier was dropping quarters into a pay phone in Grand Junction, Colorado. Since he was an independent trucker, time was money, and he had driven most of the night before stopping for a short nap. But even in his sleep he couldn't get that Alfie out of his head. Although never specific in his threats, the kid had sent signals all over the place that he was going to do something sensational at the convention. And, as Gus had finally concluded, what could be more sensational than the assassination of the President of the United States.

Gus realized that he was probably overreacting, that the kid was probably just a flake who liked to shock people. Still, there was that possibility. He could be a real psycho—the kind you read about in the papers after they've killed someone important.

When a deputy sheriff answered the telephone in Las Vegas, Gus quickly described his experience and expressed his suspicions that the boy might be bent on some crazy assassination scheme.

Deputy Ted Greeley kept grunting impatiently while Gus tried to recall the kid's precise language.

"Okay, okay, I've got all the pertinent facts down on paper. So you think this rich kid with a Ferrari is a political assassin?"

"I don't know," Gus said, realizing how foolish he must be sounding. "Maybe he's harmless, but it wouldn't hurt to have a little talk with him."

Greeley laughed harshly. "And how do I arrange that? You've got his name and phone number?"

The question surprised Meier. "Look, all you've got to do is find the Ferrari. It's on the side of the road, exactly seventy-three miles from the Monarch II. It's got license plates. His first name's Alfie—talked like his father's a big movie star, but he could've been bullshitting me."

"Tell you what, you come down here and help us draw a composite. The Secret Service boys might want to get into it."

"Out of the question," Gus said. "I have a load to deliver."

"Call your company, have them send another driver to pick up your truck, and you catch a flight down here."

"You don't understand. I'm an independent trucker."

"Tell you what we'll do. Have your dispatcher send a driver and you fly down here. We'll pick up the tab if you're on the level."

There was a long pause and Greeley heard the trucker sigh heavily.

"Oh, shit," he said. "I'll do it."

"Okay. When you get your flight number, call me and I'll pick you up at the airport myself."

"Yeah," Gus said. "I just hope I'm not making a fool of myself. See you in a few hours."

"Thanks, buddy," Greeley said, but the line was already dead.

"Oh, Daddy," Eileen gushed, throwing her arms around his neck the moment they were settled in the limousine, "you were glorious, glorious, glorious."

She kissed him on the mouth, her hard breasts pressing into his arm and chest, and for an instant Randolph was back in Cambridge with Betty and the first time he'd kissed her. Eileen didn't only look like her mother, but she kissed and tasted like her.

He laughed and pulled away. "I wasn't all that glorious."

"Oh, but you were, you really were simply, divinely, exquisitely glorious. There's just no other word for it. I'm so proud of you. I'll bet even Alicia was impressed."

Alicia was hugging the opposite corner, as far away from her father who sat in the middle as she could get. She watched them with appraising, somewhat startled eyes.

"Let's not open up that ball of wax," Randolph said. "I'd like to keep this high a little longer. For all I care, she can get the hell back to the ranch. That kind of help I can do without."

"I know, Daddy," Eileen said. "Don't let her get you down. She's just another smartass Berkeley radical. They're all the same. You never know what's going to come out of their filthy mouths."

"Whatever it is," Randolph said, continuing to talk as though Alicia weren't there, "I don't want to deal with it anymore."

" 'Oh, well,' " Eileen mimicked her sister. " 'I haven't found a political party that'll have me.' I nearly puked. And then refusing to endorse you for the Vice-Presidency. Daddy, honestly, I'm telling you, it took all my self-restraint not to slap her smartass mouth right there in front of twenty million people."

"More like sixty million," Randolph said. "Well, despite her, I think we put some big points on the scoreboard."

"Super points, Daddy."

The limo telephone buzzed and Eileen picked it up, handing it to her father.

Randolph listened with a broadening smile as his grandfather praised his performance.

"Better hurry over here," Rufus said. "The phones are jingling off the hooks. You did us proud this morning, sonny boy, and now it's time to roll up our sleeves and get set for the kill."

CHAPTER

54

The complex networks of telephone and television lines sheathed in heavy cables were strewn along the floor of the East Convention Hall like giant entrails, connecting all the delegations with the two candidates' command posts in mobile trailers parked immediately outside the convention center.

At their hotel headquarters, both Abbott and Foote had some two hundred aides with access to direct lines to their convention managers in the trailers. To facilitate the monitoring of the convention proceedings the floor was divided into sixteen regions, each covered by TV cameras and monitored by aides in the trailers.

Along with the elaborate communication systems, each candidate used secret code words. In the President's camp, he was Eagle, the First Lady, Dove, his chief of staff, Adam Baxter, Falcon, his convention manager, Senator Tom Atkins of Ohio, Kingfisher. His floor manager, Senator Paul Wiltz of Michigan, was Hawk, perched in a sky suite waiting for floor aides to send him those delegate pigeons who were soft and ripe for seduction. Hamilton Foote's people used the signs of the Zodiac for their code system with Foote as Aquarius. Randolph, who didn't have his own separate organization and was piggy-backing on Foote's, was Condor.

The command trailers were also connected by private telephone lines to the sky suites of the four television networks, high above the convention floor. Electronic security experts were kept busy sweeping the equipment and cables of both candidates and the networks for wiretaps and bugs.

Joseph Alcorn walked into the NTN sky suite and took his seat across a long table from Alistair Baker. Below them the delegates were straggling in, late as usual, most of them having waited until after

Randolph's appearance on the "Today" show before leaving their hotels. Baker watched them shuffle to their various delegations, mostly a sea of white, middle-aged faces, many of them lined and tired after a hard night of partying.

Not much had changed in the makeup of delegates since the 1960 convention when Norman Mailer had written in *Esquire* that the Republican Party was "still a party of church ushers, undertakers, choirboys, prison wardens, bank presidents, small-town police chiefs, state troopers, psychiatrists, beauty-parlor operators, corporation executives, Boy Scout leaders, fraternity presidents, tax-board assessors, community leaders, surgeons, Pullman porters, head nurses and the fat sons of rich fathers."

Alcorn was pleased with Randolph's performance on the "Today" show. At a private meeting with the senator late last night the journalist had reported almost verbatim his interview with President Abbott. Randolph had listened attentively, without interruption, as he sipped on a tall bourbon and water.

Afterward he'd smiled in appreciation. "That's sensational, Joe—I really mean it. Now tell me, how do you like your suite? They taking good care of you?"

"The greatest, Randy. There was booze in the room, flowers, fruit, even a stack of hundred-dollar chips."

"Nothing's too good for our friends," Randolph said. "Now you be in your room at midnight, like Cinderella, .and a couple of pleasant surprises will knock on your door."

"Debbi and Terri?"

Randolph stood up and offered his hand. "Your favorite little sixty-niners."

"Randy," Alcorn said, leaning dangerously forward to shake Randolph's hand, "if I can be of any service at all, don't hesitate to call me right at the booth."

"Don't worry, pal, you'll be hearing from me. And if you've got anything to report, you know how to reach me."

Randolph walked him to the door. "Oh, yes, one more thing, Joe. In your analysis try to pound away at the fact that there are a couple hundred uncommitted delegates, that others are soft, that it would be a uniting gesture if Abbott were to release his delegates and open up the convention. After all, he's been a popular President—why should he feel threatened by his own party? The delegations all watch their TV sets on the floor to find out what the hell's going on down there. They'll have you tuned in, hanging on to every word, trying to decide which way to turn. Let's help them along.

"The one thing to remember about a delegate is that he's a politician. He may be a barber from Omaha, but he thinks of himself as a sharp politician, and the worst thing that can happen to a sharp politician is to find himself backing a loser. Once they get that uncertain feeling about Abbott being a shoo-in on the first ballot, they'll start maneuvering, and that's when we move in. Also remind the uncommitted delegates of the danger of remaining uncommitted. A no vote is like a wrong vote. The idea is to create as much confusion and doubt as possible, not only in their minds, but in Abbott's, who's going to get the feedback on a minute-to-minute basis."

Randolph opened the door and Alcorn backed out, his whiplike body swaying, his dark eyes glinting with anticipation. "I hear you, Randy. You can count on it." Randolph nodded, waved, and closed the door.

Joseph Alcorn was just one of many television and print media people from whom Randolph and his staff were collecting IOUs that had accumulated over the years with free rides on his private jet, complimentary accommodations at hotels in Las Vegas, Reno, and Lake Tahoe. The collecting was a friendly and orderly process. Most of the reporters were only too happy to help. There was more involved than the repayment of past favors. There was the future to consider. Randolph and his friends were not only generous, but were men of power, with long careers ahead and even longer memories.

H. Russell Pierpont stood on the redwood deck of Henry's chalet and took deep breaths of fresh mountain air. He was a large, square-cut man with soft white skin and a freckled bald head fringed by close-cropped gray hair. Except for hard dark eyes and heavy black eyebrows, his face had no distinguishing features. He could have been a small-town mortician or butcher.

The view was spectacular and he loved the clean smell of pine needles. It reminded him of when his father had taken the whole family to Bar Harbor every summer when he was a boy. He had loved hiking in the Maine woods and sliding on the slick pine needles.

Now, standing on the deck of the chalet surrounded by tall firs under another summer sky, he longed for those days of his youth when he had been a fearless adventurer. He'd wandered alone in the woods, never afraid of getting lost, until the day he'd broken his legs skiing down a steep pine needle-covered hill and a search party hadn't found him until late that night. Lying helpless, in excruciating pain, he'd heard strange, frightening noises and seen the eyes of unknown animals glowing in the darkness. Those few hours had blotted out all the good times of his earlier years of tramping in the woods. It had changed him irrevocably.

For a fleeting moment he regretted his lost youth, but the business at hand was far too pressing to allow him the luxury of pointless reminiscence. He heard a noise behind him and turned to accept a mug of coffee from Jesse Stelk.

"Thanks," he said, taking a sip of the steaming coffee. "God, this is another world, isn't it? I'll bet it's already a hundred degrees on the Strip. I can't stand that kind of heat. Give me snow and freezing weather anytime."

Stelk was wearing a short-sleeved golf shirt, lightweight slacks, and running shoes. He went to a glass-topped table and sat in a padded wrought-iron chair. "Tell me, Russ—why wear your banker's suit and tie out here in the wilderness?"

Pierpont seemed surprised by the question. "It's what I always wear. I'd feel naked dressed like you."

"What did you think of our boy on 'Today'? Not a bad performance."

Pierpont nodded. "He's got potential. Of course, he's used to cameras, knows precisely what he's doing every moment. It's quite brilliant, because while it's totally studied, he makes it appear spontaneous, so he comes off looking sincere, warm, charming, concerned, graceful, well informed—you name it. That's quite an art, Jesse, that ability to dissemble with ease."

"I agree, Russ, he's refined it to an art form."

"As long as he doesn't fool himself."

"I would doubt that very much. He knows what he's doing and he's had one hell of a teacher in Rufus."

Pierpont nodded. "He's a most persuasive man."

Stelk laughed. "He's that, all right, but he's also one of the most dedicated and loyal members of our committee. We owe him and he wants to collect."

Pierpont tapped his coffee mug on the redwood railing. "Why don't you make the necessary arrangements to have the senator come up here for a final evaluation?"

"Good," Stelk said. "I'll pass the word to Rufus. Set it up for Wednesday morning. By then we should have a pretty good idea where we stand at this convention."

Pierpont came to the table and sat down across from Stelk. "About that conversation between Truman and Mary we overheard last night —I've been giving it some thought. It's interesting that Mary has kept her visits to Lisa's loft secret. From what our investigators tell us, Mary can't do a thing with her. Lisa really lashed into her mother a couple of months ago and they haven't spoken to each other since."

"Maybe she figures Abbott's got enough worries without adding that little bitch to them. He hasn't seen his daughter in probably two years and hasn't the slightest idea of her condition. Mary, who's a pretty tough cookie, has no doubt ordered the Secret Service to keep their mouths shut. By now they've learned she's got clout. She attends Cabinet meetings and speaks her mind. One word from her and they'll get bounced to some shitty detail. For her, I think, it's simply a question of protecting her husband."

"In a way, it works to our advantage," Pierpont said.

"Yes, and we can use all the breaks we can get. Abbott's due for one hell of a shock if he doesn't come around in time."

55

Vince Bacino, Lew Spark, George Clews, and Sid Spargo, the casino manager who represented two New York Cosa Nostra families with a joint interest in the Monarch II, missed the "Today" show. At seven o'clock that morning the four men walked down a narrow corridor and entered the casino's counting room through a secret wall panel that was electronically controlled by a combination of four remote devices with extremely sophisticated signals. It took all four devices, in proper rotation, to open and close the steel panel. This was a safeguard against any single member deciding to do some skimming on his own.

The only other entrance was through a vault door at the back of the cashier's cage. It was on a time lock, which opened at the end of each shift—six in the morning, four in the afternoon, and midnight—for the security people to deposit the large drop boxes from the gaming tables and the coins from the slot machines. And it opened again at nine every morning for the official count, giving the four men now entering the room ample time to perform their work in total privacy. The television cameras that monitored the official count were also on a time clock that automatically turned them on at nine o'clock and not a second sooner. Officials from the Gaming Control Board Audit section who wanted to monitor the count could do so from television screens in a room created for that purpose. Casino officials also monitored the count to make sure their employees didn't have sticky fingers. The employees, who had to be approved by the Control Board, wore blue, form-fitting, short-sleeved, pocketless, cuffless coveralls and were subject to occasional spot checks for which they had to strip to the buff.

On tables waiting for the four men were five hundred and ten large boxes containing the receipts for all three shifts from eighteen crap tables, eight roulette wheels, a hundred blackjack tables, four baccarat tables, seventeen poker tables, four wheels of fortune, three keno lounges, and sixteen race and sports book positions. On the floor were sacks of coins taken from twelve hundred slot machines; they would be weighed instead of counted to determine their worth.

In the two years since the hotel's opening there'd been no variation in the amount skimmed for each day of the week: $75,000 on Monday, Tuesday, Wednesday; $125,000 on Thursday; $200,000 on Friday; $250,000 on Saturday; $200,000 on Sunday. A cool million each and every week, fifty-two million a year of tax-free money. And from just one hotel. Even on weekends like the one just ended, when the play was especially heavy, the four men never exceeded their quota. Greed had nothing to do with their operation. It was strictly a business proposition. This way the play could fluctuate on the official count, as it did at other casinos. It was a foolproof system as long as it was kept under control. No Apollo of law enforcement was going to pin ass's ears on Lew Spark.

Each of the four men had a trusted nominee who substituted for him on off days, but no more than two of the principals could be absent at any one time. George Clews, because of his advanced age and length of devoted service, had been placed in charge of all of Rufus's nominees who every day collected his cut from the counting rooms of other hotels. Clews was proud of his responsible position and enjoyed the leisurely hours, the luxurious accommodations, and, most of all, the thrill of looting all that money from the boxes.

Rufus's cut at the Monarch II was twenty-five percent, as it was for each of the other three men. Rufus had this large percentage because he owned the land on which the hotel was built and had leased it for ninety-nine years. The rent was considerable and variable with the cost-of-living index.

The four men went to work, each possessing the two keys required to open the drop boxes.

"What fucking slobs," Bacino grunted as he emptied the contents of a drop box on the table in front of him.

"What're you talking about?" Spargo asked. His pale blue eyes looked out of place in that swarthy face.

"The delegates. Shit, they're going around like any other bunch of stupid conventioneers. Getting stinking drunk and throwing up in the casino and lobby. No class."

Spargo laughed. "Them fucking hookers are cleaning up. Them guys are hitting all the scumbags. Wait till they get home and their schlongs start dripping. Then they'll holler blue murder. Serves them right, the jerkoffs."

Lew Spark opened a box and lovingly ran his hands through the bills. "They're spending their money—I'll say that for them," he said, starting to stack bills in a neat pile, making sure none were counterfeit or marked. The preference was for older hundred- and thousand-dollar bills. Crisp new bills running in sequence were avoided. If there ever was a time Spark was tempted to deviate from the routine, this was it, but he knew that everybody else in town was doing fantastic business. The Republicans, slobs or not, were loaded and determined to have their go at this wide-open town. For some it was their only chance to have a real adventure.

Spark pushed the stack of bills to one side and refilled the drop box, making sure to lock it with both keys. Through a system they had devised, each knew exactly how much to take out of each box to arrive at the designated total for each day of the week.

George Clews was quick at counting money, going through the boxes at a rapid pace, but his eyes, hidden under his Neanderthal brow, were constantly watching the hands of the other three men. There were plenty of thousand-dollar bills in those boxes and it was possible that some could be stolen by sleight-of-hand tricks. Rufus had cautioned Clews about that possibility.

Sometimes even as he counted the money and his eyes kept track of the others, his mind would start wandering into the past. The more important events in which he had figured came marching right through his head.

There was the ecstatic expression on Rufus's face the night they'd met, when Rufus had heard the sound of that guy's neck snapping in that New York alley. When Clews had tried to apologize, Rufus had told him to forget it, that he wished he could have done it himself. At that moment, Clews knew his future was settled. He'd never again have to hustle for a living. Rufus Boutwell was the type of hardheaded businessman who needed a George Clews to do his dirty work. Thinking about it now, Clews smiled to himself. It was like they said about good marriages being made in heaven. They were made for each other and Fate had brought them together for precisely that purpose. That was Clews's philosophy of life. Fate arranged things and his job was to follow through. When his time came, he'd go, period. It was the same when he killed someone. Fate had decided the victim's death and Clews was merely the instrument of Fate.

That had been the case with that old one-legged miner, Yulee. But he'd been a tough old bird. Clews had worked him over for nearly two days in the abandoned line shack, trying to force the location of his gold mine from him, but the old man had taken the punishment without a whimper, the toughest old geezer Clews had ever encountered. There was something inhuman about that kind of stoical resistance. It had been freezing cold in the line shack and Clews had stripped him naked, but the old man just stood there, not even shivering. The only time his expression had changed was when Clews pressed a lighted cigar into his armpits and on the nipples of his breasts. The old man gritted his teeth and looked straight at him with those kid blue eyes. There was plenty of pain in that gaze but enough defiance to drive Clews into a frenzied rage.

At that moment Clews realized the old man's will was superior to his own ability to inflict pain. He'd never reveal the mine's location and Clews had no more time to play with him. Reaching for Yulee's neck with one hand, he slowly strangled him to prolong the agony. Then he dumped his naked corpse into an old mine shaft.

The one time George Clews had failed to carry out Rufus's instructions to the letter was the attack on Henry at the ranch. Rufus had wanted Henry immobilized with a broken leg, but Henry's strength and agility had surprised him. The first thing Clews knew he was fighting for his very life. He'd broken Henry's leg as ordered, but if he hadn't been hit in the back with that shovel, he'd have killed him, even though warned against it by Rufus. In a way the broken back was a blessing in disguise, for Rufus would never have forgiven him.

There had been many other gratifying moments when he'd faithfully served Rufus, but none could compare with the night he was given Betty. That was one picture in his brain that he saved for late at night, when sleep wouldn't come, and he needed something exciting to pass away the lonely hours.

When the count was completed, the money was divided evenly and placed into four legal briefcases. The men left the counting room, using their remote devices to close the steel panel, and walked up the narrow corridor, again using their remote devices to open the secret panel in Spark's private quarters behind his office. Bacino and Spargo sat down on facing sofas before a burning fireplace, the heat unfelt in the air conditioning, while Spark unlocked his office door and called his secretary for coffee. George Clews walked out without saying a word to anyone. Unless absolutely necessary for business purposes, the three men and Clews never exchanged words. At first they had tried to draw him out, but when he continually failed to respond, they'd stopped talking to him. And now, except for the very real money he carried away every day, it was as though he were a ghost—a dark brooding force lurking in the background.

56

No matter how much he played with the numbers, and no matter how promising they looked, Hamilton Foote had this strange feeling that none of it was real—that he would awaken at any moment and find himself back on the lecture circuit preaching about the coming renaissance of the Republican Party. A small, fastidious man in his early sixties, Foote thought of himself as a refugee from academia, having risen to the presidency of Brewster, one of the most prestigious colleges in California, during the student riots of the mid-1960s. His bold stance against student radicals had gained him national attention. The next year, backed by big-oil money, he had been elected governor of California, where his extremist views clashed violently with a Democrat-controlled legislature. But the notoriety gained him legions of devoted right-wing followers.

As he sat with members of his staff at the dining table in his Hilton suite, counting the numbers on a scoreboard, there was a roar of voices from the living room and he looked up to see Rufus and Randolph walk into the dining room.

"Well, Ham, hope you're using a pencil with a big eraser," Rufus said, shaking hands with Foote and standing aside for Randolph to follow suit. "Them numbers are going to change a thousand times between now and Wednesday night."

Foote smiled and shrugged. "I'm firming up, counting all the uncommitted delegates known to be leaning strongly toward me, and by adding Randolph's two thirty, I'm up to a thousand ninety-five."

"Sounds damn good," Rufus said. "How many hard rocks left?"

"Sixty-two, and they're holding out for the best deal. They're expecting to come out of this convention with something besides fond memories."

"Have you firmed Abbott's figure?" Randolph asked.

"Yes, eleven hundred and two."

"Just seven votes separating you two," Randolph said, turning to Rufus. "It's better than I thought it would be at this point. Hell, we've got three days to seduce these bastards."

"Not so fast," Rufus said. "Seducing goes both ways. Somehow incumbent Presidents seem to have greater sex appeal. Let's have a look at that scoreboard."

Foote picked it up and held it so that all three could examine it. "All right, you've got the South locked up pretty solid and most of the Sun Belt."

"The one sixty-seven from California looks pretty impressive," Randolph said.

"But look at Pennsylvania," Rufus said. "Seventy-three for Abbott, fourteen for Ham, and sixteen uncommitted. That's the largest block of uncommitted delegates on the board. Hawaii with ten is next. Both are going to be hard nuts to crack. Then New York with nine. I see you've got twenty in your column and one twenty-five for Abbott. Seems about right to me. Been working on numbers most of the night myself."

"With the magic number at eleven thirty you need thirty-five to win on the first ballot," Randolph said. "That is, if I release mine to you. And I will if I see they can turn the trick, but otherwise we'll go for a second ballot. Then it's going to be wide open and anybody's ball game."

Rufus smiled. "He means between you and Abbott, of course."

"Naturally," Randolph said. "There's no dark horse at this convention."

Rufus sat down at the head of the table. "Could be a real donnybrook. The worst in history was in nineteen twenty-four when McAdoo and Smith lost out on the one hundred and third ballot to Davis. Christ, can you believe it? That squabble divided the Democrats for years. About ruined the party. Let's hope nothing like that happens here. But at a convention you never know what to expect, no matter how smart you think you are at fixing things. There're too many loose ends that can strangle you."

He stood up. "Well, keep plugging away, and we'll do likewise. We've got a hell of a good shot."

"One moment, please," Foote said. "Would you step in the bedroom. There's something I'd like to say privately to both of you."

They followed him and Rufus sat on the bed, a knowing glint in his gray eyes as he studied Foote.

"First, Randolph, I want to thank you for the kind words on the 'Today' show. It was most generous of you. I think you're absolutely right about avoiding any bloodshed that might hurt the party's chances in the fall." He paused and looked directly at Randolph. "I'd be honored to have you as my running mate, Randolph. I think we'd make a powerful team. What do you say?"

Randolph and Rufus had anticipated the offer and had determined to keep all options open.

"Thanks, Ham, I appreciate the offer and will give it serious consideration, but I think we better keep it to ourselves for the time being. Let's see how the first ballot goes, or how both our numbers look just before the balloting. Announcing your Vice-Presidential choice at this point won't serve any purpose, might even be harmful."

"In what way?"

Rufus stood up. "Who knows?" he said. "As I've said, that's an unpredictable animal out there. Let's not twist its tail just yet. Let's first figure out all the angles. Then we'll make our move. But let me say right here and now, so there won't be any misunderstanding, if you get the nomination Randolph will be proud to be your running mate. Understand?"

"Understood," said Foote, offering his hand first to Rufus and then to Randolph.

In the limousine Rufus chuckled to himself. "He's running scared. Doesn't know what's coming off. Can't blame the poor bastard. He really thinks he's got a shot. I bankrolled his campaign through a dozen blind organizations just so we could twist Abbott's arm. Why, the Democrats would murder Foote in the fall. Him and his religious loonies and weirdo right-wing crackpots. They make the old Birch Society look like fucking Bolsheviks, and for all the wrong reasons."

"Then why would you want me to be his running mate?"

"Sonny boy, what else could I say? Listen, he's nervous enough without our adding to it. The longer he thinks we're behind him, the harder he's going to work. No need tipping our hand just yet. Besides, we don't need him as an enemy in the fall. Let's keep everybody nice and happy until we've really got to kick ass, then watch out."

Randolph smiled. "Rufus, I love you. I really mean it." He looked directly at his grandfather and his eyes misted, which surprised Rufus almost as much as the question. "What am I going to do when you're gone?"

"Gone! Where the fuck am I going? I'm a young man. Healthy as a bull."

Randolph reached over and gently squeezed his shoulder. "Yeah, a young octogenarian who's about a hundred pounds overweight and smokes far too many cigars."

"Well, shit, I don't drink. Now you want to take my food and cigars away from me? Don't worry about me. I feel as good as I did forty years ago."

Randolph laughed. "Want to go jogging today?"

"That exercise stuff's bullshit. I didn't go jogging forty years ago, or sixty, for that matter. In the meantime, I've buried a lot of joggers and runners. Listen, now, I'm going to make you a promise." He reached out and grabbed both of Randolph's hands. "Are you listening to me, sonny boy?"

"Yes, Rufus."

"Then look me in the eye when I tell you this. I'm going to live to see you President of these United States of America. Now that's a promise, sonny boy." He leaned forward and gripped Randolph's knee. "Now, there's something else I've got to tell you that's top secret. Wednesday morning you're going to meet the two most important men in your life, and they will be speaking for ninety-eight other men, myself included, who are the most powerful in the free world."

Randolph nodded somberly. "The Century Committee. I've often wondered if you were a member. I'm glad you are, Rufus. Now I can appreciate your confidence even more."

"Enough. Let's change the subject," Rufus said as the limousine pulled up at the Monarch II.

57

At first Garfield Stone really enjoyed himself. Hopkins had given him a list containing the last forty names of the California delegation. The rest of the list had been given to other telephone workers. Garfield had been instructed to use his name to impress the delegates with his famous father and to say that he was taking a poll for Senator Godwin to find out how they would vote if it went to a second ballot, which would automatically release them from their pledge to Foote.

Instead of using his own name, Garfield decided it would be even more interesting if he identified himself as Rocky Stone and imitated his father's voice. The reaction so far had been fantastic. His father was even more popular than he'd realized.

By late afternoon, however, the game was wearing thin. The convention had recessed at noon until the evening session, making it a hassle to find the delegates. Few stayed in their hotel or motel rooms. By the time Garfield had decided to fake the rest of the poll, a delegate named David Webber came on the line. He sounded sleepy but friendly.

"Sorry, pal, if I woke you up," Garfield said. "This is Rocky Stone and I wonder if I could have a couple minutes of your time."

"You mean you're Rocky Stone the actor?"

"Right, and I'm taking a poll of the California delegation for a pal of mine, Senator Godwin."

"Well, I appreciate your calling, but we're pledged to Governor Foote. There's this rule in California. Whoever gets the most votes wins the state's whole delegation."

"David—you don't mind if I call you by your first name—you call me Rocky, okay?—we're aware of the California rule, but first let me ask you something personal, David. What is your profession?"

"I'm an electronics engineer."

"What's your specialty?"

"Computers."

"That's fantastic, David. It takes plenty of brainpower to work with that stuff. Me, all I do is stand in front of the cameras and say a few words—takes no brains whatsoever."

"Oh, I wouldn't say that," David said. "I think you're a good actor and that takes a special talent."

"Thank you, David. Ever get down to Beverly Hills?"

"Now and then on business, but not too often."

"Well, next time why don't you drop by the house and say hello. Meet the family. You married, David? Any children?"

"Yes, two boys and a girl."

"Bring them along."

"Gee, Mr. Stone, I mean, Rocky, that's very kind of you."

"Listen, you'd be doing me a favor. Never met an electronics genius before."

"I'm no genius, Rocky."

"Let me ask you a question, David. How're you going to vote if it goes to a second ballot?"

David cleared his throat nervously. "Well, there've been some strong suggestions that we better stick with Foote no matter how many ballots it takes."

Garfield was excited again. This was the first delegate to level with him. The others had either been dyed-in-the-wool extremists or been cute in their response, but none had indicated that some form of coercion was going on. This was something that needed further exploration on a personal level. The way to gain Senator Godwin's confidence and appreciation. It could result in Garfield receiving carte blanche on the penthouse floor.

"Tell you what, David. Why don't you come to the Monarch II and we'll have an early dinner? You've got to be at the hall by six. It'll give us a little time to explore this situation a little further."

"Thank you, Rocky. Where do you want to meet?"

"How about in front of the Café Noir. That's at the far end of the casino. What do you look like?"

"I'm about five-ten, blond hair, glasses. I'll be wearing a light blue sports shirt and dark blue pants. But I'll recognize you."

"Of course," Garfield said, his heart suddenly sinking. "See you in a half hour."

He hung up and sat there dumbfounded. He'd become so caught up in the game that he'd completely forgotten that, while he could imitate his father, he couldn't pass for him. In a fit of temper he picked up the phone and smashed it against the desk. He quickly looked around to see if anyone had noticed. The place was in its usual state of bedlam and no one even turned in his direction.

The moment David Webber entered the lobby he was astonished to see his brother-in-law, Gus Meier, standing tall and looking over the crowd as though he were searching for someone.

David hurried up to him and grabbed him by the arm. "What the hell you doing here, Gus?"

Gus swung around, equally startled by David's sudden appearance. "Oh, Christ, don't ask."

"What do you mean, don't ask? Don't tell me you lost money at the tables."

Gus took David by the arm. "Let's get out of this traffic lane and I'll explain the whole thing. But you've got to promise to keep it to yourself."

The elevator doors opened and Garfield stepped out, looked across the lobby, and ducked quickly to his left until he was hidden behind a huge ficus plant. What was that truck jockey doing here? He should be in Iowa by now. And what was he doing talking to a blond man, with glasses, wearing a light blue shirt and dark blue trousers? This was sheer insanity. Things like this weren't supposed to happen except in spy movies.

As Garfield stared, a deputy sheriff—a sergeant—and a man in a light gray business suit went up to the truck jockey, and after the blond man had shaken hands with the trucker the other three walked hurriedly away.

Garfield followed the blond man and by the time he reached the Café Noir he had devised a new plan of action.

Walking up to the blond man, he said, "Are you David Webber?"

"Yes, I am."

"I'm Phil Morris, an assistant of Senator Godwin. Rocky Stone asked me to meet you here. It looks like he's going to be delayed. Had a hurried conference call from the senator, so he suggested we get started without him. We'll order dinner and go over the California situation until he joins us."

David Webber stared at this emaciated young man with the long hair, no more than in his midteens, and didn't know what to do. Still, if he worked with Senator Godwin, he was probably one of those whiz kids.

"All right," David said. "But I don't have too much time. I don't want to be late for the opening ceremony tonight. Daisy Miller is singing the National Anthem. I've never seen her in person before."

"Is that right?" Garfield said. "Well, she's performing here nightly. Would you like me to make reservations for you and your wife—as Rocky Stone's guest, of course?"

David blushed. "No, thank you, but I appreciate the offer."

Although it was early, the restaurant was nearly full. The maitre d' glanced at them and headed for a table near the kitchen doors. Garfield touched David's arm and said, "Wait here a minute."

When the maitre d' turned, Garfield was standing so close that they nearly bumped noses. "What the fuck do you think you're pulling?" Garfield asked, his eyes flashing murderously. "I'm with Senator Godwin and I'm trying to romance a delegate for him. So you'll get us a nice private booth if you like your fucking job here."

The maitre d' just stared at him.

Sensing the need for different tactics, Garfield pulled out a fifty-dollar bill and pressed it in his hand. "Look, it's no big deal, don't sweat it. Just give us a private booth."

The maitre d' looked down at the fifty in his hand, looked up at Garfield, and nodded. Garfield motioned for Webber to follow as the maitre d' led the way to a booth at the rear of the restaurant.

"This is more like it," Garfield said. "Now we can talk without all that clatter from the kitchen."

David smiled but his eyes looked puzzled. "I don't see how I can really help you," he said.

"Oh, but you can be of tremendous help," Garfield said, pausing while the busboy brought water, butter, and bread to their table. Then it was the wine steward and Garfield ordered Dom Perignon. Smiling at David, he said, "I meant to ask you, who was that big guy you were with a while ago? Noticed him being dragged away by cops when I came out of the elevator."

David swallowed with difficulty. "That's my brother-in-law, but he wasn't being arrested."

Garfield shrugged. "Looked like it to me, the way they pulled him away."

"No, no," said Webber nervously. "Just guys he knows—they needed him for something, I don't know what."

Garfield hoped that his voice wouldn't reveal the sudden fear that gripped him. There was no question about it; they were looking for him. That truck jockey had told the police about him, and now they had the FBI and Secret Service on the case, looking for a crazy kid called Alfie who they probably thought was out to kill the President. Why hadn't he kept his big mouth shut in the truck? Now he'd have to stay out of the lobby, just move from his room to the penthouse floor. Everything would be okay. They didn't know his name. He'd have to call the garage and make sure the owner didn't blow the deal.

"Is your brother-in-law also a delegate?" he asked, forcing a smile.

"No," David said, distractedly, still trying to sort out what Gus had revealed to him.

"I see—well, to get back to the business at hand, what's happening in your delegation? Is everybody ideologically committed to Foote?"

"I'm not and I know others who feel as I do, but for most of us it's our first convention and nobody wants to raise a fuss without fully understanding the consequences."

"Who's in charge?"

"Charlie Bliss, who's a former Republican National Committeeman from California and a strong supporter of Governor Foote."

"So he's pushing hard, right, to keep everybody in line?"

David smiled. "I'd say that's a fair statement."

"How many do you think would defect if they had the chance?"

"Quite a few."

"Give me a guess."

"I can't even come close. All I know is that in my group, the ones I'm sitting with, at least half would go for Abbott."

"Would any go for Godwin in the second ballot just to keep the pot boiling, see what develops?"

David Webber looked concerned. "I'm afraid I'm not too well acquainted with Senator Godwin's record."

"Has anybody mentioned Senator Godwin in your delegation?"

"Well, they say there's a possibility he could be Foote's running mate."

"What would you think of that as a ticket?"

David shook his head. "I don't think I'm going to vote for Foote. If he's on the ticket, then I'm just not going to vote in the Presidential election."

The waiter came and took their orders: prime rib for David and a watercress salad for Garfield.

As they talked, David Webber kept glancing toward the front of the restaurant. "You think he'll see us way back here?"

"Who?"

"Rocky Stone."

"Oh, sure, I told the captain. He'll bring him right to the table when he comes—that is, if he can break away in time. It's pretty hectic up there."

"I can imagine," David said, again glancing toward the front of the restaurant.

"That fucking Charlie Bliss," Randolph said when Hopkins reported Garfield's conversation with David Webber. "He's been a power in California Republican politics a long time. Got his stripes when he got behind Foote's first gubernatorial campaign. Now he's got the delegates by the throat and is holding on for dear life. His one and only shot at the brass ring. He can just see himself as Foote's chief of staff in the White House."

As Randolph talked, Daisy Miller was singing the National Anthem on the four television sets in his room, each of which was tuned to a different network. The sets were muted and Randolph pressed the sound buttons on all four remote devices. As the music blasted into the room, he said, "How's that for stereo? That lady has one sweet voice. Caught her show last night. Wonder how old she really is. Looks fantastic whatever her age. What a great lay she must be. Imagine the experience that goes with those eyes and that incredible face. That mouth and fabulous smile."

"I know what you're thinking," Hopkins laughed. "Don't ask me to fix you up. She's your daddy's girl."

"Thanks for reminding me," Randolph said sarcastically. "Daddy or no daddy, just give me one quick shot at her. Christ, imagine having her on her knees, in front of you, sucking on your cock."

"I don't even want to think about it," Hopkins said.

Randolph leaned back in his chair and plunked his feet on the coffee table. "I took her to dinner once. She was Bacino's mistress then. I went backstage after one of her shows at the old Monarch and she seemed really pleased to see me. Christ, she started asking all kinds of questions—personal stuff—and she knew about Aunt Caroline, Moses, and Holly. My guess is she was seeing Henry even then, cheating on Bacino. A woman like that—how can any one guy expect to keep her on a short leash?"

"Well, what happened at dinner?" Hopkins asked, grinning, his chipmunk cheeks quivering.

"It was more like breakfast. We were in the coffee shop until the sun came up. Then we went out and sat by the pool. There was no end to her questions. Wanted to know all about Betty and the girls. How we'd met. Then she got into the war, where I served. Finally, I said. 'Are you writing a book and looking for a screwy character to put in it?'

"She laughed and touched my hand. It was more of a caress, the way she did it. So I made my play. I said something like, 'Why don't we continue this conversation at your place or mine? Then we can lie down, kind of relax while we talk.'"

Hopkins laughed. "Oh, man, that's an original line for a former Harvard stud."

"Well, she's not an easy lady to proposition. Anyway, she almost looked sad. She said, 'But you're happily married and have lovely twin daughters.' Then I guess I really put my foot in it. I said, 'Tell you what, I won't tell them if you won't.' Christ, she looked at me like I'd just raped the Virgin Mary. I've never seen an expression like that on a woman's face before. I think she was working hard not to cry. Anyway, she stood up and looked at me with those big eyes of hers—Jesus, are they ever beautiful—and said, 'I've enjoyed our talk, up to a point, and I hope we can always be good friends.' Then we shook hands like two old buddies leaving for opposite corners of the world." He paused and laughed. "Hoppy, she left me there, high and dry, with the god-damndest hard-on you ever saw."

"Don't feel bad about it," Hopkins said. "She's probably old enough to be your mother."

Garfield stood on the terrace of Randolph's penthouse suite and looked down at the cars, mostly limousines, moving up the curved drive to the VIP entrance under the striped awning.

Hundreds of people, perhaps thousands, Garfield thought, were milling along the curved drive, with many crowded around the fountain, all waiting in the heat and congestion for an opportunity to glimpse an important politician or Hollywood star just so they could return home and say they had seen someone, anyone, in person.

Garfield wished his old man were there on the terrace with him. He'd strike him on the head with a blunt instrument and throw him over the railing, give the poor fools down there something to take home with them as souvenirs. He heard footsteps and turned nervously.

"What're you doing here?" Hopkins asked.

"Getting some fresh air and taking in this beautiful view. I'm going to get my old man to rent me out one of these penthouses. I like it up here."

Hopkins joined him at the railing. "Well, you really shouldn't be here. It's getting late and Senator Godwin likes his privacy at night."

"Sorry, I was a little bushed and—well, I understand. You want your elevator key back?"

Hopkins looked at him curiously. "No, don't take it wrong. You're doing good work. We want you back tomorrow. It's just that the senator is expecting some guests and it's my job to clear out the place."

"How high are we, do you suppose?" Garfield asked.

Hopkins leaned over and looked down. "About four hundred feet, I'd say."

"Makes you feel like you're on top of the world."

Hopkins nodded. "Okay, listen, we'll see you in the morning. Get a good night's sleep. We're going to work your ass off tomorrow."

Gloria was one of the feathered topless centerpieces in the French extravaganza playing twice nightly in the Monarch II's Parisienne Showroom. Gloria stood there in a ridiculous pose, a frozen smile on her sensuous face, while others danced their legs off all around her. If it hadn't been for the grass and coke she'd have gone stark raving mad long ago.

She'd been in Las Vegas nearly four years and she was still in her teens. In the meantime, she'd been to bed with some of the most famous male and female stars appearing on the Strip. They all loved her and told her she had a promising career, but no one so far had done a single thing to further it along. Now Gloria thought she'd found the right man in Senator Godwin, whose grandfather, everybody knew, was the richest and most powerful man in Nevada. One word from him and Gloria could become a star overnight. In the meantime, she'd been moonlighting in related fields.

At three o'clock on Tuesday morning, Randolph and Gloria were out on the terrace off his bedroom soaking in a lukewarm Jacuzzi and sucking on joints. Randolph looked so relaxed and receptive that she began to tell him the story of her short, unhappy life.

"Would you believe that I started sucking my father's cock when I was nine? I woke up one night and he was poking it in my mouth. When I tried to refuse, he grabbed me by the back of the neck with one hand, really paralyzed my jaws, and shoved it in. He said, 'Suck—it'll make your tits grow.' Can you believe it?"

She laughed and sucked on the joint. "So I did, you know. It wasn't all that big a deal. I'd seen my mother suck on it enough times to know what it was all about. In fact, I kind of got to liking it. Sometimes when he was watching football on television and my mother was cooking dinner in the kitchen, I'd sneak in there to give him a quick blow job and he'd finger me. You know, tit for tat, right?"

Randolph smiled. "He was a good teacher, furthered your career considerably, I'd say. And it looks like it helped your tits grow."

"I left home at fourteen and came here. Worked as a topless dancer in a small joint back of the Strip. I was a perfect thirty-six by then. I don't want to pat myself on the back, but I'm a very creative dancer. I'm very erotic and I really get into what I'm doing. Sometimes I get so excited people can tell I'm getting off."

"You are?"

"I worked a place one time where you danced in the nude on a stage and there were tables all around it, and when I'd get excited, I'd squat right on the edge of the stage and guys would just line up to eat me out. I'm telling you, guys all over the audience were jacking off like crazy. Boy, I had a big following at that place."

She leaned back and sucked on the joint. "Am I boring you?"

Randolph took her hand and placed it on his erect penis. "What do you think?"

She giggled. "Well, I'm sorry to say, when you dance like that some people get an attitude about you. You become a very sleazy, second-rate-citizen-type person. So I gave up nude dancing and got into porno."

"I know," Randolph said. "I've seen some of your work. Very energetic."

"Yeah, well, if you only knew how terribly boring it is to make a porno, it'd turn you right off. It's so cut and dry. It's sex with no sex in it! It's a very competitive business now and the guys in it are young and real studs, but you look up and they're in a corner trying to work themselves up. Most of the girls are lesbians, and when the photographer says, 'Let's get rolling,' some of the guys turn to the girls and say, 'Would you mind helping me out a little?' and they say, 'Get it up yourself, asshole.'"

"A woman can fake it, but what about the guys?" Randolph asked.

"Some are pretty clever at faking it. They mix egg white and powdered sugar into a solution that looks like semen. Porno films are such ripoffs. Guys hold their cock at the base to make it look like it's up, and the photographer can do a lot by virtue of the angle. They get down, shooting up, and make a guy look like a moose when basically he's only three or four inches. It's all bullshit."

"You like big cocks?" Randolph asked.

"Yeah, the bigger the better."

Randolph smiled and stood up. "What do you think?"

"It's beautiful, baby, but I mean guys twice your size."

Randolph shrugged. "Look behind you. Are they twice his size?"

She turned and saw Bryce Silver standing there, naked, his enormous penis at full mast.

"Holy fucking mother of Jesus. Is that for real?"

"Go suck on it and find out," Randolph said, helping her out of the Jacuzzi. "And while you're doing it, hold up your little ass, I'm going in the back door tonight."

"Sure, baby, but first rub a little coke on it and watch it open up like a flower in spring."

Randolph reached between her legs and pressed his thumb inside her. "Gloria, has anyone ever told you that you're a real fucking poet?"

"No, but I know a lot of real dirty limericks."

"You don't say. Can you suck and recite at the same time?"

Bryce Silver, who was aging gracefully, reached over and goosed Henry. "Guess who I saw coming out of the convention hall tonight," he said. "Ruth Bellini. Remember her?"

"Yeah, she still around? Christ, she must be in her forties."

"She's gone downhill, Randy. Was lined up with all the other scumbags hustling the delegates. Wearing bikini shorts and a halter. Body seems to be holding up, but the face is hard, baby. Christ, though, what a great cocksucker she was in her day. One of the very best ever."

"Don't make any rash judgments until glorious Gloria gets to work on your shaft."

"That's right, baby," cooed Gloria, "don't count me out till all the votes are in."

58

The door opened and Mary Abbott stepped into the makeshift conference room followed by her husband.

Standing around the table were fourteen men, including Adam Baxter, Pat Daley, Senators Tom Atkins and Paul Wiltz; Treasury Secretary Richard Crowell and Budget Director Alfred Kitzmiller.

"Gentlemen, good morning, and please be seated."

"Good morning, Mr. President and Mrs. Abbott," they chorused.

Abbott smiled. "Mary and I have been playing with your numbers most of the night and we've come to some preliminary conclusions we'd like to explore with you this morning. Pat and Adam have revised the figures, based on inputs from the entire staff, and from what our people in the enemy camp have reported, we're firming at around eleven hundred, give or take two or three votes. That's assuming, of course, that Godwin will not gain a few more votes as a favorite son. For the moment, his votes are being counted in Foote's column, which is where most will go when released. That gives Foote very close to eleven hundred. So we're in a tight horse race."

"It's more like psychological warfare," Baxter said.

Mary smiled. "Yes, Adam, and that's the part that intrigues me."

Abbott leaned back in the chair. "It's Mary's contention that all our problems would vanish if I took Senator Godwin as my running mate. Anyone here disagree with her?"

"Let's take a look at it," Atkins said. "He's got two hundred and thirty delegates committed to him for the first ballot. Even if he gives them to Foote, it's not enough to put him over the top. And that's not what Godwin and Boutwell want anyway. This whole Foote-Godwin campaign was engineered by Boutwell and his friends, not because that's what Boutwell wants for his grandson, but to pressure us. He knows a Foote-Godwin ticket can't win in the fall."

"Okay, so Foote-Godwin can't win in the fall, and Abbott-Godwin is a shoo-in," Abbott said. "At least, that's what I'm being told by a long list of persistent party leaders and contributors. And while we sit here in relative calm, delegations are caucusing: farm states are caucusing individually and together, labor union delegates are caucusing, black delegates, Southern delegates, any and every group with a cause, real or imaginary, is searching for a common front and assessing its strength, trying to devise some means of exerting pressure on us candidates."

"Granted, Mr. President," Atkins said. "But an Abbott-Godwin ticket makes you even stronger."

"Godwin is irrevocably out. Besides, what would you do? Turn Fowler into a villain?"

Daley laughed. "Well, it would make great copy. You know the press is always looking for conflict. As one noted reporter observed, a story flies best when it has a hero for one wing and a villain for another."

"Boutwell would bring powerful forces to bear on the campaign," Atkins continued. "We'd have campaign funds coming out of our ears."

"May I add, Mr. President," Crowell interjected, "that it's no secret that Boutwell and Stelk and their business associates control over a thousand corporate political action committees. There were only a third that many four years ago. The kitty, I've heard from reliable sources, is well over a hundred million, and they're going to be spending big bucks on their favorite senators and congressmen in both parties. This is a new force in national politics we must reckon with or suffer the consequences."

There was silence around the table. "I knew they were growing like Topsy," Abbott said finally, "but a thousand? And all in four years' time? I assume you've checked those figures."

"Mr. President, the figures, if anything, are growing as we sit here talking. The days of stealing elections are over. Today they're being bought by big business."

"All right, we're in the middle of a squeeze play—never mind the future," Abbott said. "So where do we stand? Godwin is out. Period. So let's go forward from there. What about the eighteen minority reports coming up before the convention today? Let me state up front, so there won't be any misunderstanding, I don't intend to get bloodied out there with a series of procedural defeats. They'll try to bludgeon us with ideological hogwash. Well, I'm not buying."

"I quite agree," Baxter said. "There's only one raw meat issue and that's Minority Report Number Two to suspend the rule binding delegates to the candidate who won them in the primaries and caucuses."

Abbott smiled. "Gentlemen, Mary and I have solved that one. First, let me say that we're not contesting Minority Report Number One requiring the Presidential nominee to pledge his support to the entire platform. After all, we all know that a platform has no purpose beyond flattering the egos of the people who worked on it and the pressure groups who need to report their valiant efforts back to their memberships. A party's real program lies in the vision and conscience of the candidate. It has nothing to do with the heated discussions and wheeling and dealing that has gone on in smoke-filled rooms during the past week."

"Tru," Mary said, "must you keep them in suspense forever?"

Abbott laughed. "All right, we fight on Two because we can't lose."

"We can't?" Baxter asked. "That's nice to know."

"I'd love to hear how you've worked that one out," Atkins said.

"All right, gentlemen," Abbott said, a gleam in his eyes. "The way the figures break down is that we're left with about sixty uncommitted delegates. I have a list of their names, as you do, and what I see is a group of ambitious men and women who know they've got this convention by the throat. They hold the power and when the time comes they expect to be generously remunerated with patronage jobs for their votes. Do you suppose for a minute that they'd chuck this away by voting for an open convention?"

Wiltz laughed. "Right on target, Mr. President. We can shift those sixty votes right in your column."

"This should give us a good bounce for Wednesday," Baxter said. "Even if we don't win on the first ballot Wednesday night, we might pick up some of Godwin's delegates who at the moment seem pretty much committed to Foote."

"Let's take one bounce at a time," Abbott said. "Get the word out, gentlemen: we gracefully accept Minority Report One and fight like hell on Two. Then let the rest of the procedural garbage slide. The delegates can have their fun. I don't want any head knocking. The word is massage. Keep stroking those little egos with promises, promises, promises. Let's turn the sky suite and this whole floor into a massage parlor. Stock up on liquor and cold cuts. And let's keep canvassing the delegates. I don't want any unpleasant surprises. Meanwhile, the word from up here is that your President will accept whatever commandments this convention wishes to carve on its great stone tablet."

"Well said, Tru," Mary said, smiling. "Gentlemen, you could say the President has just hit the ball into the other court. It will be fascinating to see whether Rufus Boutwell charges the net and kills us with a crisp volley or decides to play the baseline, thinking he can outsteady the President."

As Abbott and his staff were conferring, Henry was in Orville Fowler's suite in the North Wing, trying to dissuade him from accepting renomination as Abbott's running mate.

A rancher from eastern Oregon, Fowler had served two terms in the U.S. Senate before becoming Secretary of Agriculture in the previous administration, where his popularity with farmers and ranchers had given him the proper balancing mixture for Abbott's predominately Eastern Establishment ticket. Since then, however, Fowler had fallen into the President's shadow. It was Rufus's contention that Fowler was unhappy in his present role and might be ripe for seduction if the approach was persuasive enough.

"What are you doing in the North Wing?" Henry asked after the two men were seated in the rather small living room. Fowler's wife had discreetly remained in the bedroom. "This is like being in Siberia while the decisions are being made in Moscow."

"Aw, shucks, Henry, they've got all the brainpower they need in Moscow right now."

"Well, you ready for another four years on the shelf, Orville?" Henry asked. The two men had known each other a long time. In fact, during his first term in the Senate Fowler had been invited to join the Forum Club, and on several occasions Henry had made it possible for Fowler to receive large contributions from interested lobbyists. Later, as Agriculture Secretary, by means of secret family trusts established by associates of Stelk who were involved in grain sales to Russia, Fowler had received gifts of stock valued at almost a million.

"Yes, I am, Henry. I've given the President my word on it."

Henry smiled. "I suppose you know why I'm here?"

"I reckon so, but I don't see how I can help you, Henry."

"Have you given it serious consideration? You know, of course, that Rufus is quite set about having Randolph on Abbott's ticket."

"I figured as much. I never for a second believed he'd run with Foote. And President Abbott wants me."

"Don't bet on it, Orville. As far as Rufus is concerned, the Presidential candidate, whoever he may be, will have Randolph as his running mate. And you've known Rufus long enough to understand his kind of politics."

Fowler shrugged. "You think maybe he's going to put the screws to me if I don't back off?"

Henry stood up and went to the window. He disliked this view of the city. The growing sprawl of little houses, one on top of another, reminded him of a fungus. Every time he looked at it, it seemed to have multiplied itself.

"What would you like most in the world, Orville?" Henry asked, turning away from the window to face Fowler.

"Shucks, Henry, that's easy. To be President of these United States of America. It's every schoolboy's dream."

"And you think that after another four years in the closet you're going to be a viable candidate? That's not too realistic, Orville."

"Henry, I'm going to be down-home honest with you, so there's no misunderstanding between us. Every minute I'm Vice-President I feel like a designated hitter in the American League. Any moment somebody like the Chief Justice of the Supreme Court can come up and hand me a big old bat and say, 'Orville, it's your turn, slugger. Go put some big numbers on the scoreboard for your country.'"

There was a glint in Fowler's eyes that told Henry even more than the words. "You're quite a hard case for a good old country boy, aren't you?"

"Henry, people are always underestimating good old country boys. That's why country boys do so well when they leave home for the big city. Ain't Rufus an old country boy himself?"

"Yes, and so am I."

Fowler smiled. "Henry, you had it too soft as a country boy. It didn't stick to you. You're not in our league. Oh, you're pretty sharp, Henry, and don't mind doing a little corrupting here and there for old Rufus, but your heart ain't in it. You've got one of them queasy stomachs and a sensitive nose. How long have I known you? Twenty years? Well, most of the times I've talked to you I got the impression that only part of you was there and it wished it was somewhere else. Good old country boys, Henry, don't only go for the jugular and balls, but take a mite of pleasure while they're at it."

Henry shrugged. "You're entitled to your opinion. But believe me when I say that both parts of me are here right now. I'm telling you as plainly as I can that Rufus will get his way or this is going to be a hurting situation."

"So what's the other side of the coin?"

"Five million, Orville, any way you want it. We can do it like the million you got on the grain deal, stocks in blue chips through secret family trusts, or numbered accounts in Swiss banks, or the presidency of a large corporation with stock options that will earn you a million-plus a year for five years, or longer, if you wish."

"And the hurting, Henry. Is it the million on the grain deal? Will Rufus expose me?"

"I can't answer that, Orville. Rufus will do whatever it takes to get his way. If it means destroying you, then I suppose he'll do it."

Fowler laughed. "Burn the whole darn barn down to get one rat, right? But it don't wash, Henry. If he gets me, he dirties Abbott, and then he's stuck with Foote. The Democrats would bury him in a landslide. I'd say you're in a dilly of a pickle, Henry."

"Five million plus Secretary of Agriculture?"

"Henry, stop it. You can't buy an old country boy's dream of becoming President of these United States. It just ain't possible."

Henry walked from the window to the door. "Thanks for being down-home honest with me. You've saved us both a lot of frustration. But I think I should be down-home honest with you too. You've just thrown away five million dollars and the lucrative honor of again being Secretary of Agriculture. You've misjudged me and the gravity of the situation. And, more importantly, you've misjudged Rufus. I'll tell you now, and I've never been more serious in my life, there's no way in this world you can win this one."

Fowler chuckled. "We'll see soon enough, now, won't we?"

"Yes—in about thirty-six hours, I'd say. Fowler, ordinarily I'd feel bad about what's going to happen to you, but after what you've told me here today about your ghoulish aspirations as a designated hitter, I think you're going to get what you so richly deserve."

"Now, wait a goddamn minute, Henry Godwin. I was honest with you, now you be honest with me. Why does Rufus want the Vice-Presidency for Randolph? So that Abbott can stick him in a closet for four years? Kid yourself, Henry, but don't try to kid me. He's picking himself a designated hitter. Nobody in the whole history of this country ever accepted this job without the knowledge that he's one heartbeat away from the Presidency. Period. I'm just down-home honest enough to admit it."

Henry went to the door and opened it. For reasons he couldn't completely explain, Henry felt a sudden surge of anger and frustration. "Orville, do me a favor, go fuck yourself." Fowler laughed as Henry closed the door.

Henry took a few steps down the empty hallway and felt a sharp stabbing pain in his chest. At first it felt like a gas pain pressing against his heart, then his legs grew weak and he leaned against the wall for support. A cold sweat suddenly covered his body, followed by chills, and for a moment he thought he was going to vomit. He started taking deep breaths and became so dizzy he had to sit down. Almost in slow motion, he lowered himself by leaning his back against the wall and sliding down until he was sitting on the thick carpeting. He was glad there was no one there to see him. Remembering something he'd heard long ago, he lowered his head between his legs and continued deep breathing. The pain around his heart was hot, searing now, so sharp and penetrating it sapped his strength. He tried to raise his arms and was encouraged when they went up without too much effort, because he remembered hearing that the right or left arm of a person having a heart attack usually became paralyzed.

Perhaps it was an attack of food poisoning. He tried to remember what he'd ordered for breakfast: scrambled eggs, bacon, hash browns, tomatoes, English muffins, orange juice, coffee. The eggs could have been spoiled, the bacon rancid.

The pain was lessening and he could feel strength returning to his legs. He raised his head and the dizziness was gone. But his head began to throb. He rubbed his temples. It was just a bad headache. A couple of aspirins would take care of it. Slowly, using both hands against the wall, he pushed himself up the way he'd gone down. He stood a moment, trying to judge the strength in his legs before daring to take that first step. Then he heard the elevator doors open around the bend of the long hallway. He started walking toward the voices.

By the time he turned the corner, the hallway was empty except for the two Secret Service agents sitting facing the bank of elevators. They looked up and smiled; then their expressions turned serious. "Are you all right, Mr. Godwin?" the agent nearer him asked.

"A little upset stomach," Henry said. "I'll be okay. Thank you."

"Are you going downstairs?"

"No, back to the penthouse."

"Well, sir, these elevators don't go any higher. There's a penthouse elevator at the end of this hall and around to your left. Want one of us to go with you? You look pretty pale."

"Thank you, thank you very much, gentlemen, but I'll be fine."

"All right, Mr. Godwin," the other agent said. "But if I were you, sir, I'd go to my room and lie down for a while."

"I'll do that," Henry said.

He walked carefully down the hallway, anxious to reach the elevator while he still had the strength. If only he could go to his room and take a nap, but Rufus was waiting for him to activate the next stage of his master plan. Any nap would have to wait.

59

Rufus looked up from the pile of papers on his desk, his gray eyes narrowing into slits. "What happened to you?" he said. "Seen a ghost?"

Henry sat down in a chair beside the desk. "Just a little headache."

"Shit, you look wrung out." Rufus stared at him a moment. "How did it go with Orville?"

"Not too well. In fact, I ended up telling him to go fuck himself."

Rufus broke into raucous laughter. "You, Henry, said that to Orville? You really are under the weather. Must have given you a hard time. But before we get into that, listen to the end of the tape I just recorded of Abbott's staff meeting."

Rufus pressed the play button on the tape recorder and Henry heard Mary's remark about the ball being in Rufus's court.

Rufus smiled slyly. "It was quite a meeting. Abbott's staff would dump Fowler in a minute if Abbott gave them the word. We've got loyal friends in there. But Abbott's no dummy. He's got the strategy figured on the minority reports and the uncommitted delegates. So we've got to move fast. While old Orville was giving you a hard time, I was getting things set up at this end."

"Rufus, sometimes I wonder where I've been all these years. Why has it taken me twenty years to realize that Orville Fowler is nothing but another selfish prick?"

"Why didn't you ask me, Henry? I could've told you that twenty years ago. So he turned down the five mil. Wants to stand in the wing and wait for the crown to drop in his lap? Well, wait until this election's over and we'll fuck him real good. He's going to be the first Vice-President in history to end his days in prison. He'll learn not to buck me at the most crucial time in my life. Forget about him. Let me lay out what I've got planned. I've got a mobile trailer parked all by itself on the south side of the East Hall. And I've got six million in hundred-dollar bills. I'm going to buy me some hardhead delegates and grab this convention right by the family jewels."

Henry closed his eyes, wondering when his head would stop pounding.

"What do you want from me?"

"I'll do the buying and you'll do the paying."

"You mean we're going to personally get involved in this. You want us to join Orville in the federal pen?"

"Henry, this's for Randolph. There's no one else I'd trust. But there's no danger. Here's the way we'll work it. I'll be in the front room of the trailer, where I'll give the delegates the sales pitch—one hundred thousand each and whatever reasonable patronage job they want. Then I'll send them to you, in the back room, which is set up with a video camera to record the payoff. What you do is hand each one the money in a paper bag, push it across the table, and lean back in your chair while he counts it. Ask him if it's all there, make him repeat the amount, and let him out the back way. The camera's going to be just on him and anything you say will be edited out of the film and another voice substituted. It's foolproof."

"I still don't see why we personally have to do the dirty work."

"Because he's your son and my grandson. I'm not just buying him this election, I'm putting something of myself on the line. It's the least you can do. Remember, you and I've been working for this moment all these years."

"No, Rufus. This has been your dream, not mine. If I'd had my way, Randolph wouldn't even be in politics. He'd be on the ranch with me, enjoying a quiet, peaceful life. He wouldn't be like all the other people we've corrupted."

"Are you saying I've corrupted Randolph?"

"We both have. I'm just as much to blame as you are because I looked the other way. I didn't have the courage to stand up to you."

"You don't know what you're talking about. I did what I had to do to protect that boy from your weaknesses. I had to put some steel in his spine and some dreams in his head." Rufus stood up abruptly. "We're wasting time. Let's get to work. After tomorrow, you can retire to your ranch. I won't need you anymore."

"You don't really need me now," Henry said. "There's a hundred people you could have in here in two minutes who would not only do the job better but enjoy it a hell of a lot more."

Rufus stopped by Henry's chair and looked down at him. "Old

friend, you're not feeling good. I won't hold you responsible for what you're saying."

Henry slowly stood up, testing the strength in his legs before daring to follow Rufus, who was already halfway across the room.

The first delegate to face Rufus across a small table in the trailer was a police sergeant from Pittsburgh, a stocky man with a bull neck and suspicious thyroid eyes.

"I'm Rufus Boutwell and I'm not going to beat around the bush. I want your vote and I'm willing to pay for it. What do you think about that for a proposition?"

He laughed. "Well, Mr. Boutwell, I know you from reputation. And I know that your grandson, Senator Godwin, and his people have been active on the floor."

"Do you know that I'm a man of my word?"

"Yes, sir, I believe I do."

"All right, young man, what do you want most in the world? Just tell me and I'll tell you straight out whether or not I can get it for you."

"I'd like to be a U.S. marshal."

"Can do, no problem. In return I want your vote, and when I say that, I mean we've got a deal, no backing out or hustling on the side for something better. When I buy anybody, they stay bought. As long as you understand that, we'll get along just dandy."

He shook his head. "That's too iffy, Mr. Boutwell. If your grandson gets in then you'll have some clout, but what if he don't, where does that leave me?"

"Good point. First, I'm not only buying your vote, but all of the sixty-two hard rocks willing to sell. You know what I'm talking about? You guys now control this convention. If I control you, then I control the convention. I get what I want and so do you."

He kept shaking his head. "I don't know."

"There's a sweetener I forgot to mention. One hundred thousand dollars in hundred-dollar bills. Cold cash on the barrelhead. The money and the job are yours if you say yes. If you say no, I'll say thank you for your time and good luck with your vote. I might point out, however, that an uncommitted delegate who waits too long turns himself into a nondelegate. He's as bad off as the delegate who backed a loser. With me you get money, and that's yours no matter what happens, and if enough of you guys come around, then you'll get your job too. You tell me now, yes or no."

"It's yes, Mr. Boutwell. When do I get the money?"

"Someone will give it to you when you go through that door. First, remember this. Our code is going to be Condor XPD—that means expedite. When someone calls you with those code words, you follow his instructions to the letter."

"Got you, Mr. Boutwell. How do we go on Minority Report Two? It's coming up for a vote this afternoon."

"Against it. You want to keep your power, don't you?"

"Yes, sir, that's what I thought. Everybody uncommitted in our delegation is against it."

"Okay, go through that door and get your money. Then wait for our call."

"Thank you, Mr. Boutwell. You can count on me one thousand percent."

Rufus smiled and waited until the cop from Pittsburgh was in the other room before having the next delegate admitted.

For Henry it was completely routine. He pushed the paper bag with the money across the table and leaned back in his chair to make sure he was out of the camera's range.

"Here's the hundred thousand," he said.

The police sergeant picked up the bag and quickly opened it, his thyroid eyes growing even larger when he saw the stacks of hundred dollar bills.

"Thanks."

"Please take it out of the bag and count it."

"It looks okay."

"Please count it."

"Okay," the police sergeant said, dumping the money on the desk and quickly riffling the stacks. "Looks okay to me."

"Fine. Remember, we'll be calling you with instructions, so stay close to your delegation's phones."

"No problem," he said, waving to Henry as he went out the door.

By seven o'clock that evening Rufus had bought fifty-eight of the sixty-two delegates. Only four had refused his offer, but not even these had been shocked by it. They were holding out for bigger prizes in the event of a logjam. Rufus's only remark to each was a reminder that a good gambler always knows when to press his bet and when to pull back. He wished them luck.

CHAPTER

60

In his glass booth above the convention floor, Alistair Baker was bored as the roll calls continued on the minority reports. The only excitement had been the vote on Minority Report Number Two, which was soundly defeated. To Baker it seemed to spell the end of Foote's chances, but the NTN crew on the convention floor were sending him conflicting reports. Rumors, as always at conventions, were getting wilder by the hour. One rumor that particularly intrigued Baker was that Rufus Boutwell had gained control of the remaining uncommitted delegates. If that were the case, then the outcome of the convention might well be in Boutwell's hands.

Baker wanted to get into the Boutwell empire, but he needed something to liven his material up. During the next commercial break he called Eileen Godwin and she promised to hurry right over.

While waiting for her, he turned the microphone over to Joseph Alcorn, who went into what he considered a profound analysis of the President's reluctance to challenge any minority reports however opposed to his own philosophy of government.

Even the massive defense buildup proposed in Minority Report Number Six, a package estimated to cost nearly $2 trillion over the next five years, which was trumpeted by Foote as his most important plank, was not challenged by anyone carrying the prestige of the President's mantle.

"The President," said Alcorn, "is definitely on the defensive against this amazingly powerful challenge of Hamilton Foote. Abbott delegates await word from their leader, who remains incommunicado in his headquarters suite at the Monarch II. There's been constant polling of delegations by Abbott aides anxiously trying to stop any suspected slippage in voting patterns. Well, both camps are keeping a watchful eye on their carefully prepared charts on delegate commitments and leanings, and they are poised to pounce on anyone who shows the slightest tendency to defect.

"The latest Gallup Poll shows Foote losing decisively to Democratic candidate Robert McCall in a general election. This dilemma suggests a scenario for some kind of dark-horse ticket. The name of Senator Randolph Godwin is one that keeps cropping up on the convention floor. His showing in the few primaries in which his name was entered without his consent was quite impressive. His nomination as a favorite son tomorrow could ignite this convention. At this time it's impossible to predict what might happen if neither of the two candidates goes over the top on the first ballot. The President's failure would be a damaging psychological blow to supporters who consider him a sure winner. Delegates now legally or morally bound to his candidacy would be free . . ."

Eileen walked into the sky suite and Alcorn completely lost his train of thought. With a signal from Baker he quickly closed his commentary, and a moment later was quietly calling Randolph.

Randolph, who with his aides had been listening to Alcorn's remarks, was not surprised when he received the call because Eileen was already being introduced by Baker.

"What's he up to?" Randolph asked.

"I haven't the slightest clue," Alcorn said. "I think he wants to do some backgrounding on your grandfather."

"Joe, watch him carefully," Randolph said. "If he starts getting cute, cut in on him."

Alcorn coughed nervously. "That's impossible, Randy. He controls all the mikes. He's got me muted. I'd have to get up and walk into the picture."

"If you must, then do it."

"Randy, he'd fire me on the spot. You don't know him. He runs the show up here with the authority of a Prussian general."

"Okay, listen, I'll tell you what. If it starts going sour I'll have Lew Spark call the booth."

"Have him call me. Baker won't take calls when he's interviewing unless it's absolutely urgent. They'll put the call through to me and I'll signal him to take it."

"Are you enjoying the convention, Miss Godwin?" Baker asked.

"Tremendously," she said, "but please call me Eileen."

"Thank you. After all, you have a twin sister and we wouldn't want the viewers to confuse the two of you."

"I would hope not," Eileen said, the sweetness momentarily gone from her tone. "We may look alike, but we certainly don't think alike."

"Yes, I've noticed that, Eileen. For example, I know that you have done considerable campaigning on behalf of your father."

"Oh, no, Alistair. My father did not campaign. But I have, at various times, expressed my feelings on certain political issues and on the Republican Party in general."

"And your sister, Alicia—is she a Republican?"

Eileen shook her head. "Frankly, I haven't the faintest idea what political party she favors, if any. But I'd much rather talk about my great-grandfather, Rufus Boutwell, who unquestionably is the greatest man in Nevada history and a true American. And my father, whom I dearly love, and who's a devoted public servant."

Baker nodded. "The reason I brought up your sister is that millions of people have shared your tragedy and I'm sure are curious as to your present life-style. It comes as something of a surprise to discover that the lovely Godwin twins, who had the prayers and sympathy and admiration of so many million Americans, have somehow grown distant . . ."

"The cocksucker," Randolph shouted. "Danny, have Lew call him right now. I want her off the fucking show."

"I've got Lew on an open line. Want to talk to him? Take line twelve."

"Lew, what's his tab?" Randolph asked.

Spark laughed. "Forty-one thousand over the past ten years. Not much, but that's not counting the plane rides."

"Be diplomatic, Lew, but stick it to him. Any hookers involved?"

"Oh, sure, I've got the whole list. Quite a few are still in town."

"Freaky or straight."

"Straight arrow. In fact, I've got a notation from Ruth Bellini. Remember her? That was a few years back, but she said he actually apologized when he came too fast. Poor sap thought he'd deprived her of her well-deserved orgasm. They don't come much straighter."

"Okay, get with it. He's on a commercial break."

When Alcorn indicated the waiting phone call, Baker frowned impatiently and punched the button on his telephone console.

"Yes, make it fast. I'm on the air in thirty seconds."

"Alistair, this is Lew Spark."

"Lew, hello, what's wrong? I mean, what can I do for you?"

"Alistair. Don't play games with me. Stick that hatchet back in your hip pocket. You're not the only guy who can play dirty. That fucking microphone doesn't give you a license to insult your friends and benefactors. There's a little matter of forty-one thou you owe this hotel that I want paid in full tonight."

Baker was incensed. "Don't try that muscle stuff on me," he warned in a low voice. "I'll expose your whole dirty racket."

Spark laughed. "Do yourself a big favor and don't say another word to me. And after some nice words to your motherfucking audience about Randolph and Rufus and Eileen and Alicia, get her out of there."

The commercial break ended just as the line went dead. Baker swallowed with difficulty and readjusted his smile.

"Eileen, may I say that you and your sister have grown up to be beautiful and charming young ladies. Of course, as you know, I've known your father many years, and your grandfather and great-grandfather, and I must say you come from a family of truly distinguished Americans. Earlier this evening I was talking about famous political families. I think Rufus Boutwell, Henry Godwin, and Senator Randolph Godwin have made a profound contribution to the growth and welfare of this great state of Nevada. Their contribution transcends state lines. It is national and even international. I don't think there's anywhere on this globe you can go today where people have not heard about Las Vegas. When you travel to foreign countries in Europe and Asia and Africa and South America, the first thing they ask you if you're an American is about Las Vegas. I was in Australia . . ."

61

Of all her father's aides and close friends, Alicia's favorite was Guy Charest, her father's speechwriter. Guy had been a close family friend going back to the days when her father had been a legislative aide for Senator Elisha Toombs.

A former newspaper reporter with *The Washington Post*, Charest had left the paper years ago to become a speechwriter for Governor Nelson Rockefeller of New York before coming to work for Randolph. In his late fifties and a lifelong bachelor, Charest was from a small town in Maine, where he'd attended Bowdoin College. In his old *Post* days Charest had been a frequent visitor at the Godwins' Georgetown home. Although Alicia had been very young then, she remembered that Guy and her mother had been good friends. Today he was the only one from those days who would talk with her about her mother. He'd recall stories and events involving Betty with a clarity of detail that delighted Alicia. For reasons she couldn't understand she hungered for the tiniest morsel of information about her mother.

In light moments with Henry Alicia called her quest an obsession, but there were times when she felt it was turning into paranoia. It was during her first year in college that she started writing about her mother in a diary and had since filled countless notebooks with details about her life and death. She had spent weeks in Quincy with her grandmother, Eileen Schurtz, pumping her for all she was worth, convinced that the old woman was holding back information that Alicia needed to fill the blanks in Betty's early life.

She had consulted the Washington, D.C., police, had gone over the autopsy and investigative reports concerning the murder numerous times. She had, in fact, convinced the police to give her copies of all their reports, and they had complied just to be rid of her. The lieutenant in charge of the investigation had since died, which left her with no

one to turn to with her questions. The murderer had never been appre-
hended, and the details of her death were so strangely inconclusive
that each reading fed Alicia's suspicions, which, in turn, fed her obsession.

Early in the morning Alicia had played three hard sets of tennis with
Charest and had spent the rest of the morning lounging by the pool.
She hated Las Vegas, with its grotesque nouveau riche opulence and
its stupid tourists being led to the slaughter of the gaming tables.

For a while Charest had sat beside her, working on her father's
speech. He wore bikini swim trunks and for a man of his age he was
powerfully built, with supple muscles, a flat stomach, and slim hips, a
condition maintained through hard work and a strong narcissistic drive.

Alicia also recognized the narcissism in Daisy, but that was expected
in an entertainer, especially in someone who had remained at the top
of the heap for God only knew how long. In recent years Alicia had
seen a lot of Daisy and grown quite fond of her. She was an amazing
woman. Somewhere Daisy had found the fountain of youth. Alicia was
certain that she hadn't had any face-lifts. She'd seen her with wet hair
after a swim enough times to know there were no telltale marks behind
her ears or at her hairline. And that dazzling smile showed her own
teeth, not the porcelain caps so popular with most movie stars.

The strange thing about Daisy was her relationship with Henry and
her great curiosity about the most minute details concerning Randolph,
Betty, Eileen, and Alicia herself. At times Daisy's quest seemed almost
as obsessional as her own. There had been humorous moments when
both women had realized that they were pumping each other. By now
Alicia was convinced that Henry and Daisy had known each other
intimately for far more years than either would ever admit.

She wished she knew more about her grandfather's life. When she
was a child, during vacations at the ranch, Henry had told her and
Eileen stories about the General that had delighted Alicia. The great
enjoyment Henry seemed to derive from talking about him had
touched her even as a child. But as she'd grown older, she'd realized
that, although Henry talked a great deal about the General, he revealed very little about himself.

In early afternoon Alicia joined Daisy for brunch, which meant a tall
glass of mixed vegetables. It tasted terrible, but if that was what it took
to look like Daisy at her age, Alicia was ready to drink all the vegetables she could process in her fancy blender.

Daisy was an easy lady to be with. She always seemed to be in a cheerful frame of mind. And there was nothing pretentious about her. She never alluded to her fame, directly or indirectly, and seldom spoke about her work. She never played any of her own records, but had gone to great expense to apply modern electronic techniques to the records of Bessie Smith and Billie Holiday. Those records, along with those of Sarah Vaughan, Ella Fitzgerald, Lena Horne, Anita O'Day, Mahalia Jackson, Diana Ross, and Aretha Franklin, were on her stereo constantly. It was interesting to Alicia that all the singers she played, except O'Day, were black, and O'Day in her best work sounded black. For that matter, so did Daisy.

"You really favor black singers, don't you?" Alicia asked.

Daisy's eyes twinkled. "They sing my kind of music," she said. "Bessie was my idol. When I first started singing I was really doing an imitation of her. So one day this piano player was hired to accompany me. It was my first job, in a grubby little honky-tonk in the tenderloin. We practiced a few numbers and I thought I was doing just great until he said, 'Hey, sugar, I've heard Bessie sing plenty of times, and I don't think you're going to improve on her, so how about giving me a rendition of you?' "

Daisy laughed. "I was so young and frightened. I nearly died on the spot. Then I tried to sing and nothing came out. I had no idea what I was supposed to do. See, Bessie's records had taught me how to hold notes, how to phrase, everything, but the way she did it was unique, believe me. There's never been another Bessie and there never will be. Nor another Billie. Can you imagine what they'd sound like today with all the sophisticated electronic systems we get to work with in recording sessions. It would blow their minds and they'd blow ours."

They were sitting at an umbrella table on the terrace of Daisy's suite. Alicia was still in her bikini and Daisy was in brief shorts and tank top with the words WIN-GOD-WIN.

"So what did you do?" Alicia asked.

Daisy raised an eyebrow. "What do you think I did? I burst into tears, naturally, and that dear man was beside himself with guilt. He worked with me all afternoon and into evening right up to showtime. We teamed up after that and worked together a few months, until he got a job with a big band." She smiled. "The good Lord was looking out for me that day when he sent Benny Burns to accompany me."

"What ever happened to him? Did you ever see each other again?"

"Many times, but he's dead now. Got hooked on the hard stuff and it killed him like it's killed so many other good people. If I ever write my autobiography, I'll dedicate it to him. He was the Lord's messenger. Without him I might not be here today. He set me on the right path by teaching me an important lesson. Never be an imitation of anything in life. Good, bad, or mediocre, it's always better to be yourself. Now are you satisfied? You came here for my delicious vegetable cocktail and got a sermon to boot."

"That's right," Alicia said, assuming a serious expression. "I understand they do the same thing at skid row missions. Prayers first, then bread."

"Well, let's drink a toast to Benny Burns, if not the Lord's messenger, then my rumpled Professor Higgins."

When Alicia returned to Henry's suite later in the afternoon, she found Garfield Stone on the terrace, leaning dangerously over the railing.

"Get back from there," she called.

He pulled himself up and turned to stare at her, his face flushed from the exertion. "Oh, you're one of the twins," he said.

"Yeah, and who are you, and what were you doing hanging over the railing like a monkey?"

"I'm Garfield Stone. I'm working for your father's campaign."

"Do you realize you're thirty-six stories up?"

"I'm not afraid of heights, are you?"

"No, but I'm not about to start doing handstands on the railing."

"I'll do one," Garfield said. "Watch."

"Get back here, you little nut,"

"Hey, watch your fucking mouth," he cried, his face contorting angrily. "Who you calling a nut, you dumb cunt?"

Alicia looked at him and burst out laughing. "Now, I get it," she said. "The Beverly Hills syndrome. The typical movie star brat. I had some of you guys in my classes at Berkeley. All paranoid. Think the whole world's judging them by daddy's or mommy's achievements. Makes life real tough to be a failure at sixteen. You've really got my heartfelt sympathy."

Garfield couldn't believe his ears. "What the hell are you, a motherfucking shrink?"

"Well, I took Psych One and Two, which is more than you've done, you poor neglected child."

In a fit of rage Garfield jumped up on the railing and teetered precariously. Alicia's hand went to her mouth to stifle the scream building inside her. He regained his balance and turned to glare at her.

"Please," she pleaded softly, "come down off the railing. I'm sorry if I offended you. I thought you knew I was only kidding, having a little word game."

"Bullshit," he cried. "Now, which way do you want me to come down, this way or that way."

"For God's sake, Garfield, be reasonable. You're scaring me half to death."

"Say pretty please," asked Garfield, his rage subsiding.

"Pretty please."

"Say you'll kiss my ass."

"I'll say it, but I won't do it."

"Say it."

"I'll kiss your ass if you get off that fucking railing."

He jumped off, smirking, turned around, and bent over. "Kiss it or next time I'll do a handstand."

"Go to hell," she said, turning away. "The fastest way there is over that railing. So long, brat."

He ran after her. "Hey, what's your name?"

"Alicia."

"I'm sorry, Ali, I was just getting kicks. I like to scare people. It's my thing, you know. Did you ever play Russian roulette?"

She stopped and tapped a stiff finger against his bony chest. "Garfield, the game's over. You're sending out some very weird vibes. I think I'm going to have your ass kicked out of here. You're a walking fruitcake and a menace to the peace and tranquility of this benign convention."

His face contorted again but this time tears started streaming down his hollowed cheeks. "Hey, I'm sorry, really. Don't get me kicked out. I've got important work to do—for your father."

"Where's Hoppy?"

He grabbed her hand. "Don't, please don't. I'll really kill myself if I can't work for your father's campaign. My father would be really pissed at me. Give me a break, will you? Please!"

She looked at him and saw a frightened boy, emaciated, the dark circles under his wet eyes grotesquely magnified by the thick lenses of his glasses.

"All right, Garfield, but no more crazy antics. You promise?"

"Oh, God, on my father's head. May he burn in the fires of hell for all eternity if I ever touch that railing again."

Alicia shook her head. "Oh, Jesus, you do come on strange, Garfield. Okay, I'll see you later."

In the excitement she forgot to ask him what he was doing in Henry's suite or how he had gained entry. She would remember it later, but it would be too late.

62

The isolation tank was ten feet long, four feet wide, and just as high. Inside was one foot of water and two hundred pounds of Epsom salts. Lying on its buoyant surface, Daisy was silently repeating her secret mantra. For many years she had been into one form or another of yoga, combining vigorous exercises with meditation to achieve union with Brahma—the Ultimate Reality or Absolute.

Daisy found great comfort in yogic meditation. Twenty minutes of meditation twice a day had become a way of life with her. It was the one sure way she knew of recharging her battery. Tests performed on her by a specialist while she was in a state of meditation showed a significant drop in her blood pressure, a twenty percent drop in oxygen consumption, and a heavy increase in the alpha waves produced in her brain by electrical activity associated with a feeling of relaxation.

With the addition of the isolation tank Daisy found herself slipping into a state comparable to reentering the womb. She was so charged with energy after one of these sessions that she could perform for hours without becoming fatigued. But there were limits to her devotion. She had long ago abandoned the more severe forms of meditation that required her to give up physical and earthly pleasures. Yet she deeply believed in her mantra and had read the fourteenth-century Christian treatise *The Cloud of Unknowing*, which advised: "Clasp this word tightly in your heart so that it never leaves no matter what may happen. This word shall be your shield and your spear."

Daisy had often tried to get Henry interested in yogic meditation, even in the relatively milder TM, since she could see that he was living under enormous stress, but her efforts had been wasted. Sometimes she thought of him as a man drowning and refusing to grab the lifeline offered him.

It reminded her of a story she'd once heard about a psychologist who had drowned two wild rats. He dropped the first rat in the tank of warm water and it swam for nearly sixty hours before becoming exhausted and drowning. He held the second rat in his hand until it stopped struggling. When he dropped that one in the water, it splashed around for a few minutes, then passively sank to the bottom. The psychologist's conclusion was that the second rat had despaired of escape even before it got wet, and, in effect, died of helplessness.

Daisy had been told that there was a little of Rat Two in most people. She found a frightening amount in Henry's growing melancholia. Henry had been held in the iron grip of Rufus Boutwell until he'd stopped struggling. His frequent bouts of depression were, in effect, feelings of helplessness.

Earlier in the evening Henry had stopped by and Daisy had been shocked by his appearance. He looked like a man on the verge of total collapse.

She had just completed her series of exercises and was about ready to get into the isolation tank for her meditative period when Henry let himself in with his key and went directly to the bar to pour himself straight bourbon over ice.

Usually she would have kidded him for ignoring her in favor of a drink, but when she saw his gray face and glazed eyes she was instantly alarmed.

She went to him and kissed his forehead. It felt cold and clammy. "Henry, darling, you look like you could use a little sleep. Why don't you take your drink to the bedroom and lie down while you finish it. I'll turn the convention on and I guarantee it'll put you to sleep in two minutes flat."

"You know what I'd like to do," he said, pausing to take a deep swallow of the bourbon. "I'd like to get in my chopper and go kick those people off my mountaintop."

"Let's do it. I'll help you."

He laughed. "I think you would."

"In a minute," she said, coming to kneel by his chair. "It must have been one hell of a rotten day."

"Yeah. To give you some idea, the highlight was when I told the Vice-President of the United States to go fuck himself."

She smiled admiringly. "That's my old Henry, all right. The fighter who'd stand up to anybody. What happened to that fighter lately, do you know?"

"Oh, not you, too," he moaned.

She grabbed his free hand and kissed it. "I'm only teasing, darling. You've always been my hero." She paused a moment. "Will you tell me someday about the Pikes?"

He nodded. "Someday I'll tell you about a lot of things, but not today. I've just been told by my charming father-in-law that he's worked hard all these years to protect Randolph from my weaknesses. That—and I want this quote to be accurate—he 'had to put some steel in his spine and some dreams in his head.' Now don't say I never tell you anything."

She pressed his hand against her cheek. It too felt cold and clammy. "Why have you put up with that man all these years?"

He smiled, but his eyes remained glazed. "See, I tell you a couple of things and immediately you want to know more. You're insatiable, in all departments."

"Now you're being a comedian," she said. "How about opening my act with a stand-up routine? Go to bed, Henry, and I promise not to molest you."

He finished his drink and stood up. "Sorry, honey, but I've got work to do." He stopped and shook his head. "Christ, I must be sending out terrible vibrations. I know you have to get yourself up for these strenuous performances and I'm not helping. Next time I see you I promise to be radiating optimism from every pore. I'm going to pump you up so high you'll take that watery coffin you meditate in and throw it right out the window."

She kissed him, walked him to the door, and went to meditate in her watery coffin.

By the time Eileen had removed her clothes and stood naked before him, Alistair Baker had completely forgotten about Lew Spark's phone call. First there had been the romantic candlelight dinner in the Café Noir, with champagne and violin music. Raising their glasses for a toast, their eyes had met over the rims and locked. Baker had felt giddy. When their eyes finally disengaged, he knew for a certainty that he'd score before the night was out.

Now as she walked up to him and began unbuttoning his shirt, Baker felt his legs start to tremble. He'd been so busy watching her undress that he'd only removed his jacket and tie while she performed the most erotic strip he'd ever seen.

She was smiling, her mouth slightly open, her tongue moving slowly against moist lips. Her hands reached inside his shirt and touched his chest, her long, warm fingers caressing his nipples. He groaned and she smiled. She lowered her head and he felt her tongue lick his chest, then her lips suddenly fastened on his right nipple. It produced a sensation he'd never felt before and he struggled to control himself.

"You like that, Daddy?" she whispered against his tingling flesh.

He was startled by the word *Daddy* but quickly caught on to the game she wanted to play.

"Undress Daddy," he moaned, "so he can fuck his little girl."

She looked up and her hands went to his waist, expertly unbuckling his belt and unzipping his fly. He felt his trousers and underwear drop around his ankles and she was cupping him with both hands.

"You want me to suck on your big cock, Daddy?"

"Holy Mother of Jesus Christ," he whimpered. "Suck me, little girl."

"Come to bed, and we'll do *soixante-neuf*. I want you to eat me too, Daddy."

Holding on to his engorged penis, Eileen led Baker to the bed. A moment later her perfumed vagina was at his face and she was licking slowly on his member. He tasted her, darting his tongue between the lips of her scented mound, and tried to forget she had him in her mouth, working over him with her lips and tongue, her fingers squeezing his buttocks, flicking over his anus. He tried to control himself, wanted desperately not to be premature, but it was too late.

To his utter amazement, she held on to his throbbing penis, her lips closing tightly as she pumped his organ and continued sucking. His face was buried in her and her thighs tightened around his head. She began bucking as he licked and sucked as furiously as he could until she stopped.

"Oh, Daddy," she moaned deep in her throat, "that was divinely delicious."

He looked at her and she slithered into his arms, her mouth closing on his, her tongue pressing inside, giving him the salty taste of his own semen. Her hands clutched the back of his head tightly, and gradually he felt his tongue being sucked into her mouth. This was the most passionate woman he'd ever known. Her aggressiveness left him dizzy with desire. To his astonishment he had grown hard again, and she was straddling him now, her hands guiding him inside her, as she lowered herself slowly and exquisitely until her buttocks rested on his pelvis.

"Is my cunt tight enough, Daddy?" she whispered hoarsely, as her hips began to rotate.

"Oh, yes, little girl, it's the tightest."

Then she did something he'd never seen before. She slid a hand under one of her breasts, lowered her head, and began licking and sucking her own nipple. He reached up for the other breast, but she gently pushed his hand away. "Don't touch, Daddy—they're mine alone."

She was moving faster now, sideways, up and down, and he sank back and closed his eyes, straining to keep himself from ejaculating again prematurely.

A moment later Eileen screamed and when he opened his eyes Alistair saw the two tall, heavyset men in security uniforms, guns on their hips, standing just inside the door of the bedroom.

"Sorry for the interruption," the older of the two men said, "but you've got a little unfinished business with Mr. Spark."

"Get out of here," Eileen shouted, "or my father will have your heads."

The younger one grinned foolishly, his cold blue eyes slowly moving over her body. "What do you think of that, Charlie? A hooker with connections. You think her old man's her pimp?"

Charlie pointed to the telephone. "Dial one eleven. Mr. Spark is waiting for your call."

"All right," Baker said angrily. "I'll call him, but you two get out of here. Wait in the living room."

"Make the fucking call," the younger one said. "We're staying right here."

Eileen had remained in her sitting position. Her green eyes had turned to ice but she made no attempt to cover herself. "Dial the number, Alistair, and hand me the phone."

Baker dialed. When Spark answered, he said, "One moment, please," and handed her the phone.

"Lew, this is Eileen. There are two goons in this bedroom and if they're not out of here in ten seconds flat you're going to get the goddamnedest fireworks you ever saw."

"Calm down, honey," Spark said. "Put one of them on the horn."

She handed the phone to the younger one. He took it, listened, nodded a few times, and handed the phone back to Eileen. "Sorry, please forgive the intrusion. It was a mistake. I'm really sorry."

"You asshole," she shouted. "Get out of here, both of you."

They were already out of the room before she could get the words out of her mouth. "Lew, I want them fired. They're arrogant, filthy animals."

466

"All right, sweetheart. It was a mistake. I had no idea you were with Baker. Please, do me a favor and forget the whole thing."

"I said I want them fired."

"Okay, you've got it, sweetheart. Now, will you please hand the phone to Baker. There's something I have to discuss with him."

"No, I'm not going to hand him the phone. You leave him alone."

"Sweetheart, I'm just following your father's orders."

"Well, I've just canceled those orders. Good night, Lew!"

She tossed the receiver to Baker, who caught it and gently hung it up. He looked sheepishly at her. "I'm sorry, Eileen. I had no idea they'd break into this room."

"That's all right, darling," she said, stretching out next to him. "What pissed him off?"

"Remember the call I got while I was interviewing you?"

"Yes, I wondered about it. After that you just cut me right off."

"Your father wanted you off the show and had Lew call me."

"So what are these goons doing in your room at one in the morning?"

Baker looked away. "Spark claims I owe him forty-one thousand dollars. He's evidently been keeping tab on every time they've comped me at the two Monarchs for the past ten years."

"Oh, the creepy bastards," she cried, sitting up in bed. "Tell them to kiss your ass. Don't you pay it. I'll talk to my father. I'll straighten it out, don't worry. Now, sweet Daddy," she said, lowering her voice and snuggling against him, "where were we?"

David Webber hadn't been asleep five minutes before the phone rang. He picked it up and said, "Hello, is that you, Peggy?"

Garfield laughed. "No, David, this is Rocky Stone. Hope I didn't wake you up again."

David cleared his throat. "Not really. I'd just gone to bed."

"Well, listen, David, I'm here at the Monarch with my director and producer for my next film and we've got a little problem in arithmetic or geometry we thought you might help us solve, if you don't mind. Take only a minute for a guy with your brainpower."

Gus Meier, who had moved in with David, sat up in the other twin bed and rubbed his eyes. It was the first time he'd been in a real bed in days and he had been hoping to get a few hours' sleep before resuming his search for that loony kid.

"First, David, I want to apologize for missing that dinner, but I hope Senator Godwin's young assistant treated you all right."

"Yes, he did, very nice."

"Good, David. Now, here's our problem. We're doing a movie about a high-rise fire and we need to know how long it takes for a body to drop, let's say, four hundred feet. Could you figure it out?"

"Yes, give me a second to recall the equation. Okay, a free-falling body accelerates at thirty-two feet per second squared. So the equation is D equals one-half times A times T squared. When you square something you multiply it by itself. So it's really one-half times A times T times T. D is the distance the body drops, four hundred feet, and A is the acceleration. For natural gravity that's thirty-two."

"Is that in a vacuum, David?"

"No, no, that's just free-falling in air. T is the time it takes for it to drop." Webber reached over for the calculator he'd put on the bedside table. "Okay, so now the way our equation looks is that if you substitute four hundred for D, you have four hundred is equal to one-half times thirty-two times T times T. And playing around with the equation, you can rewrite it as being eight hundred feet is equal to thirty-two times T times T. This way we get rid of the one-half there."

"That's very clever, David. How long is that equation?"

"Quite short, really. So, you end up with T times T is equal to eight hundred divided by thirty-two. So what does that give us? T squared was equal to eight hundred divided by thirty-two and that's twenty-five, and the square root of twenty-five is five. Now we know that T is equal to five. In other words, it takes five seconds to drop the four hundred feet."

"That's really super, David. How fast will the body be traveling when it hits the firemen's net?"

"This next equation is V is equal to A times T. That's velocity is equal to acceleration times time. We know the acceleration is thirty-two feet per second squared, and the time is five seconds. So we just take five seconds times thirty-two and you end up with the speed he's going at when he hits the bottom. That's a hundred and sixty feet per second. Now we can convert that to miles per hour. You divide the one-sixty by five thousand two hundred and eighty, which is the number of feet in a mile, and you come up with point zero three zero three miles per second. Doesn't seem like much, but that's per second. There's sixty seconds in a minute and we multiply that and it gives us one point eight one eight miles per minute, multiplied by sixty minutes in an hour and we get one hundred and nine point zero nine miles per hour."

"Fantastic, David. Does the weight of the person falling make any difference?"

"No, this is all independent of weight. People are built pretty much the same aerodynamically. They all drop like a lead brick."

"David, you really are a genius. I wish I had your brain, man. I'd conquer the world. Well, good luck at the convention. Don't let that Charlie Bliss push you around. You've got ten times his brainpower, man. Well, thanks, and now you go back to sleep. I promise not to wake you up ever again."

"Don't mention it, Rocky," David said. "And good luck with your new movie."

David hung up, turned out the lights, and got back into bed. "These movie people are very meticulous about being accurate," he said.

63

At seven o'clock on Wednesday morning Henry awoke with an erection and found Daisy in his bed. She must have sneaked in after her midnight show, he thought, when she found him missing from her bed. He smiled.

She was sleeping on her side, facing away from him, and he gently pressed his naked body into the curve of hers, one hand going to caress her firm, silky-smooth breasts. She groaned softly and reached back to stroke his cheek.

"You horny old man," she said, her voice thick with sleep. "What's this object I feel pressing so urgently against my virginal derrière?"

"I may be knocking at your back door, honey," he said, "but where I hail from us white gentlemen folk always use the front door."

"Thank God for white gentlemen folk," she said, turning to face him, her hand moving to his forehead, which felt warm and dry. "Feeling much better, aren't you?"

"Feel like a million," he said. "All I needed was a good night's sleep. I was dead to the world, didn't even dream." Then he remembered his nightmare about Betty. He assumed his dream had been triggered by what Alicia had told him about the night of her mother's death. In his dream Betty was on the telephone sobbing that a man was raping and killing her. She was pleading for Henry's help. He screamed hysterically into the phone, hoping that the rapist would hear his voice and be frightened away. Betty kept begging for help, telling Henry she loved him, saying that if he loved her, he'd help her because the rapist was choking her to death. Then a hand had touched him and the dream was gone.

"You were thrashing around pretty good when I got into bed," Daisy said. "But I touched you and you stopped. A second later you were snoring to high heaven."

"Yes, I remember, now," he said. "Nightmare Henry was reviewing another horror film."

Through the years she had heard enough about his nightmares to recognize that he was a man drowning not only in helplessness but in guilt. She reached down to touch him and found that his erection had gone limp. "That didn't last very long," she said.

He kissed her and pressed his hand between her legs. "Talking about nightmares will do that to me every time," he said. "I've got a one-track mind."

She took him in her hand. "Keep moving on this track and we've got it made."

"Honey, you and me, we've got it made on all tracks, for always and forever, whichever comes last."

Two hours later Henry was in the Rolls limousine on his way to Oscar's in Charleston Park. Moses was behind the wheel, and when he heard Henry start speaking into a pocket-sized cassette recorder, he closed the glass panel to give Henry privacy.

The strange attack had shaken Henry. Although he told himself it was caused by food poisoning or the twenty-four-hour flu, a small voice in the back of his head was telling him that he was rationalizing something that was far more serious, but he refused to listen to it. Yet the attack had made him very much aware that he was indeed mortal. His time could come at any moment, but he had certain obligations to fulfill before he called it quits for good. For one thing he had to help relieve the torment Alicia was going through in her search for the truth concerning her mother's death. Because she cared so deeply, Henry decided to make a tape that would be passed on to her in the event of his sudden death. The tape might provide the link she needed to put the pieces together—as he had never been able to do—and finally put the matter to rest.

Betty's death, like Yulee's, had tormented Henry for many years. He'd gone over the details in his mind numerous times, always ending up wondering who had come in that evening while Betty was on the telephone with him. It couldn't have been the murderer, because she had died three or four hours later. No rapist would remain that long in a house with children asleep upstairs. So many questions kept revolving in his head. Why had Rufus and Randolph gone to the Stork Club that night? Both men had told the police they'd left the house around seven thirty that evening after Betty had declined to join them because of a headache. Of course, she was drunk on the telephone, and that could've been the reason, but Betty's phone call to Henry was around eight, which meant they couldn't have been there at seven thirty. After all, Betty had said she hadn't seen Randolph in four days. Why the discrepancy in time? And since Randolph and Rufus were hardly in a mood to take Betty anyplace after they learned of her background from Joey Alongi, their story about Betty declining to join them had also been a lie. There was something disturbing about the lies and sequence of events. Finally, what were the sounds Alicia had heard in her bedroom that night, and what was the real conflict between Alicia and Randolph?

Henry decided that the only way he could begin to cope with all the questions was to lay out the facts as he knew them on the tape and permit Alicia to take it from there. But once started in his dictating, he found that he wanted to talk about other events in his life, and he started another tape for Daisy. He talked about the death of Yulee, the Klan attack, the murder of the Pikes, and of Alongi. He was, he thought as the limousine came to a stop in Oscar's parking lot, unburdening his soul for the first time in his life. And it felt remarkably good.

Oscar served them breakfast out on the deck, but Henry ate sparingly. Moses ordered the works, while Henry sipped coffee and crunched on dry toast.

He looked at Moses and smiled. "On the way up here," he said, "I had a strange thought. Remember the night you broke Clews's back with the shovel?"

Moses chuckled. "Henry, that was one of the great highlights of my life. I'll *never* forget it."

"Well, I think I made a serious mistake that night."

"I do too," Moses said with a wide grin.

"You do? You reading my mind again?"

"Henry, I've got the power, what can I tell you. The good Lord said, 'Moses, I give you the power to read that white devil's mind.'" Moses slapped the table and howled with laughter.

"Let's hear it, great seer."

"Between you and me, Henry, you should've let me cut his fucking head off with that shovel. I could've buried him in the north pasture and nobody would've been the wiser. That man's the most evil devil I ever knowed, white or black."

The sound of a helicopter drowned out Moses' words, and a moment later a sleek royal blue Sikorsky S-76 with a gold crest on the doors came into view as it headed for Henry's mountaintop.

"I guess somebody's having company," Moses shouted over the noise. "But, Henry, was I right?"

"Yes, Moses," Henry said as the helicopter disappeared on the other side of the mountain. "I wonder how many lives would've been spared by that one simple act of charity?"

The Sikorsky settled gently on the circular pad. An aide opened the door and lowered the steps.

"Cut that engine and wait in here for us," Rufus said as he went out the door and down the steps, followed by Randolph.

"You okay, sonny boy?" he asked.

"Feel just great," said Randolph, whose snorts of cocaine prior to leaving for the airport had eased him into a relaxed, confident mood.

"You're about to meet the two most powerful businessmen in the world. Things have been set up, but still they want to take a closer look at you before putting their seal on the deal."

"Everything's fine, Rufus. Relax, will you?"

Rufus laughed. "Am I getting on your nerves?"

At that moment Jesse Stelk came out on the redwood deck to greet them.

"Rufus, thanks for coming," Stelk said as they shook hands. "Senator, a pleasure to see you again," he added, turning to Randolph.

They shook hands and Randolph said, "Mr. Stelk, the pleasure is mine. I had no idea who I was going to see here today. Rufus has been most mysterious about this meeting. I'm delighted it's you. When you appeared before our committee studying the tax structure of multi-nationals, I hope we treated you fairly."

"As far as it went," Stelk said, "but you were particularly gracious."

H. Russell Pierpont came out to join them and now Randolph was surprised. He'd heard a great deal about this heir to a vast banking empire, but he'd never met him. And Rufus, sly old fox that he was, had never once mentioned Pierpont in conversation.

After the introduction, the four went inside. They sat in easy chairs arranged around a circular coffee table near the massive stone fireplace that covered an entire wall, rising two stories high. There was a coffee urn on the table and the men helped themselves.

"We've been baching it," Stelk said.

"But in style," Pierpont added. "Rufus, those meals your chef has had flown in have been a lifesaver. Thank him for us, will you?"

Rufus nodded and sipped his coffee. "Do you want me to start this out? I haven't told him a thing yet."

Pierpont smiled. "Randolph, this is going to be strictly on a need-to-know basis. But before we get into the purpose of this little gathering, I should tell you and Rufus that Abbott just concluded his morning staff conference, and it was most encouraging. Wouldn't you agree, Jesse?"

Stelk laughed softly. "We've got him boxed in and he knows it. We had the information leaked to him about your control of the uncommitted delegates, and I must say he's sorely tempted to grab the bait. To use Mary's phrase, the ball is back in Abbott's court. And it was a crisp volley that caught him leaning the wrong way. Mary was a riot in there today."

Pierpont joined Stelk in the laughter. "She's a woman who understands the uses of power. I don't think she'd be the least opposed to having Randolph on the ticket. In fact, she spoke quite highly of you this morning. But Abbott is totally against you."

Stelk fixed his blue eyes on Randolph. "What did you ever do to that man that would give him such a hard-on for you? I mean besides fucking his daughter?"

Randolph shrugged. "I don't know whether it's me or that he's committed to Fowler in ways we don't understand."

"Oh, it's you," Stelk said. "If Fowler dropped dead right now, Abbott still wouldn't want you as his running mate."

"We're going to have to play more than tennis to convince him," Rufus said. "This is hardball, gentlemen, and we've got one hell of an inside curve to dust him off with."

"In fact," Pierpont said, "Jesse called Abbott immediately after the staff conference and set up a meeting in Henry's suite for two o'clock this afternoon."

"Is he coming alone?" Rufus asked. "I don't want Mary in there for the rough stuff, if it gets down to it."

"Alone," Stelk said. "Oh, he'll have his usual entourage of aides and agents, but they'll stay in the living room while we have a private discussion in the library."

Rufus smiled. He knew they'd picked Henry's library because of the electronic bugs that would make it possible for Pierpont to eavesdrop on the meeting. "I'm glad you'll be there with us, Jesse."

"Wouldn't miss it for the world. How often does a man get a chance to really twist a President's tail?"

Pierpont turned to Randolph. "Senator, we've been observing you for a long time and we like what we've seen. We were pleasantly impressed with your work on the Multilateral Commission. With due respect to modesty, we as a group—and I include Jesse and Rufus—represent the most powerful economic forces in the free world. Our long-range vision is to make this group the nucleus of a new corporate world. Now, I hope you'll bear with me if I appear to be delivering a lecture, but it's the shortest distance to where we wish to take you today." He settled back in his chair and fixed his eyes on Randolph. "In this century we've witnessed the slow strangulation of capitalism, as the egalitarian demands of democracy have expanded in a geometric ratio. We must accelerate the dismantling of the welfare state to get at these excesses of democracy, excesses that afflict all advanced capitalist nations. But nowhere is it more pronounced and flagrant than right here in our own country. Many of our conclusions and views are stated in the Multilateral Commission's last report, 'Crisis of Capitalism,' and in the Appendix, 'Targets for Action.'"

Randolph smiled confidently. "Yes, and I'm in complete agreement with both. In fact, I helped with some of the language. Just the other day someone asked me if I honestly believed there was an excess of democracy in this country and my reply was affirmative. I believe that our present democracy is a threat to itself. This nation needs to restore a more equitable relationship between governmental authority and popular control. There can be no progressive change without a strengthening of the capitalist system."

Rufus smiled admiringly. Randolph's statement was almost a verbatim rendition of what he had told Alicia during dinner on Sunday night. The boy was amazing. Had a mind like a steel trap.

"Yes, you're right, of course," Stelk said, "but there's something important to bear in mind as a Vice-Presidential candidate. As we said in our report, there's been a decline in the legitimacy of coercion, discipline, bribery, secrecy, and deception—all powerful tools of capitalism. But in your speeches and personal contacts you can't reveal these beliefs. To get elected, you must emphasize the work ethic, the family as a cultural unit, religion for the masses, and patriotism for all good Americans. Those of us who will be supporting and funding your campaign will know where you really stand, and that's all that matters."

"A successful politician must be a consummate actor," Pierpont said. "He must be able to conceal his true opinions behind carefully chosen words. He must live in a world of contradictions and never get confused."

"Randolph is aware of all this," Rufus interjected. "He knows the value of being both charming and ruthless. Nothing and no one should be allowed to interfere with the achievement of our goals. A person with a mission to benefit the world has a duty to destroy anyone that stands in his way. Corporate control of the free world is our only defense against the encroachment of Communism in Third World nations."

Pierpont nodded his approval of Rufus's summation. "Yes, and the First Amendment protection of the media must be reexamined in light of society's broader interests," Pierpont asserted with added vigor. "This government must have the right and ability to withhold information at the source."

"Along with that," Stelk added, "we must curtail the expansion of higher education, which has become a major source of creedal passion. Educational institutions must gear their programs to reasonable patterns of economic development. What's needed are programs to lower job expectations, with realistic assessments of future job opportunities. As for workers, they must be kept from participating in decision making, which only foments leftist trade unionist activity."

Randolph was nodding approvingly to everything being said. "And may I add," he said, "that the government must get out of the self-defeating practice of regulating business and let the free market take over."

"Yes, I would put that very high on the list," Pierpont said with satisfaction. "That and free trade for our multinationals, which we prefer to call transnational, since our activities transcend nations. The American industrial muscle is turning to flab because of the trade unions, which force companies to seek foreign bases to manufacture goods more cheaply. There may come a time when this country will be reduced to providing services rather than goods."

"Well put, Russ, but let me wind this up," said Stelk. "This isn't the time to get into all the nuts and bolts. Suffice it to say we need more government money in the International Monetary Fund to bail out Third World nations in danger of defaulting on enormous loans from U.S. banks. As I'm sure you know, we're not opposed to the devaluation of the dollar. It means we can charge more for our products. And wages, which are controlled by labor contracts, never rise as fast as prices. Someday we'll create our own international money, a computer memory currency, which will be a genuine currency used in exchange markets."

"A final word," Pierpont said, "and that's it. We'd want multilateral commissioners appointed to all policymaking roles in State, Defense, Treasury, the Security Council, and the World Bank."

"Randolph, how do you feel about our vision for the future?" Stelk asked.

Randolph's eyelids relaxed, widened, giving him that artless boyish look that never failed to charm those exposed to it. "I'm in total agreement. This country must undergo traumatic changes if it wishes to survive into the twenty-first century as a viable world power. I take no exception to anything you've said."

Stelk smiled at Pierpont. "I told you he was our man."

Rufus laughed. "I've been telling you that for years." He stood up and stretched. "Jesse, you coming with us now, or do you want me to send the chopper back for you around one?"

"Do that, will you, Rufus."

Pierpont stood up and they shook hands all around. "Thank you for coming this morning, Senator. I look forward to many pleasant meetings in the future."

"So do I, Mr. Pierpont," Randolph said. "Meanwhile, Rufus and I will do our damnedest to make Abbott come around to our terms."

"I'm sure you will," Pierpont said. "But I don't want you in the meeting with Abbott. It's best if you can later deny any knowledge of the meeting. Abbott doesn't like you now, and he'll like you even less if you're there while he's on the rack, so to speak." He laughed and patted Randolph on the shoulder.

In the helicopter Rufus was jubilant. "You were beautiful, sonny boy. Never blinked an eye. How did you like that little business about printing our own funny money." Rufus laughed and slapped his knee. "Legalized counterfeiting. Like making your own gold. Instead of using lead bricks, you punch the old computer and out it comes. Now that's my idea of heaven on earth."

Randolph smiled happily. "Pierpont as Rumpelstiltskin. And I'm his man."

Rufus squeezed Randolph's knee. "Before long, sonny boy, you're going to be *the* man."

"Tru," Stelk said, addressing the President of the United States, "we've known each other a long time—lots of water under the bridge and over the dam—and in all that time have you ever known me to lie to you?"

Abbott, who had just entered the library and taken the chair farthest away from Rufus, Henry, and Stelk, looked uncomfortable. "No, Jesse, not to my knowledge."

"Or anybody else's knowledge?" Stelk persisted. "I'm establishing this premise for a reason, Tru. I know you're a busy man, and so are we, so there's no sense in wasting time."

"Well, in fact, I've only got a few minutes to spare. I'm expected at a delegate reception at Lake Mead."

Stelk smiled. "Yes, they've got a little extra time on their hands with the platform out of the way so quickly. You kind of took the wind out of Foote's sails. Plan on doing a little more massaging this afternoon?"

"I'm going to press flesh, if that's what you mean."

Rufus winked at Henry. He was pleased with Stelk's direct, no-nonsense approach.

"Do you think it'll do any good, change any votes at this late stage of the game?"

Abbott shrugged. "You do what you can and hope for the best. In politics there's one thing I've learned. You never second-guess the outcome of an election until the votes are counted."

Stelk stood up and walked to the fireplace. "What would you say if I told you the votes are already counted. That the nomination is in *our* hands, not yours, that we are in complete control of this convention."

"I'd say you're blowing smoke."

"So we're back to my original premise—that I don't lie. You obviously think I do?"

"Not necessarily, Jesse. Like anyone else, you're not infallible. You can be wrong."

"Not about this, Tru. Now, let's review some hard facts. As it stands right now, you and Foote are deadlocked at about eleven hundred apiece, give or take one or two. There're sixty-two uncommitted delegates, who, by the way, won't be at Lake Mead this afternoon. So the flesh you're going to press is already in your meat wagon. It's like jacking off, Tru. It may relieve tension, but it gets you no closer to a real piece of ass. And there won't be any Foote delegates there either. He's got his own massage session slated at the Hilton. So here comes the first ballot tonight and what happens? Who gets the psychological boost from a standoff? The incumbent President who can't control his own party, or Foote the challenger, who's stopped the incumbent dead in his tracks?"

"All hypothetical," Abbott said.

"Bullshit, Tru, and you fucking well know it," Stelk said, raising his voice for the first time. "You think I'd be here wasting my time if I didn't know what I'm talking about."

"That's a good question," Abbott said, clearly angry himself. "What *are* you doing here, and why are we in this room with Rufus Boutwell and Henry Godwin?"

"That's elementary, Tru. We—and when I say we, you know I'm also speaking for forces other than ourselves—we want Randolph Godwin on the ticket as your running mate."

Abbott flushed angrily. "Yes, so I gather. But I'm sorry, Jesse—your cute little pressure game's a waste of time."

Stelk shook his head in disbelief. "I really don't understand, Tru. Why are you so dead set against Godwin? For Christ's sake, let's get it out in the open so we can deal with it."

Abbott paused and appeared to arrive at a decision. "I've got some Secret Service reports on him."

"What kind of reports?" Rufus demanded, his eyes narrowing angrily.

"I'm not at liberty to discuss them."

"Bullshit!" Rufus exploded.

Putting a hand on Rufus's shoulder to restrain him, Stelk walked to Abbott's chair and stared hard. "I think I can guess. Something about Lisa and Randolph at Aspen?"

"Leave my daughter out of this," Abbott warned, rising halfway out of his chair.

"There's nothing I'd like better," Stelk said. "So let's drop Lisa for a moment and go on with our—what do you call it? hypothetical—game plan."

Stelk moved back to the fireplace and turned to face Abbott. "If I could prove to you that we do in fact control fifty-eight of the sixty-two uncommitted delegates, would that alter your judgment of Randolph Godwin?"

"Nothing can alter my judgment of the man," Abbott said, turning to Henry. "I'm sorry, Henry, I have nothing against you. But I cannot in good conscience accept him, and I will not be coerced into it. All we're doing here today is spinning our wheels."

"Then you'll lose the nomination," said Henry quietly, already feeling uncomfortable with the way the discussion was going.

Abbott shrugged. "Then the Republicans will lose the election in the fall. It's out of my hands. You say you people control the votes, then vote them as you wish. And if that's all you have to say to me, I'll take my leave. Good day, gentlemen."

He stood up and looked directly at Stelk. "I warned you on the phone this morning that it would be a waste of time, Jesse. I knew what you had in mind. We haven't exactly been asleep on the thirty-fifth floor. We know Rufus bought himself some delegates. The FBI is already looking into it."

"Please, Tru, sit down, will you?" Stelk said, his voice growing conciliatory. He pulled a chair away from the desk and brought it close to Abbott's chair. "There's something we have to get into—something I'd rather avoid because it will involve people I know—but this has developed into a no-limit poker game. There's one thing you're not understanding, but there's no getting around it, whatever your personal distaste or objections. The Presidential candidate picked by this convention will have Senator Godwin as his running mate. Now, it can be you, or Hamilton Foote, or some dark horse. We don't care as long as Randolph's on the ticket. Why you can't understand this simple fact beats the shit out of me."

"Before you continue with your little song and dance, perhaps you could answer a question that beats the shit out of *me*," Abbott said. "Why are you and your friends so set on having Godwin on the ticket? Don't you know the man's a sexual pervert? And a sadist?" He gave Henry a helpless shrug. "I'm sorry, Henry, but it's true."

"That's bullshit, Mr. President," Stelk said. "Randolph is a normal, virile, modern male, who's simply broken the Victorian mold that still influences so many older people."

Abbott flushed angrily. "I don't just mean group sex. I said he's a sadist and I have proof in black and white."

Stelk looked at him with scorn. "Tru, I happen to know something about the incident in question and you're wrong. It's back to Aspen, right?"

"I'm not going to elaborate any further," Abbott said defiantly.

"Then let's skip it for the moment, and let me answer the first part of your question. We're for Randolph, my friends and I, because of Rufus. He's had one dream in his life and that's to see his grandson amount to something special in this world. Rufus has worked hard for his state and his country, and he's been a valued colleague to the people I call friends. Naturally, for a man from Nevada the Presidency is an unrealistic goal, but not the Vice-Presidency. It's really that simple. My associates and I are repaying years of friendship with this gesture, and we're not about to quit because of your Victorian standards of sexual behavior."

Abbott shook his head. "Flimsy, Jesse—not even close. So, let's have your dirt and get it over with."

"There's a little matter of Orville accepting over a million dollars in bribes on grain sales to Russia when he was Agriculture Secretary. All well documented."

Abbott leaned back in his chair. "I've heard rumors to that effect, but how does it serve the Republican cause to dirty me with his corruption?"

"The point, Tru, is that if we know about it, others less friendly may learn of it and blow your campaign out of the water."

"Show me your proof on Orville and he's off the ticket, but that doesn't get Randolph on it. My choice will be Tom Atkins."

"Well, we tried," Stelk said, sighing deeply. "Tru, believe me, what I have to say next I wish could've been left unsaid."

The lines around Abbott's mouth hardened and his eyes flashed angrily. "There's more? You better make it fast."

"There's more because you leave us no alternative. You're a hardheaded man and the Presidency has a way of making hardheaded men stubborn to the point of self-destruction. As a quick aside, my friends and I contributed thirty-eight million, by one means or another, not all lawful, to your first Presidential campaign. And we've gotten shit in return. Your popularity with the common people was built with our money, while you expanded the dole system and soaked the rich to pay for it. Now we come to you with a simple request and you spit on us. Why should we care whether you win or lose the election? We fared better with the Democrats. So if you're feeling impatient right now, thinking perhaps that the President of the United States shouldn't have to sit here and take this crap, just think of it as a thirty-eight-million-dollar session."

"That's unfair," Abbott said. "I brought down inflation and unemployment and kept this country at peace."

"Save the political speeches for the stump," Stelk said. "To get back to cases, what I've got to tell you isn't pretty, but it's true, truer than I ever wanted to get into. If you persist with your stubborn refusal after hearing this story and viewing the evidence, then you're a fool and don't belong in the White House. And I promise you, my friends and I will do what we can to evict you."

"Who are you to say who belongs in the White House?" Abbott asked.

Stelk stood up in disgust and went to the desk. He picked up a remote control device and leaned against a corner of the desk, "Tru, please settle down and listen carefully to what I'm going to say. Let me start with a word about a thriving industry that's gained popularity all over the world. Hardcore pornography. As you know, hundreds of theaters show nothing but X-rated movies. Porno shops in every major city sell video cassettes and discs of both full-length features and short films, running anywhere from a few minutes to an hour. Now, Tru, I'm going to show you a scene from an upcoming X-rated movie that's scheduled to open in two weeks in at least six hundred theaters all over this country. It's called *The Erotic Snow Queen*."

Stelk pressed a button on the remote device and a panel opened to reveal a large television screen. He pressed another button and an image flashed on the screen. A naked girl, kneeling on a mink bedspread, was holding a huge penis in her hands, running the tip of her tongue slowly up and down the extraordinarily thick shaft.

"It's so big," she cooed in baby talk, "I don't know if I can eat it all." Her mouth closed over the bulbous head and she looked straight up at the camera.

"My God!" Abbott cried out. "It's Lisa."

Stelk flicked the set off and looked sadly at the President. "I'm sorry, Tru. It's the last thing I wanted to show you."

"It's phony, some doctored-up job," Abbott shouted, leaping angrily to his feet.

"No, Tru, she's the star of the picture, top billing: Lisa Abbott in *The Erotic Snow Queen*."

Henry seethed inside. He had recognized the scene as shot in Randolph's bedroom on the L-1011 and the man, who was seen only from the shoulders down, was unquestionably Senator Bryce Silver. This attempt to blackmail the President was crazy and dangerous. They were placing Randolph in great jeopardy. Henry wanted to grab the cassette and walk out, but he stayed in his chair, aware that any sudden reaction on his part would upset the balance of tension in the room.

Abbott sat down again, dizzy with uncertainty. There was no doubting what he had witnessed. The woman was Lisa. If they were to release hundreds of copies of that film—and who knew how many other films they might have stockpiled—there was nothing he could do to stop them. She was an adult and the making and distribution of pornography was legal. Unless, of course, she'd been doped and tricked into it.

He tried to rise but felt a hand on his arm and saw the sympathetic expression on Stelk's face. "Please, Tru, sit down. Let me explain this whole thing before you jump to the wrong conclusion and do something foolish."

Abbott sat again and for a moment felt like weeping.

"There's nothing phony about the movie," Stelk said. "Not only did she knowingly act but she was paid for her work and endorsed the checks. The Secret Service has done a lousy job of watching her. That sadism business you brought up about Randolph—you're talking about Aspen, am I right?"

Abbott nodded in agreement.

"Well, here's what really happened. Lisa, the stud in the picture, other actors, and the film crew all went to Aspen at the time Randolph was vacationing there. Lisa went to visit him and they spent a couple days together. When the stud found out, *he* beat her up, not Randolph. To use street language, he's her old man, and he rules her life. It's not much of a life, Tru. Lisa's hooked on drugs. She's gone the whole route. From grass to pills to coke to acid and to junk in a big way. There is nothing she hasn't dipped into. She's a sick girl who's in need of professional help. If I were you I'd commit her in a safe out-of-the-way place where she'd get top professional treatment." Stelk peered at the shattered man before him. "When was the last time you saw your daughter, Tru?"

Abbott looked embarrassed. "I'm not quite sure, two years, a long time. But she's always been independent. Impossible to control. We tried to get her psychiatric help, but she wouldn't cooperate. When a child comes of age, what can you do if she decides to go on her own? You can't put her in a cage. I'm not the first President with an unruly child."

"You have a way with understatement," Stelk said. "Unruly is hardly the word."

"I know, I know, and so does the Secret Service, but they've had a hard time keeping track of her." He looked down at his hands, folded in his lap, and sighed heavily.

Stelk glanced quickly at Rufus. Both men knew the fight was out of Abbott. Stelk went to Abbott's chair and lowered himself to one knee. "The Secret Service was wrong about Randolph. As I told you, the bruises they saw on her were inflicted by her old man. In fact, Randolph liked her very much, but he recognized that she had deep psychological problems. He talked to Rufus about it and Rufus told me. That's when we started checking into it. Now this film is scheduled for release by big-time pornographers who expect to clean up on it and on a few others they've made with her. But as it happens, I have certain contacts—let's just leave it at that—who can put the clamp on these people if I give them the word."

"Please, Jesse, give them the word. It would kill Mary. She's got to be protected from this filth."

"I want to assure you again that Rufus and Randolph and I had nothing to do with the making of this film. I have the power to stop it. Sure, it'll be expensive, but my associates are willing to bear that cost if you're willing to admit you were wrong about Randolph and name him as your running mate. It will be a strong ticket, Tru."

Abbott looked up and there were tears in his eyes. "But what about Lisa—I have no idea where she is."

"I do, Tru, and here's what I recommend. I know a place in Switzerland where she'd get the best medical and psychiatric care in the world. No one would ever hear about it. For that matter, our media contacts could plant stories in the press from time to time about her skiing at Saint Moritz, attending the Cannes Film Festival, that sort of thing. We could even get pictures from the sanitarium with her all dressed up for release to the press. What do you say?"

"I'd want Mary involved," he said. "She'd have to approve everything. But please don't tell her about the movie. I think it'd kill her."

"Of course," said Stelk quietly. "Mary and I will take Lisa to Switzerland together, along with a Secret Service detail, if you feel it necessary."

"You and Mary take charge of things. I've got a country to run and a campaign to conduct. After the election I'll go see her. Plan some kind of official European trip. By then she should be recovering."

"Absolutely, Tru. I'll get to work on it right away. Do we shake on the deal."

Abbott looked up puzzled. "Deal?"

"Randolph goes on your ticket, Lisa goes to Switzerland, the producers get paid off, and all copies of the film get destroyed."

Abbott stood up and offered his hand. "You win, Jesse. I've got to protect the two persons I love most in this world."

"It's for the best, Tru. All around. When you have time to think it over, you'll realize what a service we've rendered you."

"You could be right. I don't know. Meanwhile, what do I tell Orville?"

"Tell him to go fuck himself," Rufus said. "Better still, let me tell him. As a down-home country boy, I'm sure he'll appreciate the irony."

Abbott turned for the door but stopped. "Sometimes I ask myself why I ever got involved with politics, and I never come up with a convincing answer."

"Tru, don't go soft on me," Stelk said. "You've been through the wars. You know this shit goes with the territory when you're in big business or politics."

The moment the door closed behind the President, Henry went to the video recorder and retrieved the cassette.

"What're you doing?" Rufus asked.

Henry held up his hand. "Not a goddamn word," he warned, his voice deadly. "I'm in no mood for any more of your bullshit. Or yours, Jesse."

Rufus and Stelk watched in silence as Henry stuffed the cassette into his pocket and left the room.

65

The telephone buzzed softly at his elbow and Joseph Alcorn picked it up, keeping his voice low so as not to interfere with Alistair Baker's detailed summation of what had taken place on the now empty convention floor during the past three days. It was a filler of dead time between commercials.

"Alcorn here."

"Joe, Danny Arnold. I've got an exclusive for you. Randolph says you've got at least a fifteen-minute lead on it."

"What's up?"

"Abbott just dumped Fowler and Randolph is in. Abbott's on his way to Lake Mead, where he'll make the announcement."

Garfield was lounging disconsolately on a sofa, staring vacantly at the four muted television sets, the lips of the anchormen and reporters moving silently. He couldn't stand that garbage. All day he'd been thinking about Alfie. Not Alfie the doorman. The real Alfie. Alfie March, the best friend he'd ever had and the only person in his entire life he'd ever loved.

Alfie's father was the famous movie cowboy Johnny March, a former all-American football star from USC, whom police had caught flagrante delicto with a sixteen-year-old male prostitute in the restroom of a Sunset Strip gay joint. The studio had hushed the incident, but the story had spread through the movie colony with the speed of a brushfire fanned by a Santa Ana wind, but it hadn't harmed his career.

Alfie had been eight then and had become the butt of cruel jokes at school. His father was described as having the fastest pecker in the West, and Alfie was warned to watch his asshole if he didn't want to be buggered by the fastest pecker in the West. A delicate, sensitive boy, Alfie had run home crying instead of fighting back and was too embarrassed to tell either parents or school authorities about the taunting.

If he lived to be a hundred, Garfield would never forget the last day he'd played with Alfie. Garfield had been nine that summer day and Alfie ten. There was no one at the Stone residence except the maid, and the two boys had decided to skinny-dip in the pool. They'd heard about college kids doing it and thought they'd find out what the fuss was all about.

Lying on the sofa in the Monarch II, Garfield closed his eyes and saw everything with photographic clarity. He could again feel the thrill of slipping through the water without any clothes on. They'd played in the pool for hours, swimming and diving off the springboard. Bouncing on the board, they'd laughed at the way their scrotums and penises flopped up and down. After a while they began bouncing together on the board, holding hands, attempting to touch bottom together with their feet. By holding hands neither one could cheat. Then Alfie, always full of clever ideas, thought it would be fun if instead of holding hands they held on to each other's genitals. Garfield thought it was a fine idea, and after a few jumps Alfie made a discovery that intrigued both boys.

"Look at my pecker," Alfie said, awe in his voice. "It's standing straight up like in the dirty pictures we found in your father's desk."

"Is it really hard?" Garfield asked, his own penis still hanging like a dead worm.

"Like a rock," Alfie said. "I guess it means I'm a man now."

"Jesus," Garfield said, "are you lucky."

"Here, Gar, feel it."

They were sitting by the side of the pool with their feet dangling in the water, and Garfield reached out and gently touched it.

"Jesus, it is hard."

Alfie reached down and started squeezing himself. "Boy, Gar, this feels really weird."

"What do you mean weird?"

"I don't know how to explain it. Just sort of good weird. The more I squeeze it, the more I want to keep doing it. Squeeze yours a few times—maybe it'll get hard like mine."

"Naw. I've tried it lots of times, but nothing ever happens."

"Here, let me try."

"Jesus, Alfie, you think you can make it stand up like yours?"

"I don't know. Let's see. Here, you squeeze mine while I work on yours."

The boys had been so involved in their exploration that neither one saw or heard Rocky Stone until he was standing right over them. Grabbing both boys by the scruff of the neck, he dragged them across the patio and into the house, screaming obscenities at the top of his lungs.

"Dirty, filthy, little faggots, fucking little cocksuckers. I've got a good mind to cut your pricks and balls right off." Then he'd swiped Alfie across the head. "You and your faggot father. Like father, like son. How long you been giving him hand jobs, you dirty little fag? Get the fuck out of here."

Rocky had kicked Alfie then, his large foot striking the boy at the base of the spine, knocking him down. "Now, get up and drag your ass out of here. And if I ever catch you here again, or even see you looking at Garfield, I'll beat the living shit out of you. And you can tell that to your faggot old man next time you suck his cock."

The next morning Alfie's naked body was found on the patio beneath the third story window of his bedroom, his legs soaked with blood. Moments before dropping to his death, he had tried to castrate himself with a paring knife.

Garfield, who had gone in search of Alfie shortly after sunrise, had discovered the body and gone completely berserk. Running home, he grabbed a butcher knife and burst into his father's bedroom with the full intention of slaughtering him. But his father had heard Garfield's hysterical screams, had seen his son running wildly across the back lawns toward the house, and was ready for the attack. He easily wrested the knife from Garfield's hand and then carried him, screaming and kicking, to the third-floor attic, where he locked him in a closet. Rocky's wife, who had no idea what was happening, had stood by helplessly.

Garfield was left in the closet until after Alfie's funeral, until the excitement had died down. Given one meal a day and left to wallow in his own body waste, Garfield had been strangely withdrawn when his father had finally released him from the closet and taken him to a private mental institution in Denver, where Garfield remained for nearly a year. When Garfield returned home, Rocky Stone never mentioned the incident, and the boy had understood that his freedom depended on keeping his mouth shut.

Danny Arnold and a half-dozen aides came rushing into the room to turn up the sound on the NTN channel.

Arnold glanced at Garfield and asked, "What's wrong with you?"

"Nothing."

"Then why are you crying? You sick?"

"I'm not crying. My eyes are weak, and they run."

Then Alcorn's voice blasted into the room and everyone turned to listen. What Garfield heard galvanized him into action. When Arnold turned to look at him after Alcorn's brief announcement, Garfield was gone.

"Weird kid," he said.

"What's that?" asked Guy Charest.

"I said that Garfield kid's weird. Found him bawling his head off a minute ago. Tells me his eyes are weak. Then he vanishes."

"I don't think we ought to let him stick around here anymore. The war's over. The troops can go home."

"Good idea. I'll tell Hoppy to get his elevator key."

66

H. Russell Pierpont heard the helicopter and turned up the sound on the receiver so he could still hear the conversation taking place in Henry's library. At first he thought the helicopter was just passing nearby, but when he heard it come down on the landing pad, invading his privacy, he rushed outside, leaving his electronic equipment unattended.

The chopper was the familiar royal blue Sikorsky, but when the door opened a tall, gray-haired man hurried down the steps followed by a stocky black man. As the two rushed toward him, Pierpont waited on the deck, rather at a loss for words.

"I'm Henry Godwin and this is my friend, Moses Grimes."

"Oh, of course," Pierpont said, somewhat relieved. "Randolph's father. It's an honor to meet you, sir."

"You won't think so in a minute," Henry said, pushing past Pierpont, ignoring his outstretched hand.

"I beg your pardon?"

"I own this house and I want you packed and out of here. Now! You can take your buddy Stelk's junk with you."

Pierpont followed Henry and Moses into the house. "Sir, I don't think you know who I am."

"I know who you are and I couldn't care less. Get on with it."

The banker was nonplussed. Then he remembered Henry's angry reaction to the showing of the porno film and suddenly panicked when he realized that the sound being transmitted from Henry's bugged library at the Monarch II was blasting away in the den downstairs.

"This is most unusual," he said. "May I telephone Mr. Stelk or Mr. Boutwell?"

"All I want you to do is grab your junk and hightail it out of here before I do something we'll both regret. You more than me."

"There's no need for threats. I'll honor your request if you'll give me a moment to gather my belongings."

Henry had been hearing the voice emerging from the lower floor, but had vaguely assumed the sounds came from the television. Then he recognized Stelk's voice and rushed down the stairs to his den. The electronics equipment covering his desk startled him.

Pierpont stood in the doorway, fear tightening his face. "This was your father-in-law's idea," he said.

Henry looked at him a long time, but his mind was on the words being spoken by Stelk and Rufus. "Pierpont, close the door on your way out. Moses, get him out of here, fast."

When they had left, Henry sat, listening and wondered how many times Rufus had eavesdropped on him through the years. What a prize sucker he'd been.

"What about this sadism crap?" Rufus was asking, concerned. "Don't shit me, Jesse. Did Randolph really hurt Lisa?"

"It was nothing, Rufus. He had to slap her around a little, that's all. She dropped acid and freaked out."

"Lisa's not a hooker, then," Rufus persisted, trying to assuage his own concerns about Randolph.

"Hell, no. She's too busy giving it away."

"All right, Jesse, but it's time to get very goddamned careful. Let's make sure you get every one of those fucking cassettes back. If one of them gets to the wrong people . . ."

Stelk laughed. "Rufus, you're not giving me enough credit. Henry's got the only tape in existence and he's probably burned it by now. What's important is the deal's finally airborne. We've got a launch, old friend. I'll let you tell Randolph the good news."

"When do I tell him the rest? Even he's getting curious about all the fuss over the Vice-Presidency."

"On a need-to-know basis, Rufus. You play it by ear from here on in. When you feel the timing's right, go with it. Randolph'll buy it. He's smart and ambitious and hard as nails. And what politician have you ever known who wouldn't want to be President?"

Rufus sighed. "He'll buy it or I'll break his back. A year at the outside, Jesse?"

"Absolutely. It's already in the works. Our money's on Randolph, and we know we've got a winner. The majority we'll have in Congress will give him carte blanche in instituting our programs." Stelk paused "Well, my friend, it's in your hands now. I've got to get moving."

"Thanks for everything, Jesse."

"First chance you get, I suggest you retrieve that cassette from Henry—if he hasn't destroyed it. What's with him anyway?"

"Just a little tentative lately. Not everyone stays hard with age. He probably recognized Randolph's bedroom on the plane. Henry's very protective of Randolph. Don't worry—he'll never do anything to harm that boy."

Henry heard the library door open and close as the two left the room. He sat there staring at the silent speaker. He could feel his heart pounding in his ears and he tried to get himself under control. This was not the time to get another heart attack. It was monstrous. They were actually planning to assassinate President Abbott, and Randolph would be part of the plot.

It was then that Henry noticed that Pierpont had been tape-recording the session. Why would they be recording themselves, he wondered, unless it was Pierpont's idea to make a record of the blackmailing of the President. It would give him something to hold in abeyance for the day he himself might need to blackmail Rufus or Stelk—or Randolph, for that matter. Henry shook his head. There were no limits to what they would crawl to in their pursuit of power. Deception was par for the course in that league. Then, as Henry heard the sound of the chopper lifting off, he punched the rewind button on the recorder.

President Abbott's announcement at Lake Mead that he had selected Senator Godwin as his running mate threw Daisy into an ecstatic tailspin. She ran for the telephone, but the doorbell rang before she could pick it up. She moved quickly to the door, hoping that it was Henry.

Alicia stared at her. "What are you on, speed?"

"Alicia, God, have you heard the news? President Abbott just told the whole world that your father is going to be the next Vice-President of the United States. Aren't you thrilled?"

"Should I be?"

"Oh, Ali, sometimes you really stretch one's patience."

"Okay, I'll go get my cheerleader's pom-poms and go into—"

"Oh, quiet," said Daisy, as if to an obstinate child. "I won't let you spoil this moment for me. I have to call Henry and congratulate him. But I don't even know where he is. I haven't heard from him all day."

"Why don't you call Randolph? He's the lucky one."

"Oh, of course, you're right. What's his number? I can't remember anything. I'm so excited."

"Here, let me get him on the phone for you."

Alicia dialed and asked for Guy Charest when Hopkins answered. "Hi, Guy, can you get the old Veep on the line? I have someone here who'd like to congratulate him."

"Ali, the *new* Veep is celebrating and it's a 'do not disturb.'"

"What do you mean, 'do not disturb'?"

Charest lowered his voice. "I mean he's celebrating in the boudoir."

"So, isn't there an extension, for Christ's sake?"

Charest wondered what she'd say if he told her there was an orgy in process, involving glorious Gloria, Clorice, Bryce Silver, and God only knew who else. But he quickly dismissed the thought. Lowering his voice, Charest said, "Ali, if I disturbed your father now there's a distinct possibility that he'd shove the terrific acceptance speech I've just finished right up my bunghole *sans lubricasio*. This would place me in a rather unorthodox position among the cue-card holders, and who knows of their bizarre sexual predilections."

Alicia was laughing so hard she had to sit on the floor. "Oh, Guy, what would I do without you in that grim Godwin mafia."

"Become a clown, darling. Everybody loves a clown."

"Yeah, but what does a clown love?"

"His work, and the money that goes with it, and the perks, of course. Call later, sweetheart. See you."

She handed the phone to Daisy and remained on the floor. "Daddy's busy celebrating and cannot be disturbed."

"Well, that's understandable."

"Are we going shopping?"

Daisy's hand went to her mouth. They had planned to go shopping in the vast underground mall of the Monarch II, where outrageously expensive little boutiques offered the creations, copies as well as originals, of the world's most renowned fashion designers.

"Oh, Ali, in the excitement I completely forgot. We'll go buy something truly extravagant to celebrate this moment. First, though, I'd really like to reach Henry. Just give me a minute."

But after calling all the possibilities she could think of without success, she gave up and went shopping with Alicia.

Daisy had tried the chalet, but Henry had let the phone ring.

Garfield wandered around downtown Las Vegas. There was something special he wanted to buy, but it had to be an exact replica. Otherwise the whole thing wouldn't be as perfect as he wanted it to be. He had to keep track of the time. If only he could find what he wanted and be there at the precise moment, everything would be far more spectacular than he'd planned when he'd first heard the convention was to be held in Las Vegas.

Vince Bacino, hidden behind his sunglasses, came out of Cartier and nearly bumped into Alicia.

"Excuse me—oh, Daisy, baby, what a surprise," he said, as they hugged and blew kisses across their cheeks.

"Vince, this is Alicia, Senator Godwin's daughter."

"Oh, yeah, I saw you on TV yesterday."

"That was my sister Eileen," Alicia said. "We're twins."

He laughed. "Right, your hair's different, and your voice. A little sharper edge, not as soft as your sister, but you're both real stunners. Hey, you in a hurry? Can I buy you ladies a drink at Harry's Bar?"

Daisy explained to Alicia that this was an exact duplicate of the bar in Venice where Hemingway had presided over less celebrated American expatriates.

"Thank you," Alicia said. "I think I'd enjoy a drink. Do we have time, Daisy?"

"Absolutely," she said, giving him her blinding smile. "I always have time for my old *amico*, Vince."

As they stepped inside, the maitre d' took one look at Vince Bacino and nearly jumped out of his shoes getting to him.

"Mr. Bacino, Miss Miller, what an honor."

"Pete, this is Senator Godwin's daughter, Alicia. You have my special table?"

"Yes, sir, Mr. Bacino—right this way, please."

When they were seated, Bacino, with his back to the wall, had an unobstructed view of the entire room. "Pete, tell Miss Godwin the history of this table."

Pete nodded happily. "With pleasure, Mr. Bacino." He turned to Alicia. "This is the actual table Ernest Hemingway used to write his famous novel about Venice." He gently raised the tablecloth in front of Bacino. "If you look closely at the top of the table, you can see the millions of little indentations made by his pencil. I can tell you, getting possession of this table was quite a coup."

"Thanks, Pete. Would you ladies like some champagne?"

"Not for me," Daisy said. "Perrier and lime, please."

"C.C. and water, a tall one," Alicia said.

"My usual mineral water," Bacino said. "Are you ladies hungry?"

They both declined and the maitre d', the wine steward, and the waiter bowed almost reverently as they took their leave.

"What are you, the secret owner of this place?" Alicia asked.

Bacino laughed. "Not at all—they treat everybody polite here. I guess they need the business, you know."

The waiter returned with their order and Daisy leaned toward Bacino and held out her hand. "Okay, let's see it. What did you buy at Cartier?"

He shrugged. "Just a little bauble."

"May I see it?"

He reached inside his jacket and brought out a ring box, handing it to Daisy. She opened it and both women gasped in appreciation. It was a huge opal in a platinum setting, ringed with rubies. Fire danced out of it.

"Not bad, eh?" he said.

"It's the most magnificent opal I've ever seen," Alicia said. "Daisy, look at the depth and the color."

"You like it, young lady?"

"It's exquisite."

"Then it's yours."

She looked startled. "You can't be serious? I couldn't accept a gift like this. I don't even know you."

"Alicia, I've been a close friend of your father's and grandfather's for many years. You and I are almost *famiglia.*"

She turned to Daisy and saw a look in her eyes that told her to decline the gift. "You're terribly gallant, Mr. Bacino, but I really can't accept it. But if you want to sell it for the price you paid I'll buy it from you."

The lines around his mouth suddenly hardened. "Young lady, I'm not in the jewelry business. I make gifts of it, but I don't peddle the stuff." He relaxed then, letting the unintentional insult pass. "Here, Daisy, you take it. I was going to get you a little welcome home present anyway. Consider this a down payment. I've got something else in mind for you. Knock your eyes right out of your head."

"That I'd like to see," Alicia said.

"Right," Bacino laughed. "This lady's got more ice than Tiffany and Cartier together."

Daisy ignored Bacino's outstretched arm and worked on her Perrier for a while before changing the subject. "So what do you think about Abbott picking her father for his running mate?"

"Hey, what did I tell you Sunday night when you came in? Didn't I tell you Boutwell had the Prez by the—" He paused and smiled at Alicia. "Well, you get my meaning. It was no contest. So now we can all go to the White House for tea."

"I hate to disappoint you," Alicia said, "but the Vice-President seldom gets to the White House for tea himself."

"Well, maybe someday he'll be the President—who knows? Life's unpredictable. Your father's a young man, with young ideas. He's like Kennedy. He enjoys a good time."

"Right," Alicia said, "a real swinger."

"Well, this has been delightful, Vince," Daisy said rising, "but we've got more shopping to do. Thanks for the drink."

Bacino immediately rose to his feet. "My pleasure, ladies. If you'll excuse me, I'll finish my drink. I have a couple phone calls to make." He quickly picked up the ring box and handed it to Daisy. "You take it, no argument. And, Alicia, I hope to see you again real soon. You play golf?"

"Vince, we have to go," Daisy said, dropping the ring box in her purse. "Thank you for the opal, truly." They hugged and blew kisses again and Daisy said, "I feel sorry for the poor girl who was supposed to get that ring."

"Don't worry about it," he said with a wave of his hand. "There's plenty more where that came from."

As soon as they were out in the mall, Daisy handed the ring box to Alicia. "From me to you," she said. "Not from him to you, ever, darling. You're his type. But if you're as smart as I think you are, you'll stay a million miles away from him."

"With those dark glasses and those hard lines around his mouth, he looks like Mr. Mafia. Is he?"

"Don't change the subject," Daisy said. "I saw the way he looked at you. He's going to be coming on to you, and when Vince sets his mind on getting a woman, she either gives in or finds herself fighting for her life."

"Now, don't exaggerate."

"Be prepared for the struggle of your life. Don't let your guard down for a second. Take it from someone who's been through that experience. Besides, you'd break Henry's heart."

68

Gus Meier was dead on his feet. The whole thing was getting ridiculous. How did they expect him to find one skinny kid in the midst of thousands of milling people. People were pushing and talking and yelling and drinking and waving placards and blowing on little horns. One idiot had screamed fire into a bullhorn and nearly caused a riot. The security guards had hustled him out of there in a hurry. But now FBI and Secret Service agents were moving toward the VIP area, checking the crowd, preparing for the President's arrival from Lake Mead. He was scheduled to reach the VIP entrance around six o'clock. The entire driveway was cordoned off, lined with local uniformed police and federal agents.

Gus would have liked to see the President in person, but he didn't want to go through that hassle. He kept moving and looking. At six-four, he at least had the advantage of seeing over most people's heads.

Then he saw him, just a fleeting glimpse as the doors of a penthouse elevator closed. It was definitely the same kid, carrying a large package under his arm. But what was he doing in a penthouse elevator? Well, after all, he had been driving a Ferrari. Maybe he was just another neurotic rich kid.

Gus started elbowing his way through the crowd, looking as he went for a policeman or security guard, even a bellman—anybody who could place a call to the special number he'd been given—while he continued following the kid. But there was no one. Only a lot of people who needed to be shoved aside. Several men swore at him until they saw his size, and then turned away, muttering to themselves.

Gus reached the bank of elevators, but found keyholes instead of buttons. He swore and banged his fist against the wall. What if the kid had a weapon in the package? The President was due to arrive at any moment. Meier was debating with himself—whether he should go to a telephone and call the number himself, or try to get up to the penthouse—when two women walked up, stopping before one of the elevators. The younger of the two placed a key in the hole and the doors opened.

"Excuse me, ladies, but I've got to go up with you," Gus said.

Alicia looked at Daisy and shrugged. "Don't you have a key? The penthouse floor is private."

"I know," he said, "but I'm working with the Secret Service and I'm following a crazy kid who just went up there."

"What crazy kid?" Alicia asked, knowing even before he opened his mouth that he was talking about Garfield.

"A weird-looking kid. Skinny. Thick glasses. There's a good chance he's armed and wants to kill the President."

"From the penthouse floor?" Daisy asked.

"Listen, I've got a number I'd like one of you ladies to call when we get up there. Tell whoever answers that I'm Gus and the kid's on the penthouse floor. They'll know what to do."

Gus held out the card with the number on it and Alicia handed it to Daisy. "You call. He's talking about Garfield Stone. I know what he looks like."

The elevator stopped and the doors opened. Gus stepped out, not knowing which way to turn.

"Come with me," Alicia said. "I think I know where he is."

"Okay," Gus said, "but he told me his name was Alfie."

They ran down the hall to Henry's suite, which Alicia knew overlooked the VIP entrance. She unlocked the door, ran across the living room to the terrace, and screamed.

Gus nearly fell over her when he saw the kid standing on top of the railing. Garfield was dressed in buckskins, moccasins on his feet. A black band with a single feather circled his head.

Garfield nearly lost his balance when he saw them. "Don't come near me," he screamed. "Stay where you are."

Alicia fought to control her panic. "Come on, Garfield. You're scaring me again."

"My friend Alfie was always the Lone Ranger and I was Tonto. We had so much fun together." There was a chilling madness in Garfield's eyes. "He was Kemo Sabe, my faithful friend—the only real friend I ever had."

"Where is he now, Garfield?" Alicia asked, moving a step toward him, keeping her voice calm. "Want me to call him?"

"My father killed him," he screamed hysterically, and his eyes flooded with tears, blinding him. Again he almost lost his balance. "That dirty motherfucking monster. He killed me too. You don't know what he did to me. Nobody knows."

"But, Garfield, why this?" Alicia asked.

"Kemo Sabe," he said. "Do you realize it takes one second to say it. It's like saying, thousand-one, thousand-two. But you've got to say it with just the right tempo. I've been practicing."

He looked down and everything was blurred. He removed his glasses and angrily swiped at his eyes with his fingers. His tears angered him. What was there to cry about, he asked himself? In a moment the anguish would be over. His body would become Kemo Sabe's silver bullet. With it he would kill the President of the United States. The idea was sheer genius. His feat would never be topped by anyone. Instead of just another suicide—a one-day sensation—as he had first planned, he would become part of history, something his father would never achieve. And in the process he would finally join his faithful friend, wherever he might be in the hereafter.

Gus Meier took a step toward the railing and Garfield screamed at him. The trucker quickly stepped back. Garfield looked down and saw that the President's limousine had reached the curve in the driveway. In seconds it would disappear under the striped awning.

"If you ever see my father," he said, without taking his eyes from the limousine, "tell him to suck my dead cock."

"Garfield, please! Look, I'm begging you on my knees," Alicia cried, dropping to her knees. "Please come off that railing and let's talk about this whole thing."

"I'll get to say five Kemo Sabes."

Gus yelled. "Don't! Wait!"

But Garfield was already airborne. They heard him say "Kemo Sabe" twice and then the screams welcoming the President from below drowned him out.

Alfie, in his John Paul Jones uniform, his face beet red from the heat and excitement, was beaming proudly as he reached to open the door of the President's limousine.

"Welcome back, Mr. President," he said, swinging the door open with a flair acquired through years of experience, "to the Mon—"

He never finished the word, but Garfield Stone got to say his five Kemo Sabes before his head exploded into Alfie's, killing them both instantly. Blood and bone and brain tissue splattered against the limousine and on the President, who was leaning forward, ready to step out. Within split seconds Abbott was pulled back inside, and the Secret Service agent behind the wheel was gunning the engine. But a moment later the limo slammed to a stop behind the traffic snarled in front of it. Agents and policemen rushed from all directions to surround the President's car. Men and women were screaming and crying, none with the slightest understanding of what had just happened.

Inside the limousine Mary Abbott looked at the blood and brain tissue splattered on her husband's face and shirtfront and vomited. The President moaned and vomited in the lap of the Secret Service agent who was holding his head down. The vision of the two heads exploding had been seared into his brain.

On the terrace of Henry's penthouse suite, Alicia and Gus looked down in horror.

"That crazy kid," Gus said, grasping the railing with knuckles pinched white.

"I'm going to be sick," Alicia sobbed, and slowly collapsed at Meier's feet.

The television cameras of the four networks, along with cameras of local stations, still photographers, and the foreign press, were all zeroed in on the President's car when Garfield crashed into Alfie.

All four networks were shooting live and viewers all over the world saw the disintegration of the two heads in vivid colors, and in slow motion replays that were repeated throughout the night and for days to come. Millions viewed it live as they tried to eat their dinners.

PRESIDENT ESCAPES ASSASSINATION, read a typical headline. The subheads played up the Hollywood and hero angles: ROCKY STONE'S SON LEAPS FROM BUILDING, MISSES KILLING PRESIDENT BY SPLIT SECOND. DOORMAN'S QUICK MOVE CREDITED WITH SAVING PRESIDENT'S LIFE.

In most stories Alfie's name was mentioned in the seventh or eighth paragraph, but Garfield remained Rocky Stone's son in most stories until the final paragraph, where his age was listed along with the fact that he'd once been committed to a mental institution. Rocky and Mrs. Stone went into seclusion and were not available for comment, but Rocky's personal manager issued a press release expressing the Stone family's deep sorrow and anguish over what they believed was the accidental death of their son. They thanked God the President was unharmed and were praying for his continued safety.

A subdued convention began the first ballot to nominate a Presidential candidate at eight o'clock, and by the time the roll call reached Pennsylvania, which cast 91 of its 103 votes for Abbott, the President had clinched the nomination. A few minutes later the hall shouted its approval of a motion that Abbott be declared the winner by acclamation.

The President and his wife, both under sedation, spent the evening in their suite, viewing the proceedings from bed. Every time one of the networks replayed the death scene, both closed their eyes and muted the four television sets.

"They are bloodthirsty, morbid bastards," Abbott complained after yet another replay.

"How many times do they expect people to look at this grisly scene," Mary asked in disgust. "I can't help feeling sorry for that poor boy. He was only seventeen. Had everything to live for in this world—a rich and famous father, respect in the community. What happens to children who seem to have everything going for them and turn out so badly?" She paused and sighed. "I'm glad you've found Lisa and that we'll get professional help for her. She's a sick girl, Tru. Sicker, I think, than you realize. What finally convinced you to take this step?"

Abbott groaned. "Mary, for God's sake, I'm not up to discussing Lisa tonight."

"Do you think it's possible the Stone boy fell? From what the Secret Service has learned, he was terribly strange. But perhaps it was just a crazy stunt. What do you think, Tru?"

"Mary, I know sedatives make you talkative, but please go to sleep. Take a few of the sleeping pills the doctor gave you. We both need a good night's sleep."

"We should be celebrating instead of lying in bed like a couple of comatose invalids."

"Mary, take my word for it, it's been a hard day, and I don't just mean nearly getting killed. If you don't mind, I'm going to turn the sets off, put the lights out, and try to sleep."

Alicia was furious. She couldn't forget how Garfield had stood on the railing, crying and saying that his father had murdered his best friend. Now it has been disclosed in news stories that Rocky Stone had had his son committed following the death of a boyhood friend—the friend she assumed Garfield had meant. The more she thought about it, the more she felt like complying with Garfield's last request.

Rocky Stone was in seclusion, but she knew that Lew Spark, still a top executive at TCA and a close friend of Stone's, would have a number where he could be reached.

When Spark came on the line he sounded harried. "Alicia, I've only got a minute. This place's a madhouse."

"I'd like Rocky Stone's phone number."

There was a brief pause. "I don't think I have it."

"Come on, Lew. You must have some number for him. He's a friend of yours, isn't he?"

"Look, darling, I don't think the man should be disturbed right now, especially by someone who was with his son just before the tragedy. Give him a few days. This has hit him hard."

"You won't give me the number?"

"Sorry, Ali. Not now. Call me in a week or so, after things have calmed down."

She hung up and called the hotel switchboard. "This is Alicia Godwin. Can you put me through to Mr. Bacino?"

Ten seconds later Vince Bacino was on the line. "Hey, beautiful lady, good hearing from you."

"Mr. Bacino, I need a favor."

"I'm Vince, okay? Just name it."

"I want to talk with Rocky Stone and I need the number where he can be reached tonight, now."

"You've got it. Hang on while I make a call."

Alicia could hear him dialing another phone. Rather than put her on hold, he had elected to let her hear his conversation. "Lew, I need Rocky's number. She did? Well, now it's me asking you. Thanks."

He came back on her line and gave her the number.

"Thank you, Vince, very much," she said.

"Listen, don't hang up just yet. I enjoyed meeting you today. How about lunch one of these days? I promise to be a gentleman. You see, being Italian, I like to be seen with beautiful and famous ladies. Good for my image, you know. No passes, just good friends, like me and Daisy are good friends."

"How could I refuse such an elegant invitation?"

He laughed. "You'll be hearing from me—soon."

"Good night and thanks again." She'd show Daisy she could take care of herself.

She hung up, prepared herself for the confrontation, and dialed Rocky Stone's number. He answered the phone and she immediately recognized his voice.

"I'm Alicia Godwin," she said.

There was a long pause and deep annoyed breathing. "How did you get my number?"

"Lew Spark. I said I'm Alicia Godwin."

"I know, I heard you. You're the one who was with Garfield before he fell."

"He jumped," Alicia said. "But before he jumped, he had a few words to say that might interest you."

"I don't think so. That kid was bad news all his life."

"You have my sympathy."

"Look, I don't want to be rude, but I'm going to hang up now."

"Hold it! You hang up on me and I'll call the press. Your son made what you might call a deathbed confession."

"You lousy bitch. Don't you have any sense of decency? We lost our son today."

"No, Mr. Stone, you lost your son when you murdered his childhood friend and then committed your son to a private snake pit to hide your crime." It was a wild guess, but the moment she said the words she believed them.

"You're out of your mind. I'm going to call your father and tell him about this crap."

"Be my guest. But your son had one last request that I feel obligated to pass on to you."

"Go on, spit it out, get it over with."

"His last words before he went off that railing, were, 'Tell my father to suck my dead cock.'"

At first there was silence. Then she heard Stone say, "Go fuck yourself, you degenerate bitch," followed by a dial tone.

Alicia listened to the dial tone a moment, lowered the receiver slowly, and said out loud, "Now live with it, you monster."

70

By Thursday noon Daisy was frantic. She had called and visited Henry's suite several times, had called the chalet, the ranch, the airport—every number she could think of—but Henry remained among the missing. She was convinced the attack on Tuesday had been more than indigestion. For all she knew, Henry could be dead.

She'd called both Rufus's and Randolph's suites and had been referred to a number on the thirty-fourth floor, which was answered by Blair Hopkins. With Randolph's nomination assured, the staff had been cleared from the penthouse floor. She asked to speak to Randolph, and Hopkins suggested she discuss the matter with Danny Arnold. She thanked him, hung up, and decided to take things into her own hands by going directly to Randolph's suite. Henry could be lying near death in one of the bedrooms. She knew she might be overreacting, but her nerves were frayed after the horrifying tragedy that had started on Henry's terrace. It could be that he was merely trying to avoid the press. But why wouldn't he call her? He had to know she'd be worried.

Both Rufus and Randolph were deeply shaken by the near assassination of the President. They had met with Stelk and Pierpont on Wednesday evening before the two had left for New York. Now after a late breakfast on the terrace of Randolph's suite, they repaired to the library for a private conference.

As Daisy neared the door to Randolph's suite, it opened and Eileen came out. The two exchanged polite greetings, but Daisy was obviously in a hurry. "Is Henry in there?" she asked.

"I haven't seen Grandpa for a couple of days," Eileen said. "Daddy and Rufus have been looking for him, too. Alicia usually knows where he is most of the time."

"Thanks, I'll try her," said Daisy, moving back down the hall.

Eileen pulled the door closed behind her and called after Daisy. "What do you think of Daddy's nomination? Isn't it thrilling?"

"It's marvelous," Daisy shouted back. "I'm very happy for him. I'm sure you must be terribly proud." Daisy walked out of sight around a bend in the corridor, leaving Eileen staring after her curiously.

Daisy returned to her suite to ponder Henry's vanishing act.

In the library of Randolph's suite Randolph and Rufus were comfortably ensconced in large leather chairs, smoking cigars.

"Rufus, I've been giving this serious consideration. What do you think of the idea of having the governor appoint Eileen to my Senate seat after the election? Or Henry. That's even better. Wouldn't that be a great first. Father a senator and his son Vice-President. That's one for all the record books."

Rufus growled angrily. "I wouldn't appoint Henry dog catcher of Golconda, and there's probably only two mangy curs in the whole goddamned town."

"Rufus, you're supposed to be the one with the cool head."

"Your father kicked H. Russell Pierpont off his mountain yesterday. Have you forgotten?"

"In a few months the sting will be gone. I think Pierpont will understand."

"Maybe he will, but I won't. Besides, there's more involved that I can't get into right now."

"Well, then Eileen."

"A definite possibility. She's bright and attractive and you couldn't ask for a more loyal daughter. But let me tell you something, sonny boy. You know what they say about 'the best laid plans of man,' or some such shit. Well, that crazy Stone kid about put an end to our plans. A change of one or two seconds in the timing and Foote would be this convention's candidate and we'd be up shit creek without a paddle."

"I don't want to think about it," Randolph said. "I'm the one who told Hoppy to put him to work."

Rufus lowered his voice. "Between you and me, sonny boy, if the kid had waited a year and been successful he'd have saved us the trouble."

Randolph stopped puffing on his cigar and gave Rufus a quizzical look. "I don't get it."

"Smarten up. Why do you think my friends in the Century Committee went to all this trouble to get you on the ticket?"

"So I'd get a shot at the Presidency next time around."

"Not likely. Remember when Toombs died before the election and we kept him on ice three days so the governor could appoint you to his Senate seat?"

"You're losing me, Rufus. I don't get the connection."

"It's a similar deal, except this time we make it happen. You enter the Oval Office through the back door. No election. Too iffy. Get my meaning now?"

Randolph straightened up in his chair, his eyes fixed. "Rufus, do you know something I don't know? Is Abbott dying of cancer? Is that it?"

"Not that I know of. But that would be a blessing in disguise."

"Rufus, you're beginning to scare me."

"Now, sonny boy, you listen hard—get my meaning the first time around. I don't want to go into detail or repeat myself. Abbott is mortal like the rest of us. Except that now that you're going to be his heir apparent, he's become more mortal. One way or the other, he's got one year to go. That's the bottom line. Period. End of conversation. Unless you want to voice an objection. And if you do, sonny boy, this is a hell of a lousy time for me to learn about it."

While Randolph knew that nothing was beyond the capability of the Century Committee, it was still a frightening proposition.

"Well, sonny boy, are you with us?"

Randolph nodded. "All the way."

Rufus grunted and struggled to lift his great bulk out of the chair. He walked toward the library door and Randolph watched him move —an old man in a fat, tired, worn-out body. A moment ago the thought of being involved in a conspiracy to assassinate the President had taken his breath away. But now as he watched Rufus walk painfully across the room, the thought that his grandfather might not live long enough to fulfill his promise terrified Randolph even more.

Stopping with his hand on the doorknob, Rufus turned and smiled. "Bear this in mind, sonny boy. One year from this day we'll complete the dismantling of this welfare state and begin the creation of our Corporate World. What we envision is more revolutionary than the goddamn American Revolution itself. You'll go down in history as a greater man than Washington or Lincoln. And I'll be part of that history."

CHAPTER

71

For the second day, Henry worked in his den behind a locked door. Around noon on Thursday, Moses Grimes arranged for Henry's helicopter to be delivered to the chalet's pad. He watched with interest as the pilot who had delivered it was picked up in a sling chair by another copter.

Moses returned to the house, prepared a spinach salad, and brought it to the den with a bottle of white wine. He knocked and waited patiently until Henry opened it.

Moses smiled broadly. "You afraid that soft white man's going to come back up this mountain to git you?"

"Don't be silly," Henry said. "What have I got to fear with you here to protect me?"

Henry had tried to smile, but his tone had remained sharp. There was a fixed glint in Henry's eyes that told Moses his boss was in no mood for small talk. Whatever Henry was doing behind that locked door had to be of great importance. And after all these years with Henry, Moses knew better than to ask questions at these rare moments. If Henry wanted him to know, he'd tell him in his own good time.

"Thought you might enjoy a little lunch," Moses said, still trying to keep the tone light. He placed the serving tray on the desk, next to a tape recorder, which he noticed was in the pause mode.

"Thanks," Henry said, glancing at his wristwatch. "My God, is it one o'clock already? Look, I've got more work to do in here, so why don't you just relax, take a nap. I'll call you when I'm ready to leave. And give Holly a call. Tell her to expect us back at the ranch in the morning."

"Yes, sir," Moses said, grinning happily. "Them are the words I've been waiting to hear."

Henry raised an eyebrow and almost smiled. "I'm going," Moses said, "before I spoil your happy mood."

It was after five o'clock when Henry came out of the den. He was carrying a briefcase and his step was quick as he headed for the helicopter pad with Moses trailing after him.

Both men strapped themselves in their seats and Henry started the engine. A moment later they were airborne and heading toward Las Vegas. They flew in silence, with Moses casting furtive glances at Henry. The fixed glint was still in his eyes, and now Moses noticed a slight twitching of muscles along the jawline.

"Listen, Moses," Henry said, raising his voice to be heard over the roar of the engine, "I've got two packages in the briefcase. One is addressed to Alicia and the other to Daisy. In the event something happens to me—I don't foresee anything happening, but one never knows—you make sure they get these packages, but only after they've left Las Vegas. You understand?"

"Yes, Henry," Moses said.

"All right, old friend, I know I can depend on you. Sorry if I've been a little grim lately."

Moses laughed. "We all have our ups and downs. And speaking of down, where we going? The airport's the other way."

"The roof of the Monarch II."

Moses was nervous. "I don't know, Henry. Since that boy jumped off, I heard on the radio it's full of Secret Service agents. They'll probably shoot us down."

Indeed, as they moved toward the Monarch II, Henry saw several men on the rooftop running to the hotel's landing pad, their weapons drawn. Undeterred, Henry landed the craft.

The first agent to arrive at Henry's door recognized him immediately. "Mr. Godwin, you can't land here."

"It looks like I have," Henry said, stepping down on the hotel roof.

"Yes, sir. I can see that."

"Good," Henry said, waiting for Moses to climb down with the briefcase. Without another word they strode toward a steel door that was guarded by another agent, who unlocked it as they approached. Henry thanked him and hurried down the concrete staircase to the penthouse floor. With Moses behind, he moved quickly toward his suite.

Moses unlocked the door. As Henry went up the stairs to his bedroom, Moses immediately placed the briefcase in the bottom drawer of a large walnut chest. Upstairs, Henry sat on the bed and reached for the phone. It rang before he could pick it up.

"I want to see you," Rufus shouted over the line. "Right now!"

"You know where I live," Henry said, and hung up.

Moses answered the doorbell and Rufus angrily brushed past him.

"Where is he?" he demanded.

"I'm here," Henry said from the top of the staircase.

"Have you gone completely crazy?" Rufus shouted. "What right did you have kicking a great man like H. Russell Pierpont out like a bum?"

"What right did you and your gangster friend Stelk have to involve me and Randolph in blackmailing the President?"

"Oh, Christ, Henry, you're getting so fucking sanctimonious I could puke. Where's the video cassette?"

"I've burned the goddamn thing and I've burned all the other shit you had out there. Now, tell me, my honored father-in-law and trusted colleague, how many years have you been eavesdropping on me?"

"All your . . ."

Henry took a step and a split second later he was sliding down the stairs on his back. The pain gripping his heart this time was so powerful that it toppled him backward like a man poleaxed in the forehead. He was unconscious by the time he reached the bottom of the sweeping staircase.

72

Randolph strode confidently up the podium steps and across to the lectern. His appearance was greeted by a well-orchestrated demonstration that sent delegates dancing into the aisles, waving placards with his photograph and the words WIN GOD WIN in a vertical line. The sounds of their adulation mounted as he smiled and waved both arms above his head. It was the most exhilarating moment of his life. They loved him. They really did love him.

After hearing from Rufus about Henry's heart attack, Randolph had hurried to his room for heavy snorts of cocaine that had quickly eased the tension. Rufus, still pale and shaken, was sitting on the podium behind him with Iola and the twins—Alicia had relented after Eileen had pleaded with her. But even while sitting there Alicia was wondering where Henry was. It was particularly curious that he wouldn't be here on this most important of nights.

The tumult gradually subsided, and Randolph, still smiling, began his address.

"Delegates and friends," he said, his eyes scanning the entire convention hall. "It is a great honor for me to stand before this historic convention and to have on the dais with me my two daughters, Eileen and Alicia, and my grandfather, Rufus Boutwell. Without my daughters' affection and support and the wisdom and constant guidance of my grandfather I wouldn't be here tonight.

"I am deeply touched by your vote of confidence and I am proud to accept your nomination as your candidate for Vice-President of the United States.

"I want to express my heartfelt appreciation to our President for the confidence he has shown in me. Gratified by your trust and humbled by this new opportunity to serve the nation I love so deeply, I pledge to you and to all Americans that I will strive with all my strength and heart to insure four more years of dynamic Republican leadership in the White House."

He paused while the delegates applauded and cheered and tooted their horns. He turned to smile at Rufus and saw that the old man was having difficulty breathing. Leaving the lectern during the continuing applause, Randolph went to his grandfather, going down on one knee before his chair.

"Rufus, are you ill?"

Rufus had closed his eyes against the pain, and now he struggled to open them, slits of gray suddenly filled with fear. But his lips twisted into the semblance of a smile as he reached out to touch Randolph's cheek.

"Don't worry about me, sonny boy. I'm okay." His voice wheezed and again he seemed unable to breathe.

"Lay your head back a moment," Randolph said, placing his hand on Rufus's forehead, which felt cold and clammy. "Feel a little dizzy?"

Rufus's mouth was wide open and he was noisily sucking air.

Iola and Eileen, who sat on each side of Rufus, leaned forward, each offering a hand to support his head, which seemed to be hanging from a nerveless neck. Gently they brought his head forward and both smiled anxiously at him. Alicia, who sat next to Iola, studied him with cold appraising eyes.

"Get back out there," Rufus tried to growl, but the sound was weak, barely audible. "This is your big moment. Don't fuck it up."

"Rufus, you take it easy. Want me to get a doctor?"

"No," he growled. This time there was more volume in his voice. He tried to squeeze Randolph's hand but there was no strength in his fingers. His arm fell to his side, but he continued smiling. "Go on, sonny boy, I've waited all my life for this moment. Knock 'em dead."

"You're sure you're all right?" Randolph asked, slowly rising to his feet.

"Never felt better."

"All right, you listen while I tell the world what I think of you."

Rufus nodded, unable any longer to speak.

"Keep an eye on him," Randolph said to Iola and Eileen.

"Don't worry, we will," Iola said, turning to smile lovingly at Rufus.

Randolph returned to the lectern. "This has been an exciting week for all of us," he said after the convention had quieted down. "My grandfather, who worked harder than anyone I know, is feeling the stress. He may be getting on in age, but in mind and heart he's a young man. How proud I am of what he has accomplished for our great state of Nevada . . ."

Daisy sat next to Henry's bed, holding his hand. The hotel's doctor, called by Moses, had recommended immediate hospitalization. Henry, who had regained consciousness, vetoed the idea. The doctor had warned him of the danger, explaining that it was imperative for tests to be performed that could only be carried out at a hospital. But Henry had impatiently waved him away, saying that he'd die the way he'd lived, without a lot of needles sticking out of him and without doctors cutting him open like a slab of beef. Finally the doctor conceded, after ordering various medications and giving Moses strict instructions regarding Henry's care.

Now in the bedroom with Daisy's hand in his, Henry tried to smile. "This was quick," he said. "One moment I was talking and the next I was on my ass, sliding down the stairs."

She stroked his hand lovingly. "Don't talk, darling, please rest. If you won't go to the hospital, at least follow the doctor's orders."

"To hell with his orders," he said. "We've all got to go sometime. Except you, of course, my darling—you're immortal. But for us mortals, this is the way. No fuss, no mess, just boom, and you're gone."

He squeezed his eyes shut and gritted his teeth. That hand with the steel fingers was squeezing his heart again, but a little more gently this time. He wanted to tell Daisy about the tape recordings he had made that afternoon—about what he now was convinced was a plot to assassinate the President and what he wanted her to do to prevent it. But he knew this was not the time or place to discuss it. The last thing he wanted was to place her in jeopardy. The men now controlling Randolph and Rufus were not only totally ruthless, but among the most powerful in the country. They had the means to kill anyone, to achieve any goal.

Henry opened his eyes and saw the fear in hers. "It's all right," he said. "Why don't you turn on the television. I'd like to see what's happening at the convention."

Daisy picked up the remote device and switched on the set to the NTN channel. Randolph's face came into the room and his voice, so deep and resonant, sent chills down Daisy's spine.

"In my opening remarks I used the word *historic* in reference to this convention. It is indeed an historic convention, as it is the first ever held in Nevada, and I am the first Nevadan to be nominated as a candidate for Vice-President of the United States.

"Coming from Nevada, still one of the smallest states in the Union in population but perhaps one of the best-known states in the world, I hope I can spread the good word to all our people that Nevadans, like all other Americans, are hard-working, loyal, and devoted citizens of this great nation of ours.

"My grandfather, Rufus Boutwell, came to this state as a boy. Like other pioneers with a vision, he dared to gamble his youth and energy on the future of his adopted state. He found treasures in its mountains, gold and silver, and vital minerals under its arid surface that helped this country win the war against fascism. He found great natural springs and made thousands of acres of desert land bloom. And people came, first by the hundreds, then the thousands and now by the tens of thousands, and they keep coming because Nevada is a land of opportunity . . ."

Rufus turned violently toward Iola and peered at her with glazed slits of gray. "God, I hope I don't shit my pants," he groaned, but the words were a guttural mumbling impossible for Iola to make out.

She reached for him and his head again fell back, but this time his eyes rolled up in his head. Iola gave a small cry and Eileen leaned forward, her arm going up behind Rufus's head to support it.

"Oh, we must get help right away," Iola cried.

"It's too late," Eileen said in a firm voice. "He's gone. Don't you dare spoil Daddy's big moment."

Alicia heard the exchange but kept her gaze fixed straight ahead.

"My great-grandfather was a slave owner in Mississippi who fought for the Confederacy during the War Between the States. He was a lieutenant general at the age of thirty-three. He was in charge of the defense of Vicksburg when Yankee troops—bluebellies, he called them —attacked his city. Their artillery bombardment continued for seven weeks, day and night, before the General surrendered Vicksburg, which he called the Gibraltar of the West. There is a bronze statue of him astride his famous horse Black Lightning at the entrance to the Vicksburg National Military Park. This same man, this slave owner who fought for the South, was murdered at the age of ninety-four by the Ku Klux Klan when he tried to save two black sharecroppers who worked on his plantation. Armed with two shotguns he attacked over a hun-

515

dred Klan horsemen, and they shot him down, filling his frail body with their bullets. That is how one of the South's great heroes died and he was my great-grandfather. I proudly bear his name: Randolph Harrison Godwin . . ."

Daisy felt Henry's hand tense. She looked at him and saw that he was again fighting against the pain.

"Don't you think it would be better if you tried to sleep. Why don't I get in bed with you. We can hold each other and sleep."

"Daisy, there's something you've got to promise me," he said, bringing her hand to his lips. "If I don't pull through this, there's something you must do for me and Randolph. But it will be dangerous, my love, and it could destroy your career."

"Oh, my God, Henry, you're scaring me."

"I'm sorry. No more now."

"No, please, tell me."

"I've told you all I can. If I die, you'll get something in the mail. I know you'll do the right thing."

"I will, Henry, I really will. I promise with all my heart. But can't you tell me more?"

He shook his head and closed his eyes.

It was a summer day and they stopped their horses on the edge of a bluff high over the great Mississippi. The General leaned forward in his saddle and pointed to where the artillery batteries had been placed to make the bluffs a fortress against Yankee gunboats and shipping.

"That old boy Grant tried like hell to slip by but we stopped him cold for two and a half years," he said, giving Henry a conspiratorial wink. "One time he tried to build a mile-long canal to bypass our batteries and attack from the south, but the spring rains flooded the canal and damn near drowned his troops. But that man was persistent. You've got to give the devil his due." The old man stretched his neck and leaned back in the saddle, his deeply etched face contemplative as his dark eyes narrowed to survey the gentle sweep of a river he had known all his life.

Then suddenly the eyes were blue, a bright, summer sky blue. The old man looked up and said, "Howdy, stranger," and his face seemed a hundred years old. His left hand was absently stroking the dusty hide of a dead burro lying at his side. "This is Bessie," he said. "Dang old fool stepped into a nest of rattlers." He slapped his weather-beaten cowboy hat angrily against the ground. "Had to use my hunting knife on her, had to take her out of her misery." He paused and put his hat back on his head. His shoulder-length hair was white as snow. "I knowed she trusted me. Looked me right in the eye with those big sad eyes of hers when I stuck the knife into her heart. She didn't make a sound. Just pissed and toppled over." Tears ran down into the dark creases of his sunbaked face, making them look slick and even deeper, and for a moment it seemed like he was going to lose control of himself, but suddenly he turned to look at the dead burro. "Dang your ornery hide, Randolph," he cried angrily. "You should've known better than to get mixed up with a bunch of rattlers."

"Wait a minute," Henry started to protest. "That's not Randolph. My son is only a baby." But the old man ignored him, and the steel fingers crushed Henry Godwin's heart. He gasped once, and his jaws slackened.

Daisy, who was watching television, felt the hand go limp. She let out a small, helpless cry when she saw his face—the eyes turned slightly upward, the mouth open and slack at the corners where tears had rolled down to collect in the wrinkles the years had brought.

In the sky suite at the convention hall Alistair Baker was smiling happily into the camera. "Listen to this crowd," he was saying. "This tumultuous standing ovation is for Senator Randolph Godwin, this convention's candidate for the Vice-Presidency. He's just finished a rousing speech, by turns personal and emotional, deeply touching, exciting in its vision, sprinkled with wit and wisdom . . ."

There was a victorious smile on Randolph's face when he turned to look at Rufus. What he saw sent chills of terror through him. Eileen was watching him with tears in her eyes. He stepped forward on legs that felt numb. Iola was cradling Rufus's head in her arms, like a mother holding a sleeping child, except that Randolph knew that the man who had protected him all of his life was dead.

"Goddamn you, Rufus," he cried, dropping to his knees. "What about your promise? What do I do now?" And for the first time since his mother had left home he felt lost and desperate and wept openly like a child.

In the wings President Abbott and his entourage of Secret Service agents and advisers were waiting for the convention to come to order.

And in the living rooms across the nation Americans considered the remarkable future that awaited this relatively young man. Truman Abbott had a difficult act to follow. Randolph Godwin, whose speech had been delivered with the poise and assurance of a seasoned diplomat, appeared for all the world like a man destined for the Presidency.